HT

Enthusiastic praise for
ELIZABETH GEORGE
and her spellbinding
***New York Times* bestseller**

WITH NO ONE AS WITNESS

"Stunning . . . Ms. George delivers a shocker that will change her work in ways her readers could not have expected . . . George's trademark—an unblinking eye directed toward her characters—is always in evidence, as are her psychological insight and graceful, impassioned writing. And most remarkably, she just keeps getting better, keeps pushing her work to the next level . . . *With No One As Witness* is a compelling read that works at multiple levels."

Richmond Times Dispatch

"Inspector Lynley is back in top form . . . Elizabeth George is an American master of the British mystery . . . An absorbing police procedural . . . George fully develops every nuance of the racially loaded case—and every thrill in the chase. But it's the note on which the novel ends that stuns as the series is violently wrenched onto new ground."

New York Daily News

"Ms. George provides enough twists and shocks in this detailed police procedural to startle and satisfy even the most jaded reader."

Wall Street Journal

"[A] top-notch psychological thriller/whodunit/police procedural."

San Jose Mercury News

"A riveting installment in a superb series—far more than just plain good. It's also a turning point for the series as George makes some bold, surprising decisions that permanently change the lives of the characters her fans have come to know."

Booklist (★ Starred Review ★)

"A satisfying blend of suspense and psychological case study . . . Weaving issues of race, gender, class, and politics into her skillfully crafted prose, George creates a morally complex world that illuminates the ways in which everyone's motives are suspect—even our own."

People (★★★★ "Critics Choice")

"Another spellbinder . . . All of George's characters are intensely human, and thus memorable fictional material."

Toronto Sun

"George's appetite for unerring detail, complex plotting, and probing attention to issues of class, race, character, and disenfranchisement has always made her an original, and *Witness* confirms her mastery . . . The real shocker for longtime fans is a stakes-raising, stunningly effective plot twist that changes the entire series in a heartbeat. Grade: A-."

Entertainment Weekly

"[A] juicy serial killer whodunit . . . A story that ends with not one but several shocking twists."

USA Today

"A master of riveting psychological intrigue . . . George does a superb job here of depicting seamier aspects of London's underside. The explicit evil is almost palpable . . . George has a fine ear for dialogue and permits the intricate plot to unfold slowly . . . *With No One As Witness* is frequently horrifying, always entertaining."

Nashville Tennessean

"Absorbing . . . Crime fans will find plenty of forensic minutiae and details of police bureaucracy and politics, but it's characterization at which George really excels . . . This is an outstanding and explosive addition to a popular series."

Publishers Weekly (★ Starred Review ★)

"I wouldn't miss an Elizabeth George novel . . . There simply aren't many detective novelists today who can write a scene of great brutality at one moment . . . and at another write the tenderest love scenes."

Philadelphia Inquirer

"In a word: gripping."

Melbourne Herald Sun (Australia)

Books by Elizabeth George

FICTION

A Great Deliverance
Payment in Blood
Well-Schooled in Murder
A Suitable Vengeance
For the Sake of Elena
Missing Joseph
Playing for the Ashes
In the Presence of the Enemy
Deception on His Mind
In Pursuit of the Proper Sinner
A Traitor to Memory
I, Richard
A Place of Hiding
With No One As Witness

NONFICTION

Write Away: One Novelist's Approach to Fiction and the Writing Life

ANTHOLOGY

A Moment on the Edge: 100 Years of Crime Stories by Women

Elizabeth
GEORGE

With No One As Witness

HarperTorch
An Imprint of HarperCollins*Publishers*

This is a work of fiction. Names, characters, places, and incidents are products of the author's imagination or are used fictitiously and are not to be construed as real. Any resemblance to actual events, locales, organizations, or persons, living or dead, is entirely coincidental.

HARPERTORCH
An Imprint of HarperCollins*Publishers*
10 East 53rd Street
New York, New York 10022-5299

ISBN-13: 978-0-06-054561-1
ISBN-10: 0-06-054561-5

First HarperTorch paperback printing: March 2006
First HarperTorch international printing: January 2006
First HarperCollins hardcover printing: March 2005

Printed in the United States of America

Visit HarperTorch on the World Wide Web at www.harpercollins.com

10 9 8 7 6 5 4 3 2 1

For Miss Audra Isadora, with love

. . . and if you gaze for long into the abyss,
the abyss gazes also into you.

—Nietzsche

Prologue

Kimmo Thorne liked Dietrich best of all: the hair, the legs, the cigarette holder, the top hat and tails. She was what he called the Whole Blooming Package, and as far as he was concerned, she was second to none. Oh, he could do Garland if pressed. Minnelli was simple, and he was definitely getting better with Streisand. But given his choice—and he *was* generally given it, wasn't he?—he went with Dietrich. Sultry Marlene. His number one girl. She could sing the crumbs out of a toaster, could Marlene, make no bloody mistake about it.

So he held the pose at the end of the song not because it was necessary to the act but because he loved the look of the thing. The finale to "Falling in Love Again" faded and he just kept standing there like a Marlene statue with one high-heeled foot on the seat of the chair and his cigarette holder between his fingers. The last note disappeared into silence and he remained for a five count—exulting in Marlene and in himself because she was good and he was good, he was damn *damn* good when it came down to it—before he altered his position. He switched off the karaoke machine then. He doffed his top hat and fluttered his tails. He bowed deeply to his audience of two. And Aunt Sal and Gran—ever loyal, they were—reacted appropriately, as he'd known they would. Aunt Sally cried, "Brilliant! Brilliant, lad!" Gran said, "Tha's our boy all over. A hunnert percent talent, our Kimmo. Wait'll I send some snaps to your mum and dad."

That would certainly bring them running, Kimmo thought sardonically. But he put his high-heeled foot on the chair once more, knowing Gran meant well, even if she was something of a dim bulb when it came to what she believed about his parents.

Gran directed Aunt Sally to "Move to the right. Get the boy's best side," and in a few minutes the pictures had been taken and the show was over for the evening.

"Where you off to tonight?" Aunt Sally asked as Kimmo headed for his bedroom. "You seein' anyone special, our Kim?"

He wasn't, but she needn't know that. "The Blink," he told her blithely.

"Well, you lads keep yourselfs out of trouble, then."

He winked at her and ducked into his doorway. "Always, *always*, Auntie," he lied. He eased the door shut behind him then and flicked its lock into place.

The care of the Marlene togs came first. Kimmo took them off and hung them up before turning to his dressing table. There, he examined his face and for a moment considered removing some of the makeup. But he finally shrugged the idea aside and rustled through the clothes cupboard for a change that would do. He chose a hooded sweatshirt, the leggings he liked, and his flat-soled, suede, ankle-high boots. He enjoyed the ambiguity of the ensemble. Male or female? an observer might ask. But only if Kimmo spoke would it actually show. For his voice had finally broken and when he opened his mouth now, the jig was up.

He drew the sweatshirt hood over his head and sauntered down the stairs. "I'm off, then," he called to his gran and his aunt as he grabbed his jacket from a hook near the door.

" 'Bye, darlin' boy," Gran replied.

"Keep yourself yourself, luv," Aunt Sally added.

He kissed the air at them. They kissed the air in turn. "Love you," everyone said at once.

Outside, he zipped his jacket and unlocked his bicycle from the railing. He rolled it along to the lift and pressed the button there, and as he waited, he checked the bike's saddlebags to make sure that he had everything he'd need. He maintained a mental checklist on which he ticked items off: emergency hammer, gloves, screwdriver, jemmy, pocket torch, pillowcase, one red rose. This last he liked to leave as his calling card. One really oughtn't to take without giving as well.

It was a cold night outside in the street, and Kimmo didn't look forward to the ride. He hated having to go by bike, and he hated biking even more when the temperature hovered so close to freezing. But as neither Gran nor Aunt Sally had a car, and as he himself had no driving licence to flash at a copper, along with his most appealing smile if he was stopped, he had no other choice but to pedal it. Going by bus was more or less out of the question.

His route took him along Southwark Street to the heavier traffic of Blackfriars Road till, in a crisscrossing fashion, he reached the environs of Kennington Park. From there, traffic or not, it was more or less a bullet's path to Clapham Common and his destination: a conveniently detached redbrick dwelling of three storeys, which he'd spent the last month carefully casing.

At this point, he knew the comings and goings of the family inside so thoroughly that he might as well have lived there himself. He knew they had two children. Mum got her exercise riding a bike to work, while Dad went by train from Clapham Station. They had an au pair with a regularly scheduled two nights each week off, and on one of those nights—always the same one—Mum, Dad, and the kids left as a family and went to . . . Kimmo didn't know. He assumed it was Gran's for dinner, but it just as easily could have been a lengthy church service, a session with a counselor, or lessons in yoga. Point was, they were gone for the evening, till *late* in the evening, and when they arrived home, they invariably had to lug the little ones into the house because they'd fallen asleep in the car. As for the au pair, she took her nights off with two other birds who were similarly employed. They'd leave together chatting away in Bulgarian or whatever it was, and *if* they returned before dawn, it was still long after midnight.

The signs were propitious for this particular house. The car they drove was the largest of the Range Rovers. A gardener visited them once a week. They had a cleaning service as well, and their sheets and pillowcases were laundered, ironed, and returned by a professional. This particular house, Kimmo had concluded, was ripe, and waiting.

What made it all so nice was the house next door and the lovely "To Let" sign dangling forlornly from a post near the street. What made it all so perfect was the easy access from the rear: a brick wall running along a stretch of wasteland.

Kimmo pedaled to this point after coasting by the front of the house to make sure the family were being true to their rigid schedule. Then he bumped his way across the wasteland and propped his bike against the wall. Using the pillowcase to carry his tools and the rose, he hopped up on the saddle of the bike and, with no trouble, lifted himself over the wall.

The back garden was blacker than the devil's tongue, but Kimmo had peered over the wall before and he knew what lay before him. Directly beneath was a compost heap beyond which a little zigzagging orchard of fruit trees decorated a nicely clipped lawn. To either side of this, wide flower beds made herbaceous borders. One of them curved round a gazebo. The other graced the vicinity of a garden shed. Last in the distance just before the house were a patio of uneven bricks where rainwater pooled after a storm and then a roof overhang, from which the security lights were hung.

They clicked on automatically as Kimmo approached. He gave them a nod of thanks. Security lights, he'd long ago decided, had to be the ironic inspiration of a housebreaker, since whenever they switched on, everyone appeared to assume a mere cat was passing through the garden. He'd yet to hear of a neighbour giving the cops a bell because of some lights going on. On the other hand, he'd heard plenty of stories from fellow housebreakers about how much easier those lights had made access to the rear of a property.

In this case, the lights meant nothing. The uncurtained dark windows along with the "To Let" sign told him that no one resided in the house to his right, while the house to his left had no windows on this side of it and no dog to set up a spate of barking in the nighttime cold. He was, as far as he could tell, in the clear.

French windows opened onto the patio, and Kimmo made for these. There, a quick tap with his emergency hammer—suitable in a crisis for breaking a car window—was quite sufficient to gain him access to the handle on the door. He opened this and stepped inside. The burglar alarm hooted like an air-raid siren.

The sound was earsplitting, but Kimmo ignored it. He had five minutes—perhaps more—till the phone would ring, with the security company on the line, hoping to discover that the alarm had been tripped accidentally. When they went unsatisfied, they would phone the contact numbers they'd been given. When *that* didn't suffice to bring an end to the incessant screeching of the siren, they might phone the police, who in turn might or might not show up to check matters out. But in any case, that eventuality was a good twenty minutes away, which in itself was ten minutes longer than Kimmo needed to score what he was looking for in the building.

He was a specialist in this particular field. Leave to others the computers, the laptops, the CD and DVD players, the televisions, the jewellery, the digital cameras, the Palm Pilots, and the video players. He was looking for only one kind of item in the houses he visited, and the benefit of this item he sought was that it would always be in plain sight and generally in the public rooms of a house.

Kimmo shone his pocket torch round. He was in a dining room, and there was nothing here to take. But in the sitting room, he could already see four prizes glittering on the top of a piano. He went to fetch them: silver frames that he divested of their photographs—one always wanted to be thoughtful about *some* things—before depositing them carefully in his pillowcase. He found another on one of the side tables, and he scored this as well before moving to the front of the house where, near the door, a half-moon table with a mirror above it displayed two others along with a porcelain box and a flower arrangement, both of which he left where they were.

Experience told him that chances were good he'd find the rest of what he wanted in the master bedroom, so he quickly mounted the stairs as the burglar alarm continued to blare against his eardrums. The room he sought was on the top floor, in the back, overlooking the garden, and he'd just clicked on his torch to check out its contents when the shrieking of the alarm ceased abruptly just as the telephone started to ring.

Kimmo stopped short, one hand on his torch and the other halfway to a picture frame in which a couple in wedding gear kissed beneath a bough of flowers. In a moment, the phone stopped just as abruptly as the alarm, and from below a light went on and someone said, "Hullo?," and then, "No. We've only just walked in . . . Yes. Yes. It was going off, but I haven't had a chance to—Jesus Christ! Gail, get away from that glass."

That was enough to tell Kimmo that matters had taken an unexpected turn. He didn't pause to wonder what the hell the family were doing home when they were still supposed to be at Gran's at church at yoga at counseling or *wherever* the hell they went when they went. Instead, he dived for the window to the left of the bed as below, a woman cried, "Ronald, someone's in the house!"

Kimmo didn't need to hear Ronald come tearing up the stairs or Gail shouting, "No! Stop!" to understand that he had to be out of there pronto. He fumbled with the lock on the window, threw up the sash, and heaved himself and his pillowcase out just as Ronald barreled into the room armed with what looked like a fork for turning meat on a barbecue.

Kimmo dropped with an enormous thump and a gasp onto the overhang some eight feet below, cursing the fact that there had been no convenient wisteria vine down which he could Tarzan his way to freedom. He heard Gail shouting, "He's here! He's here!," and Ronald cursing from the window above. Just before he scarpered for the rear wall of the property, he turned back to the house, giving a grin and a saucy salute to the woman who stood in the dining room with an awestruck sleepy child in her arms and another hanging on to her trousers.

Then he was off, the pillowcase bouncing against his back and laughter bubbling up inside him, only sorry he hadn't been able to leave behind the rose. As he reached the wall, he heard Ronald come roaring out of the dining-room door, but by the time the poor bloke reached the first of the trees, Kimmo was up, over, and heading across the wasteland. When the cops finally arrived—which could be anywhere from an hour to midday tomorrow—he'd be long gone, a faint memory in the mind of the missus: a painted face beneath a sweatshirt hood.

God, this was living! This was the best! If the haul proved to be sterling stuff, he'd be a few hundred quid richer come Friday morning. Did it get better than this? *Did* it? Kimmo didn't think so. So *what* that he'd said he'd go straight for a while. He couldn't throw away the time he'd already spent putting this job together. He'd be thick to do that, and the one thing Kimmo Thorne was not was thick. Not a bit of that. No way, Hoe-say.

He was pedaling along perhaps a mile from his break-in when he became aware of being followed. There was other traffic about on the streets—when wasn't there traffic in London?—and several cars had honked as they'd passed him. He first thought they were honking at him the way vehicles do to a cyclist they wish to get out of their way, but he soon came to realise that they were honking at a slow-moving vehicle close behind him, one that refused to pass him by.

He felt a little unnerved by this, wondering if Ronald had somehow managed to get it together and track him down. He turned down a side street to make sure he wasn't mistaken in his belief in being tailed, and sure enough, the headlights directly behind him turned as well. He was about to shoot off in a fury of pedaling when he heard the rumble of an engine coming up next to him and then his name spoken in a friendly voice.

"Kimmo? That you? What're you doing in this part of town?"

Kimmo coasted. He slowed. He turned to see who

was speaking to him. He smiled when he realised who the driver was, and he said, "Never mind me. What're *you* doing here?"

The other smiled back. "Looks like I'm cruising round for you. Need a lift somewhere?"

It would be convenient, Kimmo thought, if Ronald had seen him take off on the bike and if the cops were quicker to respond than they normally were. He didn't really want to be out on the street. He still had a couple more miles to go, and it was cold as Antarctica, anyway. He said, "I got the bike with me, though."

The other chuckled. "Well, that's no problem if you don't want it to be."

Chapter One

Detective Constable Barbara Havers considered herself one lucky bird: The drive was empty. She'd elected to do her weekly shop by car rather than on foot, and this was always a risky business in an area of town where anyone fortunate enough to find a parking space near their home clung to it with the devotion of the newly redeemed to the source of his redemption. But knowing she had much to purchase and shuddering at the thought of trudging in the cold back from the local grocery, she'd opted for transport and hoped for the best. So when she pulled up in front of the yellow Edwardian house behind which her tiny bungalow stood, she took the space in the drive without compunction. She listened to the coughing and gagging of her Mini's engine as she turned it off, and she made her fifteenth mental note of the month to have the car looked at by a mechanic who—one prayed—would not ask an arm, a leg, and one's firstborn child to repair whatever was causing it to belch like a dyspeptic pensioner.

She climbed out and flipped the seat forward to gather up the first of the plastic carrier bags. She'd linked four of them over her arms and was dragging them out of the car when she heard her name called.

Someone sang it out. "Barbara! Barbara! Look what I've found in the cupboard."

Barbara straightened and glanced in the direction from which the voice had chimed. She saw the young daughter of her neighbour sitting on the weathered wooden bench in front of the ground-floor flat of the old converted building. She'd removed her shoes and was in the process of struggling into a pair of inline skates. Far too large by the look of them, Barbara thought. Hadiyyah was only eight years old and the skates were clearly meant for an adult.

"These're Mummy's," Hadiyyah informed her, as if reading her mind. "I found them in a cupboard, like I said. I've never skated on them before. I expect they're going to be big on me, but I've stuffed them with kitchen towels. Dad doesn't know."

"About the kitchen towels?"

Hadiyyah giggled. "Not *that*! He doesn't know that I've found them."

"Perhaps you're not meant to be using them."

"Oh, they weren't *hidden*. Just put away. Till Mummy gets home, I expect. She's in—"

"Canada. Right," Barbara nodded. "Well, you take care with those. Your dad's not going to be chuffed if you fall and break your head. D'you have a helmet or something?"

Hadiyyah looked down at her feet—one skated and one socked—and thought about this. "Am I meant to?"

"Safety precaution," Barbara told her. "A consideration for the street sweepers, as well. Keeps people's brains off the pavement."

Hadiyyah rolled her eyes. "I know you're joking."

Barbara crossed her heart. "God's truth. Where's your dad, anyway? Are you alone today?" She kicked open the picket gate that fronted a path to the house, and she considered whether she ought to talk to Taymullah Azhar once again about leaving his daughter on her own. While it was true that he did it rarely enough, Barbara had told him that she would be pleased to look after Hadiyyah on her own time off if he had students to meet or lab work to supervise at the university. Hadiyyah was remarkably self-sufficient for an eight-year-old, but at the end of the day she was still that: an eight-year-old, and more innocent than her fellows, in part because of a culture that kept her protected and in part because of the desertion of her English mother who had now been "in Canada" for nearly a year.

"He's gone to buy me a surprise," Hadiyyah informed her matter-of-factly. "He thinks I don't know, he thinks *I* think he's running an errand, but I know what he's really doing. It's 'cause he feels bad and he thinks *I* feel bad, which I don't, but he wants to help me feel better anyway. So *he* said, 'I've an errand to run, *kushi,*' and I'm meant to think it's not about me. Have you done your shopping? C'n I help you, Barbara?"

"More bags in the car if you want to fetch them," Barbara told her.

Hadiyyah slipped off the bench and—one skate on and one skate off—hopped over to the Mini and pulled out the rest of the bags. Barbara waited at the corner of the house. When Hadiyyah joined her, bobbing up and down on her one skate, Barbara said, "What's the occasion, then?"

Hadiyyah followed her to the bottom of the property where, under a false acacia tree, Barbara's bungalow—looking much like a garden shed with delusions of grandeur—snowed flakes of green paint onto a narrow flower bed in need of planting. "Hmm?" Hadiyyah asked. Close up now, Barbara could see that the little girl wore the headphones of a CD player round her neck and the player itself attached to the waistband of her blue jeans. Some unidentifiable music was issuing tinnily from it in a feminine register. Hadiyyah appeared not to notice this.

"The surprise," Barbara said as she opened the front door of her digs. "You said your dad was out fetching you a surprise."

"Oh, *that.*" Hadiyyah clumped into the bungalow and deposited her burdens on the dining table where several days' post mingled with four copies of the *Evening Standard*, a basket of dirty laundry, and an empty bag of custard cremes. It all made an unappealing jumble at which the habitually neat little girl frowned meaningfully. "You haven't sorted out your belongings," she chided.

"Astute observation," Barbara murmured. "And the surprise? I know it's not your birthday."

Hadiyyah tapped her skate-shod foot against the floor and looked suddenly uncomfortable, a reaction entirely unusual for her. She had, Barbara noted, plaited her own dark hair today. Her parting made a series of zigzags while the red bows at the end of her plaits were lopsided, with one tied a good inch higher than the other. "Well," she said as Barbara began emptying the first of the carrier bags onto the work top of the kitchen area, "he didn't exactly say, but I expect it's 'cause Mrs. Thompson phoned him."

Barbara recognised the name of Hadiyyah's teacher. She looked over her shoulder at the little girl and raised a questioning eyebrow.

"See, there was a tea," Hadiyyah informed her. "Well, not really a tea, but that's what they called it because if they called it what it *really* was, everyone would've been too embarrassed and no one would've gone. And they did want everyone to go."

"Why? What was it really?"

Hadiyyah turned away and began unloading the

carrier bags she'd brought from the Mini. It was, she informed Barbara, more of an *event* than a tea, or really, more of a *meeting* than an event. Mrs. Thompson had a lady come to talk to them about their *bodies*, you see, and all the girls in the class and all their mums came to listen and afterwards they could ask questions and after *that* they had orange squash and biscuits and cakes. So Mrs. Thompson called it a tea although no one actually *drank* tea. Hadiyyah, having no mum to take along, had eschewed attending the event altogether. Hence the phone call from Mrs. Thompson to her father because, like she said, everyone was really meant to go.

"Dad said he would've gone," Hadiyyah said. "But that would've been *excruciating*. 'Sides, Meagan Dobson told me what it was all about anyway. Girl stuff. Babies. Boys. *Periods*." She pulled a shuddering face. "You know."

"Ah. Got it." Barbara could understand how Azhar must have reacted to the phone call from the teacher. No one she had ever met had as much pride as the Pakistani professor who was her neighbour. "Well, kiddo, if you ever need a gal pal to act as a substitute for your mother," she told Hadiyyah, "I'm happy to oblige."

"How lovely!" Hadiyyah exclaimed. For a moment Barbara thought she was referring to her offer as maternal surrogate, but she saw that her little friend was bringing forth a package from within the bag of groceries: Chocotastic Pop-Tarts. "Is this for your breakfast?" Hadiyyah sighed.

"Perfect nutrition for the professional woman on the go," Barbara told her. "Let it be our little secret, okay? One of many."

"And what're *these*?" Hadiyyah asked as if she hadn't spoken. "Oh, *wonderful*. Clotted-cream ice-cream bars! If I was a grown-up, I'd eat just like you."

"I do like to touch on all the basic food groups," Barbara told her. "Chocolate, sugar, fat, and tobacco. Have you come across the Players, by the way?"

"You mustn't keep smoking," Hadiyyah told her, rustling in one of the bags and bringing out a carton of the cigarettes. "Dad's trying to stop. Did I tell you? Mummy'll be so pleased. She asked him and *asked* him to stop. 'Hari, it'll make your lungs all nasty if you don't quit,' is what she says. *I* don't smoke."

"I should hope not," Barbara said.

"Some of the boys do, actually. They stand round down the street from school. These're the older boys. *And* they take their shirttails out of their trousers, Barbara. I expect they think it makes them look cool, but *I* think it makes them look . . ." She frowned, thoughtful. ". . . beastly," she settled on. "Perfectly beastly."

"Peacocks and their plumes," Barbara acknowledged.

"Hmm?"

"The male of the species, attracting the female. Otherwise, she'd have nothing to do with him. Interesting, no? Men should be the ones wearing makeup."

Hadiyyah giggled at this, saying, "Dad would look a sight wearing lipstick, wouldn't he?"

"He'd be fighting them off with a broomstick."

"Mummy wouldn't like *that*," Hadiyyah noted. She scooped up four tins of All Day Breakfast—Barbara's preferred dinner in a pinch after a longer than usual day at work—and carried them over to the cupboard above the sink.

"No. I don't expect she would," Barbara agreed. "Hadiyyah, what *is* that bloody-awful screeching going on round your neck?" She took the tins from the little girl and nodded at her headphones, from which some sort of questionable pop music was continuing to issue.

"Nobanzi," Hadiyyah said obscurely.

"No-whatie?"

"Nobanzi. They're brilliant. Look." From out of her

jacket pocket she brought the plastic cover of a CD. On it, three anorexic twentysomethings posed in crop tops the size of Scrooge's generosity and blue jeans so tight that the only thing left to imagine was how they'd managed to cram themselves into them.

"Ah," Barbara said. "Role models for our young. Give that over, then. Let's have a listen."

Hadiyyah willingly handed over the earphones, which Barbara set on her head. She absently reached for a packet of Players and shook one out despite Hadiyyah's moue of disapproval. She lit one as what sounded like the chorus to a song—if it could be called that—assailed her eardrums. The Vandellas Nobanzi definitely was not, with or without Martha, Barbara decided. There was a chorus of unintelligible words. Lots of orgasmic groaning in the background appeared to take the place of both the bass line and the drums.

Barbara removed the headphones, and handed them over. She drew in on her fag and speculatively cocked her head at Hadiyyah.

Hadiyyah said, "Aren't they *brilliant*?" She took the CD cover and pointed to the girl in the middle, who had dual-colored dreadlocks and a smoking pistol tattooed on her right breast. "This's Juno. She's my favourite. She's got a baby called Nefertiti. Isn't she lovely?"

"The very word I'd use." Barbara screwed up the emptied carrier bags and shoved them in the cupboard beneath the sink. She opened her cutlery drawer and found at the back of it a pad of sticky notes that she generally used to remind herself of important upcoming events like Consider Plucking Eyebrows or Clean This Disgusting Toilet. This time, however, she scribbled three words and said to her little friend, "Come with me. It's time to see to your education," before grabbing up her shoulder bag and leading her back to the front of the house, where Hadiyyah's shoes lay beneath the bench in the flagstoned area just outside the door to the ground-floor flat. Barbara told her to put on her shoes while she herself posted the sticky note on the door.

When Hadiyyah was ready, Barbara said, "Follow me. I've let your dad know," and she headed off the property and in the direction of Chalk Farm Road.

"Where're we going?" Hadiyyah asked. "Are we having an adventure?"

Barbara said, "Let me ask you a question. Nod if any of these names are familiar. Buddy Holly. No? Richie Valens. No? The Big Bopper. No? Elvis. Well, of course. Who wouldn't know Elvis, but that hardly counts. What about Chuck Berry? Little Richard? Jerry Lee Lewis? 'Great Balls of Fire.' Ring any bells? No? Bloody hell, what're they teaching you at school?"

"You shouldn't swear," Hadiyyah said.

On Chalk Farm Road, it was not an overlong walk to their destination: the Virgin Megastore in Camden High Street. To get there, though, they had to negotiate the shopping district, which, as far as Barbara had ever been able to ascertain, was unlike any shopping precinct in the city: packed shopfront to street with young people of every colour, persuasion, and manner of bodily adornment; flooded by a blaring cacophony of music from every direction; scented with everything from patchouli oil to fish and chips. Here shops had mascots crawling up the front of them in the form of super-huge cats, the gigantic bottom of a torso wearing blue jeans, enormous boots, an aeroplane nose down . . . Only vaguely did the mascots have anything to do with the wares within the individual shops, since most of these were given over to anything black and many things leather. Black leather. Black faux leather. Black faux fur on black faux leather.

Hadiyyah, Barbara saw, was taking everything in

with the expression of a novice, the first indication Barbara had that the little girl had never before been to Camden High Street, despite its proximity to their respective homes. Hadiyyah followed along, eyes the size of hubcaps, lips parted, face rapt. Barbara had to steer her in and out of the crowd, one hand on her shoulder, to make sure they didn't become separated in the crush.

"Brilliant, *brilliant*," Hadiyyah breathed, hands clasped to her chest. "Oh, Barbara, this is so much *better* than a surprise."

"Glad you like it," Barbara said.

"Will we go into the shops?"

"When I've seen to your education."

She took her into the megastore, to classic rock 'n' roll. "This," Barbara told her, "is music. Now . . . Where to start you off . . . ? Well, there's no question, really, is there? Because at the end of the day, we have the Great One and then we have everyone else. So . . ." She scanned the section for the H's and then the H's themselves for the only H that counted. She examined the selections, flipping each over to read the songs while next to her Hadiyyah studied the photos of Buddy Holly on the CD covers.

"Bit odd looking," she remarked.

"Bite your tongue. Here. This'll do. It's got 'Raining in My Heart,' which I guarantee will make you swoon and 'Rave On,' which'll make you want to dance on the work top. *This,* kiddo, is rock 'n' roll. People'll be listening to Buddy Holly in one hundred years, I guarantee it. As for Nobuki—"

"Nobanzi," Hadiyyah corrected her patiently.

"They'll be gone next week. Gone and forgotten while the Great One will rave on into eternity. This, my girl, is *music*."

Hadiyyah looked doubtful. "He wears awfully strange specs," she noted.

"Well, yeah. But that was the style. He's been dead forever. Plane crash. Bad weather. Trying to get home to the pregnant wife." Too young, Barbara thought. Too much in a hurry.

"How sad." Hadiyyah looked at the photo of Buddy Holly with awakened eyes.

Barbara paid for their purchase and peeled off its wrapper. She brought out the CD and replaced Nobanzi with Buddy Holly. She said, "Feast your ears on this," and when the music started, she led Hadiyyah back out to the street.

As promised, Barbara took her into several of the shops where the here-today-passé-in-thirty-minutes fashions were crammed onto clothing racks and hung from the walls. Scores of teenagers were spending money as if news of Armageddon had just been broadcast, and there was a sameness to them that caused Barbara to look at her companion and pray Hadiyyah always maintained the air of artlessness that made her such a pleasure to be around. Barbara couldn't imagine her transformed into a London teenager in a tearing hurry to arrive at adulthood, mobile phone pressed to her ear, lipstick and eye shadow colouring her face, blue jeans sculpting her little arse, and high-heeled boots destroying her feet. And she certainly couldn't imagine the little girl's father allowing her out in public so arrayed.

For her part, Hadiyyah took everything in like a child on her first trip to a fun fair, with Buddy Holly raining in her heart. It was only when they'd progressed upwards to Chalk Farm Road, where the crowds were if anything thicker, louder, and more decorated than in the shops below, that Hadiyyah removed her earphones and finally spoke.

"I want to come back here *every* week from now on," she announced. "Will you come with me, Barbara? I could save all my money and we could have lunch and then we could go in *all* of the shops. We can't today 'cause I ought to be home before Dad gets there. He'll be cross if he knows where we've been."

"Will he? Why?"

"Oh, 'cause I'm forbidden to come here," Hadiyyah said pleasantly. "Dad says if he *ever* saw me out in Camden High Street, he'd wallop me properly till I couldn't sit down. Your note didn't say we were coming here, did it?"

Barbara gave an inward curse. She hadn't considered the ramifications of what she'd intended as only an innocent jaunt to the music shop. She felt for a moment as if she'd corrupted the innocent, but she allowed herself to experience the relief of having written a note to Taymullah Azhar that had employed three words only—"Kiddo's with me"—along with her signature. Now if she could just depend on Hadiyyah's discretion . . . although from the little girl's excitement—despite her intention of keeping her father in the dark as to her whereabouts while he was on his errand—Barbara had to admit it was highly unlikely that she'd be able to hide from Azhar the pleasure attendant on their adventure.

"I didn't exactly tell him where we'd be," Barbara admitted.

"Oh, that's brilliant," Hadiyyah said. " 'Cause if he knew . . . I don't much fancy being walloped, Barbara. Do you?"

"D'you think he'd actually—"

"Oh look, *look,*" Hadiyyah cried. "What's this place called, then? And it smells so *heavenly*. Are they cooking somewhere? C'n we go in?"

"This place" was Camden Lock Market, which they had come up to in their journey homeward. It stood on the edge of the Grand Union Canal, and the fragrance of the food stalls within it had reached them all the way on the pavement. Within, and mixing with the noise of rap music emanating from one of the shops, one could just discern the barking of food vendors hawking everything from stuffed jacket potatoes to chicken tikka masala.

"Barbara, c'n we go inside this place?" Hadiyyah asked again. "Oh, it's so *special*. And Dad'll *never* know. We won't be walloped. I promise, Barbara."

Barbara looked down at her shining face and knew she couldn't deny her the simple pleasure of a wander through the market. How much trouble could it cause, indeed, if they were to take half an hour more and poke about among the candles, the incense, the T-shirts, and the scarves? She could distract Hadiyyah from the drug paraphernalia and the body-piercing stalls if they came upon them. As to the rest of what Camden Lock Market offered, it was all fairly innocent.

Barbara smiled at her little companion. "What the hell," she said with a shrug. "Let's go."

They'd taken only two steps in their intended direction when Barbara's mobile phone rang, however. Barbara said, "Hang on," to Hadiyyah and read the incoming number. When she saw who it was, she knew the news was unlikely to be good.

"THE GAME'S AFOOT." It was Acting Superintendent Thomas Lynley's voice, and it bore an underlying note of tension the source of which he made clear when he added, "Get over to Hillier's office as quickly as you can."

"*Hillier*?" Barbara studied the mobile like an alien object while Hadiyyah waited patiently at her side, toeing a crack in the pavement and watching the mass of humanity part round them as it heaved its way towards one market or another. "AC Hillier can't have asked for me."

"You've got an hour," Lynley told her.

"But, sir—"

"He wanted thirty minutes, but we negotiated. Where are you?"

"Camden Lock Market."

"Can you get here in an hour?"

"I'll do my best." Barbara snapped the phone off and shoved it into her bag. She said, "Kiddo, we've got to save this for another day. Something's up at the Yard."

"Something bad?" Hadiyyah asked.

"Maybe yes, maybe no."

Barbara hoped for no. She hoped that what was up was an end to her period of punishment. She'd been suffering the mortification of demotion for months now, and she couldn't help anticipating an end to what she considered her professional ostracism every time Assistant Commissioner Sir David Hillier's name came up in conversation.

And now she was wanted. Wanted in AC Hillier's office. Wanted there by Hillier himself and by Lynley, who, Barbara knew, had been manoeuvring to get her back to her rank almost as soon as she'd had it stripped from her.

She and Hadiyyah virtually trotted all the way back to Eton Villas. They parted where the flagstone path divided at the corner of the house. Hadiyyah gave a wave before she skipped over to the ground-floor flat, where Barbara could see that the sticky note she'd left for the little girl's father had been removed from the door. She concluded that Azhar had returned with the surprise for his daughter, so she went to her bungalow for a hasty change of clothes.

The first decision she had to make—and quickly, because the hour Lynley had spoken of on the mobile was now forty-five minutes after her dash from the markets on Chalk Farm Road—was what to wear. Her choice needed to be professional without being an obvious ploy to win Hillier's approval. Trousers and a matching jacket would do the first without teetering too close to the second. So trousers and matching jacket it would be.

She found them where she'd last left them, in a ball behind the television set. She couldn't recall exactly how they'd got there, and she shook them out to survey the damage. Ah the beauty of polyester, she thought. One could be the victim of stampeding buffalo and still not bear a wrinkle to show it.

She set about changing into an ensemble of sorts. This was less about making a fashion statement and more about throwing on the trousers and rooting for a blouse without too many obvious creases in it. She decided on the least offensive shoes she owned—a pair of scuffed brogues that she donned in place of the red high-top trainers she preferred—and within five minutes she was able to grab two Chocotastic Pop-Tarts. She shoved them into her shoulder bag on her way out of the door.

Outside, there remained the question of transport: car, bus, or underground. All of them were risky: A bus would have to lumber through the clogged artery of Chalk Farm Road, a car meant engaging in creative rat running, and as for the underground . . . the underground line serving Chalk Farm was the notoriously unreliable Northern line. On the best of days, the wait alone could be twenty minutes.

Barbara opted for the car. She fashioned herself a route that would have done justice to Daedalus, and she managed to get herself down to Westminster only eleven and a half minutes behind schedule. Still, she knew that Hillier was not going to be chuffed with anything other than punctuality, so she blasted round the corner when she got to Victoria Street, and once she'd parked, she headed for the lifts at a run.

She stopped on the floor where Lynley had his temporary office, in the hope that he might have held off Hillier for the extra eleven and a half minutes it had taken her to get there. He hadn't done, or so his empty office suggested. Dorothea Harriman, the departmental secretary, confirmed Barbara's conclusion.

"He's up with the assistant commissioner, Detective Constable," she said. "He said you're to go up and join them. D'you know the hem's coming out of your trousers?"

"Is it? Damn," Barbara said.

"I've a needle if you want it."

"No time, Dee. D'you have a safety pin?"

Dorothea went to her desk. Barbara knew how unlikely it was that the other woman would have a pin. Indeed, Dee was always turned out so perfectly that it was tough to imagine her even in possession of a needle. She said, "No pin, Detective Constable. Sorry. But there's always this." She held up a stapler.

Barbara said, "Go for it. But be quick. I'm late."

"I know. You're missing a button from your cuff as well," Dorothea noted. "And there's . . . Detective Constable, you've got . . . Is this slut's wool on your backside?"

"Oh damn, *damn*," Barbara said. "Never mind. He'll have to take me as I am."

Which wasn't likely to be with open arms, she thought as she crossed over to Tower Block and took the lift up to Hillier's office. He'd been wanting to sack her for at least four years, and only the intervention of others had kept him from it.

Hillier's secretary—who always referred to herself as Judi-with-an-i-MacIntosh—told Barbara to go straight in. Sir David, she said, was waiting for her. *Had* been waiting with Acting Superintendent Lynley for a good many minutes, she added. She smiled insincerely and pointed to the door.

Inside, Barbara found Hillier and Lynley concluding a conference call with someone who was on Hillier's speakerphone talking about "preparing to engage in damage limitation."

"I expect we'll want a press conference, then," Hillier said. "And soon, so we don't end up seeming as if we're doing it just to appease Fleet Street. When can you manage it?"

"We'll be sorting that out directly. How closely do you want to be involved?"

"Very. And with an appropriate companion at hand."

"Fine. I'll be in touch then, David."

David and damage limitation, Barbara thought. The speaker was obviously a muckety-muck from the DPA.

Hillier ended the conversation. He looked at Lynley, said, "Well?" and then noticed Barbara, just inside the door. He said, "Where the hell have you been, Constable?"

So much, Barbara thought, for having a chance to polish anyone's apples. She said, "Sorry, sir," as Lynley turned in his chair. "Traffic was deadly."

"Life is deadly," Hillier said. "But that doesn't stop any of us from living it."

Absolute monarch of the flaming non sequitur, Barbara thought. She glanced at Lynley, who raised a warning index finger approximately half an inch. She said, "Yes, sir," and she joined the two officers at the conference table where Lynley was sitting and where Hillier had moved when he'd ended his phone call. She eased a chair out and slid onto it as unobtrusively as possible.

The table, she saw with a glance, held four sets of photographs. In them, four bodies lay. From where she sat, they appeared to be young adolescent boys, arranged on their backs, with their hands folded high on their chests in the manner of effigies on tombs. They would have looked like boys asleep had they not been cyanotic of face and necklaced with the mark of ligatures.

Barbara pursed her lips. "Holy hell," she said. "When did they . . . ?"

"Over the past three months," Hillier said.

"Three months? But why hasn't anyone . . . ?" Barbara looked from Hillier to Lynley. Lynley, she saw, looked deeply concerned; Hillier, always the most political of animals, looked wary. "I haven't heard a whisper about this. Or read a word in the papers. Or seen any reports on the telly. Four deaths. The same MO. All victims young. All victims male."

"Please try to sound a little less like an hysterical newsreader on cable television," Hillier said.

Lynley shifted position in his chair. He cast a look Barbara's way. His brown eyes were telling her to hold back from saying what they all were thinking until the two of them managed to get alone somewhere.

All right, Barbara thought. She would play it that way. She said in a careful, professional voice, "Who are they, then?"

"A, B, C, and D. We haven't any names."

"*No one* reported them missing? In three months?"

"That's evidently part of the problem," Lynley said.

"What d'you mean? Where were they found?"

Hillier indicated one of the photographs as he spoke. "The first . . . in Gunnersbury Park. September tenth. Found at eight-fifteen in the morning by a jogger needing to have a piss. There's an old garden inside the park, partially walled, not far off Gunnersbury Avenue. That looks to be the means of access. There're two boarded-up entrances there, right on the street."

"But he didn't die in the park," Barbara noted, with a nod at the photo in which the boy had been positioned supine on a mattress of weeds that grew at the juncture of two brick walls. There was nothing that suggested a struggle had taken place in the vicinity. There was also, in the entire stack of pictures from that crime scene, no photograph of the sort of evidence one expected to find where a murder occurs.

"No. He didn't die there. Nor did this one." Hillier picked up another batch of photographs. In it, the body of another slender boy was draped across the bonnet of a car, positioned as neatly as the first in Gunnersbury Park. "This one was found in an NCP car park at the top of Queensway. Just over five weeks later."

"What's the murder squad over there saying? Anything from CCTV?"

"The car park doesn't have closed-circuit cameras." Lynley answered Barbara's question. "There's a sign posted that there 'may' be cameras on the premises. But that's it. That's supposed to do the job of security."

"This one was in Quaker Street," Hillier went on, indicating a third set of photos. "An abandoned warehouse not far from Brick Lane. November twenty-fifth. And this—" he picked up the final batch and handed them over to Barbara—"is the latest. He was found in St. George's Gardens. Today."

Barbara glanced at the final set of pictures. In them, the body of an adolescent boy lay naked on the top of a lichen-covered tomb. The tomb itself sat on a lawn not far from a serpentine path. Beyond this, a brick wall fenced off not a cemetery—as one would expect from the tomb's presence—but a garden. Beyond the wall appeared to be a mews of garages and a block of flats behind them.

"St. George's Gardens?" Barbara asked. "Where is this place?"

"Not far from Russell Square."

"Who found the body?"

"The warden who opens the park every day. Our killer got access from the gates on Handel Street. They were chained up properly, but bolt cutters did the trick. He opened up, drove a vehicle inside, made his deposit on the tomb, and took off. Stopped to wrap the chain back round the gate so anyone passing wouldn't notice."

"Tyre prints in the garden?"

"Two decent ones. Casts are being made."

"Witnesses?" Barbara indicated the flats that lined the garden just beyond the mews.

"We've constables from the Theobald's Road station doing the door-to-door."

Barbara pulled all of the photographs towards her and laid the four victims in a row. She immediately took note of the differences—all of them major ones—between the final dead boy and the first three. All of them were young teenagers who'd died in an identical fashion, but unlike the first three boys, the latest victim was not only naked but also had a copious amount of makeup on: lipstick, eye shadow, liner, and mascara smeared across his face. Additionally, the killer had marked his body by slicing it open from sternum to waist and by drawing with blood an odd circular symbol on his forehead. The most potentially explosive political detail, however, had to do with race: Only the final victim was white. Of the earlier three, one was black and the two others were clearly mixed race: black and Asian, perhaps, black and Filipino, black and a blend of God only knew what.

Seeing this last feature, Barbara understood: why there had been no front-page newspaper coverage, why no television, and worst of all, why no whispers round New Scotland Yard. She raised her head. "Institutionalised racism. That's what they're going to claim, isn't it? No one across London—in any of the stations involved, right?—even twigged there's a serial killer at work. No one got round to comparing notes. This kid—" here she raised the photograph of the black youth—"might've been reported missing in Peckham. Maybe in Kilburn. Or Lewisham. Or anywhere. But his body wasn't dumped where he lived and disappeared from, was it, so the rozzers on his home patch called him a runaway, left it at that, and never matched him up to a murder that got reported in another station's patch. Is that what happened?"

"You can see the need for both delicacy and immediate action," Hillier said.

"Cheap murders, hardly worth investigating, all because of their race. That's what they're going to call the first three when the story gets out. The tabloids, television and radio news, the whole flaming lot."

"We intend to get the jump on what they call anything. If the truth be told, the tabloids, the broadsheets, the radio, and the television news—had they been attuned to what's going on and not intent on pursuing scandals among celebrities, the government, and the bloody royal family—might have broken this story themselves and crucified us on their front pages. As it is, they can hardly claim institutionalised racism for our failure to see what they themselves could have seen and did not. Rest assured that when each station's press officer released the news of a body being found, the story was judged a nonstarter by the media because of the victim: just another dead black boy. Cheap news. Not worth reporting. Ho-hum."

"With respect, sir," Barbara pointed out, "that's hardly going to stop them braying now."

"We'll see about that. Ah." Hillier smiled expansively as his office door swung open again. "Here's the gentleman we've been waiting for. Have they sorted out your paperwork, Winston? May we call you Sergeant Nkata officially?"

Barbara felt the question come at her like an unexpected blow. She looked at Lynley, but he was standing to greet Winston Nkata, who'd paused just inside the door. Unlike her, Nkata was dressed with the care he habitually employed: Everything about him was crisp and clean. In his presence—in the presence of all of them, come to that—Barbara felt like Cinderella in advance of the fairy godmother's visit.

She got to her feet. She was about to do the very worst thing for her career, but she didn't see any other way out . . . except the way out, which she decided to take. She said to her colleague, "Winnie. Brilliant. Cheers. I didn't know." And then to the other two ranking officers, "I've just remembered a phone call I'm meant to return."

Then she left the room.

ACTING SUPERINTENDENT Thomas Lynley felt the distinct need to follow Havers. At the same time, he recognised the wisdom of staying put. Ultimately, he knew, he'd probably be better able to do her service if at least one of them managed to remain in AC Hillier's good graces.

That, unfortunately, was never easy. The assistant commissioner's style of command generally existed on the border between Machiavellian and despotic, and rational individuals gave the man a very wide berth if they could. Lynley's own immediate superior—Malcolm Webberly, who'd been on medical leave for some time—had been running interference for both Lynley and Havers since the day he'd assigned them to their first case together. Without Webberly at New Scotland Yard, it fell to Lynley to recognise which side of the bread bore the butter.

The present situation was trying Lynley's determination to remain a disinterested party in his every interaction with Hillier. There'd been a moment early on when the AC could have easily told him about Winston Nkata's promotion: the very same moment when the man had refused to restore Barbara Havers to her rank.

What Hillier had said with little enough grace was, "I want you heading up this investigation, Lynley. Acting superintendent . . . I can hardly give it to anyone else. Malcolm would have wanted you on it anyway, so put together the team you need."

Lynley had mistakenly put the AC's laconism down to distress. Superintendent Malcolm Webberly was

Hillier's brother-in-law, after all, and the victim of an attempted homicide. Hillier doubtless worried about his recovery from the hit-and-run that had nearly killed him. So he said, "How's the superintendent's progress, sir?"

"This isn't the time to talk about the superintendent's progress," was Hillier's reply. "Are you heading this investigation or am I handing it over to one of your colleagues?"

"I'd like to have Barbara Havers back as sergeant to be part of the team."

"Would you. Well, this isn't a bargaining session. It's a Yes, I'll get to work directly, sir, or a Sorry, I'm going on an extended holiday."

So Lynley had been left with the Yes, I'll get to work directly, and no room to manoeuvre for Havers. He made a quick plan, though, which involved assigning his colleague to certain aspects of the investigation that would be guaranteed to highlight her strengths. Certainly, within the next few months he'd be able to right the wrongs that had been done to Barbara since the previous June.

Then, of course, he'd been blindsided by Hillier. Winston Nkata arrived, newly minted as sergeant, blocking Havers from promotion in the near future, and unaware of what his role was likely to be in the ensuing drama.

Lynley burned at all this, but he kept his features neutral. He was curious to see how Hillier was going to dance round the obvious when he assigned Nkata to be his right-hand man. Because there was no doubt in Lynley's mind that this was what AC Hillier intended to do. With one parent from Jamaica and the other from the Ivory Coast, Nkata was decidedly, handsomely, and suitably black. And once the news broke of a string of racial killings that had not been connected to one another when they damn well should have been, the black community was going to ignite. Not one Stephen Lawrence but three. With no excuse to be had but the most obvious, which Barbara Havers herself had stated in her usual, politically unastute manner: institutionalised racism that resulted in the police not actively pursuing the killers of young mixed-race boys and blacks. Just because.

Hillier was carefully oiling the skids in preparation. He seated Nkata at the conference table and brought him into the picture. He made no mention of the race of the first three victims, but Winston Nkata was nobody's fool.

"So you got trouble," was his cool observation at the end of Hillier's comments.

Hillier replied with studied calm. "The situation being what it is, we're trying to avoid trouble."

"Which's where I come in, right?"

"In a manner of speaking."

"What manner of speaking is that?" Nkata inquired. "How're you planning to keep this under the carpet? Not the fact of the killings, mind you, but the fact of nothing being done 'bout the killings."

Lynley controlled his need to smile. Ah, Winston, he thought. No one's dancing, blue-eyed boy.

"Investigations have been mounted on all the relevant patches," was Hillier's reply. "Admittedly, connections should have been made between the murders, and they weren't. Because of that, we at the Yard have taken over. I've instructed Acting Superintendent Lynley to put together a team. I want you playing a prominent role on it."

"You mean a token role," Nkata said.

"I mean a highly responsible, crucial—"

"—visible," Nkata cut in.

"—yes, all right. A visible role." Hillier's generally florid face was becoming quite ruddy. It was clear that the meeting wasn't following his preconceived scenario. Had he asked in advance, Lynley would have been happy to tell him that, having once done a stint as chief battle counsel for the Brixton Warriors and bearing the scars to show it, Winston Nkata was the last person one ought to fail to take seriously when devising one's political machinations. As it was, Lynley found himself enjoying the spectacle of the assistant commissioner floundering. He'd clearly expected the black man to snap joyfully at the chance to play a significant role in what was going to become a high-profile investigation. Since he wasn't doing that, Hillier was left walking a tightrope between the displeasure of an authority being questioned by such an underling and the political correctness of an ostensibly moderate English white man who, at heart, truly believed that rivers of blood were imminently due to flow in the streets of London.

Lynley decided to let them go at it alone. He got to his feet, saying, "I'll leave you to explain all the finer points of the case to Sergeant Nkata, sir. There're going to be countless details to organise: men to bring off rota and the like. I'd like to get Dee Harriman on all that straightaway." He gathered up the relevant documents and photographs and said to Nkata, "I'll be in my office when you're through here, Winnie."

"Sure," Nkata said. "Soon's we got the fine print read."

Lynley left the office and managed to keep himself from chuckling till he was some distance down the corridor. Havers, he knew, would have been difficult for Hillier to stomach as a detective sergeant once again. But Nkata was going to be a real challenge: proud, intelligent, clever, and quick. He was a man first, a black man second, and a cop only a distant third. Hillier, Lynley thought, had got every part of him in the wrong order.

He decided to use the stairs to descend to his office

once he crossed to Victoria Block, and that was where he found Barbara Havers. She was sitting on the top step, one flight down, smoking and picking at a loose thread on the cuff of her jacket.

Lynley said, "You're out of order, doing that here. You know that, don't you?" He joined her on the step.

She studied the glowing tip of the tobacco, then returned the cigarette to her mouth. She inhaled with showy satisfaction. "Maybe they'll sack me."

"Havers—"

"Did you know?" she asked abruptly.

He gave her the courtesy of not pretending to misunderstand. "Of course I didn't know. I would have told you. Got a message to you before you arrived. Something. He took me by surprise as well. As he doubtless intended."

She shrugged. "What the hell. It's not as if Winnie doesn't deserve it. He's good. Clever. Works well with everyone."

"He's putting Hillier through the paces, though. At least, he was when I left them."

"Has he twigged that he's to be window dressing? Black face at press conferences front and centre? No colour problems here, and look at this, everyone: We've got the proof in person? Hillier's so bloody obvious."

"Winston's five or six steps ahead of Hillier, I'd say."

"I should've stayed to see it."

"You should have done, Barbara. If nothing else, it would have been wise."

She tossed her cigarette to the landing below them. It rolled, stopped against the wall, and sent a lazy plume of smoke upwards. "When have I ever been that?"

Lynley looked her up and down. "With the ensemble today, as a matter of fact. Except . . ." He leaned forward to look towards her feet. "Are you actually holding the trousers together with staples, Barbara?"

"Quick, easy, and temporary. I'm a bird who hates commitment. I'd've used Sellotape but Dee recommended this. I shouldn't've bothered one way or the other."

Lynley rose from the step and extended his hand to help her up as well. "Apart from the staples, you've done yourself proud."

"Right. That's me. Today the Yard, tomorrow the catwalk," Havers said.

They descended to his temporary office. Dorothea Harriman came to the door once he and Havers were spreading the case materials out on the conference table. She said, "Sh'll I start phoning them in, Acting Superintendent Lynley?"

"The secretarial grapevine round here is, as ever, a model of efficiency," Lynley noted. "Bring Stewart off rota to run the incident room. Hale's in Scotland and MacPherson's involved with that forged-documents situation, so leave them be. And send Winston through when he gets down from Hillier."

"Detective Sergeant Nkata, right." Harriman was making her usual competent notes on a sticky pad.

"You know about Winnie as well?" Havers asked, impressed. "Already? Have you got a snout up there or something, Dee?"

"The cultivation of resources should be the aim of every dutiful police employee," Harriman said piously.

"Cultivate someone across the river, then," Lynley said. "I want all the forensic material SO7 has on the older cases. Then phone each police borough where a body was found and get every scrap of every report and every statement they have on these crimes. Havers, in the meantime, you'll need to get on to the PNC—grab at least two DCs from Stewart to help you—and pull out every missing-persons report filed in the last three months for adolescent boys ages . . ." He looked at the photos. "I think twelve to sixteen should do it." He tapped the picture of the most recent victim, the boy with makeup smeared across his face. "And I think we'll want to check with Vice on this one. It's a route to go with all of them, in fact."

Havers picked up on the direction his thoughts were taking. "If they're rent boys, sir—runaways who happened to fall into the game, say—then it may be there's no missing-person report filed for any one of them. At least not in the same month they were killed."

"Indeed," Lynley said. "So we'll work backwards in time if we have to. But we've got to start somewhere, so let's keep it at three months for now."

Havers and Harriman left to see to their respective assignments. Lynley sat at the table and felt in his jacket pocket for his reading spectacles. He took another look at the photographs, spending the most time on those pictures of the final killing. They could not, he knew, accurately portray the understated enormity of the crime itself as he'd seen it earlier that day.

When he had arrived at St. George's Gardens, the scythe-shaped area held a full complement of detectives, uniformed constables, and scenes-of-crime officers. The forensic pathologist was still on the scene, bundled against the grey-day cold in a mustard anorak, and the police photographer and videographer had just completed their work. Outside the tall wrought-iron gates of the gardens, the public had begun to gather, and from the windows of the buildings just beyond the garden's brick wall and the mews behind it, more spectators were observing the activity taking place: the careful fingertip search for evidence, the minute examination of a discarded bicycle that sprawled near a statue of Minerva, the collection of silver objects that were scattered on the ground round a tomb.

Lynley hadn't known what to expect when he showed his ID at the gate and followed the path to the professionals. The phone call he'd received had used the phrase "possible serial killing" and because of this, as he walked, he steeled himself to see something terrible: a disembowelment in the manner of Jack the Ripper, perhaps, a decapitation or dismemberment. He'd assumed it would be the horrific that he would be gazing upon when he worked his way to look at the top of the tomb in question. What he hadn't assumed was that it would be the sinister.

Yet that was what the body represented to him: the sinister, left hand of evil. Ritualistic killings always struck him that way. And that this murder had been a ritual was something that he did not doubt.

The effigylike arrangement of the body served to encourage that deduction, but so did the mark in blood on the forehead: a crude circle crisscrossed by two lines that each bore cruciforms at the top and the bottom. Additionally, the element of a loincloth added support to this conclusion: an odd, lace-edged piece of fabric, which had been tucked, as if lovingly, round the genitals.

As Lynley donned the latex gloves and stepped to the side of the tomb to gaze more closely upon the body, he saw and learned of the rest of the signs that pointed to some sort of arcane rite having been carried out upon it. "What've we got?" he murmured to the forensic pathologist, who'd been snapping off his gloves and shoving them into his pocket.

"Two A.M. or thereabouts," was the succinct reply. "Strangulation, obviously. Incised wounds all inflicted after death. One cut for the primary incision down the torso, with no hesitation. Then . . . see the separation here? Just at the area of the sternum? It looks like our knife man dipped his hands inside and forced a bigger opening, like a quack surgeon. We won't know if anything's missing inside him till we cut him open ourselves. Looks doubtful, though."

Lynley noticed the inflection the pathologist had given to the word *inside.* He glanced quickly at the victim's folded hands and his feet. All digits accounted for. He said, "As to outside the body? Is something missing?"

"The navel. It's been chopped right off. Have a look."

"Christ."

"Yes. Ope's got a dodgy one on her hands."

Ope turned out to be a grey-haired woman in scarlet earmuffs and matching mittens who came striding towards Lynley from a group of uniformed constables who'd been in some sort of discussion when he'd arrived on the scene. She introduced herself as DCI Opal Towers, from Theobald's Road police station, in whose patch they were currently standing. She'd taken just one look at the body and concluded they had a killer who "could definitely go serial," she'd explained. She'd mistakenly thought that the boy on the tomb was the unfortunate initial victim of someone they could identify quickly and stop before he struck again. "But then DC Hartell over there"—with a nod towards a baby-faced detective constable who chewed gum compulsively and watched them with the nervous eyes of someone expecting a dressing down—"said he'd seen a killing something like this in Tower Hamlets when he worked out of the Brick Lane station a while back. I phoned his former guv and we had a few words. We think we're looking at the same killer in both cases."

At the time, Lynley hadn't asked why she'd then phoned the Met. He hadn't known till he met with Hillier that there were additional victims. He hadn't known that three of the victims were racial minorities. And he hadn't known that not a single one of them had yet been identified by the police. All that was later spelled out to him by Hillier. In St. George's Gardens, he merely reached the conclusion that reinforcements were called for and that someone was needed to coordinate an investigation that was going to involve turf in two radically different parts of town: Brick Lane in Tower Hamlets was the centre of the Bangladeshi community, containing remnants of the West Indian population who had once been its majority, while the area of St. Pancras, where St. George's Gardens formed a green oasis among distinguished Georgian conversions, was decidedly monochromatic, the colour in question being white.

He said to DCI Towers, "How far has Brick Lane got in their investigation?"

She shook her head and looked towards the wrought-iron gates through which Lynley had come. He followed her gaze and saw that members of the press and television news—distinguished by their notebooks, their handheld tape recorders, and the vans from which video cameras were being unloaded—had begun to gather. A press officer was directing them to one side. She said, "According to Hartell, Brick Lane did sod all, which is why he wanted out of the place. He says it's an endemic problem. Now, could be he just has an axe he's grinding on the reputation of his ex-guv over there, or could be those blokes've been sleeping at the wheel. But in either case, we've got some sorting to do." She hunched her shoulders and drove her mittened hands into the pockets of her down jacket. She nodded at the news people. "To say they're going to have a field day if they twig all that . . . Between you, me, and the footpath, I thought it best we look like we've got coppers from bottom to top crawling all over this."

Lynley eyed her with some interest. She certainly didn't look like a political animal, but it was clear that she was quick on her feet. Nonetheless he felt it wise to ask, "You're sure about what Constable Hartell is claiming, then?"

"Wasn't at first," she admitted. "But he convinced me quick enough."

"How?"

"He didn't get as close a look at the body as I did, but he took me aside and asked about the hands."

"The hands? What about the hands?"

She gave him a glance. "You didn't see them? You best come with me, Superintendent."

Chapter Two

Despite the early hour at which he rose the next morning, Lynley found that his wife was already up. He found her in what was going to be their baby's nursery, where yellow, white, and green were the colours of choice, a cot and changing table comprised the furniture delivered so far, and photographs clipped from magazines and catalogues indicated the placement of everything else: a toy chest here, a rocking chair there, and a chest of drawers moved daily from point A to point B. In her first trimester, Helen was nothing if not changeable when it came to the appearance of their son's nursery.

She was standing before the changing table, her hands massaging the small of her back. Lynley joined her, brushing her hair away from her neck, making a bare spot for his kiss. She leaned back against him. She said, "You know, Tommy, I never expected impending parenthood to be so political an event."

"Is it? How?"

She gestured to the surface of the changing table. There, Lynley saw, the remains of a package lay. It had obviously come by post on the previous day, and Helen had opened it and spread its contents upon the table. These consisted of an infant's snowy christening garments: gown, shawl, cap, and shoes. Next to them lay yet *another* set of christening garments: another gown, shawl, and cap. Lynley picked up the postal wrapping that had covered the box. He saw the name and the return address. "Daphne Amalfini," he read. She lived in Italy, one of Helen's four sisters.

He said, "What's going on?"

"Battle lines are being drawn. I hate to tell you, but I'm afraid that soon we'll have to choose a side."

"Ah. Right. I take it that these . . . ?" Lynley indicated the set of garments most recently unpacked.

"Yes. Daphne sent them along. With a rather sweet note, by the way, but there's no mistaking the meaningful subtext. She knows that your sister *must* have sent us the ancestral Lynley baptismal regalia, being so far the only reproductive Lynley of the current generation. But Daph seems to think that five Clyde sisters procreating like bunnies is reason enough why the Clyde apparel should be sufficient unto the christening day. No, that's not right. Not sufficient unto the day at all. More like de rigueur for the day. It's all ridiculous—believe me, I *know*—but it's one of those family situations that ends up being blown out of proportion if one doesn't handle it correctly." She looked at him and offered a quirky smile. "It's utterly stupid, isn't it? Hardly comparable to what you're dealing with. What time did you actually get home last night? Did you find your dinner in the fridge?"

"I thought I'd eat it for breakfast, actually."

"Take-away garlic chicken?"

"Well. Perhaps not."

"Any suggestions you care to make about the christening clothes, then? And don't suggest we forego the christening altogether, because I don't want to be responsible for my father's having a stroke."

Lynley thought about the situation. On the one hand, the christening garments from his own family had been used for at least five—if not six—generations of infant Lynleys as they were ushered into Christendom, so there was a tradition established in using them. On the other hand, if the truth were told, the clothes were beginning to *look* as if five or six generations of infant Lynleys had worn them. On the other, other hand—presuming three hands were possible in this matter—every child of every one of the five Clyde sisters had worn the more recently vintaged Clyde family raiment, and thus a tradition was being *started* there, and it would be pleasant to uphold it. So . . . what to do?

Helen was right. It was just the sort of idiotic situation that bent everyone out of shape. Some sort of diplomatic resolution was called for.

"We can claim both sets were lost in the post," he offered.

"I had no idea you were such a moral coward. Your sister already knows hers arrived, and in any case, I'm a dreadful liar."

"Then I must leave you to work out a Solomon-like solution."

"A distinct possibility, now that you mention it," Helen remarked. "A careful application of the scissors first, right up the middle of each. Then needle, thread, and everyone's happy."

"And a new tradition's begun into the bargain."

They both gazed at the two christening ensembles and then at each other. Helen looked mischievous. Lynley laughed. "We don't dare," he said. "You'll work it out in your inimitable fashion."

"Two christenings, then?"

"You're on the path to solution already."

"And what path are you on? You're up early. Our Jasper Felix awakened me doing gymnastics in my stomach. What's your excuse?"

"I'd like to head off Hillier if I can. The Press Bureau

are setting up a meeting with the media, and Hillier wants Winston there, right at his side. I'm not going to be able to talk him out of that, but I'm hoping to get him to keep it low key."

He maintained that hope all the way to New Scotland Yard. There, however, he soon enough saw that forces superior even to AC Hillier were at work, making Big Plans in the person of Stephenson Deacon, head of the Press Bureau and intent upon justifying his present job and possibly his entire career. He was doing this by means of orchestrating the assistant commissioner's first meeting with the press, which apparently involved not only the presence of Winston Nkata at Hillier's side but also a dais set up before a curtained background with the Union Jack draped artfully nearby, as well as detailed press kits manufactured to present a dizzying amount of noninformation. At the rear of the conference room, someone had also arranged a table that looked suspiciously intended for refreshments.

Lynley evaluated all of this bleakly. Whatever hopes he'd had of talking Hillier into a subtler approach were thoroughly dashed. The Directorate of Public Affairs were involved now, and that division of the Met reported not to AC Hillier but to *his* superior, the deputy comissioner. The lower downs—Lynley among them—were obviously being transformed into cogs in the vast machinery of public relations. Lynley realised that the best he could do was to protect Nkata from the exposure as much as possible.

The new detective sergeant had already been there. He'd been told where to sit when the press conference took place and what to say should he be asked any questions. Lynley found him steaming in the corridor. The Caribbean in his voice, child of his West Indian mother, always came out in moments of stress. *Th* became either *d* or *t*. *Man*—pronounced *mon*—worked its way forward as interjection of choice.

"I di'n't get into this to be some dancing monkey," Nkata said. "My job i'n't meant to be all about my mum turning on the telly and seeing my mug on the screen. He thinks I'm dim, that's what he thinks. I'm here to tell him I'm not."

"This goes beyond Hillier," Lynley said, with a nod of greeting to one of the sound technicians, who was ducking into the conference room. "Stay calm and put up with it for the moment, Winnie. It'll be to your advantage in the long run, depending on what you want to do with your career."

"But you know why I'm here. You bloody *know* why."

"Put it down to Deacon," Lynley said. "The Press Bureau are cynical enough to think the public will leap to a preordained conclusion when they see you on the dais elbow to elbow with the assistant commissioner of the Met. Just now Deacon's arrogant enough to think your appearance there will quiet speculation in the press. But none of that is a reflection on you, either personally or professionally. You've got to remember that in order to get through this."

"Yeah? Well, I don't believe it, man. And if there's speculation out there, then it's deserved. How many more dead is't going to take? Black-on-black crime is *still* that: crime. With next to no one looking into it. An' if this partic'lar situation happens to be *white*-on-black crime and it's gone ignored, having me acting like Hillier's right-hand man when you and he both know he wouldn't've even promoted me if the circumstances'd been different . . ." Here Nkata paused, drawing breath as he seemed to search for just the right peroration to his remarks.

"Murder as politics," Lynley said. "Yes. That's it. Is that nasty? Undoubtedly. Is it cynical? Yes. Unpleasant? Yes. Machiavellian? Yes. But at the end of the day, it doesn't mean you need to be—or are—anything less than a decent officer."

Hillier came out of the room then. He looked pleased with whatever Stephenson Deacon had set up for the coming press briefing. "We'll be buying at least forty-eight hours once we've met with them," he said to Lynley and Nkata. "Winston, mind you remember your part."

Lynley waited to see how Nkata would react. To his credit, Winston did nothing but nod neutrally. But when Hillier walked off in the direction of the lifts, he said to Lynley, "These're kids we're talking about. Dead *kids*, man."

"Winston," Lynley said, "I know."

"What's he doing, then?"

"I believe he's positioning the press to take a fall."

Nkata looked in the direction Hillier had taken. "How's he going to manage that?"

"By waiting long enough for them to expose their bias before he talks to them. He knows the papers will get on to the fact that the earlier victims were black and mixed race, and when they do, they'll start baying for our blood. What were we doing, asleep at the wheel, et cetera, et cetera. At that point, he'll counter with piously wondering why it's taken *them* so long to glean what the cops knew—and told the press—from the first. This last death makes page one of every paper. It runs near the front of the evening news. But what about the others? he'll ask. Why weren't they considered top stories?"

"Hillier's taking the offensive, then," Nkata said.

"It's why he's good at what he does, most of the time."

Nkata looked disgusted. "Four white boys killed in different parts of town and the coppers'd be liaising themselves like the bloody dickens from the first."

"They probably would."

"Then—"

"We can't correct their failures, Winston. We can

loathe them and try to change them for the future. But we can't go back and make them different."

"We c'n keep them from being swept under the rug."

"We could champion that cause. Yes. I agree." And as Nkata started to say more, Lynley plunged on with, "But while we do that, a killer goes on killing. So what have we gained? Have we unburied the dead? Brought anyone to justice? Believe me, Winston, the press will recover from Hillier's allegations about the pot and the kettle shortly after he makes them, and when they do, they'll be all over him, like gnats on fruit. In the meantime, we've got four killings to deal with properly, and we won't be able to do that if we don't have the cooperation of those very same murder squads you're hot to expose as bigoted and corrupt. Does that make sense to you?"

Nkata thought about this. He finally said, "I want a real role in all this. I got no plans to be Hillier's *lad* at press conferences, man."

"Understood and agreed," Lynley said. "You're a DS now. No one's likely to forget that. Let's get to work."

The incident room had been set up a short distance from Lynley's office, where uniformed PCs were already at the computer terminals, logging information that was coming in per Lynley's request to the police boroughs where the earlier bodies had been found. China boards held crime-scene photographs along with a large schedule containing team members' names and the identifying numbers of the actions assigned to them. Technicians had set up three video machines so that someone could review all relevant CCTV tapes—where and if they existed—from every area where the bodies had been dumped, and their flexes and cords snaked along the floor. The telephones were already ringing. Manning them at the moment were Lynley's longtime colleague, DI John Stewart and two DCs. The former was seated at a desk already compulsively organised.

Barbara Havers was in the midst of highlighting data sheets with a yellow marker when Lynley and Nkata walked in. At her elbow sat an opened package of Mr. Kipling strawberry jam tarts and a cup of coffee, which she drained with a grimace, and a "Bloody hell. Cold," after which she looked longingly at a packet of Players half-buried beneath a pile of printouts.

"Don't even think of it," Lynley told her. "What've you got from SO5?"

She set down her marker pen and worked the muscles of her shoulders. "You're going to want to keep this one away from the press."

"Now that's a fine beginning," Lynley commented. "Let's have it, then."

"Going back three months, Juvenile Index and Missing Persons together coughed up fifteen hundred and seventy-four names."

"Damn." Lynley took the data sheets from her and flipped through them impatiently. Across the room, DI Stewart rang off and finished his notes.

"You ask me," Havers said, "it looks like things haven't changed much since the last time SO5 faced the press about not keeping their systems up to date. You'd think they wouldn't want egg on their neckties again."

"You'd think so," Lynley agreed. As a matter of course, the names of children reported missing went into the system at once. But often, when the child was found, the name was not then *removed* from the system. Nor was it necessarily removed when children who might have started out missing ended up either incarcerated as youth offenders or placed in the care of Social Services. It was a case of the left and right hands not knowing, and more than once this sort of inefficiency on the part of Missing Persons had created a logjam in an investigation.

"I'm reading the news on your face," Havers said,

"but no way can I do this alone, sir. More than fifteen hundred names? By the time I get through them all, this bloke"—with a jerk of her head towards the photographs posted on the china board—"he'll have his next seven victims dispatched."

"We'll get you some help," Lynley said. To Stewart, "John? Get some additional manpower for this. Put half on the phones checking to see if these kids have turned up since they went missing and have the other half go for a match: our four bodies to descriptions in the paperwork. Anything remotely possible that could allow us to tie a name to a corpse, run with it. And what've we heard from Vice on the most recent body? Has Theobald's Road given us anything on the boy in St. George's Gardens? Has King's Cross? What about Tolpuddle Street?"

DI Stewart took up a notebook. "According to Vice, the description doesn't fit any boy recently on the job anywhere. Among the regulars, no one's missing. So far."

"Get on to Vice where the other bodies were found as well," Lynley said to Havers. "See if you can make a match with anyone reported missing there." He went to the china board, where he gazed at the photos of the most recent victim. John Stewart joined him. As usual, the DI was nervous energy combined with an obsession for detail. The notebook he carried was open to an outline, which he'd done in various colours significant only to himself. Lynley said to him, "What've we got from across the river?"

"No reports yet," Stewart said. "I checked with Dee Harriman not ten minutes ago."

"We'll want them to test the makeup this boy's wearing, John. See if we can track down the manufacturer. Could be our victim didn't put it on himself. If that's the case and if the makeup's not something available at every Boots in town, the point of sale could move us in the right direction. In the meantime, run a check on recent releases from prison and from mental hospitals. Recent releases from every youth facility within one hundred miles as well. And this works in both directions, so keep that in mind."

"Both directions?" Stewart looked up from his furious writing.

"Our killer could come from one of them. But so could our victims. And until we have a positive identification on all four of these boys, we don't know exactly what we're dealing with, except the most obvious."

"One sick bastard."

"There's enough evidence on the last body to attest to that," Lynley agreed. His gaze went to that evidence even as he spoke, as if drawn there without his intention: the long postmortem incision on the torso, the blood-drawn symbol on the forehead, the missing navel, and what hadn't been noted or photographed until the body was moved for the very first time: the palms of the hands burned so thoroughly that the flesh was black.

He shifted his gaze to the list of actions he'd already assigned on the previous long night of setting up the team: There were men and women knocking on doors in the vicinity where every one of the first three bodies had been found; additional officers were studying prior arrests to see if any lesser crimes had been documented that bore the hallmark of escalating behaviour which might lead to such murders as they now had on their hands. This was well and good, but they also needed to get someone on to the loincloth that had dressed the final body, someone to deal with the bicycle and the pieces of silver that had been left at the scene, someone to triangulate and analyse all of the crime scenes, someone to run down all sex offenders and their alibis, and someone to check throughout the rest of the country to see if there were similar unsolved murders elsewhere. They knew they had four, but there was every possibility that they had fourteen. Or forty.

Eighteen police detectives and six police constables were working the case at this moment, but Lynley knew without a doubt they were going to need more. There was only one way to get them.

Sir David Hillier, Lynley thought sardonically, was going to love and hate that fact simultaneously. He'd be pleased as punch to announce to the press that thirty-plus officers were working the case. But he'd hate like the dickens having to authorise the overtime for them all.

Such, however, was Hillier's lot in life. Such were the disadvantages of ambition.

BY THE NEXT AFTERNOON, Lynley had in hand from SO7 the complete autopsies of the first three victims and the preliminary postmortem information from the most recent killing. He combined this with an extra set of photographs from all four of the murder scenes. He packed this material into his briefcase, went for his car, and set out from Victoria Street in a light mist that was blowing in from the river. Traffic was stop and start, but when he finally got over to Millbank, he had the river to contemplate . . . or what he could see of it, which was mostly the wall built along the pavement and the old iron street lamps that cast a glow against the gloom.

He veered to the right when he came to Cheyne Walk, where he found a place to park that was being vacated by someone leaving the King's Head and Eight Bells at the bottom of Cheyne Row. It was a short distance from there to the house at the corner of this street and Lordship Place. Less than five minutes found him ringing the bell.

He anticipated the barking of one very protective long-haired dachshund, but that didn't happen. Instead the door was opened by a tallish red-haired woman with a pair of scissors in one hand and a roll of yellow ribbon in the other. Her face brightened when she saw him.

"Tommy!" Deborah St. James said. "Perfect timing. I need help and here you are."

Lynley entered the house, shedding his overcoat and setting his briefcase by the umbrella stand. "What sort of help? Where's Simon?"

"I've already roped him into something else. And one can only ask husbands for so much assistance before they run off with the local floozy from the pub."

Lynley smiled. "What am I to do?"

"Come with me." She led him to the dining room, where an old bronze chandelier was lit over a table spread with wrapping materials. A large package there was already brightly wrapped, and Deborah seemed to have been caught in the midst of designing a complicated bow for it.

"This," Lynley said, "is not going to be my métier."

"Oh, the plans are laid," Deborah told him. "You're only going to need to hand over the Sellotape and press where indicated. It shouldn't defeat you. I've started with the yellow, but there's green and white to add."

"Those are the colours Helen's chosen . . ." Lynley stopped. "Is this for her? For us? By any chance?"

"How vulgar, Tommy," Deborah said. "I never saw you as someone who'd hint round for a present. Here, take this ribbon. I'm going to need three lengths of forty inches each. How's work, by the way? Is that why you've come? I expect you're wanting Simon."

"Peach will do. Where is she?"

"Walkies," Deborah said. "Rather reluctant walkies because of the weather. Dad's taken her, but I expect they're battling it out somewhere to see who's going to walk and who's going to get carried. You didn't see them?"

"Not a sign."

"Peach has probably won, then. I expect they've gone into the pub."

Lynley watched as Deborah coiled the lengths of ribbon together. She was concentrating on her design, which gave him a chance to concentrate on her, his onetime lover, the woman who'd been meant to be his wife. She'd found herself face-to-face with a killer recently, and she still hadn't healed completely from the stitches that had patched up her face. A scar from the sutures ran along her jaw and, typical of Deborah—who'd always been a woman almost completely devoid of ordinary vanity—she was doing nothing to hide it.

She looked up and caught him observing her. "What?" she said.

"I love you," he told her frankly. "Differently from before. But there it is."

Her features softened. "And I love you, Tommy. We've crossed over, haven't we? New territory but still somchow familiar."

"That's exactly how it is."

They heard footsteps then, coming along the corridor, and the uneven nature of them identified Deborah's husband. He came to the door of the dining room with a stack of large photographs in his hands. He said, "Tommy. Hullo. I didn't hear you come in."

"No Peach," Deborah and Lynley said together, then laughed companionably.

"I knew that dog was good for something." Simon St. James came to the table and laid the photographs down. "It wasn't an easy choice," he told his wife.

St. James was referring to the photographs which, as far as Lynley could see, were all of the same subject: a windmill in a landscape comprising field, trees, background hillsides, and foreground cottage tumbling to ruins. He said, "May I . . . ," and when Deborah nodded, he looked at the pictures more closely. The exposure, he saw, was slightly different in each, but what was remarkable about them all was the manner in which the photographer had managed to catch all the variations of light and dark while at the same time not losing the definition of a single subject.

"I've gone for the one where you've enhanced the moonlight on the windmill's sails," St. James told his wife.

"I thought that was the best one as well. Thank you, love. Always my best critic." She completed her task with the bow and had Lynley assist with the Sellotape. When she was done, she stood back to admire her work, after which she took a sealed envelope from the sideboard and slipped it into place on the package. She handed it over to Lynley. "With our fondest wishes, Tommy," she said. "Truly and completely."

Lynley knew the journey Deborah had traveled in order to be able to say those words. Having a child of her own was something denied her.

"Thank you." He found that his voice was rougher than usual. "Both of you."

There was a moment of silence among them, which St. James broke by saying lightly, "A drink is in order, I think."

Deborah said she would join them as soon as she'd sorted out the mess she'd made in the dining room. St. James led Lynley from there to his study, just along the corridor and overlooking the street. Lynley fetched his briefcase from the entry then, leaving the wrapped package in its place. When he joined his old friend, St. James was at the drinks cart beneath the window, a decanter in his hand.

"Sherry?" he said. "Whisky?"

"Have you gone through all the Lagavullin yet?"

"Too hard to come by. I'm pacing myself."

"I'll assist you."

St. James poured them both a whisky and added a sherry for Deborah, which he left on the cart. He joined Lynley by the fireplace and eased himself into one of the two old leather chairs to one side of it, something of an awkward business for him, owing to the brace he'd worn for years on his left leg.

He said, "I picked up an *Evening Standard* this afternoon. It looks like a messy business, Tommy, if my reading between the lines is any good."

"So you know why I've come."

"Who's working on the case with you?"

"The usual suspects. I'm after clearance to add to the team. Hillier will give it, reluctantly, but what choice has he? We're going to need fifty officers, but we'll be lucky to end up with thirty. Will you help?"

"You expect Hillier to give clearance for me?"

"I've a feeling he'll greet you with open arms. We need your expertise, Simon. And the Press Bureau will be only too happy to have Hillier announcing to the media the inclusion of independent forensic scientist Simon Allcourt-St. James, formerly of the Metropolitan police, now an expert witness, university lecturer, public speaker, et cetera. Just the sort of thing to restore public confidence. But don't let that pressure you."

"What would you have me do? My crime-scene days are far and away gone. And God willing, you won't have further crime scenes anyway."

"You'd consult. I won't lie to you and say it wouldn't impinge on everything else you have on your plate. But I'd try to keep the requests to a minimum."

"Let me see what you have, then. You've brought copies of everything?"

Lynley opened his briefcase and handed over what he'd gathered before leaving Scotland Yard. St. James set the paperwork to one side and went through the photographs. He whistled silently. When he looked up at last, he said to Lynley, "They didn't jump to serial killing at once?"

"So you see the problem."

"But these have all the hallmarks of a ritual. The burnt hands alone . . ."

"Just on the final three."

"Still, with the similarities all along in the positioning of the bodies, they're as good as advertising themselves as serial killings."

"For the latest one—the body in St. George's Gardens?—the DCI on scene marked it as a serial killing at once."

"As to the others?"

"Each body was left on the patch of a different station. In every case, they appear to have gone through the motions of an investigation, but it seems it was easy to call each of them a one-off crime. Gang related because of the race of the victims. Gang related because of the condition of the bodies. Marked in some way with the signature of a gang. As a warning to others."

"That's nonsense."

"I'm not excusing it."

"It's a PR nightmare for the Met, I daresay."

"Yes. Will you help?"

"Can you fetch my glass from the desk? It's in the top drawer."

Lynley did so. A chamois pouch held the magnifying glass, and he brought this to his friend and watched while St. James studied the photographs of the corpses more closely. He spent the most time over the recent crime, and he gazed long upon the face of the victim before he spoke. Even then it seemed he spoke more to himself than to Lynley.

"The abdominal incision on the final body is obviously postmortem," he said. "But the burning of the hands . . . ?"

"Before death," Lynley agreed.

"That makes it very interesting, doesn't it?" St. James looked up for a moment, thoughtfully, his gaze on the window, before he examined victim four another time. "He's not particularly good with the knife. No indecision about *where* to cut, but surprised to discover it wasn't easy."

"Not a medical student or a doctor, then."

"I shouldn't think so."

"What sort of implement?"

"A very sharp knife will have worked just fine. A kitchen knife, perhaps. That and a certain amount of strength because of all the abdominal muscles involved. And to create this aperture . . . That can't have been easy. He's quite strong."

"He's taken the navel, Simon. On the final body."

"Gruesome," St. James acknowledged. "One would think he's made the incision just to get enough blood to make the mark on the forehead, but taking the navel discounts that theory, doesn't it? What d'you make of the forehead mark, by the way?"

"A symbol, obviously."

"The killer's signature?"

"In part, I'd say so. But more than that. If the entire crime is part of a ritual—"

"And it looks like that, doesn't it?"

"Then I'd say this is the final part of the ceremony. A full stop after the victim dies."

"It's saying something, then."

"Definitely."

"But to whom? To the police who've failed to grasp that a serial killer's at work in the community? To the victim who's just completed a real trial by fire? To someone else?"

"That's the question, isn't it?"

St. James nodded. He laid the pictures to one side and took up his whisky. "Then that's where I'll begin," he said.

Chapter Three

When she turned off the ignition that evening, Barbara Havers remained inside the Mini, once again listening disconsolately to its sputtering engine. She rested her head on the steering wheel. She was knackered. Odd to think that spending hours upon hours on computers and telephones was more exhausting than hoofing round London to track down witnesses, suspects, reports, and background information, but that was the case. There was something about staring at a computer terminal, reading and highlighting printouts, and running through the same monologue on the phone with one desperate set of parents after another that made her long for baked beans on toast—bring on a tin of Heinz, that ultimate comfort food—followed by a horizontal position on the daybed with the television remote tucked in her hand. Simply put, she hadn't had an easy time for one moment during the first two endless days.

First there was the subject of Winston Nkata. Detective *Sergeant* Winston Nkata. It was one thing to know why Hillier had promoted her colleague at this particular point in time. It was quite another to realise that, victim of political machination or not, Winston actually did deserve the rank. What made it all worse was having to work with him in spite of this knowledge, realising that he was just as uneasy with the whole situation as she was.

Had Winston been smug, she would have known how to cope. Had he been arrogant, she would have had a bloody good time taking the piss. Had he been ostentatiously humble, she could have dealt with that in a satisfyingly biting fashion. But he was none of that, just a quieter version of regular Winston, a version that affirmed what Lynley had indicated: Winnie was nobody's fool; he knew perfectly well what Hillier and the DPA were trying to do.

So ultimately, Barbara felt sympathy for her colleague, and that sympathy had inspired her to fetch him a cup of tea when she fetched one for herself, saying, "Well done on the promotion, Winnie," as she placed it next to him.

Along with the constables assigned by DI Stewart, Barbara had spent two days and two evenings coping with the overwhelming number of missing-persons reports that she had pulled from SO5. Ultimately Nkata had joined the project. They had managed to cross off the list a good number of names in that time: kids who had returned to their homes or had contacted their families in some way, making their whereabouts known. A few of them—as expected—had turned up incarcerated. Others had been tracked down in care. But there were hundreds upon hundreds unaccounted for, which took the detectives to the job of comparing descriptions of missing adolescents with descriptions of the unidentified corpses. Part of this could be done by computer. Part of it had to be done by hand.

They had the photographs and the autopsy reports from the first three victims to work from, and both parents and guardians of the missing kids were almost universally cooperative. Eventually, they even had one possible identity established, but the likelihood was remote that the missing boy in question was truly one of the bodies they had.

Thirteen years old, mixed race, black and Filipino, shaved head, nose flattened on the end and broken at the bridge. . . . He was called Jared Salvatore, and he'd been gone nearly two months, reported missing by his older brother who—so it was noted in the paperwork—had made the call to the cops from Pentonville Prison where he himself was banged up for armed robbery. How the older brother had come to know young Jared was missing was not documented in the report.

But that was it. Sorting out identities for each corpse from the vast number of missing kids they had was thus going to be like picking fly poo out of pepper if they couldn't come up with some kind of connection between the murder victims. And considering how widespread the body sites were, a connection seemed unlikely.

When she'd had enough—or at least as much as she could handle for the day—Barbara had said to Nkata, "I'm out of here, Winnie. You staying or what?"

Nkata had pushed back his chair, rubbed his neck, and said, "I'll stay for a while."

She nodded but didn't leave at once. It seemed to her that they both needed to say something, although she wasn't sure what. Nkata was the one who took the plunge.

"What d'we do with all this, Barb?" He set his biro on a legal pad. "Question is, how do we *be*? We can't 'xactly ignore the situation."

Barbara sat back down. There was a magnetic paperclip holder on the desk, and she picked this up and played with it. "I think we just do what needs doing. I expect the rest will sort itself out."

He nodded thoughtfully. "I don't sit easy with this. I know why I'm here. I want you to unnerstan that."

"Got it," Barbara said. "But don't be rough on yourself. You deserve—"

"Hillier wouldn't know sod all 'bout what I deserve," Nkata cut in. "Not to mention DPA. Not before this, not now, and not later."

Barbara was silent. She couldn't dispute what they both knew to be the truth. She finally said, "You know, Winnie, we're sort of in the same position."

"How d'you mean? Woman cop, black cop?"

"Not that. It's more about vision. Hillier doesn't really see either one of us. Fact is, you can apply that to everyone on this team. He doesn't see any of us, just how we can either help him or hurt him."

Nkata considered this. "I s'pose you're right."

"So none of what he says and does matters because we have the same job at the end of the day. Question is: Are we up for that? 'Cause it means letting go of how much we loathe him and just getting on with what we do best."

"I'm on for that," Nkata said. "But, Barb, you still deserve—"

"Hey," she interrupted, "so do you."

Now, she yawned widely and shoved her shoulder against the recalcitrant door of the Mini. She'd found a parking space along Steeles Road, round the corner from Eton Villas. She plodded back to the yellow house, hunched into a cold wind that had come up in the late afternoon, and went along the path to her bungalow.

Inside, she flipped on the lights, tossed her shoulder bag on the table, and dug the desired tin of Heinz from a cupboard. She dumped its contents unceremoniously into a pan. Under other circumstances, she'd have eaten the beans cold. But tonight, she decided she deserved the full treatment. She popped bread into the toaster and from the fridge took a Stella Artois. It wasn't her night to drink, but she'd had a tough day.

As her meal was preparing itself, she went for the television remote, which, as usual, she couldn't find. She was searching the wrinkled linens of the unmade daybed when someone rapped at her door. She glanced over her shoulder and saw through the open blinds on the window two shadowy forms on her front step: one quite small, the other taller, both of them slender. Hadiyyah and her father had come calling.

Barbara gave up her search for the remote and opened the door to her neighbours. She said, "Just in time for a Barbara Special. I've two pieces of toast, but if you behave yourselves, we can divide them three ways." She held the door wider to admit them, giving a glance over her shoulder to check that she'd tossed her dirty knickers in the laundry basket sometime during the last forty-eight hours.

Taymullah Azhar smiled with his usual grave courtesy. He said, "We cannot stay, Barbara. This will only take a moment, if you do not mind."

He sounded so sombre that Barbara glanced warily from him to his daughter. Hadiyyah was hanging her head, her hands clasped behind her back. A few wisps of hair escaped from her plaits, brushing against her cheeks, and her cheeks themselves were flushed. She looked as if she'd been crying.

"What's wrong? Is something . . . ?" Barbara felt dread from a dozen different sources, none of which she particularly cared to name. "What's going on, Azhar?"

Azhar said, "Hadiyyah?" His daughter looked up at him imploringly. His face was implacable. "We have come for a reason. You know what it is."

Hadiyyah gulped so loudly that Barbara could hear it. She brought her hands from round her back and extended them to Barbara. In them, she held the Buddy Holly CD. She said, "Dad says I'm to give this back to you, Barbara."

Barbara took it from her. She looked at Azhar. She said, "But . . . Sorry, but is it not allowed, or something?" That seemed unlikely. She knew a little about their customs, and gift giving was one of them.

"And?" Azhar said to his daughter without answering Barbara's question. "There is more, is there not?"

Hadiyyah lowered her head again. Barbara could see that her lips were trembling.

Her father said, "Hadiyyah. I shall not ask you—"

"I fibbed," the little girl blurted out. "I fibbed to my dad and he found out and I'm meant to give this back to you in consee . . . con . . . *con*sequence." She raised her head. She'd begun to cry. "But thank you, because I thought it was lovely. I liked 'Peggy Sue' especially." Then she spun on her heel and fled, back towards the front of the house. Barbara heard her sob.

She looked to her neighbour. She said, "Listen, Azhar. This is actually my fault. I had no idea Hadiyyah wasn't supposed to go to Camden High Street. And she didn't know where we were going when we set off. It was something of a joke anyway. She was listening to some pop group and I was giving her aggro about them and she was saying how great they are and I decided to show her some real rock 'n' rock and I took her down to the Virgin Megastore but I didn't know it was forbidden and she didn't know where we were going." Barbara was out of breath. She felt like an adolescent getting caught for being out after curfew. She didn't much like it. She calmed herself and said, "If I'd *known* you'd forbidden her to go to Camden High Street, I never would have taken her there. I'm dead sorry, Azhar. She didn't mention it straightaway."

"Which is the source of my irritation with Hadiyyah," Azhar said. "She should have done so."

"But, like I said, she didn't know where we were going till we got there."

"Once you arrived, was she wearing a blindfold?"

"Of course not. But then it was too late. I didn't exactly give her a chance to say something."

"Hadiyyah should not need an invitation to be truthful."

"Okay. Agreed. It happened, and it won't happen again. At least let her keep the CD."

Azhar glanced away. His dark fingers—so slender, they looked like a girl's—moved beneath his trim jacket to the pocket of his pristine white shirt. He felt there and brought forth a packet of cigarettes. He shook one out, appeared to think about what to do next, and then offered the packet to Barbara. She took this as a positive sign. Their fingers brushed as she took a cigarette from him, and he lit a match that he shared with her.

"She wants you to stop smoking," Barbara told him.

"She wants many things. As do we all."

"You're angry. Come in. Let's talk about this."

He remained where he was.

"Azhar, listen. I know what you're worried about, Camden High Street and all that. But you can't protect her from everything. It's impossible."

He shook his head. "I don't seek to protect her from everything. I merely seek to do what's right. But I find that I don't always know what that is."

"Being exposed to Camden High Street isn't going to pollute her. And Buddy Holly"—here Barbara gestured with the CD—"isn't going to pollute her either."

"It's not Camden High Street or Buddy Holly that comprises my concern," Azhar said. "It is the lie, Barbara."

"Okay. I can see that. But it was only a lie of omission. She just didn't tell me when she could have told me. Or should have told me. Or whatever."

"That is not it at all."

"What is it, then?"

"She lied to me, Barbara."

"To you? About—"

"And this is something I will not accept."

"But when? When did she lie to you?"

"When I asked her about the CD. She said you had given it to her—"

"Azhar, that was *true*."

"—but she failed to include the information about where it had come from. That in itself slipped out when she was chatting about CDs in general. About how many there were to choose from at the Virgin Megastore."

"Bloody hell, Azhar, that's not a lie, is it?"

"No. But the outright denial of having been in the Virgin Megastore is. And this is something that I will not accept. Hadiyyah is not to start that with me. She will not begin lying. She will not. Not to me." His voice was so controlled and his features so rigid that Barbara realised far more was being discussed than his daughter's initial venture into prevarication.

She said, "Okay. I get it. But she feels wretched. Whatever your point is, I think you made it."

"I hope so. She must learn that there are consequences to the decisions she makes, and she must learn this as a child."

"I don't disagree. But . . ." Barbara drew in on her cigarette before she dropped it to the front step and ground it out. "It seems like making her admit her wrongdoing to me—sort of like in public?—is punishment enough. I think you should let her keep the CD."

"I've decided the consequences."

"You can bend, though, can't you?"

"Too far," he said, "and you break on the wheel of your own inconsistencies."

"What happens then?" Barbara asked him. When he didn't reply, she went on quietly with, "Hadiyyah and lying . . . This isn't really what it's all about. Is it, Azhar."

He replied, "I will not have her start," and he

stepped back, preparatory to leaving. He added politely, "I have kept you from your toast long enough," before he returned to the front of the property.

NO MATTER HIS conversation with Barbara Havers and her reassurance on the subject, Winston Nkata didn't rest easily beneath the mantle of detective sergeant. He'd thought he would—that was the hell of it—but it wasn't happening, and the comfort he wanted in his employment hadn't materialised for most of his career.

He hadn't started out in police work feeling uneasy about his job. But it hadn't been long before the reality of being a black cop in a world dominated by white men had begun to sink in. He'd noticed it first in the canteen, in the way that glances sidled over to him and then slid onto someone else; then he felt it in the conversations, how they became ever so slightly more guarded when he joined his colleagues. After that it was in the manner that he was greeted: with just a shade *more* welcome than was given the white cops when he sat with a group at table. He hated that deliberate effort people made to appear tolerant when he was near. The very act of diligently treating him like one of the lads made him feel like the last thing he'd ever become was one of the lads.

At first he'd told himself he didn't want that anyway. It was rough enough round Loughborough Estate hearing himself called a fucking coconut. It would be that much worse if he actually ended up *becoming* part of the white establishment. Still, he hated being marked as phony by his own people. While he kept in mind his mother's admonition that "it doesn't make you a chair 'f some ignoramus calls you a chair," he found it increasingly difficult just to keep himself moving in the direction he wanted to go. On the estate, that meant to and from his parents' flat and nowhere else. Otherwise, it meant upward in his career.

"Jewel, luv," his mother had said when he phoned her with the news of his promotion. "Doesn't matter one bit why they promoted you. What matters is they *did,* and now the opening's there. You walk through it. And you don't look back."

But he couldn't do that. Instead, he continued to feel weighed down by AC Hillier's sudden notice of him when before he'd been nothing more to the man than a passing face to which the assistant commissioner could not have put a name if his continued existence had depended upon it.

Yet, there was still so much truth to what his mother had said. Just walk through the opening. He had to learn how to do it. And the entire subject of openings applied to more than one area of his life, which was what he was left thinking about once Barb Havers departed for the day.

He took a final look at the pictures of the dead boys before he too left the Yard. He did it to remind himself that they were young—terribly young—and as a consequence of their racial background, he had obligations that went beyond merely bringing their killer to justice.

Below, in the underground carpark, he sat for a moment in his Escort and thought about those obligations and what they called for: action in the face of fear. He wanted to slap himself stupid for even *having* that fear. He was twenty-nine years old, for God's sake. He was an officer of the police.

That alone should have counted for something, and it would have done in other instances. But it counted for nothing in this situation, when being a cop was the single profession in life least designed to impress. Yet . . . It couldn't be helped that he was a cop. He was also a man, and a man's presence was called for.

Nkata finally set off with a deep breath. He followed

a route across the river to South London. But instead of heading home, he took a detour round the curved brick shell of the Oval and drove down Kennington Road in the direction of Kennington Station.

The tube itself marked his destination, and he found a place to park nearby. He bought an *Evening Standard* from a vendor on the pavement, using the activity to build up his courage for walking the length of Braganza Street.

At its bottom, Arnold House—part of Doddington Grove Estate—rose out of a lumpy carpark. Across from this building, a horticultural centre grew behind a chain-link fence, and it was against this fence that Nkata chose to lean, with his newspaper folded beneath his arm and his gaze on the third-floor covered walk that led to the fifth flat from the left.

It wouldn't take much effort to cross over the street and weave his way through the carpark. Once there, he was fairly certain the lift would be available since, more often than not, the security panel giving access to it was broken. How much trouble would it be, then, to cross, to weave, to punch the button, and then to make his way to that flat? He had a reason to do so. There were boys being murdered across London—mixed-race boys—and inside that flat lived Daniel Edwards, whose white father was dead but whose black mother was very much alive. But then that was the problem, wasn't it. She was the problem. Yasmin Edwards.

"Ex-*con*vict, Jewel?" his mother would have said had he ever had the nerve to tell her about Yasmin. "What'n God's name you *thinking*?"

But that was easy enough to answer. Thinking of her skin, Mum, and how it looks when a lamp shines against it. Thinking of her legs, which ought to be wrapped round a man who wants her. Thinking of her mouth and the curve of her bum and the way her breasts rise and fall when she's angry. Tall she is, Mum. Tall to my tall. Good woman who made one very big mistake, which she'd paid for like she ought.

And anyway, Yasmin Edwards wasn't really the point. Nor was she the target of duty. That was Daniel, who at nearly twelve could well be in the sights of a killer. Because who knew how their killer was choosing his victims? No one. And until they *did* know, how could he—Winston Nkata—walk away from giving a warning where it might be needed?

All that was required of him was to walk across the street, dodge a few cars in the wretched carpark, depend upon the security panel being broken, ring the bell for the lift, and knock on that door. He was fully capable of doing that.

And he was going to. Later, he swore that to himself. But just as he was about to lift his foot in step number one of however many it was going to take to get to Yasmin Edwards' front door, the woman herself came along the pavement.

She wasn't walking from the underground station as Nkata himself had done. Rather, she was coming from the opposite direction, from beyond the gardens at the bottom of Braganza Street where, from her little shop in Manor Place, she offered hope in the form of makeup, wigs, and makeovers to black women suffering from disorders of the body and the soul.

In reaction to seeing her, Nkata found himself fading back against the chain-link fence and into a pool of shadow. He hated himself the moment he did it, but he just couldn't move forward as he ought to have done.

For her part, Yasmin Edwards walked steadily towards Doddington Grove Estate. She didn't see him in the shadows, and that alone was reason to talk to her. Good-looking woman on the street alone in this neighbourhood after dark? Need to be cautious, Yas. Need to be on the lookout. Someone jump you . . . hurt you . . .

rape you . . . rob you . . . ? What's Daniel going to do if his mum goes the way of his dad and dies on him?

But Nkata couldn't say that. Not with Yasmin Edwards herself being the reason why Daniel's father was dead. So he stayed in the shadows and he watched her, even as he felt the terrible shame of his breath going faster and his heart beating harder than it ought.

Yasmin moved forward along the pavement. He saw that her 101 plaits with their beaded ends were gone now, her hair close cropped and no longer making the soft chorus that he would otherwise have heard from where he stood. She shifted the carrier bags she held from one hand to the other, and she felt in the pocket of her jacket. He knew that she was seeking her keys. End of the day, a meal to be got for her boy, life going on.

She reached the carpark and crisscrossed through the ill-defined bays. At the lift, she punched the security code that would give her access, and then she punched the button to call it. She quickly disappeared within.

She came out again on the third floor and strode towards her door. When she put her key in its lock, it opened before she had a chance to unlock it. And there was Daniel, backlit by a shifting glow that would be coming from the television set. He took the carrier bags from his mother, but as he was about to move off, she stopped him. Hands on hips, she stood. Head cocked. Weight on one of her long, lithe legs. She said something and Daniel came back to her. He set the bags down and submitted to a hug. Just at the point when it looked like the hug was being only endured and not enjoyed, his own arms went round his mother's waist. Then Yasmin kissed the top of his head.

After that, Daniel took the carrier bags inside and Yasmin followed him. She shut the door. A moment later, she appeared at the window which, Nkata knew, looked out from the sitting room. She reached for the curtains to shut them against the night, but before she did that, she stood for twenty seconds or so, gazing into the darkness, her expression set.

He was still in the shadows, but he could sense it, he could *feel* it: She hadn't looked his way once, but Nkata could swear that Yasmin Edwards had known all along that he was there.

Chapter Four

A day later, Stephenson Deacon and the Directorate of Public Affairs decided the time had ripened enough for the first press briefing. Assistant Commissioner Hillier, given the word from above, instructed Lynley to be there for the big event, with "our new detective sergeant" in tow. Lynley wanted to be there as little as Nkata, but he knew the wisdom of at least appearing to cooperate. He and the DS descended via the stairs to arrive promptly at the conference. They encountered Hillier in the corridor.

"Ready?" The AC spoke to Lynley and Nkata as he paused to examine his impressive head of grey hair in the glass cover of a notice board. Unlike the other two men, he looked pleased to be there and he seemed to be restraining himself from rubbing his hands in anticipation of the coming confrontation. Clearly, he expected the briefing to click along like the well-oiled machine it was designed to be.

He didn't wait for a response to his question. Instead, he ducked into the room. They followed.

The print and broadcasting journalists had been relegated to the rows of seats fanning out before the dais. The television cameras were set to shoot over their heads. This would illustrate later for the public—via the nightly news—that the Met was making all possible efforts to keep the citizenry in the picture through an ostensibly open and welcoming venue for their human conduits of information.

Stephenson Deacon, the head of the Press Bureau, had himself chosen to make the prefatory remarks at this first briefing. His appearance not only signaled the importance of what was about to be announced, but it also telegraphed to the general public the appropriate level of police concern. Only the presence of the head of the DPA could have made a more impressive statement.

The newspapers had, of course, jumped upon the story of a body found on the top of a tomb in St. George's Gardens, as anyone with a brain at New Scotland Yard had known they would. The reticence of the police at the crime scene, the arrival there of an officer from New Scotland Yard long before the removal of the body, the lapse of time between the body's discovery and this press conference . . . All of it had whetted the appetite of the journalists and spoke of a much bigger story to come.

When Deacon turned the meeting over to him, Hillier played on this. He began with the larger purpose of the press conference, which was, he declared, "to make our young people aware of the dangers they face in the streets." He went on to sketch out the crime under investigation, and just at the point at which anyone might have logically wondered why a briefing was being held to inform the media of a killing they'd already featured at the top of the news and on the first pages of their papers, he said, "At this juncture, we're looking for witnesses to what appears to be a series of potentially related crimes against young men."

It took less than five seconds for the word *series* to lead ineluctably to *serial*, at which point the reporters jumped aboard like commuters leaping on the night's final train. Their questions erupted like pheasants from beaten bushes.

Lynley could see the pleasure in Hillier's features as the reporters asked just the sort of questions that he and the Press Bureau had hoped they would ask, leaving unspoken the very topics that he and the Press Bureau had wished to avoid. Hillier held up a hand with an expression that communicated both his understanding and his tolerance of their outburst. He then went on to say precisely what he had planned to say, regardless of their questions.

The individual crimes, he explained, had initially been investigated by the murder squads most closely associated with the locations in which the bodies had been found. Doubtless their brother and sister journalists who were responsible for gathering the news at each of these relevant stations would be *happy* to supply the notes they themselves had already assembled on the killings, which would save everyone valuable time just now. For its part, the Met was going to press forward with a thorough investigation of this most recent murder, tying it to the others if there was a clear indication that the crimes were related. In the meantime, the Met's immediate concern—as he'd already mentioned—was the safety of the young people who populated the streets, and it was crucial that the message get out to them at once: Adolescent boys appeared to be the target of one or more killers. They needed to be aware of that and take appropriate precautions when away from home.

Hillier then introduced the "two leading officers" in the investigation. Acting Detective Superintendent Thomas Lynley would be heading it and coordinating all previous investigations done by the local stations, he said. He would be assisted by Detective Sergeant Winston Nkata. No mention was made of DI John Stewart or anyone else.

There followed more questions, these about the composition, size, and strength of the squad, which Lynley answered. After that, Hillier deftly resumed control. He said, as if it had just crossed his mind, "While we're on the subject of the constitution of the squad . . . ," and he went on to tell the journalists that he'd personally brought aboard forensic specialist Simon Allcourt-St. James, and to enhance his work and the work of the officers from the Met, a forensic psychologist—otherwise more commonly known as a profiler—would be contributing his services as well. For professional reasons, the profiler preferred to remain in the background, but suffice it to say that he had trained in the U.S. at Quantico, Virginia, home of the Federal Bureau of Investigation's profiling unit.

Hillier then drew the meeting to a practised close, telling the journalists that the Press Bureau would be offering them daily briefings. He switched off his mike and led Lynley and Nkata out of the room, leaving the reporters with Deacon, who signaled a minion to pass out the sheaves of additional information that had previously been determined suitable for media consumption.

In the corridor, Hillier gave a satisfied smile. "Time bought," he said. "See that you use it well." His attention then went to a man who was waiting nearby in the company of Hillier's secretary, a visitor's badge pinned to his baggy green cardigan. Hillier said to him, "Ah. Excellent. You've arrived already," and he set about making the introductions. This was Hamish Robson, he told Lynley and Nkata, the clinical and forensic psychologist he'd just been speaking about to the journalists. Otherwise employed at the Fischer Psychiatric Hospital for the Criminally Insane in Dagenham, Dr. Robson had kindly agreed to be of assistance by joining Lynley's murder squad.

Lynley felt his spine stiffen. He realised he'd been

blindsided yet again, having erroneously assumed during the press conference that Hillier had been lying through his teeth about an unnamed forensic psychologist. He went through the motions of shaking Dr. Robson's hand, however, while he said to Hillier, "If we could have a word, sir," in as agreeable a voice as he could manage.

Hillier made much of glancing at his watch. He made even more of telling Lynley that the deputy commissioner was waiting for a report on the conference they'd only just concluded.

Lynley said, "This will take less than five minutes and I consider it essential," adding the word *sir* as a deliberate afterthought whose tone and meaning Hillier could not avoid comprehending.

"Very well," Hillier said. "Hamish, if you'll excuse us . . . ? DS Nkata will show you where the incident room—"

"I'll need Winston for the moment," Lynley said, not because this was strictly the truth but because somewhere along the line he knew he was going to have to drive home to Hillier the point that the assistant commissioner of police was not running the investigation.

There was a tight little silence during which Hillier appeared to be evaluating Lynley for his level of insubordination. He finally said, "Hamish, if you'll wait here for a moment," and he ushered Lynley and Nkata not to an office, not to the stairs, not to the lift to take them above to his own quarters, but into the men's toilet where he told a uniformed constable in the act of emptying his bladder to vacate the premises and stand before the door, allowing no one to enter.

Before Lynley could speak, Hillier said pleasantly, "Don't do that again, please. If you do, you'll find yourself back in uniform so fast that you'll wonder who zipped your trousers."

Seeing what the temperature of this conversation

was likely to become despite Hillier's momentarily affable tone, Lynley said to Nkata, "Winston, would you leave us, please? Sir David and I need to have some words I'd prefer you not hear. Go back to the incident room and see where Havers has got to with Missing Persons, particularly with the one that looks like a possibility."

Nkata nodded. He didn't ask if he was meant to take Hamish Robson with him as previously ordered by Hillier. Instead, he looked glad of the command that gave him the opportunity to demonstrate where his loyalties lay.

When he was gone, Hillier was the one to speak. "You're out of order."

"With due respect," Lynley returned, although he felt little enough of it, "I believe you are."

"How dare you—"

"Sir, I'll bring you up to the minute daily," Lynley said patiently. "I'll face the television cameras if you like and sit at your side and force DS Nkata to do the same. But I'm not going to hand over the direction of this investigation to you. You need to stay out of it. That's the only way this is going to work."

"Do you want to be up for review? Believe me, that can be arranged."

"If you need to do it, you'll have to do it," Lynley replied. "But, sir, you've got to see that at the end of the day, there has to be only one of us heading this inquiry. If you want to be that person, then be him and have done with pretending I'm in charge. But if you want me to be that person, you're going to have to back off. You've blindsided me twice now, and I don't want a third surprise."

Hillier's face went the red of sunset. But he said nothing as he evidently registered the lengths Lynley had gone to to remain calm as he simultaneously evaluated the ramifications of Lynley's words. He finally said, "I want daily briefings."

"You've been getting them. You'll continue to get them."

"And the profiler stays."

"Sir, we don't need psychic mumbo jumbo at this point."

"We need all the help we can get!" Hillier's voice grew loud. "The papers are twenty-four hours away from starting the hue and cry. You damn well know that."

"I do. But we also both know that's going to happen eventually, now that the other murders have been mentioned."

"Are you accusing me—"

"No. *No.* You said what had to be said in there. But once they start digging, they'll go after us, and there's plenty of truth in what they're going to allege about the Met."

"Where the hell are your loyalties?" Hillier demanded. "Those buggers are going to go back and look up the other murders and then they'll put it down to *us*—not to themselves—that not one of them ever made the front page. At which point they'll wave the racism flag, and when they do, the whole community's going to blow. Like it or not, we have to stay one step ahead of them. The profiler's one way to do it. And that, as you might say, is that."

Lynley considered this. He hated the idea of having a profiler onboard, but he had to admit that his presence did serve the purpose of buoying up the investigation in the eyes of the journalists who were covering it. And while he ordinarily had no use for either newspapers or television—seeing the collection and dissemination of information as something that was yearly becoming more opprobrious—he could understand the necessity of keeping their focus on the progress of the current investigation. If they started to rave about the Met's failure to see the relationships among three prior killings, they would put the police in the position of having to waste time attempting to excuse the lapse. This served no one and nothing but the coffers of the newspapers, who might be able to increase their sales by fanning the flames of a public indignation that always lay like a dragon in repose.

"All right," Lynley said. "The profiler stays. But I determine what he sees and what he doesn't."

"Agreed," Hillier said.

They returned to the corridor, where Hamish Robson waited for them unaccompanied. The profiler had taken himself down to a notice board some distance from the toilets. Lynley had to admire the man for that.

He said, "Dr. Robson?," to which Robson replied, "Hamish. Please."

Hillier said, "The superintendent will take you in hand at this point, Hamish. Good luck. We're relying on you."

Robson glanced from Hillier to Lynley. Behind his gold-rimmed spectacles, his eyes looked wary. The rest of his expression was muted by his greying goatee, and as he nodded, a lock of thinning hair flopped onto his forehead. He brushed it off. The glint of a gold signet ring caught the light. "I'm happy to do what I can," he said. "I'll need the police reports, the crime-scene photos . . ."

"The superintendent will give you what you need," Hillier said. And to Lynley, "Keep me up to speed." He nodded to Robson and strode off in the direction of the lifts.

As Robson observed Hillier walking off, Lynley observed Robson and decided he looked harmless enough. There was, indeed, something vaguely comforting about his dark green cardigan and his pale yellow shirt. He wore a conservative, solid-brown tie with this, the same colour as his trousers, which were worn and lived in. He was podgy of body and looked like everyone's favourite uncle.

"You work with the criminally insane," Lynley said as he led the other man to the stairwell.

"I work with minds whose only outlet for torment is the commission of a crime."

"Isn't the one the same as the other?" Lynley asked.

Robson smiled sadly. "If that were only the case."

LYNLEY BRIEFLY INTRODUCED Robson to the team before he took him from the incident room to his office. There he gave the psychologist copies of the crime-scene photographs, the police reports, and the preliminary post-mortem information from the forensic pathologists who'd examined the bodies at the scene of each crime. He held back the autopsy reports. Robson took a cursory look through the material, then explained that it would take him at least twenty-four hours to evaluate it.

That was no problem, Lynley told him. There was plenty for the team to do while they were waiting for his . . . Lynley wanted to say *performance,* as if the man were a psychic come to bend spoons in their presence. He settled on *information* instead. *Report* gave Robson too much legitimacy.

"The investigators seemed . . ." Robson appeared to look for a word. "Rather wary to have me among them."

"They're used to the old-fashioned way of doing things," Lynley told him.

"I believe they'll find what I have to say useful, Superintendent."

"I'm glad to hear that," Lynley said, and he called Dee Harriman to see Dr. Robson on his way.

When the profiler had departed, Lynley returned to the incident room and the work at hand. What did they have? he wanted to know.

DI Stewart was, as ever, ready with his report, which he stood to present like a schoolboy hoping for high marks from the teacher. He announced he'd subdivided his officers into teams, the better to deploy them in different areas. At this, a few eyes rolled heavenward in the incident room. Stewart did most things like a frustrated Wellington.

They were inching forward, engaging in the tedious plodwork of a complicated investigation. Stewart had two officers from team one—"They'll be doing background," he reported—covering the mental hospitals and the prisons. They had unearthed a number of potential leads that they were following up: paedophiles having finished their time in open conditions within the last six months, paroled murderers of adolescents, gang members in remand awaiting trial—

"And from youth offenders?" Lynley asked.

Stewart shook his head. Sod all appeared useful from that end of things. All the youth offenders recently released were accounted for.

"What are we getting from the door-to-doors at the body sites?" Lynley asked.

Little enough. Stewart had constables reinterviewing everyone in those areas, seeking witnesses to anything at all. They knew the drill: It wasn't so much the unusual that they were looking for, but the ordinary that, upon reflection, made one stop and think. Since serial killers by their very nature faded into the woodwork, the woodwork itself had to be examined, inch by tedious inch.

He'd directed enquiries to hauling companies as well, Stewart explained, and he'd so far come up with fifty-seven lorry drivers who would have been on Gunnersbury Road on the night when the first victim had been left in Gunnersbury Park. A DC was in the process of contacting them, to see if she could jump-start their memories about any kind of vehicle that might have been parked alongside the brick wall of the park, on the road into London. In the meantime, another DC was in touch with every taxi and minicab service, looking for much the same result. As to the door-to-door, a line of houses stood directly across the road from the park, albeit separated from it by four lanes of traffic and a central reservation. There were hopes of getting something from one of them. One never knew who might have been suffering insomnia and gazing out of the window on the night in question. The same went for Quaker Street, by the way, where a block of flats stood opposite the abandoned warehouse in which the third body had been found.

On the other hand, the multi-story carpark location—site of the second body—was going to be more difficult. The only person who might have seen anything inside it was the attendant on duty that night, but he swore he'd seen nothing between one in the morning and six-twenty, when the body was discovered by a nurse heading to an early shift at Chelsea and Westminster Hospital. That didn't, of course, mean he hadn't slept right through the entire circumstance. The carpark in question had no central kiosk at which an attendant sat day and night, but rather an office tucked away deep in the interior of the structure and furnished with a reclining chair and a television set to make the long hours of the night shift seem moderately less so.

"And St. George's Gardens?" Lynley asked.

That was somewhat more hopeful, Stewart reported. According to Theobald's Road's DC who'd canvassed the vicinity, a woman living on the third floor of the building at the junction of Henrietta Mews and Handel Street heard what she thought was the sound of the garden's gate being opened sometime round three in the morning. She'd thought it was the park warden at first, but upon reflection she'd realised it was far too early for him to be unlocking the gates. By the time she got herself out of bed, swathed in her dressing gown, and in place at her window, she was just in time to see a van driving off. It passed beneath a streetlamp as she watched. It was "large-ish," as she described it. She thought the colour of the van was red.

"That's taken it down to a few hundred thousand vans across the city, however," Stewart added regretfully. He flipped his notebook closed, his report complete.

"We need to get someone on to Swansea, pulling vehicle records anyway," Barbara Havers said to Lynley.

"That, Constable, is a complete nonstarter, and you ought to know it," Stewart informed her.

Havers bristled and began to respond.

Lynley cut her off. "John." He said the DI's name in a minatory tone. Stewart subsided, but he didn't look happy to have Havers—lowly DC that she was—offering her opinion.

Stewart said, "Fine. I'll see to it. I'll put someone on to the old bat in Handel Street as well. We may be able to jog something else from her memory about what she saw from that window."

"What about the piece of lace on body four?" Lynley asked.

Nkata was the one to reply. "Looks like tatting, you ask me."

"What?"

"Tatting. That's what it's called. My mum does it. Knotting up string along the edges of a mat. For putting on antique furniture or under a piece of porcelain or something."

"Are you talking about an antimacassar?" John Stewart asked.

"Anti-what?" one of the DCs asked.

"It's antique lacework," Lynley explained. "The sort of thing ladies used to do for their bottom drawers."

"Bloody hell," Barbara Havers said. "Our killer's an *Antiques Roadshow* freak?"

Guffaws all round greeted this remark.

Lynley said, "What about the bicycle left in St. George's Gardens?"

"Prints on it are the kid's. There's some sort of residue on the pedals and the gear shift, but SO7's not done with it yet."

"The silver at the scene?"

Aside from the fact that the silver comprised only photo frames, no one knew anything else about it. Someone made reference to the *Antiques Roadshow* once again, but the comment was less humorous the second time round.

Lynley told them all to carry on. He directed Nkata to continue trying to make contact with the family of the one missing boy who looked like a possible match, he told Havers to continue with the missing-persons reports—an order she did not embrace with a full heart, if her expression was any indication—and he himself returned to his office and sat down with the autopsies. He put on his reading spectacles and went over the reports with eyes that he tried to make fresh. He also created a crib sheet for himself. On this, he wrote:

Means of death: strangulation by ligature in all four cases; ligature missing.

Torture prior to death: palms of both hands burnt in three of four cases.

Marks of restraints: across the forearms and at ankles in all four cases, suggesting victim tied to an armchair of some kind or possibly supine and restrained another way.

Fibre analysis corroborates this: same leather fibres on the arms and ankles in all four cases.

Contents of stomach: a small amount of food eaten within an hour preceding death in all four cases.

Gagging device: duct-tape residue over the mouth in all four cases.

Blood analysis: nothing unusual.
Postmortem mutilation: abdominal incision and removal of navel in victim four.
Marking: forehead marked in blood in victim four.
Trace evidence on the bodies: black residue (under analysis), hairs, an oil (under analysis) in all four cases.
DNA evidence: nothing.

Lynley went through it all once, then a second time. He picked up the phone and called SO7, the forensic lab on the south bank of the Thames. It had been ages since the first of the murders. Surely by now they had an analysis of both the oil and the residue they'd found on the first of the bodies, no matter how overwhelmed with work they were.

Maddeningly, they had nothing yet on the residue, but "Whale" was the single answer he was given when he finally tracked down the responsible party in Lambeth Road. She was called Dr. Okerlund, and she was apparently given to monosyllables unless pressed for more information.

"Whale?" Lynley asked. "Do you mean the fish?"

"For God's sake, mammal," she corrected him. "Sperm whale, to be exact. Official name—the oil, not the whale—is ambergris."

"Ambergris? What's it used for?"

"Perfume. All you need from me, Superintendent?"

"Perfume?"

"Are we playing at echoes here? That's what I said."

"Nothing else?"

"What else d'you want me to say?"

"I mean the oil, Dr. Okerlund. Is it used for anything besides perfume?"

"Couldn't tell you," she said. "That's your job."

He thanked her for the reminder as pleasantly as he could manage. Then he rang off. He added the word *ambergris* in the section for trace evidence, and he returned to the incident room. He called out, "Anyone familiar with ambergris oil? It was found on the bodies. It's from whales."

"Cardiff, I reckon," a DC noted.

"Not Wales," Lynley said. "Whales. The ocean. Moby-Dick."

"Moby-who?"

"Christ, Phil," someone called out. "Try elevating your reading beyond page three."

Ribald remarks greeted this comment. Lynley let them feed off one another. To his way of thinking, the work they had to engage in was time consuming, wearisome, and gut wrenching, weighing on the shoulders of the officers involved and often causing trouble in their homes. If they needed to relieve the stress of it with humour, that was fine by him.

Nonetheless, what happened next was more than welcome. Barbara Havers looked up from a phone call she had just completed.

"We've got a positive ID on St. George's Gardens," she announced. "He's a kid called Kimmo Thorne and he lived in Southwark."

BARBARA HAVERS INSISTED that they take her car, not Nkata's. She saw Lynley's assigning her to the interview of Kimmo Thorne's relations as an opportunity for a celebratory cigarette, and she didn't want to pollute the interior of Winston's pristinely kept Escort with her ash or smoke. She lit up as soon as they hit the underground carpark, and she watched with some amusement as her colleague folded his six-feet, four-inch frame into her Mini. He was left grumbling, with his knees pressed into his chest and his head scraping the ceiling.

Once she finally got the car started, they lurched in

the direction of Broadway. From there, Parliament Square opened onto Westminster Bridge and their route across the river. This was more Winston's territory than it was Barbara's, and he acted the part of navigator once York Road loomed in front of them on the left. From that point, she found it short work to weave over to Southwark, where Kimmo Thorne's aunt and grandmother lived in one of the many nondescript blocks of flats that had been thrown up south of the river after the Second World War. The building's only distinction turned out to be its proximity to the Globe Theatre. But as Barbara sardonically pointed out to Nkata as they alighted into the cramped street, it wasn't as if anyone who lived in the vicinity could actually afford a ticket.

When they presented themselves at the Thorne establishment, they found Gran and Aunt Sal sitting dully before three framed photographs that had been placed on a coffee table in front of their sofa. They'd identified the body, Aunt Sal explained. "I di'n't want Mum to go, but she wasn't having any of that from me. It's done her in proper, seeing our Kimmo laid out like that. He was a good boy. I hope they hang who did this to him."

Gran said nothing. She looked shell-shocked. In her hand she clutched a white handkerchief that was embroidered round the edges with lavender bunnies. She gazed on one of the pictures of her grandson—in it he appeared curiously attired as if for a fancy dress party, wearing an odd combination of lipstick, a Mohawk, green tights, and a Robin Hood tunic with Doc Marten boots—and she pressed the handkerchief beneath her eyes when tears welled up in them during the course of their interview.

The police, Barbara told Kimmo Thorne's gran and aunt, were doing everything they could to find the young man's killer. It would help enormously if Miss and Mrs. Thorne would tell them everything they could about the last day of Kimmo's life.

After she said all this, Barbara realised that she'd automatically assumed the role that had once been hers, the very role that now belonged to Nkata. She gave a tiny grimace of chagrin and looked in his direction. He lifted a hand, telegraphing "It's okay" in a gesture that was unnervingly like one Lynley might have made in the same circumstances. She dug out her notebook.

Aunt Sal took the request seriously. She started with Kimmo's rising in the morning. He dressed in his usual—

"Leggings, boots, an outsize sweater, that nice Brazilian scarf knotted round his waist . . . the one his mum and dad sent over at Christmas, do you remember it, Mum?"

—and put on his makeup. He had his breakfast of cornflakes and tea, and he went to school.

Barbara exchanged a glance with Nkata. Considering the description of the boy, along with the pictures on the coffee table and their proximity to the Globe, the next question rose naturally. Nkata asked it. Was Kimmo taking courses at the theatre? Acting classes or the like?

Oh, their Kimmo was made for drama and make no mistake about *that*, Aunt Sal replied. But no, he wasn't doing a course at the Globe or anywhere else. As things turned out, this was his regular getup when he left the flat. Or when he stayed in the flat, if it came down to that.

Setting aside the issue of his clothing, Barbara said, "He wore makeup regularly, then?" When the two women nodded, she did a mental cross off on one of their working theories: that the killer might have bought cosmetics somewhere and smeared them across the most recent victim's face. Yet it was hardly likely that Kimmo was attempting to attend school thus arrayed. Certainly, his aunt and gran would have heard from the head teacher if that had been the case. Still, she asked them if Kimmo had returned home from school—or wherever he'd been, she added mentally—at the usual time on the day of his death.

They said he'd been back by six o'clock as usual, and they'd had dinner together as usual as well. Gran did a fry-up, which Kimmo didn't much like because he was watching his figure, and afterwards Aunt Sal did the washing up while Kimmo applied the tea towel to the cutlery and crockery.

"He was the same as always," Aunt Sal said. "Chatting, telling stories, making me laugh till my insides hurt. He had a real way with words. Wasn't a thing in life he couldn't make a drama of and act it out. And sing and dance . . . the boy could do them like magic."

"'Do them'?" Nkata asked.

"Judy Garland. Liza. Barbra. Dietrich. Even Carol Channing when he put on the wig." He'd been working hard lately at Sarah Brightman, Aunt Sal said, only the high notes were a trial for him and he'd not got the hands quite right. But he would've, he *would've,* God love the boy, only now . . .

Finally, Aunt Sal broke down. She began to sob when she tried to speak, and Barbara glanced Nkata's way to see if he was making the same assessment of this little family: It was clear that as odd as Kimmo Thorne had looked and might have been, he'd also been night and day to his aunt and his gran.

Gran took her daughter's hand and pressed the bunny-edged handkerchief into it. She took up the story.

He did Marlene Dietrich for them after supper: "Falling in Love Again." The tails, the mesh stockings, the heels, the hat . . . Even the platinum hair, with its little scoop of a wave. He had it all down perfect, had Kimmo. And then after the show, he went out.

"What time was this?" Barbara asked.

Gran looked at an electric clock that sat atop the television set. She said, "Half ten? Sally?"

Aunt Sal dabbed her eyes. "Somewhere round there."

"Where was he going?"

They didn't know. But he said he'd be messing about with Blinker.

"Blinker?" Barbara and Nkata said together.

Blinker, they confirmed. They didn't know the boy's last name—apparently Blinker was male and of the human species—but what they did know was that he was *definitely* the cause of any trouble their Kimmo *ever* got into.

The word *trouble* struck Barbara, but she let Nkata do the honours. "What sort of trouble?"

No *real* trouble, Aunt Sal assured them. And nothing he'd ever started on his own. It was just that that bloody Blinker—"Sorry, Mum," she said hastily—had passed along something of some kind to their Kimmo, which Kimmo had flogged somewhere, only to be caught out selling stolen property. "But it was that Blinker responsible," Aunt Sal said. "Our Kimmo'd never been in trouble before."

That certainly remained to be seen, Barbara thought. She asked if the Thornes could direct them to Blinker.

They had no phone number for him, but they knew where he lived. They said it shouldn't be hard to find him on any morning because the one thing they knew about him was that he was up all night hanging about Leicester Square and he slept till one in the afternoon. He kipped on his sister's sofa, and she lived with her husband on Kipling Estate, near Bermondsey Square. Aunt Sal didn't know the sister's name—nor did she have the first idea of Blinker's Christian name, but she expected if the police went round asking where a bloke called Blinker might be, someone would know for certain. Blinker was someone who *always* managed to get known.

Barbara asked if they might have a look through Kimmo's belongings, then. Aunt Sal took them to his room. This was crowded with bed, dressing table, wardrobe, chest of drawers, television, and music system. The dressing table held a display of makeup that would have done Boy George proud. The top of the chest of drawers served as a location for wig stands, of which there were five. And the walls held dozens of professional head shots of Kimmo's sources of apparent inspiration: from Edith Piaf to Madonna. The boy was nothing if not eclectic in his taste.

"Where'd he get the dosh for all this?" Barbara asked once Aunt Sal had left them to look through the dead boy's lumber. "She didn't mention anything about employment, did she?"

"Makes you think about what Blinker was really giving him to sell," Nkata replied.

"Drugs?"

He waggled his hand: maybe yes, maybe no. "A lot of something," he said.

"We need to find that bloke, Winnie."

"Shouldn't be tough. Someone'll know him on the estate, ask round enough. Someone always does."

Ultimately, they got little joy from their efforts in Kimmo's room. A small stack of cards—birthday, Christmas, and the odd Easter thrown in, all signed "Lovekins, darling, from Mummy and Dad"—were hidden away in a drawer along with a photo of a well-tanned thirtysomething couple on a sunny, foreign balcony. A yellowed newspaper article about a transgender professional model who'd been outed by the tabloids in the distant past surfaced beneath a knot of costume jewellery on the dressing table. A hair-styling magazine—at least in other circumstances—could have indicated a future career.

Otherwise, much of it was what one would expect in the bedroom of a fifteen-year-old boy. Malodorous shoes, underpants screwed up beneath the bed, stray socks. It would have been ordinary, except for the presence of all the items that made it into a hermaphroditic curiosity.

When they'd seen it all, Barbara stood back and said to Nkata, "Winnie, what d'you reckon he was really into?"

Nkata joined her in assessing the room. "I got a feeling this Blinker can tell us."

They both knew there was no point in looking up Blinker at the moment. They'd be better off trying in the morning just about the time those who had jobs would be setting off for work from the housing estate where Blinker lived. They returned to Aunt Sal and Gran, then, and Barbara asked about Kimmo's parents. It was the small and pathetic hoard of postcards in the boy's room that prompted her question, rather than a need to know for purposes of their investigation. It was also what that hoard of postcards said about people's priorities in life.

Oh, they were in South America, Gran said. They'd been there since just before Kimmo's eighth birthday. His dad was in the hotel business, you see, and they'd gone there to manage a luxury spa. They intended to send for Kimmo when they got settled in. But Mum wanted to learn the language first, and it was taking her longer than she'd thought it would.

Had they been informed of Kimmo's death? Barbara asked. Because—

Gran and Aunt Sal had exchanged a look.

—surely there were arrangements they'd want to be making to come home straightaway.

She said this in part because she wanted them to have to acknowledge what she assumed: Kimmo's parents were parents only because of an egg, a sperm, and an accidental inception. They had more important concerns than what had come of that flesh-rubbing moment between them.

Which led her to think of the other victims. And of what it was that might tie all of them together.

Chapter Five

By the next day, two pieces of news from SO7 gave cause for what went for good cheer. The two tyre prints at the scene of the St. George's Gardens body had been identified by manufacturer. They'd also been characterised by a peculiar wearing pattern on one of them that was going to please the Crown prosecutors, when and if the Met made an arrest of someone in possession of those tyres and a vehicle to which they might be attached. The other piece of news had to do with the residue on the pedals and the gears of the bicycle in St. George's Gardens as well as the residue on all four of the bodies they were dealing with: It was all identical. From this, the murder squad concluded that Kimmo Thorne had been picked up somewhere—bike and all—and murdered somewhere else, after which his killer dumped the body, the bike, and probably the silver photo frames in St. George's Gardens. All of this constituted meagre progress, but progress all the same. So when Hamish Robson returned to them with his report, Lynley was inclined to forgive him for showing up three and a half hours later than the promised twenty-four hours he'd thought it would take him to assemble some usable information.

Dee Harriman fetched him from reception and returned him to Lynley's office. He said no to the offer of an afternoon cup of tea and instead he nodded towards the conference table rather than taking one of the two chairs in front of the desk. It seemed a subtle way of telegraphing equality to Lynley. Despite his apparent reticence, Robson didn't appear to be a man who was going to be easily cowed by anyone.

He carried with him a legal pad, a manila folder, and the paperwork Lynley had given him on the previous day. He folded his hands neatly across the top of it all and asked Lynley what he knew about profiling. Lynley told him he'd never yet had an occasion to use a profiler, although he was aware of what profilers did. He didn't add any comments about his reluctance to use one or about his belief that, in truth, Robson had only been called in in the first place to give Hillier something to hand to that ravenous dog the media.

"Would you like some background on profiling, then?" Robson asked.

"Not particularly, to tell you the truth."

Robson observed him evenly. His eyes behind his spectacles looked shrewd, but he made no remark other than to say obscurely, "Right. We'll see about it, won't we." He took up his legal pad without further ado.

They were looking, he told Lynley, for a white male between twenty-five and thirty-five. He would be neat in his appearance: close shaven, short haired, in good physical condition, which was possibly the result of weight training. He would be known to the victims, but not well known. He would be of high intelligence but low achievement, a man with a decent school record but with disciplinary problems stemming from a chronic failure to obey. He would likely possess a history of job losses, and while he would probably be working at this time, it would be in employment below his capabilities. They would find criminal behaviour in his childhood and adolescence: possibly petty arson or cruelty to animals. He would be at this time unmarried and living either alone or with a dominant parent.

Despite what he already knew about profiling, Lynley felt doubtful about the number of details Robson had provided. He said, "How can you know all this, Dr. Robson?"

Robson's lips moved in a smile that tried—and failed—not to look satisfied. He said, "I *do* assume you know what profilers do, Superintendent, but do you know how and why profiling actually works? It's rarely inaccurate, and it's nothing to do with crystal balls, tarot cards, or the entrails of sacrificed animals."

At this, smacking of the gentle correction a parent gives to a wayward child, Lynley considered half a dozen ways to regain dominance. They were all a waste of time, he concluded. So he said, "Should we begin again with each other?"

Robson smiled, genuinely this time. "Thank you," he said. He went on to tell Lynley that to know a killer, one merely had to look at the crime committed, which was what the Americans had begun doing when the FBI had developed their Behavioural Science Unit. By gathering information over the decades of pursuing serial killers and by actually interviewing incarcerated serial killers by the dozens, they'd discovered there were certain commonalities that could be depended upon to be present in the profile of the perpetrator of a certain kind of crime. In this particular crime, for example, they could rely upon the fact that the killings were bids for power although their killer would tell himself that the killings had another reason entirely.

"Not just killing for the thrill of it?"

"Not at all," Robson answered. "This actually has nothing to do with thrill. This man's striking out because he's been frustrated, contradicted, or thwarted. Whatever thrill there is, is secondary."

"Thwarted by the victim?"

"No. A stressor has set him on this course, but its source isn't the victim."

"Who is it, then? What?"

"A recent job loss that the killer thinks is unfair. The breakup of a marriage or another amorous relationship. The death of a loved one. The rejection of a proposal of marriage. A court injunction. A sudden loss of money. The destruction of a home by fire, flood, earthquake, hurricane. Think of something that would put your world or anyone's world into chaos and you'll have a stressor."

"We all have them in our lives," Lynley said.

"But not all of us are psychopaths. It's the combination of the psychopathic personality and the stressor that's deadly, not the stressor alone." Robson fanned out the crime-scene photographs.

Despite the aspects of the crime suggesting sadism—the burnt hands, for example—their killer felt a certain amount of remorse for what he'd done once he'd done it, Robson said. The body in each case told them that: its position traditional to corpses placed in coffins prior to burial, not to mention the fact that the final victim wore what amounted to a loincloth. This, he said, was called psychic erasure or psychic restitution.

"It's as if the killing were a sad duty that the perpetrator believes and tells himself he must perform."

Lynley felt this was going too far. The rest he could swallow; there was sense to it. But this . . . restitution? Penance? Sorrow? Why do it four times if he felt remorse afterwards?

"The conflict for him," Robson said, as if in reply to the questions Lynley hadn't asked, "is the compulsion to kill, which has been triggered by the stressor and can only be relieved by the act of killing itself, versus the knowledge that what he's doing is wrong. And he *does* know that, even as he is driven to do it again and again."

"So you believe he'll strike another time," Lynley said.

"There's no question about it. This is going to escalate. It's actually escalated from the first. You can see that in how he's been upping the stakes. Not only in where he's put the bodies—taking bigger risks of discovery every time he positions one—but also in what he's done to the bodies."

"Increasing the marking on them?"

"What we call making his signature more apparent. It's as if he believes the police are too stupid to catch him, so he's going to taunt you a bit. He's burned the hands three times, and you've failed to make the connection between the killings. So he's had to do more."

"But why so much more? Wouldn't it have been enough just to slice open the final victim? Why add the mark on the forehead? Why the loincloth? Why take the navel?"

"If we discount the loincloth as psychic restitution, we're left with the slice, the missing navel, and the mark on the forehead. If we see the slice as part of a ritual that we as yet don't understand and the missing navel as a gruesome souvenir that allows him to relive the event, then what we really have is the mark on the forehead to serve as a *conscious* escalation of the crime."

"What do you make of that mark?" Lynley asked him.

Robson took up one of the photographs that featured it particularly. "It's rather like a cattle brand, isn't it? I mean the mark itself, not how it was made. A circle with two two-headed crosses quadrisecting it. It clearly stands for something."

"So you're saying it's not a signature on the crime like the other indicators?"

"I'm saying it's more than a signature because it's too deliberate a choice to be merely a signature. Why not use a simple X if you just want your mark on the body? Why not a cross? Why not one of your initials?

Any of those would be quicker to put on your victim than this. Especially when time is probably of the essence."

"You're saying this mark serves a dual purpose, then?"

"I'd say so. No artist signs a painting till it's done, and the fact that this mark was made with the victim's blood tells us that it was likely put on his forehead after death. So yes, it's a signature, but it's something more. I think it's a direct communication."

"With the police?"

"Or with the victim. Or the victim's family." Robson handed the photographs back to Lynley. "Your killer has an enormous need to be noticed, Superintendent. If it isn't satisfied by the current publicity—which it won't be because his sort of need is never actually satisfied by anything, you see—then he'll strike again."

"Soon?"

"I'd say you can depend upon that." He handed Lynley the reports as well. He included with them his own report, which he took from the manila folder, neatly typed and official, with a cover sheet on the letterhead of Fischer Psychiatric Hospital for the Criminally Insane.

Lynley added the reports to the photographs Robson had already handed over, along with his card. He thought about everything the profiler had said. He knew other officers who believed completely in the art—or perhaps it *was* a real science based on irrefutable empirical evidence—of psychological profiling, but he had never been one of them. Put to the test, he'd always preferred his own mind and a sifting through concrete facts to trying to take those same facts and from them create a portrait of someone utterly unknown to him. Besides, he couldn't see how it actually *helped* the situation. At the end of the day, they still had to locate a killer among the ten million people who lived in Greater London, and he wasn't clear on how the profile Robson had provided was going to help do that. The psychologist appeared to know this, however. He added a final detail, as if to put a full stop to his report.

"You also need to prepare yourself for contact," he said.

"What sort?" Lynley asked.

"From the killer himself."

ALONE, He was Fu, Creature Divine, eternal Deity of what must be. He was the truth and His was the way, but the knowledge of this was no longer enough.

The need was upon Him again. It had come far sooner than He had expected. It had come in days instead of in weeks, possessing Him with the call to act. Yet despite the pressure to judge and avenge, to redeem and release, He still moved with care. It was essential He choose correctly. A sign would tell, and so He waited. For there had always been a sign.

A loner was best. He knew that much. And naturally, there were loners aplenty to choose from in a city like London, but following one of them was the only way to confirm His selection as right and apt.

Secure in the camouflage of other passengers, Fu performed this task by bus. His chosen one climbed aboard ahead of Him, immediately making for the curve of stairs to the upper saloon. Fu did not follow him there. Instead, once onboard, He remained below, where He took a position two poles away from the exit door with a view of the stairs.

Their journey turned out to be a long one. They inched along congested streets. At each of the stops, Fu kept His attention fixed on the exit. Between the stops, He entertained Himself by studying His companions in the lower saloon: the tired mother with the screaming toddler, the ageing spinster with sagging ankles, the schoolgirls with coats unbuttoned and blouses hanging out of their skirts, the Asian youths with their heads together making plans, the black youths with their earphones on and their shoulders moving to the beat of music no one else could hear. All of them were in need, but most of them didn't know it. And none of them knew Who stood among them, for anonymity was the greatest gift of living in this place.

Someone somewhere pressed the button that would alert the driver to pull over at the next request stop. A clatter from the stairs and a large mixed group of youths descended. Fu saw that the chosen one was among them, and He eased His own way down the aisle to the door. He ended up directly behind His prey and He could smell the scent of him when He stood on the steps before they disembarked. It was the rank odour of the boy's early adolescence, restless and randy.

Out on the street, Fu hung back, giving the boy a good twenty yards. The pavement wasn't as crowded here as it had been elsewhere, and Fu looked round to get an idea of exactly where He was.

The area was mixed race: black, white, Asian, and Oriental. The voices here spoke a dozen languages, and while no one group looked completely out of place, somehow every individual did.

Fear did that to people, Fu thought. Distrust. Caution. Expect the unexpected from any quarter. Be ready either to flee or to fight. Or to go unnoticed, if that was possible.

The chosen one adhered to this latter principle. He walked, head down, and appeared to acknowledge no one he passed. This, Fu thought, was all to the good when it came to His own intentions.

When the boy reached his destination, though, it was not his home, as Fu had thought it might be. Instead, he walked from the bus stop down the length of a commercial area of markets, video shops, and betting parlours till he came to a small shop with soap-covered windows, and there he entered.

Fu crossed the street so that He could observe from the shadows of the doorway to a bicycle shop. The place the boy had entered was well lit, and despite the cold the door was propped open. Brightly clad men and women stood about chatting while among them children darted noisily. The boy himself was talking to a tall man in a colourful collarless shirt that hung to his hips. He had skin the hue of white coffee, and round his neck hung a carved wooden necklace. There appeared to be some sort of connection between this individual and the boy, but it was something less than father and son. For there was no father. Fu knew that. So this man . . . this particular man . . . Perhaps, Fu thought, He had not chosen wisely after all.

He was soon reassured. The crowd took seats and began singing. They did so haltingly. Taped music accompanied their efforts, heavy on drums and suggesting Africa. Their leader—the man the boy had spoken to—repeatedly stopped and started them again. While this was going on, the boy himself slipped out. He came back into the street, zipping his jacket, and he headed in the shadows farther along the commercial area. Fu followed, unseen.

Up ahead, the boy turned a corner and headed down another street. Fu hurried His own pace and was just in time to see him duck inside the doorway of a windowless brick building next to a scruffy workman's café. Fu paused, assessing. He didn't wish to risk being seen but He needed to know if His choice of the boy was legitimate.

He sidled up to the door. He found it unlocked, so He eased it open. An unlit corridor led to the doorway of a large room that was fully illuminated. From this room came the sounds of thuds, grunts, and the occasional guttural noise of a man ordering someone to "Jab, God damn it" and "Use an upper cut, for Christ's sake."

Fu entered this place. Immediately, He smelled the dust and the sweat, the leather and the mildew, the unwashed male clothes. Along the walls of the corridor, posters hung, and midway to the bright room beyond, a trophy cabinet stood. Fu snaked along the wall with care. He had nearly gained the doorway when someone spoke from out of nowhere.

"You need something, man?"

It was a black male voice and none too friendly. Fu allowed Himself to diminish in size before He turned to see who owned it. A refrigerator made flesh stood on the bottom step of a darkened stairway that Fu had not noticed. He was dressed for outdoors and he was slapping a pair of gloves against his palm. He repeated his question.

"Wha' you need, man? This's private premises."

Fu had to be rid of him, but He also had to see. Somehow, He knew, this building contained the affirmation He needed before He could act. He said, "Sorry. I didn't know it was private. I saw a few blokes come out and I wondered what this place was. I'm new round here."

The man observed him, saying nothing.

Fu added, "I'm looking for new digs," and He smiled affably. "Just doing a recce of the area. Sorry. I didn't mean to offend." He gave His shoulders a little hunch for effect. He moved towards the front door although He had no intention of leaving, and even if He *was* forced out to the street by this lout, He would return as soon as the other man was gone.

The black said, "You c'n have a look, then. But don't be bothering no one, you got that?"

Fu felt a bubble of anger rising. The tone of voice, the audacity of the order. He breathed in calm with the stale air of the corridor, and He said, "What is this place?"

"Boxing gym. You c'n have a look. Just try not to look like a punch bag." The black left then, laughing at his weak attempt at wit. Fu watched him depart. He found that He was longing to follow, to give in to the temptation to let the other learn with whom he had just spoken. The longing fast grew into a hunger, but He refused to submit. Instead, He went to the bright doorway and, keeping to the darkness, He gazed into the room from which the grunts and thuds were coming.

Punch bags, speed bags, two boxing rings. Free weights. A treadmill. Skipping ropes. Two video cameras. Equipment was everywhere. So were the men using the equipment. Mostly blacks, but there were half a dozen white youths among them. And the man who'd been doing the shouting was also white: bald as a baby and wearing a grey towel round his shoulders. He was instructing two boxers in the ring. They were black, sweating, panting like overheated dogs.

Fu sought out the boy. He found him pounding a punch bag. He'd changed his clothes and was wearing a tracksuit. Already, it bore large crescents of sweat.

Fu watched as he pummeled the bag without either style or precision. He hurled himself upon it and pounded ferociously, ignoring everything else around him.

Ah, Fu thought. The journey across London had been well worth the risk after all. What He witnessed now had been worth even the brief interlude with the lout on the stairs. For unlike any other moment before this when Fu had been able to study the boy, this time the chosen one stood revealed.

He had an anger within him to match Fu's own. He was indeed in need of redemption.

* * *

For a second time, Winston Nkata didn't go straight home. Instead, he followed the river to Vauxhall Bridge, where he crossed and circled round the Oval once again. He did it all without thinking, simply telling himself that it was time. The press conference made everything easier. Yasmin Edwards would know something about the murders at this point, so his purpose in calling would be to emphasise those details whose importance she might not have fully understood.

It was only when he'd parked across from Doddington Grove Estate that Nkata came fully to what he considered to be his senses. And that didn't turn out to be an ideal situation, because coming to his senses also meant coming to his sensations, and the one he felt as he drummed his fingers on the steering wheel was again largely cowardice.

On the one hand, he *did* have the excuse he'd been looking for. More than that, he had the duty he'd taken the attestation to perform. Surely it was a small enough matter to impart the necessary information to her. So why he should be feeling nerved out about doing his *job* . . . It was way beyond him to suss that one out.

Except, Nkata knew that he was lying to himself even as he allowed himself thirty seconds to do so. There were half a dozen reasons for his being reluctant to ride the lift up to that third-floor flat, and not the least of them was what he'd deliberately done to the woman who lived within it.

He hadn't really come to terms with why he'd assigned himself the job of making Yasmin Edwards aware of her lover's infidelity. It was one thing to be in honest pursuit of a killer; it was quite another to want the killer to be someone who stood in the way of Nkata *himself* achieving . . . what? He didn't want to consider the answer to that question.

He said, "Come *on*, man," and shoved open the car door. Yasmin Edwards might have knifed her own husband and done time for it. But the one thing he knew for certain was that if it came to knives between them, he had far more experience in wielding one.

There had been a time when he would have rung a different flat to gain access to the lift, telling the occupant at the other end of the buzzer that he was a cop so he could ride up to the third floor and knock on Yasmin Edwards' door without her knowing he was on his way. But he didn't allow himself to do that now. Instead, he buzzed her flat and when he heard her voice asking who was there, he said, "Police, Missus Edwards. I'll need a word please."

A hesitation made him wonder if she'd recognised his voice. A moment later, though, she released the lock on the lift. Its doors slid open and he stepped inside.

He thought she might meet him at the door to her flat, but it was as firmly closed as ever—with the curtains drawn for the evening at the sitting-room window—when he strode down the outdoor corridor to it. She answered quickly enough when he knocked, though, which told him she must have been standing just inside, waiting for his arrival.

She observed him expressionlessly, and she didn't have to lift her head much to do so. For Yasmin Edwards was an elegant six feet tall and as imposing a presence as she'd been when he'd first met her. She'd changed out of her work clothes and was wearing striped pyjamas. She wore nothing else, and he knew her well enough to recognise that she'd deliberately put on no dressing gown when she'd heard who'd come calling, which was her way of signaling to the police that she feared nothing from them, having experienced the worst at their hands already.

Yas, Yas, he wanted to say. That's not the way it has to be.

But instead, he said, "Missus Edwards," and reached

for his identification, as if he believed she didn't remember who he was.

She said, "What is it, man? 'Nother murderer you're sniffing up round here? No one in this flat capable of that but me, so when is it I need the alibi for?"

He shoved his warrant card back into his pocket. He didn't sigh, although he wanted to. He said, "Could I have a word, Missus Edwards? Truth to tell, it's about Dan."

She looked alarmed, in spite of herself. But as if she suspected a trick of some kind, she remained where she was, blocking his entrance. She said, "You best tell me what's about Daniel, Constable."

"Sergeant now," Nkata said. "Or does that make it worse?"

She cocked her head. He found he missed the sight and the sound of her 101 beaded plaits, although her close-cropped hair suited her just as well. She said, "Sergeant, is it? That what you come to tell Daniel?"

"I didn't come to talk to Daniel," he said patiently. "I come to talk to you. About Daniel. I c'n do it outside if that's what you want, Missus Edwards, but you're gonna get colder if you stand there much longer." He felt his face get hot because of what his words implied about what he'd noticed: the tips of her breasts peaking against the flannel of the pyjama top, her exposed skin the colour of walnut goose-fleshing where the top formed a V. As best he could, Nkata avoided looking at the vulnerable parts of her that were open to the winter air, but still he could see the smooth and stately curve of her neck, the mole he'd never noticed before, beneath her right ear.

She shot him a look of contempt and reached behind the door where, he knew, she kept a line of hooks for coats. She brought from it a heavy cardigan, which she took her time about donning and buttoning to the throat. When she was garbed to her liking, she gave him her attention again. "Better?" she asked.

"Whatever's best for you."

"Mum?" It was her son's voice, coming from his bedroom doorway, which, Nkata knew, was to the left of the front door. "Wha's going on? Who's—" Daniel Edwards stepped into view just beyond Yasmin's shoulders. His eyes widened when he saw who was calling on them, and his grin was contagious, exposing those perfect white teeth of his, so adult in his twelve-year-old face.

Nkata said, " 'Lo, Dan. Wha's happening?"

"Hey!" Daniel said. "You 'member my name."

"He's got it in his records," Yasmin Edwards said to her son. "Tha's what cops do. Are you ready for the cocoa yet? It's in the kitchen if you want it. Homework finished?"

"You coming in?" Daniel said to Nkata. "We got cocoa. Mum makes it fresh. I have enough to share 'f you like."

"Dan! Is your hearing—"

"Sorry, Mum," Daniel said. That grin again, though. Daniel disappeared through the kitchen doorway. The opening and closing of cupboards ensued from that direction.

"In?" Nkata said to the boy's mother, with a nod at the interior of the flat. "This'll take five minutes. I c'n promise that, cos I got to get home."

"I don't want you trying to get Dan—"

Nkata raised his hands in a sign of surrender. "Missus Edwards, I bother you since what happened happened? No, right? I think you c'n trust me."

She seemed to think this over while, behind her, the cheerful clatter continued in the kitchen. Finally, she swung the door open. Nkata stepped inside and shut it behind him before she had a chance to change her mind.

He gave a quick look round. He'd determined not to

care about what he might find inside, but he couldn't help his curiosity. When he'd met Yasmin Edwards, she'd been living as lovers with a German woman, a lag like herself who'd done time for murder, also like herself. So he wondered if the German had been replaced.

There was no sign of this being the case. Everything was much as it had been before. He turned to Yasmin and found her watching him. She held her arms crossed beneath her breasts and her face read, Satisfied?

He hated being off balance with her. He wasn't used to that with women. He said, "There's a boy been murdered. Body was put up in St. George's Gardens, near Russell Square, Missus Edwards."

She said with a shrug, "North of the river," as if she meant, How can that affect this part of town?

He said, "No. It's more than that. This's one of a string of boys been found all over town. Gunnersbury Park, Tower Hamlets, carpark in Bayswater, and now the garden. One in the garden's white, but the rest of them, looks like all been mixed race. And young, Missus Edwards. Kids."

She shot a look towards the kitchen. He knew what she was thinking: Her Daniel fitted the profile he'd just described. He was young; he was mixed race. Still, she shifted her weight to one hip and said to Nkata, "All north of the river. Don't affect us over here. And why're you really here, 'f you don't mind my asking?," as if everything she said and the abrupt way she said it could protect her from fearing for her boy's safety.

Before Nkata could answer, Daniel returned to them, a cup of steaming cocoa in his hand. He appeared to avoid his mother's look as he said to Nkata, "I brought you this anyway. It's made from scratch. You c'n have more sugar in it if you want."

"Cheers, Dan." Nkata took the mug from the boy and clasped him on the shoulder. Daniel grinned and shifted from one bare foot to the other. "Look like you grown since I saw you," Nkata added.

"Did," Daniel said. "We measured. We got marks on a wall in the kitchen. You c'n see if you want. Mum marks me first of every month. I grew two inches."

"Sprouting up like that," Nkata said, "make your bones hurt?"

"Yeah! How'd you know? Oh, I 'xpect cos you grew fast as well."

"Tha's right," Nkata said. "Five inches one summer. Ouch."

Daniel laughed. He appeared ready to settle in for a chat, but his mother stopped this by saying his name sharply. Daniel looked from Nkata to her, then back to Nkata.

"Have your cocoa," Nkata said. "See you later."

"Yeah?" The boy's face asked that a promise be made.

Yasmin Edwards didn't allow it, saying, "Daniel, this man's here on business, nothing else." That was enough. The boy scooted back to the kitchen, casting one final look over his shoulder. Yasmin waited till he was gone before she said to Nkata, "Anything else?"

He took a gulp of the cocoa and set the mug on the iron-legged coffee table where the same red high-heel-shaped ashtray still sat, empty now that the German woman who'd used it was gone from Yasmin Edwards' life. He said, "You got to have more of a care right now. With Dan."

Her lips flattened. "You trying to tell me—"

"No," he said. "You the best mum that boy could have in the world, and I mean it, Yasmin." He startled himself with his use of her given name, and he was grateful when she pretended not to notice. He hurried on. "I know you got stuff to do coming out 'f your ears, what with the wig business an' all that. Dan spends time on his own, not cos that's the way you want it but cos that's how it is. All I'm saying is, this bleeder's picking up boys Dan's age and he's killing them, and I don't want that to happen to Dan."

"He's not stupid," Yasmin said curtly, although Nkata could tell this was all bravado. She wasn't stupid, either.

"I know that, Yas. But he's . . ." Nkata searched for the words. "You c'n tell he needs a man. 'S obvious. An' from what we c'n tell 'bout the boys been killed . . . They're going with him. They're not fighting it. No one sees anything cos there's nothing to see cos they trust him, okay?"

"Daniel *i'n't* about to go with some—"

"We think he uses a van," Nkata cut in, persisting in spite of her evident scorn. "We think it's red."

"I'm saying. Daniel doesn't take rides. Not from people he doesn' know." She cast a look in the direction of the kitchen. She lowered her voice. "What're you saying? You think I di'n't teach him that?"

"I know you taught him. Like I said, I c'n see you're a good mum to the boy. But that doesn' change what the fact is inside of him, Yas. And the fact is, he needs a man."

"Thinkin' you're going to be it or something?"

"Yas." Now that he'd begun saying her name, Nkata found he couldn't say it enough. It was an addiction for him, one he knew he had to be rid of in very short order or he would be lost, like a needle freak dossing in a doorway in the Strand. So he tried again. "Missus Edwards, I know Dan spends time on his own cos you're busy. And tha's not good and tha's not bad. It's just how it is. All I want you to unnerstan is wha's going on in your neighbourhood, see?"

"Fine," she said. "I un'erstand now." She moved past him to the door and reached for the knob, saying, "You did what you come for, and now you can—"

"Yas!" Nkata wouldn't be dismissed. He was there

to do the woman a service whether she liked it or not, and that service was to *impress* upon her the danger and urgency of the situation, neither of which she apparently wished to grasp. "There's a bugger out there going after boys just like Daniel," Nkata said rather more hotly than he would have liked. "He's getting them in a van and he's burning their hands till the skin goes black. Then he's strangling them and he's slicing them open." He had her attention now, and that spurred him to continue, as if each word were a way he proved something to her, although what that something was he didn't want to consider at the moment. "Then he marks them up a bit more with their own blood. And then he puts their bodies on display. Boys go with him and we don't know why and *till* we know . . ." He saw that her face had changed. Anger, horror, and fear had metamorphosed into . . . What was it he was seeing?

She was looking beyond him, her gaze fixed on the kitchen. And he knew. Just like that—as if fingers had snapped in front of his face and he suddenly returned to consciousness, he knew. He didn't have to turn. He only had to wonder how long Daniel had been standing in the doorway and how much he had heard.

Aside from having given Yasmin Edwards a wealth of information that she did not need and that he was not authorised to give to anyone, he'd frightened her son, and he knew that without looking, just as he knew he'd long outstayed whatever welcome he might have had in Doddington Grove Estate.

"Done enough?" Yasmin Edwards whispered fiercely, moving her gaze from her son to Nkata. "Said enough? Seen enough?"

Nkata tore his gaze from her, moving it to take in Daniel. He was standing in the doorway with a piece of toast in his hand, one leg crossed over the other and squeezing as if he needed the toilet. His eyes were big, and what Nkata felt was sorrow that he'd had to see or hear his mum in anything resembling an altercation with a man. He said to Daniel, "I d'n't want you to hear that, man. No need and I'm sorry. You just be careful on the street. There's a killer going after boys your age. I don't want him going after you."

Daniel nodded. He looked solemn. He said, " 'Kay." And then when Nkata turned to leave, "You come round again or what?"

Nkata didn't answer him directly. He said, "You just keep safe, okay?" And as he stepped out of the flat, he ventured a final look at Daniel Edwards' mother. His expression said to her, What did I tell you, Yasmin? Daniel needs a man.

Her expression responded just as clearly, Whatever you're thinking, that man i'n't you.

Chapter Six

Five more days passed. They comprised what every investigation into murder comprised, cubed by the fact that the squad was dealing with multiple killings. So the hours that stacked upon hours, which worked their way into long days, longer nights, and meals grabbed on the run, ended up being devoted to 80 percent slog. This involved endless phone calls, record checks, fact gathering, statements taking, and reports making. Another 15 percent went to coalescing all the data and trying to make some sense of it. Three percent went to revisiting every piece of information dozens of times to make sure nothing had been misunderstood, misplaced, or missed altogether, and 2 percent went to the occasional feeling that progress was actually being made. Staying power was necessary for the first 80 percent. Caffeine worked well for the rest.

During this time, the Press Bureau did its promised part to keep the media informed, and at these events AC Hillier continued to require DS Winston Nkata—and frequently Lynley as well—to serve as window dressing for the Met's display of Your Taxes at Work. Despite the maddening nature of the press conferences, Lynley had to admit that, so far, Hillier's performances in front of the journalists appeared to be paying off, since the press had not begun baying yet. But that didn't make the time spent with them any less onerous.

"My efforts might best be devoted to other pursuits, sir," he informed Hillier as diplomatically as possible after his third appearance on the dais.

"This is part of the job," was Hillier's reply. "Cope."

There was little enough to report to the journalists. DI John Stewart having divided his allocation of officers into teams, they were working with a military precision that could not be anything but pleasing to the man. Team one had completed their study of the alibis given by the possible suspects they'd dug up after looking into releases from mental hospitals and prisons. They'd done the same for sex offenders set free within the last six months. They'd documented who was working in open conditions prior to discharge, and they'd added homeless shelters to their list, to see if anyone behaving suspiciously had been hanging about on any of the murder nights. So far they'd uncovered nothing.

In the meantime, team two had taken over beating the bushes in an effort to roust out witnesses . . . to anything. Gunnersbury Park still looked like their best bet for this, and DI Stewart was, as he put it, damn well determined to find *something* in that direction. Surely, he had lectured the team, someone *had* to have seen a vehicle parked on Gunnersbury Road in the early hours of the morning when victim number one had been left inside, for it remained that the only two means of access into the park after hours were over the wall—which at eight feet high seemed an unlikely route for someone carrying a body—or through one of the two boarded-up sections of that wall on Gunnersbury Road. But so far, a canvassing of houses across the street had given team two nothing, and interviews with nearly all the lorry drivers who would have been on that route hadn't unearthed anything either. Nor had conversations—still ongoing—with taxi and minicab companies.

They were left with the red van seen in the area of St. George's Gardens. But when Swansea delivered a list of such vehicles registered to owners in the Greater London area, the total was an impossible 79,387. Even Hamish Robson's profile of the killer—suggesting that they limit their interest to those vehicle owners who were male, single, and between the ages of twenty-five and thirty-five—didn't make that number remotely manageable.

The entire situation made Lynley long for the cinematic version of the detective's life: a brief period of slog, a slightly longer period of cogitation, and then great scenes of action in which the hero chased the villain over land, over sea, through back alleys, and beneath elevated railway tracks, finally clobbering him into submission and securing his exhausted confession. But that wasn't how it was.

It was after yet another appearance in front of the press that three hopeful developments occurred within moments of each other, however.

Lynley returned to his office in time to pick up the phone and receive a call from SO7. The analysis of the black residue on all of the bodies and on the bicycle had coughed up a valuable piece of information. The van they were looking for was likely a Ford Transit. The residue came from the disintegration of a type of optional rubber lining that had been offered for use on the floor of this vehicle between ten and fifteen years ago. The Ford Transit detail was going to go some way towards narrowing down the list they'd received from Swansea, although they wouldn't know by how much until they fed the data into the computer.

When Lynley returned to the incident room with this news, he was greeted by the second development.

They'd had a positive identification on the body left in the Bayswater carpark. Winston Nkata had taken a jaunt to Pentonville Prison to show photographs of their killer's second victim to Felipe Salvatore—doing time for armed robbery and assault—and Salvatore had sobbed like a five-year-old when he declared the dead boy to be his little brother Jared whom he'd reported missing the first time he'd skipped a regular visit to the clink. As for any other members of Jared's family . . . They were proving more difficult to locate, a fact apparently having to do with the cocaine addiction and peripatetic nature of the dead boy's mother.

The final development also came from Winston Nkata, who'd spent two mornings on Kipling Estate, attempting to unearth someone whom they knew only as Blinker. His perseverance—not to mention his good manners—had finally paid off: One Charlie Burov, aka Blinker, had been located and was willing to talk to someone about his relationship with Kimmo Thorne, the St. George's Gardens victim. He didn't want to meet up on the housing estate where he dossed at his sister's, though. Instead he would meet someone—not in uniform, he'd apparently stressed—inside Southwark Cathedral, five pews from the back on the left-hand side, at precisely 3:20 in the afternoon.

Lynley grasped the opportunity to get out of the building for a few hours. He phoned the assistant commissioner with an update that offered fodder for the next press conference, and he himself effected an escape to Southwark Cathedral. He tapped DC Havers to go along. He told Nkata to check Jared Salvatore's name with Vice in the last police borough in which he'd lived, and after that to get on to the present location of the boy's family. Then he set off with Havers in the direction of Westminster Bridge.

It was a straightforward affair to get to Southwark Cathedral once the general confusion round Tenison

Way was mastered. Fifteen minutes after setting off from Victoria Street, Lynley and the detective constable were in the nave of the church.

Voices came from the direction of the chancel, where a group of what appeared to be students stood round someone pointing out details on the tester above the pulpit. Three out-of-season tourists were flipping through postcards at a bookstall directly across from the entrance, but no one appeared to be waiting for a meeting with anyone. The situation was exacerbated by the fact that, like most medieval cathedrals, Southwark had no regular pews, so there was no fifth-row-from-the-back-and-on-the-left seating where Charlie Burov, aka Blinker, might have slouched in anticipation of their arrival.

"So much for his churchgoing proclivities," Lynley murmured. As Havers looked round, sighed, and muttered a curse, he added, "Mind the mouth, Constable. Lightning is never a dear commodity when it comes to the Lord."

"He might've at *least* sussed out the place first," she groused.

"In the best of all worlds." Lynley finally spied a spindly, black-garbed figure near the baptismal font, who was darting looks in their general direction. "Ah. Over there, Havers. That could be our man."

He didn't run off as they approached him, although he cast a nervous glance towards the group at the pulpit and then another towards the people at the bookstall. When Lynley asked politely if he was Mr. Burov, the boy said, "'S Blinker. You the fuzz, then?" out of the side of his mouth like a character in a bad film noir.

Lynley introduced himself and Havers while he gave the boy a quick appraisal. Blinker appeared to be round twenty years old with a face that would have been completely nondescript had not head shaving and body piercing been in vogue. As it was, studs erupted from his face like a visitation of smallpox in silver and when he spoke, which was with some difficulty, it was to reveal half a dozen additional studs lined up along the edge of his tongue. Lynley didn't want to think about the difficulty they presented the boy in eating. Hearing the difficulty they presented him in speaking was bad enough.

"This might not be the best place to have our conversation," Lynley noted. "Is there somewhere nearby . . ."

Blinker agreed to a coffee. They managed to find a suitable café not far from St. Mary Overy Dock, and Blinker slid onto a chair at one of the grubby, Formica-topped tables where he studied the menu, and said, "C'n I get a spag bol, then?"

Lynley eased a malodorous ashtray towards Havers and said to the boy, "Be my guest," although he shuddered at the thought of personally ingesting any kind of food—not to mention any kind of pasta—served up in a place where one's shoes adhered to the lino and the menus looked in need of disinfectant.

Blinker apparently took Lynley's reply as licence for liberality, for when the waitress came for their order he added gammon steak, two eggs, chips, and mushrooms along with a tuna and sweet-corn sandwich to the spaghetti. Havers ordered an orange juice, Lynley a coffee. Blinker grabbed the plastic salt shaker and began rolling it between his palms.

He didn't want to talk until he'd "had a nosh," he told them. So they waited in silence for the first of his plates to arrive, Havers taking the opportunity for another smoke, Lynley nursing his coffee and steeling himself to the spectacle of the boy working food past his tongue studs.

He'd apparently had plenty of practice, as things turned out. When the first plate was deposited in front of him, Blinker made quick work of the gammon steak and its companions, with minimum fuss and—blessedly—even less display. When he'd sopped up the remaining egg yolk and gammon grease with a triangle of toast, he said, "Better, that," and appeared ready to give himself over for conversation and a cigarette, which he cadged from Havers while he waited for the pasta's arrival on the scene.

He was "that torn up" about Kimmo, he told them. But he'd warned his mate—he'd warned him a hundred million times—about taking it up the chute from blokes he didn't know. Kimmo always claimed the risk was worth it, though. And he *always* made them use a spunk bag . . . even if, admittedly, he didn't always turn round at the vital moment to make sure it was on.

"I tol' him it wa'n't *about* some bloke *infectin'* him, for God's sake," Blinker said. "It was about 'xactly what happened to him anyways. I *never* wanted him out there alone. Never. When Kimmo was on the streets, *I* was on the streets wif him. Tha's the way it was s'posed to be."

"Ah," Lynley said. "I'm getting the picture. You were Kimmo Thorne's pimp, then?"

"Hey. It wa'n't like that." Blinker sounded affronted.

"So you *weren't* his pimp?" Barbara Havers put in. "What would you call it when it was home with its mother?"

"I was his mate," Blinker said. "I kept watch for any nasty sort of business 'at might be going on, like some bloke wif more on his mind than a bit 'f fun wif Kimmo. We worked together, like a team. It wa'n't *my* fault, was it, Kimmo being the one they fancied?"

Lynley wanted to say that Blinker's appearance might have had something to do with who was being fancied by the punters, but he let the subject go. He said, "The night Kimmo disappeared, he didn't start out with you, then?"

"I di'n't even know he was going out, did I. We'd done Leicester Square the night before, see, and we'd found a party wanting some entertainment over in Hollen Street, so we did a bit of business wif them. We had enough dosh off that that we di'n't need to be out again and Kimmo said his gran wanted him home for a night anyways."

"Was that normal?" Lynley asked.

"Nah. So I should've known summat was up when he said it, but I didn't cos it was fine wif me not to go out. I had the telly . . . and other things to do."

"Such as?" Havers asked. When Blinker didn't respond, merely looking in the direction of the kitchen for his spaghetti Bolognese to put in an appearance, she said, "What else were you two into besides prostitution, Charlie?"

"Hey. Like I said. We *never* were into—"

"Let's not play games," Havers cut in. "Tart it up any way you want, but the truth is, if you get paid for it, Charlie, it's not true love. And you did get paid for it, right? Isn't that what you said? And isn't that why you didn't need to be going out another night? Because Kimmo had earned you enough cash for a week probably, providing 'entertainment' in Hollen Street. I'm wondering what you did with the lolly, though. Smoke it, shoot it, snort it? What?"

"You know, I don' *have* to talk to you lot," Blinker said hotly. "I could get up right now and be out of that door faster'n—"

"And miss your spaghetti Bolognese?" Havers asked. "Holy hell, *not* that."

Lynley said, "Havers," in the tone he generally used—with limited success—to restrain her. And to Blinker, "Would it have been like Kimmo to go off on his own? Despite your usual arrangement?"

"He did sometimes, yeah. Like I said. I tol' him not to, but he did it anyways. I said it wa'n't safe. He wa'n't a big bloke, was he, an' if he misjudged who he let do him . . ." Blinker crushed his cigarette and looked away. His eyes grew watery. "Stupid little bugger," he muttered.

His spaghetti Bolognese showed up, along with a dispenser of cheese that looked like sawdust deficient in iron. This he sprinkled delicately over the pasta and tucked in, his emotion subdued by his appetite. The café door opened and two workmen entered, jeans whitened by plaster dust and thick-soled shoes crusted with cement. They called out familiar hellos to the cook who was visible by means of a serving hatch, and they chose a table in a corner where they placed their orders for a multicourse meal not unlike the one Blinker himself had requested.

"I tol' him this would happen if he went it alone," Blinker said when he had finished wolfing down the pasta and was waiting for his tuna and sweet-corn sandwich. "I tol' him over an' over, but he never listened, did he. He said he could tell about blokes, he could. The bad ones, he said, they have this kind of smell 'bout them. Like they been thinking too long what they want to do to you and it makes their skin all oily and cooked up, like. I tol' him that was rubbish and he had to take me wif him no matter what, but he wasn't having any of that, was he, so look what happened."

"So you think this is the work of a punter," Lynley said. "Kimmo making a bad judgment call when he was alone."

"What else could it be?"

"Kimmo's gran said you've got him in trouble," Havers said. "She claims he was flogging stolen property you handed over to him. What d'you know about that?"

Blinker rose in his chair as if he'd been mortally wounded. "I never!" he said. "She's a bloody liar, she is. Flaming old cow. She di'n't like me from the first and now she's tryin to get me under the cosh, i'n't she. Well, any trouble Kimmo got in di'n't have nothing to do wif me. You ask round Bermondsey and see who knows Blinker and who knows Kimmo. Tha's what you do."

"Bermondsey?" Lynley asked.

But Blinker was saying nothing else. He was, instead, fuming at the idea that someone had fingered him as a thief instead of as what he really was, a common chili chump on the street, promoting the services of a fifteen-year-old boy.

Lynley said, "Were you and Kimmo lovers, by the way?"

Blinker shrugged, as if the question were unimportant. He looked round for his tuna sandwich, saw it waiting for delivery on the sill of the serving hatch, and went to fetch it himself. The waitress said, "Hang on, mate. I'll get to you soon 'nough."

Blinker ignored her and took the sandwich to the table. There, he didn't sit again. Nor did he eat. Instead, he wrapped the sandwich in his used paper napkin and shoved the package into the pocket of his worn leather jacket.

Lynley watched him and saw that the young man wasn't so much piqued by his final question as he was grieved in a way that he clearly had not expected to be. In a quivering muscle visible on his jaw, the answer lay. He and the dead boy had indeed been lovers, if not recently then initially, and probably before they had set off on a course of making money through the use of Kimmo's body.

Blinker looked at them as he zipped his jacket. He said, "Like I said. Kimmo wouldn't've had no trouble if he stayed wif me. But he didn't, did he? He went his own way when I tol' him not to. Thought he knew the world, he did. And look where it got him." That said, he was gone, making for the door and leaving Lynley and Havers studying the remains of his spaghetti Bolognese like high priests searching for auguries.

Havers said, "Didn't even say cheers for the meal." She picked up his fork and twirled two strands of the pasta onto it. This she then raised to the level of her eyes. "The body, though. Kimmo's body. None of the reports claim sex before he died, do they?"

"None of the reports," Lynley agreed.

"Which could mean . . . ?"

"That his death has nothing to do with working the streets. Unless, of course, what happened that night happened *before* they ever got to the sex." Lynley pushed his coffee cup to the centre of the table, most of it undrunk.

"But if we have to eliminate sex as part . . . ?" Havers asked.

"Then the question is: How are you at getting up before dawn?"

She looked at him. "Bermondsey?"

"I'd say that's our next direction." Lynley watched her as she considered this, the fork still dangling from her fingers.

She finally nodded, but she didn't look pleased. "I hope you're planning to be part of that party."

"I'd hardly let a lady prowl round South London in the dark on her own," Lynley replied.

"That's good news, then."

"I'm glad you're reassured. Havers, what are you intending to do with that pasta?"

She glanced at him, then back at the fork still dangling in the air. "This?" she said. She popped the spaghetti into her mouth and chewed it thoughtfully. "They definitely need to do some work on their al dente," she told him.

JARED SALVATORE, the second victim of their murderer—to whom they'd begun referring as Red Van for want of another sobriquet—had lived in Peckham, some eight miles as the crow flies from where his body had been found in Bayswater. Since from Pentonville Prison Felipe Salvatore had not been able to provide a recent address for his family, Nkata went first to their last-known abode, which was a flat in the wilderness of North Peckham Estate. This was a place where no one wandered unarmed after dark, where cops were not welcome, where turf was marked. It offered the worst there was in communal living: dismal lines of washing hanging from balconies and from drainpipes, broken and tyreless bicycles, shopping trolleys given over to rust, and every kind of rubbish imaginable. The North Peckham area made Nkata's own housing estate look like Utopia on opening day.

At the address he'd been given for the Salvatore family, Nkata found no one at home. He knocked up neighbours who either knew nothing or were willing to say nothing, until he found one who offered the information that the "crackhead cow and her snivellers" had finally been evicted after a monumental battle with Navina Cryer and her crew, all of whom hailed from Clifton Estate. That was the extent of the information available on the family. But having been given a new name—that of Navina Cryer—Nkata next went to Clifton Estate to seek her and whatever information she could give him of the Salvatores.

Navina turned out to be a sixteen-year-old girl who was hugely pregnant. She lived with her mother and her two younger sisters, along with two toddlers in nappies who, during Nkata's conversation with the girl, were never identified as belonging to anyone. Unlike the denizens of North Peckham Estate, Navina was only too happy to talk to the police. She took a long look at Nkata's warrant card, took a longer look at Nkata himself, and ushered him inside the flat. Her mother was at work, she informed him, and the rest of that lot—by which he reckoned she meant the other children—could look after themselves. She led him to the kitchen. There a table held several loads of unwashed laundry, and the air was ripe with the scent of disposable nappies in need of disposal.

Navina lit a cigarette on one of the grimy stove's gas burners, and she leaned against it rather than taking a seat at the table. Her stomach protruded so far that it was difficult to see how she actually remained upright, and beneath the taut material of her leggings, her veins stood out like worms after rainfall. She said abruptly, "'Bout time, innit. Wha' was it lit the fire under you lot? I'd like to know, so nex' time I got the right approach."

Nkata sorted through these remarks. He concluded from them that she'd been expecting the police. Considering the information he'd gleaned from the one neighbour willing to talk on North Peckam Estate, he assumed she was referring to the outcome—whatever it had been—of her reported altercation with Mrs. Salvatore.

He said, "Woman over North Peckham . . . ? She told me you might know the whereabouts of Jared Salvatore's mum. 'S that right?"

Navina narrowed her eyes. She took a deep hit on her cigarette—deep enough to make Nkata shudder for her unborn child—and as she blew the smoke out, she studied him, then studied the ends of her fingernails, which were painted fuchsia and matched her toenails. She said slowly, "Wha' 'bout Jared? You got word on him?"

"Word for his mum, you can tell me where she is," Nkata replied.

"Like she going t' care, you mean?" Navina sounded scornful. "Like he mean more to her than flake? That cunt di'n't even know he was *gone* till I tol' her, mister, an' if you find her under wha'ever car she been dossin since they got done wif her on North Peckham, you c'n tell her I said she c'n die an' I spit on her coffin an' be glad to do it." She took another hit on the cigarette. Nkata saw that her fingers were shaking.

He said, "Navina, c'n we reverse things here? I'm in the dark."

"How? Wha' more do I got to tell you lot? He been gone an' gone an' it ain't like him, which is what I been sayin over and over. Only no one's listenin an' I just 'bout ready—"

"Hang *on*," Nkata said. "C'n I get you to sit over here? I'm sorting this, but you're going too quick." He pulled a chair from beneath the table and indicated she should take it. One of the toddlers trundled into the kitchen at that point, nappy hanging nearly to his knees, and Navina took a moment to change him, which consisted of ripping the nappy off, tossing it into a swing bin—with its load mercifully intact—and strapping him into another without undo ceremony, the remains of his droppings still clinging to his flesh. After that, she rooted out a boxed Ribena for the child and handed it over, leaving him to suss out a manner of detaching its straw and driving it into the small carton. Then she lowered herself into the chair. All along her cigarette had dangled from her lips, but now she stubbed it out in an ashtray that she took from beneath the pile of dirty laundry.

Nkata said to her, "You reported Jared missing? Tha's what you're telling me?"

"I tol' the cops d'rectly he di'n't show up for the antenatal. I knew right then there was summat wrong 'cause he always come, di'n't he, to see 'bout his baby."

Nkata said, "He's the dad, then? Jared Salvatore's your baby's dad?"

"An' proud to be from the first, he was. Thirteen years old, not many blokes get started so fast, and he liked that, Jared. It made him swell up bigger 'n you would've believed, the day I tol' him."

Nkata wanted to know what she'd been doing messing with a mere boy who should have been at school making a future and not out on the loose making babies, but he did not ask. Navina herself should have been at school, if it came to that, or at least she should have been doing something more useful than offering herself to a randy adolescent at least three years her junior. She also had to have been doing the job with Jared since the boy had been twelve. It made Nkata's head swim, just thinking about it. And knowing that at twelve years old, with a willing female, he too might have happily plunged away his life, hot for that fleshy moment of contact and thinking about nothing else.

He said to Navina, "We got the report from his brother Felipe, in the Ville. Jared di'n't show for visiting when he should've, and Felipe called him in missing. This was something like five, six weeks ago."

"I went to them louts two days later!" Navina cried. "Two days af'er he di'n't show at the antenatal like he was s'posed to. I tol' the cops and they di'n't listen. They weren't havin none of it off me."

"When was this?"

"More'n a month ago," she said. "I go to the station and tell that bloke in reception I got someone missin. He say who and I say Jared. I tell him he di'n't come to the antenatal and he di'n't ever give me a bell about that or nothin which wa'n't *like* him. They figger he done a runner 'cause of the baby, see. They say wait 'nother day or two and when I go back, they say wait 'nother. An' I keep goin an' I keep tellin them an' they jot down my name an' Jared's an' no one does *nothing*." She began to cry.

Nkata got up from his own chair and went to hers. He put his hand on the back of her neck. He could feel how slender it was beneath his fingers and how warm her flesh was where it touched his own, and from that he guessed what the girl's appeal had been prior to being made hugely swollen and ungainly with a thirteen-year-old's child. He said, "I'm sorry. They should've listened, the locals. I'm not from there."

She raised her wet face. "But you said a cop . . . Then where?"

He told her. Then as gently as he could, he told her the rest: that the father of her baby was dead at the hands of a serial killer, that he'd probably already been dead on the day of the antenatal appointment he'd missed, that he was one of four victims who, like himself, were adolescent boys whose bodies had been found too far from their homes for anyone in the vicinity to recognise them.

Navina listened and her dark skin shone beneath the tears that continued to roll down her cheeks. Nkata felt torn between the need to comfort her and the desire to lecture some sense into her. What did she actually *think*, he wondered and wanted to say, that a thirteen-year-old boy would be around forever? Not so much because he'd die, although God knew enough of their young men never made it to thirty, but because he'd come to his senses eventually and realise there was more to life than fathering babies and he wanted whatever that *more* was?

The need to comfort won out. Nkata fished a handkerchief from his jacket pocket and pressed it on her. He said, "They should've listened and they di'n't, Navina. I can't 'xplain why. I'm that sorry 'bout it."

"*Can't* you 'xplain?" she asked bitterly. "What'm I to them? Cow up the spout, done to by the kid got caught wif two nicked credit cards and *tha's* what they remember 'bout him, innit? Snatched a purse once'r twice. Wif some blokes, tried to carjack a Mercedes one night. Some rude boy, so we don't plan on lookin for *him* nowhere, so get out of here, girl, and stop pollutin our precious atmosphere, thank you. Well I loved him, I did, and we meant to have a life together and he was makin that life. He was learning cookin and he meant to be a real chef. You ask round about that. You see what they say."

Cooking. Chef. Nkata took out the slender leather diary he used as a notebook, and he jotted the words down in pencil. He didn't have the heart to press Navina for more information. From what she'd already said, he reckoned there was going to be a treasure trove of facts about Jared Salvatore at the Peckham police station.

He said, "You be all right, Navina? You got someone I c'n ring for you?"

She said, "My mum," and for the first time she seemed sixteen and also what she probably was at heart, which was afraid, like so many of the girls who grew up in an environment where no one was safe and everyone was suspect.

Her mum worked in the kitchen at St. Giles Hospital, and when Nkata spoke to her by phone, she said she'd be home at once. "She i'n't startin, is she?" the woman asked anxiously and then said, "Thank Jesus for that, at least," when Nkata told her it was something of a different nature entirely but her presence would be a great comfort to the girl.

He left Navina in anticipation of her mother's arrival, and he went from Clifton Estate to Peckham police station, which was only a short distance along the High Street. In reception, a white special constable was working behind the counter, and he spent just a shade longer than seemed necessary at his tasks before he acknowledged Nkata. Then he said, "Help you?," with a face that managed to be perfectly blank.

Nkata took a certain pleasure in saying, "DS Nkata," as he showed his warrant card to the man. He explained why he'd come. As soon as he mentioned the Salvatore family name, it seemed he would need no further introduction. Finding someone at the station who *didn't* know the Salvatores would have been more challenging than finding someone who'd mixed with them at one time or another. Aside from Felipe doing time in Pentonville, there was another brother languishing in remand on a charge of assault. The mother had a record going back to her adolescence and the other boys in the family were apparently doing what they could to better it before they reached their twenties. So the real question was, who in the station did DS Nkata want to talk to, because just about anyone could give him an earful.

Nkata said that whoever had taken Navina Cryer's missing-persons report about Jared Salvatore would do. This, of course, brought up the delicate question of why no one had bothered to *file* such a report, but he didn't want to travel that road. Surely someone had listened to the girl if not formally recording what she'd said. That was the person he wanted to find.

Constable Joshua Silver turned out to be the man. He came to fetch Nkata from reception and ushered him into an office shared by seven other officers, where space was at a minimum and noise was at a maximum. He had something of a cubby hole carved out between a bank of perpetually ringing phones and a row of ancient filing cabinets, and he guided Nkata to this. Yes, he admitted, he'd been the person to whom Navina Cryer had spoken. Not the first time she'd come to the station, when she hadn't apparently got beyond reception, but the second and third times. Yes, he'd written down the information she'd offered, but truth to tell, he hadn't taken her seriously. The Salvatore yobbo was thirteen years old. Silver reckoned the boy'd done a runner, what with the girl on her way to popping. There was nothing in his past that suggested he'd be apt to hang round waiting for any blessed events to be occurring.

"Kid's been in trouble since he was eight years old," the constable said. "He came up before the magistrate first when he was nine—bag snatching from an old lady, this was—and the last time we hauled his bum through the door, it was for breaking into a Dixon's. Planned to sell the takings in one of the street markets, our Jared."

"You knew him personally?"

"As good as anyone round here, yeah."

Nkata handed over a photo of the body that Felipe Salvatore had named as that of his brother. Constable Silver examined it and nodded his confirmation of Felipe's identification. It was Jared, all right. The almond eyes, the squashed-tip nose. All the Salvatore kids had them, gift of the racial mix of their parents.

"Dad's Filipino. Mum's black. A crackhead." Silver looked up quickly as he said this last, as if he'd suddenly realised he might have given offence.

"I sorted that." Nkata took the picture back. He asked about the cooking that Jared was supposedly learning.

Silver knew nothing about this and declared it the product of either Navina Cryer's wishful thinking or Jared Salvatore's outright prevaricating. All he knew was that Jared had been turned over to Youth Offenders, where a social worker had tried—and obviously failed—to make something of him.

"Youth Offenders over here," Nkata said, "could they've arranged some training for the boy? D'they get jobs for kids?"

"When pigs fly," Silver said. "Our Jared frying fish in your local Little Chef? Don't know I'd've eaten a meal that bloke put on a plate if I was starving." Silver took a staple remover from the top of his desk and used it to dig some grime from beneath his thumbnail as he concluded, "Here's the real truth about scum like the Salvatores, Sergeant. Most of them end up where they're heading all along, and it was going to be no different for Jared, which was something Navina Cryer couldn't accept. Felipe's locked up already; Matteo's in remand. Jared was third in line of the kids, so he was next in line for the nick. Do-gooders over at Youth Offenders might've done their best to stop that from happening, but they had everything set against it from the start."

"Everything being . . . ?" Nkata inquired.

Silver eyed him over the staple remover and flicked the detritus from beneath his thumbnail onto the floor. "No offence meant, but you're the exception, man. You're not the rule. And I expect you had some advantages along the way. But there're times when people don't add up to much, and this is one of those times. You start out bad, you end up worse. That's just how it is."

Not if someone takes an interest, was what Nkata wanted to reply. Nothing was written in stone.

But he said nothing. He had the information he'd come for. He had no greater understanding of why Jared Salvatore's disappearance had gone largely unremarked by the police, but he needed no greater understanding. As Constable Silver himself had put it: That's just how it was.

Chapter Seven

When she got back to Chalk Farm at the end of the day, Barbara Havers was feeling almost jaunty. Not only had the interview with Charlie Burov—aka Blinker—seemed like a moment of actual progress, but being out of the incident room and engaged in the *human* end of the investigation in Lynley's company made her feel as though regaining her rank was not a pipe dream after all. She was, in fact, blithely humming "It's So Easy" when she hiked homeward from the spot she'd found to park the Mini. Even when rain began to fall and was driven into her face by the wind, she was not bothered. She merely stepped up her pace—and the tempo of her tune—and hurried towards Eton Villas.

She glanced quickly at the ground-floor flat when she went up the drive. Lights were on inside Azhar's digs, and through the French windows she could see Hadiyyah sitting at a table with her head bent over an open notebook.

Homework, Barbara thought. Hadiyyah was a dutiful pupil. She stood for a moment and watched the little girl. As she did so, Azhar came into the room and walked by the table. Hadiyyah looked up and followed him longingly with her gaze. He didn't acknowledge her, and she didn't speak, merely ducking her head again to her work.

Barbara felt a sharp twinge at the sight of this, struck by an unexpected anger whose source she didn't want to examine. She went along the path to her bungalow. Inside, she flipped on the lights, tossed her shoulder bag on the table, and dug out a tin of All Day Breakfast, which she dumped unceremoniously into a pan. She popped bread into the toaster and from the fridge took a Stella Artois, making a mental note to cut back on the drinking since this was yet another night when she was not supposed to be imbibing at all. But she felt like celebrating the interview with Blinker.

As her meal was doing what it could to prepare itself without her participation, she went as usual for the television remote, which again as usual she couldn't find. She was searching for it when she noticed that her answer machine was blinking. She punched it to play as she continued her search.

Hadiyyah's voice came to her, tense and low, sounding as if she was trying to keep someone else from hearing her. "I got gated, Barbara," she said. "This's the first chance I had to ring you 'cause I'm not meant even to use the phone. Dad said I'm gated 'till further notice' an' I don't think it's fair at *all*."

"Damn," Barbara muttered, studying the grey box from which her little friend's voice came.

"Dad said it's owing to my arguing with him. I di'n't really want to give back the Buddy Holly CD, see. Then when he said I had to, I said could I just leave it for you with a note. And he said no, I had to do it in person. And I said I di'n't think that was *fair*. And he said I was to do what he told me and since I 'clearly di'n't *want* to do it' he'd make sure it was done properly, which's why he came with me. And then I said he was mean, mean, mean and I *hated* him. And he . . ." A silence as if she were listening to something nearby. She hurried on. "I'm not meant to argue with him *ever* is what he said and he gated me. So I can't use the phone and I can't watch telly and I can't do anything but go to school and come home and it's not *fair*." She began to cry. "Gotta go. 'Bye," she managed to say with a hiccup. Then the message was over.

Barbara sighed. She had not expected this of Taymullah Azhar. He had broken rules himself: leaving an arranged marriage and two small children to take up with an English girl with whom he'd fallen in love. He'd been ousted from his family as a result, forever a pariah to his own kin. Of all the people on earth, he was the *last* person she would have anticipated being so inflexible and unforgiving.

She was going to have to have a talk with him. Punishments, she thought, should match their crimes. But she knew she would have to come up with an approach that didn't *seem* like actually talking to him, by which of course she really meant giving him a piece of her mind. No, she was going to have to dress it in the guise of a natural part of a conversation, which meant she was going to have to develop a *subject* of conversation that would allow the topics of Hadiyyah, lying, being gated, and unreasonable parents to arise naturally. At the moment, though, the very thought of all that verbal manoeuvring made Barbara's head feel like a balloon too full of air. She made a mental note to seek out a reasonable excuse to talk to Azhar, and she uncapped her Stella Artois.

There was a good chance, she thought, that she would need to consume two bottles of lager tonight.

FU MADE THE necessary preparations. These did not take long because He had laid the groundwork well. Once the chosen boy had proved himself worthy, He had watched him until He knew all his routines and movements. So when the time was right, He was able to make a quick choice of the environs in which He would finally act. He chose the gym.

He felt confident. He'd found a place where He'd been able to park without difficulty each time he'd been in the vicinity. It was in a street where on one side a stained brick wall formed the boundary of a schoolyard and on the other a cricket ground lay in darkness. The street wasn't particularly close to the gym, but Fu didn't expect that to present much trouble because, more important than anything else, the place He parked was on the route the boy would have to take to get to his home.

When he emerged from the gym, Fu was waiting although He made it seem as though their meeting were a coincidence.

"Hey," Fu said, all pleased surprise. "Is that... What're you *doing* here?"

The boy was three steps ahead of Him, shoulders hunched, as they always were, head hanging down. When he turned, Fu waited for recognition to dawn. It did quickly enough to satisfy.

The boy looked left and right, but it didn't seem so much because he wanted to escape what was coming, as to see if anyone else was there to witness the circumstance of such a person being in such a place where that person patently didn't belong. But there was no one nearby, for the gym's entrance was on the side of the building, not the front on the main route more used by pedestrians.

The boy jerked his head in that age-old male adolescent form of hello. His short dreadlocks bounced round his dark face. "Hey. What're *you* doing round here?"

Fu offered the excuse He'd planned. "Trying to make peace with my dad and getting nowhere, as usual." It meant nothing at all in the general scheme of life, but Fu knew it would mean everything to the boy. It told a tale of brotherhood in twelve brief words, obvious enough to be understood by a thirteen-year-old, subtle enough to suggest that a bond of the unspoken might actually exist between them. "Heading back to the banger. What about you? D'you live round here?"

"Up past the station. Finchley Road and Frognal."

"I'm parked in that direction. I'll give you a lift if you like."

He moved along, keeping His pace somewhere between a stroll and a brisk, wintertime walk. Like a regular mate, He lit a cigarette, offered one to the boy, and confided that He'd parked a bit of a distance from where He'd met His dad because He'd known He'd want to clear His head afterwards with a walk. "Never works out with the two of us talking," Fu said. "Mum says she only wants us to *relate* to each other but I keep telling her you can't relate to a bloke who walked out before you were born." He felt the boy's eyes on Him, but they suggested interest and not suspicion.

"I met my dad once. Works on German cars over in North Kensington, he does. I went to see him."

"Waste of time?"

"Bloody waste." The boy kicked a squashed Fanta can that lay in their path.

"Loser?"

"Bugger."

"Wanker?"

"Yeah. No one else'll prob'ly touch it."

Fu gave a bark of laughter. "Motor's just over that way," He said. "Come on." He crossed over the road, careful not to watch to see if the boy was following. He took His keys from His pocket and jangled them in His hand, the better to telegraph the nearness of the van should his companion begin to feel uneasy. He said, "Heard you've been doing well, by the way."

The boy shrugged. Fu could tell he was pleased by the compliment, though.

"What're you on to now?"

"Doing a design."

"What sort?"

There was no reply. Fu glanced the boy's way, thinking He might have pushed too far, invading what was delicate territory for some reason. And the boy *did* look embarrassed and reluctant to speak, but when he finally replied, Fu understood his hesitation: the discomfiture of a teenager afraid of being labelled uncool. He said, "For a church thing meets in a shop down Finchley Road."

"That sounds good." But it didn't, really. The idea of the boy's being attached to a church group gave Fu pause because the disenfranchised were what He wanted. A moment later, however, the boy clarified the level—or lack thereof—of both his virtue and his connection with others. "Rev Savidge's got me in care at his house."

"The . . . vicar is it? . . . of the church group?"

"Him and his wife. Oni. She's from Ghana."

"From Ghana? Recently?"

The boy shrugged. It seemed a habit with him. "Don' know. It's where his own people're from. Rev Savidge's people. It's where they came from before they got sent to Jamaica on a slave ship. Oni, she's called. Rev Savidge's wife. Oni."

Ah. The second and third time he'd said her name. Here, then, was a *real* something to be mined, several nuggets at once. Fu said, "Oni. That's a brilliant name."

"Yeah. She's a star."

"Like to live with them, then? Reverend Savidge and Oni?"

The shoulders again, that casual lift of them that hid what the boy no doubt was feeling, not to mention what he was wanting. "All right," he said. "Better than with my mum anyway." And before Fu could press, asking the boy questions that would reveal his mum's imprisonment, thereby allowing Fu to forge yet another false bond with him, the boy said, "So where's your car, then?" in a restless manner, which could be interpreted as a very bad sign.

Thankfully, though, they were nearly upon it, parked in the shadows of an enormous plane tree. "Right there," Fu said, and He gave a look round to make sure the street was as deserted as it had been on His every recce of the site. It was. Perfect. He tossed his cigarette into the street, and when the boy had done the same, He unlocked the passenger door. "Hop in," He said. "You hungry? I've some takeaway in that bag on the floor."

Roast beef, although it should have been lamb. Lamb would have been richer with appropriate associations.

Fu shut the door when the boy was inside and going for the bag of food as required of him. He tucked right in. Happily, he didn't notice that his door had no interior handle and that his seat belt had been removed. Fu joined him, heaving Himself into the driver's seat and thrusting the ignition key into its home. He started the van, but He did not put it into gear, nor did He release its hand brake. He said to the boy, "Grab us something to drink, okay? I've a cooler back there. Behind my seat. I could do with a lager. There's Cokes if you want one. Or have a beer yourself if you'd rather."

"Cheers." The boy twisted in his seat. He peered into the back where, because the van was carefully panelled and thoroughly insulated, it was conveniently dark as the devil's bum. He said, "Behind where?" as required of him.

Fu said, "Hang on. I've got a torch here somewhere," and He made much of searching round His seat till He put His hands on the torch in its special hidden spot. He said, "Got it. Have some light, then," and He flicked it on.

Focused on the cooler and the promise of beer within it, the boy didn't notice the rest of the van's interior: the body board firmly in its brackets, the wrist and ankle restraints curled to either side on the floor, the stove from the vehicle's former days, the roll of tape, the washing line, and the knife. Especially that. The boy saw none of this because like the others who'd preceded him, he was just a male adolescent with the male adolescent's appetites for the illicit and in this moment the illicit was represented by beer. In another moment, an earlier moment, the illicit had been represented by crime. It was that for which he now stood doomed to punishment.

Turned in his seat and bending to the back of the van, the boy reached towards the cooler. This exposed his torso. It was a movement designed to aid what followed.

Fu turned the torch and pressed it into the boy. Two hundred thousand volts scrambled his nervous system.

The rest was easy.

LYNLEY WAS STANDING at the work top in the kitchen, downing a cup of the strongest coffee he'd been able to manage at half past four in the morning, when his wife joined him. In the doorway, Helen blinked against the overhead lights as she tied the belt of her dressing gown round her. She looked extremely weary.

"Bad night?" he asked her and added with a smile, "All that worry over christening clothes?"

"Stop," she grumbled. "I dreamed our Jasper Felix was doing backflips in my stomach."

She came to him and slipped her arms round his waist, yawning as she rested her head against his shoulder. "What are you doing dressed at this hour? The Press Bureau haven't taken to offering predawn press briefings, have they? You know what I mean: See how diligently we work at the Met; we're up before the sun on the scent of malefactors."

"Hillier would ask for that if he thought of it," Lynley replied. "Wait another week. It'll occur to him."

"Misbehaving, is he?"

"Just being Hillier. He's parading Winston in front of the press like Rod Hull. Except poor Emu doesn't get to speak."

Helen looked up at him. "You're angry about this, aren't you? It's not like you not to be philosophical. Is this about Barbara? Winston's getting the promotion instead of her?"

"That was rotten of Hillier, but I should have seen it coming," Lynley said. "He'd love to get rid of her."

"Still?"

"Always. I've never known quite how to protect her, Helen. Even doing the superintendent bit temporarily, I feel at a loss. I haven't a quarter of Webberly's skill at this sort of thing."

She released herself from his embrace and went to the cupboard where she took out a mug, which she filled with skimmed milk and put into the microwave to heat. She said, "Malcolm Webberly has the advantage of being Sir David's brother-in-law, darling. That would have counted for something when they knocked heads on an issue, wouldn't it?"

Lynley grumbled, neither agreement nor dissent. He watched his wife take her warmed milk from the microwave and stir a spoonful of Horlicks into it. He finished off his coffee and was rinsing out the cup when the front doorbell buzzed.

Helen turned from the work top, saying, "Who on earth . . . ?" as she looked towards the wall clock.

"That'll be Havers."

"You *are* going to work, then? Really? At this hour?"

"Going to Bermondsey." He left the kitchen and she followed, Horlicks in hand. "The market."

"*Tell* me it's not to shop," she said. "Bargains are bargains, and you know I'd never turn away from one myself, but surely one ought to draw the line at bargains reached before the sun comes up."

Lynley chuckled. "Are you sure you don't want to come with us? The odd piece of priceless porcelain for twenty-five pounds? The Peter Paul Rubens hidden beneath two centuries of grime, with nineteenth-century household cats painted over it by a six-year-old?" He crossed the marble tiles of the entrance and opened the door to find Barbara Havers leaning against the iron railing, a knitted cap pulled low on her brow and a donkey jacket wrapped round her stubby body.

Havers said to Helen, "If you're seeing him off at this hour, the honeymoon has definitely gone on too long."

"My restless dreams are seeing him off," Helen said. "That and general anxiety over the future, according to my husband."

"Haven't decided on the christening clobber yet?"

Helen looked at Lynley. "Did you actually tell her, Tommy?"

"Was it confidential?"

"No. Just inane. The situation, that is, not your telling it." And then to Barbara, "We may have a small fire in the nursery. It will, unfortunately, burn both sets of clothes beyond use and recognition. What do you think?"

"Sounds just the ticket to me," Havers said. "Why go for family compromise when you can have arson?"

"Our very thought."

"Better and better," Lynley said. He put his arm round his wife's shoulders and kissed the side of her head. "Lock up behind me," he instructed her. "And go back to bed."

Helen spoke to her small bump. "Do not haunt my dreams again, young man. Mind your mummy." And then to Lynley and Barbara, "And you mind how you go," before she shut the door behind them.

Lynley waited to hear the bolts shoot into place. Next to him, Barbara Havers was lighting a cigarette. He eyed her with disapproval, saying, "At half past four in the morning? Even in my worst days, Havers, I couldn't have managed that."

"Are you aware there's nothing more sanctimonious than a reformed smoker, sir?"

"I don't believe it," he replied, leading them down the street in the direction of the mews, where his car was garaged. "There must be something else."

"Nothing," she said. "There've been studies done on it. Even your basic Mary Magdalenes living now as nuns don't rate a sausage compared to your former weed fiends."

"It must be our concern for the health of our fellows."

"More like your desire to inflict your misery on everyone else. Give it up, sir. I know you want to rip this out of my hand and smoke it to the nub. How long have you gone without at this point?"

"So long I can't even remember, actually."

"Oh, bloody right," she said to the sky.

They set off in the blessing of early morning London: There was virtually no other vehicle on the streets. Because of this, they zipped through Sloane Square with all traffic lights in their favour, and in less than five minutes they saw the lights of Chelsea Bridge and the tall brick smokestacks of Battersea Power Station rising into the charcoal sky across the Thames.

Lynley chose a route along the embankment that kept them on the wrong side of the river as long as possible, where he was more familiar with the turf. Here too there were very few vehicles, just the odd cab heading into the centre of town for the day's work and the occasional lorry getting a head start on deliveries. Thus they wended their way to the massive grey fortress that was the Tower of London before crossing over, and from there it was no difficult feat to find Bermondsey Market, not overly far along Tower Bridge Road.

Using the illumination of tall streetlamps, as well as torches, fairy lights strung round the occasional stall, and other localised lights of dubious origin and weak wattage, vendors were in the final stages of setting up for business. Their day would begin shortly—for the market opened at five in the morning and was a thing of memory by two in the afternoon—so they were intent upon the assembly of the poles and tables that defined their stalls. Around them in the darkness waited boxes of countless treasures, which were stacked on carts that had been wheeled into position from vans and cars along the nearby streets.

Already, there were people waiting to be the first to browse through everything from hairbrushes to high-button shoes. No one officially held them back, but it was clear from watching the vendors at work that customers would not be welcome until the goods were fully displayed beneath the predawn sky.

As in most London markets, the vendors occupied the same general area every time Bermondsey was open for business. So Lynley and Havers began at the north end and worked their way south, asking for someone who could talk to them about Kimmo Thorne. The fact that they were police did not garner them the quick cooperation they had hoped for under circumstances that involved the death of one of the vendors' own. But this they knew was likely due to Bermondsey's reputation for being a clearing ground for stolen property, a place where the *trade* part of "in the trade" frequently meant breaking and entering.

They'd spent more than an hour quizzing vendors when a seller of ersatz Victorian dressing-table sets ("This's guaranteed one hunderd p'rcent the genuine article, sir and madam") recognised Kimmo's name, and after declaring both the name and the person in possession of it, "an odd l'tle sod, you ask me," he directed Lynley and Havers to an elderly couple at a silver stall. "You talk to the Grabinskis over there," he said, using his chin to indicate the direction. "They'll be able to tell you what's what with Kimmo. Dead sorry about wha' happened to the l'tle sod. Read about it in the *News of the World.*"

So, evidently, had the Grabinskis, who turned out to be a couple whose only son had died years in the past but at something near the same age as Kimmo Thorne. They'd quite taken to the boy, they explained, not so much because he reminded them physically of their dear Mike but because he had something of Mike's enterprising nature. This quality the Grabinskis both admired in Kimmo and deeply missed in their departed son, so when Kimmo had turned up on occasion with the odd something or other or a bagful of somethings he wanted to sell, they shared their stall with him and he gave them a portion of his profit.

Not that they'd ever asked him for it, Mrs. Grabinski said hastily. Her name was Elaine and she wore sage green Wellingtons with red wool kneesocks gaily turned over their tops. She was polishing an impressive epergne, and the moment Lynley had said Kimmo Thorne's name, she'd said, "Kimmo? Who's come to ask about Kimmo, then? 'Bout time, innit," and she made herself available to help them. As did her husband, who was hanging a display of silver teapots on strings that dangled from one of the horizontal poles of the stall.

The boy had come to them first, hoping they would buy from him, Mr. Grabinksi—"Call me Ray"—informed them. But he asked a price they weren't willing to pay, and when no one else in the market was willing to pay it either, Kimmo had returned to them with another offer: to sell from the stall himself and to give them a portion of the takings.

They'd liked the boy—"He was that cheeky," Elaine confided—so they gave him a quarter of one of the tables along the side of the stall, and there he did his business. He sold silver pieces—some plate, some sterling—with a speciality in photo frames.

"We've been told he got into some trouble with that," Lynley said. "Evidently he sold something that shouldn't have been on sale in the first place."

"Having been lifted off someone else," Havers put in.

Oh, they knew nothing about *that*, both Grabinskis hastened to say. As far as they were concerned, it was someone wanting to get Kimmo in trouble who told that tale to the local rozzers. Doubtless, in fact, it was their chief competitor in the market: one Reginald Lewis, to whom Kimmo had also gone trying to sell his silver before returning to them. Reg Lewis was that jealous of *anyone* wanting to set up business round early morning Bermondsey, wasn't he? He'd tried to keep the Grabinskis out twenty-two years back when they first started, he'd done the same to Maurice Fletcher and to Jackie Hoon when they started up.

"So there was no truth to Kimmo's goods being stolen?" Havers asked, looking up from her notebook. "Because, when you think of it, how else would a kid like Kimmo be coming across valuable pieces of silver for sale?"

They had assumed he was selling off family pieces, Elaine Grabinski said. They did ask him and that's what he told them: He was helping out his gran by offering the family silver to the public.

To Lynley it looked like a case of the Grabinskis believing what they had wanted to believe because they liked the boy, rather than a case of Kimmo being a sophisticated liar who pulled the wool over the eyes of an elderly couple. They had to have known at some level that he wasn't the legitimate article, but at that same level, they had to have not cared.

"We told the police we'd speak up for the boy if it came to court," Ray Grabinski asserted. "But once they carted poor Kimmo off, we didn't hear 'nother word about him. Till we saw the *News of the World*, that is."

"An' you ask Reg Lewis 'bout *that*, you lot," Elaine Grabinski said, returning to the epergne with renewed vigour. She added ominously, "What I wouldn't put past *him* fits in a teaspoon," and her husband said, "Now, pet," and patted her shoulder.

Reg Lewis turned out to be only slightly less antique than his wares. He wore bright tartan braces beneath his jacket and they held up a pair of ancient plus fours. His spectacles were as thick as the bottom of whisky tumblers. Overlarge hearing aids protruded from his ears. He fit the profile of their serial killer as well as a sheep fit the profile of a genius.

He "weren't s'prised none" when the cops had come calling for Kimmo, he told them. Something was off with the bugger first time Reg Lewis laid eyes on the creature. Dressed half man, half woman he did, with them tights of his or whatever they were, and those poncey ankle boots and the like. So when the cops showed up with a list of stolen property in their mitts, he—Reg Lewis, mind you—was *not* gobsmacked that they found what they were looking for in the possession of one Kimmo Thorne. Carted him off then and there, they did, and good riddance it was. Besmirching the reputation of the market, he was, flogging pinched silver. And not any pinched silver, mind you, but pinched silver that he'd been too thick to notice had personal and *immediately* identifiable engraving upon it.

What happened to Kimmo after that, Reg Lewis didn't know and didn't much care. The only good thing the little nancy boy did at the end of the day was not drag the Grabinskis down with him. And weren't those two blind as bats in the daylight? Anyone with sense would've known that boy was up to no good when he first showed his mug in the market. Reg warned the Grabinskis off him, he did, but would they listen to someone with their best interests at heart? Not bloody likely. Yet who turned out to be right at the end of the day, eh? And who never heard a word of you-were-right-Reg-and-we-apologise-for-our-nastiness from anyone, eh?

Reg Lewis had nothing more to add. Kimmo had vanished that day with the coppers. Perhaps he'd done a stretch in borstal. Perhaps he'd had the fear of God put into him at the police station. All Reg knew was that the boy hadn't brought any more stolen silver to sell in Bermondsey Market, which was fine by Reg. Cops over in Borough High Street could fill anyone in on the rest, couldn't they.

Reg Lewis said everything but "good riddance to bad rubbish," and if he'd read about or heard about Kimmo Thorne's murder, he made no mention of the fact. But it was clear that the boy had done nothing to enhance the reputation of the market in Reg's eyes. More than that, as he had pointed out, they would have to suss out from the local police.

They were on their way to do so—wending their way through the market, back to Lynley's car—when his mobile rang.

The message was terse, its meaning unmistakable: He was wanted immediately on Shand Street, where a tunnel beneath the railway took the narrow little thoroughfare to Crucifix Lane. They had another body.

Lynley flipped off the phone and looked at Havers. "Crucifix Lane," he said. "Do you know where it is?"

A vendor at a nearby stall answered the question. Right up Tower Bridge Road, he told them. Less than half a mile from where they stood.

A RAILWAY VIADUCT shooting out from London Bridge station comprised the north perimeter of Crucifix

Lane. Bricks formed it, so deeply stained with more than a century of soot and grime that whatever their original colour had been, it was now a distant memory. What remained in that memory's place was a bleak wall done up in variations of carbonaceous sediment.

Into this structure's supporting arches had been built various places of business: lockups for hire, warehouses, wine cellars, car-repair establishments. But one of the arches created a tunnel through which ran a single lane that was Shand Street. The north part of this street served as the address of several small businesses closed at this hour of the morning and the south part of it—the longer part—curved under the railway viaduct and disappeared into the darkness. The tunnel here was some sixty yards long, a place of deep shadows whose cavernous roof was bandaged with corrugated steel plates from which water dripped, soundless against the consistent rumble of early morning trains heading into and out of London. More water ran down the walls, seeping from the rusty iron gutters at a height of eight feet, collecting in greasy pools below. The scent of urine made the tunnel's air rank. Broken lights made its atmosphere chilling.

When Lynley and Havers arrived, they found the tunnel completely sealed off at either end, with a constable at the Crucifix Lane end who—clipboard in hand—was restricting entrance. He had apparently met his match in the early representatives of the news media, however, those hungry journalists who monitored every police station's patch in the hope of being first with a breaking story. Five of them had already assembled at the police barrier, and they were shouting questions into the tunnel. Three photographers accompanied them, creating strobe-like lighting as they shot above and around the constable who was trying vainly to control them. As Lynley and Havers showed their identification, the first of the television news vans pulled up, disgorging camera and soundmen onto the pavement as well. A media officer was needed desperately.

". . . serial killer?" Lynley heard one of the journalists call out as he crossed the barrier with Havers behind him.

". . . kid? Adult? Male? Female?"

"Hang on, mate. Give us bloody *something*."

Lynley ignored them, Havers muttered, "Vultures," and they moved in the direction of a low-slung, paintless, and abandoned sports car sitting midway through the tunnel. Here, they learned, the body had been discovered by a taxi driver on his way from Bermondsey to Heathrow, from which he would spend the day driving transatlantic fares into London for an exorbitant price made more exorbitant by the perennial tailback on the east side of the Hammersmith Flyover. That driver was long gone, his statement taken. In his place the SOCO team already worked, and a DI from the Borough High Street station waited for Lynley and Havers to join him. He was called Hogarth, he said, and his DCI had given the word to make no moves till someone from Scotland Yard checked out the crime scene. It was clear he wasn't happy about that.

Lynley couldn't be troubled with unruffling the DI's feathers. If this was indeed another victim of their serial killer, there would be far greater concerns than someone's not liking having his patch invaded by New Scotland Yard.

He said to Hogarth, "What have we got?" as he donned a pair of latex gloves handed over by one of the scenes-of-crime officers.

"Black kid," Hogarth replied. "Boy. Young. Twelve or thirteen? Hard to tell. Doesn't fit the MO of the serial, you ask me. Don't know why you lot got a call."

Lynley knew. The victim was black. Hillier was covering his well-tailored backside in advance of his next press briefing. "Let's see him," he said, and he stepped past Hogarth. Havers followed.

The body had been deposited unceremoniously in the abandoned car, where the driver's seat had over time disintegrated down to metal frame and springs. There, with its legs splayed out and its head lolling to one side, it joined Coke bottles, Styrofoam cups, carrier bags of rubbish, McDonald's take-away containers, and a single rubber glove that lay on what had once been the rim of the car's back window. The boy's eyes were open, staring sightlessly at what remained of the car's rusted steering column, short dreadlocks springing out of his head. With smooth walnut skin and perfectly balanced features, he had been quite lovely. He was also naked.

"Hell," Havers murmured at Lynley's side.

"Young," Lynley said. "He looks younger than the last. Christ, Barbara. Why in God's name . . . " He didn't finish, letting the unanswerable go unasked. He felt Havers' glance graze him.

She said with a prescience that came from working with him for years, "There're no guarantees. No matter what you do. Or what you decide. Or how. Or with whom."

"You're right," he said. "There are never guarantees. But he's still somebody's son. All of them were that. We can't forget it."

"Think he's one of ours?"

Lynley took a closer look at the boy, and upon a first glance, he found himself agreeing with Hogarth. While the victim was naked as had been Kimmo Thorne, his body clearly had been dumped without ceremony and not laid out like all the others. He had no piece of tatting as a modesty wrap on his genitalia, and there was no distinguishing mark on his forehead, both additional features of Kimmo Thorne's body. His abdomen did not appear to be incised, but perhaps more important, the position of the body itself suggested haste and a lack of planning that were uncharacteristic of the other murders.

As the SOCO team moved round him with their evidence bags and collection kits, Lynley made a closer inspection. This proved to tell him a more complete tale. He said, "Have a look at this, Barbara," as he gently lifted one of the boy's hands. The flesh was deeply burned, and the marks of a restraint dug into the wrist.

There was much about any serial killing that was known only by its perpetrator, held back by the police for the dual reason of protecting the victims' families from unnecessarily heartbreaking knowledge and of winnowing out false confessions from the attention seekers who plagued any investigation. In this particular case, there was much that still remained police knowledge only, and both the burns and the restraints were part of that knowledge.

Havers said, "That's a pretty good indication of what's what, isn't it?"

"It is." Lynley straightened up and glanced over to Hogarth. "He's one of ours," he said. "Where's the pathologist?"

"Been and gone," Hogarth replied. "Photographer and videographer as well. We've just been waiting for you lot before we clear him out of here."

The rebuke was implied. Lynley ignored it. He asked for the time of death, for any witnesses, for the taxi driver's statement.

"Pathologist's given us a time of death between ten and midnight," Hogarth said. "No witnesses to anything so far as we can tell, but that's not surprising, is it. Not a place you'd find anyone with brains after dark."

"As for the taxi driver?"

Hogarth consulted an envelope that he took from his jacket pocket. It evidently did duty as his notepad.

He read off the name of the driver, his address, and the number of his mobile phone. He'd had no fare with him, the DI added, and the Shand Street tunnel was part of his regular route to work. "Goes past between five and half past every morning," Hogarth told them. "Said this"—with a nod at the abandoned car—"has been here for months. Complained about it more'n once, he said. Banged on about how it's asking for trouble when Traffic Division can't seem to get round to—" Hogarth's attention went from Lynley to the Crucifix Lane end of the tunnel. He frowned. "Who's this? You lot expecting a colleague?"

Lynley turned. A figure was coming along the tunnel towards them, backlit from the lights for the television cameras that were rolling in the street. There was something familiar about the shape of him: big and bulky, with a slight stoop to the shoulders.

Havers was saying cautiously, "Sir, isn't that . . ." when Lynley himself realised who it was. He drew in a breath so sharp that he felt its pressure beat within his eyes. The interloper on the crime scene was Hillier's profiler, Hamish Robson, and there could be only one way he'd gained access to the tunnel.

Lynley didn't hesitate before striding towards the man. He took Robson by the arm without preamble. "You need to leave at once," he said. "I don't know how you managed to cross that barrier, but you've no business here, Dr. Robson."

Robson was clearly surprised by the greeting. He glanced over his shoulder in the direction of the barrier through which he'd just come. He said, "I had a phone call from Assistant—"

"I've no doubt of that. But the assistant commissioner was out of order. I want you to clear out. Immediately."

Behind his glasses, Robson's eyes assessed. Lynley could feel the evaluation going on. He could read the profiler's conclusion as well: subject experiencing understandable stress. True enough, Lynley thought. Each time the serial killer struck, the bar would be raised. Robson hadn't *seen* stress yet, compared to what he'd see if the killer snuffed out someone else before the police got to him.

Robson said, "I can't pretend to know what's going on between you and AC Hillier. But now that I'm here, I might be of use to you if I have a look. I'll keep my distance. There's no risk I'll contaminate your crime scene. I'll wear what you need me to wear: gloves, overalls, cap, whatever. Now I'm here, use me. I can help you if you'll let me."

"Sir . . . ?" Havers spoke.

Lynley saw that from the opposite end of the tunnel, a trolley had been wheeled, the body bag upon it ready to be used. A SOCO team member stood with paper bags prepared for the victim's hands. All that was required was a nod from Lynley and part of the problem engendered by Robson's presence would be taken care of: There would be nothing for him to see.

Havers said, "Ready?"

Robson said quietly, "I'm already here. Forget how and why. Forget Hillier altogether. For God's sake, use me."

The man's voice was as kind as it was insistent, and Lynley knew there was truth in what he said. He could hold rigidly to the arrangement he'd negotiated with Hillier or he could use the moment and refuse to let it mean anything else than simply that: seizing an opportunity in front of him, one that presented a chance to have a bit more insight into the mind of a killer.

Abruptly, he said to the team members waiting to bag the body, "Hang on for a moment." And then to Robson, "Have a look, then."

Robson nodded, murmured, "Good man," and approached the paintless car. He went no closer than four feet from it and when he wanted to examine the hands, he did not touch them but rather asked DI Hogarth to do it. For his part, Hogarth shook his head in disbelief but cooperated. Having Scotland Yard there at all was bad enough; having a civilian on the scene was unthinkable. He lifted the hands with an expression that said the world had gone mad.

After several minutes of contemplation, Robson returned to Lynley's side. He said first what Lynley and Havers had themselves said, "So young. God. This can't be easy for any of you. No matter what you've seen in your careers."

"It isn't," Lynley said.

Havers came to join them. By the car, the preparations began for transferring the body onto the trolley, to remove it for postmortem examination.

Robson said, "There's a change. Things are escalating now. You can see he's treated the body completely differently: no covering of the genitals, no respectful positioning. There's no regret at all, no psychic restitution. Instead, there's a real need to humiliate the boy: legs spread out, genitalia exposed, seated with the rubbish deposited by vagrants. His interaction with this boy *prior* to death was unlike his interactions with the others. With them, something occurred to stir him to regret. With this boy, that didn't happen. Rather, its opposite did. Not regret, then, but pleasure. And pride in the accomplishment as well. He's confident now. He's sure he won't be caught."

Havers said, "How can he think that? He's put this kid on a public street, for God's sake."

"That's just the point." Robson gestured to the far end of the tunnel, where Shand Street opened up to the small businesses that lined it in a few dozen yards of South London redevelopment that took the form of modern brick buildings with decorative security gates in front of them. "He's placed the body where he could easily have been seen doing so."

"Couldn't you argue the same of the other locations?" Lynley asked.

"You could do, but consider this. In the other locations, there was far less risk for him. He could have used something no witness would question as he transported the body from his vehicle to the dump site: a wheelbarrow, for example, a large duffel bag, a street sweeper's trolley. *Anything* that wouldn't seem out of place in that particular area. All he had to do was get the body from his vehicle to the dump site itself, and under cover of darkness, using that reasonable means of transport, he'd be fairly safe. But here, he's out in the open the moment he puts the body into that derelict car. And he didn't just dump it there, Superintendent. It only looks dumped. But make no mistake. He *arranged* it. And he was confident he wouldn't be caught at his work."

"Cocky bastard," Havers muttered.

"Yes. He's proud of what he's been able to accomplish. I expect he's somewhere nearby even now, watching all the activity he's managed to provoke and enjoying every bit of it."

"What d'you make of the missing incision? The fact that he didn't mark the forehead. Can we conclude he's backing off now?"

Robson shook his head. "I expect the missing incision merely means that, for him, this killing was different to the others."

"Different in what way?"

"Superintendent Lynley?" It was Hogarth, who'd been supervising the transfer of the body from the car to the trolley. He'd stopped the action prior to the body bag being zipped round the corpse. "You might want a look at this."

They went back to him. He was gesturing to the

boy's midsection. There, what had been obscured before by the body's slumped position in the seat was visible now that it was stretched on the trolley. While the incision from sternum to navel had indeed not been made on this most recent victim, the navel itself had been removed. Their killer had taken another souvenir.

That he'd done so after death was evident in the lack of blood from the wound. That he'd done so in anger—or possibly in haste—was evident in the slash across the stomach. Deep and uneven, it provided access to the navel, which a pair of secateurs or scissors had then removed.

"Souvenir," Lynley said.

"Psychopath," Robson added. "I suggest you post surveillance at all the previous crime scenes, Superintendent. He's likely to return to any one of them."

Chapter Eight

Fu was careful with the reliquary. He carried it before Him like a priest with a chalice and set it down on a tabletop. Gently, He removed the lid. A vaguely putrescent odour wafted upward, but He found that the smell did not bother Him nearly as much as it had done at first. The scent of decay would fade soon enough. But the achievement would be there forever.

He looked down upon the relics, satisfied. There were two of them now, nestling like shells in a rain cloud. With the slightest of shakes, the cloud subsumed them, and that was the beauty of where He'd placed them. The relics were gone, but still they were there, like something hidden within the altar of a church. In fact, the activity of reverently moving the reliquary from one place to another was indeed just like *being* in a church, but without the social restrictions that churchgoing always placed upon members of the congregation.

You'll sit up straight. You'll stop the fidgeting. D'you need a lesson in how to behave? *When you're told to kneel, you do it, boy. Put your palms together. God damn it. Pray.*

Fu blinked. The voice. At once distant and present, telling him a maggot had slunk into his head. In through His ear and onward to His brain. He'd been less than careful, and the thought of church had given it entry at last. A snicker initially. Then an outright laugh. Then the echo of *pray, pray* and *pray*.

And, *Finally looking for a job, are you? Where d'you expect to find one, stupid git? And you get out of the way, Charlene, or do you want some of this for yourself?*

It was yammer and yammer. It was shout and shout. It sometimes went on for hours at a time. He'd thought He'd finally rid Himself of the worm, but thinking of church had been His mistake.

I want you out of this house, you hear? Sleep in a doorway if that's what it takes. Or don't you have the bottle for that?

You drove her there, blast you. You did her in.

Fu squeezed His eyes shut. He reached out blindly. His hands found an object, and His fingers felt buttons. He pushed them indiscriminately until sound roared forth.

He found Himself staring at the television set, where a picture came into focus as the voice of the maggot faded away. It took Him a moment to understand what He was looking at: The morning news was assaulting His ears.

Fu gazed at the screen. Things began to make sense. A female reporter with wind-tousled hair stood in front of a police barricade. Behind her, the black arch of the Shand Street tunnel gaped like the upper jaw of Hades, and deep within that piss-scented cavern, temporary lights illuminated the back end of the abandoned Mazda.

Fu relaxed into the sight of that car, released and *released*. It was, He thought, unfortunate that the barrier had been set up at the south end of the tunnel. From this position, the body could not be seen. And He'd taken such *pains* to make the message clear: The boy doomed *himself*, don't you see? Not to retribution, from which there had never once been a realistic hope of escape, but from release. Until the end, the boy had both protested and denied.

Fu had expected to wake from the night with a sense of disquiet, born of the boy's refusal to admit his shame. True, He hadn't felt any such sense at the moment of his death, experiencing instead the momentary loosing of the vice that had His brain in its grasp, tighter and tighter with each passing day. But He *had* assumed He'd feel it later on, when clarity and personal honesty demanded that He evaluate His choice of subject. Yet upon waking He hadn't felt anything remotely like unease at all. Instead, until the arrival of the maggot, well-being had continued to suffuse Him, like the sense of repletion after a good meal.

". . . not releasing any other information at the moment," the reporter was saying earnestly. "We know there's a body, we've heard—and let me stress that we've only *heard,* and it has not been confirmed—that it's the body of a boy, and we've been *told* that officers have arrived from the Met police squad already investigating the last murder in St. George's Gardens. But as to whether this latest killing is related to the earlier murders . . . We're going to have to wait for word on that."

As she spoke, several individuals came out of the tunnel behind her: plainclothes cops by the look of them. A dumpy woman with pudding-basin hair took some direction from a blond officer in an overcoat that had the look of old money about it. She nodded once and headed out of sight, whereupon the officer stood in conversation with a bloke in a mustard anorak and another with concave shoulders and a crumpled mac.

The reporter said, "I'll just see if I can have a word . . . ," and advanced as close to the barricade as she could get. But every other reporter had the same idea, and so much jostling and shouting ensued that no one got an answer to anything. The cops ignored the lot of them, but the telly cameraman zoomed in anyway. Fu got a good look at His adversaries. The dumpy woman was gone, but He had time to study Overcoat, Anorak, and Crumpled Mac. He knew He was more than a match for them.

"Five and counting," He murmured to the television. "Don't touch that dial."

Nearby, He had a cup of tea that He'd made upon waking, and He saluted the television with it before He replaced it on a nearby table. Around Him, the house creaked as its pipes supplied the old radiators with water to heat the rooms, and He heard in those creaks an announcement of the maggot's imminent return.

Look at this, He would instruct as He pointed to the television where the police discussed Him and His handiwork. I leave the message, and they must read. Every step of it planned in exquisite detail.

The stertorous breathing behind Him, then. That eternal signal of the maggot's presence. Not in His head now, but here in this room.

What're you doing, boy?

Fu didn't need to have even a look. The shirt would be white, as it always was, but worn at both the collar and cuffs. The trousers would be charcoal or brown, the tie knotted perfectly and the cardigan buttoned. He'd have polished his shoes, polished his specs, and polished his round bald head as well.

The question again: *What're you doing?* with the threat implicit in the tone.

Fu made no reply since the answer was obvious: He was watching the news and experiencing the unfolding of His personal history. He was making His mark, and wasn't that exactly what He'd been instructed to do?

You best answer me when I speak to you. I asked what're you doing and I want a reply.

And then, *Where the* hell *were you brought up? Get that teacup off the bloody wood. You want to polish the furniture in your spare time since you've got so much of it? What're you* thinking *about anyway? Or are you out of practice in that department?*

Fu fixed His attention on the television. He could wait him out. He knew what came next because some things were written: bran in warm milk, soaked into slop, a glass of fibre dissolved in juice, those prayers sent heavenward for a quick movement of the bowels so he wouldn't have to experience said movement in a public place like the gents' loo at school. And if movement was achieved, a triumphant notation on the calendar hanging inside the cupboard door. *R* for *regular* when regular was the last thing a maggot could ever hope to be.

But something was different this morning. Fu could feel him charging, a horseman directly from Revelations.

Saying, *Where are they? What've you bloody done . . . I told you to keep your filthy mitts off. Didn't I say? Didn't I* expressly *tell you? You turn off that God damn telly and look at me when I'm talking to you.*

He wanted the remote. Fu would not hand it over.

You defying me, Charlene? You *defying* me?

What if He was? Fu thought. What if she was? What if they were? What if He did? What if *everyone* did? Amazingly, He found Himself unafraid, wary nevermore, utterly at ease, even a bit amused. The maggot's power was nothing in comparison with His own now that He'd finally taken it up, and the beauty of it all was that the maggot had no idea who or what he was dealing with. Fu felt such a *presence* in His veins, such capability, such sureness and knowledge. He rose from the chair, and He allowed His body to come into its fullness, undisguised. He said, "I wanted and I took. That's what it was."

Then nothing. *Nothing*. It was as if the maggot read Fu's power. He sensed a sea change.

"Good on you," Fu said to him. Self-preservation tended to gain you very high marks round here.

But the maggot couldn't leave it completely alone,

not when his way of simply *being* had long been so thoroughly ingrained in him. So he watched Fu's every move and he waited, eager for an indication that it was safe to speak.

Fu went to put the kettle on to boil. Perhaps, He thought, He would have a whole bloody *pot* of tea. And He would choose a blend possessing something of a vaguely celebratory air. He studied the boxes of tea in the cupboard. Imperial gunpowder? He thought. Too weak, although He had to admit that He found the name attractive. He settled on one that had been His mother's favourite: Lady Grey, with its hint of fruit.

And then, *What are you doing up? Before nine a.m. the first time in . . . how long? When're you planning to do something useful? That's what I really want to know.*

Fu looked up from spooning Lady Grey into the teapot. "*No one* knows," he said. "Not you, not anyone."

That's what you think? Taking a slash in public, but no one knows? Your name on the charge sheet three or four times and that's fine, isn't it? Who's going to care? And don't you touch Charlene! Anyone *touches the stupid cow, it's going to be me.*

Now they were in familiar territory: the open-palm slapping so as not to leave a mark, the grip on the hair and the head jerked back, the shove into the wall and the kick in places where it wouldn't show.

Punctured lung, Fu thought. Was that what it was? Saying, You watch, boy. You learn from this.

Fu felt the urge come upon Him, then. His fingertips tingled and the muscles throughout His body made Him ready to strike. But no. The time was not right. When the day came, though, it was going to be such a pleasure to lower the pudgy, soft, never-known-hard-work hands to the pan, to its burning surface. His face hovering above the maggot and *His* lips hurling the curses this time. . . .

He would beg like all the others. But Fu would not relent. He would take him to the edge, like the others. And just like the others, He would hurl him over.

See my power. Know my name.

Detective Constable Barbara Havers made her way over to Borough police station and found it on the High Street, which in this part of town and at this time of morning was funneling commuters through its narrow canyon. The noise level was intense, and the cold air was heavy with diesel exhaust fumes. These were doing their best to deposit even more grime upon the already grimy buildings that sat back from pavements littered with everything from beer cans to condoms limp with use. It was that kind of neighbourhood.

Barbara was beginning to feel the stress. She'd never worked on a serial killing before, and while she'd always known the sensation of urgency attendant on getting to a killer and making an arrest, she'd never actually experienced what she was experiencing now, which was the feeling that she was somehow personally responsible for this latest murder. Five now, with no one held to an accounting. Whatever else, they weren't working fast enough.

She was finding it difficult to keep her focus on Kimmo Thorne, victim number four. With number five dead and number six out there, somewhere innocently going about his daily affairs, it was all she could do to stay calm as she entered the Borough High Street station and flashed her identification.

She needed to speak to whoever had nabbed a kid called Kimmo Thorne in Bermondsey Market, she told the special. The matter was urgent.

She watched as he placed three telephone calls. He spoke low, keeping his eye upon her and no doubt evaluating her as a representative of New Scotland Yard. She didn't look the part—disheveled and ill dressed, with all the glamour of a wheelie bin—and this morning she knew she was particularly unkempt. One did not rise before four A.M., spend several hours in the grime of South London, and still manage to swan about looking like the catwalk was in one's afternoon diary. She'd thought her red high-top trainers had added a cheerful touch to her ensemble. But they seemed to be causing the special constable the most concern, considering the disapproving looks he kept casting in their direction.

She paced over to a notice board and read about community-action committees and neighbourhood watch programmes. She considered adopting two sad-looking dogs whose pictures were posted, and she memorised the phone number of someone willing to sell her the secrets of instant weight loss while allowing her to continue to eat whatever she wanted. She went on to read all about "Taking the Offensive When Walking at Night" and was halfway through this when a door opened and a male voice said, "Constable Havers? You're wanting me, I believe." She turned and saw a middle-aged Sikh in the doorway, his turban blindingly white and his dark eyes deeply soulful. He was called DS Gill, he told her. Would she accompany him to the canteen? He'd been having his breakfast, and if she didn't mind his finishing it . . . Mushrooms on toast with baked beans. He had become more English than the English, he said.

She took a coffee and a chocolate croissant from the food on offer, eschewing the wiser and decidedly more nutritious possibilities. Why indulge in a virtuous half grapefruit when she was soon to learn the secret of weight loss while continuing to eat whatever she wanted, which was usually something laced with lard? She paid for her goodies and carried them to the table where DS Gill was once again tucking into the breakfast she had interrupted.

He told her that everyone at the Borough High Street station knew *about* Kimmo Thorne, even if not everyone had met the boy. Kimmo had long been one of those individuals whose doings were never far from the police radar screen. When his aunt and his gran had reported him missing, no one at the station had been surprised, although to have him turn up as a murder victim whose body was dumped in St. George's Gardens . . . That had shaken a few of the less hardened officers at the station, making them wonder if they had done enough to try to keep Kimmo on the straight and narrow.

"You see, we quite liked the boy here, Constable Havers," Gill confided in his pleasant Eastern voice. "My gracious, he was a character, Kimmo: always ready with the chat, whatever his circumstances happened to be. To be honest, it was very difficult not to like him, despite the cross-dressing and soliciting. Although, to be frank, we never actually caught him in the act of soliciting, no matter how we went about it. That boy had such a sense for when someone was undercover . . . If I may say so, he was streetwise beyond his years, and for that reason we may have fallen derelict in our duty to apprehend him by a more advanced means, which could in turn have saved him. And for this, I personally"—he touched his chest—"do feel responsible."

"His mate—a bloke called Blinker . . . one Charlie Burov—says they worked it as a pair across the river. Out of Leicester Square and not round here. Kimmo did the deed while Blinker kept watch."

"That explains some of it," Gill noted.

"Some?"

"Well, you see, he was not a stupid boy. We'd had him in for warnings. We tried to tell him time and again that it was only luck that was keeping him out of trouble, but he would not hear us."

"Kids," Barbara said. She was trying to be delicate with her croissant, but it was defying her attempts at social nicety, dissolving into delicious flakes that she restrained herself from licking from her fingers, not to mention from the table. "What're you going to do about them, anyway? They think they're immortal. Didn't you?"

"At that age?" Gill shook his head. "I was far too hungry then to think immortality was in store for me, Constable." He'd finished his breakfast and folded his paper napkin neatly. He placed his plate to one side and brought his cup of tea closer. "For Kimmo, it was more than a sense that he could not be hurt, that he could not fall into danger by making the wrong choice. He had to believe himself an astute judge of whom to go with and whom to refuse because he had plans, and soliciting was a means to make them happen. He could not—and would not—give it up."

"What sort of plans?"

Gill looked momentarily embarrassed, as if against his will he were about to confide an offensive secret to a lady. "Actually, he wished to have a sexual change. He was saving for that. He told us the first time we had him into the station."

"A bloke over in the market said you lot finally sent him down for selling stolen goods," Barbara said. "But what I don't get is why Kimmo Thorne? There's got to be dozens over there flogging lumber they've nicked."

"This is true," Gill said. "But as you and I well know, we do not have the manpower to sort through every stall in every market in London to ascertain which products are legitimately on offer and which are not. In this particular case, however, Kimmo was selling items that—without his knowledge—had all been engraved with infinitesimal serial numbers. And the last thing he expected was to find the owners of the items seeking them out Friday after Friday in the market. When they found him with their belongings for sale, they rang us up directly. I was called out and . . ." He raised his fingers. The gesture said, The rest is history.

"You'd never twigged before that that he was breaking and entering?"

"He was rather like a canine in that," Gill said. "He did not foul his own den. When he wished to break the law, he did so in another station's jurisdiction. He was clever that way."

Thus, Gill explained, Kimmo's arrest for selling stolen property went down as his first offence. Because of that, when he went in front of the magistrate, he was put on probation. This too the DS deeply regretted. Had Kimmo Thorne been taken seriously, had he been given more than a slap on the hand and a probation officer in Youth Offenders to report to, he might have changed his ways and still been walking the streets today. But alas, that had not happened. Instead, he'd been sent to an organisation for youth at risk and they'd tried to work with him.

Barbara's ears pricked up. Organisation? she asked. What? Where?

It was a charity called Colossus, Gill told her. "A fine project, right here, south of the river," he said. "They offer young people alternatives to street life, crime, and drugs. With recreational programmes, community activities, life-skills classes . . . And not just for youth at risk with the law, but for the homeless, for truants, for those in care . . . I admit to having relaxed my own vigilance on Kimmo's behalf when I knew he had been assigned to Colossus. Surely, I thought, someone there would take him under a protective wing."

"As a mentor?" Barbara asked. "Is that what they do?"

"That's what he needed," Gill said. "Someone to take an interest in him. Someone to assist him towards seeing he had a degree of value that he did not quite believe he actually had. Someone to turn to. Someone to . . ." The DS seemed to bring himself up short, perhaps realising he'd gone from relaying information as an officer of the law to advocating action like a social militant. He loosened the tight grip he had on his teacup.

Small wonder that he was upset by the boy's death, Barbara thought. With his present mind-set, she wondered not only how long Gill had been a cop but also how he managed to stay one, facing what he had to face at work every day. She said, "It's not your fault, you know. You did what you could. Fact is, you did more than most cops would've done."

"But as things turned out, I did not do enough. And that is what I must live with now. A boy is dead because Detective Sergeant Gill could not bring himself to do enough."

"But there are millions of kids like Kimmo," Barbara protested.

"And most of them are alive at this moment."

"You can't help them all. You can't save each one."

"That is what we tell ourselves, isn't it?"

"What else should we tell ourselves?"

"That saving all of them is not required of us. What *is* required is helping the ones whom we come across. And this, Constable, I failed to do."

"Bloody hell. Don't be so hard on yourself."

"Who else," he said, "is there to do so? Tell me that if you will. Because here is exactly what I believe: If more of us were hard on ourselves, more children would live lives all children deserve."

At this, Barbara dropped her gaze from his. She knew she couldn't argue with that. But the fact that she wanted to do so told her how close she herself was to caring too much. And this, she knew, made her more like Gill than she, as part of the team investigating these crimes, could afford to be.

That was the irony about police work. Care too little and more people died. Care too much and you couldn't catch their killer.

"I'D LIKE A WORD," Lynley said. "Now." He didn't add *sir* and he made no real effort to modulate his voice. Had he been present, Hamish Robson no doubt would have taken note of everything his tone implied about aggression and the need to settle a score, but Lynley didn't care about that. They'd negotiated an arrangement. Hillier hadn't upheld it.

The AC had just concluded a meeting with Stephenson Deacon. The head of the Press Bureau had left Hillier's office looking as grim as Lynley felt. Things were obviously not going smoothly at that end of things, and for a moment Lynley took a perverse pleasure in this. The thought of Hillier eventually dangling in the wind of the Press Bureau's machinations before a pack of baying journalists was deeply gratifying just now.

Hillier said, as if he hadn't spoken, "Where the hell is Nkata? We've a meeting with the media coming up and I want him here in advance." He gathered up an array of papers spread out on his conference table and shoved them at an underling who was still seated there, having attended the meeting that had gone on prior to Lynley's arrival. He was a razor-thin twenty-something in John Lennon spectacles who was continuing to take notes as he apparently tried to avoid becoming the focus of Hillier's exasperation. "They're on to colour," the AC said curtly. "So who the *hell* over there"—he jerked his finger in what Lynley decided was supposed to be a southerly direction, meaning south of the river, meaning the Shand Street tunnel—"leaked that bit to those predators? I want to know and I want that bugger's head on a dish. You, Powers."

The underling jumped to, leaning in to say, "Sir? Yes, sir?"

"Get that halfwit Rodney Aronson on the phone. He's running *The Source* these days, and the colour question came in by phone from someone on that rotten little rag. Trace it back to us that way. Put pressure on Aronson. On anyone else you come across as well. I want every leak plugged by the end of the day. Get on to it."

"Sir." Powers scooted from the room.

Hillier went to his desk. He picked up the phone and punched in a few numbers, either oblivious of or indifferent to Lynley's presence and his state of mind. Unbelievably, he began to book himself a massage.

Lynley felt as if battery acid were running through his veins. He strode across the room to Hillier's desk, and he pushed the button to disconnect the AC from his phone call. Hillier snapped, "What the *bloody* hell do you think you're—"

"I said I want a word," Lynley cut in. "You and I had an arrangement, and you've violated it."

"Do you *know* who you're talking to?"

"Only too well. You brought Robson in as window dressing, and I allowed it."

Hillier's florid face went crimson. "No one *bloody* allows—"

"Our agreement was that I would decide what he saw and what he didn't see. He had no business at anyone's crime scene, but there he was, given access. There's only one way that sort of thing happens."

"That's right," Hillier said. "Keep it in mind. There's only one way anything happens round here and you are not that way. I'll decide who has access to what, when, and how, Superintendent, and if it comes to me that it might advance the investigation by having the Queen turn up to shake hands with the corpse, then prepare yourself to tug your forelock because her Roller's going to drop her off for a look. Robson's part of the team. Cope with it."

Lynley was incredulous. One moment the assistant commissioner was frothing at the mouth about locating leaks within the investigation; the next moment he was happily welcoming a potential snout right into their midst. But the problem went beyond what Hamish Robson might deliberately or inadvertently reveal to the media. He said, "Had it occurred to you that you're putting this man at risk? That you're exposing him to danger just for the hell of it? You're making yourself look good at his expense, and if anything goes wrong, it's down to the Met. Have you thought of that?"

"You're so far out of order—"

"Answer my question!" Lynley said. "There's a killer out there who's taken five lives, and for all we know he was standing behind the barrier this morning, among the gawkers, taking note of everyone who came and went."

"You're being hysterical," Hillier said. "Get out of this office. I've no intention of listening to you rant like a common lout. If you can't handle the pressure of this case, then take yourself off it. Or I'll do it for you. Now where the *hell* is Nkata? He's meant to be here when I talk to the press."

"Are you listening to me? Have you any idea . . ." Lynley wanted to pound his fist on the top of the AC's desk, just to feel something beyond outrage for a moment. He tried to calm himself. He lowered his voice. "Listen to me, sir. It's one thing for a killer to mark one of us. That's part of the risk we face when we take the job. But to put someone in the sight lines of a psychopath just to protect your political backside—"

"That's enough!" Hillier looked apoplectic. "That's

bloody well enough. I've put up with your insolence for years but you're so far out of order at this point . . ." He came round the desk, stopping within three inches of Lynley. "Get out of this office," he hissed. "Get back to work. For the moment, we're going to pretend this conversation never happened. You're going to go about your business, you're going to obey every order that comes in your direction, you're going to get to the bottom of this mess, and you're going to make a prompt arrest. After that"—here Hillier poked Lynley's chest and Lynley's vision went red although he managed to restrain himself from reacting—"we'll decide what's going to happen to you. Have I made myself clear? Yes? Good. Now get back to work and get a result."

Lynley allowed the AC the last word although it felt like swallowing poison to do so. He turned on his heel and left Hillier to his political scheming. He used the stairs to descend to the incident room, cursing himself for thinking he could make a difference in Hillier's way of doing business. He needed to keep his focus on matters that counted, he realised, and the AC's use of Hamish Robson was going to have to be eliminated from that list.

All the members of the murder squad were in the picture with regard to the Shand Street tunnel body, and when Lynley joined them it was to find them as subdued as he expected. All counted, they numbered thirty-three now: from the constables on the street to the secretaries keeping track of all the reports and relevant documentation. Being defeated by a single individual when they had the power of the Met behind them—with everything from sophisticated communications systems and CCTV films to forensic labs and databases—was more than disheartening. It was humiliating. And worse, it had failed to stop a killer.

So they were much subdued when Lynley entered.

The only noise among them was the tapping of computer keys. That too ceased when Lynley said quietly, "What's the form?"

DI John Stewart spoke from one of his multicoloured outlines. Triangulating the crime scenes wasn't proving fruitful, he said. The killer was, literally, all over the London map. This suggested a confident knowledge of the city, which in turn suggested someone whose day job would give him that knowledge.

"Taxi driver comes to mind, obviously," Stewart said. "Minicab driver. Bus driver as well, since not one body site is particularly far off a bus route either."

"The profiler's saying he's working a job below his ability," Lynley acknowledged, although he was loath even to mention Hamish Robson after his contretemps with Hillier.

"Courier works as well," one of the DCs pointed out. "Riding round on a motorbike'd give you the Knowledge as good as studying to drive a black cab."

"Even a bicycle," someone else said.

"But, then, where does the van come in?"

"Personal transport? He doesn't use it for his job?"

"What do we have on the van?" Lynley asked. "Who talked to the St. George's Gardens witness?"

A team two constable spoke up. Careful massaging of the witness had initially gleaned nothing, but she'd phoned in late last night with a sudden memory, which, she said, she *hoped* was a real memory and not a combination of imagination and her desire to help the police. At any rate, she felt she could say with confidence that it was a full-size van they were looking for. It had faded white lettering on the side, suggesting it was or had once been a business van.

"Confirmation for the Ford Transit, essentially," Stewart said. "We're working with the DVLA list, looking for a red one that belongs to a business."

"And?" Lynley said.

"Takes time, Tommy."

"We haven't *got* time." Lynley heard the agitation in his voice and he knew the others heard it as well. He was reminded at the worst possible moment that he wasn't Malcolm Webberly, that he didn't possess the former superintendent's calm, nor his steady approach when under pressure. He saw in the faces gathered round him that the other officers were thinking this as well. He said more evenly, "Move forward on that front, John. The moment you've got something, I'll want to know."

"As to that . . . ," Stewart hadn't made eye contact at Lynley's outburst, instead making a notation that he underscored three times partway down his precise outline. "We've got two sources from the Net. For the ambergris oil."

"Only two?"

"It's not your everyday purchase." The two sources were in opposite directions: a shop called Crystal Moon on Gabriel's Wharf—

"That's a south-of-the-river location for us," someone noted hopefully.

—and a stall in Camden Lock Market called Wendy's Cloud. Someone would need to suss out each place.

"Barbara lives up in the Camden Lock area," Lynley said. "She can deal with that. Winston can . . . Where is he, by the way?"

"Hiding from Dave the Knave, probably," was the reply, an irreverent reference to Hillier. "He's started getting fan mail from the telly watchers, has Winnie. All those lonely birds looking for a man with promise."

"Is he in the building?"

No one knew. "Get him on his mobile. Havers as well."

As he spoke, Barbara Havers arrived. Winston Nkata followed in her wake seconds later. The others greeted them with tension-diffusing hoots and ribald greetings that suggested their dual advent had a personal explanation behind it.

Havers gave them two fingers. "Sod you lot," she said affably. "I'm surprised to find you outside of the canteen."

For his part, Nkata merely said, "Sorry. Trying to track down a social worker for the Salvatore boy."

"Success?" Lynley asked.

"Sod all."

"Keep with it. Hillier's looking for you, by the way."

Nkata scowled. He said, "Got something on Jared Salvatore from Peckham police." He relayed all the information he'd gathered, while the others listened and made relevant notes. "Girlfriend said he was learning to cook somewhere, but the blokes at the station aren't giving that credence," he concluded.

"Have someone check the cookery schools," Lynley told DI Stewart. Stewart nodded and made a note. Lynley said, "Havers? What about Kimmo Thorne?"

She said that everything they'd been told by Blinker and then by the Grabinskis and Reg Lewis in Bermondsey Market had checked out with the Borough police. She went on to add that Kimmo Thorne had evidently been involved in a programme called Colossus, which she called "Bunch of do-gooders south of the river." She'd gone there to check out the place: a renovated manufacturing plant not far from the knot of streets that merged at Elephant and Castle. "They weren't open yet," Havers concluded. "The place was locked up tight, but there were some kids hanging about, waiting for someone to show up and let them in."

"What did they give you?" Lynley asked her.

"Not a bloody thing," Havers said. "I said, 'You lot involved in this place?' and they twigged I was a copper. That was that."

"Look into it, then."

"Will do, sir."

Lynley filled them in, then, on what Hamish Robson had had to say about the latest killing. He didn't tell them that the profiler had been sent to the scene by Hillier. There was no sense in getting them worked up about something over which they had no control. Thus, he mentioned the killer's change in attitude towards the most recent victim and the indications that he could reappear at any of the crime scenes.

Hearing this, DI Stewart set about arranging surveillance at the body sites before he went on to another report: The officers who'd been slogging through all of the relevant CCTV tapes from the areas near the body-dump sites were continuing that tedious job. It wasn't exactly gripping drama, but the constables in question were soldiering on, supported by vats of hot coffee. They were looking not only for a van but for another means of transporting a body from point A to point B, and one that wouldn't necessarily be noticed by people living in the vicinity: milk float, street-sweeping trolley, and the like.

To this information, he added that they'd had a report from SO7 on the makeup worn by Kimmo Thorne. The brand was No. Seven, commonly sold at Boots. Did the superintendent want them to start observing all the CCTV films from the Boots outlets nearest Kimmo Thorne's home? He didn't sound thrilled with this possibility. Still, he pointed out, "That might give us something. Bloke at the till disapproving how the Thorne kid was bent and wanting to do him in? That sort of thing."

Lynley didn't want to count anything out at this point. So he gave the nod for Stewart to assign a team to get on to the security tapes from the Boots outlets in the vicinity of Kimmo Thorne's Southwark home. He himself assigned the two outlets for oil of ambergris to

Nkata and to Havers, telling Havers to look in on Wendy's Cloud when she headed home at the end of the day. In the meantime, she would accompany him to Elephant and Castle. He was determined to see himself what could be gained from a call upon Colossus. If one of the boys had been associated with it, what was to say the rest of the victims—still unidentified—might not have been allied with it as well?

"Couldn't this last've been a copycat killing?" Havers asked. "That's something we haven't talked about yet. I mean, I know how Robson explained the differences between this body and the others, but those differences *could* be owing to someone knowing something about the crime scene but not everything, right?"

That couldn't be discounted, Lynley agreed. But the truth was that copycat killings came from information generated by the news media, and despite the fact that they had a leak somewhere in the investigation, he knew that it was a recent one. The press jumping on the fact that the latest body was black was evidence of that since there were far more sensational details to exploit on the front pages of the tabloids than that one. And Lynley knew how the media worked: They weren't about to withhold something gruesome if it had the potential to sell another two hundred thousand copies of their papers. So indications were strong that they didn't have anything gruesome on record yet, which suggested this killing wasn't a copy of the earlier ones but rather another death in a line of similar deaths, all bearing the signature of a single killer.

That was the person they had to find, quickly. For Lynley was perfectly capable of making the psychological jump implied by everything Hamish Robson had told him that morning about the man they were looking for: If he'd treated this last body with contempt and without remorse, things were escalating now.

Chapter Nine

Nkata managed to depart Victoria Street without a run-in with Hillier. He'd had a message on his mobile from the AC's secretary advising him of "Sir David's wish to confer prior to the next press briefing," but he decided to ignore it. Hillier no more wanted to confer with him than he wanted to be exposed to the Ebola virus, and that was a fact, one which Nkata had been reading between the lines of his every meeting with the man. He was tired of being Hillier's token nod-of-head to equal opportunities for minorities at the Met. He knew if he continued to play along with the propaganda, he was going to end up despising his profession, his associates, and himself. That wasn't fair on anyone. So he escaped from New Scotland Yard directly upon the conclusion of the meeting in the incident room. He used oil of ambergris as his excuse.

He made his way across the river to Gabriel's Wharf, an expensive square of riverfront tarmac which stood just beyond the midway point between two of the bridges that spanned the Thames: Waterloo and Blackfriars. It was a summertime kind of place, completely open to the air. Despite the cheery lights strung above it in crisscross fashion—and lit, even though it was still daylight—in winter the wharf was experiencing little custom. No one at all was doing business in the shop hiring out bicycles and inline skates, and while there were a few browsers in the small, ramshackle galleries that defined the wharf's boundaries, the other enterprises were virtually deserted. These comprised restaurants and food stalls, which in summer would be hard pressed to keep up with the demand for the crepes, pizzas, sandwiches, jacket potatoes, and ices that were largely going ignored at present.

Nkata found Crystal Moon lodged between two take-aways: crepes on the left and sandwiches on the right. It was part of the eastern portion of the wharf, where shantylike shops and galleries backed right up to a line of tenements. The upper floors of these had long ago been painted with trompe l'oeil windows, each of a style so different from the last that the overall feeling was one of speeding round Europe on foot. Georgian London windows gave way within four paces to rococo Paris, which in turn faded fast to the doge's Venice. It was nothing if not fanciful, in keeping with the wharf itself.

Crystal Moon maintained the whimsical atmosphere, inviting one to enter through a beaded curtain fashioned to look like a galaxy dominated by a slice of lunar green cheese. Nkata ducked through this and opened the door beyond it, expecting to be greeted inside by a pyramid- wearing hippie hopeful who called herself something like Aphrodite but whose real name was Kylie from Essex. Instead, he found a grandmotherly type seated on a tall stool next to the till. She was wearing a soft pink twin set and purple beads and she was leafing through a glossy magazine. A stick of incense burning next to her spread the scent of jasmine into the air.

Nkata nodded but did not immediately approach her. Rather, he took stock of what was on offer. Crystals abounded, as one might expect: hanging from cords, decorating small lamp shades, worked into candle-holders, loose in small baskets. But so did incense, tarot cards, dream catchers, fragrant oils, flutes, recorders, and—for some reason not immediately apparent—decorated chopsticks. He went to the oils.

Black man in the shop. White woman alone. At another time, Nkata might have set her mind at rest by introducing himself and proffering his identification. Today, however, with Hillier and everything Hillier stood for on his mind, he just wasn't in the mood for adding to the peace of any white person, old lady or not.

He did a little browsing. Anise. Benzoin. Klinden. Chamomile. Almond. He picked up one, read the label, and noted the multitude of uses. He replaced it and picked up another. Behind him the pages of the magazine continued to turn with no alteration in pace. Finally, after stirring on her stool, the proprietor of the shop spoke.

Only, it turned out she wasn't the proprietor at all, which she revealed to Nkata with an embarrassed little laugh as she offered to assist him. "I don't know how much help I can *be*," she told him, "but I'm willing to try. I just come in once a week for the afternoon, you see, while Gigi—that's my granddaughter—has her singing lessons. This is her little place, what she's doing till she's broken into the business . . . Isn't that how they say it? May I *be* any help, by the way? Looking for anything special?"

"What's all this for, then?" Nkata indicated the display of small bottles that contained the oils.

"Oh, many things, dear," the old lady said. She eased herself off the stool and came over to the display to stand beside him. He towered over her, but she didn't seem to be disconcerted to discover this. She crossed her arms beneath her breasts, said, "My goodness, you've taken your vitamins, haven't you?," and went on amiably. "Some of them have medicinal uses, dear. Some are for magic. Some are for alchemy. This is according to Gigi, naturally. I don't actually know if they're good for anything. Why d'you ask? D'you need something special?"

Nkata reached for the bottle of ambergris oil. "What about this one?"

She took it from him and said, "Ambergris . . . Let's see, shall we?" She carried the bottle back to the counter and from beneath it she brought forth a volume.

If she herself hadn't been what Nkata expected to find inside a shop called Crystal Moon, the enormous book she heaved to the counter was. It looked like something from the prop room at Elstree Studios: large, leather bound, with dog-eared pages. Nkata expected moths to fly out when she opened it.

She seemed to read his mind because she laughed in an embarrassed fashion and said, "Yes. A bit silly, I know. But people expect this sort of thing, don't they?" She flipped through some pages and began to read. Nkata joined her at the counter. She started tut-tutting, shaking her head and fingering her beads.

"What?" he asked.

"It's a bit unpleasant, actually. Its associations, I mean." Pointing to the page, she went on to tell him that not only did some poor sweet whale have to die in order for people to get their hands on the oil, but the substance itself was used in doing works of wrath or vengeance. She frowned and looked up at him earnestly. "Now, I *must* ask. Forgive me, please. Gigi would be appalled, but there are some things . . . Why would you be wanting the ambergris? Lovely man like you. Is it something to do with the scar, dear? It's unfortunate you have it, but if I might say . . . Well, it does give your face a certain distinction. So *if* I might guide you in another direction . . . ?"

She told him that a man like himself should think instead about calamint oil, which would help keep women away because surely he was mobbed by them on a daily basis. On the other hand, bryony could be used in love potions if there was a special woman out there who had struck his fancy. Or agrimony, which would banish negativity. Or eucalyptus for healing. Or sage for immortality. There were so *many* choices with far more positive uses than the ambergris, dear, and if she could possibly do anything at all to guide him in a direction that would assist him in an outcome having *positive* repercussions in his life . . .

Nkata realised it was time. He brought out his identification. He told her that ambergris oil had been associated with a murder.

"Murder?" Her eyes—their blue faded with age—widened as one hand went to her chest. "My dear, you don't think . . . Has someone been *poisoned*? Because I don't believe . . . it can't be possible . . . the bottle would be marked in some way . . . I know that . . . it would have to be . . ."

Nkata hastened to reassure her. No one had been poisoned, and even if someone had, the shop would only be responsible if the shop had administered the substance. That wasn't the case, was it?

"Of course not. Of *course* not," she said. "But, my dear, when Gigi hears about this, she'll be devastated. To be even remotely connected to a murder . . . She is the most peaceable young woman. Truly. If you could see her in here with her customers. If you could hear the music she plays. I've the CDs right here and you're welcome to look through them. See? *The God Within, Spiritual Journeys*. And there are others. All about meditations and the like."

It was her mention of the word *customers* that Nkata brought her back to. He asked if the shop had sold any of the ambergris oil recently. She told him that she didn't quite know. They probably had done. Gigi did a respectable business, even at this time of year. But they had no records of individual purchases. There were the credit card receipts, of course, so the police might go at things from that end. Otherwise there was only the notebook that customers signed if they wanted a copy of Crystal Moon's newsletter. Would that help at all?

Nkata doubted it, but he accepted the offer and took it from the woman. He gave her his card and told her that if she remembered anything at all . . . Or if Gigi could add to what her grandmother knew . . .

Yes, yes. Of course. Anything at all. And as a matter of fact . . .

"Heaven knows what help it might be, dear, but there *is* a list Gigi's been keeping," her grandmother said. "It's only postal codes. She's been keen to open Crystal Moon Two on the other side of the river—Notting Hill?—and she's been keeping the postal codes of her customers to buoy her case for a loan from the bank. Would that help at all?"

Nkata didn't see how, but he was willing to take the list anyway. He thanked Gigi's gran and started to leave but found himself pausing, in spite of himself, in front of the display of oils once again.

"Is there anything else, then?" Gigi's gran asked.

He had to admit to himself that there was. He said, "Which one 'd you say banishes negativity?"

"That was the agrimony, dear."

He scooped up a bottle and carried it to the counter. "This'll do, then," he said.

ELEPHANT AND CASTLE existed as a place apparently oblivious of the other Londons that had, over the years, developed and died around it. The Swinging London of miniskirts, vinyl boots, the King's Road, and Carnaby Street had decades ago passed it by. The catwalks of Fashion Week London had never been laid anywhere near its environs. And while the London

Eye, the Millennium Footbridge, and the Tate Modern all stood as examples of the dawn of a brand new century in town, Elephant and Castle remained locked in the past. True, the area was struggling to be redeveloped, as were many places south of the river. But its struggle was one against the odds, and the odds comprised drug users and suppliers doing business on the streets, as well as poverty, ignorance, and despair. It was into this milieu that its founders had set Colossus, taking what had been a derelict structure designed for the manufacture of mattresses and modestly renovating the place to serve the community in an entirely different way.

Barbara Havers directed Lynley to the spot on New Kent Road, where a small carpark behind the jaundiced brick structure offered a place for participants in Colossus to have a smoke. A crowd of them stood round doing just that as Lynley guided his car into one of the parking bays. As he put on the brake and shut down the engine, Havers pointed out that a Bentley was, perhaps, not the best choice of transport to be bringing into the neighbourhood.

Lynley couldn't disagree. He hadn't quite thought things through when, in the underground carpark on Victoria Street, Havers had said, "Why don't we take my motor, sir?" At that moment he'd just wanted to assert some control over things, and one part of getting that control was putting distance between himself and any edifice that happened to shelter the assistant commissioner of police. Another part had been making the decision about how that distance was going to be effected. But now he saw that Havers had been right. It wasn't so much that they put themselves at risk, driving a posh car into this kind of place. It was more that they made a statement about themselves, which didn't need making.

On the other hand, he told himself, at least they

weren't announcing the fact that they were coppers to all and sundry. But he was disabused of that notion the moment he stepped out of the Bentley and locked it behind him.

"The filth," someone muttered, and this caution passed quickly throughout the smokers until all conversation had died among them. So much for the value of vehicular incognito, Lynley thought.

As if he'd spoken, Havers replied in a low voice, "It's me, sir, not you. They've got rozzer radar, this lot. They knew who I was straightaway when they saw me earlier." She glanced his way. "But you c'n act like my driver if you want. We still might be able to pull the wool. Let's start with a fag. You c'n light it for me." Lynley shot her a look. She grinned. "Just a thought."

They made their way through the silent group to a flight of iron stairs that climbed the back of the building. On the first floor, a broad green door bore "Colossus" inscribed on a small plaque of polished brass. A window set high above this showed a bank of lights along a corridor within. Lynley and Havers entered and found themselves in a combination gallery and modest gift shop.

The gallery constituted a pictorial history of the organisation: its founding, its development of the site that housed it, and its impact on the inhabitants of the area. The gift shop—which was essentially a single display case of reasonably priced items—offered T-shirts, sweatshirts, caps, coffee mugs, shot glasses, and stationery, all with identical logos. These consisted of the organisation's mythological namesake surmounted by dozens of tiny figures who used his massive arms and shoulders as a means to cross from destitution to achievement. Beneath the giant was the word *together*, forming a half circle that was completed by *Colossus*, which created the other half above him. Within this case also was a signed photograph of the Duke and

Duchess of Kent, lending their royal patronage to some event connected with Colossus. This, apparently, was not for sale.

On the far side of the display case, a door led into the reception room. There, Lynley and Havers found themselves being immediately eyed by three individuals who fell into silence the moment they approached. Two of the three—a slender, youngish man in a EuroDisney baseball cap and a mixed-race boy perhaps fourteen years old—were playing cards at a low table between two sofas. The third—a large young man with neat ginger hair and a wispy beard, nicely trimmed but still barely covering pockmarked cheeks—sat behind the reception desk, a turquoise cross dangling from one earlobe. He wore one of the Colossus sweatshirts, and at the otherwise spotless desk, he'd apparently been making notations in blue pencil upon a calendar while soft jazz came from speakers positioned above him. He did not look friendly once his glance took in Havers. Next to him, Lynley heard the DC sigh.

"I need a bloody makeover," she muttered.

"You might want to lose the shoes," he suggested.

"Help you?" the young man asked. From beneath the desk he brought forth a bright yellow bag with "Mr. Sandwich" printed on it. From this he took a sausage roll and crisps, and he set about eating without further ado. Cops, his actions telegraphed to them, would not get in the way of his daily routine.

Although it appeared to be entirely unnecessary, Lynley produced his ID for the ginger-haired young man, ignoring the two others for the moment. A plastic nameplate at the desk's edge indicated he was introducing himself and Havers to one Jack Veness, who seemed to be deeply unimpressed that the two rozzers standing before him were representing New Scotland Yard.

Giving a glance to the cardplayers, as if for approval, Veness simply waited for more to be said. He chewed his sausage roll, dipped into his crisps, and glanced at the wall clock above the door. Or perhaps it was to the door itself that he looked, Lynley thought, through which Mr. Veness might be waiting for rescue. He seemed all right superficially, but there was an air of unease about him.

They were there to speak to the director of Colossus, Lynley told Jack Veness, or, for that matter, to anyone else who could talk to them about one of their clients . . . if that was the proper term, he added: Kimmo Thorne.

The name had just about the same effect as a stranger walking into a barroom in an old-time American Western. In other circumstances, Lynley might have been amused: The two cardplayers ceased their game altogether, setting their cards on the table and making no secret of the fact that they intended to listen to everything that was said from that moment on, while Jack Veness ceased chewing his sausage roll. He set it on its Mr. Sandwich bag and pushed his chair away from his desk. Lynley thought he intended to fetch someone for them, but instead he went to a water cooler. There, he filled a Colossus mug from the hot spigot provided, after which he grabbed a tea bag and gave it a few douses inside.

Next to Lynley, Havers rolled her eyes. She said, " 'Scuse us, mate. Your hearing aid just blow a fuse or something?"

Veness returned and put his mug on the desk. "I c'n hear you lot fine. I'm just trying to decide if it's worth giving you an answer."

Across the room, EuroDisney gave a low whistle. His companion ducked his head. Veness looked pleased that he'd managed to obtain their approval. Lynley decided this was enough.

"You can make that decision in an interview room if you like," he said to Veness.

To which Havers added, "We're happy to oblige. Here to serve and all that, you know."

Veness sat. He wadded a hunk of sausage roll into his mouth and said past it, "Everyone knows everyone else at Colossus. Thorne included. That's how it works. That's why it works."

"That goes for you as well, I take it?" Lynley said. "Regarding Kimmo Thorne?"

"You take it right," Veness agreed.

"What about you two?" Havers asked the cardplayers. "Did you know Kimmo Thorne as well?" She took out her notebook as she asked the questions. "What're your names, by the way?"

EuroDisney looked startled to be suddenly questioned at all, but he said cooperatively that he was called Robbie Kilfoyle. He added that he didn't actually *work* at Colossus like Jack but merely volunteered several days each week, this being one of those days. For his part, the boy identified himself as Mark Connor. He said he was in day four of assessment.

"That makes him new round here," Veness explained.

"So he won't have known Kimmo," Kilfoyle added.

"But you did know him?" Havers asked Kilfoyle. "Even though you don't work here?"

"Hey, you know, he didn't say that," Veness said.

"You his brief?" Havers retorted. "No? Then I expect he can answer for himself." And again to Kilfoyle: "Did you know Kimmo Thorne? Where do you work?"

Unaccountably, Veness persisted. "Drop it. He brings in the bloody sandwiches, all right?"

Kilfoyle scowled, perhaps offended by the dismissive tone. He said, "Like I said already. I volunteer. On the phones. In the kichen. I work in the kit room when things pile up. So I saw Kimmo round. I knew him."

"Didn't everyone," Veness said. "And speaking of which . . . There's a group going out on the river this afternoon. D'you have time to handle that, Rob?" He gave Kilfoyle a long look, as if some sort of double message were being sent.

"I c'n help you, Rob," Mark Connor offered.

"Sure," Kilfoyle said. And to Jack Veness, "You want me to set things up now or what?"

"Now would be brilliant."

"Well, then." Kilfoyle gathered up the cards and, accompanied by Mark, he headed for an interior door. Unlike the others, he wore a windbreaker rather than a sweatshirt, and instead of "Colossus" written on it, it bore a logo of a stuffed baguette with arms and legs and the words "Mr. Sandwich" below it.

The departure of these two effected a complete change in Jack Veness for some reason. As if an unseen switch had been suddenly turned off—or on—in him, the young man altered on the head of a pin. He said to Lynley and Havers, "Right then. Sorry. I can be a real streak of piss when I want. Y'know, I wanted to be a cop, but I couldn't make it. It's easier to blame you than to look at myself and work out why I didn't cut it." He snapped his fingers, offered a smile. "How's that for instant psychoanalysis? Five years of therapy and the man is cured."

The change in Veness was disconcerting, like discovering two personalities inside one body. It was impossible not to wonder if the presence of Kilfoyle and Connor had had something to do with who he'd portrayed himself to be earlier. But Lynley went with the change in the man and brought up Kimmo Thorne again. Next to him, Havers flipped open her notebook. The newly minted Jack Veness didn't quiver an eyelash.

He told them frankly that he knew Kimmo and had known him from the time of Kimmo's assignment to Colossus. He, after all, was the organisation's receptionist. Everyone who came, who went, and who remained was someone he quickly got to know. He made it his *business* to know, he emphasised. It was, he told them, part of his *job* to know.

Why was this? Lynley asked.

Because, Veness said, you never knew, did you?

Knew what, exactly? Havers put in.

What you were dealing with.

"That lot." With this, Veness indicated the young people smoking outside in the carpark. "They come from everything, don't they? The streets, care, Youth Offenders, drug rehab, gangs, turning tricks, running weapons, selling drugs. Doesn't make sense to trust them till they give me a reason to trust them. So I keep an eye out."

"Did this apply to Kimmo as well?" Lynley asked.

"Applies to everyone," Veness said. "Winners and losers alike."

Havers took up the ball at that remark. She said, "How's that apply to Kimmo? He get on your bad side some way?"

"Not mine," he said.

"Someone else's then?"

Veness contemplatively fingered his sausage roll.

"If there's something we should know," Lynley began.

"He was a tosser," Veness said. "A loser. Look, it happens, sometimes. Kid's got something here. All's that's needed is climbing aboard. But sometimes they just stop coming—even Kimmo, who's *supposed* to show up or he'll be back in borstal in a wink—and I can't get my brain round that, see. You'd think he'd grab on to anything that'd help him out of that one. But he didn't, did he? He just stopped showing up."

"When did he stop?"

Jack Veness thought for a moment. He took a spiral book from the middle drawer of his desk and examined the signatures that crawled down a dozen or more pages. It was, Lynley saw, a signing-in register, and when Veness replied to Lynley's question, the date he gave for Kimmo's final appearance at Colossus matched up with his murder, within forty-eight hours.

"Dumb fuck," Veness said, shoving the signing-in book to one side. "Didn't know when he was well off. Trouble is, kids can't wait for the payoff, can they? Some kids, mind you, not all of them. They want the result but not the process that leads to the result. I expect he's quit. Like I said, that happens."

"He was murdered, actually," Lynley said. "That's why he stopped coming."

"But you'd worked that out, hadn't you?" Havers added. "Else why would you be talking about him in the past tense from the start? And why else would the rozzers be dropping in on you? And twice in one day because one of that lot"—as Veness himself had done, she indicated the group who were gathered outside—"must've told someone in here that I stopped by earlier, before you opened up."

Veness shook his head vehemently. "I didn't . . . No. No. I didn't know." He shot his gaze over to a doorway and a corridor off which brightly lit rooms opened. He appeared to think something over for a moment before he said, "That kid over in St. Pancras? In the gardens?"

"Bingo," Havers said. "You're definitely no dummy when you're breathing, Jack."

"That was Kimmo Thorne," Lynley added. "His is one of five deaths we're investigating."

"*Five*? Hey now. Wait. You can't be thinking Colossus—"

"We're not drawing any conclusions," Lynley said.

"Hell. Sorry, then. About what I said. Tosser and loser. Hell." Veness picked up his sausage roll, then put it back down. He wrapped it up and returned it to its take-away bag. He said, "Some kids just drop out, see. They have a chance, but they still walk away. They go for what looks like the easy route. It's frustrating as hell to watch." He blew out a breath. "But damn. I'm sorry. Was it in the papers? I don't read 'em much and—"

"Not his name at first," Lynley said. "Just the fact of

his body being found in St. George's Gardens." He didn't add that chances were good to excellent that the papers were going to become *full* of the serial killings now: names, places, and dates as well. A young white victim had piqued the tabloids' interest; this morning's young black victim gave them the opportunity they needed to cover their own backsides. Mixed race, cheap news of little interest, they'd decided about the earlier killings. All that had changed with Kimmo Thorne. And now with the black boy . . . The tabloids were going to grab on to the opportunity to make up for lost time and overlooked responsibility.

"The death of a boy associated with Colossus brings up a number of questions," Lynley pointed out to Jack Veness, "as you can no doubt imagine. And we've identified another boy who might be associated with Colossus as well. Jared Salvatore. Sound familiar?"

"Salvatore. Salvatore." Veness mumbled the name. "No. I don't think so. I'd remember."

"Then we'll need to speak to your director—"

"Yeah, yeah, yeah." Veness surged to his feet. "You'll want to talk to Ulrike. She runs the whole operation. Hang on, then. I'll see . . ." That said, he shot off through the doorway that led to the interior of the building. He turned a corner and quickly disappeared.

Lynley looked at Havers. "Now that was interesting."

She agreed. "We don't even have to look for still waters in that bloke."

"I got that impression as well."

"So I s'pose the question is how deep're things really running with him?" Havers asked.

Lynley reached across the desk and snagged the signing-in book that Jack had been using. He handed it to Havers.

"Salvatore?" she said.

"It's a thought," he replied.

Chapter Ten

In very short order, Lynley and Havers discovered that not only was the director of Colossus *also* in the dark about Kimmo Thorne's death but additionally, for some reason, Jack Veness had not put her in the picture with regard to the matter when he went to find her. Evidently, he had told her only that two cops from New Scotland Yard wanted to see her. It was an intriguing omission.

Ulrike Ellis turned out to be a pleasant-looking young woman in the vicinity of thirty, with sandy cornrow plaits gathered back from her face and enough brass bangles on her wrists to qualify her as the prisoner of Zenda. She wore a heavy black turtleneck, blue jeans, and boots, and she came to reception herself to fetch Lynley and Havers to her office. As Jack Veness resumed his place behind the reception desk, Ulrike led the way down a corridor on the walls of which bulletin boards held neighbourhood announcements, photographs of young people, classes on offer, and schedules of Colossus events. Once in her office, she scooped a small stack of the *Big Issue* off a chair in front of her desk and shoved the magazines onto a space on a bookshelf crowded with volumes and with files needing replacement in a cabinet. This, standing near her desk, already overflowed with other files.

She said, "I keep buying these," in reference to copies of the *Big Issue*, "and then I never get a chance to read them. Take a few if you like. Or do you buy them yourselves?" She glanced over her shoulder and added, "Ah. Well, *everyone* ought, you know. Oh, I know what people think: If I buy one, this unwashed sod'll go off and spend the profit on drugs or booze, won't he, and how will *that* be of help to him? But what I say is that people might want to stop assuming the worst and start pitching in to make a difference in this country." She looked round the office as if seeking other employment and said, "Well, that didn't much help, did it. One of you still has to stand. Or shall we all stand? Is that better? Tell me this: Is TO31 *finally* going to take notice of us?"

Actually, Lynley told her as Barbara Havers wandered to the bookshelf to have a look at Ulrike Ellis's many volumes, he and DC Havers were not there representing Community Affairs. Rather, they'd come to talk to the director of Colossus about Kimmo Thorne. Did Ms. Ellis know the boy?

Ulrike sat behind her desk. Lynley took the chair. Havers remained at the volumes, reaching for one of several framed photographs that stood among them. Ulrike said, "Has Kimmo done something? See here, we're not responsible for the kids' staying out of trouble. We don't even claim to be able to do that. Colossus is about showing them alternatives, but sometimes they still choose the wrong ones."

"Kimmo's dead," Lynley said. "You may have read about the body that was found in St. George's Gardens, up in St. Pancras. He's been identified in the press by now."

Ulrike said nothing in reply at first. She merely

stared at Lynley for a good five seconds before her glance went to Havers, still in possession of one of her photographs. She said, "Put that down, please," in the calmest possible voice. She loosed her plaits from their binding and refastened them tightly before she said more. Then it was merely, "I phoned . . . I *did* phone the moment I was told."

"So you knew he was dead?" Havers put the photograph back in place but facing outward so Lynley could see it: a very young Ulrike, an older man in minister's garb who might have been her father, and between them the brightly clad figure of Nelson Mandela.

Ulrike said, "No. No. I didn't mean . . . When Kimmo failed to come to day five of his assessment course, Griff Strong reported him, as he was meant to do. I phoned Kimmo's probation officer straightaway. That's how we do it if one of our kids is ordered here by the magistrate or by Social Services."

"Griff Strong is . . . ?"

"A social worker. Trained as a social worker, I mean. We're not social workers per se at Colossus. Griff leads one of our assessment courses. He does extremely well with the kids. Very few of them drop out once they've had Griff."

Lynley saw Havers take down this information. He said, "Is Griff Strong here as well today? If he knew Kimmo, we're going to want to speak to him."

"To Griff?" Ulrike looked at her phone for some reason, as if this would give her the answer. "No. No, he's not in. He's bringing in a delivery . . ." She seemed to feel the need to toss her plaits into a more comfortable position. "He said he'd be late today, so we're not expecting him until . . . You see, he does our T-shirts and sweatshirts. A sideline of his. You may have seen them outside reception. In the glass case. He's an excellent social worker. We're very lucky to have him."

Lynley felt Havers looking his way. He knew what she was thinking: more depths to plumb here.

He said, "We've another dead boy as well. Jared Salvatore. Was he also one of yours?"

"*Another . . .*"

"There are five deaths we're investigating in all, Ms. Ellis."

Havers added, "Do you read the newspapers, by any chance? Does anyone round here, if it comes to that?"

Ulrike looked at her. "I hardly think that question's fair."

"Which one?" Havers said, but she didn't wait for an answer. "This is a serial killer we're talking about. He's going after boys round the age of those you've got standing in your carpark smoking fags. One of them could be next, so pardon my manners, but I don't care what you think is fair."

In other circumstances, Lynley would have reined the constable in at this point. But he could see that Havers' demonstration of impatience had had a positive effect. Ulrike got to her feet and went over to the filing cabinet. She squatted and jerked out one of the crammed drawers, which she fingered through rapidly. She said, "Of *course* I read . . . I look at the *Guardian*. Every day. Or as often as I can."

"But not recently, right?" Havers said. "Why is that?"

Ulrike didn't reply. She continued going through her files. She finally slammed the drawer closed and rose, empty handed. She said, "There is no Salvatore among our kids. I hope that satisfies you. And now let me ask you something in turn: Who sent you to Colossus in the first place?"

"Who?" Lynley asked. "What do you mean?"

"Oh, come on. We have enemies. Any organisation like this . . . trying to make the slightest degree of *change* in this bloody backward country . . . Do you honestly think there aren't people out there who want us to fail? Who put you on to Colossus?"

"Police work put us on to Colossus," Lynley said.

"The Borough High Street station, to be specific," Havers added.

"You actually want me to believe . . . You've come here because you think Kimmo's death has something to do with Colossus, haven't you? Well, you wouldn't even be thinking that if it hadn't been suggested by someone outside these walls, be that someone from Borough High Street station or someone from Kimmo's life."

Like Blinker, Lynley thought. Except Kimmo's stud-faced mate hadn't once mentioned Colossus, if he even had known about it. He said, "Tell us what happens in the assessment course."

Ulrike went back to her desk. For a moment, she stood there looking down at her phone, as if waiting for a prearranged deliverance. Beyond her, Havers had moved to a wall of degrees, certificates, and commendations, where she'd been jotting down salient details from the objects on display. Ulrike watched her. She said quietly, "We *care* about these kids. We want to make a difference for them. We believe that the only way to do that is through connection: one life to one life."

"Is that the assessment, then?" Lynley asked. "The attempt to connect with the young people who come here?"

It was that and far more than that, she told them. It was the young people's first experience with Colossus: a fortnight in which they met daily in a group of ten other young people with an assessment leader: Griffin Strong, in Kimmo's case. The object was to engage their interest, to prove to them that they could achieve success in one area or another, to establish in them a sense of trust, and to encourage them to commit to taking part in the Colossus programme. They began with developing a personal code of conduct for the group, and each day they assessed what had gone on—and been learned—the day before.

"Ice-breaking games at first," Ulrike said. "Then trust activities. Then a personal challenge, like climbing the rock wall out the back. Then a trip which they plan and take together. Somewhere into the countryside or to the sea. Hiking in the Pennines. Something like that. At the end, we invite them back for classes. Computers. Cookery. Single living. Health. From learning to earning."

"Jobs, you mean?" Havers asked.

"They aren't ready for jobs. Not when they first get here. Most of them are monosyllabic if not completely nonverbal. They're beaten down. What we try to do is show them there's another way from what they've been doing in the streets. There's returning to school, learning to read, completing college, walking away from drugs. There's having a belief in their future. There's managing their feelings. There's *having* feelings in the first place. There's developing a sense of self-esteem." She looked sharply at them both, as if trying to read them. "Oh, I know what you're thinking. Such touchy-feely crap. The ultimate in psychobabble. But the truth is that if behaviour is going to change, it's going to do it from the inside out. No one chooses a different path till he feels differently about himself."

"That was the plan for Kimmo?" Lynley asked. "From what we've learned, he seemed to feel fairly good about himself already, despite the choices he made."

"No one making Kimmo's choices feels good about himself at heart, Superintendent."

"So you expected him to change through time and exposure to Colossus?"

"We have," she said, "a high level of success. Despite what you're obviously thinking about us. Despite our not knowing Kimmo was murdered. We did what we were meant to do when he failed to show up."

"As you said," Lynley agreed. "And what do you do about the others?"

"The others?"

"Does everyone come to you via Youth Offenders?"

"Not at all. Most of them come because they've heard about us in another way entirely. Through church or school, through someone already involved in the programme. If they stay, it's because they begin to trust us and they start to believe in themselves."

"What happens with those who don't?" Havers asked.

"Don't what?"

"Start to believe in themselves?"

"Obviously, this programme doesn't work for them all. How can it? We're up against everything in their backgrounds, from abuse to xenophobia. Sometimes, a kid can't cope here any better than he can cope anywhere else. So he dips in and then out and that's how it is. We don't force anyone to stay who isn't required to by a court order. As for the rest, as long as they obey the rules, we don't force them to leave either. They can be here for years, if they like."

"And are they?"

"Occasionally, yes."

"Like who?"

"I'm afraid that's confidential."

"Ulrike?" It was Jack Veness. He'd come to the doorway of Ulrike's office, quiet as the fog. "Phone. I tried to tell him you were busy, but he wasn't having it. Sorry. What d'you want me . . . ?" He raised his shoulders as a way of completing the question.

"Who is it, then?"

"Reverend Savidge. He's in a state. Says Sean Lavery's gone missing. Says he didn't turn up at home last night when he was due back from the computer course. Should I—"

"No!" Ulrike said. "Put him through, Jack."

Jack left her office. She closed her fingers into a fist. She didn't look up as she waited for the phone to ring.

"There was another body this morning, Ms. Ellis," Lynley said.

"Then I'll put him on the speakerphone," she replied. "Please God this has nothing to do with us." While she waited for the phone call to ring through, she told them that the caller was the foster parent of one of the boys in their programme: He was called Sean Lavery, and he was black. She looked at Lynley, the question hanging unasked between them. He merely nodded, confirming her unspoken fears about the body found that morning in the Shand Street tunnel.

When the phone rang, Ulrike punched the button for the speaker. Reverend Savidge's voice came through, deep and anxious. Where was Sean? he wanted to know. Why hadn't Sean returned from Colossus last night?

Ulrike told him what little she knew. As far as she understood, Reverend Savidge's foster son Sean Lavery had been at Colossus as usual on the previous day and had left as usual on his regular bus. She'd heard nothing contrary to that from his computer instructor, and his instructor hadn't reported him as absent, which he definitely would have done because Sean had come to them via a social worker, and Colossus always kept in touch.

Where the hell *was* he, then? Reverend Savidge demanded. There were boys going missing all over London. Was Ulrike Ellis aware of that? Or did it not count to her if the boy in question happened to be black?

Ulrike assured him that she'd speak with the computer instructor the first chance she had but in the meantime . . . Had Reverend Savidge phoned round to see if Sean had perhaps gone home with a friend? Or gone to his dad's? Or gone to see his mum? She was still in Holloway, wasn't she, which wasn't a particularly difficult trip for a boy Sean's age to make. Sometimes boys do just go off for a bit, she'd said to Savidge.

He said, "Not this boy, madam," and he rang off abruptly.

Ulrike said, "Oh Lord," and Lynley knew it was a prayer.

He said one himself. Reverend Savidge's next call, Lynley reckoned, was going to be to his local police.

ONLY ONE OF THE two detectives left the building after the phone call from Reverend Savidge. The other—the unattractive woman with the chipped front teeth and the ridiculous red high-top trainers—remained behind. The man, Detective Superintendent Lynley, was going to head up to South Hampstead to talk to Sean Lavery's foster father. His subordinate, Detective Constable Barbara Havers, was going to hang round as long as it was necessary to have a word with Griffin Strong. Ulrike Ellis processed all this in a matter of seconds once the cops had finished with her: Lynley asked for Bram Savidge's address; Havers asked could she have a wander round the premises, the better to manage a word here and there.

Ulrike knew she could hardly say no. Things were bad enough without her being anything less than cooperative. So she agreed to the constable's request. For no matter what had happened beyond the walls of this place, Colossus and what Colossus represented were larger than the life of one boy or a dozen boys.

But even as she reassured herself that Colossus would emerge unscathed from this setback, Ulrike worried about Griff. He should have shown up at least two hours ago, no matter what she'd told the cops about the putative delivery of T-shirts and sweatshirts. The fact that he hadn't . . .

There was nothing to do but phone him on his mobile and warn him what to expect when he arrived. She wouldn't be blatant about it, however. She didn't trust the security of mobile phones. Instead she would tell him to meet her at the Charlie Chaplin pub. Or in the shopping centre up on the corner. Or at one of the market stalls just outside. Or even in the subway that led to the underground station because what did it matter when what was important was simply that they meet so she could warn him . . . Of what? she asked herself. And *why*?

Her chest was hurting. It had been hurting for days, but it had suddenly become worse. Did one have heart attacks at thirty years old? When she'd squatted in front of the filing drawer, she'd experienced a combination of light-headedness and increased chest pain that nearly overcame her. She'd thought she would swoon. God. *Swoon*. Where had *that* word come from?

Ulrike told herself to stop it. She picked up the phone and dialed for an outside line. When she had it, she tapped in the number of Griff Strong's mobile. She'd interrupt him doing *whatever* he was doing, but that couldn't be helped.

Griff said, "Yes?," on the other end. He sounded impatient, and what was *that* about? He worked at Colossus. She was his boss. Deal with it, Griff.

She said, "Where are you?"

He said, "Ulrike . . ." in a voice whose tone was a message in itself.

But the fact he'd used her name told her he was in a place of safety. She said, "The police have been. I can't say more. We need to meet before you get here."

"*Police*?" His previous impatience was gone. Ulrike could hear the fear that replaced it. She herself felt a corresponding frisson.

She said, "Two detectives. One of them is still in the building. She's waiting for you."

"For me? Shall I—"

"No. You must come in. If you don't . . . Look, let's not have this conversation on a mobile. How soon can you meet at . . . say, at Charlie Chaplin?" And then because it was more than reasonable, "Where are you?," so she could determine how long it would take him to get there.

Even the thought of the police at Colossus didn't put Griffin off his stride, however. He said, "Fifteen minutes."

Not at home, then. But she'd deduced that much when he'd said her name. She knew she wouldn't get anything more from him.

"Charlie Chaplin, then," she said. "Fifteen minutes." She rang off.

What remained was the waiting. That and wondering what the constable was doing as she had her ostensible look round the premises. Ulrike had determined in a flash that it benefitted Colossus for the DC to have this look unattended. Allowing her to wander freely sent a message about Colossus having nothing to hide.

But Lord, *Lord,* her chest was *pounding*. Her cornrow plaits were far too tight. She knew if she pulled on one of them, the whole lot would detach from her scalp, rendering her bald. What did they call it? Stress causing one's hair to fall out? Alopecia, that was it. Was there something called spontaneous alopecia? Probably. She'd be afflicted with that next.

She got up from her desk. From a rack next to the door, she plucked her coat, her scarf, and her hat. She slung these over her arm and left her office. She ducked down the corridor and slid into the loo.

There she prepared. She wore no makeup, so there was nothing to check save the condition of her skin, which she blotted with toilet tissue. Her cheeks bore the faint pockmarks of an adolescence given over to outbreaks of acne, but she felt it was an overt mark of self-absorption to use some sort of foundation to cover them. That smacked of a lack of self-acceptance and sent the wrong message to the board of trustees who'd hired her for the strength of her character.

Which was what she was going to need if Colossus was to get through this bad period. Strength. Plans had long been laid for the organisation's expansion to a second location—this one in North London—and the last thing the development committee needed over at the administration and fund-raising offices was the news that Colossus was being mentioned in the same sentence as a murder investigation. That would bring expansion to a screeching halt, and they *needed* to expand. The urgency was everywhere. Kids in care. Kids on the street. Kids selling their bodies. Kids dying from drugs. Colossus had the answer for them, so Colossus had to be able to grow. The entire situation they were in at the moment had to be dealt with expeditiously.

She had no lipstick, but she did carry gloss. She rooted this out of her bag and smoothed it across her lips. She adjusted the neck of her sweater a bit higher and shrugged on her coat. She put on the hat and the scarf and decided she looked enough like a supervisor to get through the meeting with Griffin Strong without being accused of personifying carpe diem in the worst possible way. This was about Colossus, she reminded herself and would remind Griff when she finally saw him. Everything else was secondary.

BARBARA HAVERS WASN'T about to cool her heels in her wait for Griffin Strong. Instead, after she told Ulrike Ellis that she'd "poke round a bit, if no one minds," she left the director's office to do so before Ulrike could assign her a watchdog. She then had a proper wander round the building, which was filling up with Colossus participants newly returned from late lunch, from cigarettes in the carpark, or from whatever dubious else they'd been doing. She watched them drift off to various activities: Some went to a computer room, some to a large educational kitchen, some to small classrooms, some to a conference room where they sat in a circle and talked earnestly, overseen by an adult who documented their ideas or concerns on a flip chart. The adults in question Barbara took close note of. She would need to get the name of each one. Each one's past—not to mention his present—would have to be checked out. Just because. Grunt work, all of it, but it had to be done.

She got aggro from no one as she had her wander. Most everyone simply and in some cases studiously ignored her. Eventually, she made her way into the computer room, where a mixed bag of adolescents appeared to be working on Web designs and a tubby male instructor round Barbara's own age was guiding an Asian youth through the use of a scanner. When he said, "You try it this time," and stepped away, he saw Barbara and came over to her.

"Help you?" he said quietly. He kept it friendly enough, but there was no disguising the fact that he knew who she was and what she was there for. The news was apparently traveling at a jackrabbit pace.

"Grass doesn't grow here, does it?" Barbara said. "Who's spreading the word? That bloke Jack in reception?"

"It would be part of his job," the man replied. He introduced himself as Neil Greenham, and he offered his hand to shake. It was soft, feminine, and a little too warm. He went on to say that Jack's information had been largely unnecessary. "I would have known you were a cop anyway."

"Personal experience? Clairvoyance? My fashion sense?"

"You're famous. Well, relatively. As these things go." Greenham went to a teacher's desk in one corner of the room. From there, he took a folded newspaper. He returned to her and handed it over. "I picked up the latest *Evening Standard* on my way back from lunch. Like I said, you're famous."

Curiously, Barbara unfolded it. There on the front page, the headline shrieked the news of the early morning discovery in the Shand Street tunnel. Beneath it, were two photographs: One was a grainy picture of the tunnel's interior, in which several figures round a sports car were silhouetted by the stark portable lights brought in by the SOCO team; the other was a fine, clear shot of Barbara herself, along with Lynley, Hamish Robson, and the local DI, as they spoke outside the tunnel and in view of the press. Only Lynley was identified by name. There was, Barbara thought, little blessing in that.

She handed the paper back to Greenham. "DC Havers," she said. "New Scotland Yard."

He nodded at the paper. "Don't you want that for your scrapbook?"

"I'll buy three dozen on my way home tonight. Could we have a word?"

He gestured to the classroom and the young people at work. "I'm in the middle of something. Can it wait?"

"They look like they're coping without you."

Greenham ran his gaze over them as if checking for the truth of this statement. He gave a nod then and indicated they could speak in the corridor.

"One of yours is gone missing," Barbara told him. "Have you heard that yet? Has Ulrike told you?"

Greenham's eyes shifted from Barbara to the corridor; he looked in the direction of Ulrike Ellis's office. Here, Barbara thought, was a piece of news that apparently hadn't traveled on the jackrabbit express. And that was curious, considering Ulrike's telephone promise to Reverend Savidge to talk to the computer instructor about the newly missing boy.

Greenham said, "Sean Lavery?"

"Bingo."

"He just hasn't come in yet today."

"Aren't you meant to report him?"

"At the end of the day, yes. He could merely be late."

"As the *Evening Standard*'s pointing out, a dead boy was found in the London Bridge area round half past five this morning."

"Sean?"

"We don't know yet. But if it is, that's two."

"Kimmo Thorne as well. The same killer, you mean. Serial . . ."

"Ah. Someone *does* read the newspapers round here. I was getting a little curious about that, why no one seemed to know Kimmo's dead. You knew, but you didn't talk about it with any of the others?"

Greenham shifted weight from one leg onto the other. He said, sounding not too comfortable about the admission, "There's a bit of a divide. Ulrike and the assessment people on one side; the rest of us on the other."

"And Kimmo was still at the assessment level."

"Right."

"Yet you knew him."

Greenham wasn't about to be caught by the undercurrent of accusation in the remark. He said, "I knew who he was. But who *wouldn't* have known who Kimmo was? Cross-dresser? Eye shadow, lipstick? He was hard to miss and harder to forget, if you know what I mean. So it wasn't only me. Everyone knew Kimmo five minutes after he walked through the door."

"And this other kid? Sean?"

"Loner. A bit hostile. Didn't want to be here, but he

was willing to give computers a try. In time, I think we could've got through."

"Past tense," Barbara said.

Greenham's upper lip looked damp. "That body . . ."

"We don't know who it is."

"I suppose I assumed . . . with you here and all . . ."

"Not a good idea, assuming." Barbara took out her notebook. She saw the look of alarm pass across Greenham's pudgy face. She said, "Tell me about yourself, Mr. Greenham."

He recovered quickly. "Address? Education? Background? Hobbies? Do I kill adolescent boys in my spare time?"

"Start with how you fit in the hierarchy round here."

"There is no hierarchy."

"You said there was a divide. Ulrike and assessment on one side. Everyone else on the other. How did that come about?"

He said, "You misunderstand. The divide has to do with information and how it's shared. That's all. Otherwise, we're all on the same page at Colossus. We're about saving kids. That's what we do."

Barbara nodded thoughtfully. "Tell that to Kimmo Thorne. How long have you been here?"

"Four years," he replied.

"And before?"

"I'm a teacher. I worked in North London." He gave the name of a primary school in Kilburn. Before she could ask, he told her he'd left that employment because he'd come to realise he preferred to work with older children. He added that he'd also had issues with the head teacher. When Barbara asked what sort of issues, he told her forthrightly that they were about discipline.

"Which side of the fence did you happen to reside on?" Barbara asked. "Sparing and spoiling or as the twig is bent?"

"You're rather full of clichés, aren't you?"

"I'm a walking encyclopaedia of them. So . . . ?"

"It wasn't corporal punishment," he told her. "It was classroom discipline: the removal of privileges, a thorough talking to, a brief spate of social ostracism. That sort of thing."

"Public ridicule? A day in the stocks?"

He coloured. "I'm trying to be frank with you. You'll phone them up, I know. They're going to tell you we had our differences. But that's only natural. People are always of different opinions."

"Right," Barbara said. "Well, we all have those, don't we, our different opinions? You have them here as well? Difference of opinions leading to conflicts leading to . . . Who knows what? Perhaps the divide you mentioned?"

"I'll repeat the point I tried to make before. We're all on the same page. Colossus is about the kids. The more people you talk to, the more you're going to understand that. Now, if you'll excuse me, I see that Yusuf needs my help." He left her then, returning to his classroom where the Asian boy was bent over the scanner looking as if he wished to hammer it. Barbara knew the feeling.

She left Greenham to his students. Her further exploration of the premises—still unimpeded—took her to the very back of the building. There she found the kit room where a group of kids were being set up with appropriate dress and equipment for winter kayaking on the Thames. Robbie Kilfoyle—he of the earlier cardplaying and the Euro-Disney baseball cap—had them lined up, and he was measuring them for wetsuits, a row of which hung along one wall. He'd pulled life jackets from a shelf as well, and those who were done being measured were sorting through these, finding one that fitted. Conversation among them was muted. It appeared they'd all finally got the word: either about Kimmo Thorne or about the cops asking questions.

Kilfoyle dismissed them to the game room when they had their wet suits and their life jackets. Wait there for Griffin Strong, he told them. He would be assisting their assessment leader on the river trip, and he was going to grouse about it if he didn't find them all ready when he showed up. Then, as they filed out, Kilfoyle went on to sort through a mound of Wellingtons piled on the floor. He began to pair them and slide them onto shelves that were marked with sizes. He gave Barbara a nod of recognition. "Still here?" he said.

"As ever. Seems we're all waiting for Griffin Strong."

"Truth to that, all right." There was an airiness to his voice suggesting double meanings. Barbara took note.

"Volunteer here long?" she asked him.

Kilfoyle thought about that one. "Two years?" he said. "Bit more. Something like twenty-nine months."

"What about before that?"

He gave her a look, one that said he knew this was no simple chat on her part. "This's my first spate of volunteering anywhere."

"Why?"

"Which? The first-time part or the volunteering-at-all part?"

"Volunteering at all."

He stopped his work, a set of Wellingtons in his hand. "I do their sandwich deliveries, like I said in reception. That's how I met them. I could see they needed help because—between you and me—they pay their actual employees shit, so they can never find enough help or keep them long when they do find them. I started hanging about after my lunch deliveries were done for the day. Doing this, doing that, and hey, presto, I was a volunteer."

"Nice of you."

He shrugged. "Good cause. Besides, I'd like to be taken on eventually."

"Even though they pay their employees shit?"

"I like the kids. And anyway, Colossus pays more than I'm currently making, believe me."

"So how do you make them?"

"What?"

"Your deliveries."

"Bicycle," he replied. "There's a cart that gets attached to the back."

"Going where?"

"The cart? The deliveries?" He didn't wait for an answer. "Round South London, mostly. A bit in the City. Why? What're you looking for?"

A van, Barbara thought. Deliveries by van. She noted that Kilfoyle had started to flush, but she didn't want to put that down as any more significant than Greenham's damp upper lip or his too soft hands. This bloke was ruddy skinned anyway, in the way of many Englishmen, and he had the doughy face, narrow nose, and knobby chin that would mark him out as British no matter where he went.

Barbara realised then how badly she wanted to read *one* of these blokes as a serial killer behind their ordinary exteriors. But the truth was, she'd so far wanted to read just about everyone she'd come across exactly the same and, no doubt when he finally showed his mug, Griff Strong was going to look bloody good to her as a serial killer, as well. She needed to keep things slow and easy at this point, she thought. Piece details together, she told herself, don't cram them into position simply because you want them to be there.

"So how do they keep body and soul together?" Barbara asked. "Not to mention roofs over their heads?"

"Who?"

"You said wages were bad here . . . ?"

"Oh. That. Mostly they've got second jobs."

"Such as?"

He considered. "Don't know them all. But Jack's got a weekend job in a pub, and Griff and his wife have a silk-screen business. Fact is, I think only Ulrike's making enough not to have something else going on at the weekends or at night. It's the only way anyone can actually do this and still eat." He looked past Barbara to the doorway and added, "Hey, mate. I was just about to set the hounds on you."

Barbara turned and saw the same boy who'd been playing cards with Kilfoyle earlier in reception. He was slouching in the doorway, baggy blue jeans crotched at the knees and boxer shorts bulging at the waist. He shuffled into the kit room, where Kilfoyle set him up sorting through a tangle of climbing ropes. He began pulling them out of a plastic barrel and coiling them neatly round his arm.

"Do you happen to know Sean Lavery?" Barbara asked Kilfoyle.

He thought about this. "Been through assessment?"

"He's on a computer course with Neil Greenham."

"Then I probably know him. By sight if not by name. Back here"—He used his chin to indicate the kit room—"I only see the kids close up when there's an activity scheduled and they come in for supplies. Otherwise, they're just faces to me. I don't always put a name to them or keep a name on them once they've moved beyond the assessment level."

"Because only assessment-level kids use this stuff?" Barbara asked him, referring to the supplies in the kit room.

"Generally speaking, yes," he said.

"Neil Greenham tells me there's a divide between the assessment people and everyone else round here, with Ulrike on the assessment side. He indicated that's a trouble spot."

"That's just Neil," Kilfoyle said. He shot a look towards his helper and lowered his voice. "He hates being out of the loop. He takes offence easy. He's keen to have more responsibility and—"

"Why?"

"What?"

"Why's he keen to have more responsibility?"

Kilfoyle moved from the Wellingtons to the remaining life jackets that had not been chosen for wear by the team going out on the Thames. "Most people want that in their jobs, don't they? It's a power thing."

"Neil likes power?"

"I don't know him well, but I get the feeling he'd like to have more say about how things are run round here."

"And what about you? You've got to have bigger plans for yourself than volunteering in this kit room."

"You mean here at Colossus?" He thought about this, then gave a shrug. "Okay, I'll play. I wouldn't mind being hired to do outreach when they open the Colossus branch north of the river. But Griff Strong's angling for that. And if Griff wants it, it's going to be his."

"Why?"

Kilfoyle hesitated, weighing a life jacket between one hand and another as if he were also weighing his words. He finally replied, "Let's just say Neil was right about one thing: Everyone knows everyone else at Colossus. But Ulrike's going to make the decision on the outreach job, and she knows some people better than others."

FROM THE BENTLEY, Lynley phoned the police station in South Hampstead and brought them into the picture: the body found that morning south of the river, which was possibly one of a series of killings . . . if the station would allow him a conversation with a certain Reverend Savidge who might soon be phoning them about a missing boy . . . Arrangements were made as he crossed the river, heading diagonally through the city.

He found Bram Savidge at his ministry, which turned out to be a former shop for electrical goods whose whimsical name Plugged Inn had been economically used as part of the church's moniker, Plugged Inn to the Lord. In the Swiss Cottage area of Finchley Road, it appeared to be part church and part soup kitchen. At the moment, it was operating as the latter.

When Lynley walked in, he felt like an overweight nudist in a crowd wearing overcoats: He was the only white face in the establishment, and the black faces looking him over were doing so without much welcome. He asked for Reverend Savidge, please, and a woman who'd been dishing out a savoury stew to a line of the hungry went to fetch him. When Savidge turned up, Lynley found himself face-to-face with six feet, five inches of solid Africa, which was hardly what he'd expected from the public school sound of the man's voice on the speakerphone in Ulrike Ellis's office.

Reverend Savidge appeared in a caftan of red, orange, and black, while on his feet were roughly made sandals, which he wore without socks despite the winter weather. An intricately carved wooden necklace lay on his chest, and a single earring of shell, bone, or something very like dangled just below the height of Lynley's eyes. Savidge might have just stepped off the plane from Nairobi, except his clipped beard framed a face not as dark as one would have expected. Aside from Lynley, he was actually the lightest-skinned person in the room.

"You're the police?" That accent again, speaking not only of public schools and a university degree, but also of an upbringing in an area that was a far cry from his present community. His eyes—they were hazel, Lynley noted—took in Lynley's suit, shirt, tie, and shoes. He made his evaluation in an instant, and it wasn't good. So be it, Lynley thought. He showed his identification and asked if there was somewhere private for them to speak.

Savidge led the way to an office at the back of the building. They wound there through long tables set up for use in eating the meal being dished out by women wearing garb not unlike Savidge's own. At these, perhaps two dozen men and half as many women wolfed down the stew, drank from small cartons of milk, and slathered bread with butter. Music played low to entertain them, a chant of some sort in an African tongue.

Savidge closed the door on all this when they got to his office. He said, "Scotland Yard. Why? I phoned the local station. They said someone would come. I assumed . . . What's happening? What's this all about?"

"I was in Ms. Ellis's office when you phoned Colossus."

"What's happened to Sean?" Savidge demanded. "He didn't come home. You must know something. Tell me."

Lynley could see the reverend was used to being instantly obeyed. There was little doubt why this was the case: He dominated by simple virtue of being alive. Lynley couldn't remember the last time he'd seen a man who so effortlessly exuded such authority.

He said, "I understand Sean Lavery lives with you?"

"I'd like to know—"

"Reverend Savidge, I'm going to need some information. One way or the other."

They engaged in a brief battle of eyes and wills before Savidge said, "With me and my wife. Yes. Sean lives with us. In care."

"His own parents?"

"His mum's in prison. Attempted murder of a cop." Savidge paused, as if registering Lynley's reaction to this. Lynley took care not to give him one. "Dad's a mechanic over in North Kensington. They were never married, and he had no interest in the boy, before or after Mum's arrest. When she went inside, Sean went into the system."

"And how did you end up with him?"

"I've had boys in my home for nearly two decades."

"Boys? Are there others, then?"

"Not now. Just Sean."

"Why?"

Reverend Savidge went to a Thermos, out of which he poured himself a cup of something fragrant and steaming. He offered this to Lynley, who demurred. He took it to his desk and sat, nodding Lynley into a chair. On the desk, a legal pad held jottings, things listed and crossed out, circled and underlined. "Sermon," Savidge said, apparently noticing the direction of Lynley's gaze. "It doesn't come easy."

"The other boys, Reverend Savidge?"

"I have a wife now. Oni's English isn't good. She felt overwhelmed and a bit overrun, so I had three of the boys placed elsewhere. Temporarily. Till Oni settles in."

"But not Sean Lavery. He's not been placed elsewhere. Why?"

"He's younger than the others. It didn't feel right to move him."

Lynley wondered what else hadn't felt right. He couldn't help concluding it might have been the new Mrs. Savidge, inadequate in English and home alone with a household of adolescent boys.

"How did Sean come to be involved in Colossus?" he asked. "It's quite a distance for him to go there from here."

"Colossus do-gooders came to the church. They called it outreach, but what it amounted to was talking up their programme. An alternative to what they obviously believe every child of colour would get up to, given half the chance and absent their intervention."

"You don't approve of them, then."

"This community's going to help itself from within, Superintendent. It's not going to improve by having help imposed upon it by a group of liberal, guilt-ridden social activists. They need to toddle back to whichever of the Home Counties they came from, hockey sticks and cricket bats well in hand."

"Yet somehow Sean Lavery ended up there, despite your feelings."

"I had no choice in the matter. Neither did Sean. It was all down to his social worker."

"But surely, as his guardian, you have a strong say in how he spends his free time."

"Under other circumstances. But there was an incident with a bicycle as well." Savidge went on to explain: It was a complete misunderstanding, he said. Sean had taken an expensive mountain bike from a boy in the neighbourhood. He'd thought he'd been given permission to use it; the boy had thought otherwise. He reported it stolen and the cops found it in Sean's possession. The situation was considered a first offence, and Sean's social worker suggested nipping any potential for illegal behaviour in the bud. So Colossus came into the picture. Savidge had initially, if reluctantly, approved the idea: Of all his boys, Sean had been the first to come to the notice of the police. He was also the first who wouldn't attend school. Colossus was supposed to remedy all this.

"He's been there how long?" Lynley asked.

"Closing in on a year."

"Attending regularly?"

"He has to. It's part of his probation." Savidge lifted his mug and drank. He wiped his mouth carefully. He went on with, "Sean's said from the first that he didn't steal that bike, and I believe him. At the same time, I want to keep him out of trouble, which you and I know he's going to get into if he doesn't go to school and doesn't get involved with something. He hasn't exactly looked forward to Colossus every day—from what I can tell—but he goes. He managed the assessment course, and he's actually had some good words to say about the computer course he's doing now."

"Who was his assessment leader?"

"Griffin Strong. Social worker. Sean liked him well enough. Or at least well enough not to complain about him."

"Has he ever failed to come home before, Reverend Savidge?"

"Never. He's been late a few times, but he's phoned to let us know. That's it."

"Is there any reason he might have decided to run off?"

Savidge thought about this. He circled his hands round his mug and rolled it between his palms. He finally said, "Once he managed to track down his dad without telling me—"

"In North Kensington?"

"Yes. Munro Mews, a car-repair shop. Sean tracked him down a few months ago. I don't know exactly what happened. He's never said. But I don't expect it was anything positive. His dad's moved on in his life. He has a wife and kids, which is all I know from Sean's social worker. So if Sean went hoping to get Dad's attention . . . That would have been a real nonstarter. But not enough to cause Sean to run off."

"The dad's name?"

Savidge gave it to him: one Sol Oliver. But then he ran out of the willingness to cooperate and self-subordinate. He was clearly not used to doing either. He said, "Now, Superintendent Lynley. I've told you what I know. I want you to tell me what you're going to do. And not what you're going to do in forty-eight hours or however long you expect me to wait because Sean might have run off. He doesn't run off. He phones if he's going to be late. He leaves Colossus and he checks in here on his way to the gym. He pounds the punch bag and then he goes home."

The gym? Lynley took note of this. What gym? Where? How often did he go? And how did Sean get from Plugged Inn to the Lord to the gym and from there to home? On foot? By bus? Did he ever hitch-hike? Did someone drive him?

Savidge regarded him curiously but answered willingly enough. Sean walked, he told Lynley. It wasn't far. Either from here or from home. It was called Square Four Gym.

Did the boy have a mentor there? Lynley asked. Someone he admired? Someone he spoke of?

Savidge shook his head. He said that Sean went to the gym as part of coping with his anger and upon his social worker's recommendation. He had no ambition to be a body builder, a boxer, a wrestler, or anything else along those lines, as far as Savidge knew.

What about friends? Lynley asked. Who were they?

Savidge thought about this for a moment before he admitted that Sean Lavery didn't seem to have friends. But he was a good boy and he was responsible, Savidge insisted. And the one thing he could vouch for was that Sean wouldn't fail to come home without phoning and explaining why.

And then because somehow Savidge knew that New Scotland Yard would not have come in place of the local police without more of a reason than having been in Ulrike Ellis's office when he phoned, he said, "Perhaps it's time you told me why you're really here, Superintendent."

In reply, Lynley asked Reverend Savidge if he had a photo of the boy.

Not there in his office, Savidge told him. For that, they would need to go to his home.

Chapter Eleven

Even if Robbie Kilfoyle in his EuroDisney cap hadn't alluded to the fact, Barbara Havers would have twigged that something was going on between Griffin Strong and Ulrike Ellis about fifteen seconds into seeing them together. Whether it was merely a case of angst-filled love going unacknowledged, of footsie in the local canteen, or Kama Sutra under the stars, she couldn't have said. Nor could she tell if it was just a one-way street with Ulrike doing all the driving in a car she was piloting to nowhere. But that there was *something* in the air between them—some sort of electrical charge that usually meant naked bodies and moaning exchanges of bodily fluids but could really mean anything in between handshakes and the primal act—only a deaf-mute alien life form would have thought to deny.

The director of Colossus personally brought Griffin Strong to Barbara. She made the introductions, and the way she said his name—not to mention the way she looked at him, with an expression not unlike the one Barbara felt on her own face whenever she gazed upon a fruit-topped cheesecake—pretty much put neon lights round whatever secret she or they were supposed to be keeping. And obviously, there had to be a secret. Not only had Robbie Kilfoyle earlier mentioned the word *wife* in connection with Strong, but the man himself wore a wedding band the approximate size of a lorry tyre. Which in itself was a wise idea, Barbara thought. Strong was just about the most gorgeous thing she'd ever seen walking unmolested on the streets of London. He no doubt needed *something* to ward off the hordes of females whose jaws probably dropped to their chests when he passed them. He looked like a film star. He looked better than a film star. He looked like a god.

He also, Barbara realised, looked uneasy. She couldn't decide if this counted in his favour or marked him down for further study.

He said, "Ulrike's told me about Kimmo Thorne and Sean Lavery. You might as well know: They were both mine. Sean went through assessment with me ten months ago and Kimmo was going through assessment now. I let Ulrike know straightaway when he—Kimmo—didn't turn up. Obviously, I didn't know Sean was missing, as he's not currently one of mine."

Barbara nodded. Helpful, she thought. And the bit about Sean was an interesting wrinkle.

She asked was there a spot where they could talk. They didn't exactly need Ulrike Ellis hanging upon their every word.

Strong said he shared an office with two other assessment leaders. They were off with their kids today, though, and if she'd follow him there, they'd have some privacy. He himself didn't have a lot of time, though, because he was due to help take some kids out on the river. He gave Ulrike a quick glance and motioned Barbara to follow him.

For her part, Barbara tried to interpret that glance

and the nervous smile that quivered on Ulrike's lips as she received it. *You and me, babe. Our secret, darling. We'll talk later. I want you naked. Rescue me in five minutes, please.* The possibilities seemed endless.

Barbara followed Griffin Strong—"It's Griff," he said—to an office just the other side of reception. It displayed the same decorating sense as Ulrike's: heavy on clutter and light on available space. Bookshelves, filing cabinets, one shared desk. The walls held posters intended to influence young people in a positive direction: illiterate football stars with curious hairdos, pretending to read Charles Dickens, and pop singers doing thirty seconds of public service in soup kitchens. Colossus posters joined these. On them, the familiar logo appeared, that giant allowing himself to be used by the smaller and the less fortunate.

Strong went to one of the filing cabinets and fingered through a packed drawer to pull out two files. He consulted them and told her that Kimmo Thorne had come to Colossus via the magistrate's court, Youth Offenders, and his predilection for selling stolen goods. Sean had come via Social Services and something about a hijacked mountain bike.

Again, that demonstration of helpfulness. Strong returned the files and went to the desk, where he sat and rubbed his forehead.

"You look tired," Barbara noted.

"I've a baby with colic," he said, "and a wife with postnatal blues. I'm coping. But only just."

That at least partially explained whatever might be going on with Ulrike, Barbara decided. It fell into the poor-misunderstood-and-neglected-husband class of extramarital whatevers. "Tough times," she said in acknowledgement.

He flashed her a smile of—what else would it be?—perfect, white teeth. "It's worth it. I'll get through them."

Bet you will, Barbara thought. She asked him about Kimmo Thorne. What did Strong know about his time at Colossus? About his associates here? His friends, mentors, acquaintances, teachers, and the like. Having had him in the assessment course—which she was given to understand would provide the most intimate of the interactions that the kids would engage in at Colossus—he probably knew Kimmo better than anyone else did.

Good kid, Strong told her. Oh, he'd been in trouble, but he wasn't cut out for criminality. He just did it as a means to an end, not for kicks and not as an unconscious social statement. And he'd rejected that sort of life, anyway. . . . Well, at least that was how it had seemed so far. It had been too soon to tell which way Kimmo would actually go, which was generally the case during a young person's first weeks at Colossus.

What sort of boy was he? Barbara then asked.

Well liked, Griff told her. Pleasant, affable. He was just the sort of boy who stood a good chance of actually making something of himself. He had real potential and real talent. It was a bloody shame some bastard out there had targeted him.

Barbara took down all of this information, despite knowing most of it already, despite feeling it was all somehow rehearsed. Doing this gave her the opportunity not to look at the man who was passing the details along to her. She evaluated his voice while not distracted by his GQ looks. He *sounded* sincere enough. Very forthcoming and all that. But there was nothing in what he was telling her that indicated he knew Kimmo better than anyone else, and that didn't make sense. He was *supposed* to know him well, or at least to be getting to know him well. Yet there was nothing here to indicate that, and she had to wonder why.

"Any special friends here?" she asked.

He said, "What?" And then, "Do you actually think someone from *Colossus* may have killed him?"

"It's a possibility," Barbara said.

"Ulrike'll tell you everyone's thoroughly vetted before they come to work here. The idea that somehow a serial killer—"

"Had a good chat with Ulrike before you and I met, then?" Barbara looked up from her notes. He had a deer-in-the-headlights expression on his face.

"Of course she told me you were here when she told me about Kimmo and Sean. But she said there were several other deaths you're investigating, so it *can't* have anything to do with Colossus. And no one knows if Sean's just bunked off for the day anyway."

"True," Barbara said. "Any special friends?"

"Mine?"

"We were talking about Kimmo."

"Kimmo. Right. Everyone liked him. And you'd think the opposite would be the case, considering how he got himself up and how most kids feel about their sexuality in adolescence."

"How's that, then?"

"You know, a bit ill at ease, unsure at first about their own proclivities and consequently unwilling to have anything to do with someone who might cast a questionable light upon them in the eyes of their peers. But no one seemed to shun Kimmo. He didn't allow it. As to special friends, there was no one he singled out and no one who singled out him more than anyone else. But that's not something that would happen in assessment anyway. The kids are supposed to bond as a group."

"What about Sean?" she asked him.

"What about Sean?"

"Friends?"

Strong hesitated. Then, "He had a rougher time than

Kimmo, as I recall," he said reflectively. "He didn't get close to the group he went through assessment with. But he seemed more standoffish in general. An introvert. Things on his mind."

"Such as?"

"I don't know. Except he was angry, and he didn't try to hide it."

"About what?"

"Being here, I expect. In my experience, most kids are angry when they come to us through Social Services. They generally break down sometime during their assessment weeks, but Sean never did."

How long had Griffin Strong been an assessment leader at Colossus? Barbara asked.

Unlike Kilfoyle and Greenham, who'd had to think about how long they'd been associated with the organisation, Griff said, "Fourteen months," at once.

"And before?" Barbara asked.

"Social work. I'd started out in medicine—thought I'd be a pathologist till I found I couldn't abide the sight of a dead body—then I switched over to psychology. And sociology. I've a first in each."

That was impressive enough, as well as easily checked out. "Where'd you work?" Barbara asked him.

He didn't respond at once, so again Barbara lifted her head from her notebook. She found him staring at her, and she knew that he'd intended her to raise her head and that he enjoyed the sensation of having forced her into doing so. Flatly, she repeated her question.

He finally said, "Stockwell, for a time."

"Before that?"

"Lewisham. Is this important?"

"Just now, everything's important." Barbara took her time writing "Stockwell" and "Lewisham" into her notebook. She said, "What sort, anyway?" when she'd put a little flourish on the final letter.

"What sort of what?"

"Social work. Kids in care? Lags on the loose? Single mums? What?"

He didn't answer a second time. Barbara thought he might be playing the power game again, but she raised her head anyway. This time, though, he wasn't looking at her but rather at the football player on the poster, ostensibly enraptured by his leather-bound copy of *Bleak House*. Barbara was about to repeat her question when Griff appeared to come to a decision about something.

He said, "You might as well know. You'll find out anyway. I was sacked from both jobs."

"For?"

"I don't always get on with supervisors, especially if they're female. Sometimes . . ." He gave his attention fully back to her, two dark deep eyes compelling her to keep her gaze locked upon him. "There are always disagreements in this sort of work. There have to be. We're dealing with human lives and each life is different from the last, isn't it."

"You could say that," Barbara said, curious about where he was going with all this. He showed her in short order.

"Yes. Well. I have a tendency to express myself strongly, and women have a tendency not to take that well. I end up getting . . . let's call it misunderstood for want of a better term."

Ah, there it was, Barbara thought, the misunderstood business. It just wasn't being applied where she'd expected it to be. "But Ulrike doesn't have that problem with you?"

"Not so far," he said. "But then, Ulrike likes discussion. She's not afraid of a healthy debate among the team."

Or a healthy something else as well, Barbara thought. Especially that. She said, "You and Ulrike are close, then?"

He wasn't about to get into that. "She runs the organisation."

"What about when you're not here at Colossus?"

"What are you asking?"

"If you're bonking your boss. I guess I'm wondering how the other assessment leaders might feel about it if you and Ulrike happen to be making the beast with two backs after hours. Or how anyone else might feel about it, for that matter. Is that how you lost your other two jobs, by the way?"

He said evenly, "You're not very nice, are you?"

"Not with five dead bodies to account for."

"Five . . . ? You can't possibly conclude . . . I was told . . . Ulrike said you'd come here—"

"About Kimmo, yeah. But that's just one of two dead bodies with names," Barbara said.

"But you said that Sean . . . Sean's only *missing*, isn't he? He's not dead . . . You don't know . . ."

"We've a body this morning that could be Sean, and I'm sure Ulrike clued you in on that. Beyond that, we've got a kid called Jared Salvatore identified and three others in line to be claimed by someone. Five in all."

He didn't say anything, but he seemed to be holding his breath for some reason, and Barbara wondered what that meant. He finally murmured, "Jesus."

"What's happened to the rest of your assessment kids, Mr. Strong?" Barbara asked.

"What do you mean?"

"How closely do you follow them when they're done with their first two weeks at this place?"

"I don't. I haven't. I mean, they go on to their instructors next. If they *want* to go on, that is. The instructors keep tabs on how they're doing, and they report in to Ulrike. The whole team meets every two weeks and we talk, and Ulrike herself counsels the kids having trouble." He frowned. He tapped his knuckles on his desk. "If these other kids turn out to be ours . . . Someone's trying to discredit Colossus," he told her. "Or one of us. Someone's trying to get at one of us."

"You think that's the case?" Barbara asked.

"If even one other of the bodies comes from here, what else is there to think?"

"That kids are in danger all over London," Barbara said, "but that they're really up against it if they end up here."

"Like we're setting *out* to kill them, you mean?" Strong's question was outraged.

Barbara smiled and flipped her notebook closed. "Your words, not mine, Mr. Strong," she said.

REVEREND BRAM SAVIDGE and his wife lived in a West Hampstead neighbourhood that belied the church leader's we-are-of-the-people demeanour. It was a small house, true. But it was far more than anyone whom Lynley had seen either dishing out the food or eating it at Plugged Inn to the Lord could afford. And Savidge led the way there in a late-model Saab. As DC Havers would have happily pointed out: Someone round here wasn't hurting for lolly.

Savidge waited for Lynley to find a place for the Bentley on the tree-lined street. He stood on the front step of his house, looking vaguely biblical with his caftan blowing in the winter breeze, coatless despite the frigid winter weather. When Lynley finally joined him, he sorted out three locks on the front door and opened it. He called, "Oni? I've brought a visitor, darling."

He didn't call out about Sean, Lynley noted. Not "Has the boy phoned?" Not "Any word from Sean?" Just "I've brought a visitor, darling," and in a tentative manner that sounded somehow like a warning and was completely out of character for the man Lynley had been speaking with so far.

There was no immediate reply to Savidge's call. He

said to Lynley, "Wait here," and directed him to the sitting room. He himself went to a staircase and climbed quickly to the first floor. Lynley heard him moving along a corridor.

He took a moment to gaze round the sitting room, which was simply fitted out with well-made furniture and a brightly patterned rug. The walls held old documents, framed and mounted, and as above him doors opened and closed in rapid succession, Lynley went to examine these. One was an antique bill of lading, apparently from a ship called the *Valiant Sheba* whose cargo had been twenty males, thirty-two females—eighteen of whom were documented as "breeding"—and thirteen children. Another was a letter written in copperplate on stationery that bore "Ash Grove, nr Kingston" as its letterhead. Faded with time, this proved difficult to read, but Lynley made out "excellent stud potential" and "if you can control the brute."

"My thrice-great-grandfather, Superintendent. He didn't quite take to slavery."

Lynley turned. In the doorway, Savidge stood with a girl at his side. "Oni, my wife," he said. "She's asked to be introduced."

It was hard for Lynley to believe he was looking at Savidge's wife, for Oni appeared no older than sixteen, if that. She was thin, long necked, and African to the core. Like her husband, her manner of dress was ethnic, and she carried an unusual musical instrument in her arms, its belly not unlike a banjo, but with a tall bridge that lifted more than a dozen strings high up.

One glance at her explained a great deal to Lynley. Oni was exquisite: like midnight unblemished, with hundreds of years of blood untarnished by miscegenation. She was what Savidge himself could never be because of the *Valiant Sheba*. She was also the last thing a rational man would want to leave alone with a group of teenage boys.

Lynley said, "Mrs. Savidge."

The girl smiled and nodded. She looked to her husband as if for guidance. She said, "You might wanting?," and halted, as if sorting through a catalogue of words that she knew and grammar whose rules she barely understood.

He said, "This is about Sean, darling. We don't mean to disturb your practice with the kora. Why don't you go on with it down here while I take the policeman up to Sean's room?"

"Yes," she agreed. "I will be playing, then." She went to the sofa and placed the kora carefully on the floor. As they were about to leave her, she said, "It is very sunless today, no? Another month passes. Bram, I . . . discover . . . No, not discover isn't . . . I *learn* this morning . . ."

Savidge hesitated. Lynley discerned a change in him, like tension released. He said, "We'll talk later, then, Oni."

She said, "Yes. And the other as well? Again?"

"Perhaps. The other." Quickly, he directed Lynley to the stairs. He led the way to a room at the back of the house. When they were within it, he seemed to feel the need to explain. He shut the door and said, "We're trying for a baby. No luck so far. That's what she meant."

"That's rough," Lynley said.

"She's worried about it. Worried that I might . . . I don't know . . . discard her or something? But she's perfectly healthy. She's perfectly formed. She's—" Savidge stopped, as if he realised how close he was to describing someone's breeding potential himself. He settled on changing course altogether, and he said, "Anyway. This is Sean's room."

"Did you ask your wife if he's turned up? Phoned? Sent a message?"

"She doesn't answer the phone," Savidge said. "Her English isn't good enough. She lacks confidence."

"Anything else?"

"What do you mean?"

"I mean did you ask her about Sean?"

"I didn't need to. She would have told me. She knows I'm worried."

"What's her relationship with the boy?"

"What's that got to do with—"

"Mr. Savidge, I've got to ask," Lynley said, his gaze steady. "She's obviously much younger than you."

"She's nineteen years old."

"Much closer in age to the boys you've sheltered than to yourself, am I right?"

"This isn't *about* my marriage, my wife, or my situation, Superintendent."

Oh, but it is, Lynley thought. He said, "You're what? Twenty years older than she? Twenty-five years older? And the boys were what age?"

Savidge seemed to grow larger, indignation colouring his reply. "This is about a missing boy. In a circumstance in which *other* boys of a similar age have gone missing, if the newspapers are anything to go by. So if you think I'm going to let you misdirect my concerns because you lot have botched an investigation, you'd better change course." He didn't wait for an answer. Instead, he went to a bookcase that held a small CD player and a rank of paperback books that looked untouched. From the top of this, he took up a photograph in a plain wooden frame. He thrust it at Lynley.

In the picture, Savidge himself in his African garb stood with his arm round the shoulders of a solemn-looking boy wearing an overlarge tracksuit. The boy had a head of germinant dreadlocks and a wary expression, like a dog's too often returned to his cage at the Battersea shelter after a walk. He was very dark, only a little lighter than Savidge's wife. He was also, unmistakably, the boy whose body they'd found that morning.

Lynley looked up. Beyond Savidge's shoulder, he saw that the walls of Sean's room had posters on them: Louis Farrakhan in passionate exhortation, Elijah Mohammed backed by neat-suited members of the Nation. A young Muhammad Ali, perhaps the most famous of the converted. He said, "Mr. Savidge . . ." And then, for a moment, he found himself in the position of not knowing exactly how to go on. A body in a tunnel became all too human the moment you placed it in a home. At that point, a body altered *from* a body to a person whose death could not go unmarked by a desire for revenge or a need for justice or the duty to express the simplest form of regret. He said, "I'm sorry. We've got a body you're going to have to look at. It was found this morning, south of the river."

Savidge said, "Oh my God. Is it . . ."

"I hope it isn't," Lynley said, although he knew it was. He took the other man's arm to give him support. There were questions he was going to have to ask Savidge eventually, but at the moment there was nothing more to say.

ULRIKE MANAGED to cool her heels in her office till Jack Veness closed down the phones and tidied up the reception room for the day. Once she'd acknowledged his good night and heard the outer door slam behind him, she went in search of Griff.

She found Robbie Kilfoyle instead. He was in the entry corridor, emptying two rubbish bags of Colossus T-shirts and sweatshirts into the storage cupboard beneath the display case of goods for sale. At least, she saw, Griff had told the truth in this. He *had* spent several hours at his silk-screening business today.

She'd doubted that. When they'd met at the Charlie Chaplin, the first thing she'd said was, "Where've you *been* all day, Griffin?," and then winced at the tone of her voice because she knew what she sounded like and he knew she knew, which was why he'd said, "Don't," before he told her. A piece of equipment had needed repair at the silk-screening shop and he'd seen to it, he said. "I told you I'd be going by the business on my way in. You wanted me to bring more shirts, remember?" That was a quintessential Griffin reply. I was doing what *you* asked, he implied.

Ulrike said to Robbie Kilfoyle, "Have you seen Griff? I need a word with him."

Squatting on the floor, Robbie rested back on his heels and tipped his cap to the back of his head. He said, "He's helping take that new group of assessment kids onto the river. They went off in the vans . . . round two hours ago?" Robbie's expression told her he thought she—as director—ought to be aware of this piece of information. He said, "He left this stuff"—with a nod at the rubbish bags—"back in the kit room. I reckoned it was best to pack it all in here. C'n I help you with something?"

"Help me?"

"Well, if you want Griff and Griff's not here, I might be able to . . ." He shrugged.

"I said I wanted a *word* with him, Robbie." Ulrike was at once aware of how curt she sounded. She said, "Sorry. That was rude of me. I'm frazzled. The police. First Kimmo. Now . . ."

"Sean," Robbie said. "Yeah. I know. He's not dead, though, is he? Sean Lavery?"

Ulrike looked at him sharply. "I didn't say his name. How d'you know about Sean?"

Robbie seemed taken aback. "That cop asked if I knew him, Ulrike. That woman cop. She came by the kit room. She said Sean was in one of the computer courses, so when I had a chance, I asked Neil what was going on. He said Sean Lavery didn't turn up today. That was it." Then he added, "Okay, Ulrike?," as an afterthought, but he didn't sound deferential when he said it.

She couldn't blame him. She said, "I'm . . . Look, I didn't *mean* to sound so . . . I don't know . . . so suspicious. I'm on edge. First Kimmo. Now Sean. And the police. D'you know what time Griff and the kids will be back?"

Robbie took a moment, seeming to evaluate her apology, before he replied. This, she decided, was a wee bit much. He was, after all, only a volunteer. He said, "I don't know. They'll probably stop for a coffee afterwards. Half seven p'rhaps? Eight? He's got his own keys to the place, right?"

True, she thought. He could come and go as he liked, which had been convenient in the past when they'd wanted to have a political powwow. Planning strategies before staff meetings and after hours. Here's where I stand on an issue, Griffin. What about you?

"I suppose you're right," she said. "They could be gone hours."

"Not too late, though. The dark and all that. And it must be cold as hell on the river. Between you and me, I can't think why assessment chose kayaking at all for their group activity this time round. Seems a hike would've been better. A footpath in the Cotswolds or something. Going between villages. They could've stopped for a meal at the end." He went back to stowing the T-shirts and sweatshirts away in the cupboard.

"Is that what you would have done?" she asked him. "Taken them on a hike? Somewhere safe?"

He looked over his shoulder. "It's probably nothing, you know."

"What?"

"Sean Lavery. They bunk off sometimes, these kids."

Ulrike wanted to ask him why he thought he knew the kids at Colossus better than she. But the truth was, he likely *did* know them better because she'd been distracted for months on end. Kids had come into and gone from Colossus, but her mind had been elsewhere.

Which could cost her her job, if it came down to the board of directors looking for someone culpable for what was going on . . . *if* something was going on. All those hours, days, weeks, months, and years given to this organisation: down the toilet in one hardy flush. She'd be able to get another job somewhere, but it wouldn't be at a place like Colossus, with all of Colossus's potential to do exactly what she so fervently believed *needed* to be done in England: to make change at a grass-roots level, which was at the level of the individual child's psyche.

Where had it all gone? She'd come into her job at Colossus believing that she could make a difference and she *had* done just that, right up till the time Griffin Charles Strong had planted his CV on her desk and his mesmerising dark eyes on her face. And even *then* she'd managed to maintain an air of cool professionalism for months on end, knowing full well the dangers represented by becoming involved with anyone at her place of employment.

Her resolve had weakened over time. Perhaps just to touch him, she'd thought. The gorgeous head of hair, wavy and thick. Or the broad oarsman's shoulders beneath the fisherman's sweater he favoured. Or the lower arm whose wrist was banded by a leather plait. Touching him had eventually become such an obsession that the only way possible to rid herself of the preoccupation with her hand grazing some part of his body was simply to *do* it. Just reach across the conference table and grasp his wrist to emphasise her agreement with some remark he'd made during a staff meeting and then feel the rush of surprise when he briefly closed his other hand over hers and squeezed. She told herself it was merely a sign that he appreciated her support of his ideas. Except there were signs . . . and then there were signs.

She said to Robbie Kilfoyle, "When you're finished here, make sure the doors are locked, won't you?"

"Will do," he said, and she felt his gaze fixed on her speculatively as she returned to her office.

There, she went to the filing cabinet. She squatted in front of the bottom drawer that she'd opened before, in the presence of the detectives. She fingered through the manila folders and brought out the one she needed, which she shoved into the canvas book bag she used as a briefcase. That done, she grabbed up her bicycle clothing and went to change for the long ride home.

She did her changing in the ladies' toilet, taking her time and all the while listening for the hopeful sounds of Griff Strong and the assessment kids returning from the river. But the only thing she heard was Robbie Kilfoyle leaving, and then she herself was alone at Colossus.

She couldn't risk Griff's mobile this time round, not when she knew he was with a group. There was nothing left but to write him a note. Rather than deposit it on his desk, however, where he could use the excuse of not having seen it, she took it outside to the carpark and shoved it beneath the windscreen wiper of his vehicle. On the driver's side. She even took a piece of Sellotape to make sure the note didn't blow away. Then she went for her bike, unlocked it, and headed for St. George's Road, the first part of the crisscrossing route that would take her from Elephant and Castle up to Paddington.

The ride took her nearly an hour in the bitter cold. Her mask prevented her from breathing the worst of the traffic fumes, but there was nothing to protect her from the constant noise. She reached Gloucester Terrace more exhausted than usual, but at least grateful that the ride itself—and the need to be on guard against traffic—had kept her mind occupied.

She chained her bicycle to the railing in front of number 258, where she unlocked the front door to the usual cooking smells emanating from the ground-floor flat. Cumin, sesame oil, fish. Overcooked sprouts. Rotting onions. She held her breath and went for the stairs. She was up five of them when behind her, the front-door buzzer sounded sharply. The door had a rectangle of glass on top, and through it she saw the shape of his head. She descended quickly.

"I rang your mobile." Griff sounded irritated. "Why didn't you answer? Fuck it, Ulrike. If you're going to leave me a note like that—"

"I was on my bike," she told him. "I can hardly answer it when I'm riding home. I turn it off. You know that." She held the door open and turned from it. He would have no choice but to follow her upstairs.

On the first floor, she switched on the timed light and went for the door of her flat. Inside, she dumped her canvas holdall on the lumpy sofa and turned on a single lamp. She said, "Wait here," and went into her bedroom, where she took off her bike-riding clothes, sniffed her armpits, and found them wanting. A damp flannel took care of that problem, after which she examined herself in the mirror and was satisfied with the heightened colour the ride across London had brought to her cheeks. She slid into a dressing gown and tied its belt. She returned to the sitting room.

Griff had turned on the brighter overhead lights. She chose to ignore that. She went to the kitchen where the fridge held a chilled bottle of white Burgundy. She took out two glasses and fetched the corkscrew.

Seeing this, Griff said, "Ulrike, I've just got off the river. I'm knackered and there's just no way—"

She turned round. "That wouldn't have stopped you a month ago. Anytime, anywhere. Man the torpedoes and damn the consequences. You can't have forgotten."

"I haven't."

"Good." She poured the wine and carried a glass over to him. "I like to think of you as eternally ready." She hooked her arm round his neck and drew him to her. An instant of resistance and then his mouth was on hers. Tongues, more tongues, a lengthy caress, and after a moment his hand sliding from her waist to the side of her breast. Fingers reaching for her nipple. Squeezing. Coaxing her to groan. Heat shooting into her genitals. Yes. Very nice stuff, Griff. She released him abruptly and moved away.

He had the grace to look flustered. He went to a chair—not the sofa—and sat. He said, "You said this was urgent. Emergency. Twenty-five-line whip. Crisis. Chaos. That's why I came. This is exactly the opposite direction from home, by the way, which means I'll not even *get* home now till God knows what time."

"How unfortunate," she said. "With duty calling you and all that. And I'm fully aware of your address, Griffin. As you well know."

"I don't want a row. Have you brought me here for a row?"

"Why would you think that? Where were you all day?"

He raised his head to the ceiling, one of those martyred male looks of the sort one saw in paintings of dying early Christian saints. He said, "Ulrike, you know my situation. You've always known it. You can't have . . . What would you have me do? Now *or* then? Walk out on Arabella when she was five months pregnant? While she was in labour? Now she's got an infant to contend with? I *never* gave you the slightest indication—"

"You're right." She produced a brittle smile. She could actually *feel* how frangible it was, and she loathed herself for reacting to him. She saluted him with her wineglass in a mock toast. "You never did. Bully for you. Everything always in the open and on the up-and-up. Don't ask anyone to wear a blindfold. That's a very good way to sidestep responsibility."

He put his wineglass on the table, its contents untouched. He said, "All right. I surrender. White flag. Whatever you want. Why am I here?"

"What did she want?"

"Look, I was late today because I went to the silk-screening shop. I told you that. Not that it's actually any of your business what Arabella and I—"

Ulrike laughed, although it was somewhat forced, a bad actress on an overlit stage. "I have a fine idea of what Arabella wanted and what you probably gave her . . . all seven and a half inches of it. But I'm not talking about you and the darling wife. I'm talking about the policewoman. Constable Whatsername with the broken teeth and bad hair."

"Are you trying to back me into a corner?"

"What are you talking about?"

"I'm talking about your whole approach. I protest, I call a halt to the way you're behaving just now, I say enough, I tell you to fuck off, and you've got what you want."

"Which is?"

"My head on a bloody charger, no dancing and no seven veils required."

"Is that what you think? Is that why you *actually* think I've asked you to come here?" She drained her glass of wine and felt the effect of it almost immediately.

"Are you saying you wouldn't sack me, given half the chance?"

"In an instant," she replied. "But that's not why we're talking."

"Then why . . . ?"

"What did she talk to you about?"

"Exactly what you thought she'd talk to me about."

"And?"

"And?"

"And what did you tell her?"

"What d'you think I told her? Kimmo was Kimmo. Sean was Sean. One was a free-spirit transvestite with the personality of a vaudeville queen, a kid no one in his right mind would want to harm. The other looked like someone who wanted to chew screws for breakfast. I let you know when Kimmo missed a day of assessment. Sean was out of my orbit and on to something else, so I wouldn't have known if he stopped turning up."

"That's all you told her?" She studied him as she asked the question, wondering about what kind of trust could possibly exist between two people who'd betrayed a third.

His eyes had narrowed. He said only, "We agreed." And as she openly evaluated him, he added, "Or don't you trust me?"

She didn't, of course. How could she trust someone who lived by betrayal? But there was a way to test him, and not only that, but a way to fix him in position so that he *had* to maintain the pretence of cooperation with her, if it was a pretence in the first place.

She went to her canvas holdall. From it, she took the file she'd removed from her office. She handed this over to him.

She watched as his gaze dropped to it, as his eyes took in the label at the top. He looked up at her once he'd read it. "I did what you asked. What am I supposed to do with this, then?"

"What you have to," she said. "I think you know what I mean."

Chapter Twelve

When Detective Constable Barbara Havers pulled into the underground carpark at New Scotland Yard the next morning, she was already on her fourth cigarette, not counting the one she'd lit up and sucked down as she made her way from bed to shower. She'd been smoking steadily since leaving her digs, and the always maddening trip from North London had done nothing to improve either her nerves or her mood.

She was used to rows. She'd had run-ins with everyone she'd ever worked with, and she'd even gone so far as to shoot at a superior officer, in the truly *advanced* row that had cost her her rank and very nearly her job. But nothing that had gone before in her patchy career—not to mention in her life—had affected her as she'd been affected in five minutes of conversation with her neighbour.

She hadn't intended to take on Taymullah Azhar. Her objective had been to extend a simple invitation to his daughter. Careful research—well, what went for careful research on her part, which was to buy a copy of *What's On*, like a tourist come to see the Queen—had informed her that a place called the Jeffrye Museum offered glimpses into social history via models of sitting rooms through the centuries. Wouldn't it be brilliant for Hadiyyah to accompany Barbara there in order to feed her eager little mind with something other than considerations of the belly rings currently being worn by female pop singers? It would be a journey from North to East London. It would, in short, be edu-bloody-cational. How could Azhar, a sophisticated educator himself, object to that?

Quite easily, as it turned out. When Barbara knocked him up on her way out to her car, he opened the door and he listened politely, as was his habit, with the fragrance of a well-balanced and nutritional breakfast floating out from the flat behind him like an accusation against Barbara's own morning ritual of Pop-Tart and Players.

"Sort of a double whammy, you could call it," Barbara finished the invitation, and even as she said it, she wondered where the hell *double whammy* had come from. "I mean, the museum's built in a row of old almshouses, so there's historical and social architecture involved as well. The sort of thing kids pass without knowing what they're passing, if you know what I mean. Anyway, I thought it might be . . ." What, she asked herself? A good idea? An opportunity for Hadiyyah? An escape from further punishment?

That last was it, of course. Barbara had passed Hadiyyah's solemn little gated face in the window one time too many. Enough was bleeding *enough,* she'd thought. Azhar had made his point. He didn't need to beat the poor kid over the head with it.

"This is very kind of you, Barbara," Azhar had said with his usual grave courtesy. "However, in the circumstance in which Hadiyyah and I find ourselves . . ."

She'd appeared behind him then, having apparently heard their voices. She cried, "Barbara! Hello, hello," and she peered round her father's slender body. She said, "Dad, can Barbara not come in? We're having our breakfast, Barbara. Dad's made French toast and scrambled eggs. That's what I'm having. With syrup. He's having yogurt." She wrinkled her nose, but not evidently at her father's choice of food because she went on to say, "Barbara, have you been smoking *already?* Dad, can Barbara not come in?"

"Can't, kiddo," Barbara said hastily so Azhar wouldn't have to issue an invitation he might not want to issue. "I'm on my way to work. Keeping London safe for women, children, and small furry animals. You know the drill."

Hadiyyah bounced from foot to foot. "I got a good mark in my maths exam," she confided. "Dad said he was proud when he saw it."

Barbara looked at Azhar. His dark face was sombre. "School is very important," he said to his daughter, although he looked at Barbara as he spoke. "Hadiyyah, please go back to your breakfast."

"But can't Barbara come—"

"Hadiyyah." The voice was sharp. "Have I not just spoken to you? And has Barbara herself not told you that she must go to work? Do you listen to others or merely desire and hear nothing that precludes desire's fulfillment?"

This seemed a little harsh, even by Azhar's standards. Hadiyyah's face, which had been glowing, altered in an instant. Her eyes widened, but not with surprise. Barbara could see she did it to contain her tears. She backed away with a gulp and scooted in the direction of the kitchen.

Azhar and Barbara were left together eyeball to eyeball, he looking like a disinterested witness to a car crash, she feeling the warning sign of heat seeping into her gut. That was the moment when she should have said, "Well. Right. That's that, then. P'rhaps I'll see you both later. Ta-ta," and gone on her way, knowing she was wading out of her depth and mindlessly swimming into someone else's business. But instead she'd held her neighbour's gaze and allowed herself to feel the heat and its progression from her stomach to her chest, where it formed a burning knot. When it got there, she spoke.

"That was a bit out of order, don't you think? She's just a kid. When're you planning to give her a break?"

"Hadiyyah knows what she is meant to do," Azhar replied. "She also knows there are consequences when she goes her own way in defiance."

"Okay. All right. Got it. Written in stone. Tattooed on my forehead. Whatever you want. But how about punishments fitting the crime? And while we're at it, how about not humiliating her in front of me?"

"She is not—"

"She is," Barbara hissed. "You didn't see her face. And let me tell you this for a lark, all right? Life's hard enough, especially for little girls. What they don't need is parents making it harder."

"She needs to—"

"You want her brought down a peg or two? Want her sorted? Want her to know she's not numero uno in anyone's life and she never will be? Just let her out in society, Azhar, and she'll get the message. She bloody well doesn't need to hear it from her father."

Barbara could see she'd gone too far with that. Azhar's face—always composed—shuttered completely. "You have no children," he replied. "If one day you find yourself fortunate enough to be a mother, Barbara, you will think otherwise about how and when your child should be disciplined."

It was the word *fortunate* and all it implied that allowed Barbara to see her neighbour in an entirely new light. Dirty fighter, she thought. But two could play at that game.

"No wonder she walked out, Azhar. How long did it actually take her to get a reading on you? Too long, I'd guess. But that's not much of a surprise, is it? After all, she was an English girl, and none of us English girls play the game with all fifty-two cards in the deck, do we?"

That said, she turned and left him, enjoying the coward's brief triumph at having had the last word. But it was the simple fact that she'd *had* that word that kept Barbara in raging and internal conversation, with an Azhar who wasn't present, all the way into Central London. So when she pulled into a parking bay beneath New Scotland Yard, she was still in a state and hardly in the proper frame of mind for a day's productive employment. She was also light-headed from nicotine.

She stopped in the ladies' loo to splash some water on her face. She looked in the mirror and hated herself for stooping to examine her image for evidence of what she realized Taymullah Azhar had been seeing for all these months they'd been neighbours: Unfortunate female Homo sapiens, a perfect specimen of everything gone wrong. No chance for a normal life, Barbara. Whatever the hell that was.

"Sod him," she whispered. Who was he, anyway? Who the bloody hell did he think he was?

She ran her fingers through her chopped-up hair, and she straightened the collar of her blouse, realising she should have ironed it . . . had she owned an iron. She looked three quarters of the journey towards a fright, but that couldn't be helped and it didn't matter. There was a job to do.

In the incident room, she found that the morning briefing was already going on. Superintendent Lynley glanced her way in the middle of listening to something being said by Winston Nkata, and he did not look particularly chuffed as his gaze traveled beyond her to the clock on the wall.

Winston was saying, ". . . works of wrath or vengeance, 'cording to what the lady at Crystal Moon told me. She looked it up in a book. She handed over a register of shop visitors wanting to be on their newsletter list, and she's got credit card purchases and postal codes of customers as well."

"Let's match the postal codes with the body sites," Lynley said to him. "Do the same with the register and the credit card purchases. We may get some joy there. What about Camden Lock Market?" Lynley looked towards Barbara. "What did you get from that stall, Constable? Did you stop there this morning?" Which was his way of saying, I trust that's your reason for walking in here late.

Barbara thought, Holy hell. The run-in with Azhar had wiped every other consideration from her mind. She fumbled round her head for an excuse, but the course of wisdom brought her back from the brink at the last moment. She opted for the truth. "I dropped the ball on that," she admitted. "Sorry, sir. When I was finished with Colossus yesterday, I . . . Never mind. I'll get on to it directly."

She saw the looks exchanged round her. She saw Lynley's lips get thin for an instant, so she went on hastily in an attempt to smooth over the moment. "I think the direction we need to take is Colossus anyway, sir."

"Do you." Lynley's voice was even, too even, but she chose to ignore that.

She said, "I do. We've got possibles and counting over there that need looking into. Aside from Jack Veness, who seems to know something about everyone, there's a bloke called Neil Greenham who's a bit overly helpful. He had a copy of the *Standard* that he was dead chuffed to show me, by the way. And that Robbie Kilfoyle—he was in reception yesterday, playing cards with that kid?—he volunteers in the kit room. He does lunch deliveries as a second job—"

"Van?" Lynley asked.

"Bike. Sorry," Barbara said regretfully. "But he admitted he's aiming for a real job at Colossus if it expands across the river, which gives him a motive to make someone else look—"

"Killing off the customers is hardly going to get him that, is it, Havers?" John Stewart cut in acerbically.

Barbara ignored the dig, going on to say, "His competition could be a bloke called Griff Strong, who's lost his last two jobs in Stockwell and Lewisham because, according to him, he didn't get along with female coworkers. That's four possibles, and they're all in the age range of the profile, sir."

"We'll look into them," Lynley agreed. And just as Barbara thought she'd redeemed herself, Lynley asked John Stewart to hand out that assignment and he went on to tell Nkata to dig round in the background of Reverend Bram Savidge and to deal with the goings-on at Square Four Gym in Swiss Cottage, and a car repair shop in North Kensington, while he was at it. Then he made additional assignments involving the taxi driver who'd called 999 about the body in the Shand Street tunnel and the abandoned car where that body had been deposited. He took in a report about the cookery schools in London—no Jared Salvatore enrolled in any of them—before he turned to Barbara and said, "I'll see you in my office, Constable." He strode out of the incident room with a "Get on with it, then" to the rest of the team, leaving Barbara to follow. She noted that no one looked at her as she trailed after Lynley.

She found herself scurrying to keep up with him, and she didn't like the dog-and-master feeling this evoked. She knew she'd muffed it by forgetting to check the stall in Camden Lock Market and she supposed she deserved a dressing-down for that, but on the other hand, she'd given them a new direction with Strong, Greenham, Veness, and Kilfoyle, hadn't she, so that had to count for something.

Once in the superintendent's office, however, it seemed that Lynley didn't see things this way. He said, "Shut the door, Havers," and when she had done so, he went to his desk. Instead of sitting, however, he merely leaned his hips against it and faced her. He gestured her to a chair, and he loomed above her.

She absolutely loathed the way this made her feel, but she was determined that loathing would not rule her. She said, "Your picture was on the front page of the *Standard*, sir. Yesterday afternoon. So was mine. So was Hamish Robson's. We were standing just outside of the Shand Street tunnel. You were named. That's not good."

"It happens."

"But with a serial killer—"

Lynley broke in. "Constable, tell me this: Are you deliberately attempting to shoot yourself in the foot or is all of this part of your unconscious?"

"All of this . . . ? What?"

"You were given the assignment. Camden Lock Market. On your route home, for the love of God. Or, for that matter, on your route here. Do you realise how you appear to the others when—as you put it—you 'drop the ball'? If you want your rank back, which I assume you do and which I also assume you know depends upon your being able to function as part of a team, how do you expect to achieve that if you're going to make your own decisions about what's important in this investigation and what is not?"

"Sir, that's not fair," Barbara protested.

"And this isn't the first time you've operated on your own," Lynley said, as if she hadn't spoken. "If ever an officer had a professional death wish . . . What the *hell* were you thinking? Don't you see I can't keep running interference for you? Just when I begin to think I've got you sorted, you begin it all again."

"All what?"

"Your infernal bloody-mindedness. Your taking the reins in your hands instead of the bit in your mouth. Your constant insubordination. Your unwillingness even to make a pretence of being part of a larger team. We've been through this before. Time and again. I'm doing my best to protect you, but I swear to you if this doesn't stop . . ." He threw up his hands. "Get over to Camden Lock Market, Havers. To Wendy's Rainbow or whatever the hell it was called."

"Wendy's Cloud," Barbara said numbly. "But she may not be open because—"

"Then you can bloody well track her down! And until you do, I don't want to see your face, hear your voice, or know you exist on the planet. Is that clear?"

Barbara stared at him. Her stare turned into an observation. She'd worked with Lynley for long enough to know how wildly out of character his outburst was, no matter how richly she deserved being sorted. She did a mental riffling through the reasons he was on the edge: another murder, a row with Helen, a run-in with Hillier, trouble with his younger brother, flat tyre on the way to work, too much caffeine, not enough sleep . . . But then it came to her, as easily as knowing who Lynley was.

She said, "He's got in touch with you, hasn't he? He saw your name in the paper and he bloody got in touch."

Lynley observed her for a moment before making his decision. He moved round his desk. There he took a paper out of a manila folder. He handed it to her, and Barbara saw it was a copy of an original, which, she presumed, was already on its way to forensics.

THERE IS NO DENIAL, ONLY SALVATION was printed neatly in block letters on a single line across the page. Beneath this was not a signature but rather a marking that looked not unlike two squared-off but separated sections of a maze.

"How'd it get here?" Barbara asked, returning it to Lynley.

"By post," Lynley said. "Plain envelope. Same printing."

"What d'you make of the marking? A signature?"

"Of sorts."

"Could be some bugger just wanting to play games, couldn't it? I mean, he doesn't actually tell us anything to show he knows something only the killer would know."

"Except the salvation bit," Lynley said. "It suggests he knows that the boys—at least the ones we've identified—have been in trouble with the law one way or another. Only the killer knows that."

"Plus everyone at Colossus," Barbara pointed out. "Sir, that bloke Neil Greenham had a copy of the *Standard*."

"Neil Greenham and everyone else in London."

"But you were named in the *Standard*, and that's the edition he showed me. Let me dig around his—"

"Barbara." Lynley's voice was patient.

"What?"

"You're doing it again."

" 'It'?"

"Handle Camden Lock Market. I'll deal with the rest."

She was about to protest—better judgement be damned—when the phone rang and Lynley picked it up. He said, "Yes, Dee?," to the departmental secretary. He listened for a moment, then said, "Bring him up here, if you will," before ringing off.

"Robson?" Barbara asked.

"Simon St. James," Lynley replied. "He's got something for us."

HE RECOGNISED that his wife, at this point, was his anchor. His wife and the separate reality that she represented. It was, to Lynley, nothing short of miraculous that he could go home and—for the few hours he was there—become, if not consumed, then at least diverted by something as ridiculous as the drama of trying to keep peace between their families over the idiotic question of christening clothes.

"Tommy," Helen had said from the bed as she'd watched him dressing for the day, an early morning cup of tea balanced on her growing bump, "did I mention your mother phoned yesterday? She wanted to report that she'd finally found the christening booties after spending days rooting round the apparently spider-and-poisonous-snake-infested attics in Cornwall. She's sending them along—the booties, not the spiders and the snakes—so be prepared to find them in the post, she said. A little yellowed with age, I'm afraid, she said. But certainly nothing that a good launderer couldn't sort out. Of course, I didn't know what to tell her. I mean, if we don't use your family's christening clothes, will Jasper Felix even *be* a proper Lynley?" She yawned. "Lord, not that tie, darling. How old is it? You look like an Etonian on the loose. First free weekend across the bridge to Windsor and trying to look like one of the lads. Wherever did you get it?"

Lynley unlooped it and replaced it in the wardrobe, saying, "The astonishing thing is that, as bachelors, men actually dress themselves for years not knowing they're completely incompetent without a woman at their sides." He took out another two ties and held them up for her approval.

"The green," she said. "You know I love the green for work. It makes you look so Sherlockian."

"I wore the green yesterday, Helen."

"Pooh," she said. "No one will notice. Believe me. No one ever notices men's ties."

He didn't point out to Helen that she was contradicting herself. He merely smiled. He went across to the bed and sat on the edge of it. "What've you got on for today?" he asked her.

"I've promised Simon to work a few hours. He's overextended himself again—"

"When has he not?"

"Well, he's begging for help preparing a paper on a chemical whatsit applied to whosit to produce thisorthat. It's all beyond me. I just go where he points and attempt to look decorative. Although"—and here she gazed fondly at her bump—"that's soon going to be impossible."

He kissed her forehead and then her mouth. "You'll always look decorative to me," he told her. "Even when you're eighty-five and toothless."

"I plan to keep my teeth right to the grave," she informed him. "They'll be perfectly white, completely straight, and my gums will not have receded so much as a millimeter."

"I'm impressed," he told her.

"A woman," she replied, "should always have *some* kind of ambition."

He laughed, then. She could *always* make him laugh. It was why she was a necessity to him. Indeed, he could have done with her this morning, diverting his thoughts from what was clearly Barbara Havers' death wish.

If Helen was a miracle to him, Barbara was a puzzle. Every time he thought he'd got her on the road to professional redemption at last, she did something to disabuse him of that notion. A team player she was not. Assign her to any action like any other member of an investigation and she was likely to go one of two ways: embellish upon the activity until it was unrecognisable or drift her own way and ignore it altogether. But right now, with five murders demanding action before there was a sixth, there was too much at stake for Barbara to do anything but what she was told to do when she was told to do it.

Still, for all her maddening ways, Lynley had learned the wisdom of valuing Barbara's opinion. Quite simply, she'd never been anyone's fool. So he allowed her to remain in his office as Dee Harriman went to fetch St. James up from the lobby.

When the three of them were together and St. James's demurral to Dee's offer of coffee had sent her on her way, Lynley indicated the round conference table, and they sat there as they'd done so often in the past in other locations. Lynley's first words were the same, as well.

"What do we have?"

St. James took a sheaf of papers from the manila envelope he'd carried with him. He made two piles of them. One held autopsy reports. The other consisted of an enlargement of the marking that had been made in blood on the forehead of Kimmo Thorne, a photocopy of a similar symbol, and a neatly typed, albeit brief, report.

"It took a while," St. James said. "There're an inordinate number of symbols out there. Everything from universal road signs to hieroglyphics. But on the whole, I'd say it's a fairly straightforward business."

He handed Lynley the photocopy and the enlargement of the mark that had been made upon Kimmo Thorne. Lynley laid them side by side as he reached in his jacket for his reading glasses. The parts of the symbol were all present in both of the documents: the circle, the two lines crisscrossing each other within and then extending beyond the circle, the cruciform tips at the end of the two lines.

"The same," Barbara Havers said, craning her neck to see the two documents. "What is it, Simon?"

"An alchemical symbol," St. James said.

"What does it mean?" Lynley asked.

"Purification," he replied. "Specifically, a purification process achieved by burning out impurities. I'd say that's why he's scorching their hands."

Barbara gave a low whistle. "'There is no denial, only salvation,'" she murmured. And to Lynley, "Burning out their impurities. Sir, I think he's saving their souls."

St. James said, "What's this?," and looked to Lynley, who fetched him the copy of the note he'd received. St. James read it, frowned, and gazed towards the windows in thought. "It could explain why there's no sexual component to the crime, couldn't it?"

"Is the symbol he's used on the note familiar to you?" Lynley asked his friend.

St. James studied it again. "You'd think it would be, after all the icons I've been looking at. May I take this with me?"

"Have at it," Lynley said. "We've other copies."

St. James put the paper into his manila envelope. He said, "There's something else, Tommy."

"What's that?"

"Call it professional curiosity. The autopsies refer to a consistent bruiselike wound on each of the bodies, on the left side, between two and six inches beneath the armpit. Apart from one of the bodies where the wound also included two small burns in the centre, the description is the same every time: pale in the middle, darker—nearly red in the case of the body from St. George's Gardens—"

"Kimmo Thorne," Havers said.

"Right. Darker, then, round the edges. I'd like to have a look at that wound. A photograph will do, although I'd prefer to see one of the bodies. Can that be arranged? On Kimmo Thorne perhaps? Has his body been released to the family yet?"

"I can arrange it. But where are you heading with this?"

"I'm not entirely sure," St. James admitted. "But I think it might have to do with how the boys were subdued. There's no trace of any drug from toxicology, so they weren't sedated. There's no evidence of a struggle prior to placing restraints round the wrists and ankles, so there wasn't an initial assault. Assuming this isn't some sort of S and M ritual—a young boy being seduced into kinky sex by an older man who murders him ahead of the sex act—"

"And we can't discount that," Lynley noted.

"Right. We can't. But assuming this has no overt sexual component to it, then there has to be a way your killer is managing to tie them up prior to the torture and the killing."

"These are streetwise kids," Havers noted. "They're not likely to have cooperated with some bloke wanting to tie them up for a lark."

"That's very much the case," St. James agreed. "And the presence of this consistent wound suggests that the killer knew to expect that from the very first. So not only must there be a connection among all the victims—"

"Which we've already found," Havers cut in. She was beginning to sound excited, which, Lynley knew, was never a good sign when it came to keeping her on track. "Simon, there's an outreach group called Colossus. Do-gooders working with inner-city youth, kids at risk, young offenders. It's near Elephant and Castle, and two of these dead kids were involved over there."

"Two of the *identified* bodies," Lynley corrected her. "One other identified body isn't connected to Colossus. And there are others still not identified at all, Barbara."

"Yeah, but I say this," Havers argued, "dig through the records and find out which kids stopped showing up at Colossus round the time of those other deaths we're dealing with and I'd say Bob's your mum's little brother when it comes to identifying the other bodies.

This is a Colossus situation, sir. One of those blokes has got to be our man."

"There's a strong suggestion they knew their killer," St. James said, as if in agreement with Havers. "There's a good possibility that they trusted him as well."

"And that's another key to what goes on at Colossus," Havers added. "Trust. Learning to trust. Sir, Griff Strong told me that's even part of their assessment course. And *he* leads the trust games that some of them do together. Bloody hell, we ought to take a team over there and grill the hell out of him. And those three other blokes. Veness, Kilfolye, and Greenham. They've all got a connection to at least one of the victims. *One* of them's dirty. I swear it."

"That might be the case, and I appreciate your enthusiasm for the task," Lynley said dryly. "But you've got an assignment already. Camden Lock Market, I believe."

Havers had the grace to look chastened. She said, "Oh. Right."

"So perhaps now would be a good time to do it?"

She didn't appear pleased, but she didn't argue. She got to her feet and plodded towards the door. "Good to see you, Simon," she said to St. James. "Cheers."

"And you," St. James said as she left them. He turned back to Lynley. "Trouble on that front?"

"When is there anything else when it comes to Havers?"

"I've always thought you considered her worth it."

"I do. She is. Generally."

"Close to getting her rank back?"

"I'd give it back to her, despite her bloody-mindedness. But I'm not the one making the decision."

"Hillier?"

"As ever." Lynley leaned back in his chair and took off his glasses. "He pigeonholed me this morning before I even got to the lift. He's been trying to run the investigation through the machinations of the Press Bureau, but the reporters aren't being as cooperative as they were in the beginning, grateful for the coffee, croissants, and the scraps of information Hillier's been supplying them. It seems they've put it all together now: three mixed-race boys murdered in a similar fashion prior to Kimmo Thorne, and so far no appearance on *Crimewatch* by anyone from the Met. What's *that* about? they want to know. What does *that* say to the community about the relative importance of these deaths to others in which the victim was white, blond, blue-eyed, and decidedly Anglo-Saxon? They're starting to ask the hard questions, and he's ruing his decision not to fight to keep the Press Bureau at a greater distance in all this."

"Hubris," St. James noted.

"Someone's hubris run amok," Lynley added. "And things are about to get worse. The last murdered boy—Sean Lavery—was in care, living up in Swiss Cottage with a community-activist type who—Hillier told me—is having a press conference himself round noon today. One can only anticipate what that's going to do to the collective blood lust of the media."

"Making Hillier his usual pleasure to work with?"

"Amen. The pressure's on everywhere." Lynley looked at the photocopy of the alchemical sign, considering the possibilities it offered of shedding light on the situation. He said to St. James, "I'm going to make a phone call. I'd like you to listen in, if you've time."

He looked for the number for Hamish Robson and found it on the cover sheet of the report that the profiler had given him. When he had Robson on the phone, he switched it to the speaker and introduced him to St. James. He went through the information that St. James had provided, and to this he added an acknowledgement of Robson's prescience: He told him the killer had been in contact.

"Has he indeed?" Robson said. "By phone? By post?"

Lynley read him the note. He said, "We're concluding that the purification symbol on the forehead and the burning of the hands are connected. And we've tracked down some information on ambergris oil, which was found on the bodies. Evidently, it's used for works of wrath or vengeance."

"Wrath, vengeance, purity, and salvation," Robson said. "I'd say he's broadcasting his message fairly clearly, wouldn't you?"

"There's thought here that this is all coming from an outreach programme across the river," Lynley said. "It's called Colossus. They work with troubled youth. Do you want to add anything at this point?"

There was silence for a moment as Robson thought this over. He finally said, "We know he's above average intelligence, but he's frustrated that the world doesn't see his potential. If you've come close to him in the investigation, he's not going to put a foot wrong to let you get any nearer. So if he's taking boys from one source—"

"Like Colossus," Lynley added.

"Yes. If he's taking boys from Colossus, I very much doubt he'll carry on doing so when he sees you there asking questions."

"Are you saying the killings themselves will stop?"

"They might. But only for a time. Killing provides him too much gratification to stop entirely, Superintendent. The compulsion to kill and the pleasure it yields will always overwhelm the fear of capture. But I expect he'll take far more care now. He may change ground, move farther afield."

"If he thinks the police are closing in," St. James said, "why get in touch by post?"

"Ah, that's part of the psychopath's sense of invincibility, Mr. St. James," Robson said. "It's evidence of what he sees as his omnipotence."

"The sort of thing that leads to his downfall?" St. James said.

"The sort of thing that convinces him he can't make the one mistake that will doom him. It's rather like Brady attempting to bring the brother-in-law into the fun and games: He thinks he's so mighty a force of personality that no one who knows him would think of turning him in, let alone dare to do it. It's the great flaw in the psychopath's already flawed personality. Your killer in this case believes you can't touch him no matter how close you get. He'll ask you outright what evidence you have against him should you question him, and he's going to be careful not to give you any henceforth."

"We're thinking there's no sexual component to the crimes," Lynley said, "which rules out previous Category A offenders."

"This is about power," Robson agreed, "but so are sex crimes. So you may well find something sexual down the line, perhaps a sexual degrading of the body should the murder itself not continue to provide the killer his required degree of satisfaction and release."

"Is that normally the case?" St. James asked. "In murders like these?"

"It's a form of addiction," Robson said. "Each time he indulges his fantasy of salvation via torture, he needs a little bit more to satisfy him. The body grows tolerant of the drug—whatever the drug—and more is necessary to achieve nirvana."

"So you're saying to expect more. With possible variations on the theme."

"Yes. That's exactly what I'm saying."

HE WANTED TO feel it again: the soaring that came from within. He wanted the sense of freedom that engulfed

Him in the final moment. He wanted to hear His soul cry *Yes!* even as the muted shriek below Him strained out its last weak *No!* He needed this. More, He was owed it. But when the hunger rose in Him as an exigent presence, He knew that He couldn't be hasty. This left Him with the wanting and a bubbling mixture of necessity and duty that He could feel in His veins. He was like a diver ascending to the surface too quickly. The longing was fast transforming into pain.

He took some time to attempt a mitigation. He drove to the marshes, where He could walk the tow path along the River Lea. There, He thought, He could seek relief.

They always panicked when they regained their senses and found themselves strapped down to the board, their hands and feet bound, and their mouths taped silver. As He drove them through the night, He could hear them struggling vainly behind Him, some of them in terror, others in anger. By the time He reached the appointed place, though, they had all passed through their preliminary and instinctive reaction and they'd arrived at the bargaining table. I'll do what you want. Just let me live.

They never said this directly. But it was there, in their frenzied eyes. I'll do anything, be anything, say anything, think anything. Just let me live.

He always stopped in the same safe spot, where a dogleg in the ice rink's carpark protected him from view from the street. There, a spot was wildly overgrown with shrubbery and the security lamp above the area had long ago burnt out. He switched off the lights—both inside and out—and climbed into the back. He squatted next to the immobilised form and waited till His eyes adjusted to the darkness. What He said then was always the same, although His voice was gentle as well as regretful. *You've done wrong.* And then, *I shall remove this—* with his fingers on the tape—*but only silence will keep you safe and ensure your release. Can you be silent for me?*

They would nod, always, desperate to talk. To reason, to admit, sometimes to threaten or to demand. But no matter where they began or what they felt, they were reduced to supplication.

They felt His power. They could catch the strong scent of it in the oil He'd used to anoint His body. They saw it in the glint of the knife He brought forth. They felt it in the heat from the stove. They heard it in the crackle of the pan.

I don't need to hurt you, He would tell them. *We must talk, and if our talk goes well, this can end in your freedom.*

Talk they would. Indeed, they would babble. His recitation of their crimes generally elicited nothing but anxious agreement from them. Yes, I did this. Yes, I am sorry. Yes, I swear . . . to whatever it is you will have me swear, just let me go.

But they added to that mentally, and He could read their thoughts. You filthy bastard, they concluded. I'll see you sent to hell for this.

So, of course, He could not possibly release them. At least, not in the way they hoped to be released. But He was nothing if not a man of His word.

The burning came first, just of the hands, to show them His wrath as well as His mercy. Their declarations of guilt opened the door to their redemption, but they had to suffer in order to be cleansed. So He taped their mouths again and He held their hands to the white-hot heat till He smelled the odour of searing meat. Their backs arched for escape, and their bladders and their bowels gave way. Some passed out and did not then feel the garrotte first slide and then tighten round their necks. Others did not, and it was with these that Fu felt Himself truly exulting as their lives left their bodies and transported His.

And then He always meant to free their souls, using the knife against their earthbound flesh, opening them for their final release. It was what He had promised them, after all. They merely had to admit their guilt and express a true desire for redemption. But most of them did only the first. Most of them didn't begin to understand the second.

The last had done neither. To the end, he'd denied. I didn't do nothing, you freaking bastard, I didn't do nothing, you got that straight? Fuck you, motherfucker, let me *go.*

Release, then, was impossible for him. Freedom, redemption, anything Fu offered, the boy both spat upon and cursed. He went unpurified, with his soul unreleased, a failure on the part of the Creature Divine.

But the infinite pleasure of the moment itself . . . That had actually remained for Fu. And that was what He wanted again. The seductive narcotic of utter command.

Walking the River Lea did not provide it. Nor did memory. Only one thing ever could.

Chapter Thirteen

Barbara Havers was in a foul mood when she finally reached Camden Lock Market. She was angry with herself for having allowed personal considerations to get in the way of properly doing her job. She was on edge having to drive all the way back to North London shortly after having *already* suffered through the morning traffic on the way into the centre of town. She was irritated that parking restrictions made it impossible for her to get anywhere close to the market without engaging in a hike. And she was self-righteously positive that this entire engagement was an absolute waste of her time.

The answers resided within the walls of Colossus, not here. Despite the fact that at heart she believed the profiling report was rubbish, she was willing to accept at least *part* of it, and that part was the description of their serial killer. Since at least four men fitted that description—all of them employed across the Thames at Colossus—she knew that she was unlikely to find anyone else so described wandering round the stalls and the shops near Camden Lock. And she certainly didn't expect to find any trace of a suspect at Wendy's Cloud. But she knew the wisdom of appearing to walk the straight and narrow for Lynley at this point. So she fought the traffic and found a distant parking space into which she crammed her Mini like the foot of one of the ugly stepsisters. Then she hoofed it back in the direction of Camden Lock with its shops, its stalls, and its restaurants strung along the water and away from Chalk Farm Road.

Wendy's Cloud was not easy to find, as it possessed no signage. After reading a directional board and asking round, Barbara finally located it: a simple stall within one of the permanent shops in the market. The shop sold candles and candleholders, greeting cards, jewellery, and handmade stationery. Wendy's Cloud had massage and aromatherapy oils, incense, soap, and bath crystals on offer.

The eponymous owner of the establishment sat in a beanbag chair, hidden from view behind the counter. Barbara thought at first she was keeping an eye out for light-fingered customers, but when she called, "Excuse me, c'n I have a word?," it turned out that Wendy was nodding off on a substance that was probably not for sale on her stall. Her eyelids hung well below half-staff. She didn't so much stagger as claw her way to her feet, using one of the legs of the counter and resting her chin for a moment among the bath crystals.

Barbara cursed inwardly. With her stringy grey hair and Indian bedspread caftan, Wendy didn't look like a promising wellspring of information. Instead, she looked like a refugee from the hip generation. Only the love beads round her neck were missing.

Nonetheless, Barbara introduced herself, showed her identification, and attempted to stimulate the aging woman's brain by mentioning New Scotland Yard and the words *serial* and *killer* in rapid succession. She went on to talk about ambergris oil, and she asked hopefully about Wendy's record keeping. For a moment, she thought that only a quick trip to a long, cold shower would bring Wendy round, but just at the point when she was considering where she might find water with which to douse the woman, Wendy finally spoke.

"Cash 'n' carry," was what she said. She followed this with, "Sorry."

Barbara took her comments to mean that she did not keep a record of purchases made. Wendy nodded. She went on to add that when she had only one bottle of an oil left in stock, she ordered another. *If,* of course, she remembered to look over the stock at the end of the day when she closed. Fact was, she often forgot to do that and it was only when a customer asked for something specifically that she sometimes realised she needed to place another order.

This sounded relatively hopeful. Barbara asked her if she could recall anyone asking for ambergris oil recently.

Wendy frowned. Then her eyeballs went heavenward into her head, as she apparently disappeared into the recesses of her own mind to sort this one out.

"Hello?" Barbara called. "Hey. Wendy. You still with me?"

"Don't bother with her, luv," someone said from nearby. "She's been doping up for thirty-odd years. Not much furniture left in her attic, if you know what I mean."

Barbara glanced round and saw that the speaker was sitting at the till of the larger shop in which Wendy kept her stall. As Wendy herself disappeared in the direction of the beanbag chair once more, Barbara joined the other woman who introduced herself as Wendy's long-suffering sister, Pet. Short for Petula, she explained. She'd been allowing Wendy to keep her stall in the shop forever, but whether she showed up on a given day was something open to chance.

Barbara asked what happened on a day when Wendy didn't appear. What if someone wanted to buy goods from her then? Did Pet—Barbara hoped—make the sale for her sister?

Pet shook her head, grey like Wendy's but permed to such a point that it resembled steel wool. No, dearie, she'd long ago learned her lesson about enabling the abuser, hadn't she. Wendy was welcome to her space in the shop as long as she paid for it, but if she wanted to make money and keep herself out of the gutter in which she'd apparently resided for a decade or two prior to Wendy's Cloud, she had to suit up, show up, open up, and make the sales. Her baby sister wasn't about to do it for her.

"So you wouldn't know if someone's been purchasing ambergris oil from her?" Barbara said.

She wouldn't, Pet told her. People came and went all the time in Camden Lock Market. Weekends, as the constable might know, were mad round here. Tourists, teenagers, dating couples, families with small children looking for an inexpensive means of entertainment, regular customers, pickpockets, shoplifters, thieves . . . One could hardly be expected to remember who purchased what from one's own shop, let alone who was making a purchase from one's sister's establishment. No, truth of the matter was that if anyone could tell the constable who had made a purchase from Wendy's Cloud, it would be Wendy herself. The unfortunate circumstance was, however, that Wendy spent most of her time *in* the cloud . . . if the constable knew what Petula meant.

Barbara did. Further, she knew there was nothing more to be gained from this useless trip across town. She bade Pet farewell, leaving her mobile number in the unlikely event that Wendy happened to descend to earth long enough to recall something pertinent, and then she decamped.

So that the entire adventure would not be a waste, Barbara made two additional stops. The first was at a stall along one of the passageways. Her collection of motto-bearing T-shirts always in need of expansion, she inspected the offerings at Pig & Co. She rejected "Princess in Training" and "My Mum and Dad Went to Camden Lock Market and All I Got Was a Lousy T-shirt," and she settled on "I Brake for Alien Life Forms," which was printed below a caricature of the prime minister caught beneath the wheels of a London taxi.

She made her purchase and decided a quick meal was in order. A pause at a stall selling jacket potatoes took care of this. She chose a filling of coleslaw, prawns, and sweet corn—one *had* to make sure one's basic food groups were being addressed at all times—and she took it, along with a plastic fork, back outside the market where she ate as she engaged in the hike back to her car.

This took her in the direction of her own home, northwest along Chalk Farm Road. She'd got barely 100 yards from the entrance to Camden Lock Market, however, when her mobile chimed deep in her shoulder bag, forcing her to pause, to balance her jacket potato on the top of a rubbish bin at the first street corner, and to dig the mobile out. Perhaps Wendy had come round and given her sister some useful information that Pet wished to pass along. . . . One lived in hope.

Barbara said, "Havers," encouragingly, and she looked up in time to see a van drive past and park illegally at the side entrance to the Stables Market, an old housing for artillery horses that had long since been put to commercial use just along the street from Camden Lock. She watched it idly as Lynley spoke.

"Where are you, Constable?"

"Camden Lock as commanded," Barbara said. "No result, I'm afraid." Ahead of her, a man clambered out of the van. He was oddly garbed, even by cold-weather standards, in a red elfinlike stocking cap, sunglasses, fingerless gloves, and a bulky black coat dangling to his ankles. Too bulky a coat, Barbara thought, and she watched him curiously. It was the sort of coat one could hide explosives under. She gave a closer inspection to his van as he came round to the back of it. It was purple—odd enough colour, that was—with white lettering on the side. Barbara positioned herself for a better look at it. In her ear, Lynley continued to speak.

"So get on that directly," he was saying. "You may be right about Colossus after all."

"Sorry," Barbara said hastily. "Lost you for a moment, sir. Bad reception. Bloody mobiles. Try again?"

Lynley said that someone on DI Stewart's team two had come up with some information on Griffin Strong. Evidently, Mr. Strong hadn't been as forthcoming as he might have been on the subject of leaving Social Services prior to his employment at Colossus. A child had died in care while Strong was his social worker at his last posting, in Stockwell. It was time to dig round Strong a little deeper. Lynley gave her the man's home address and told her to begin there. He lived in a housing estate on Hopetown Street. East One, Lynley told her. It would be a bit of a drive to get there. He could send someone else, but as Havers had been the one who was most insistent about Colossus . . .

Did he sound regretful? Barbara wondered. Making amends? Suddenly realising that *his* bad day didn't have to become everyone else's as well?

It didn't matter. She'd take what she could get. She told him a maddening zigzag down to Whitechapel would be *just* the ticket. She'd get right on it, she said. She was, in fact, trotting back to her car even as they spoke.

"Fine," Lynley said. "See to it, then." He rang off before Barbara could tell him what she'd been considering as she watched the purple van ahead of her and the man at its rear, unloading a few boxes from inside.

Purple, Barbara had been thinking. Darkness, illumination provided only by a streetlamp some yards away, and a woman half asleep at a window above.

She walked over to the van and gave it a look. Lettering on the side indicated that the vehicle was operated by Mr. Magic, with a London phone number. That would be the man in the overcoat, Barbara thought, because in addition to concealing explosives, the garment was surely suitable for hiding everything from doves to Dobermans.

As she'd been sauntering over, jacket potato in hand, the man had used his foot to slam home the rear doors of the van. He'd left his hazard lights on, no doubt hopeful that this would prevent an enthusiastic traffic warden from ticketing him. He saw Barbara and said, "Excuse me. Could I ask you . . . I'll just be a minute inside. Taking this"—nodding at the two boxes he had in his arms—"to the stall. Would you keep an eye out? They're heartless round here when it comes to parking."

"Sure," Barbara said. "You're Mr. Magic?"

He made a wry face. "Barry Minshall, actually. I won't be a tick. Cheers." He went in the side entrance to the Stables—one of at least four markets in the immediate area—and Barbara took the opportunity to walk round his van. It wasn't a Ford Transit, but that didn't matter because she wasn't considering it as the one they were looking for. She knew how long the odds were that an officer on the case would providentially in the street run into the serial killer she happened to be seeking. But the idea of the van's *colour* intrigued her with all it suggested about misinformation wearing the guise of truth.

Barry Minshall returned, expressing his thanks. Barbara took the opportunity to ask him what he sold on his stall. He spoke of magic tricks, videos, and gag items. He made no mention of any kind of oil. Barbara listened, wondering about the sunglasses he wore, considering the weather, but after her interlude with Wendy, she knew the sky was the limit on what one could expect to see in the area.

She took herself off to her car, thoughtful. Someone had said a red van, so they'd been thinking in red throughout the investigation. But red was only part of a larger spectrum of colour, wasn't it? Why not something closer to blue? It was definitely something they needed to consider.

WHEN DS WINSTON NKATA went up to Plugged Inn to the Lord, he went prepared: In advance he did the requisite digging round in the background of Reverend Bram Savidge. The information he found was enough to arm him to meet the man, who'd been called the Champion of Finchley Road by both the *Sunday Times* magazine and the *Mail on Sunday* in special reports about his ministry.

A press conference was in full swing when Nkata entered the shopfront-church cum soup kitchen. The poor and the homeless usually served by the kitchen during the day had formed themselves into a dispirited queue outside along the pavement. Most of them had sunk onto their haunches with the sort of inevitable patience evidenced by people who'd lived too long on the edge of society.

Nkata felt a twinge as he passed them. It was only a twist of circumstance, he thought, the stalwart love of his parents, and the long-ago intervention of one concerned cop that had kept him from a life among them. He experienced the same constriction in his chest that he always experienced when he had to carry out one duty or another among his own people. He wondered if he'd ever get over it: the feeling that somehow he'd betrayed them by following a course that most of them did not understand.

He'd seen the same reaction in the eyes of Sol Oliver

when he'd walked into his ramshackle car repair shop less than an hour earlier. It was part of a shantytown of buildings comprising the narrow street of Munro Mews in North Kensington, heavily marked by taggers and graffiti artists, blackened with generations of soot and the residue of a fire, which had gutted the structure next door. The mews itself backed onto Golberne Road, where Nkata had left his Escort. There, traffic trundled through a neighbourhood of dingy shops and grubby market stalls, between cracked pavements and gutters littered with rubbish.

Sol Oliver had been working on an antique Volkswagen Beetle when Nkata came upon him. Hearing his name, the mechanic lifted himself from a contemplation of the car's minuscule engine. His gaze had taken in Nkata from head to toe and, when shown the DS's warrant card, whatever Sol Oliver had suspected about Nkata settled his features into a permanent expression of distrust.

Yeah, he'd been put in the picture about Sean Lavery, Oliver told him in short order, although he didn't sound particularly distressed about the news. Reverend Savidge had phoned with the information. He didn't have anything to tell the cops about Sean in the days leading up to his death. He hadn't seen his son in months.

"When was the last time?" Nkata asked.

Oliver looked at a calendar on the wall as if to stimulate his memory. It was hanging below a veritable hammock of cobwebs and above a grimy coffeemaker. A mug sat next to this, painted in a child's hand with footballs and the single word "Daddy."

"End of August," Oliver said.

"You sure?" Nkata asked.

"Why? You think I killed him or summick?" Oliver set down the crescent wrench he was holding. He wiped his hands on a limp blue rag that was bruised with stains. "Look, man, I di'n't even know the kid. I d'n't even *want* to know him. I got a family now and what went on wif me and his mum was just what happens. I tol' the kid I'm sorry Cleo's doing time, but no way could I take him in, no matter what he wanted. Tha's how it is. Not like we were married or nuffink."

Nkata did his best to keep his face dispassionate, although the last thing he actually felt was disinterest. Oliver epitomised what was wrong with their men: Plant the seed because the woman was willing; walk away from the consequences with a shrug. Indifference became the legacy that was passed along from father to son.

He said, "What'd he want from you, then? I can't think he was calling round just to chat."

"Like I said. Wanted to come live wif us, di'n't he? Me, the wife, the kids. I got two. But I couldn't take him. I don't got the room an' even if I did . . ." He looked round, as if seeking an explanation hidden within the pungent confines of the old garage. "We 'as *strangers*, man. Him and me. He was 'xpecting I just take him on cos we share blood but I couldn't do that, see. He needed to get on wif his life. Tha's what I did. Tha's what we all do." He seemed to read censure on Nkata's face, because he went on with, "It's not like his mum wanted me round, innit. She's in the club, i'n't she, but it's not like she tol' me till I run into her on the street when she's 'bout ready to pop. Tha's when she says it's my kid, right? But how do I know? Anyways, she never comes to me af'er he's born either. She goes her way. I go mine. Then he's thirteen and comes round wanting me as a dad. But I don't *feel* like his dad. I don't know him." Oliver picked up his crescent wrench again, obviously ready to go back to work. "Like I say, I'm sorry 'bout his mum getting herself locked up, but it's not like I'm responsible for it."

Right, Nkata thought now as he entered Plugged Inn

to the Lord and took a position to one side of the room. He felt certain they could cross Sol Oliver from whatever list of suspects they were generating. The mechanic hadn't possessed enough interest in Sean Lavery's life to have seen to his death.

The same, however, couldn't be said for Reverend Bram Savidge. When Nkata had done his homework on the man, he'd found there were elements of his background that needed exploration, not the least of which was why he'd lied to Superintendent Lynley about the removal from his home of three boys who'd once been in his care.

Dressed in African garb of caftan and head covering, Savidge was at a lectern that held three microphones. The bright lights needed by a television crew shone upon him as he spoke directly to journalists who occupied four rows of chairs. He'd managed to pull together a good audience, and he was making the most of it.

"So we're left with nothing but questions," he was saying. "They're the reasonable questions of *any* concerned community, but they're also the questions that habitually go ignored in circumstances where the police response is defined by the community's colour. Well, we demand an *end* to that. Five deaths and counting, ladies and gentlemen, with the Metropolitan police waiting until death number *four* to finally get round to setting up a task force to investigate. And why is that?" His gaze swept over them. "Only the Metropolitan police can tell us." He began to thunder at this point, touching on every topic that any reasonable person of colour would be asking: everything from why the earlier murders weren't investigated thoroughly to why no warnings had been posted on the streets. There was an appropriate murmur among the journalists in response to this, but Savidge didn't rest on any laurels. Instead he said, "And *you* lot, for shame. You are the whited sepulchres of our society, for you have abnegated your responsibility to the public every bit as much as have the police. These killings have ranked as news not worthy enough to merit front-page attention. So what's it going to take for you to acknowledge that a life is a life, no matter its colour? That *any* life's worthy. That it's loved and mourned. The sin of indifference should weigh on your shoulders every bit as heavily as it weighs on the shoulders of the police. The blood of these boys cries out for justice and the black community will *not* rest till justice is done. That's all I have to say."

Reporters leapt to their feet, of course. The entire enterprise had been designed for that. They clamoured for Reverend Savidge's attention, but he did everything save bathe his hands in their presence before he disappeared through a door leading to somewhere at the back of the establishment. He left behind a man who stepped to the lectern and identified himself as the solicitor for Cleopatra Lavery, the incarcerated mother of the fifth murder victim whose interests he was representing. She too had a message for the media, and he would read it to them forthwith.

Nkata didn't remain to hear Cleopatra Lavery's words. Instead, he skirted round the side of the room, and he made his way to the door Bram Savidge had used. It was guarded by a man in hieratic black robes. He shook his head at Nkata and crossed his arms.

Nkata showed him his identification. "Scotland Yard," he said.

The guard took a moment to evaluate this before he told Nkata to wait. He went through to an office, returning in a moment to say that Reverend Savidge would see him.

Behind the door, Nkata found Savidge waiting for him, positioned in a corner of the small room. On either side of him framed photographs hung: Savidge in Africa, one black face among millions.

The reverend asked to see his identification, as if not believing what his bodyguard had told him. Nkata handed it over and inspected Savidge much as Savidge inspected him. He wondered if the minister's background was sufficient explanation for his adoption of all things African: Nkata knew that Savidge had grown up in Ruislip, the decidedly middle-class child of an air-traffic controller and a science teacher.

Savidge handed Nkata's ID back to him. "So you're the sop, are you?" he asked. "How stupid does the Met actually think I am?"

Nkata met Savidge's eyes, and he held them for five seconds before he spoke, telling himself the other man was angry and with very good reason. There was truth to what he was saying as well.

He said, "We got something wants clarifying, Mr. Savidge. Thought it best 'f I come to do it in person."

Savidge didn't reply at once, as if he were taking the measure of Nkata's refusal to rise to his baiting. He finally said, "What wants clarifying?"

"The boys you had in care. You told my guv that you had three of the four boys you were foster dad to placed in other homes cos of your wife. Her not speaking good English or something, I think you said."

"Yes," Savidge said, although he sounded wary. "Oni's learning the language. If you'd like to see for yourself . . ."

Nkata moved his hand in a not-what-I-want gesture. He said, "I'm sure she's learning English, all right. But fact is, Reverend, you di'n't have the boys put somewhere else. They were taken away by Social Services before you ever married your wife, and what I don't unnerstan is why you lied 'bout that to Superintendent Lynley when you must've figured we'd be looking into you."

Reverend Savidge didn't answer at once. A knock sounded at the door. It opened and the guard stuck his head inside. "Sky News want to know will you give them a word on camera with their reporter."

"They've had my word," Savidge replied. "Clear the whole lot out of here. We've people to feed."

The man said, "Right," and closed the door again. Savidge went to his desk and sat behind it. He gestured to a chair for Nkata.

Nkata said, "You want to tell me about it? Arrest for lewd conduct was what the records said. How'd you get the matter settled without more in the files?"

"It was a misunderstanding."

"What sort of misunderstanding ends up with 'n arrest for lewd conduct, Mr. Savidge?"

"The sort that comes from having neighbours who're waiting with bated breath for the black man to put a step wrong."

"Meaning?"

"I sunbathe in the nude in the summer, when we actually have a summer. A neighbour saw me. One of the boys had come out of the house, and he decided to join me. That was it."

"What? Two blokes lying starkers on the lawn or something?"

"Not exactly."

"Then what?"

Savidge pressed his fingers together beneath his chin, as if considering whether to go on. He made his decision. "The neighbour . . . It was ridiculous. She saw the boy undressing. She saw me helping him. With his shirt or his trousers. I don't know which. She leapt to an hysterical conclusion and she made a phone call. The result was an unpleasant few hours with the local authorities in the person of an aging police constable whose brains didn't equal the leaps his imagination was making. Social Services swept in and took the boys off, and I ended up explaining myself to a magistrate. By the time the matter was officially sorted out, the boys were in other homes and it seemed heartless to uproot them once again. Sean was my first placement since then."

"That's it?"

"That's it. A naked male adult, a naked male adolescent. A rare bit of sunshine. End of story."

Not quite, of course, Nkata thought. There was the reason, as well, but he reckoned he knew what it was. Savidge was black enough for a white society to label him a minority, but he was far from black enough to be enthusiastically embraced by his brothers. The reverend was hoping that the summer sun could give him briefly what nature and genetics had denied him, and the rest of the year in a tanning bed could do much the same. Nkata thought about the irony of it and about how mankind's behaviour was so often dictated by the sheer and lunatic misperception that went by the name Not Good Enough. Not white enough here, not black enough there, too ethnic for one group, too English for another. At the end of the day, he believed Savidge's story of naked suntans in the garden. It was just on the right side of madness to be true.

He said, "I had a word with Sol Oliver over in North Kensington. He says Sean came asking to live with him."

"That doesn't surprise me. Life wasn't easy for Sean. He'd lost his mother to prison, and he'd been shuffled round the system for two years by the time I got him. I was his fifth placement, and he was tired of it all. If he could talk his dad into taking him in, at least he'd be somewhere permanently. That's what he wanted. It's hardly an unreasonable hope."

"How'd he find out about Oliver?"

"From Cleopatra, I suppose. His mum. She's in Holloway. He visited her every chance he got. When it could be arranged."

"Anyplace else he went? Aside from Colossus?"

"Bodybuilding. There's a gym up Finchley Road just a bit. Square Four Gym. I told your superintendent about it. After Colossus, Sean would stop here to check in with me—say hello and whatever—and then he'd head either home or to that gym." Savidge seemed to reflect on this piece of information for a moment. Then he went on, reflectively, "I expect it was the men that drew him there, although I didn't think about that at the time."

"What did you think about?"

"Just that it was good he had an outlet. He was angry. He felt he'd been dealt a rotten hand in life and he wanted to change it. But now I see . . . the gym . . . It could have been how he was trying to make that change. Through the men who go there."

Nkata sharpened to this. "In what way?"

"Not in the way you're thinking," Savidge said.

"Then how?"

"How? In the way of all boys. Sean had a hunger and a thirst for men that he could admire. That's normal enough. I just pray to God that wasn't what killed him."

HOPETOWN ROAD glided east off Brick Lane, deep within a crowded area of London that had been through at least three incarnations within Barbara Havers' lifetime. The neighbourhood still held a multitude of grimy-looking wholesale garment shops and at least one brewery belching the scent of yeast into the air, but over the years its inhabitants had altered from Jewish to Caribbean to Bengali.

Brick Lane was attempting to make the most of its current ethnicity. Foreign restaurants abounded and along the pavement, and the streetlamps—heralded at the bottom of the street by a fanciful archway wrought of iron with a vaguely mosquelike shape—bore ornate fixtures suspended among filigree-iron decoration. Not what you'd see in Chalk Farm, Barbara thought.

She found Griffin Strong's home directly across from a little green where hillocks offered children an area in which to play and a wooden bench offered their minders a place to sit. The Strong residence was one of a line of redbrick, plain terraced houses, their individuality expressed in their choice of front doors and front fences and in what they'd decided to do with their patch of front gardens. The Strongs had opted for a draughts-board pattern of large tiles on the ground, and they'd covered them with an array of pot plants that someone had been tending with devotion. Their fence was brick like the house and their door was oak with an oval of stained glass in the middle. All very nice, Barbara noted.

When she rang the bell, a woman answered. She had a crying baby on her shoulder and magenta workout attire on her body. She said, "Yes?," over the sound of an exercise programme coming from within the house. Barbara showed her identification. She said she'd appreciate a word with Mr. Strong, if he was about. "Are you Mrs. Strong?" she added.

"I'm Arabella Strong," the woman said. "Come in, please. Just let me get Tatiana settled," and she carried the squalling infant into the reaches of the house, leaving Barbara to mouth *Tatiana?* and to follow in her wake.

In the sitting room, Arabella laid the baby on a leather sofa, where a small pink blanket was topped by a smaller pink hot-water bottle. She put the baby on her back, wedged her in place with pillows, and set the hot-water bottle on her abdomen. "Colic," she said to Barbara over the noise, "the warm seems to help."

That proved to be true. In a few moments, Tatiana's screaming subsided to whimpering so that the remaining din in the room came only from the telly. There, via video and to the accompanying *ka-boom-diddy-boom* of music, an impossibly sculpted woman was panting "lower abs, come on, lower abs, come on," as she rhythmically thrust her legs and hips into the air from a supine position. As Barbara watched, the woman suddenly leaped to her feet and gave the camera a sideways view of her stomach. It was as flat as a Dutch horizon gone vertical. She was obviously someone who ignored the better things in life. Like Pop-Tarts, Kettle Crisps, battered cod, and chips soaked in vinegar. Miserable cow.

Arabella used the remote to switch off the television and the video recorder. She said, "I expect she's at that at least sixteen hours a day. What do you think?"

"Rubens is rolling in his grave, you ask me. And *she* needs to be put out of my misery."

Arabella chuckled. She sank onto the sofa next to her baby and motioned to a chair for Barbara. She reached for a towel and pressed it against her forehead. She said, "Griff isn't here. He's at the factory. We've a silk-screen business."

"Where is it, exactly?" Barbara sat and dug her notebook from her shoulder bag. She flipped it open to take down the address.

Arabella gave it to her—it was in Quaker Street—and watched as Barbara wrote this down. She said, "This is about that boy, isn't it? The one who was murdered? Griff told me about him. Kimmo Thorne, he was called. And about the other boy who's gone missing. Sean."

"Sean's dead as well. His foster dad's identified him."

Arabella glanced at her baby, as if in reaction to this. "I'm sorry. Griff's devastated about Kimmo. He'll feel the same when he hears about Sean."

"Not the first time someone died on his watch, I understand."

Arabella smoothed Tatiana's hairless head, her expression soft, before she replied. "As I said, he's devastated. And he had nothing to do with either boy's death. With any death. At Colossus or otherwise."

"It makes him look a bit careless, though, if you know what I mean."

"As it happens, I don't."

"Careless with other people's lives. Or bloody unlucky. Which do you reckon it is?"

Arabella stood. She went to a metal bookshelf at one side of the room and took up a packet of cigarettes. She lit one jerkily and just as jerkily inhaled. Virginia Slims, Barbara saw. That figured. Mental imaging, or something. And Arabella needed it: She had her work cut out for her, getting back into shape. She was pretty enough—good skin, nice eyes, dark, silky hair—but she looked as if she'd gained a few stone too many during her pregnancy. Eating for two, she'd probably told herself.

"If it's alibis you're after—that *is* what your sort look for, isn't it?—then Griff's got one. Her name is Ulrike Ellis. If you've been to Colossus, you've met her."

This was a *truly* interesting turn. Not the fact of Ulrike and Griff, which Barbara had already assumed was a probability, but the fact that Arabella knew about Ulrike and Griff. *And* didn't appear upset about them. What was *that* all about?

Arabella seemed to read her mind. "My husband's weak," she said. "But all men are weak. When a woman marries, she marries knowing this and she decides in advance what she's going to accept when it eventually crops up. She never knows how the weakness is going to manifest itself, but I suppose that's part of the . . . the journey of discovery. Will it be drink, food, gambling, excessive work, other women, pornography, football hooliganism, addiction to sports, addiction to drugs? In Griff's case, it turned out to be an inability to say no to women. But that's hardly a surprise, considering how they throw themselves at him."

"Tough to be married to someone so . . ." Barbara looked for the right word.

"Beautiful? Godlike?" Arabella offered. "Apollo? Narcissus? Whoever? No, it's not difficult at all. Griff and I plan to stay married to each other. We're both from broken homes, and we don't intend that for Tatiana. As it happens, I've been able to put it all in perspective. There are worse things than a man who gives in to women's advances. Griff's been through this before, Constable. Doubtless, he'll go through it again."

Hearing this, Barbara wanted to shake the bewilderment out of her head. She was used to the idea of women fighting for their men or women seeking revenge after an infidelity or women harming themselves—or others, for that matter—when faced with an adulterous spouse. But this? Calm analysis, acceptance, and *c'est la vie*? Barbara couldn't decide if Arabella Strong was mature, philosophical, desperate, or simply mad as a hatter.

She said, "So how's Ulrike his alibi?"

"Compare the dates of the murders with his absences from home. He'll have been with her."

"All night?"

"Enough of it."

And wasn't that just bloody convenient? Barbara wondered how many phone calls had been placed among the three of them to cook this one up. She also wondered how much of Arabella's placid acceptance *was* placid acceptance and how much was actually the result of the vulnerability a woman felt once she had a child to care for. Arabella needed her man to bring home the bacon if she herself wanted to stay home and care for Tatiana.

Barbara flipped her notebook closed and thanked Arabella for her time and her willingness to speak openly about her husband. She knew that if anything more was to be gained from this journey to East London, it wasn't going to turn up here.

Back at her car, she dug out the *A to Z* and looked up

Quaker Street. Luck was with her for once. She found it was just south of the railway tracks leading to Liverpool Street Station. It appeared to be a short one-way thoroughfare that connected Brick Lane to Commercial Street. She could walk there and work off at least one mouthful of her morning's Pop-Tart. The jacket potato she'd inhaled at Camden Lock would have to wait.

"WE'RE HAVING a devil of a time with all the phone calls, Tommy," John Stewart said. The DI had laid a neatly clipped document precisely in front of him. As he spoke, he lined up the corners of it within the curve of the conference table. He straightened his tie, checked his fingernails, and gazed round the room as if to assess its condition, reminding Lynley as he always did, that Stewart's wife had probably had more than one reason for ending their marriage. "We've got parents clamouring from all over the country," he went on. "Two hundred with missing kids at this point. We need more help on the phones."

They were in Lynley's office, trying to work out a change in the deployment of the personnel. They didn't have enough manpower, and Stewart was right. But Hillier had refused to give them more without the magical production of a "result." Lynley thought he'd had that with the identification of yet another body: fourteen-year-old Anton Reid, who'd been the first victim of their killer, his body left in Gunnersbury Park. A mixed-race boy, Anton had disappeared from Furzedown on the eighth of September. He'd been a gang member with arrests for malicious mischief, trespassing, petty theft, and assault, all of which had been relayed to New Scotland Yard earlier in the day by the Mitcham Road police station, who'd admitted having written Anton off as yet another runaway when his parents first reported him missing. The newspapers were going to be in a filthy uproar over *that* piece of data, Hillier had told Lynley at some considerable volume on the phone when he was given the news. So when the hell did the superintendent intend to have something to present to the press office other than a bleeding identity for another sodding body?

"Get on it," had been the AC's parting remark. "I don't expect you lot need me down there wiping your arses. Or do you?"

Lynley had held his tongue and his temper. He'd called Stewart into his office and there they sat, sorting through the action reports.

Finally and definitively, there was nothing from Vice on any of the identified boys beyond Kimmo Thorne. Aside from Kimmo, none of them were engaged in illicit sex as rent boys, transvestites, or streetwalkers. And despite their otherwise chequered histories, none of them could be associated with either the sale or the purchase of drugs.

The interview with the taxi driver who'd discovered Sean Lavery's body in the Shand Street tunnel had given them nothing. A background check on the man had shown a perfectly clean record without even a parking ticket to mar his reputation.

The Mazda in the tunnel could be associated with no one even tangentially involved in the investigation. With its number plates missing, its engine gone, and its body torched, there was no way to tell whose it was, and no witness could attest to how it had ended up in the tunnel in the first place or even how long it had been there. "That's a real nonstarter" was how Stewart put it. "We're better off using the manpower elsewhere. I suggest we have a rethink on those blokes surveilling the crime scenes as well."

"Nothing there?"

"Sod all."

"Christ, how can no one not have *seen* anything worth reporting?" Lynley knew his question would be taken as rhetorical, and it was. He also knew the answer. Big city. People on the underground and in the street all avoiding each other's eyes. The public's philosophy of see nothing, hear nothing, leave me alone was the very plague of their jobs as cops. "You'd think someone would at least have seen a car being torched. Or a car on fire, for the love of God."

"As to that . . ." Stewart flipped through his neatly assembled paperwork. "We've had a wee bit of joy from background. To the point, Robbie Kilfoyle and Jack Veness. Two of the blokes from Colossus."

Both of the Colossus men, as things turned out, had juvenile records. Kilfoyle's stuff was relatively minor. Stewart offered a list of truancy problems, vandalism reported by neighbours, and looking in windows where he didn't belong, saying, "All meagre pickings. Except for the fact that he was dishonourably discharged from the army."

"For?"

"Continually going AWOL."

"How does that relate?"

"I was thinking of the profile. Disciplinary problems, failure to obey orders. It seems to fit."

"If you stretch it," Lynley said. Before Stewart could take offence, he added, "What else? More on Kilfoyle?"

"He's got a job delivering sandwiches by bicycle round lunchtime. With an organisation called . . ." He referred to his notes. "Mr. Sandwich. That's how he ended up at Colossus, by the way. He delivered there, got to know them, and started working as a volunteer after his sandwich hours. He's been there for the last few years."

"Where is this place?" Lynley asked.

"Mr. Sandwich? It's on Gabriel's Wharf." And when Lynley looked up at this, Stewart smiled. "Right you are. Home of Crystal Moon."

"Well done, John. What about Veness?"

"Even more joy. He's a former Colossus boy. Been there since he was thirteen years old. A little arsonist, he was. Started out with small fires in the neighbourhood, but he escalated things to torching vehicles and then a whole squat. Got caught for that one, did some time in borstal, hooked up with Colossus afterwards. He's their shining example now. Trot him out to their fund-raisers, they do. He gives the official spiel on how Colossus saved his life after which the hat's passed round or whatever."

"His living situation?"

"Veness . . ." Stewart referred to his notes. "He's got a room over in Bermondsey. He's not far from the market, as it happens. Kimmo Thorne flogging stolen silver and all that, if you recall. As for Kilfoyle . . . He's got digs in Granville Square. Islington."

"Smart part of town for a sandwich-delivery boy," Lynley remarked. "Check on it. Get on to the other bloke, Neil Greenham, as well. According to Barbara's report—"

"She actually *made* a report?" Stewart asked. "What miracle brought that about?"

"—he taught at a primary school in North London," Lynley plunged on. "Had a disagreement of some sort with his superior. About discipline, apparently. It resulted in his resignation. Have someone get on to that."

"Will do." Stewart made a note.

A knock on the door brought Barbara Havers into the office then. Close on her heels was Winston Nkata with whom she was in terse conversation. She looked excited. Nkata looked interested. Lynley grew momentarily heartened by the idea that progress might actually be about to occur.

Havers said, "It's Colossus. Got to be. Listen to this. Griffin Strong's silk-screening business just happens to be in Quaker Street. Sound familiar? It did to me.

Turns out he's got a smallish factory in one of the warehouses, and when I asked round in the area to suss out which one, an old bloke on the pavement shook his head, made some grave mutterings like the ghost of Christmas past, and pointed out the spot where—as he put it—the 'devil made his presence known.' "

"Which meant?" Lynley asked.

"That one of the bodies was found not two doors down from our Mr. Strong's secondary means of employment, guv. The third of the bodies, as it turned out. Which sounded too bloody coincidental to be coincidental, so I checked out the rest. And listen to this . . ." She stuck half of her arm into her enormous shoulder bag and, after some struggle, pulled out her tattered spiral notebook. She ran a hand through her hair—doing nothing to improve its overall dishevelled look—and went on. "Jack Veness: number eight Grange Walk, not even a mile from the Shand Street tunnel. Robbie Kilfoyle: sixteen Granville Square, sneezing distance from St. George's Gardens. Ulrike Ellis: two-five-eight Gloucester Terrace, just round two corners from a multi-storey carpark. *The* multi-storey carpark, if you know what I mean. This has got to be a Colossus situation, start to finish. If the bodies themselves didn't scream that at us, where the bodies were put bloody well does."

"The Gunnersbury Park body?" John Stewart asked. He'd been listening with his head cocked, and his face wore an expression of paternal indulgence which Lynley knew that Havers would particularly loathe.

"I haven't got to that one yet," she admitted. "But odds are that body from Gunnersbury Park is someone else from Colossus. And bigger odds are that Gunnersbury Park is a hop and a jump from where a Colossus employee lives. So all we have to do is get the names and addresses of everyone who works there. Of volunteers as well. Because believe me, sir, someone inside's trying to paint the place black."

John Stewart shook his head. "I don't like it, Tommy. A serial killer choosing his victims from within his immediate sphere? I can't see how that plays with what we know about serial killers in general and this one in particular. We know this is an intelligent bloke we're dealing with, and it's damned lunacy to think he'd work there, volunteer there, or do anything else there. He'd know we'd twig it eventually, and then what? When we're hot on his tail, what's he going to do?"

Havers countered. "You *can't* be thinking it's some major coincidence that every body we've been able to identify just *happens* to be associated with Colossus." Stewart shot her a look, and she added, "Sir," as an afterthought. "With respect, that doesn't make sense." She pulled out another notebook from her battered shoulder bag. Lynley saw it was the signing-in register they'd taken surreptitiously from the reception desk at Colossus earlier. She opened it, riffling through a few pages as she said, "And listen to this. I had a look through this on my way back from the East End just now. You're not going to believe . . . Bloody *hell,* what liars." She leafed through the book and read aloud as she flipped through the pages, "Jared Salvatore, eleven A.M. Jared Salvatore, two-ten P.M. Jared Salvatore, nine-forty A.M. Jared Bloody Blooming Salvatore, three twenty-two P.M." She slapped the notebook down on the conference table. It slithered across and knocked John Stewart's neatly compiled notes to the floor. "Am I right that no cookery school in London knows the first thing about Jared Salvatore? Well, why would they when he was doing his cookery course at Colossus all along? Our killer's *right there* inside that place. He's picking and choosing. He's setting things up like a pro, and he doesn't expect us to catch him at *any* of it."

"That fits in with something Robson pointed out," Lynley said. "The sense of omnipotence the killer must have. How big a leap is it from putting bodies in public places to be working within the walls of Colossus? In both cases, he doesn't expect to be caught."

"We need to get every one of these blokes under surveillance," Havers said. "And we need to do it now."

"We haven't the manpower for that," John Stewart said.

"Then we've got to get it. And we've also got to grill each one of them, dig into their backgrounds, ask them—"

"As I've said, we've a manpower issue here." DI Stewart turned away from Havers. He didn't look pleased to have her grabbing control of the meeting. "Let's not forget that, Tommy. And if our killer's inside Colossus as the constable's suggesting, then we'd better start looking at everyone else who works there as well. And at the other 'clients' who're attached to the place: the participants or patients, whatever the hell they call themselves. I expect there are enough junior-level villains running round that place to fuel a dozen killings."

"That's a waste of our time," Havers insisted, and, "Sir, listen to me," to Lynley.

He cut in. "Your points are well taken, Havers. What did you get from Griffin Strong about the child who died on his watch in Stockwell?"

The constable hesitated. She looked abashed.

"Bloody *hell,*" DI John Stewart said. "Havers, did you not—"

"Look. When I heard about the body in the warehouse—" she began quickly, only to be cut off by Stewart.

"So you haven't looked into the other yet? It's a *death* on Strong's watch in Stockwell, woman. Does that ring any damn bells for you?"

"I'm getting on to it. I came straight back. I went to the files for this other information first because I thought—"

"You thought. You *thought*." Stewart's voice was sharp. "It's not your job to do the bloody thinking. When you're given an order . . ." His fist hit the table. "Jesus. What the *hell* is it that keeps them from giving you the sack, Havers? I'd damn well like to know your secret, because whatever's keeping you here isn't between your ears and I sure as hell don't think it's between your legs."

Havers' face went completely white. She said, "You completely sodding piece of—"

"That'll *do*," Lynley said sharply. "You're both out of order."

"She's—"

"That bastard just said—"

"Enough! Keep it out of this office and out of this investigation or both of you are permanently off the case. Christ but we have enough trouble already without you two going for each other's throats." He paused, waiting for his blood to cool. In the silence, Stewart shot Havers a look that clearly assessed her as an impossible cow, and Havers herself seethed openly back at him, a man with whom she'd long ago managed to work for only three weeks before charging him with sexual harassment. Meanwhile Winston Nkata remained by the door in the position he nearly always adopted when placed in a room with more than two white colleagues: He stood with his arms crossed and merely observed, as he had been doing since he'd walked in.

Lynley turned to him wearily. "What have you got for us, Winnie?"

Nkata reported on his meetings: first with Sol Oliver in his car repair shop, then with Bram Savidge. He went on with his visit to the gym where Sean Lavery did his workouts. He concluded with something that diffused the tension in the room: He might have found someone who'd actually seen the killer.

"There was some white bloke hanging round the gym not long before Sean went missing," Nkata said. "He got noticed 'cause not many whites use the place. Seems one night he was lurking in the corridor just outside the workout room, and when one of the lifters asked him what did he want, he said he was new to the neighbourhood and just looking round for a place to work out. He never did go in, though. Not to the gym, not to the locker room, not to the steam room. Didn't ask about membership or anything like it. Just showed up in the corridor."

"Did you get a description?"

"Arranging for an e-fit. Bloke at the gym thinks he might be able to come up with a drawing of this bugger. Right off he was able to tell me no way did the villain belong there. Not a lifter at all, he said, smallish and thin. Long face. I think we got a chance here, Super."

"Well done, Winnie," Lynley said.

"That's what I call good work," John Stewart put in pointedly. "I'll have you on my team anytime, Winston. And congratulations on the promotion. I don't think I mentioned it earlier."

"John." Lynley tried for patience. He waited till he found it before he went on. "Take the salt outside please. Phone Hillier. See if you can get manpower for surveillance. Winston, we've got Kilfoyle working at a place called Mr. Sandwich, back at Gabriel's Wharf. Try to make a connection between him and Crystal Moon."

There was a general shuffling as the men went on their way, leaving Havers behind for Lynley to deal with. He waited till the door was shut to do so.

She spoke first, her voice low but still hot. "I don't have to *bloody* put up with—"

"I know," Lynley said. "Barbara. I know. He was out of order. You were in the right to react. But the other side of the coin, whether you want to see it or not, is that you provoked him."

"*I* provoked *him? I* provoked *him* to say . . . ?" She seemed unable to finish. She sank into a chair. "Sometimes I don't even know you."

"Sometimes," he replied, "I don't know myself."

"Then—"

"You didn't provoke the words," Lynley interrupted. "They were inexcusable. But you provoked the *fact* of the words. Their existence, if you will." He joined her at the table. He was feeling exasperated, and that was not a good sign. Exasperation meant he might soon run out of ideas on how to get Barbara Havers back into her position as a detective sergeant. It also meant he might soon run out of the willingness to do so. He said, "Barbara, you know the drill. Teamwork. Responsibility. Taking an action that's been assigned and completing it. Turning over the report. Waiting for the next assignment. When you have a situation like this, one in which thirty-odd people are relying upon you to do what you've been told to do . . ." He lifted a hand and then dropped it.

Havers watched him. He watched her. And then it was as if a veil somehow lifted between them and she understood. She said, "I'm sorry, sir. What can I say? You don't need more pressure, and I pile it on, don't I?" She moved restlessly in her chair and Lynley knew she was longing for a cigarette, for something to do with her hands, for something to jolt her brain. He felt like giving her permission to smoke; he also felt like allowing her to squirm. Something had to give somewhere in the damn woman or she was going to be lost for good. She said, "Sometimes I get so bloody sick of everything in life being such a struggle. You know?"

He said, "What's going on at home?"

She chuckled. She was slumped in her chair, and she straightened her back. "No. We're not taking a stroll on that path. You've enough to cope with, Superintendent."

"All things considered, a family dispute over two sets of christening clothes is hardly something to cope with," Lynley said dryly. "And I've a wife politically adept enough to negotiate a truce between the in-laws."

Havers smiled, it seemed, in spite of herself. "I didn't mean at home and you know it."

He smiled in turn. "Yes. I know."

"You're getting a platterful from upstairs, I expect."

"Suffice it to say I'm learning how much Malcolm Webberly actually had to put up with to keep Hillier and everyone else off our backs all these years."

"Hillier sees you hot on his tail," Havers said. "A few more steps up the ladder and whammo . . . You're heading up the Met and he's pulling his forelock."

"I don't want to head up the Met," Lynley said. "Sometimes . . ." He looked round the office he'd agreed to inhabit temporarily: the two sets of windows that ludicrously indicated a rise in rank, the conference table at which he and Havers sat, carpet tiles on the floor instead of lino, and outside beyond the door the men and women under his command for the moment. It was meaningless, really, at the end of the day. And it was far less important than what faced him now. He said, "Havers, I think you're right."

"Of course, I'm right," she replied. "Anyone watching—"

"I don't mean about Hillier. I mean about Colossus. He's choosing kids from there, so he has to be connected somehow. It flies in the face of what we usually expect from a serial killer but on the other hand, how different is it, really, from Peter Sutcliffe picking up prostitutes or the Wests going for hitchhiking girls? Or someone targeting women walking dogs across parks or on commons? Or someone else always choosing an open window at nighttime and an elderly woman he knows is alone within? Our man's doing what's worked for him. And considering he's managed to pull it off five times without getting caught—without, for the love of God, even being *noticed*—why shouldn't he simply keep on doing it?"

"So you think the rest of the bodies are Colossus boys as well?"

"I do," he said. "And since the boys we've identified so far have been throwaways to everyone but their families, our killer hasn't had to worry about detection."

"So what's next?"

"Gather more information." Lynley rose and considered her: disastrous of appearance and utterly headstrong. Maddening unto the death of him. But she was quick as well, which was why he'd learned to value having her at his side. He said, "Here's the irony, Barbara."

"What?" she said.

"John Stewart agreed with your assessment. He said as much before you walked into the office. He thinks it may be Colossus as well. You might have discovered that—"

"Had I kept my mug plugged." Havers shoved her chair back, preparatory to getting to her feet. "So am I supposed to crawl? Curry favour? Create my *own* forelock to pull? Bring in coffee at eleven and tea at four? What?"

"Try staying out of trouble for once," Lynley said. "Try doing what you're told."

"Which is what at this point?"

"Griffin Strong and the boy who died while Strong was with Social Services in Stockwell."

"But the other bodies—"

"Havers. No one's arguing with you about the other bodies. But we're not going to leapfrog through this investigation no matter how much you'd like to do so. You've won a round. Now see to the rest."

"Right," she said, although she sounded reluctant even as she picked up her shoulder bag to get back to work. She headed for the door and then stopped, turned back to face him. "Which round was that?" she asked him.

"You know which round," he told her in reply. "No boy's safe if he ends up getting assigned to a spell at Colossus."

Chapter Fourteen

"Anton what?" Ulrike Ellis said into the telephone. "Could you spell the surname, please?"

On the other end of the line the detective, whose name Ulrike had already schooled herself to forget, spelled out R-e-i-d. He added that the parents of Anton Reid, who'd gone missing from Furzedown and had finally been identified as the first victim of the serial killer who'd so far murdered five boys in London, had listed Colossus as one of the places that their son had frequented in the months leading up to his death. Could the director confirm that, please? And a list of all Anton Reid's contacts within Colossus would be necessary, madam.

Ulrike did not indulge in a misinterpretation of the courtesy behind the request. But she temporised, nonetheless. "Furzedown is south of the river, and as we're well known here, Constable . . . ?" She waited for a name.

"Eyre," he said.

"Constable Eyre," she repeated. "What I'm saying is that it's a possibility that this boy—Anton Reid—merely *told* his parents he was involved with Colossus while using the time to do something else. It happens, you know."

"He came to you through Youth Offenders, according to the parents. You should have the records."

"Youth Offenders, is it? Then I'll have to check. If you could give me your number, I'll go through the files."

"We do know he's one of yours, madam."

"You may know that, Constable . . . ?"

"Eyre," he said.

"Yes. Of course. You may know that, Constable Eyre. But at this moment, I do not. Now I shall have to go through our files, so if you give me your number, I'll get back to you."

He had no choice. He could get a search warrant, but that would take time. And she was cooperating. No one could claim otherwise. She was merely cooperating within the structure of *her* schedule, not within the structure of his.

The detective constable recited his phone number and Ulrike took it down. She had no intention of using it—reporting to him like a schoolgirl hauled onto the headmistress's carpet—but she wanted to have it to wave in front of whomever turned up to gather information on Anton Reid. Because someone *would* definitely turn up at Colossus. Her job was to develop a plan to handle things when the moment arrived.

Off the phone, she went to the filing cabinet. She rued the system she had developed: the hard-copy backup to computer files. Pressed to it, she could have done *something* about material left upon hard drives, even if she'd had to reformat every miserable computer in the building. But the cops who'd come to Colossus had already seen her fingering through files in an ostensible search for Jared Salvatore's paperwork, so they'd be highly unlikely to believe that some boys had electronic documents while others did not. Still, Anton's folder could go the way of Jared's. The rest was easy enough to accomplish.

She had Anton's file halfway out of the drawer when she heard Jack Veness just outside her door. He said, "Ulrike? Could I have a word . . . ?," and he opened the door without further ado.

She said, "Do *not* do that, Jack. I've told you before."

"I knocked," he protested.

"Step one, yes. You knocked. Very nice. Now let's work on step two, which is all about waiting for me to tell you to come in."

His nostrils moved, white round the edges. He said, "Whatever you say, Ulrike," and he turned to go, always the manipulative, petulant adolescent despite his age, which was what? Twenty-seven? Twenty-eight?

Damn the man. She didn't *need* this now. She said, "What do you want, Jack?"

"Nothing," he said. "Just something I thought you might like to know."

Games, games, games. "Yes? Well, if I might like to know, why don't you tell me?"

He turned back. "It's gone. That's all."

"What's gone?"

"The signing-in book from reception. I thought I must've misplaced it when I packed up last night. But I've looked everywhere. It's definitely gone."

"Gone."

"Gone. Vanished. Disappeared. Abracadabra. Into thin air."

Ulrike rested back on her heels. Her mind wheeled through the possibilities, and she disliked every one of them.

Jack said helpfully, "Robbie might have taken it for some reason. Or maybe Griff has it. He's got a key to be in here after hours, doesn't he?"

This was too much. She said, "What would Robbie, Griff, or anyone else want with a signing-in book?"

Jack shrugged elaborately and drove his fists into the pockets of his jeans.

"When did you notice it was missing?"

"Not till the first kids got here today. I went for the book but it wasn't there. Like I said, I figured I misplaced it last night when I was packing up. So I just started another one till I could find the one that's missing. Which I couldn't. So I reckon someone nicked it off my desk."

Ulrike thought about the previous day. "The police," she said. "When you came to fetch me. You left them alone in reception."

"Yeah. That's what I reckoned 's well. Only here's the thing. I can't suss out what they want with our signing-in book, can you?"

Ulrike turned from his smug and comprehending face. She said, "Thank you for letting me know, Jack."

"Do you want me to—"

"Thank you," she repeated firmly. "Is there anything else? No? Then you can get back to work."

When Jack left her, after a little mock salute and a click of the heels that she was meant to take as amusing and did not, Ulrike shoved Anton Reid's paperwork back into place. She slammed the filing drawer home and went for the phone. She punched in Griffin Strong's mobile number. He was meeting with a new assessment group, their first day together, ice-breaking activities. He didn't like to be interrupted whenever the kids were "in circle" as they called it. But this interruption couldn't be helped and he would know that when he heard what she had to say.

He said, "Yeah?" impatiently.

"What did you do with the file?" she asked him.

"As . . . ordered."

She could tell he chose the word deliberately, as mocking as was Jack's sarcastic salute. He hadn't yet twigged who stood in jeopardy here. But he would presently.

He said, "That all?"

Dead silence in the background told her every member of his assessment group was listening to his end of the exchange. She found a bitter satisfaction in that. Fine, Griffin, she thought. Let's see how well you can carry on now.

"No," she told him. "The police know, Griff."

"Know what exactly?"

"That Jared Salvatore was one of ours. They took the reception book yesterday. They'll have seen his name."

Silence. Then, "Shit," on a breath. Then a whisper, "God *damn* it. Why didn't you think of that?"

"I might ask the same of you."

"What's *that* supposed to mean?"

"Anton Reid," she said.

Silence again.

"Griffin," she told him, "you need to understand something. You've been an exceptional fuck, but I won't let anyone destroy Colossus."

She replaced the phone, carefully and quietly. Let him hang there, she thought.

She turned to her computer. On it, she accessed the electronic information they had on Jared Salvatore. It wasn't as extensive as had been the documents in his file, but it would do. She chose the print option. Then she picked up the number that Detective Constable Eyre had given her only minutes ago.

He answered immediately, saying, "Eyre."

She said, "Constable, I've come up with some information. You'll probably want to pass this along."

NKATA LET THE computer do the work for him on the postal codes amassed by the owner of Crystal Moon. While Gigi—the shop's owner—would use them to prove the need for a branch of her business in a second location somewhere in London, Nkata intended to use them to make a match between the customers of Crystal Moon and the body sites. After reflecting on what

Barb Havers had said on the subject of body sites, however, he decided to expand his search to include a comparison between the postal codes gathered by Crystal Moon and the postal codes of all Colossus employees. This took him more time than he'd expected. At the Colossus end of things, giving out postal codes to the cops was not an idea that anyone immediately embraced.

When he finally had what he wanted, he printed out the document and studied it contemplatively. Ultimately, he passed it over to DI Stewart to relay along to Hillier when he made his request for the manpower to run more surveillance. He was donning his overcoat to head back out, over to Gabriel's Wharf to see to the next part of his assignment, when Lynley came to the door of the incident room and said his name quietly, adding, "We're wanted upstairs."

We're wanted upstairs meant only one thing. The fact that Hillier was asking for them now—a few hours after the press conference called by Reverend Bram Savidge—suggested the meeting was not going to be pleasant.

Nkata joined Lynley, but he did not remove his overcoat. "I was heading to Gabriel's Wharf," he told the acting superintendent, hoping this would be enough to get him off the hook.

"This won't hold you up long," Lynley said. It sounded like a promise.

They took the stairs. Nkata said as they climbed, "I think Barb's right, guv."

"About?"

"Colossus. I got a match on one of the postal codes from Crystal Moon. I passed it along to DI Stewart."

"And?"

"Robbie Kilfoyle. He's got the same postal code as someone who shopped in Crystal Moon."

"Does he indeed?" Lynley stopped on the stairs. He

seemed to think about the information for a moment. Then he said, "Still, it's only a postal code, Winnie. He shares it with . . . what? How many thousand people? And his employment is on the wharf as well, isn't it?"

"Directly next to Crystal Moon," Nkata admitted. "The sandwich shop."

"Then I don't know how much weight we can give it, as much as we'd like to. It's something, I agree—"

"Which is what we *need*," Nkata cut in. "Something."

"But unless we know *what* he bought . . . You see the difficulty, don't you?"

"Yeah. He works there on the wharf for God knows how long. He's prob'ly bought something off that shop and every other shop over time."

"Exactly. But speak to them, all the same."

In Hillier's suite, Judi MacIntosh ushered them in at once. Hillier was waiting for them, standing framed by the multiple panes of his windows and the view they offered of St. James's Park. He was studying this view as they entered. At his fingertips on the credenza beneath the window, a newspaper lay neatly folded.

Hillier turned. As if for an unseen camera, he picked up the paper and let it fall open so that he held the front page like a towel that covered his genitals. He said evenly, "How did this happen?"

Nkata saw it was the latest *Evening Standard*. The story on the front page dealt with the press conference that Bram Savidge had called earlier in the day. The headline spoke of a foster father's anguish.

Anguish had not been among the reactions to Sean Lavery's death that Nkata would have ascribed to Savidge. But he realised that "anguish" was more likely to sell copies of the paper than was "justifiable fury at police incompetence." Although, truth to tell, it would have been close.

Hillier went on, tossing the *Standard* onto his desk. He said to Lynley, "You, Superintendent, are supposed to be managing the victims' families, not giving them access to the media. It's part of the job, so why aren't you doing it? Have you any idea what he's said to the press?" Hillier stabbed at the paper as he made each following declaration: "Institutional racism. Police incompetence. Endemic corruption. All accompanied by calls for a thorough investigation by the Home Office, a Parliamentary sub committee, the Prime Minister, or anyone else who's willing to take up the subject of house sweeping, which is what he accuses us of needing round here." He brushed the paper off of his desk and into the rubbish basket next to it. "This bugger's got their attention," he said. "I want that changed."

There was something self-satisfied about Hillier's expression that was out of keeping both with his tone and with what he was saying. It came to Nkata as he observed this that Hillier's look had to do with the performance that he was giving, rather than with his outrage. He *wanted* to dress Lynley down in front of a subordinate officer, Nkata realised. He had the excuse of making that subordinate officer Nkata because of the press briefings that had gone before when Nkata had sat obediently at his side, second cousin to a performing dog.

He said to Hillier before Lynley could respond, " 'Scuse me, guv. I was at that briefing. Truth to tell, I di'n't even think to stop it. My thought was he c'n call the press whenever he wants to call the press. His right to do it."

Lynley glanced his way. Nkata wondered if Lynley's pride would allow him to carry off an intervention like this. He wasn't sure, so before there was an opportunity for the acting superintendent to add something, Nkata went on.

"I could've stepped up to the mike right after, 'f course, when Savidge was done with his piece. Could be that's what I should've done 's well. But I di'n't think it'd be something you'd really want me to do. Not without you being there." He smiled affably at the end of this: Little Black Sambo come to London.

Next to him, Lynley cleared his throat. Hillier shot him a look, then one at Nkata. He said, "Get things under control, Lynley. I don't want every Tom, Dick, and Harry running to the press over this."

"We'll work on that angle specifically," Lynley said. "Is that all, sir?"

"The next press briefing—" Hillier gestured rudely towards Nkata. "I want you down there ten minutes prior."

"Got it," Nkata said, tapping his skull with his index finger.

Hillier started to say more, but then he dismissed them. Lynley made no comment till they were out of the office, beyond Hillier's secretary, and crossing to Victoria Block. Then it was only, "Winston. Listen," as his footsteps slowed. "Don't do that again."

There was the pride, Nkata thought. He'd expected as much.

But then Lynley surprised him. "There's too much risk for you in taking Hillier on, even obliquely. I appreciate the loyalty, but it's more important for you to watch your back than to watch mine. He's a dangerous enemy. Don't make him into one."

"He wanted to make you look bad in front of me," Nkata said. "I don't like that. Just thought I'd return the favour and let him see how it feels."

"That presupposes the AC might think he could ever look bad in front of anyone," Lynley said wryly. They went to the lift. Lynley pushed the down button. He examined it for a moment before he went on. "On the other hand," he said, "it's a suitable irony."

"What's that, guv?"

"That in giving the rank of sergeant to you and denying it to Barbara, Hillier got more than he bargained for."

Nkata thought about this. The lift doors slid open. They entered and punched for the floors they needed. "D'you s'pose he reckoned I'd yes-guv him right to the grave?" he asked curiously.

"Yes. I think that's what he assumed."

"Why?"

"Because he has no idea who you are," Lynley replied. "But I expect that's something you've already realised."

They descended to the floor for the incident room, where Lynley got off, leaving Nkata to ride to the underground carpark. Before the doors closed upon him, however, the acting superintendent stopped them, his hand holding one of them back.

"Winston—" He didn't say anything else for a moment and Nkata waited for him to go on. When he finally did, it was to say, "Thank you all the same." He released the lift door and let it slide closed. His dark eyes met Nkata's for an instant, then were gone.

It was raining when Nkata emerged from the underground carpark. Daylight was fast fading, and the rain exacerbated the gloom. Traffic lights gleamed against the wet streets; taillights of vehicles winked in the prisms of the raindrops hitting his windscreen. Nkata worked his way over to Parliament Square and inched towards Westminster Bridge in a queue of taxis, buses, and government cars. As he crossed, the river heaved in a grey mass below him, puckered with rain and rippled by the incoming tide. There a single barge chugged its way in the direction of Lambeth, and in its wheelhouse a solitary figure kept the craft on its course.

Nkata parked illegally at the south end of Gabriel's Wharf and put a police placard in the window. Turning up the collar of his coat against the rain, he strode into the wharf area, where the overhead lights made a cheerful crisscrossing pattern above him and the owner of the bicycle rental shop was wisely wheeling his wares indoors.

At Crystal Moon, it was Gigi this time and not her grandmother who was perched on a stool, reading behind the till. Nkata approached her and showed his police identification. She didn't look at it, however. Instead, she said, "Gran told me you'd probably be back. She's good that way. A real intuitive. In another time, she'd've been done for a witch. Did the agrimony work?"

"Not sure what I'm meant to do with it."

"Is that why you're back, then?"

He shook his head. "Wanted to have a word about a bloke called Kilfoyle."

She said, "Rob?," and closed her book. It was, he saw, one of the Harry Potters. "What about Rob?"

"You know him, then?"

"Yeah." She said the word on two notes, a combination of confirmation and question. She looked wary.

"How well?"

"I'm not sure how I'm meant to take this," she said. "Has Rob done something?"

"He buy stuff here?"

"Occasionally. But so do lots of other people. What's this about?"

"What's he buy off you, then?"

"I don't know. He hasn't been in in a while. And I don't write down what people buy."

"But you know he bought something."

"Because I know *him*. I also know that two of the waitresses from Riviera Restaurant have made purchases as well. So have the head cook at Pizza Express and a collection of shop assistants from the wharf. But it's the same as for Rob: I don't recall what they bought. Except for the bloke at Pizza Express. He wanted a love potion for a girl he met. I remember that because we got into the whole love thing."

"Know him how?" Nkata asked her.

"Who?"

"You said you know Kilfoyle. I'm wondering how."

"You mean is he my boyfriend or something?" Nkata could see the colour deepen round the hollow of her throat. "No. He isn't. I mean, we had a drink once, but it wasn't a date. Is he in some sort of trouble?"

Nkata didn't reply to this. It had always been a long shot, anyway, that the owner of Crystal Moon would remember what someone had bought. But the fact that Kilfoyle had indeed *made* a purchase gave the investigation grist to move forward, which was what they needed. He told Gigi that he appreciated her help and he gave her his card and told her to phone should she remember anything particular about Kilfoyle that she thought he should know. He realised that chances were good she'd hand over the card to Kilfoyle himself the next time she saw him, but he didn't see that as a problem. If Kilfoyle *was* their killer, the fact that the cops were on to him would surely slow him down. At this point, that was nearly as gratifying as nabbing him. They had enough victims on their hands already.

He headed for the door, where he paused to ask another question of Gigi. "How'm I meant to use it, then?"

"What?"

"The agrimony."

"Oh," she said. "You burn or anoint."

"Meaning?"

"Meaning: Burn the oil in her presence or anoint her body with it. I take it it's a *her* we're talking about?"

Nkata thought about and then dismissed the likelihood of his being able to accomplish either task. But he also thought about the serial killer: burning and anointing. He was doing both. He thanked Gigi and left the shop. He went next door to Mr. Sandwich.

The little eatery was closed for the day, and the sign

said that its hours of business were from ten till three. He looked through the windows but could make nothing out in the semidarkness save the counter and, on the wall behind it, a list of sandwiches and their prices. There was nothing more to be gained in this spot, he decided. It was time to go.

But he didn't head homeward. Instead, he felt himself compelled to drive yet another time in the general direction of the Oval, weaving over to Kennington Park Road as soon as he was able to do so. He parked again in Braganza Street, but rather than wait for her or enter Doddington Grove Estate to see if she was already home, he walked up to the dispirited patch of green that was Surrey Gardens. From there, he headed into Manor Place, a spot still trying to make a choice between decrepitude and renaissance.

He hadn't been to her shop since November, but there was no way he could have forgotten where it was. He found her within, just as she'd been the last time he visited. She was at a desk at the back, her head bent over what looked like an accounts book. She had a pencil in her mouth, which made her look vulnerable, like a schoolgirl having trouble doing her sums. When she glanced up as he entered and the buzzer went off, though, she looked adult enough. And equally unfriendly. She set her pencil down and closed the book. She came to the counter and made sure, it seemed, that it stood like a bulwark between them.

He said, "A black boy was killed this time. His body got dumped near London Bridge Station. We got an ID on an earlier boy 's well. Mixed race, he was. From Furzedown. That's two boys south of the river now, Yas. Where's Daniel?"

She said, "If you think—"

He cut her off impatiently. "Yas, Daniel have anything to do with a group of kids meeting up at Elephant and Castle?"

"Dan doesn't do gangs," she protested.

"Isn't a gang, this, Yas. This's an outreach group. They offer kids activities, kids at . . . kids at risk." He hurried on. "I know. I know you'll say Dan i'n't at risk, and I'm not here to argue that. The group's called Colossus, though, and I need to know. You ever talk to them about seeing to Dan after school? While you're still working? Giving him a place to go?"

"I don't let Dan up at Elephant and Castle."

"And he never said Colossus to you?"

"He never . . . Why're you *doing* this?" she demanded. "We don't want you round us. You've done enough."

She was getting agitated. He could see as much from the rise and fall of her breasts beneath her jersey. It was cropped like all the jerseys he'd ever seen her wear, showing off her smooth stomach, which was flat like a palm. She'd had her navel pierced, he saw. A bit of gold glittered against her skin.

His throat felt dry, but he knew there were things that he had to say to her, no matter how she was likely to receive them. He said, "Yas"—and he thought, What *is* it about the sound of her name?—"Yas, would you've rather not known what was going on? She was cheating on you, had been from the first, and you got to admit that no matter what you think of me."

"You di'n't have the right—"

"Would you rather've been kept in the dark about her? What good's that supposed to do, then, Yas? And you and I know you're not bent like that anyways."

She pushed away from the counter. "That all? Cos if it is, I got work needs finishing before I go home."

"No," he returned. "Not all. There's this. What I did was right and you know it somewhere."

"You—"

"But," he continued, "how I did it was wrong. And—" He'd come to the hard part now, the tell-the-truth part,

when he didn't want to admit that truth even to himself. But he plunged forward. "And why I did it, Yasmin. That was wrong 's well. And it was wrong that I lied to myself about why I did it too. And I'm sorry for all of it. I'm dead sorry. I want to make things right."

She was silent. There was nothing that could be called kind in her stare. A car pulled up to the kerb outside and her eyes flicked to it, then back to him. "Then stop using Daniel," she said.

"Using . . . ? Yas, I'm—"

"Stop using Daniel to get to me."

"Tha's what you think?"

"I don't want you. I *had* a man. I married him, an' every time I look in the mirror I get to see what he did to me an' I get to think what I did back to him an' I'm *never* going to that place again."

She'd begun to tremble. Nkata wanted to reach across the counter that separated them and offer her comfort and the assurance that not all men . . . But he knew she would not believe him and he wasn't sure if he believed himself. And as he tried to think what to say to her, the door opened, the buzzer went off, and another black man came into the shop. His gaze lit upon Yasmin, made a quick assessment, and flicked to Nkata.

"Yasmin," he said, and he pronounced it differently. Yas*meen*, he said in a soft foreign voice. "Is there trouble here, Yasmin? Are you here alone?"

It was the way he talked to her. It was the tone and the look that went with it. Nkata felt every which way a fool.

He said to the other man, "She is now," and he left the two of them together.

BARBARA HAVERS decided a fag was in order. She considered it a little reward, the carrot she'd held out in front of herself during her long slog on the computer, followed by her further slogs on the phone. She'd managed this spate of unwelcome work with what she liked to think of as extreme good grace, when all the time what she *really* wanted to do was have a *real* slog over to Elephant and Castle so that she might engage the decidedly more *pleasant* slog of shaking things up at Colossus. During all this time, she'd done her best to ignore her feelings: her outrage at DI Stewart's remarks, her impatience with the grunt work she was being assigned, her schoolgirl envy—bloody hell, was that what it *really* was?—seeing Winston Nkata chosen by Lynley to accompany him to duel with the assistant commissioner. So, as far as she was concerned, at this late hour of the day she was owed the metaphorical rosette-on-her-lapel, which she decided a fag would represent.

On the other hand, she had to admit, however much she disliked doing so, that the computer and telephone slog had actually produced more ammunition for her to use when she made her next appearance across the river. So she gave grudging acknowledgement to the wisdom of completing activities assigned to her, and she even considered writing up her report in a timely manner as a way of admitting her earlier error in judgement. But she discarded that notion in favour of a fag. She told herself that, if she had her smoke surreptitiously in the stairwell, she'd be that much closer to the incident room and thus that much closer to a location in which she could fill out the appropriate paperwork . . . once she had the shot-in-the-eyeball of nicotine for which her body was crying out.

So she decamped to the stairwell, plopped down, lit up, and inhaled. Bliss. Not the plate of lasagne and chips she would have preferred at this hour. But a decent second.

"Havers, exactly what are you doing?"

Bloody hell. Barbara scrambled to her feet. Lynley

had just come through the doorway, preparatory to climbing or descending the stairs. He had his overcoat slung over one shoulder, so she assumed descending was the order of the day. It was something of a journey down to the carpark, but the stairwell always gave one time to think, which was probably what he'd planned unless his intention had been to escape without detection, which was also an option that the stairwell afforded.

She said, "Composing my thoughts. I did the Griffin Strong stuff, and I was sorting through how best to present the information." She offered him the notes she'd taken from both the computer and the telephone calls. She'd begun scribbling them in her spiral book but unfortunately had run out of paper. She'd been reduced to using whatever lay at hand, which had turned out to be two used envelopes from the wastepaper basket and a paper napkin she'd rummaged out of her bag.

Lynley looked from all this to her.

She said, "Hey. Before you give me aggro—"

"I'm beyond it," he said. "What have you got?"

Barbara happily settled in for a natter, fag dangling from her lips as she spoke. "First of all, according to his wife, Griffin Strong's doing the mattress polka with Ulrike Ellis. Arabella—that's the wife—puts him with Ulrike for every killing no matter when it was. Without a second to think it over, mind you. I don't know about you, but that tells me she's dead desperate to keep him bringing home the dosh while she cares for the baby and does jumping jacks in front of the telly all day. Fine. That's understandable, I suppose. *But* it turns out our Griff has a history of taking up with the ladies at all his places of employment, getting in too deep—if you'll pardon the pun—then losing his way and letting the ball drop with reference to his responsibilities."

Lynley leaned against the stair rail, listening tolerantly to her metaphor mixing. He had his eyes fixed on hers, so she entertained the idea that she might actually be on the way to resurrecting something of her reputation, not to mention something of her career. She waxed enthusiastic on her topic.

"Turns out he was sacked from Social Services in Lewisham for falsifying his reports."

"That's an interesting twist."

"He was supposedly checking up on kids in care but in reality only managing to get to one in ten."

"Why?"

"The obvious. He was too busy bonking his cubicle mate. He got warned off once and written up twice before the axe finally fell, and it seems the only reason he got taken on over in Stockwell was that none of the kids on his roster at Lewisham actually suffered from his neglect."

"In this day and age, though . . . There were no repercussions?"

"Not a whisper. I talked to his Lewisham supervisor, who'd got convinced by someone—and for that I wager you can read Griffin Strong—that Griff was far more pursued than pursuer. Beating this bird off with a nail-studded stick for months on end, to hear the way Strong's guv told the tale. 'Anyone would have succumbed to her eventually,' was how he put it."

"His supervisor being male, I take it?"

"Naturally. And you should've heard him talk about this bird. Like she was the sexual equivalent of the bubonic plague."

"What about at Stockwell?" Lynley said.

"The kid that died under Strong's care was attacked."

"By whom?"

"A gang with an initiation rite involving chasing down twelve-year-olds and cutting them up with broken bottles. They caught him crossing Angell Park, and what was s'posed to be a cut on the thigh hit an artery and he bled to death before he could get home."

"Christ," Lynley said. "But that was hardly Strong's fault, was it?"

"When you consider the kid who cut him up was his own foster brother . . . ?"

Lynley raised his head heavenward. He looked done in. "How old was the foster brother, then?"

Barbara glanced at her notes. "Eleven," she said.

"What happened to him?"

She continued to read. "Psychiatric lockup till he's eighteen. For all the good it'll do." She knocked the growing tube of ash from her fag. "It all made me think . . ."

"About?"

"The killer. Seems to me that he sees himself ridding the flock of black sheep. Like it's sort of a religion to him. When you think of all the aspects of ritual that're part of the killings . . ." She let him finish the thought for himself.

Lynley rubbed his forehead and leaned against the handrail of the stairs. He said, "Barbara, I don't care what he's thinking. These are *children* we're talking about, not genetic mutations. Children need guidance when they go wrong, and they need protection the rest of the time. Full stop. End of story."

"Sir, we're on the same page," Barbara said. "Start to finish." She dropped the nub of her cigarette on the stairs and crushed it out. To cover the trace of her malefaction, she picked up the dog end and placed it, along with her notes, in her shoulder bag. She said, "Trouble upstairs?," with reference to Lynley's meeting with Hillier.

"No more than usual," Lynley said. "Winston isn't turning out to be the blue-eyed boy the AC thought he'd be, though."

"Now that's gratifying," Barbara said.

"To an extent, yes." He studied her. A little silence

lingered between them during which Barbara looked away, picking at a fuzz ball that needed removing from the arm of her baggy pullover . . . along with all the other fuzz balls that adorned the garment. "Barbara," Lynley finally said, "I wouldn't have it this way."

She looked up. "What?"

"I think you know. Have you ever considered you'd make better progress towards reinstatement if you worked with someone less . . . less objectionable to people in power?"

"Like who, for example? John Stewart? Now that would be chummy."

"MacPherson, possibly. Or Philip Hale. Even out of here altogether, in one of the borough stations. Because as long as you're in my sphere—not to mention in Hillier's—with Webberly no longer here to be a buffer for either one of us . . ." He made a gesture. It said, Finish the thought in a logical manner.

She didn't need to. She heaved her bag higher on her shoulder and began to head back up to the incident room. She said, "That's not how this is going to play out. At the end of the day, I know what's important and what isn't."

"Which means?"

She paused at the door to the corridor. She offered him the response he'd given her. "I think you know, sir. Have a good night. I've got work to do before I can go home."

Chapter Fifteen

In his mind, he put a body before him: lying on the floor, crucified by restraints and the board. It was a soundless but not a lifeless body and when its senses returned, what it knew was that it was in the presence of a power it could not hope to escape. So fear descended in the guise of anger, and in the presence of that fear, Fu's heart grew large. Blood engorged His muscles, and He rose above Himself. It was the kind of ecstasy that only came from being a god.

Having had it that way, He wanted it again. Once He had experienced the sensation of who He actually was, bursting from the chrysalis of who He only appeared to be, it could not be laid aside. It was forever.

He had attempted to hold on to the feeling for as long as possible once the first boy died. Time and again, He had put Himself into darkness and there He slowly relived each moment that had taken Him from selection to judgement, and from there to admission, onward to punishment, and then to release. But still the sheer *exultation* of the experience had faded, as all things do. To recapture it, He had no choice but to make another selection, to perform once again.

He told Himself that He was not like the others who had gone before Him: swine like Brady, Sutcliffe, and

West. They had all been cheap thrill seekers, cold-blooded killers who preyed on the vulnerable for no other reason than to shore themselves up. They shouted their insignificance to the world through acts the world was not likely to forget.

But for Fu things were different. Not for Him were innocent children at play, streetwalkers chosen at random off the pavement, female hitchhikers taking a fatal decision to climb into a car with a man and his wife . . .

In the sphere of those killers, the possession, the terror, and the slaughter were all. But Fu trod a different path to theirs, and that was what made His current state far more difficult to cope with. Had He been willing to join the swine, He knew that He would be resting easier now: He'd have only to scour the streets and within hours . . . ecstasy once again. Because that wasn't who He was, Fu sought the darkness as an aid to relief.

Once He was there, though, He discerned intrusion. He drew a breath and held it, His senses alert. He listened. He thought of impossibility. But there was no mistaking what His body told Him.

He dispelled the gloom. He looked for the evidence. The light was dim as He preferred it, but enough to show Him that there were no obvious signs of intrusion into this place. Yet still He knew. He had learned to trust the nerve endings at the nape of His neck, and they were murmuring caution.

A book lay discarded on the floor near a chair. A magazine had its cover wrinkled. A stack of newspapers crisscrossed one on top of the other. Words. Words. Words upon words. All of them chattered, all accused. A maggot, they chorused. Here, here.

The reliquary, Fu realised. That was what he wanted. For only through the reliquary would it be possible for the maggot to speak once more. And what he would say . . .

Don't tell me you've not bought brown sauce, cow. What else have you got to think about all day?

Dear, please. The boy—

Are you trying to tell *me . . . ? Get your arse down to the shops for that sauce. And leave the boy. I said leave him. Something wrong with your ears as well as your brain?*

Now, dearest . . .

As if the tone and the words could somehow make a difference to the walking lightly and the loose-boweled fear. Both of which would return if He lost possession of the reliquary or its contents.

Yet He could see that the reliquary stood where He had left it, in its hiding place that was no place of hiding at all. And when He carefully removed the top, He found that the contents seemed to be undisturbed. Even the contents *within* the contents—carefully buried, preserved, and treasured—were as He'd left them. Or so they appeared.

He went to the pile of crisscrossed papers. He loomed above them, but they spoke only what He could see: a man in African garb. A headline declared the man "Foster Dad in Anguish," and the story that accompanied the headline told the rest: all the deaths round London and they'd finally sussed out that there was a serial killer at work.

Fu felt Himself relax. He felt His hands warm, and the sickness within Him began to recede as He fingered fondly through the stack of tabloids. Perhaps, He thought, they would suffice.

He sat. He drew the entire stack closer, like Father Christmas embracing a child. How odd it was, He thought, that only with the last boy—the lying, denying, and accusing Sean who had forfeited redemption and release because he'd stubbornly refused to admit his guilt—had the police realised they were dealing with something superior to and larger than what they were used to. He had been giving them clues all along, but they'd refused to see. Now, though, they knew. Not His purpose, of course, but the *fact* of Him as a single and singular force of justice. Always a step ahead of those who sought Him. Supreme and supreme.

He lifted the most recent copy of the *Evening Standard* and set it aside. He went down the stack till He found the *Mirror,* which featured a photo of the tunnel in which He'd left the last body. He laid His hands on the photograph of the scene, and He dropped His gaze to encompass the other pictures on the page: cops because who else could they be? And one of them named so that now He knew who wished to thwart Him, who fruitlessly directed everyone else to turn Him from the course He followed. Lynley, detective superintendent. The name would be easy enough to remember.

Fu closed His eyes and conjured up the image of Himself and this Lynley in confrontation. But not the sort in which He faced him alone. Instead, the image displayed a moment of redemption in which the detective watched, helpless to do anything to stop the cycle of punishment and salvation as it played out before his eyes. *That* would indeed be something, Fu thought. That would be a statement that no one—no Brady, no Sutcliffe, no West, no anyone else—had *ever* been able to make.

Fu took in the pleasure of the thought, in the hope it would bring Him close to the heady sensation—what He called the very *yesness*—of those final moments of the act of redemption. Wanting the swelling of success to possess Him, wanting the knowledge of fully *being* to fill Him, wanting wanting wanting to feel the emotional and sensual explosion that occurred at the impact of desire and accomplishment . . . *Please.*

But nothing happened.

He opened His eyes, every nerve alive. The maggot *had* been here, defiling this place, and that was why He could not recapture any of the moments in which He'd been most fully alive.

He could not afford the despair that threatened, so He turned it to anger, and the anger itself He lasered on the maggot. Keep out of here, wanker. Keep out. Keep away.

But His nerves still tingled, telling a tale that revealed He would never have peace in this way. Peace could now be generated only by the act that brought another soul to its redemption.

The boy and the act itself, He thought.

What was needed was what would be.

RAIN FELL for the next five days, a heavy midwinter rain of the sort that generally made one despair of ever seeing the sun again. By the sixth morning, the worst of the storm had passed, but the glowering sky heralded the arrival of yet another as the day wore on.

Lynley didn't go directly into the Yard as he normally would have done. Instead, he drove in the opposite direction, working his way over to the A4, heading out of Central London. Helen had suggested this journey to him. She'd gazed at him over a glass of breakfast orange juice and said, "Tommy, have you considered going out to Osterley? I think it's what you need."

He'd said in reply, "Is my self-doubt becoming that obvious?"

"I wouldn't call it self-doubt. And I think you're being too hard on yourself if that's what you're calling it, by the way."

"What would you call it, then?"

Helen thought about this, head cocked to one side as she observed him. She hadn't yet dressed for the day, hadn't even bothered to comb her hair, and Lynley found he liked her tousled like this. She looked . . . She looked *wifely,* he thought, that was the word, although he'd have cut out his tongue before telling her that. She said, "I'd call it a ripple on the surface of your peace of mind, courtesy of the tabloids and the assistant commissioner of police. David Hillier wants you to fail, Tommy. You ought to know that by now. Even as he blusters on about bringing in a result, you're the last person on earth he wants to do that."

Lynley knew she was right. He said, "Which makes me wonder why he put me in this position in the first place."

"Acting superintendent or heading this investigation?"

"Both."

"It's all to do with Malcolm Webberly, of course. Hillier told you himself that he *knows* what Malcolm would have wanted him to do, so he's doing it. It's his . . . his homage to him, for want of a better word. It's his way of doing his part to ensure Malcolm's recovery. But his *own* will—Hillier's, I mean—gets in the way of his intention of helping Malcolm. So while you have the elevation to acting superintendent and you have the assignment to head this investigation, you also have Hillier's bad wishes to go along with both."

Lynley considered this. There was good sense to it. But that was Helen. Scratch the surface of her habitual insouciance and she was both sensible and intuitive to her core. "I'd no idea you'd become so adept at instant psychoanalysis," he told her.

"Oh." Lightly, she saluted him with her teacup. "It all comes of watching chat shows, darling."

"Really? I'd never have thought of you as a covert chat-show viewer."

"You flatter me. I'm becoming quite fond of the American ones. You know the sort: Someone sits on a sofa, pouring out his heart to the host and half a billion viewers, after which he's given advice and sent off to slay dragons. It's confession, catharsis, resolution, and renewal all in a tidy fifty-minute package. I adore the way they solve life's problems on American television, Tommy. It's rather the way Americans do most things, isn't it? That gunslinger approach: Draw the gun, blast away, and the difficulty's gone. Supposedly."

"You aren't recommending I shoot Hillier, are you?"

"Only as a last resort. In the meantime, I suggest a trip to Osterley."

So he took up her suggestion. It was an ungodly hour for visiting a convalescent hospital, but he reckoned his police identification would be enough to get him inside.

It was. Most of the patients were still at their breakfasts, but Malcolm Webberly's bed was empty. However, a helpful orderly directed him to the physiotherapy room. There, Lynley found Detective Superintendent Webberly working his way between two parallel bars.

Lynley watched him from the doorway. The fact that the superintendent was alive was miraculous. He'd survived a laundry list of injuries, all of them brought about by a hit-and-run driver. He'd endured the removal of his spleen and a good portion of his liver, a fractured skull and the removal of a blood clot on his brain, nearly six weeks of drug-induced coma, a broken hip, a broken arm, five broken ribs, and a heart attack in the midst of his slow recovery from everything else. He was nothing if not a warrior in the battle to regain his strength. He was also the one man at New Scotland Yard with whom Lynley had long felt he could be unguarded.

Webberly inched along the bars, encouraged by the therapist, who insisted upon calling him *luv* despite the scowls Webberly sent in her direction. She was approximately the size of a canary, and Lynley wondered how she would approach supporting the burly superintendent should he begin to topple. But it appeared that Webberly had no intention of doing anything other than making his way to the end of the apparatus. When he'd managed that, he said without looking in Lynley's direction, "You'd think they'd let me have a bloody cigar on occasion, wouldn't you, Tommy? Their idea of a celebration round here is an enema administered to the sound of Mozart."

"How are you, sir?" Lynley asked, coming farther into the room. "Have you lost a few stone?"

"Are you saying I needed to?" Webberly looked shrewdly in his direction. He was pale and unshaven and he looked quite tentative about the titanium acting the part of his new hip. He wore a tracksuit instead of hospital garb. The words "Top Cop" decorated its jacket.

"Just a casual observation," Lynley said. "To me you were always a picture needing no revision."

"What cock." Webberly grunted as he reached the end of the bars and made the turn that was necessary for his descent to the wheelchair, which the therapist brought to him. "Wouldn't trust you as far as I could throw you."

"Cup of tea, luv?" Webberly's therapist asked him once he'd lowered himself to his chair. "Nice ginger biscuit? You did very well."

"She thinks I'm a performing dog," Webberly informed Lynley. He said to the woman, "Bring the whole damn tin of biscuits, thank you."

She smiled serenely and patted his shoulder. "Cup of tea and a biscuit it is. And for you?" This last was directed to Lynley, who told her he'd do nicely with nothing. She disappeared into an adjoining room.

Webberly wheeled himself over to a window, where he raised the blinds and looked out at the day. "Bloody weather," he growled. "I'm that ready for Spain, Tommy. The thought of it . . . That's what's keeping me going."

"Taking your pension, then?" Lynley tried to make

the question light, not a reflection of what he felt at the thought of the superintendent's permanent removal from the force.

He didn't fool Webberly with his tone, however. The superintendent gave him a look, cast over his shoulder from his perusal of the day. "David behaving badly, is he? You've got to come up with a strategy for coping with him. That's all I can tell you."

Lynley joined him at the window. There, they both looked morosely out at the grey day and what the window offered of it, which was a distant view of bare branches, the supplicant winter arms of trees in Osterley Park. Closer in, they had the carpark to gaze upon.

"For myself, I can do it," Lynley said.

"That's all anyone asks of you."

"It's the others I'm worried about. Barbara and Winston mostly. I've not done either of them any favours, taking on your position. It was madness to think I could."

Webberly was silent. Lynley knew that the other man would see his point. Havers' boat of dreams at the Yard would doubtless continue to take on water as long as she maintained her association with him. As for Nkata . . . Lynley knew that *any* other officer elevated to the rank of acting superintendent would have done a better job of keeping Winston out of Hillier's clutches. Instead, Havers was looking more professionally doomed every day, while Nkata knew he was being used as a token and might end up carrying round a load of bitterness that could blight his career for years. No matter how he looked at the matter, Lynley felt it was all down to him that Nkata and Havers were in the positions they were in at the moment.

"Tommy," Webberly said, as if Lynley had spoken all this, "you don't have that power."

"Don't I? You did. You do. I ought to be able—"

"Stop. I'm not talking about the power to be a buffer

between David and his targets. I'm talking about the power to change him, to un-David him. Which is what you'd like to do, if you'll admit it. But he has his own set of demons, just like you. And there's not a thing in the world that you can do to remove them from him."

"So how do you cope with him?"

Webberly rested his arms on the windowsill. He was looking, Lynley saw, much older these days. His thin hair—once the faded sand of the redhead going grey—had now reached that destination, while the flesh under his eyes was baggy and the skin beneath his chin was wattled. Seeing this, Lynley was reminded of Ulysses' rumination, faced with knowledge of his mortality: "Old age hath yet his honour and his toil." He wanted to recite it to Webberly. Anything, he thought, to postpone the inevitable.

"It's down to the knighthood, I reckon," Webberly said. "You think David wears it comfortably. I believe he wears it like a suit of armour, which as we both know, has comfort as the least of its purposes. He wanted it, and he didn't want it. He schemed to get it, and now he has to live with that."

"The scheming? But that's what he does best."

"Too right. So think about having that on your gravestone. Tommy, you *know* all this. And if you can let the knowledge just get past that nasty temper of yours, you'll be able to deal with him."

There it was, Lynley thought. The dominant truth of his life. He could hear his father comment upon it, though the man had been dead nearly twenty years: *Temper, Tommy. You're allowing passion not only to blind you but to rule you, son.*

What had it been at the time? A football match and a wild disagreement with a referee? A call in rugby he hadn't liked? A row with his sister over a board game? What? And what did it matter now?

But that had been his father's point. That, full stop.

The black passion of the moment did not matter once the moment passed. He merely failed to see that fact, over and over again, resulting in everyone else having to pay for his fatal flaw. He was Othello without the excuse of Iago; he was Hamlet sans ghost. Helen was right. Hillier set traps and he walked right into them.

It was all he could do not to groan aloud. Webberly looked at him. "There's a learning curve involved with the job," the superintendent said kindly. "Why don't you let yourself travel it?"

"Easier said than done when at the other end of the curve is someone waiting with a battle-axe."

Webberly shrugged. "You can't stop David from arming himself. Who you have to become is the person who can dodge the blows."

The canary therapist came back into the room, tea in one hand and paper napkin in the other. On this rested a lone ginger biscuit, the superintendent's reward for managing the parallel bars. "Here you go, luvvie," she said to Webberly. "Nice hot cuppa with milk and sugar . . . I've made it just the way you like it."

"I hate tea," Webberly informed her as he took the cup and the biscuit.

"Oh, go on with you," she replied. "You're being quite naughty this morning. Is that because of your visitor?" She patted his shoulder. "Well, it's good to see you showing some life. But stop pulling my leg, luv, or I'll give you what for."

"You're the reason I'm trying to get the hell *out* of here, woman," Webberly told her.

"That," she said placidly, "is my whole objective." She wagged her fingers and headed out of the room, scooping up a medical chart on her way.

"You've got Hillier, I've got her," Webberly groused as he bit into his biscuit.

"But at least she offers refreshments," Lynley said.

Nothing was resolved in the visit to Osterley, but

Helen's prescription did work as she'd thought it would. When Lynley left the superintendent back in his room, he felt ready for another round of his professional life.

What that round brought was information from a number of sources. He met the squad in the incident room, where phones were ringing and constables were typing information into the computers. Stewart was compiling action reports from one of his teams, and—mirabile dictu, as things turned out—Barbara Havers had, in his absence, apparently managed to take direction from the DI without episode. When Lynley called the group together, the first thing he learned was that, upon Stewart's orders, Havers had traveled across the river to Colossus for another set-to with Ulrike Ellis.

"It's amazing how quickly she was able to locate information on Jared Salvatore once she twigged we had the book from reception with his name blazed all over it," Havers reported, "*and* she's managed to unearth all sorts of useful details on Anton Reid. She's onboard now, sir, cooperation incarnate. She's provided the name of every kid who's dropped out of Colossus for the last twelve months, and I've been seeing if we can match any of them with the rest of the bodies."

"What about the other two boys' personal connections to anyone at Colossus?"

"Jared and Anton? Griffin Strong was their assessment leader, surprise, surprise. Anton Reid also did some time on Greenham's computer course."

"What about Kilfoyle and Veness? Any relationship between the boys and them?"

Havers consulted her report which—perhaps as evidence of her dubious intention of being a model cop from this moment forward—appeared to be typed for once. "Both of them knew Jared Salvatore. Evidently, he was quite the whiz at creating recipes. He couldn't read, so he couldn't follow cookbooks, but he'd manage to whip up something without instructions and serve it round, with the staff at Colossus doing the guinea-pig thing. Everyone knew him, as things turn out. My mistake earlier"—she shot a look round the room as if anticipating a reaction from someone to her admission—"was asking only Ulrike Ellis and Griff Strong about Jared. When they said he wasn't one of theirs, I believed them because they'd admitted to Kimmo Thorne right up front. Sorry."

"What are Kilfoyle and Veness saying about Anton Reid, then?"

"Kilfoyle says he doesn't remember Anton. Veness is vague about it. Thinks he *may*, he says. Neil Greenham remembers him well enough."

"As to Greenham, Tommy," John Stewart weighed in, "he's got a real temper, according to the head teacher up in Kilburn where he taught. He lost it with kids a few times and he shoved one against the blackboard once. He heard about *that* from the parents straightaway and he apologised for it, but that doesn't mean he was genuine about the apology."

"So much for his theories on discipline," Havers noted.

"Have we laid on surveillance for these blokes?" Lynley asked.

"We're stretched too thin, Tommy. Hillier's not authorising any more men till we've got a result."

"God damn—"

"*But* we've done some snooping, so we've got an idea of their nighttime activities."

"Which are?"

Stewart gave the nod to his team three officers. So far, very little looked suspicious. After his day at Colossus, Jack Veness evidently went regularly to the Miller and Grindstone, his local in Bermondsey, where he also had a second job behind the bar at the weekends. He drank, smoked, and made the occasional call from a phone box outside—

"That sounds promising," someone pointed out.

—but that was it. Then he went home or to a take-away curry shop near Bermondsey Square. Griffin Strong, on the other hand, seemed to alternate between his silk-screening business in Quaker Street and his home. He also, however, appeared to have a liking for a Bengali restaurant in Brick Lane, where he went to dine alone occasionally.

As for Kilfoyle and Greenham, team three were gathering information telling them that Kilfoyle spent many of his evenings in the Othello Bar of the London Ryan Hotel, which was at the base of the Gwynne Place Steps. These led up to Granville Square. Otherwise, he was at home in the square.

"Living with whom?" Lynley asked. "Do we know?"

"Deed poll says the property belongs to Victor Kilfoyle. His dad, I reckon."

"What about Greenham?"

"The only thing he's done of interest is take Mummy to the Royal Opera House. And he apparently has a lady friend he meets on the side. We know they've done cheap Chinese in Lisle Street and a gallery opening in Upper Brook Street. Other than that, he's at home with Mummy." Stewart smiled. "In Gunnersbury, by the way."

"Is anyone surprised by that?" Lynley commented. He glanced at Havers. She was doing her best, he saw, not to crow *I was right*, and he had to give her marks for that. She'd made the connection between employees at Colossus and the dump sites of bodies from the start.

Nkata joined them then, fresh from a meeting with Hillier. They were set to film *Crimewatch*, he reported, and he scowled at the good-natured comments about a star being born, which rose when he made this announcement. They'd be using the e-fit of the interloper seen at Square Four Gym, he informed them, which had been developed in concert with the bodybuilder who'd seen their potential suspect. To this, they would add the photographs of all identified victims as well as a dramatic reconstruction of what they now presumed to be Kimmo Thorne's manner of encountering his killer: a red Ford Transit stopping a bicycle rider with stolen goods in his possession, the van's driver helping to load the bicycle and the goods into the vehicle.

"We've something to add to that as well," Stewart put in when Nkata was done. He sounded pleased. "CCTV footage. I won't say we've hit gold, but we've had a little luck at last with a CCTV camera mounted on one of the buildings near St. George's Gardens: the image of a van driving down the street."

"Time and date?"

"Matching up with Kimmo Thorne's death."

"Christ in heaven, John, why's it taken this long to get to it?"

"We had it early on," Stewart said, "but it wasn't clear. We needed an enhancement, and that took time. But the wait was worth it. You'd better have a look and give the word on how you want it used. *Crimewatch* might get some mileage from it."

"I'll look at it straightway," Lynley told him. "What about surveillance at the body sites. Anything?"

Nothing, as it turned out. If their killer was considering a nocturnal visit to the shrine of his criminal accomplishment—as contended in Hamish Robson's remarks about him—he had not yet done so. Which brought up the profile itself. Barbara Havers said she'd had another look at it, and she wanted to point out part of Robson's description: the section which claimed the killer probably lived with a dominant parent. They had two suspects so far with parents in the home: Kilfoyle and Greenham. One with Dad, one with Mum. And wasn't it dodgy that Greenham was taking Mum to the

Royal Opera House but the woman friend only got cheap Chinese and a gratis gallery opening? What did *that* mean?

It was worth looking at, Lynley told her, and he said, "Who's got the information on who Veness lives with?"

John Stewart responded. "There's a landlady. Mary Alice Atkins-Ward. A distant relation."

"Do we tighten up on Kilfoyle and Greenham, then?" a DC asked, pencil at the ready.

"Let me look at the CCTV film first." Lynley told them to get back to their assigned actions. He himself followed John Stewart to a video recorder. He signaled Nkata to accompany them. He saw Havers glower at this but chose to ignore it.

He had high hopes of the CCTV footage. The e-fit had provided little enough inspiration. To him, it looked like Everyman and No Man. The suspect had worn a cap of some sort—didn't they all?—and while upon an initial glimpse of it, Barbara Havers had pointed out gleefully that Robbie Kilfoyle wore a EuroDisney cap, that was hardly a damning piece of evidence. For Lynley's money, the e-fit was on the borderline of worthless, and he reckoned *Crimewatch* would prove him right on that.

Stewart snatched up the remote for the video recorder and switched on the television. Onto the corner of the screen, the time and date popped up along with a section of mews beyond which the wall of St. George's Gardens curved. As they watched, the front of a van pulled into the picture at the end of the mews, which appeared to be some thirty yards from the CCTV camera guarding the mews itself. The vehicle stopped, lights out, and a figure emerged. He carried a tool and disappeared round the curve of the wall, presumably to apply his implement to something out of sight of the camera. This would, Lynley thought, be the padlock on the chain that held the gate closed at night.

As they watched, the figure came back into view, too distant and, even on the enhanced film, too grainy to be distinguishable. He climbed into the van and it rolled smoothly forward. Before it disappeared behind the wall, Stewart paused the film. He said, "Have a look at that lovely little picture, Tommy." He sounded pleased.

As well he might, Lynley thought. For on the film, they'd managed to capture writing on the side of the van. The miracle would have been a complete identification, which was more than they got. But half of a miracle would do. Three partial lines of faded printing were visible:

waf
bile
chen

Below them a number was rendered: 873-61.

"That last looks like part of a phone number," Nkata said.

"My money says the rest is the name of a business," Stewart added. "Question is: Do we go with it on *Crimewatch*?"

"Who've you got working on the van right now?" Lynley asked. "What are they doing?"

"Trying to get something on that partial phone number from BT, checking business licences to see if we can find a match for those letters we can see in the name, running things through Swansea another time."

"That'll take a century," Nkata pointed out. "But how many million people see this 'f we put it on the telly?"

Lynley considered the ramifications of running the video on *Crimewatch*. Millions watched the show, and it had been useful on dozens of occasions in accelerating the speed of an investigation. But there were inherent risks in broadcasting the film countrywide, not the least of which was tipping their hand to the killer. For there was every chance that their man would be watching and would put the van through such a high-powered cleaning and scouring that all evidence of any of their dead boys having been in it would be forever obliterated. And there was the additional chance that their man would dump the van immediately, taking it to one of a hundred places far out of London where it wouldn't be found for years. Or he might put it in a lockup somewhere with the same result.

It was Lynley's decision. He decided to hold off making it. He said, "I want to think about this," and to Winston, "Tell *Crimewatch* we may have something for them, but we're working on it."

Nkata looked uneasy, but he went for the phone. Stewart looked pleased as he returned to his desk.

Lynley nodded to Havers, an I'll-see-you-now look. She grabbed up what looked like a pristine notebook and followed him out of the incident room.

"Good work," he told her. He noted that she'd even dressed more suitably today, in a tweed suit and brogues. The suit had a stain on the skirt and the brogues weren't polished, but it was otherwise a remarkable change in a woman who usually favoured drawstring trousers and T-shirts bearing groan-inducing puns.

She shrugged. "I'm capable of taking the hint when I'm clubbed with it, sir."

"I'm glad to hear that. Get your things and come with me."

Her face altered, its hopeful brightness betraying her even as it deeply touched him. He wanted to tell her not to wear her professional heart on her sleeve, but he held his tongue. Havers was who Havers was.

SHE DIDN'T ASK where they were going till they were in the Bentley and heading in the direction of Vauxhall Bridge Road. Then she said, "Are we doing a runner, sir?"

He said, "Believe me, I've thought about it more than once. But Webberly tells me there's a route to dealing with Hillier. I've just not discovered it yet."

"That must be like searching for the Holy Grail." She examined her brogues and appeared to note their sad condition. She wet her fingers on her tongue and rubbed the damp against a scuff, without result. She said, "How is he, then?"

"Webberly? Slow progress, but progress."

"Well, that's good, isn't it?"

"Everything but the slow part. We need him back before Hillier self-destructs and takes us all down with him."

"D'you think it'll come to that?"

"Sometimes," he said, "I don't know what to think."

At their destination, parking was its usual nightmare. He squeezed the Bentley in front of the entrance to the Kings Head and Eight Bells pub, directly beneath a "Do NOT Block This Entrance" sign, to which "You Will Die If You Do" had been added. Havers raised her eyebrow.

"What's life without risk?" Lynley asked. But he put a police placard prominently on the dashboard.

"Now *that's* living dangerously," Havers noted.

They walked the few yards up Cheyne Row to the house at the corner of Lordship Place, where they found St. James being regaled by both Deborah and Helen, who were leafing through magazines as they chatted about "The absolute solution to everything. Simon, you've married a genius." They were all in the lab.

"Logic," Deborah replied. "It was nothing more." She looked up and saw Lynley and Havers in the doorway. She said, "Just in time. Look who's here. You won't even have to go home to talk him into it, Helen."

"Talk me into what?" Lynley went to his wife, tilting

back her chin to examine her face. "You're looking tired."

"Don't be a mother hen," she chided. "You've got worry lines coming out on your forehead."

"That's down to Hillier," Havers said. "We'll all look ten years older in another month."

"Isn't he due to retire?" Deborah asked.

"Assistant commissioners don't retire, my love," St. James told his wife. "Not until the last hope of being made commissioner is finally beaten out of them." He looked at Lynley. "I take it that doesn't seem likely to happen soon?"

"You take it correctly. Have you got anything for us, Simon?"

"I expect you mean information and not whisky," St. James said. He added, "Fu."

"Phoo?" Havers said. "As in . . . what? Phooey? Typhoo tea?"

"As in the letters *F* and *U*." On a china board, St. James had been working on a diagram with splotches of faux blood, but he left it and went to his desk where he took from the top drawer a paper on which was drawn the same symbol that had been on the bottom of the note they'd received at the Yard, purporting to be from the serial killer. "It's a Chinese symbol," St. James explained. "It means authority, divine power, and the ability to judge. It stands, in fact, for justice. And it's pronounced Fu."

Helen said, "Is that helpful, Tommy?"

"It's in keeping with the message of the note he sent. And to some extent, with the mark on Kimmo Thorne's forehead as well."

"Because it *is* a mark?" Havers asked.

"I expect that would be Dr. Robson's point."

"Even if the other mark's from alchemy?" Deborah asked the last question of her husband.

"It's the fact of the marking, I daresay," St. James replied. "Two distinct symbols with interpretations readily available. Is that what you mean, Tommy?"

"Hmm. Yes." Lynley studied the piece of paper on which the mark had been reproduced and an explanation of the mark appeared. He said, "Simon, where did you get the information?"

"Internet search," he said. "It wasn't difficult."

"So our boy's got access to a computer as well," Havers noted.

"That narrows it down to half the population of London," Lynley said grimly.

"I think I can eliminate at least a portion of that group. There's something else." St. James had moved to a worktable where he was laying out a line of photographs. Lynley and Havers joined him, while Deborah and Helen remained at the other worktable, a selection of magazines open between them.

"I had these from SO7," St. James said, in reference to the pictures, which Lynley saw were of each of the dead boys, along with respective enlargements of one small portion of each boy's torso. "D'you recall the autopsy reports, Tommy, how they all mention a specific area of what they called 'woundlike bruising' on every one of the bodies? Well, have a look at this. Deborah did the enlargements for me last night." He reached for one of the larger photos.

Lynley examined it, Havers looking over his shoulder. In the picture, he saw the bruising that St. James was talking about. He discerned that it was actually more of a pattern than a bruise, most distinguishable on Kimmo Thorne's body because he was the only white youth. On Kimmo, a central pale area was ringed by dark bruiselike flesh. In the centre of the pale portion of this, two small marks had the look of burns. With variations due to the pigment of each boy, this distinctive mark was the same on every successive photograph that St. James handed over. Lynley looked up once he'd seen them all.

"Did SO7 actually *miss* this?" he asked. What he thought was, Christ. What a *bloody* cock-up.

"They mention it in the autopsies. The problem was in their term of reference. Calling it a bruise."

"What do you make of it yourself? It looks something between a bruise and a burn."

"I had a good idea, but I wasn't entirely sure initially. So I scanned the photos and sent them over to a colleague in the States for a second opinion."

"Why the States?" Havers had taken up one of the pictures and had been frowning down at it, but now she looked up curiously.

"Because, like nearly anything else you might imagine as a weapon, they're legal in America."

"What?"

"Stun guns. I think that's how he's incapacitating the boys. Before he does the rest." St. James went on to explain how the characteristics of the bruiselike wounds on the bodies compared point by point to the kind of bruise that was the result of being jolted by the fifty thousand to two hundred thousand volts of electricity that such a weapon discharged. "Each of the boys was hit in relatively the same place on the body, on the left side of the torso. That tells us that the killer's using the gun in the same way each time."

"If you've got something that works, why mess about with it," Havers said.

"Exactly," St. James agreed. "The electricity from the stun gun scrambles the body's nervous system, leaving the victim—as the name implies—literally stunned, unable to move even if he wants to. His muscles work rapidly but without any efficiency. His blood sugar is converted to lactic acid, which depletes him of energy. His neurological impulses are interrupted. He's weak, confused, and disoriented."

"While he's in that condition, the killer has time to immobilise him," Lynley added.

"And if he starts to come round . . . ?" Havers said.

"The killer uses the gun on him again. By the time he's back to normal, he's gagged and restrained, and the killer can do what he wants with him." Lynley handed the pictures back to St. James. "Yes. I think that's exactly what's happening."

"Except . . ." Havers handed her own photograph back to St. James although she spoke to Lynley. "These are streetwise kids. You'd think they'd notice someone about to shove a gun in their ribs, wouldn't you?"

"As to that, Barbara . . ." St. James dug out a few sheets of paper from an in basket on the top of a filing cabinet. He handed over to Lynley what first appeared to be an advertisement. On closer inspection, however, Lynley saw that the document had come from the Internet. On a site called PersonalSecurity.com, stun guns were offered for sale. But these were stun guns of an entirely different order from the pistol-shaped weapon one might associate with the name. Indeed, these didn't appear to be guns at all, which was probably the point of owning one of them. Some of them were manufactured to look like mobile phones. Others looked like torches. All of them worked identically, however: The user had to make physical contact with the victim in order for the electrical charge to pass from the gun into the victim's body.

Havers gave a quiet whistle. "I'm impressed," she said. "And I reckon we can suss out how these things get into the country in the first place."

"No difficult feat to smuggle them into the UK," St. James agreed, "not looking like that."

"And from there on to the black market," Lynley

said. "Well done, Simon. Thank you. Progress. I feel moderately encouraged."

"We can't give this to Hillier, though," Havers pointed out. "He'll put it on *Crimewatch*. Or hand it over to the press before you could say 'Kiss my arse.' Not," she added hastily, "that you'd say that, sir."

"Not," Lynley said, "that I wouldn't want to. Although I tend to like something a little more subtle."

"Then we may have a difficulty with our plan." Helen spoke from the table where she and Deborah had been flipping through their magazines. She held up one of them and Lynley saw that it featured clothing for infants and children. She said, "I have to say it's not subtle at all. Deborah's suggested a solution, Tommy. To the christening situation."

"Ah. That."

"Yes. Ah that. Shall we tell you, then? Or shall I wait till later? You *could* consider it a break from the grim realities of the case, if you'd like."

"By switching to the grim realities of our families, you mean?" Lynley asked. "Now that's diverting."

"Don't tease," Helen said. "Frankly, I'd christen our Jasper Felix in a dishcloth if I had my way. But since I don't—certainly not with two hundred and fifty years of Lynley history bearing down on me—I've wanted to come up with a compromise that will please everyone."

"Hardly likely to happen with your sister Iris marshalling the rest of the girls to her side in favour of Clyde family history," Lynley said.

"Well, yes of course, Iris is rather daunting when she sets her mind to something, isn't she? Which is what Deborah and I were discussing when Deborah made the most obvious suggestion in the world."

"Dare I ask?" Lynley looked at Deborah.

"New clothes," she said.

"But not just new," Helen added. "And not the usual gown, blanket, shawl, and whatever. The point is to get something that announces itself as a *new* tradition being established. By you and me. So naturally, that's going to take a bit more effort. No simple dash through Peter Jones."

"That'll be a crushing blow to you, darling," Lynley said.

"He's being sarcastic," Helen told the rest of them. And then to Lynley, "You do see it's the answer, don't you? Something new, something different, something that we can pass along—or at least claim we're going to pass along—to our children so that they can use it as well. And you know it's out there: what we're looking for. Deborah's actually volunteered to help me find it."

"Thank you," Lynley said to Deborah.

"D'you like the idea?" she asked him.

"I like anything with the promise of peace," he said. "Even if it's only momentary. Now if we can only resolve—"

His mobile chirped. As he reached for it in the breast pocket of his coat, Havers' mobile went off as well.

The rest of them watched as the information was passed from New Scotland Yard to Lynley and Havers simultaneously. It wasn't good news.

Queen's Wood. In North London.

Someone had found yet another body.

Chapter Sixteen

Helen went down to the car with them. She stopped Lynley, saying only, "Tommy darling, please listen to me," before he got inside. She cast a look towards Havers, who was already buckling herself into the passenger seat, and then said quietly to Lynley, "You'll solve it, Tommy. Please don't be so hard on yourself."

He let out a breath. How well she knew him. He said just as quietly, "How can I be otherwise? *Another* one, Helen."

"You must remember: You're only one man."

"I'm not. I'm more than thirty men and women, and we've done bloody sod all to stop him. *He's* one man."

"That's not true."

"Which part?"

"You know which part. You're doing this the only way possible."

"While boys—*young* boys, Helen, children barely into their teens—are dying out here in the street. No matter what they've done, no matter what their crimes, if they've even committed any, they don't deserve this. I feel as if we're all asleep at the wheel without knowing it."

"I know," she said.

Lynley could see the love and concern on his wife's face. He was momentarily comforted by it. Still, as he got into the car, he said bitterly, "Please God don't think so well of me, Helen."

"I can't think anything else. Go carefully please." And then to Havers, "Barbara, will you see that he has a meal sometime today? You know him. He's likely not to eat."

Havers nodded. "I'll find him a decent fry-up somewhere. Lots of grease. That'll set him up proper."

Helen smiled. She touched Lynley's cheek and then stepped away from the car. Lynley could see her through the rearview mirror, still standing in place as they drove away.

They made fairly good time by using Park Lane and the Edgware Road, heading northwest initially. They skirted Regent's Park on its north side, shooting towards Kentish Town. They were approaching Queen's Wood from Highgate station when the day's promised rain finally began to fall. Lynley cursed. Rain and a crime scene: a recipe for forensic nightmares.

Queen's Wood was an anomaly in London: a bona fide woodland that had once been a park like any other park but had long ago been left to grow, thrive, or fail as it might. The result was acres of unbridled nature in the middle of urban sprawl. Houses and the occasional block of flats backed onto it, but within ten feet of the fences and walls of their back gardens, the woods burst out of the earth in an eruption of beech trees, bracken, shrubs, and ferns, all struggling with each other to survive just as they would in the countryside.

There were no lawns. No park benches. No duck ponds. No swans floating serenely on a lake or river. There were, instead, ill-marked paths, overfull rubbish bins sprouting everything from take-away containers to nappies, the odd signpost pointing vaguely to a route to Highgate station, and a hillside down which the woodland dropped towards a bank of allotments to the west.

The easiest access to Queen's Wood lay beyond Muswell Hill Road. There, Wood Lane veered to the northeast, bisecting the southern portion of the park. The local police made a strong presence at the scene, having blocked off the end of the street with sawhorses where four police constables kitted out in rain gear held back the curious who were bobbing round beneath their umbrellas like a collection of mobile mushrooms.

Lynley showed his ID to one of the constables, who signaled to the others to move the roadblock long enough for the Bentley to pass. Before he did so, Lynley said to the man, "Don't let anyone other than SOCO inside. Anyone. I don't care who they are or what they tell you. No one passes who isn't police with proper police ID."

The constable nodded. The flash of camera lights told Lynley that the press was already hot on the story.

The first stretch of Wood Lane comprised housing: an amalgamation of nineteenth- and twentieth-century buildings that consisted of conversions, apartments, and single homes. Perhaps two hundred yards along, however, the buildings stopped abruptly and on either side of the street the woods spread out, completely unfenced, utterly accessible, looking in this weather both brooding and dangerous.

"Good choice," Havers muttered as she and Lynley alighted from the car. "He has a way, hasn't he? You've got to give him that." She turned up the collar of her donkey jacket against the rain. "Like a set from a thriller film, this is."

Lynley didn't disagree. In the summer, the area was probably a paradise, a natural oasis that afforded an escape from the prison of concrete, stone, brick, and tarmac that had long ago enveloped the rest of the native environment. But in the winter, it was a melancholy spot in which everything was in the process of decay. Layers of decomposing leaves covered the ground and sent forth the odour of peat. Beeches toppled by storms over the years lay in various stages of rot right where they had fallen, while branches severed from trees by the wind punctuated the slope, growing moss and lichen.

Activity centred on the south side of Wood Lane, where the park dipped down towards the allotments and then up again towards Priory Gardens, which was the street beyond them. A large square of translucent plastic suspended from poles formed a rough shelter for an area perhaps fifty yards to the west of the allotments. There, an enormous beech had been torn from the ground more recently than the others, for where its roots had been there was still a hollow that time, earth, wind, small creatures, ferns, and bracken had not yet filled in.

The killer had placed the body in this hollow. At the moment, a forensic pathologist was attending it while a SOCO team worked with silent efficiency in the immediate area. Beneath a tall beech some thirty yards away, an adolescent boy was watching the activity, one trainer-shod foot up on the trunk behind him to prop him up and a rucksack at his feet. A ginger-haired man in a trench coat stood with him, and he jerked his head at Lynley and Havers in a signal to come over and join him.

Ginger Hair introduced himself as DI Widdison from the Archway police station. His companion, he said, was Ruff.

"Ruff?" Lynley glanced at the boy, who glowered at him from beneath the hood of a sweatshirt that was covered by an outsize anorak.

"No surname at present." Widdison walked five paces away from the boy and took Lynley and Havers with him. "Found the body," he said. "He's a tough little bugger, but it's shaken him up. Sicked up on his way to get help."

"Where did he go for that?" Lynley asked.

Widdison tossed a nonexistent ball back in the direction of Wood Lane. "Walden Lodge. Eight or ten flats in there. He leaned on the bells till someone let him inside to use the phone."

"What was he doing here, anyway?" Havers asked.

"Tagging," Widdison told her. "Course, he doesn't want us to know that, but he was shaken up and gave us his tag by mistake, which is why he doesn't want to give us his real name now. We've been trying to catch him for some eight months. He's put 'Ruff' on every available surface round here: signs, dustbins, trees. Silver."

"Silver?"

"His tagging colour. Silver. He's got the cans of paint in that rucksack of his. Didn't have the presence of mind to chuck them before he phoned us."

Lynley said, "What's he given you?"

"Sod all. You can talk to him if you'd like, but I don't think he saw a thing. I don't think there was anything *to* see." He tilted his head in the direction of the intense circle of work surrounding the body. "I'll be over there when you're ready." He strode off.

Lynley and Havers returned to the boy, Havers digging into her bag. Lynley said to her, "I expect he's right, Barbara. I don't imagine taking notes—"

"Not going for the notes, sir," she replied, and she offered the boy her crumpled packet of Players when they joined him.

Ruff looked from the cigarettes to her, back to the cigarettes. He finally mumbled, "Cheers," and took one, which she lit for him with a plastic lighter.

"Anyone about when you found the body?" Lynley asked the boy once he'd had time to suck hungrily on the cigarette. His fingers were dirty, with grime crusted beneath the nails and the cuticles. His face was spotty but otherwise pale.

Ruff shook his head. "Someone in the 'lotments, is all," he said. "Old bloke turning the earth with a shovel like he's looking for something. I seen him when I come down through Priory Gardens. On the path. Tha's all, innit."

"Were you by yourself tagging?" Lynley asked.

The boy's eyes flashed. "Hey, I di'n't say—"

"Sorry. Did you come into the park by yourself?"

"Yeah."

"See anything unusual? A car or van that didn't look right, up on Wood Lane? Perhaps when you went to phone for help?"

"I di'n't see fuck," Ruff said. "Anyways, there's lots 'f cars parked up there all the time in daytime. Cos people come into town from outside and they take the tube rest of the way, don't they? Cos tube's just over there. Highgate station. Look, I tol' the dibble all this. They ack like *I* did summat. An' they won't let me go."

"That might have something to do with your not giving them your name," Havers told the boy. "If they want to talk to you again, they won't know where to find you."

Ruff looked at her suspiciously, a bloke trying to suss out a trick from among her words. She said reassuringly, "We're from Scotland Yard. We're not going to drag you to the nick for spraying your name about. We've bigger fish to fry."

He sniffed, wiped his nose on the back of his hand, and relented. He was called Elliott Augustus Greenberry, he finally admitted, eyeing them sharply, as if watching for incredulous expressions to cross their faces. "Double ell, double tee, double ee, double ar. An' don' tell me how fuckin stupid, it is. I know, don' I. Look, c'n I go now?"

"In a moment," Lynley said. "Did you recognise the boy?"

Ruff brushed a greasy lock of hair off his face, tucking it into the hood of the sweatshirt. "Wha,' him, you mean? The . . . it?"

"The dead boy, yes," Lynley said. "Do you know him?"

"I never," Ruff said. "Nobody I ever seen. Could be he's from round here somewheres, like up on the street over there behind the 'lotments, but I don't know him. Like I said, I don't know fuck. C'n I go?"

"Once we have your address," Havers said.

"Why?"

"Because we'll want you to sign a statement eventually, and we need to know where to find you, don't we."

"But I said I *di'n't*—"

"It's routine, Elliott," Lynley said.

The boy scowled but cooperated, and they released him. He shed the anorak, handed it over, and took off down the slope, west towards the path that would lead him up again to Priory Gardens.

"Anything from him?" DI Widdison said when Lynley and Havers joined him.

"Nothing," Lynley said, handing over the anorak, which Widdison passed to a sodden constable, who donned it gratefully. "A man digging in the allotments."

"That's what he told me as well," Widdison said. "We've got a door-to-door going on up there now."

"And along Wood Lane?"

"The same. I'm reckoning our best bet is Walden Lodge." Once again, Widdison indicated a modern and solid-looking block of flats that squatted at the edge of the woods. It was the last building on Wood Lane before the park, and on every side it presented balconies. Most of them were empty save for the occasional barbecue and garden furniture covered for the winter, but on four of them, watchers stood. One of them held up binoculars. "I can't think the killer brought the body down here without a torch," Widdison said. "Someone up there might have seen that."

"Unless he brought it just after dawn," Havers pointed out.

"Too risky," Widdison said. "Commuters park on the lane and use the underground to get into town from here. He'd have to know that and plan accordingly. But he'd still run the risk of being seen by someone who decided to make the journey earlier than usual."

"He does his homework, though," Havers pointed out. "We know that from where he's left the rest of them."

Widdison looked unconvinced. He took them under the shelter and over to the body. It lay on its side but was otherwise dumped carelessly in the hollow created by the unearthed roots of the fallen beech. Its head was tucked into its chest; its arms windmilled out like someone frozen in the act of giving a signal.

This boy, Lynley saw, seemed younger than the others, although not by much. He was white as well: blond and extremely fair skinned, small and not particularly developed. At first glance, Lynley concluded—with relief—that he wasn't one of theirs at all, that he and Havers needn't have come this distance across London on someone's whim. But when he squatted to have a better look, he saw the postmortem incision running down the boy's chest and disappearing into the fold of his waist, while on his forehead, a crude symbol had been drawn in blood, brother to the symbol found on Kimmo Thorne.

Lynley glanced at the forensic pathologist, who was speaking into the microphone of a handheld tape recorder. "I'd like a look at his hands," he said.

The man nodded. "I've done my bit. We're ready to bag him," and one of the team came forward to do so.

They'd start by bagging the hands in paper, preserving any trace evidence from the killer that might be under the boy's fingernails. From there they'd do the rest and when they moved the body, Lynley reckoned he'd get a better look at it.

That turned out to be the case. Rigor was present, but enough of the surface of the hands became visible when the body was lifted out of the hollow for Lynley to see that the palms were blackened from having been burnt. The navel was missing as well, chopped crudely out of the body.

"The Z that stands for Zorro," Havers murmured.

She was right. They were indeed the signatures of their killer, despite the differences that Lynley could see were present on the body: There were no restraint marks on the wrists and the ankles, and the strangulation had been manual this time, leaving ugly dark bruises round the boy's neck. There were other bruises as well, on the upper arms, extending down to the elbows, and along the spine, the thighs, and the waist. The largest bruise coloured the flesh from the temple down to the chin as well.

Unlike the others, Lynley concluded, this one boy had not gone gentle, which told him the killer had made his first error in his choice of victim. Lynley could only hope that the miscalculation left behind him a pile of evidence.

"He put up a fight," Lynley murmured.

"No stun gun this time?" Havers asked.

They checked the body for the signature of that weapon as well. Lynley said, "It doesn't appear so."

"What d'you reckon that means? Would it be out of juice? *Do* they run out of it? They must, no?"

"Perhaps," he said. "Or perhaps there wasn't the chance to use it. It looks like things might not have gone according to plan." He stood, nodded to those who stood waiting to bag the body, and returned to Widdison. "Anything in the area?" he asked.

"Two footprints beneath the boy's head," he said. "Protected from the rain. Could have been there earlier, but we're taking casts anyway. We're doing a perimeter search, but I reckon our real evidence is going to come from the body."

Lynley left the DI with the instruction to get every statement from every house on Wood Lane over to him at New Scotland Yard as soon as possible. "That block of flats especially," he said. "I agree with you. Someone has to have seen something. Or heard something. And have constables in place the rest of the day on either end of the street to grill commuters who come down from the underground station to fetch their cars."

"Don't expect to get much joy from that," Widdison warned.

"Anything goes for joy at this point," Lynley told him. He added the information about the van they were looking for. "Someone may have seen it," he said.

Then he and Havers set off up the slope. Back on Wood Lane, they could see that the house-to-house was well in progress. Uniformed police were knocking on doors; others were standing in the shelter of porches, talking to inhabitants. Otherwise, no one else was on the pavement or in any front garden. The persistent rain was keeping everyone inside.

That was not the case at the barricade, however. More gawkers had gathered. Lynley waited while the sawhorse was moved once more, and he was thinking about what they'd seen in Queen's Wood when Havers muttered, "Bloody *hell*, sir. He did it again," and roused him from his thoughts.

He quickly saw what she was talking about. Just to the other side of the barricade, Hamish Robson gestured to them. At least, Lynley thought grimly, they'd managed to thwart AC Hillier in this: The constable standing watch had followed Lynley's orders to the letter. Robson had no police identification; he would not be allowed beyond the barrier no matter what Sir David Hillier had told him to do.

Lynley lowered the window, and Robson worked his way over to the car. He said, "The constable here wouldn't—"

"Those were my orders. You can't go onto this crime scene, Dr. Robson. You shouldn't have been allowed onto the last one."

"But the assistant commissioner—"

"I've no doubt he rang you, but it's just not on. I know you mean well. I also know you're caught in the middle, one of us a rock and the other a hard place. I apologise for that. For that and the inconvenience to you, coming all this way. But as it is—"

"Superintendent." Robson shivered, shoved his hands into his pockets. He'd obviously come in a hurry, without umbrella or raincoat. Great patches of damp extended across his shoulders, his spectacles were spotted with rain, and what little hair he had was sagging wetly round his face and into his forehead. "Let me help," he said urgently. "It's completely pointless to send me back to Dagenham when I'm already here, available to you."

"That's something you'll have to take up with AC Hillier," Lynley said, "the pointlessness of it."

"It doesn't have to be that way." Robson glanced round and nodded a few yards down the road. "Will you pull over there for a moment so we can talk about this?"

"I have nothing more to say."

"Understood. But I have, you see, and I'd very much like you to hear me out." He stepped back from the car in what seemed like a gesture of goodwill, one that left the decision up to Lynley: Drive off or cooperate. Robson said, "A few words. That's all," and he gave a wry smile. "I wouldn't mind getting out of this rain. If you'll let me get in the car, I promise to be gone the moment I've said my bit and heard your response to it."

"And if I have no response?"

"You're not that sort. So may I . . . ?"

Lynley considered, then nodded sharply once. Havers said, "Sir," in that uncharacteristically beseeching manner she used when she disapproved of a decision he'd taken. He said, "We may as well, Barbara. He's here. He may have something we can use."

"Crikey, are you—" She bit off her words as the back door opened and Hamish Robson sank into the car.

Lynley drove a short distance away, beyond the crowd. He pulled to the kerb, the engine still running and the wipers still moving rhythmically across the windscreen.

Robson didn't fail to take notice of this. He said, "I'll be quick, then."I'd expect this crime scene to be different to the others. Not in all ways but in some. Am I right?"

"Why?" Lynley asked. "Were you anticipating as much?"

"Is it different?" Robson persisted. "Because, you see, with profiling, we often see—"

"With respect, Dr. Robson, your profiling has got us nowhere so far. Nowhere important, and not one step closer to the killer."

"Are you sure?" Before Lynley could answer, Robson leaned forward in his seat. He went on, his voice kind. "I can't imagine having your job. It must be more draining than anyone can picture. But you must *not* blame yourself for this death, Superintendent. You're doing your best. No one could ask more of you than that, so you mustn't ask more than your best of yourself. That's the road to madness."

"Professional opinion?" Lynley asked sardonically.

Robson took the two words at their face value and ignored Lynley's tone, saying, "Completely. So let me give you a fuller opinion. Let me see the crime scene. Let me give you some guidance that you'll be able to use. Superintendent, in a psychopath the compulsion to kill only grows stronger. With each crime, it escalates; it does not subside. But each time, to achieve pleasure it takes more and more of *whatever* the killer's been doing during the commission of the crime to fulfill himself. So understand me. There's profound danger here. To young men, to boys, to little children, to . . . we don't *know* for sure, so for God's sake let me help you."

Lynley had been watching Robson through his rear-view mirror, Havers from her seat where she'd turned to observe the psychologist as he spoke. The man looked as if he'd shaken himself with the passion of his words, and he turned from them to look out of the window when he'd finally finished speaking.

Lynley said, "What's your own background, Dr. Robson?"

Robson was gazing to his left, in the direction of a yew hedge dripping small pools of water onto the pavement. He said, "Sorry. I can't abide what's done to children in the name of love. Or play. Or discipline. Or whatever." Then he was silent. Only the soft whirr of the wipers brushing off the windscreen and the purr of the Bentley's engine broke the quiet. He finally said, "For me it was my maternal uncle. Wrestling, he called it. But it wasn't. That sort of thing rarely is between an adult and a male child when it's the adult's idea. But the child, of course, never understands."

"I'm sorry," Lynley said. He too turned in his seat then and looked at the psychologist directly. "But perhaps that makes you less objective than—"

"No. Believe me, it makes me someone who knows exactly what to look for," Robson said. "So let me see the crime scene. I'll tell you what I think and what I know. The decision to act is up to you."

"I'm afraid that's not possible."

"God *damn* it—"

"The body's been moved, Dr. Robson," Lynley cut in. "The only crime scene for you to look at is a fallen beech tree and a hollow beneath it."

Robson sank back into the seat. He gazed out at the street, where an ambulance had come along Wood Lane up to the barrier erected by the police. It drove without lights whirling or siren blaring. One of the constables went out into the street and halted traffic—already slowed to a curious crawl anyway—long enough for the ambulance to pass. It did so unhurriedly; there was no urgency to get its burden to hospital quickly. This gave the photojournalists time to record the moment for the newspapers. Perhaps it was the sight of them that prompted Robson to ask his next question.

"Will you let me look at the photos, then?"

Lynley considered this. The police photographer had completed his work by the time he and Havers had arrived on the scene, and a videographer had been recording the body, the site, and the ensuing activity round the body and the site when they'd descended the slope. The incident caravan was not that far from where they were sitting at this moment. Doubtless, in that caravan there would be a visual record of the crime scene already suitable for Robson's viewing.

It wouldn't hurt at this point to let the profiler look at what they had: video footage, digital pictures, or whatever else the murder squad had so far produced. It would also act as a compromise between what Hillier wanted and what Lynley was determined not to give him.

On the other hand, the psychologist wasn't wanted here. No one at the scene had requested him and it was only down to Hillier's interference and his desire for something to feed to the media that had brought Robson here in the first place. If Lynley gave in to Hillier now, the AC would probably bring in a psychic next. And after that, what? Someone to read tea leaves? Or the entrails of a lamb? It couldn't be allowed to happen. Someone had to gain control over the lurching, runaway wagon of this entire situation, and this was the moment to do it.

Lynley said, "I'm sorry, Dr. Robson."

Robson looked deflated. He said, "Your last word on the subject?"

"Yes."

"Are you certain that's wise?"

"I'm not certain of anything."

"That's really the hell of it, isn't it?"

Robson got out of the car, then. He headed back towards the barricade. He passed DI Widdison on his route, but he made no attempt to speak to him. For his part, Widdison saw Lynley's car and raised a hand as if to stop him from leaving the scene. Lynley lowered the window as the DI hurried over.

"We've had a call from the Hornsey Road station," Widdison said when he reached the car. "A boy's gone missing, reported by his parents last night. He fits the general description of our victim."

"We'll take it," Lynley said as Havers emptied her shoulder bag on the floor to find her notebook and take down the address.

IT WAS IN Upper Holloway, on a small housing estate just off Junction Road. There, round the corner from William Beckett Funeral Directors and Yildiz Supermarket, they found a serpentine stretch of tarmac splendidly called Bovingdon Close. It was a pedestrian precinct, so they left the Bentley on Hargrave Road where a bearded vagrant with a guitar in one hand and a wet sleeping bag dragging on the pavement behind him offered to keep an eye on the car for the price of a pint. Or a bottle of wine, if they felt so inclined and he did a good job of keeping the local riffraff away from "s'ch a fine motor as yairs is, master." He wore a large green rubbish bag as a mackintosh in the rain, and he sounded like a character from a costume drama, someone who'd spent far too much of his youth tuned in to BBC1. "They's ferrinners plenty round here," he informed them. "You can't leave nothin' lying 'bout what they don't put their mitts on it, sir." He appeared to search vaguely in the direction of his head for something to tug respectfully as he concluded. When he spoke, the air became heavy with the scent of teeth in need of extraction.

Lynley told the man he was welcome to keep his eyes glued to the car. The vagrant hunkered down on the nearest stairs to one of the terrace houses, and—rain or not—he began to pluck at the three strings remaining on his guitar. Sourly, he eyed a pack of young black kids wearing rucksacks on their backs, trotting along the pavement across the street.

Lynley and Havers left the man to it and set off into Bovingdon Close. They accessed this by means of a tunnel-like opening in the cinnamon-coloured brick buildings that comprised the housing estate itself. They were looking for number 30, and they found it not far from the estate's sole recreational area: a triangular green with dormant rosebushes languishing in each of the three corners and a small bench set against one side. Other than four saplings struggling for life in the green's patch of lawn, there were no trees in Bovingdon Close, and the houses that didn't face the tiny recreational area faced each other across a width of tarmac that didn't measure more than fifteen feet. In the summer when the windows were open, everyone would doubtless be into everyone else's business.

Each of the houses had been given a sandwich-size plot of earth in front of its door that the more optimistic inhabitants were treating as their gardens. In front of number 30, the patch of earth in question was a rough triangle of dying grass, and a child's bike lay on its side upon it, next to a green plastic garden chair. Near this a tattered shuttlecock looked as if a dog had been chewing on it. The accompanying racquets leaned against the wall by the front door, most of their strings broken.

When Lynley rang the bell, a man in miniature opened the door. He was not even eye to eye with Havers, top heavy with the look of someone who weight trained to compensate for his lack of height. He was red eyed and unshaven, and he glanced from them to the tarmac beyond them as if expecting someone else.

He said, "Cops," like the answer to a question no one had asked.

"That's who we are." Lynley introduced himself and Havers and waited for the man—they knew only that his name was Benton—to ask them in. Beyond him, Lynley could see the doorway to a darkened sitting room and the shapes of people seated inside. A child's querulous voice asked why couldn't they open the curtains, why couldn't he play, and a woman shushed him.

Benton said harshly over his shoulder in that direction, "You mind what I told you." Then he gave his attention back to Lynley. "Where's the uniform?"

Lynley said they weren't part of the uniformed patrol but rather they worked in a different department and were from New Scotland Yard. "May we come in?" he asked. "It's your son that's gone missing?"

"Didn't come home last night." Benton's lips were dry and flaky. He licked them.

He stepped back from the door and led them into the sitting room, at the end of a corridor of no more than fifteen feet. In the semidarkness there, five people were arrayed on chairs, the sofa, a footstool, and the floor. Two young boys, two adolescent girls, and a woman. She was Bev Benton, she said. Her husband was Max. And these were four of their children. Sherry and Brenda the girls, Rory and Stevie the boys. Their Davey was the one gone missing.

All of them, Lynley noted, were uncommonly small. To one degree or another, all of them also resembled the body in Queen's Wood.

The boys were meant to be at school, Bev told them; the girls were meant to be at work in the food stalls at Camden Lock Market. Max and Bev themselves were meant to be serving the public from their fish van in Chapel Street. But no one was going anywhere from this house till they had word about Davey.

"Something's happened to him," Max Benton said. "They would've sent regular coppers otherwise. We're none of us so thick 's we don't know that much. What is it, then?"

"It might be best for us to speak without the children here," Lynley said.

Bev Benton keened two words, "Oh God."

Max barked at her, "We'll have none of that," and then said to Lynley, "They stay. If it's an object lesson they're about to have, then I by God want them having it."

"Mr. Benton—"

"There'll be no Mr. Benton about it," Benton said. "Give us the brief."

Lynley wasn't about to go at it that way. He said, "Have you a photograph of your son?"

Bev Benton spoke. "Sherry, pet, fetch Davey's school picture from the fridge for the officer."

One of the two girls—blonde like the body in the woods, and identically fair skinned, delicate featured, and small boned—left them quickly and just as quickly returned. She handed over the picture to Lynley, her eyes cast down to his shoes, and then returned to the footstool, which she shared with her sister. Lynley dropped his gaze to the picture. A cheeky-looking boy grinned up at him, his fair hair darkened by the gel that formed it into little spikes. He had a sprinkling of freckles across his nose and headphones slung round his neck, above his school-uniform pullover.

"Slipped them on at the last minute, he did," Bev Benton commented, as if in explanation of the headphones, which were hardly part of his regulation school attire. "Likes his music, Davey. Rap music. Mostly those blacks from America with the p'culiar names."

The boy in the photo resembled the body they had, but only an identification made by one of the parents could confirm this. Still, no matter what sort of lesson Max Benton wanted the rest of his children to have, Lynley had no intention of offering it to them. He said, "When was the last time you saw Davey?"

"Yesterday morning." Max was the one to answer. "He got off to school like always."

"Didn't come home when he was due, though," Bev Benton said. "He was meant to mind Rory and Stevie here."

"I went to tae kwon do to see was he there," Max added. "Last time he bunked off doing something he was meant to do, that's where he claimed he went instead."

"Claimed?" Barbara Havers asked. She'd remained in the doorway, and she was writing in her new spiral notebook.

"He was meant to come to our fish stall in Chapel Market one day," Bev explained. "To help his dad. When he didn't come, he said he'd gone to tae kwon do and lost the time. There's a bloke he's had some trouble with—"

"Andy Crickleworth," Max put in. "Little sod's trying to sort Davey out and set himself up as head of the crew Davey runs with."

"Not a gang," Bev added hastily. "Just boys. They been mates for ages."

"But this Crickleworth's new. When Davey said he wanted to see the tae kwon do, I thought . . ." Max had been standing, but now he went to the sofa to join his wife. He dropped down onto it and scrubbed his hands across his face. The smaller children reacted to this evidence of their dad's upset by huddling together at the knees of one of their sisters, who put her hands on their shoulders as if to comfort them. Max brought himself under control, saying, "Tae kwon do people? They never heard of Davey. Never seen him. Didn't know him. So I phoned the school to see had he been going truant without them telling us, only he hadn't, see. Today's the only day he didn't show up. All term."

"Has he been in trouble with the police before?" Havers asked. "Ever face the magistrates? Ever been assigned to a young people's group for straightening him out?"

"Our Davey doesn't need straightening out," Bev Benton said. "He never even misses school. And he's that good in his classes, he is."

"Doesn't like anyone to know that, Mum," Sherry murmured, as if believing her mother had betrayed a confidence in her final remark.

Max added to this. "He was meant to be tough. Tough louts don't care much for school."

"So Davey acted the part," Bev explained. "But he wasn't like that."

"And he's never been in trouble with the police? Never had a social worker?"

"Why d'you keep *asking* that? Max . . ." Bev turned to her husband as if for explanation.

Lynley intervened. "Have you phoned his friends? The boys you mentioned?"

"No one's seen him," Bev replied.

"And this other boy? This Andy Crickleworth?"

No one in the family had met him. No one in the family even knew where to find him.

"Any chance Davey might've made him up?" Havers asked, looking up from her notebook. "Covering for something else he was up to?"

There was a little silence at this. Either no one knew or no one wanted to answer. Lynley waited, curious, and saw Bev Benton glance at her husband. She seemed reluctant to say anything else. Lynley let the silence continue till Max Benton broke it.

"Bullies di'n't ever go after him, did they. They knew our Davey'd sort them if they picked a fight. He was small and . . ." Benton seemed to realise he'd slipped into the past tense and he stopped himself, looking shaken. His daughter Sherry supplied the conclusion to his thought.

"Pretty," she said. "Our Davey's dead pretty."

They all were that, Lynley thought: pretty and small, very nearly doll-like. The boys especially would have to do something to compensate for that. Like fight back furiously if someone tried to harm them. Like end up getting bruised and banged about before they were throttled, sliced, and discarded in the woods.

Lynley said, "May we see your son's bedroom, Mr. Benton?"

"Why?"

"There might be some indication where he's gone off to," Havers said. "Sometimes kids don't tell their parents everything. If there's a mate you don't know about . . ."

Max exchanged a look with his wife. It was the first time he'd seemed anything but master of the family.

Bev nodded encouragingly. Max told Lynley and Havers to come with him, then.

He took them upstairs where three bedrooms opened onto a simple square landing. In one of the rooms, two sets of bunk beds stood against opposite walls, a chest of drawers between them. Over one of the bed sets a shelf high on the wall held a collection of CDs and a small, neat stack of baseball caps. Beneath the upper bed, the lower one had been removed altogether and in its place a private lair had been fashioned. Part of it was given over to clothes: baggy trousers, trainers, jumpers, and T-shirts featuring graphics of the American rap artists Bev Benton had spoken about. Part of it contained a set of cheap metal bookshelves that, upon inspection, held all fantasy novels. At the far end of the lair stood a small chest of drawers. All of this, Max Benton told them, was Davey's.

As Lynley and Havers ducked within, each of them making for a different part, Max said in a voice no longer authoritarian but instead desperate and very much afraid, "You got to tell me. Wouldn't be here, would you, unless there was something more. Course I see why you di'n't want to say in front of the wife and the little ones. But now . . . They would've sent uniforms, not you lot."

Lynley had slid his hands into the pockets of the first pair of trousers as Max Benton was speaking. He stopped, though, and came back out of the lair as Havers continued searching within it. He said, "You're right. We have a body, Mr. Benton. It was found in Queen's Wood, not far from Highgate station."

Max Benton sagged a little, but he waved Lynley off when Lynley would have taken his arm and led him to the lower of the two beds across the room. He said, "Davey?"

"We're going to ask you to look at the body. It's the only way to be absolutely sure. I'm terribly sorry."

He said again, "Davey?"

"Mr. Benton, it may not be Davey."

"But you think . . . Else why would you be troubling to come up here wanting to see his things?"

"Sir . . ." From within the lair, Havers spoke. Lynley turned to see that she was holding out something for his inspection. It was a set of handcuffs, but not ordinary ones. They were not metal but formed from heavy plastic and in the dim light beneath the upper mattress, the handcuffs glowed. Havers said, "Could be—" But she was cut off by Max Benton, who said harshly, "I told him to *return* them things. He said he did. Swore to me because he di'n't want me taking him along to make sure he handed them over."

"To who?" Havers asked.

"He got 'em off a stall in the Stables Market, di'n't he. Over by Camden Lock. *He* said they were a present from a vendor there, but what vendor hands out goods to kids hanging about, you tell me. So I reckoned he nicked them and I told him to take them back straightaway. Little bugger must've hid them instead."

"What stall in the market? Did he tell you?" Lynley asked.

"Magic stall, he said. I don't know the bloke's name. He never said and I di'n't ask. I just told him to take the handcuffs back and to bloody well stop pinching clobber not belonging to him."

"Magic stall?" Barbara Havers asked. "Are you sure about that, Mr. Benton?"

"That's what he said."

Havers came out of the lair then. She said to Lynley, "Could I have a word, sir?" She didn't wait for him to reply. She left the bedroom and went onto the landing.

She said to Lynley in a quiet, terse voice, "Bloody

hell. I may've been wrong. Tunnel vision. Whatever you want to call it."

"Havers, this isn't the moment for sharing your epiphanies," Lynley said.

"Wait. I've been thinking all along of Colossus. But I never thought of magic. What kid fifteen and under doesn't like magic? No. Sir. *Wait*—" as Lynley was about to leave her to her stream-of-consciousness monologue. "Wendy's Cloud is in Camden Lock Market, right next door to the Stables. Now, she's hopped up on something much of the time and she can't say what she's selling or when she's selling it. But she's carried ambergris oil in the past—we know that—and when I finished talking to her the other day and was hiking back to my car, I saw this bloke at the Stables . . ."

"What bloke?"

"He was unloading boxes. He was taking them into a magic stall or something *like* a magic stall and he was a magician. That's what he said. There can't be more than one of them at the Stables, can there? And listen to this, sir. He was driving a van."

"Red?"

"Purple. But in the light of a streetlamp at three A.M. or whenever . . . You're at your window. You catch a glimpse. You don't even think about it because, after all, this is a huge city we're talking about and why would you think you were meant to notice everything about it if a van's on the street at three A.M.?"

"Lettering on the van?"

"Yeah. It was a magician advert."

"That's not what we're looking for, Havers. That's not what we saw on the CCTV tape from St. George's Gardens."

"But we don't *know* what that van was, the St. George's Gardens one. It could have been the warden opening up. Or someone there to make a repair."

"At three in the morning? Carrying a suspicious-looking tool that very well could have cut the lock from the gate? Havers—"

"Just hang on. Please. For all we know that could have a logical explanation that'll be sorted out in another hour. Bloody hell, the bloke could've had legitimate business in the garden and what you thought was a tool was something to do with that business. He could have been doing *anything*: making a repair, taking a piss, making an early newspaper delivery, testing out a new sort of milk float. Anything. My point is . . ."

"All right. Yes. I see."

She went on as if Lynley were still not onboard. "And I *talked* to this bloke. This magician. I saw him. So if this body in Queen's Wood is Davey and if this bloke I saw is the one who had the handcuffs nicked by Davey . . ." She let him finish her thought.

Which he did, in short order. "He damn well better have an alibi for last night. Yes, all right, Barbara. I see how you're putting it together."

"And it's him, sir. Davey. You know it."

"The body? Yes. I think it is. But we can't go further without the formality. I'll deal with that."

"And sh'll I . . . ?"

"Get on to the Stables Market. Make the connection between Davey and this magician if you can. Once you do that, get him in for questioning."

"I think we've got our first real break, sir."

"I hope you're right," Lynley replied.

Chapter Seventeen

Barbara Havers took the glow-in-the-dark handcuffs with her to the Stables Market, which was, as suggested by its name, an enormous old artillery stable of grimy brick. It ran along a section of Chalk Farm Road, but she entered by means of Camden Lock Place, and began asking the whereabouts of the magic stall at the very first shop. This was an establishment selling furniture and fabrics from the subcontinent. The air was acrid with the scent of patchouli, and sitar music blared forth from speakers insufficient to handle the volume.

The shop assistant didn't know anything about a magic stall, but she reckoned Tara Powell over at body piercing could direct Barbara wherever she needed to go. "Does fine work, Tara," the shop assistant said. She herself had a silver stud beneath her lower lip.

Barbara found the body-piercing stall without any trouble. Tara Powell turned out to be a cheerful twenty-something girl with appalling teeth. Her bow to her employment consisted of half a dozen holes from the lobe to the top of her right ear as well as a thin gold ring through her left eyebrow. She was in the middle of driving a needle through the septum of an adolescent girl's nose while her boyfriend stood by with the chosen piece of jewellery in his palm. It was a thick ring not unlike those used on cows. That, Barbara thought, was going to be attractive.

Tara was nattering on about—of all things—the Prime Minister's hairline. She apparently had done some considerable research into the subject of the burden of power and responsibility and its effect on hair loss. She could not, however, apparently apply much of her theory to Lady Thatcher.

It turned out that Tara did indeed know where the magic stall was. She said that Barbara would find it in the alley. When Barbara asked what alley, she said *the* alley and rolled her eyes in such a way as to communicate that the information ought to be sufficient. Then she turned to her customer and said, "This'll pinch a bit, luv," and with one deft thrust she drove the needle through the girl's nose.

Barbara beat a hasty retreat as the girl screamed, slumped over, and Tara cried, "Smelling salts! Quick!" to someone. It was, Barbara thought, an edgy kind of employment.

Although Barbara lived not far from Camden High Street and its markets and although she'd been in the Stables many times, she hadn't known that the narrow passage in which she finally found the magic stall had a name. It wasn't so much an actual alley as it was a gap, lined on one side by the brick wall of one of the old artillery buildings and on the other by a long row of holdings from which vendors sold their wares: everything from books to boots.

The place was dimly lit by bare bulbs dangling from a cord that ran the length of the alley. They broke into a gloom that was accentuated by the sooty stable wall and the darkly stained stalls opposite. Not all of them were open, this being a weekday. But the magic stall was. As Barbara approached it, she could see the same oddly dressed man she'd earlier seen unloading his van in the street. He was doing a rope trick to entertain a group of enthralled young boys who, instead of being at school, were gathered round his stall. They were just about the size—and the age—of the dead boy in Queen's Wood, Barbara noted.

She stood at the side of the group, watching the magician interact with the boys at the same time as she studied his stall. It wasn't large—about the size of a wardrobe—but he'd managed to cram it with magic tricks, with practical jokes along the lines of artificial vomit suitable for laying on mum's new carpet, with videos of magic acts, books on illusions, and old magazines. Among the items for sale were handcuffs identical to those Barbara had in her pocket. They were part of a sideline in saucy bedroom toys that were on offer as well.

Barbara worked her way round to the back of the group, to have a better look at the magician. He was dressed as he'd been when she'd last seen him, and she noted that his red stocking cap not only covered his head completely but also came down over his eyebrows as well. With the addition of his dark glasses to complete the ensemble, the magician had successfully obscured the upper half of his face and head. Under normal circumstances, Barbara wouldn't have thought too much about this detail. Under the conditions of a murder inquiry, however, a quirky costume going along with a pair of handcuffs, a dead boy, and a van made the bloke doubly suspicious. Barbara wanted to get him alone.

She eased her way round to the front of the group and began to look over the magic tricks for sale. The goods here seemed suitable for kids: magic colouring books, linking rings, flying coins and the like. This put Barbara in mind of Hadiyyah and Hadiyyah's solemn little face and sorrowful wave behind the French windows whenever Barbara passed the ground-floor flat in

Eton Villas. And that put Barbara in mind of Azhar, of the unpleasant words they'd exchanged the last time they'd seen each other. They'd been scrupulously avoiding each other ever since. A peace offering was called for, but Barbara wasn't sure which one of them ought to be offering it.

She picked up the pencil-penetration kit and read the scanty directions (borrow a five-pound note from someone in your audience, push the pencil into its centre, rip it sideways and ta-duh! the five-pound note remained intact). She was reflecting on its suitability as a peace offering when she heard the magician say, "That'll be all for now. Run along, you lot. I've work to do." A few of the children protested, asking for just one more trick, but he was adamant. "Next time," he said and shooed them off. He wore, Barbara saw, fingerless gloves on his pasty hands.

The kids departed—although not before Mr. Magic separated one boy from the flying coin trick he'd attempted to pinch as he drifted away—and then the magician was all Barbara's. Was there something he could help her with? he asked.

Barbara purchased the pencil-penetration kit, an investment of less than two quid in the cause of neighbourly peace. She said, "You're good with the kids. You must have them hanging round all the time."

"Magic," he said with a shrug as he put the kit neatly into a small plastic bag. "Magic and boys. They seem to go together."

"Just like Marmite and toast."

His lips curved in an I-can't-help-my-own-popularity smile.

Barbara said, "They must get on your nerves after a time, all these little blokes hanging about and wanting you to perform for them."

"It's good for business," he said. "They go home, talk to Mum and Dad about what they've seen, and when a birthday party comes up, they know what they want for the entertainment."

"A magic show?"

He swept off the stocking cap and bowed. "Mr. Magic, at their service. Or yours. Birthday parties, bar mitzvahs, the odd christening, New Year's Eve. Et cetera."

Barbara blinked, then made a quick recovery as the man drew his cap back over his head. He was using it, she saw, for the same reason he was probably also using the dark glasses and the gloves. He appeared to be an albino. Dressed as he was at the moment, he would garner the occasional look in the street. Dressed otherwise—with the colourless hair revealed and the eyes unshaded—he'd have been gawped at, not to mention tormented by the very kids who admired him now.

He handed his business card over to Barbara. She did him the same courtesy and watched what she could see of his face to note a reaction. He said, "Police?"

"New Scotland Yard. At your service."

"Ah. Well. They can't be wanting a magic show there."

Good recovery, Barbara thought. She brought the glow-in-the-dark handcuffs out of her shoulder bag. They were encased in a plastic evidence bag, on their way to be fingerprinted.

"These came from your stall, I understand," Barbara said. "Recognise them?"

"I sell something like," the magician replied. "You can see for yourself. I keep them over with the saucy items."

"A kid called Davey Benton had these off you, according to his dad when we called at his house. Pinched them, he did. He was meant to bring them back and turn them over to you."

The dark glasses prevented Barbara from reading any reaction in the magician's eyes. She was reliant on the tone of his voice, which was perfectly even as he said pleasantly, "Obviously, he dropped the ball on that."

"Which part?" Barbara asked. "Pinching them or returning them?"

"Since you found them in his things, I expect we can say he dropped the ball on returning them."

"Yeah. I expect," Barbara said. "Only I didn't quite say I'd found them among his things, did I?"

The magician turned his back and coiled the rope from the rope trick into a neat and snakelike mound. Barbara smiled inwardly when he did this. Gotcha, she thought. In her experience, every smooth customer had a rough edge somewhere.

Mr. Magic gave his attention back to her. "The handcuffs may have come from me. You can see I sell them. But I'm hardly the only person in London with saucy items for purchase or for pinching."

"No. But I expect you're the closest to Davey's home, aren't you?"

"I'd hardly know. Has something happened to this boy?"

"Something's happened to him, yes," Barbara said. "He's pretty much dead."

"Dead?"

"Dead. But let's not play echoes. When we went through his things and came up with these and his dad told us where they'd come from because Davey told *him* . . . You can see how I ended up wanting to know if they look familiar to you, Mr. . . . What's your real name? I know it's not Magic. We've met before, by the way."

He didn't ask where. His name was Minshall, he said. It was Barry Minshall. And yes, all right, it seemed that the handcuffs had come from his stall if the boy had claimed as much to his dad. But the fact was that kids pinched things, didn't they. Kids *always* pinched things. It was part of being kids. They pushed the envelope. Nothing ventured, nothing gained, and since all the cops seemed to do round here was give them a talking to if they were caught misbehaving, what did they stand to lose by having a go, eh? Oh, he tried to keep an eye out for that sort of thing, but sometimes he missed a set of sticky fingers adhering to an article like glow-in-the-dark handcuffs. Sometimes, he said, a kid was just too bloody good, a regular Artful Dodger.

Barbara listened to all this, nodding and doing her best to look thoughtful and open-minded. But she could hear the slow building of anxiety in Barry Minshall's voice, and it acted on her the way the scent of fox acts on a pack of hounds. This bloke was lying through his teeth and out of his nostrils, she thought. He was the sort who saw himself cool as a lettuce leaf, which was just how she liked it since lettuce was always so easy to wilt.

She said, "You've got a van somewhere. I saw you unloading it last time I was here. I'd like to have a look at it, if you don't mind."

"Why?"

"Let's call it curiosity."

"I don't think I'm obliged to show it to you. Not without a warrant, at least."

"Right you are. But if we go that route—which, of course, is your right—I'm going to wonder like hell if you've got something in that van that you don't want me finding."

"I'll be wanting to ring my solicitor about this."

"Ring away, Barry. Here. I've got a mobile you can use." She thrust half of her arm into her capacious bag and dug round enthusiastically.

Minshall said, "I have my own. Look. I can't leave the stall. You'll need to come back later."

"No need for you to leave the stall at all, mate," Barbara said. "Hand over the keys to the van, and I'll have a browse through it on my own."

He thought this one over behind his dark glasses and beneath the Dickensian stocking cap. Barbara could imagine the wheels turning furiously in his head as he tried to decide which route to take. Demanding both a solicitor and a search warrant was the sensible and the wise thing to do. But people were seldom either sensible or wise when they had something to hide and the cops turned up unexpectedly asking questions and wanting answers on the spot. That was when people made the foolish decision to bluff their way through a few difficult moments, mistakenly assuming that Inspector Plod had come calling and concluding they were more than a match for him. They thought that if they asked for their solicitor immediately—doing what those American police dramas always called "lawyering up"—they'd be marking themselves forever with a scarlet *G* for Guilty across their chests. Truth was, they'd be marking themselves with the scarlet *I* for Intelligent. But they seldom thought that way under pressure, which was what Barbara was depending upon now.

Minshall reached his decision. He said, "This is a waste of your time. Worse, it's a waste of mine. But if you believe it's necessary for whatever reason . . ."

Barbara smiled. "Trust me. I'm one of the lot who serve, protect, and do no ill."

"Fine. All right. But you'll have to wait while I close up the stall, and then I'll take you to the van. It'll take a few minutes, I'm afraid. I hope you have the time."

"Mr. Minshall," Barbara said, "you are one lucky sod. Because time is exactly what I have today."

WHEN LYNLEY arrived back at New Scotland Yard, he discovered that the media were already gathering, setting up shop in the little park that covered the corner where Victoria Street met Broadway. There, two distinct television crews—recognisable by the logos on their vans and on their equipment—were in the process of constructing what appeared to be a broadcasting point while nearby beneath the dripping trees in the park, several reporters milled about, distinguishable from the crew by their manner of dress.

Lynley observed this with a hollow heart. It was, he knew, too much to hope for that the media were here for any reason other than the killing of a sixth adolescent boy. A sixth killing warranted their immediate attention. It also made them unlikely to go along with how the DPA wanted them to cover the situation.

He negotiated the confusion in the street and pulled into the entrance that would take him down to the carpark. There, however, the officer in the kiosk didn't employ his usual one finger acknowledgement and lift the barrier for him. Instead, he sauntered out to the Bentley and waited while Lynley lowered the window.

He bent to the interior. "Message for you," he said. "You're to go straight to the assistant commissioner's office. Do not pass go and all the trappings, if you know what I mean. AC made the call personally. Making sure there was no ifs, ands, and buts about it. I'm to phone to tell him you've arrived, 's well. Question is, how much time d'you want? We can make it anything, only he doesn't want you stopping to talk to your team on the way."

Lynley muttered, "Christ." Then after a moment's thought, "Wait ten minutes."

"Right you are." The officer stepped back and admitted Lynley to the carpark. In the subdued light and the silence, Lynley used the ten minutes to close his eyes, remaining in the Bentley with his head pressed against the headrest.

It was never easy, he thought. You believed it might become so eventually if you were exposed to enough of horror and its aftermath. But just at the point where you thought you had mastered insentience, something occurred to remind you that you were still fully human, no matter what you'd previously thought.

That had been the case while standing alongside Max Benton as he'd identified the body of his oldest son. No Polaroid picture would do for him, no viewing from behind a glass partition, a safe distance from which there would always be certain aspects of the boy's death that he would not have to know or at least not have to see firsthand. Instead he'd insisted upon seeing it all, refusing to say whether it was his missing boy until he'd been a witness to everything that marked the way Davey had gone to his death.

Then what he'd said was, "He fought him, then. Like he was meant to. Like I taught him. He fought the bastard."

"This is your son, Mr. Benton?" Lynley asked, the formality not only an automatic question but also a way to avoid the onslaught of restrained emotion—that could never actually be adequately restrained—that he felt trying to burst from the other man.

"Said from the first that the world can't be trusted," Benton replied. "Said from the first it's a brutal place. But he never wanted to listen like I tried to get him to listen, did he. And this is what happens. *This.* I want 'em here, the rest 'f 'em. I want 'em to *see.*" His voice broke then and he went on in anguish. "Bloke tries his best to teach his kids what's what out there. Bloke lives to make them understand that they got to take a care, be on their guard, know what could happen . . . Tha's what I told him, our Davey. And no coddling from Bev either 'cause they're meant to be tough, the lot of them. You look like that and you got to be tough, you got to be aware, you got to know . . . You got to understand . . . *Listen* to me, you little sod. Why don't you see it's for your own bloody good . . . ?" He wept then, collapsing against a wall and then hitting that wall with his fist, saying, "Damn you to *hell,*" with his voice catching as his sobbing trapped the words in his throat.

There was no comfort, and Lynley honoured Max Benton's grief by not offering him any. He just said, "I'm so sorry, Mr. Benton," before he guided the broken man away.

Now, in the carpark, Lynley took the time he needed to recover, knowing he had been touched more deeply than ever before in the face of a parent's loss of a child because he too would soon join the ranks of men with sons in whom their fathers sometimes unwisely invest their dreams. Benton was right, and Lynley knew it. A man's duty was to protect his offspring. When he failed in that duty—failed spectacularly, as was the failure felt by any parent who lost a child to murder—his guilt was second only to his grief. Marriages broke down as a result; loving families were torn asunder. And everything once held dear and secure was shattered by the advent of an evil every parent feared might alight upon his child, but one that no one could anticipate.

There was no recovering from such an event. There was no waking up some future morning, having successfully swum all night in the Lethe. That did not happen—ever—to the parents of a child whose life was taken by a killer.

Six now, Lynley thought. Six children, six sets of parents, six families. Six and all the media counting.

He went, as requested, up to AC Hillier's office. By now Robson would have informed the assistant commissioner of Lynley's refusal to allow him onto the crime scene, and Hillier would doubtless be in a state about that.

The AC was in a meeting with the head of the Press Bureau. So Hillier's secretary informed Lynley. However, the AC had left explicit orders that, on the off chance that Acting Superintendent Lynley put in an appearance whilst the meeting was ongoing, he should join them at once. "He's bearing . . ." Judi MacIntosh hesitated. It seemed more for effect than out of the necessity to find the perfect words. "He's bearing a certain degree of animosity towards you at the moment, Superintendent. Forewarned and so on?"

Lynley acknowledged her with a polite nod. He often wondered how Hillier had managed to acquire a secretary so perfectly matched to his style of leadership.

Stephenson Deacon had brought two young assistants with him to his meeting with Hillier, Lynley discovered when he joined them. One male and one female, they both looked like interns: fresh scrubbed, eager, and solicitous. Neither Hillier nor the acidulous Deacon—who'd come along from the Directorate of Public Affairs bearing a litre of soda water for some reason—offered any introductions.

"You've seen the circus, I take it," Hillier said to Lynley without preamble. "The established briefings aren't giving satisfaction. We're countering with something to head them off."

The male intern, Lynley noted, was religiously writing down Hillier's every word. The female, on the other hand, was studying Lynley with a discomfiting intensity, giving the job the rapt attention of a predator.

"I thought you were doing *Crimewatch*, sir," Lynley said.

"The *Crimewatch* decision was before all this. Obviously, it's not going to suffice by itself."

"Then what?" Lynley hadn't given the assistant commissioner the information about the CCTV footage, and he didn't do so now. He wanted to wait till he heard from Havers about her interview at the Stables. "You're not going to feed them misinformation, I hope."

Hillier didn't look pleased with this remark, and Lynley realised it had been ill advised. "That's not my habit, Superintendent," the AC said. And then to the head of the Press Bureau, "Tell him, Mr. Deacon."

"Embedding." Deacon uncapped his soda water and took a swig. "Buggers'll have sod all to complain about then. Begging your pardon, Miss Clapp," he added to the young woman, who looked nonplussed to be on the receiving end of this social nicety.

Lynley thought he understood, but he didn't want to. He said, "I beg your pardon?"

"Embedding," Deacon repeated, his tone impatient. "Placing a journalist inside the inquiry. A firsthand witness to how the police investigate on crime of this scale. The sort of thing they sometimes do in wartime, if you know what I mean."

"Surely you've heard of this, Superintendent?" Hillier asked.

Lynley had, of course. He merely couldn't believe that the Press Bureau was considering adopting something so foolhardy. He said to Hillier, "We can't do that, sir," endeavouring to be as polite as possible, which was something of an effort. "It's unheard of and—"

"Certainly it's never been done, Superintendent," Stephenson Deacon said with a specious smile. "But that's not to say that it can't be done. We have in the past, after all, invited the media along on coordinated arrests. This merely takes it one step further. Placement of a diligently chosen reporter—from a broadsheet, mind you, we'll draw the line at tabloid journalists—can turn the tide of public opinion. Not only towards this particular investigation but also towards the entire Met. I don't have to point out to you how agitated the public are becoming over this case. The front page of today's *Daily Mail,* for example—"

"—will be used to line someone's rubbish bin tomorrow," Lynley said. He addressed his next remarks to Hillier, and he tried to sound as rational as Deacon. "Sir, this sort of thing could create unimaginable difficulties for us. How could the team—at a morning meeting, for example—speak freely when they know that any word they say might end up on the front page of the next edition of the *Guardian*? And how do we address the problem of the Contempt of Court Act if a journalist's among us?"

"That," Hillier said quite evenly, although he was keeping his eyes on Lynley and had been doing so from the moment Lynley had entered the room, "is the journalist's problem, not ours."

"Have you any idea how often we toss about names?" Although Lynley could feel himself losing the edge he had on his temper, he believed the issues involved were more important than his ability to express them with Holmesian dispassion. "Can you imagine what the reaction is going to be from an individual who finds himself named as 'helping with police inquiries' when that isn't the case at all?"

"That would be down to the broadsheet involved, Superintendent," Deacon said smugly.

"And in the meantime, if the individual named is actually the killer we're looking for? If he then goes to ground?"

"Surely you're not suggesting that you wish him to keep on killing so that you might find him," Deacon said.

"What I'm suggesting is that this isn't a bloody game. I've just been with the father of a thirteen-year-old boy whose body—"

"We need words about that," Hillier interrupted. He finally took his gaze off Lynley and directed it to Deacon. He said, "Come up with the list of names, Stephenson. I'd like CVs on them all. Sample articles as well. I'll have a decision for you in—" He looked at his watch and then consulted the diary on his desk, "—I should think forty-eight hours will be sufficient."

"D'you want a word leaked to the proper ears?" This came from the male minion, who'd finally looked up from his note taking. The female continued to say nothing, and her inspection of Lynley did not shift.

"Not at the moment," Hillier said. "I'll be in touch."

"That's that, then," Deacon said.

Lynley watched as the three of them gathered up notebooks, manila folders, briefcases, and bags. They left the room in a line, with Deacon at the head. Lynley didn't follow but rather used the time in an attempt to marshall tranquility.

He finally said, "Malcolm Webberly was a miracle worker."

Hillier sat behind his desk and observed Lynley over steepled fingers. "Don't let's talk about my brother-in-law."

"I think we need to," Lynley went on. "It's only just come to me the lengths he must have gone to to keep you under wraps."

"Watch yourself."

"I don't think it benefits either of us if I do."

"You can be replaced."

"Which you couldn't do to Webberly? Because he's your brother-in-law, and there was no way on earth that your wife would see you sacking her sister's husband? Not when she knew her sister's husband was the only thing standing between you and the end of your career?"

"That's quite enough."

"You've got everything the wrong way round in this investigation. You've probably always been like that, with only Webberly standing between you and the discovery of—"

Hillier surged to his feet. "I said that's enough!"

"But now he's not here and you're exposed. And I'm left with the option of seeing you hang us all or just yourself. So which course do you expect me to take?"

"I expect you to obey the orders you're given. As they're given and when they're given."

"Not when they're senseless." Lynley tried to calm himself. He managed to say in a quieter tone, "Sir, I can't let you interfere any longer. I'm going to have to demand that you either stop meddling in the investigation or I'll have to . . ." And there Lynley stopped, halted in midstride by the satisfied expression that flitted briefly across Hillier's face.

He suddenly realised that his own myopia had propelled him into the AC's trap. And that realisation prompted his understanding of why Superintendent Webberly had always made it known to his brother-in-law which of his officers ought to succeed him, even if such succession were only to be a temporary measure. Lynley *could* walk off the job at the drop of a hat without suffering a moment's hardship. The others couldn't. He had an income independent of the Met. For the other DIs, the Met put food on their families' table and a roof over their heads. Circumstances would force them time and again to submit to Hillier's directives without argument because none of them could afford to be sacked. Webberly had seen Lynley as the only one of them with the slightest chance of keeping at least some kind of rein on his brother-in-law.

God knew he owed the superintendent that favour, Lynley thought. Webberly had often enough been willing to do the same for him.

"Or?" Hillier's voice was deadly.

Lynley sought a new direction. "Sir, we've got another killing to contend with. We can't be asked to contend with journalists as well."

"Yes," Hillier said. "Another killing. You've acted in

direct defiance of an order, Superintendent, and you'd better have a good explanation for that."

They were finally down to it, Lynley thought: his refusal to let Hamish Robson view the scene of the crime. He didn't obfuscate by getting on to something else. He said, "I left word at the barrier. No one without ID onto the crime scene. Robson had no ID and the constables at the barrier hadn't a clue who he was. He might have been anyone, and specifically, he might have been a reporter."

"And when you saw him? When you spoke to him? When he made the request to see the photos, the video, what remained of the scene or anything else . . . ?"

"I refused," Lynley said, "but you know that already or we wouldn't be talking about it now."

"That's right. And now you're going to listen to what Robson has to say."

"Sir, if you'll excuse me, I've a team to see and work to be getting on with. This is more important than—"

"My authority trumps yours," Hillier said, "and you're face-to-face with a direct order now."

"I understand that," Lynley said, "but if he hasn't seen the photos, we can't waste time while he—"

"He's seen the video. He's read the preliminary reports." Hillier smiled thinly when he saw Lynley's surprise. "As I said. My authority trumps yours, Superintendent. So sit down. You're going to be here awhile."

HAMISH ROBSON had the grace to look apologetic. He also had the grace to look as uncomfortable as any intuitive man might have looked in the same situation. He came into the office with a yellow legal pad in his hand and a small stack of paperwork. The latter he handed over to Hillier. He cocked his head at Lynley and raised one shoulder in a quick, diffident movement that said "Not my idea."

Lynley nodded in turn. He bore the man no animosity. As far as he was concerned, both of them were doing their jobs under extremely difficult conditions.

Hillier obviously wanted dominance to be the theme of the meeting: He did not move from behind his desk to go to the conference table at which he'd held his colloquy with the press chief and his cohorts, and he motioned Robson to join Lynley in sitting before him. Together they ended up resembling two supplicants come before the throne of Pharaoh. Only the prostration was missing.

"What have you come up with, Hamish?" Hillier asked, eschewing any polite preliminaries.

Robson used his thumbs to hold his legal pad across his knees. His face appeared feverish, and Lynley felt a momentary surge of sympathy for the man. It was the rock and the hard place for him once again.

"With the earlier crimes," Robson said, and he sounded unsure about how exactly to negotiate the landscape of tension between the two Met officers, "the killer achieved the sense of omnipotence he was after through the overt mechanics of the crime: I mean the abduction of the victim, the restraining and the gagging, the rituals of burning and incising. But in this case, in Queen's Wood, those earlier behaviours weren't enough. Whatever he gained from the earlier crimes—let's continue to posit it was power—was denied to him with this one. That triggered a rage within him that he hasn't so far felt. And it was a rage that surprised him, I expect, since he's no doubt come up with an elaborate rationale for why he's been murdering these boys and rage has never come into the equation. But now he feels it because he's being thwarted in his desire for power, so he feels the full brunt of a sudden need to punish what he sees as defiance in his victim. This victim becomes responsible for not giving the killer what he's got from every other victim so far."

Robson had been looking at his notes as he spoke, but now he raised his head, as if needing to be told he could continue. Lynley said nothing. Hillier nodded curtly.

"So he turns to physical abuse with this boy," Robson said, "in advance of the killing. And he feels no remorse for the crime afterwards: The body's not laid out and arranged like an effigy. Instead, it's dumped. And it's placed where it might have been days before anyone stumbled upon it, so we can assume the killer's keeping watch over the investigation and making an effort now not only to leave no evidence at the scene but also to run no risk of being seen. I expect you've talked to him already. He knows you're closing in and he has no intention of giving you anything henceforth to connect him to the crime."

"Is that why there are no restraints this time round?" Lynley asked.

"I don't think so. Rather, prior to this particular murder, the killer thought he'd achieved the degree of omnipotence he's been seeking for most of his life. This delusional sense of power led him to believe he didn't even *need* to immobilize his next victim. But without the restraints, as things turned out, the boy fought him, and that required a personal means of dispatching him. So instead of the garrotte, the killer uses his hands. Only through this personal means can he regain the sense of power, the need for which motivates him to kill in the first place."

"Your conclusion, then?" Hillier asked.

"You're dealing with an inadequate personality. He's either dominated by others or he *pictures* himself as dominated by others. He has no idea how to get out of any situation in which he perceives himself as less powerful than the people round him, and he particularly has no idea how to get out of the situation he's currently in."

"The situation of the killing, you mean?" Hillier clarified.

"Oh no," Robson said. "He feels perfectly capable of leading the police on a merry chase when it comes to murder. But in his personal life, he's caught by something. And in such a way as to perceive no escape. This might be employment, a failing marriage, a parental relationship in which he has more responsibility than he likes, a parental relationship in which he has long been the underdog, some sort of financial failure he's hiding from a wife or life partner. That sort of thing."

"But you say he knows we're on to him?" Hillier said. "We've spoken to him? Been in touch in some way?"

Robson nodded. "Any one of those is possible," he said. "And this latest body, Superintendent?" This last he said to Lynley alone. "Everything about this body suggests you've come closer to the killer than you realise."

Chapter Eighteen

Barbara Havers watched as Barry Minshall—aka Mr. Magic—closed up his stall in the alley. He took his time about it, every movement designed to communicate how much trouble the rozzers were causing him. Down came the display of saucy playthings, all of which had to be placed with undo gentleness in collapsible cardboard boxes that he kept stashed in a pile in a cubbyhole designed for this express purpose above the stall. Put away were the gag items in a similar fashion, as well as a number of the magic tricks. Every object had its particular storage spot, and Minshall made certain it was deposited there in an exact position known only to him. Through all this, Barbara waited in ease. She had all the time he was intent upon demonstrating that he needed. And if he happened to be using that time to concoct a story about Davey Benton and the handcuffs, she herself used it to note those features about the alley that promised to assist her in the coming exchange with Mr. Magic. For there would be an exchange, she knew. This bloke didn't look the type to stand by idly as she rooted through his van. He was heading for too much trouble for that.

So in the minutes he took to shut up shop, she saw what could help her when the time came to put the thumbscrews on the magician: the CCTV cameras mounted at the mouth of the alley near a Chinese food stall and a bath-salts vendor some six yards away, who was watching Minshall with a great deal of interest even as the vendor devoured a samosa, the grease from which dripped down his hand and into the cuff of his shirt. That bloke, Barbara decided, looked like someone with a tale to tell.

He did, in a manner of speaking, when they passed him a few minutes later on their way out of the alley. He said, "Gotcherself a *lady* friend, Bar? Now that's a change, innit? I thought you liked the boys."

Minshall said pleasantly, "Do go fuck yourself, Miller," and passed by the stall.

Barbara said, "Hang on," and paused. She showed her ID to the bath-salts vendor. "Think you could identify some pictures of boys who might've hung about his stall in the past few months?" she asked him.

Miller was suddenly cautious. "What sort of boys?"

"The sort who've turned up dead all round London."

He flicked a glance at Minshall. "I don't want no trouble. I di'n't know you were a cop when I said—"

"What difference does that make?"

"I di'n't see anything." He turned and busied himself with his wares. "It's dim along here. Wouldn't know one boy from another anyway."

"Sure you would, John," Minshall said. "You spend enough time ogling them, don't you?" And then to Havers, "Constable, you were interested in my van . . . ?" He continued on his way.

Barbara took note of the vendor's name. She knew that his remarks about Barry Minshall could mean nothing, as could Minshall's remarks about him: just the natural animosity that males sometimes have for each other. Or they could have been the result of Minshall's oddity of appearance and Miller's schoolboy reaction to that. But in either case, they were worth looking into.

Barry Minshall led her in the direction of the main entrance to the Stables Market. They emerged into Chalk Farm Road as a train rumbled by on the overhead tracks. In the fading light of the late afternoon, the streetlamps glowed against the wet pavement, and the diesel fumes of a passing lorry scented the air with the heavy bouquet that was quintessentially winter London in the rain.

Because of the cold and the damp, the usual suspects—Goths head to toe in black and old-age pensioners wondering what the hell had happened to the neighbourhood—were absent from the pavements. In their places, commuters hurried home from work and shop owners began to move their wares inside. Barbara noted the looks that Barry Minshall got as they passed these people. Even in an area of town known for the general weirdness of its inhabitants, the magician stood out, either for the dark glasses, long coat, and stocking cap he wore, or for an emanation of malevolence that formed an aura round him. Barbara knew which she believed it was. Stripped of the patina of purity suggested by the innocence of his magic tricks, Barry Minshall was a nasty piece of business.

She said to him, "Tell me, Mr. Minshall. What sorts of places do you usually perform? The magic, I mean. Can't be you only use it to entertain the kids who stop at your stall. I expect you'd get a little rusty round the fingers if you left it to that."

Minshall shot her a glance. She reckoned he was evaluating not only the question but also the various reactions she might have to his answers.

She offered him options. "Cocktail parties, for example? Ladies' clubs? Private organisations?"

He made no reply.

"Birthday parties?" she went on. "I expect you're quite the thing at them. What about at schools, as a special treat for the kids? Church functions? Boy Scouts? Girl Guides?"

He plodded onward.

"What about south of the river, Mr. Minshall? Ever do anything there? Round Elephant and Castle? What about youth organisations? Trips to borstal in the holidays?"

He gave her nothing. He didn't intend to phone his solicitor about her request to see his van, but he clearly wasn't going to say a word that might put him in further jeopardy. So he was only half a fool, she decided. No problem. Half was probably enough.

His van turned out to be on Jamestown Road, parked with one tyre on the kerb, facing the oncoming traffic. Fortunately, Minshall had left it beneath a streetlamp, and a pool of yellow light fell directly upon it, enhanced by a security system that switched on brightly at the front of a house some fifteen feet away. That, in addition to the daylight still lingering, made further illumination unnecessary.

"Let's have a look, then," Barbara said, with a nod at the van's rear doors. "D'you want to do the honours, or shall I?" She dug round in her bag and brought out a pair of latex gloves as she spoke.

This, it seemed, prompted him to speak. "I hope you see my cooperation for what it is, Constable."

"And what would that be?"

"A fairly good indication that I wish to be helpful. I haven't done anything to anyone."

"Mr. Minshall, I'm dead chuffed to hear it," Barbara said. "Open her up, please."

Minshall fished a set of keys out of his overcoat. He opened the van and stepped back to let Barbara inspect its contents. These comprised boxes. Boxes upon boxes. The magician, in fact, appeared to be keeping the entire cardboard industry in business. Felt-pen markings identified the putative contents of what seemed like three dozen containers: "Cards & Coins"; "Cups, Dice, Hankie, Scarf & Rope"; "Videos"; "Books & Mags"; "Sex Toys"; "Gags." Beneath all of these, however, Barbara could see that the floor of the van was carpeted. The carpet was frayed, and a curious dark stain shaped like antlers reached out from beneath the cards and coins box, suggesting not only more of a stain beneath but also—possibly—an attempt to hide it in the first place.

Barbara stepped back. She swung the doors closed. Minshall said, "Satisfied?," and he sounded—to her ears—like a man relieved.

She said, "Not quite. Let's have a look up front."

He seemed as if he wanted to protest but thought better of it. With a mutter, he unlocked the driver's door and opened it. Barbara said, "Not that one," and indicated the passenger's door instead.

Inside, the front of the van was a mobile rubbish tip, and Barbara sifted her way through food wrappers, Coke cans, ticket stubs, carpark stubs, and handouts of the sort one found placed beneath windscreen wipers after a stint of parking on a public street. It was, in short, a treasure trove of evidence. If Davey Benton—or any one of the other dead boys—had been in this van, there were going to be dozens of signs indicating that.

Barbara slid her hand under the passenger seat to see if there were more goodies hidden from the eye. She brought forth a plastic disk of the sort one gets when checking a coat somewhere, along with a pencil, two biros, and an empty videocassette case. She moved round to the other side of the car, where Minshall stood at the driver's door, perhaps mistakenly thinking she intended to let him drive off into the sunset. She gave him the nod and he opened it for her. She slid her hand under the driver's seat.

Her fingers made contact with several objects here as well. She brought out a small pocket torch—operational—and a pair of scissors—dull and suitable for cutting only butter. And finally a black-and-white photograph.

She looked down at this and then up at Barry Minshall. She turned it round, facing him, and held it to her chest. "D'you want to give me the story on this, Bar?" she asked him amiably. "Or shall I guess?"

His reply was immediate, and she could have laid money on its coming. He said, "I don't know how that—"

"Barry, save the line for later. You're going to need it."

She told him to hand over his keys and she pulled her mobile phone from her bag. She punched in the numbers and waited for Lynley to take the call.

"UNTIL WE FIND that van from the CCTV film," Lynley said, "and until we know why it was going into St. George's Gardens in the middle of the night, I don't want it broadcast."

Winston Nkata looked up from the notes he was taking in his small, leather-bound book. He said, "Hillier's going to blow—"

"That's the risk we'll have to take," Lynley cut in. "We run a bigger risk—a double risk—if the news of that van goes out prematurely. We tip our hand to the killer or, if that van on the tape *does* have a reason for being there, we've just predisposed the public to be thinking in terms of a red van when the actual vehicle could be something else."

"That residue on the bodies, though," Nkata said. "It says Ford Transit, doesn' it?"

"But not the colour. So I'd like to avoid the whole matter for now."

Nkata still didn't look convinced. He'd come to Lynley's office for the final word on what was going to be broadcast on *Crimewatch*—having been entrusted with the task by AC Hillier who, it appeared, had given up micromanaging the investigation for the time it was probably going to take him to decide what he wanted to wear on television in a few hours—and he looked down at his meagre notes and no doubt wondered how he was going to relay this information to their superior officer without raising his ire.

That, Lynley decided, could not be his worry. They'd given Hillier plenty of details to use on the programme, and he trusted that Hillier's need to seem liberal in matters of race would keep him from taking out whatever frustration he had on Nkata. Nonetheless, he said, "I'll take the heat on this, Winnie," and added as a means of giving the DS further ammunition, "Until we hear from Barbara about that van she saw the magician driving, we hold back. So go with that e-fit from Square Four Gym and the reconstruction of Kimmo Thorne's abduction. I expect we'll get a result from that."

A sharp knock on the door, and DI Stewart popped his head inside Lynley's office. He said, "A word, Tommy?" and nodded a hello to Nkata, adding, "Got your face powdered for the cameras? Word has it your fan mail's doubling every day."

Nkata took the teasing with resignation. He said, "I'm forwarding it all on to you, man. Since the wife's had enough, you'll need a dating service, right? Fact, there's a special letter come from a bird in Leeds. Twenty stone, she says, but I 'xpect you can handle that much woman."

Stewart didn't smile. "Sod you," he said.

"Honours returned." Nkata got to his feet and headed out of the office. Stewart took his place in one of the two chairs in front of Lynley's desk. He tapped his fingers against his thigh, in the rhythmical pattern he adopted whenever he didn't have something in his hands to play with. He was, Lynley knew from experience, a man who could dish it out but not take it. "That was a bit below the belt," Stewart said.

"We're all losing our sense of humour, John."

"I don't like my personal life—"

"No one does. Have you got something for me?"

Stewart appeared to consider this before he spoke, pinching the crease in his trousers and removing a speck of lint from his knee. "Two pieces of news. An ID on the Quaker Street body, courtesy of Ulrike Ellis's list of missing Colossus kids. He was called Dennis Butcher. Fourteen years old. From Bromley."

"Did we have him on the list of missing persons?"

Stewart shook his head. "Parents are divorced. Dad thought he was with Mum and her lover. Mum thought he was with Dad, Dad's girlfriend, her two kids, and their new baby. So he was never reported missing. At least, that's the story they tell."

"Whereas the truth is . . . ?"

"Good riddance, as far as they were concerned. We had the devil of a time getting either one of them to help ID the body, Tommy."

Lynley looked away from Stewart and out of the window, through which the lights of nighttime London were beginning to glow. "I'd very much like someone to explain the human race to me. Fourteen years old. Why was he sent to Colossus?"

"Assault with a flick knife. He went to Youth Offenders first."

"Another soul needing purification, then. He fits the mould." Lynley turned back to the DI. "And the other piece of news?"

"We've finally come up with the Boots where Kimmo Thorne bought his makeup."

"Have you indeed? Where is it? Southwark?"

Stewart shook his head. "We watched every tape from every Boots in the vicinity of his home and then in the area of Colossus. We got nothing. So we had another look at the paperwork on Kimmo and saw he hung round Leicester Square. It didn't take long from there. Plotted out a quarter-mile radius from the square and found a Boots in James Street. There he was, buying his slap in the company of some bloke looking like the Grim Reaper gone Gothic."

"That would be Charlie Burov," Lynley said. "Blinker, as he's commonly called. A mate of Kimmo's."

"Well, he was there. Big as life, both of them. Quite the pair, Kimmo and Charlie. Hard to miss. The person at the till was female, by the way, and there was a queue. Four people waiting to be served."

"Anyone matching our e-fit from Square Four Gym?"

"Not so you could tell. But it's CCTV film, Tommy. You know what that's like."

"What about the profiler's description?"

"What about it? It's vague enough to match three-quarters of the under-forty male population of London. The way I see it, we're dotting and crossing. Enough *i*'s and *t*'s and we may stumble across what we're looking for."

There was truth to that: the endless slog that left no stone unturned. For it was often the least expected stone that, upended, revealed a vital piece of information.

Lynley said, "We'll want Havers to have a look at the film, then."

Stewart frowned. "Havers? Why?"

"She's the only person so far who's seen everyone we're interested in at Colossus."

"So you're taking her theory on board?" Stewart asked the question casually—and it wasn't an illogical inquiry—but there was something in the tone of it as well as in the attention Stewart suddenly gave to a thread on the seam of his trousers that made Lynley look more sharply at the DI.

"I'm taking every theory onboard," he replied. "Have you a problem with that?"

"No problem, no," Stewart said.

"Then . . . ?"

The DI moved restlessly in his chair. He seemed to consider how best to answer, and he finally decided, saying, "There's some muttering about favoritism, Tommy. Among the rest of the team. And there's also the matter of . . ." He hesitated, and Lynley thought for a moment that Stewart was going to suggest ludicrously that there was talk of his having some sort of personal interest in Barbara Havers. But then Stewart said, "It's the championing of her that's misunderstood."

"By everyone?" Lynley asked. "Or just by you?" He didn't wait for an answer. He knew how deep DI Stewart's dislike of Havers ran. He said lightly, "John, I'm a glutton for punishment. I've sinned, and Barbara's my purgatory. If I can mould her into a cop who can work as part of a team, I'm saved."

Stewart smiled, in spite of himself, it seemed. "She's clever enough if she weren't so bloody maddening. I'll give you that. And God knows she's tenacious."

"There's that," Lynley said. "It's a case of her good points outweighing her bad."

"Hell of a dress sense, though," Stewart pointed out. "I think she shops at Oxfam."

"I've no doubt she'd say there are worse places," Lynley said. The phone on his desk rang as he was speaking and he lifted the receiver as Stewart stood to go. It was, he found, a case of speak of the devil.

"Minshall's van," Havers said without preamble. "It's a SOCO wet dream, sir."

Lynley nodded at Stewart as he left the office. He

gave his attention to the telephone. "What've you got?" he asked Havers.

"Treasure. There's so much lumber in his van that it'll take a month to sort it all out. But there's one item in particular that's going to ring your chimes. It was under the driver's seat."

"And?"

"Child porn, sir. Dodgy photo of a naked kid with two blokes: taking at one end and giving at the other. You fill in the blanks. I say we get a warrant to search his place and another to tear his van apart. Get a SOCO team over here with fine-tooth combs."

"Where is he now? Where are you?"

"Still in Camden Town."

"Take him to the Holmes Street station, then. Put him in an interview room and get his address. I'll meet you at his digs."

"The warrants?"

"That's not going to be a problem."

THE MEETING had gone on far too long, and Ulrike Ellis was feeling the strain. Every extremity in her body tingled, with buzzing little impulses on the nerve endings running up and down her arms and her legs. She was trying to stay calm and professional—the personification of leadership, intelligence, foresight, and wisdom. But as the discussion among the board droned on, she grew ever more desperate to get out of the room.

This was the part she hated about her work: having to put up with the seven do-gooders who constituted the board of trustees and who absolved whatever guilty consciences they had about their obscene wealth by writing out the occasional cheque to the charity of their choice—in this case, Colossus—and corralling their equally well-heeled friends to do the same. Because of this, they tended to take their responsibility more seriously than Ulrike would have liked. So their monthly meetings in the Oxo Tower dragged on for hours as every penny was accounted for and tedious plans for the future were laid.

Today the gathering was worse than usual: They were all teetering on the edge without knowing it while she attempted to hide that fact from them. For meeting their long-term goal to raise enough money to open a branch of Colossus in North London was going to come to nothing if any scandal became associated with the organisation. And the need for Colossus was truly desperate across the river. Kilburn, Cricklewood, Shepherd's Bush, Kensal Rise. Disenfranchised youth lived lives exposed to drugs, shootings, muggings, and robberies every day over there. Colossus could offer them an alternative to a lifestyle that doomed them to addictions, sexual diseases, incarceration, or an early death, and they *deserved* the opportunity to experience what Colossus had to offer.

In order for any of this to happen, though, it was essential that no connection exist between the organisation and a killer. And no connection *did* exist save the coincidence of five troubled boys dying at the same time as they ceased coming to classes and activities near Elephant and Castle. Ulrike was convinced of this, for there was no other path she could take and continue to live with herself.

So she put on a show of cooperation during the endless meeting. She nodded, took notes, murmured things like "Excellent idea" and "I'll get on to that straightaway." Through this means, she eked out yet another successful encounter with the trustees until one of them finally made the blessed motion to adjourn.

She'd ridden her bicycle to the Oxo Tower, so she hurried down to it. It wasn't far to Elephant and Castle, but the narrow streets and the growing darkness made the way treacherous. By rights, she should have missed the news vendor's placard altogether as she passed down Waterloo Road. But the phrase "Sixth Murder!" leapt out at her in front of a tobacconist's shop, and she ground to a halt and pulled her bike onto the pavement.

Heart seizing up, she went inside and snatched up the *Evening Standard.* She read as she scraped a few coins out of her purse and handed them over at the till.

My God, my *God.* She couldn't believe it. Another body. Another boy. Queen's Wood, North London this time. Found that morning. He hadn't yet been identified—at least no name had been given out by the police—so there was still the hope that this was a coincidental killing bearing no relationship to the other five murders . . . Except that Ulrike couldn't quite bring herself to believe that. The age was similar: The paper used the term "young adolescent" to refer to the victim, and obviously they knew he hadn't died of natural causes or even accidentally since they were calling it a murder. But still, *couldn't* it be . . . ?

She needed this killing to be unrelated to Colossus. She was desperate for that. If it was not, then she needed to be *clearly* seen as assisting the police in any way she could. There was absolutely no middle ground in this situation. She could temporise or outright prevaricate, but all that would do was prolong the inevitable if she'd accidentally hired a murderer as an employee and then refused to take action to root him out. If that *was* the case, she was done for. And so, probably, was Colossus.

Back at Elephant and Castle, she went straight to her office. She riffled through the contents of the top drawer in her desk for the card that the Scotland Yard detective had given to her. She punched in the numbers but was told that he was in a meeting and could not be interrupted. Was there a message or could someone else help her . . . ?

Yes, she told the DC on the line. She identified herself. She mentioned Colossus. She wanted the dates when each of the bodies had been found. It was a matter of connecting the dead boys with activities at Colossus and the individuals who led those activities. She wanted to provide Superintendent Lynley with a fuller report than she'd previously given him, and those dates were the keys to meeting that self-imposed obligation.

The DC put her on hold for several minutes, no doubt seeking a superior officer to approve this request. When he came back, it was with the dates. She wrote them down, double-checked them against the names of the victims, and then rang off. Then she looked at them thoughtfully, and she considered them in the light of someone's desire to discredit and ruin Colossus.

If there was a connection between Colossus and the dead boys, aside from the obvious one, she thought, it would have to be about reducing the organisation to rubble. So perhaps someone inside this place hated these types of kids in their every manifestation. Or perhaps someone inside had been thwarted in his desire to advance, to make a change in the workings of the programme, to succeed at a high level with a previously unheard of number of clients, to . . . anything. Or perhaps someone wanted to take *her* place and this was the route to get there. Or perhaps someone was mad as a hatter and only posing as a normal human being. Or perhaps—

"Ulrike?"

She looked up from the list of dates. She'd taken a calendar out of her drawer in order to compare those dates with scheduled activities and the location of those activities. Neil Greenham was standing there, his odd round head poked just inside her door, looking deferential.

Ulrike said, "Yes, Neil? May I help you?"

He blushed for some reason, his pudgy face going an unattractive shade that climbed all the way to his scalp and highlighted the scarcity of his hair. What was *that* all about? "Wanted you to know I'll need to leave early tomorrow. Mum's got to see the doctor about her hip, and I'm the only one who can drive her."

Ulrike frowned. "She can't go by cab?"

Neil looked markedly less deferential at this. "As it happens, she can't. It's too expensive. And I won't have her taking the bus. I've already told the kids to come two hours earlier." And then he added, "If that's okay with you," although he didn't sound like someone who was going to alter his plans if they weren't okay with his superior.

Ulrike thought about this. Neil had been manoeuvring for an administrative position since he'd come to work for them. He had to prove himself first, but he didn't want to. His sort never did. He needed putting in his place. She said, "It's fine, Neil. But in future, please check with me before you alter your schedule, will you?" She looked back down at her list, dismissing him.

He didn't get the message, or he chose to ignore it. He said, "Ulrike."

She looked up again. "What else?" She knew she sounded impatient because she *was* impatient. She tried to temper that with a smile and a gesture to her paperwork.

He observed this solemnly, then raised his gaze to her. "Sorry. I thought you might want to know about Dennis Butcher."

"Who?"

"Dennis Butcher. He was doing Learn to Earn when he dis . . ."—Neil made an obvious correction in course—"when he stopped coming. Jack Veness told me the cops called while you were at the board meeting. That body found over in Quaker Street . . . ? It was Dennis."

Ulrike breathed only one word in reply. "God."

"And now there's another today. So I was wondering . . ."

"What? What were you wondering?"

"If you've considered . . ."

His significant pauses were maddening. "What?" she said. "What? What? I've got a load of work to do, so if you've something you need to say, Neil, then say it."

"Yes. Of course. I was just thinking it's time we called in all the kids and warned them, isn't it? If victims are being chosen from Colossus, it seems that our only recourse—"

"Nothing indicates that victims are being *chosen* from Colossus," Ulrike said, despite what she herself had been thinking a moment before Neil Greenham interrupted her. "These kids live their lives on the edge. They take and sell drugs, they're involved with street muggings, burglaries, robberies, prostitution. They meet and mingle with the wrong sort of people every single day, so if they end up dead, it's because of that and *not* because they've spent time with us."

He was looking at her curiously. He let a silence hang between them, during which Ulrike heard Griff's voice coming from the shared office of the assessment leaders. She wanted to be rid of Neil. She wanted to look at her lists and make some decisions.

Neil finally said, "If that's what you think . . ."

"It's what I think," she lied. "So if there's nothing else . . . ?"

Again that silence and that look. Speculative. Suggestive. Wondering how best to use her obduracy to his own advantage. "Well," he said, "I suppose that's all. I'll be off, then." Still he looked at her. She wanted to slap him.

"Safe trip to the doctor tomorrow," she told him evenly.

"Yes," he said. "I'll make sure it is, won't I."

That said, he left her. When he was gone, she rested her forehead in her fingers. God. God. Dennis Butcher, she thought. Five of them now. And until Kimmo Thorne, she hadn't even been *aware* of what was happening under her very nose. Because the only thing her nose could even begin to smell was the scent of Griff Strong's aftershave.

And then he was there too. Not hesitating at the door as Neil had done, but barging right in.

He said, "Ulrike, you've heard about Dennis Butcher?"

Ulrike knotted her eyebrows. Did he actually sound *pleased?* "Neil told me just now."

"Did he?" Griff sat on the only chair in the room besides her own. He wore that ivory fisherman's sweater that set off his dark hair and the blue jeans that emphasised the Michelangelo shape of his thighs. How typical. "I'm glad you know," he added. "It can't be what we thought, then, can it?"

We? she thought. *What* we *thought?* She said, "About what?"

"What?"

"What did we think? About what?"

"That it's to do with me. With someone wanting to set me up by killing these boys. Dennis Butcher didn't go through assessment with me, Ulrike. He belonged to one of the other leaders." Griff offered a smile. "It's a relief. With the cops breathing down my neck . . . Well, I didn't want that and I can't think you did either."

"Why?"

"Why what?"

"The police? Breathing down someone's neck? Are you suggesting *I've* been involved in the deaths of these kids? Or that the police will *think* I've been involved?"

"Jesus, no. I just meant . . . You and I . . ." He made that gesture of his that was meant to seem boyish, the hand through the hair. It tousled nicely. He no doubt had it cut to do so. "I can't think you want it getting about that you and I . . . Some things are best left private. So . . ." He flashed her that smile again. He looked over the top of her desk to the dates and the calendar. "What're you up to? How'd the board meeting go, by the way?"

"You'd better leave," she told him.

He looked confused. "Why?"

"Because I've work to do. Your day may have ended, but mine has not."

"What's wrong?" The boyish hand-to-hair again. She'd once thought it charming. She'd once seen it as an invitation to touch his hair herself. She'd reached to do so and she'd actually grown wet at the contact: her humble fingers, his glorious locks, prelude to both the kiss and the hungry pressure of his body against hers.

She said, "Five of our boys are dead, Griff. Possibly six, because there's another been found this morning. That's what's wrong."

"But there's no connection."

"How can you say that? Five boys dead and what they all have in common besides trouble with the law is enrollment here."

"Yes, yes," he said. "I know that. I meant this Dennis Butcher thing. There's no connection. He wasn't one of mine. I didn't even know him. So you and I . . . well, no one's going to need to know."

She stared at him. She wondered how she had failed to see . . . What *was* it about physical beauty? she asked herself. Did it make the beholder stupid as well as blind and deaf?

She said, "Yes. Well." And added, "Have a nice evening, won't you," and picked up her pen and bent her head to her work.

He said her name once more, but she didn't respond. And she didn't look up as he left the office.

But his message remained with her after he was gone. These murders had nothing to do with him. She thought about this. Couldn't it also be the case that they had nothing to do with Colossus? And if that *was* the case, wasn't it true that by attempting to root out a killer from the organisation, Ulrike was turning a spotlight upon all of them, encouraging the police to dig deeper into everyone's background and movements? And if she did that, wasn't she also thereby asking the police to ignore everything that could point to the *real* killer, who would go on killing as the fancy took him?

The truth was that there had to be yet another connection among the boys, and it *had* to be a connection beyond Colossus. The police had so far failed to see this, but they would. They definitely would. Just so long as she held them off and kept their noses out of Elephant and Castle.

Not a soul was on the pavement when Lynley made the turn into Lady Margaret Road in Kentish Town. He parked in the first available space he came to, in front of an RC church on the corner, and he walked up the street in search of Havers. He found her smoking in front of Barry Minshall's home. She said, "He called for the duty solicitor straightaway once I got him to the station," and handed over a photo in a plastic evidence bag.

Lynley looked at it. It was much as Havers had picturesquely described it on the phone to him. Sodomy and fellatio. The boy appeared to be about ten.

Lynley felt ill. The child could be anyone, anywhere, anytime, and the men taking their pleasure from him were completely unidentifiable. But that would be the point, wouldn't it. Satisfying the urge was all there was to monsters. To them, it was merely a case of hunter and prey. He gave the picture back to Havers and waited for his stomach to settle before he gazed at the house.

Number 16 Lady Margaret Road was a sad affair, a brick-and-masonry building of three floors and a basement with every inch of its masonry and wood in need of paint. It had no formal house number attached to its door or to the squared-off columns that defined its front porch. Rather, *16* had been scrawled in marking pen on one of these pillars, along with the letters *A*, *B*, *C*, and *D* and the appropriate up and down arrows indicating where those respective flats could be found: in the basement or in the house proper. One of London's great plane trees stood along the pavement, filling the small front garden with a covering of dead and decomposing leaves as thick as a mattress. The leaves obscured everything: from the sagging, low front wall of brick to the narrow path leading up to the steps, to the steps themselves: five of them which climbed to a blue front door. Two panels of translucent glass ran vertically up the middle half of this, one of them badly cracked and asking to be broken altogether. There was no knob, only a dead bolt surrounded by wood worn down by thousands of hands having pushed the door inward.

Minshall lived in flat A, which was in the basement. Its means of access was down a flight of steps, round the side of the house, and along a narrow passage where rainwater pooled and mould grew at the base of the building. Just outside the door was a cage holding birds. Doves. They cooed softly at the human presence.

Lynley had the warrants; Havers had the keys. She handed them over and let him do the honours. They stepped inside into utter darkness.

Finding a light was a matter of stumbling through what seemed to be a sitting room that had been thoroughly turned over by a burglar. But when Havers said, "Got a light here, sir," and switched on a dim bulb on a desk, Lynley saw that the condition of the place was due only to slovenly housekeeping.

"What d'you reckon that smell is?" Havers asked.

"Unwashed male, dodgy plumbing, semen, and poor ventilation." Lynley donned latex gloves; she did the same. "That boy was here," he said. "I can feel it."

"The one in the picture?"

"Davey Benton. What's Minshall claiming?"

"He's plugged it. I thought we'd get him on the CCTV cameras in the market, but the cops in Holmes Street told me they're just for show. No film inside them. There's a bloke there—he's called John Miller—who could probably ID a photo of Davey, though. *If* he'll talk at all."

"Why wouldn't he?"

"I think he's bent himself. Towards underage boys. I got the impression if he fingers Minshall, Minshall fingers him. Scratch mine, scratch yours."

"Wonderful," Lynley murmured grimly. He worked his way across the room and found another light by a sagging sofa. He switched it on and turned to look at what they had.

"Pay dirt in a saucepan," Havers said.

He couldn't disagree. A computer that doubtless had an Internet connection. A video player with racks of tapes beneath it. Magazines with graphic pictures of sex, others filled with S&M photos. Unwashed crockery. The paraphernalia of magic. They picked through this at different parts of the room till Havers said, "Sir? Do you make of these what I make of these? They were on the floor beneath the desk."

She was holding up what appeared to be several tea towels. They were stiffened in spots, as if they'd been used while sitting at the computer, for matters having nothing to do with drying plates and glasses.

"He's a piece of work, isn't he?" Lynley moved into

what was a sleeping alcove, where a bed bore sheets of much the same appearance and condition as the tea towels. The place was a treasure trove of DNA evidence. If Minshall had engaged in his frolics with anyone other than his computer and the palm of his hand, there was going to be enough indication of that here to send him away for decades, if the *anyone* in question was an underage boy.

On the floor next to the bed was yet another magazine, limp with someone's continual inspection of it. Lynley picked it up and leafed through it quickly. Raw photos of women, nude, legs splayed. Come-hither looks, wet lips, fingers stimulating, entering, caressing. It was sex reduced to base release and nothing else. It depressed Lynley to his core.

"Sir, I've got something."

Lynley returned to the sitting room, where Havers had been going through the desk. She'd found a stack of Polaroid pictures, which she handed over.

They were not pornography. Instead, in each of them a different young boy was kitted out in magician's togs: cape, top hat, black trousers and shirt. Occasionally a wand under the arm for effect. They were all engaged in what seemed to be the same trick: something with scarves and a dove. There were thirteen of them altogether: white boys, black boys, mixed-race boys. Davey Benton was not among them. As for the others, the parents and relatives of the dead boys would have to look them over.

"What's he said about that photo in his van?" Lynley asked when he had flipped through the Polaroids a second time.

"Doesn't know how it got there," Havers said. "Wasn't *him* put it there. He's completely innocent. It's some mistake. Yadda yadda more yadda."

"He could be telling the truth."

"You're joking."

Lynley looked round the flat. "So far there's no child pornography in here."

"So far," Havers said. She indicated the VCR and its accompanying cassettes. "You can't tell me those videos are by Disney, sir."

"I'll give you that. But tell me: Why would he have a photo in his van and none where it's infinitely safer for him to have it: here inside his flat? And why would all indication of what he's been up to sexually be referenced to women?"

"Because he won't take a trip to the nick for that. And he's smart enough to know it," she replied. "As for the rest, give me ten minutes to find it on that computer. If it takes that long."

Lynley told her to have at it. He went down a corridor beyond the sitting room and found a grimy bathroom and beyond it a kitchen. More of the same in both of the locations. A SOCO team would have to delve into it. There were going to be fingerprints galore, in addition to trace evidence deposited by anyone who'd been inside the place.

He left Havers to the computer and went back outside, following the path to the front of the house. There, he climbed the steps to the porch and rang each of the bells for the flats within. Only one yielded an answer. Flat C on the first floor was occupied, and the voice of an Indian woman told him to come up. She would be happy to talk to the police as long as he had identification that he would be willing to slide under her door when he got there.

This sufficed to gain him entry to a flat with a view of the street. A sari-clad middle-aged woman admitted him, handing back his warrant card with a formal little bow. "One cannot be too careful, I find," she told him. "It is the way of the world." She introduced herself as Mrs. Singh. She was a widow, she revealed, of no children, straitened circumstances, and little opportunity to marry again. "Alas, my child-bearing years are over. I would serve only to care for someone else's children now. Would you have tea with me, sir?"

Lynley demurred. Winter was long and she was lonely and he otherwise would have stopped long enough to give her a pleasant half hour or so. But the temperature in her flat was tropical and even if that hadn't been the case, what he needed from her was a matter of a few minutes' conversation, and he could afford no more time than that. He told her he'd come to inquire about the gentleman in the basement flat. Barry Minshall, by name. Did she know him?

"The odd man with the stocking hat, oh yes," Mrs. Singh replied. "Has he been arrested?"

She asked the question as if the word *finally* were understood between them.

"Why do you ask that?" Lynley said.

"The young boys," she said. "They came and they went from that basement flat. Day and night. I did phone the police three times about it. I believe you must investigate this man, I told them. Something clearly is not right. But I fear that they saw me as a meddlesome woman, getting into business that was not my own."

Lynley showed her the picture of Davey Benton he'd had from the boy's father. "Was this boy one of them?"

She studied it. She carried it to the window overlooking the street and she gazed from the picture to the ground below, as if trying to see Davey Benton in memory as he might have been: entering the front garden and going down the steps to the path to the basement flat. She said, "Yes. Yes. I have seen this boy. One day that man met him out there on the street. I saw this. He wore a cap, this boy. But I saw his face. I did."

"You're sure of that?"

"Oh yes. I am certain. It is the headphones in this picture, you see. He had them as well, from a player of some kind. He was quite small and very pretty, just like this boy in the picture."

"Did he and Minshall go into the basement flat?"

They went down the stairs and round the side of the house, she told him. She hadn't *seen* them go into the flat, but one could assume . . . She had no idea how long they were there. She didn't spend all of her time at the window, she explained with an apologetic laugh.

But what she'd said was enough, and Lynley thanked her for it. He turned down yet another offer of tea and descended the outer stairs to the basement flat once more. Havers met him at the door. She said, "Got him," and led Lynley to the computer. On the screen was a list of the sites that Barry Minshall had visited. It didn't take a degree in cryptology to read their titles and know what they were all about.

"Let's get SOCO over here," Lynley said.

"What about Minshall?"

"Let him languish till morning. I want him to think about us crawling round his flat, uncovering the slime trail of his existence."

Chapter Nineteen

Winston Nkata was in no hurry to get to work the next morning. He knew he was going to take good-humoured heat from his colleagues over his appearance on *Crimewatch*, and he didn't feel like facing it yet. Nor did he really have to because *Crimewatch* had actually produced a possible break in the case, and he would be tracking that break down before he headed over the river for the day.

From the sitting room, his mother's usual morning fare—*BBC Breakfast*—was doing its regular bit of recycling the news, traffic, weather, and special reports every thirty minutes on the telly. They'd reached the part where they were informing the public of what was on the front page of every national broadsheet and tabloid. From this, he was able to assess the temperature of the press regarding the serial killings.

According to *BBC Breakfast*, the tabloids were making the most of the Queen's Wood body, which at least had driven Bram Savidge and his accusations of institutional racism off their front pages. But Savidge still had a spot relegated to him, and those reporters not attempting to unearth more data about the body in the woods appeared to be conducting interviews wherever they could find them with people bearing grievances against the police. Navina Cryer shared space with the Queen's Wood body on the front of the *Mirror,* telling her tale of being ignored when she reported Jared Salvatore missing shortly after his disappearance. Cleopatra Lavery had managed to conduct a telephone interview from inside Holloway Prison with *News of the World,* and she had much to say on the subject of the criminal-justice system and what it had done to "her lovely Sean." Savidge and his African wife had been interviewed at home by the *Daily Mail,* complete with half-page photos of the wife playing a musical instrument of some sort under the fond eye of her husband. And according to what he was able to pick up from the presenters' comments on the telly as they nattered on about the other papers, Nkata could tell that the rest of the press were not going softly on the Met in the face of another boy's murder. One killer and *how* many cops? was the rhetorical question being asked by the news media with lofty irony.

Which was why *Crimewatch* and the manner in which the programme depicted the Met's endeavours in the investigation had been so crucial. Which was also why AC Hillier had attempted to usurp the director's job prior to the broadcast on the previous evening.

He wanted a split-screen effect, he'd told the men in the studio. DS Nkata would be identifying the dead boys by name and by photograph during the course of the programme, and having a head shot of Nkata speaking on one side of the screen while he identified photos of the victims of the serial killer on the other side of the screen would drive home to the viewers—by means of DS Nkata's sombre demeanour—how seriously the Met was taking the situation and the pursuit of this killer. That, of course, was utter cock. What Hillier wanted front and centre was what he and the Directorate of Public Affairs had wanted front and centre from the first: a black face attached to a rank senior to that of detective constable.

The assistant commissioner didn't get his way. They didn't go for anything fancy on *Crimewatch*, he'd been told. Just video footage if it was available, e-fits, photographs, dramatic reconstructions, and interviews with investigators. The people in makeup would buff away the shine on the face of anyone in front of the camera, and the sound blokes would clip a microphone onto the lapel of a jacket so it looked like something other than an insect about to crawl onto the presenter's chin, but Steven Spielberg this group was not. This was a low-budget operation, thank you very much. So who was going to say what to whom and in what order, please?

Hillier wasn't happy, but he could do nothing about it. He made sure that DS Winston Nkata was introduced by name, however, and he made doubly certain he repeated that name during the course of the broadcast. Other than that, he explained the nature of the crimes, gave the relevant dates, showed the locations where the bodies had been found, and sketched out a few details of the ongoing investigation in a manner that suggested he and Nkata were working it shoulder to shoulder. That plus the e-fit of the Square Four Gym mystery man, the reconstruction of Kimmo Thorne's abduction, and Nkata's recitation of the names of the dead boys comprised the programme's entirety.

The endeavour bore fruit. This, at least, made the whole enterprise worthwhile. It even made the prospect of having the piss taken out of him by his fellow officers somewhat bearable since Nkata intended to enter the incident room with solid information later that morning.

He finished his breakfast as the BBC was doing yet another traffic round-up. He ducked out of the flat to his mum's "Mind how you go, Jewel" and his dad's chin nod and soft "Proud of you, son," and he made his way along the outdoor corridor and down the stairs as he buttoned his overcoat against the chill. Across the grounds of Loughborough Estate, he met no one save a mum shepherding three small children in the general direction of the primary school. He made it to his car and began to climb inside, only to see that the right front tyre had been slashed.

He sighed. It was not just flat, of course. That could have been ascribed to anything: from a slow leak to a nail picked up in a street somewhere and dislodged after the damage was done. That sort of disagreeable start to his day would have been an irritant, but it wouldn't have had the cachet that a knifing had. A knifing suggested that the car's owner ought to watch his back, not only right now when he had to break out the jack and the spare but also anytime he was on the estate.

Nkata looked round automatically before he set to changing the tyre. Naturally, there was no one about. This damage had been done on the previous night, sometime after he'd arrived home post *Crimewatch*. Whoever had done this didn't have the bottle to face him squarely. At the end of the day, while he was a cop to them and consequently the enemy, he was also an alumnus of the Brixton Warriors, among whom he'd spilt his own blood and the blood of others.

Fifteen minutes later and he was on his way. His route took him past the Brixton police station, whose interview rooms he knew only too well from his adolescence, and he made a right turn into Acre Lane, with little traffic moving in the direction he was traveling.

This was towards Clapham, for it was from Clapham that the phone call had come at the end of *Crimewatch*. The caller was Ronald X. Ritucci—"It's for Xavier," he'd said—and he thought he had some information that might help the police in their investigation of the death of "that kid with the bicycle in the gardens." He and his wife had been watching the show without thinking how it might relate to them when Gail—"that's the wife"—pointed out that the night they'd been burgled corresponded to the night of that boy's death. And he—Ronald X.—had had a glimpse of the little thug just before he leapt out of the first-floor bedroom window of their house. He'd definitely worn makeup. So if the police were interested . . .

They were. Someone would call in the morning.

That someone was Nkata, and he found the Ritucci home not far to the south of Clapham Common. It was in a street of similar post-Edwardian houses, distinguished from so many of those north of the river by being detached dwellings in a city where land was at a premium.

When he rang the bell, he heard the sound of a child clattering along a corridor to the door. The inside bolt was messed about a bit, unsuccessfully, while a little voice called out, "Mummy! The doorbell! Did you hear?"

In a moment, a man said, "Gillian, get away from there. If I've told you once about answering the door, I've told you a thousand . . ." He jerked it open. A small girl in patent-leather tap shoes, tights, and a ballerina's tutu peered round his leg, one arm clinging to his thigh.

Nkata had his identification ready. The man didn't look at it. "Saw you on the telly," he said. "I'm Ronald X. Ritucci. Come in. D'you mind the kitchen? Gail's still feeding the baby. Au pair's down with flu, unfortunately."

Nkata said he didn't mind, and he followed Ritucci, after the man had closed, bolted, and tested the security of the front door. They went to a modernised kitchen at the back of the house, where a glassed-in nook held a pine table and matching chairs. There a harried-looking woman in a business suit was trying to spoon something into the mouth of a child perhaps one year old. This would be Gail, making a heroic attempt in the absence of her au pair to do the mother thing before she dashed off to work.

She said, like her husband, "You were on the television."

The child Gillian put in a clear, bell-like observation. "He's a black man, Daddy, isn't he?"

Ritucci looked mortified, as if the identification of Nkata's race were akin to mentioning a social disease that polite individuals would know to ignore. He said, "Gillian! That's quite enough." And to Nkata, "Tea, then? I can brew you a cup in a tick. No problem."

Nkata told him no thanks. He'd just had his own breakfast and wanted nothing. He nodded towards one of the pine chairs and said, "C'n I . . ."

"Of course," Gail Ritucci said.

Gillian said, "What did you eat, then? I had boiled egg 'n' soldiers."

Her father said to her, "Gillian, what did I just say?"

Nkata said to the child, "Eggs but no soldiers. My mum thinks I'm too old for them, but I 'xpect she'd make them if I asked nice enough. I had sausage 's well. Some mushrooms and tomatoes."

"All *that?*" the child asked.

"I'm a growing boy."

"C'n I sit on your lap?"

This was apparently the limit. The parents said Gillian's name in simultaneous horror, and the father swept her into his arms and out of the room. The mother shoved a spoonful of porridge into the gaping mouth of the toddler and said to Nkata, "She's . . . It's not you, Sergeant. We're trying to teach her about strangers."

Nkata said, "Mums and dads can't ever be too careful in that department," and geared up his pen to take down notes.

Ritucci returned almost immediately, having deposited his older child somewhere in the house, out of sight. Like his wife, he apologised, and Nkata found himself wishing there were actually something he could do to make them more comfortable.

He reminded them that they'd phoned the *Crimewatch* number. They'd reported a boy wearing makeup who'd burgled them . . . ?

Gail Ritucci was the one who told the first part of the story, handing over the spoon and the porridge to her husband who took up feeding their other child. They'd been out for the evening, she explained, having dinner in Fulham with old friends and their children. When they got back to Clapham, they found themselves behind a van in their street. It was moving slowly, and at first they'd thought it was looking for a space to park. But when it passed one space and then another, they became uneasy.

"We'd got a notice about break-ins in the neighbourhood," she said and turned to her husband. "When was that, Ron?"

He paused in his feeding of the toddler, spoon poised in the air. "Early autumn?" he said.

"I think that's right." She went back to Nkata. "So when the van crept along, it looked suspicious. I took down its number plates."

"Well done," Nkata told her.

She said, "Then we got home and the alarm was going off. Ron ran upstairs and saw the boy just as he went out of the window and onto the roof. Of course, we phoned the police at once, but he was long gone by the time they got here."

"Took them two hours," her husband said grimly. "Makes you wonder."

Gail looked apologetic. "Well, naturally, there must have been other things . . . more important . . . an accident or serious crime . . . not that it wasn't serious to *us,* to come home and find someone inside our house. But to the police . . ."

"Don't make excuses for them," her husband told her. He set down the porridge bowl and the spoon and used the edge of a tea towel to wipe the residue from his young child's face. "Law enforcement's going down the toilet. Has been for years."

"Ron!"

"No offence intended," he said to Nkata. "It's probably not down to you."

Nkata said no offence was taken, and he asked them if they'd given the number plates of that van to their local police.

They had done, they said. The very night they phoned. When the police finally showed up on their doorstep—"Must have been two A.M. then," Ritucci said—it was in the person of two female constables. They took a report and tried to look sympathetic. They said they would be in touch and in the meantime to come down to the station in a few days and pick up their report for insurance purposes.

"That was the end of it," Gail Ritucci told Nkata.

"Cops didn't do a bloody thing," her husband added.

ON HER WAY to meet Lynley in Upper Holloway, Barbara Havers stopped by the ground-floor flat, which she'd been passing assiduously with her eyes directed forward for ages by this point. She carried with her the peace offering she'd bought off Barry Minshall's stall: the pencil-through-the-five-pound-note trick meant to amuse and delight one's friends.

She missed both Taymullah Azhar and Hadiyyah. She missed the casual friendship they shared, dropping by one another's digs for a chat whenever the fancy took them. They weren't family. She couldn't even say they were the next best thing to family. But they were . . . something, a piece of familiarity and a comfort. She wanted both back, and she was willing to eat humble pie if that was what it was going to take to put things right between them.

She knocked on their door and said, "Azhar? It's me. Have you got a few minutes?" Then she stood back. A dim light shone through the curtains, so she knew they were up and about, perhaps shrugging into dressing gowns or something.

No one answered. Music's on, she told herself. A radio alarm that hadn't been shut off after it awoke the sleeper. She'd been too quiet in her attempt. So she knocked again, harder this time. She listened and tried to decide if what she heard behind the door was the rustle of someone disturbing the curtains to see who'd come calling so early in the morning. She looked towards the window; she studied the panel of material that covered the panes of the French door. Nothing.

Then she felt embarrassed. She stood back another step. She said more quietly, "Well, all right then," and she moved off to her car. If that was the way he wanted it . . . If she'd hit him so far below the belt with her remark about his wife taking off . . . But she'd said nothing but the truth, hadn't she? And anyway, they'd both played dirty and he hadn't been trotting to the bottom of the garden to apologise to *her.*

She forced herself to shrug the matter off and she used even more determination to leave the vicinity without looking back to see if one of them was watching her from a parted curtain. She went to where she'd left her car, all the way over in Parkhill Road, which was the closest space she'd been able to find upon her return the previous night.

From there she drove to Upper Holloway and found the comprehensive whose address Lynley had phoned to her while she'd still been in bed, trying to make herself rise to the irresistible oldies beat of Diana Ross and the Supremes ordering someone to "set me free why doanchew babe" on her radio alarm. She'd reached for the phone, attempted to sound chipper, and taken down the information on the inside bodice-ripping cover of *Torn by Desire,* which had kept her awake far into the night with the burning question of whether the hero and heroine would give in to their fatal passion for each other. *That* would take some heavy guesswork, she'd told herself sardonically.

The comprehensive in question wasn't too far from Bovingdon Close, where Davey Benton's family lived. It looked like a minimum-security prison, one whose occasional visual relief had been supplied courtesy of a David Hockney wanna-be.

Despite the distance he'd had to travel to get there in comparison with her own, Lynley was already waiting for her. He looked dead grim. He'd been to call upon the Bentons, he explained.

"How're they doing?"

"As you'd expect. As anyone would be doing in the same situation." Lynley's words were terse, even more than she would have expected them to be. She looked at him curiously and was about to ask him what was up when he nodded at the front of the school. "Ready, then?" he asked her.

Barbara was. They were there to talk to one Andy Crickleworth, supposed mate of Davey Benton. Lynley had said on the phone that he wanted as much ammunition as possible when they finally spoke to Barry Minshall in an interview room at the Holmes Street police station, and he had a feeling that Andy Crickleworth would be the person to supply it.

He'd phoned ahead so the comprehensive's administrators would be aware of the police interest in one of their pupils. Thus it was a matter of a few minutes only before Lynley and Barbara found themselves in the company of the school's headteacher, his secretary, and a thirteen-year-old boy. The secretary looked grey and defeated, and the headteacher had the used-up appearance of a man for whom a pension couldn't come too soon. For his part, the boy had braces on his teeth, spots on his face, and hair slicked back in the manner of a 1930s gigolo. By raising one half of his upper lip as he entered the room, he managed to look scornful about the whole matter of meeting the police. But the rehearsed snarl couldn't stop the fidgeting of his hands, which pressed down into his groin throughout the interview, as if they wished to stop him from wetting himself.

The headteacher—Mr. Fairbairn—made the introductions. They held their meeting in a conference room, round an institutional table that was itself surrounded by uncomfortable institutional chairs. His secretary sat in a corner, taking notes furiously, as if they'd need to be compared to Barbara's in an eventual lawsuit.

Lynley began by asking Andy Crickleworth if he knew that Davey Benton was dead. Davey's name was due to be released to the press that morning, but the grapevine is a powerful plant. If the school had been informed of the murder via Davey's parents, there was a high probability the word was out.

Andy said, "Yeah. Everyone knows. Least everyone in year eight knows." He didn't sound regretful about the matter. He clarified this by saying, "He got murdered, right?," and the tone of the question suggested being murdered was a higher form of leaving life than falling ill or dying in an accident, achieving a coolness unavailable to the others.

That belief would be typical of almost any thirteen-year-old boy, Barbara thought. Sudden death was a seven-day wonder to them, happening to someone else and never to you. She said lightly, "Throttled first, discarded second, Andy," to see if that would shake him. "You know there's a serial killer working round London, don't you?"

"He got Davey?" If anything, Andy sounded impressed, not chastened. "You want me to help you catch him or summat?"

Mr. Fairbairn said to the boy, "You're to answer their questions, Crickleworth. That will be the limit to the matter."

Andy gave him a *sod you* look.

Lynley said, "Tell us about the Stables Market."

Andy looked wary. "Wha' about it, then?"

"We're told by his parents that Davey went there. And if he went, I expect his whole crew went as well. You were part of his crew, weren't you?"

Andy shrugged. "Might've gone there. But it wouldn't've been to do nothing wrong."

"Davey's dad says he nicked a pair of handcuffs off a magic stall there. Do you know about that?"

"I didn't nick *nothing*," Andy said. "If Davey did, he did. Wouldn't surprise me, though. Davey liked nicking things. Videos from the shop in Junction Road. Sweets off the newsagent. Banana from the market. He thought it was cool. *I* told him he was asking to be caught sometime and dragged off to the nick, but he wouldn't listen. Tha' was Davey all over. He liked the lads to think he was hard."

"What about the magic stall?" Barbara put in.

"Wha' about it, then?"

"Did you go there with Davey?"

"Hey, I *said* I never nicked—"

"This isn't about you," Lynley cut in. "It isn't about what you did or did not steal and where you might or might not have stolen it. Are we clear on that? We have the word of Davey's parents that he visited a magic stall in the Stables Market, but that's all we have, aside from your name, which they also gave us."

"I di'n't even know them!" Andy sounded panicked.

"We realise that. We also realise that you and Davey had some difficulty getting on with each other."

"Superintendent," Mr. Fairbairn said in a monitory tone, as if understanding how easily "difficulty getting on" could lead them into an accusation he did not intend to allow spoken in his conference room.

Lynley held up his hand, stopping him from saying anything further. "But none of that is important now, Andy. Do you understand? What is important is what you can tell us about the market, the magic stall, and anything else that might help us find Davey Benton's killer. Is that clear enough for you?"

Andy said reluctantly that it was, although Barbara doubted it. He seemed more fixed on the drama of the situation than on the grim reality behind it.

Lynley said, "Did you ever accompany Davey to the magic stall in the Stables Market?"

Andy nodded. "Once," he said. "We all went down there. Wasn't my idea or nothing, mind you. I can't remember who said let's go. But we did."

"And?" Barbara asked.

"And Davey tried to pinch some handcuffs off that weird bloke runs the magic stall. He got caught and the rest of us scarpered."

"Who caught him?"

"The bloke. The weird one. *Dead* weird, he is. He wants sorting, you ask me." Andy seemed to make a sudden connection between the questions and Davey's death. He said, "D'you think *that* wanker killed our Davey?"

"Did you ever see them together after that day?" Lynley asked. "Davey and the magician?"

Andy shook his head. "I never." He frowned and then added after a moment, " 'Cept they must've."

"Must have what?" Barbara asked.

"Must've seen each other." He squirmed in his seat to look at Lynley, and he told the rest of his tale to him. Davey, he said, did some magic tricks at school. They were dead-stupid tricks—prob'ly *anyone* could've done them, really—but Davey'd *never* done any tricks before the day the crew went to that stall in the Stables Market. After, though, he did a trick with a ball: making it disappear, although anyone with a brain bigger than a pea could've seen how he did it. And then he did a trick with a rope: He cut it in half and then produced it uncut. He *might've* taught himself off the telly or something or even out of a book, but p'rhaps that wanker magician'd taught him the tricks, in which case Davey had prob'ly seen him more than once.

Andy sounded proud of this deduction and he looked round as if waiting for someone to shout, "Holmes, you amaze me."

Instead, Lynley said, "Had you ever been to the magic stall before that day?"

Andy said, "No. I never. Never," but as he spoke, he pressed his hands down into his crotch and held them there, and his glance went to Barbara's biro.

Lying, she thought. She wondered why. "Do you like magic yourself, then, Andy?"

" 'S all right. But not that baby stuff with balls an' ropes. I like the sort makes jets disappear. Or tigers. Not th' other shit."

"Crickleworth," Mr. Fairbairn said in warning.

Andy shot him a look. "Sorry. I don't like the sort Davey did. Tha's for little kids, innit. It don't suit me."

"But it suited Davey?" Lynley said.

"Davey," Andy said, "was a little kid."

Just the sort, Barbara thought, to appeal to a sod like Barry Minshall.

There was nothing more that Andy could tell them. They had what they needed: confirmation that Minshall and Davey Benton had had an interaction. Even if the magician claimed that his prints were on the handcuffs because they *had* belonged to him although he hadn't seen Davey steal them off his stall, the police would be able to thwart him there. Not only had he seen Davey attempt to steal the handcuffs, but he'd also caught the boy in the act. As far as Barbara could see, they had Minshall coming and going.

As she and Lynley left the comprehensive, she said, "La-dee-dah-dah, Superintendent. Barry Minshall's about to become our breakfast."

"If it were only that easy." Lynley's voice sounded heavy, not at all as she'd expected it to sound.

"Why wouldn't it be?" Barbara asked him. "We've the kid's statement now, and you know we can get the rest of Davey's crew onboard if we need them. We've got the Indian woman putting Davey at Minshall's flat, and his prints are going to be all over it. So I'd say things are looking up. What would you say?" She looked at him closely. "Has something else happened, sir?"

Lynley paused by his car. Hers was farther along the street. He didn't say anything for a moment and she was wondering if he would when he uttered one word, "Sodomised."

She said, "What?"

"Davey Benton was sodomised, Barbara."

She muttered, "Hell. It's just like he said."

"Who?"

"Robson told us things would escalate. That whatever gave the killer his kicks at first would fail after a while. He'd need more. Now we know what it was."

Lynley nodded. "We do." Then he roused himself to add, "I couldn't bring myself to tell the parents about it. I went to do so—they have a right to know what happened to their son—but when it came down to it . . ." He glanced away from her, across the street to an old-age pensioner who was hobbling along, pulling a wheeled grocery trolley behind him. "It was his father's worst fear. I couldn't realise it for him. I didn't have the heart. They're going to have to know eventually. If nothing else, it'll come out during the trial. But when I looked at his face . . ." He shook his head. "I'm losing the will to keep doing this, Havers."

Barbara found her Players and brought the packet out. She offered him one and hoped he'd hold firm and refuse, which he did. She lit up herself. The smell of burning tobacco was sharp and bitter in the cold winter air. "It doesn't make you less of a cop," she said, "just because you've become more of a human being."

"It's the marriage thing," he said to her. "It's the fatherhood business. It makes one feel—" He corrected himself. "It makes *me* feel too exposed. I see how fleeting life can be. It can go in an instant, and this . . . what you and I are doing . . . it underscores that. And . . . Barbara, here's what I never expected to feel."

"What?"

"That I can't bear it. And that dragging someone by his bollocks to justice isn't going to change that for me any longer."

She took a deep hit on the fag and held it long. It was all a crap shoot, she wanted to tell him. Life had strings but no guarantees. But he knew that already. Every cop knew it. Just as every cop knew that one didn't safeguard a wife, a husband, or a family just by working every day on the side of good guys. Kids still went bad. Wives committed adultery. Husbands had heart attacks. Everything one possessed could easily be wiped out in an instant. Life was life.

She said, "Let's just muddle through today. That's

what I say. We can't take care of tomorrow till it gets here."

BARRY MINSHALL didn't look as if he'd had an easy night of it, which was what Lynley had had in mind when he'd decided to wait until morning to interview the magician. He was disheveled and stooped. He came into the interview room in the company of the duty solicitor—James Barty, he said his name was as he led Minshall to the table and lowered him into a chair—and when the magician sat, he squinted in the bright lights and asked if he could have his dark glasses returned to him.

"You'll get nothing of use from looking at my eyes, if that's what you hope," he informed Lynley, and to make his point he raised his head and gave an illustration of his meaning. His eyes were slightly darker than the colour of smoke when dry wood burns, and they moved back and forth rapidly and incessantly. He took only a moment for this before he lowered his head. "Nystagmus and photophobia," he said. "That's what it's called. Or do I need a note from my doctor to prove it to you lot? I need those glasses, all right? I can't cope with the lights and I *can't* bloody see without them anyway."

Lynley nodded at Havers. She left the room to fetch Minshall's glasses. Lynley took the time to make ready the tape recorder and to study their suspect. He'd not seen albinism in the flesh before. It wasn't what, in his ignorance, he'd thought it would be. No pink eyes. No snow-white hair. Rather, the greyish eyes and a dense look to the hair, as if a buildup of deposits had been laid upon it over time, causing it to bear a yellow tint. He wore this hair long, although it was drawn back from his face and banded at his neck. His skin was completely without pigmentation. Not even a freckle dotted its surface.

When Havers returned with Minshall's dark glasses, he put them on at once. This allowed him to raise his head although he kept it tilted throughout their interview, perhaps the better to control the dancing movement of his eyes.

Lynley began with the preliminaries spoken for the sake of the tape recording that was being made. He went on to give the formal caution in order to snare Minshall's complete attention and in case the magician did not understand the extent of his jeopardy, which was unlikely. Then he said, "Tell us about your relationship with Davey Benton," as next to him, Havers took out her notebook for good measure.

"Considering the present circumstances, I don't think I'll be telling you anything." Barry Minshall's words were even, sounding well rehearsed.

His solicitor rested back in his chair, apparently at ease with that answer. He would have had the entire night to advise his client of his rights had Minshall asked for them.

"Davey's dead, Mr. Minshall," Lynley said, "as you know. I'd advise you to take a more cooperative approach. Will you tell us where you were two nights ago?"

There was a marked hesitation as Minshall thought about all the ramifications of remaining silent or offering an answer to this question. He finally said, "At what hour, Superintendent?," and gestured to his solicitor when Barty made a move, as if to stop him from speaking at all.

"At all hours," Lynley told him.

"You can't be more specific than that?"

"Are you that much in demand in the evenings?"

Minshall's lips curved. Lynley found it was disconcerting to interview someone whose eyes were protected by dark lenses, but he schooled himself to look for other signs: in the movement of the Adam's apple, the twitch of fingers, the alteration in posture.

"I closed my stall at the usual hour of half past five. No doubt John Miller—the bath-salts vendor—will confirm that, as he spends an inordinate amount of time observing the children who dawdle round me. I went from there to a café near my home, where I regularly eat my dinner. It's called Sofia's Cupboard although there's no Sofia and the coziness implied by *cupboard* is absent. But the price is reasonable and they leave me alone, which is how I prefer it. I went from there to my home. I went out again briefly to buy milk and coffee. That was it."

"And while you were home during the evening?" Lynley said.

"What about it?"

"What did you do? Watch your videos? Surf the Internet? Read a few magazines? Entertain visitors? Practise your magic?"

This took him some time to think about. He said, "Well, as I recall . . . ," and then spent a long while doing his recalling. Too long for Lynley's liking. Doubtless, what Minshall was doing was trying to assess how much the police would be able to confirm depending upon what he claimed to have been doing. Phone calls? There would be records of them. Mobile phone? The same. Internet use? The computer would show it. Visits to the local pub? There would be witnesses. Considering the state of his digs, he could hardly claim to have been cleaning the house, so it was down to television—in which case he'd have to name the programmes—his magazines, or his videos.

He finally said, "I had an early night. I had a bath and went straight to bed. I don't sleep well and occasionally it catches up with me, so I turn in early."

"Alone?" Havers asked the question.

"Alone," Minshall said.

Lynley took out the Polaroid photos they'd found in

his flat. He said, "Tell us about these boys, Mr. Minshall."

Minshall glanced down. After a moment he said, "Those would be the prize winners."

"The prize winners?"

Minshall pulled the plastic case of Polaroids towards himself. "Birthday parties. They're part of how I make my living, along with the stall in the market. I tell the hosts to have a game prepared for the children to play, and you're looking at the prize."

"Which is?"

"A magician's costume. I have them made in Limehouse if you'd like the address."

"The names of these boys? And why is the winner always a boy? Are there no girls where you perform?"

"One doesn't actually find many girls who're interested in magic. It doesn't attract them as it does boys." Minshall made much of examining the photos again. He held them closer to his face than was normal. He shook his head and put the pictures down. "I may have known their names at one time, but they're gone now. In some cases, I don't think I ever caught names at all. I didn't think to. I never thought I'd have to name them to anyone. And certainly not to the police."

"Why did you photograph them at all?"

"To show parents when arranging the next party," he said. "It's advertising, Superintendent. Nothing more sinister than that."

Smooth, Lynley thought. He had to give Minshall credit. It was not in vain that the magician had spent his night locked up in the Holmes Street station. But all his smoothness wrote *guilt* large upon his person. The job now was to discover a crack in the confident persona.

Lynley said, "Mr. Minshall, we have Davey Benton placed at your stall. We have him stealing handcuffs from you. We have a witness to your catching him in the act. So I'll ask you again to explain your relationship with the boy."

"Catching him in the act of pinching something from the stall doesn't constitute a relationship," Minshall said. "Children try to pinch things from me all the time. Sometimes I catch them. Sometimes I don't. In the case of this boy . . . the constable here"—with a nod at Barbara—"did tell me you'd come *across* some handcuffs related to him, and they might have come from my stall at some point in time. But *if* they did, doesn't that suggest to you that I didn't catch him in the act of pinching them at all? Because why would I catch him in the act and then let him go off with the handcuffs afterwards?"

"You may have had a very good reason for that."

"What would that be?"

Lynley was not about to allow the suspect to start asking his own questions at this point or any other point in the interview. He knew they'd got all they were going to get from Minshall, but not all that was available. So he said, "A SOCO team is taking evidence from your flat as we speak, Mr. Minshall, and I daresay you and I both know what's going to be found inside that place. Another officer has your computer in hand, and I've little doubt what sort of pretty pictures are going to turn up on it in short order when we begin logging on to the Web sites you've visited. In the meantime, forensic specialists are examining your van, your neighbour—I expect you know Mrs. Singh—positively identified Davey Benton as a child who visited you in Lady Margaret Road, and when she has a look at photos of some other dead boys . . . well, I expect you can fill the blanks there yourself. And this doesn't begin to address the manner in which your fellow vendors in the Stables Market are going to dig your grave for you when we talk to them."

"About what?" Minshall said, although he sounded less full of himself now and he glanced at the solicitor as if for some kind of support.

"About what's about to happen now, Mr. Minshall. I'm arresting you on a charge of murder. One charge and counting. This interview is concluded for the moment."

Lynley leaned forward, gave the date and the time, and switched off the recorder. He handed over his card to James Barty and said to the solicitor, "I'm available should your client wish to expatiate on any answers, Mr. Barty. In the meantime, we've got work to do. I'm sure the duty sergeant will make Mr. Minshall quite comfortable here before he's moved to a remand centre."

Outside, Lynley said to Havers, "We need to find the boys in those Polaroids. If there's a tale to be told about Barry Minshall, one of them is going to tell it. We need to compare them to the photos of the dead boys as well."

She looked back at the station. "He's dirty, sir. I can feel it. Can you?"

"He's what Robson told us to look for, isn't he. That air of confidence. He's up against it, and he's not even worried. Check into his background. Go back as far as you can manage. If he was warned off biking on the pavement when he was eight years old, I want to know about it." Lynley's mobile rang as he was speaking. He waited till Havers had her actions jotted down in her notebook before he answered.

The caller was Winston Nkata, and his voice had the sound of someone who was being careful to control his excitement. "We got the van, guv. Night of Kimmo Thorne's last break-in, a van was cruising down the street too slow, like it was doing a recce of the area. Cavendish Road station took the information, but nothing came of it. Couldn't relate it to the break-in, they said. They said the witness had to be mistaken on the number plates."

"Why?"

" 'Cause the owner had an alibi. Confirmed by nuns from that Mother Teresa group."

"An unimpeachable source, I'd say."

"But listen to this. Van belongs to a bloke called Muwaffaq Masoud. His phone number matches the numbers we c'n see on the video of that van in St. George's Gardens too."

"Where can we find him?"

"Hayes. In Middlesex."

"Give me the address. I'll meet you there."

Nkata did so. Lynley motioned to Havers to hand over her notebook and biro, and he jotted the address down in it. He ended the call from Nkata and thought about what this new development implied. Tentacles, he concluded. They were reaching out in all directions.

He said to Havers, "Get on to Minshall and the rest at the Yard."

"Are we close to something?"

"Sometimes I think so," he answered honestly, "and other times I think we've barely begun."

Chapter Twenty

Lynley used the A40 to make his way out to the address in Middlesex that Nkata supplied him. It wasn't easy to find, and the journey there encompassed wrong turns, route retracing, and the negotiation of a crossing place over the Grand Union Canal. Ultimately, the house in question turned out to be part of a small estate that was tucked within the embrace of two sports grounds, two playing fields, three lakes, and a marina. Part of Greater London, it still felt like the country, and the distant planes taking off from Heathrow couldn't dispel the sensation that somehow one had cleaner air and the possibility of freer and safer movement here.

Muwaffaq Masoud lived in Telford Way, a narrow street comprising terrace houses of amber brick. He lived at the end of one of the terraces, and he was at home to answer the door when Lynley and Nkata rang the bell.

He blinked at them from behind heavy-framed spectacles, a slice of toast in his hand. He was not yet dressed for the day, and he wore a dressing gown fashioned like the robe boxers might don before their bouts, complete with a hood and the sobriquet "Killer" embroidered on the breast and across the back.

Lynley offered his identification. "Mr. Masoud?" he said. And when the man bobbed his head in nervous affirmation, "May we have a word, please?" He introduced Nkata and said his own name. Masoud shot a look that went from one of them to the other before he stepped back from the door.

This gave immediately into a sitting room. It was not much larger than a refrigerator box, and a wooden staircase dominated its far end. Closer, a wool-covered sofa stood on one side of the room, facing a faux fireplace on the other. In the corner, a metal curio stand held the room's only decorations: perhaps a dozen photographs of what seemed to be a multitude of young adults and their offspring. Atop the stand, an additional picture formed part of a shrine, with silk flowers lying neatly at the base of a chrome-framed photograph of Princess Diana.

Lynley looked at the curio stand and then back at Muwaffaq Masoud. He was bearded, between fifty and sixty years old. The belt of his dressing gown suggested something of a paunch beneath it.

"Your children?" Lynley asked, nodding at the photos.

"I have five children and eighteen grandchildren," the man replied. "There you see them. Except for the new baby, third child of my eldest daughter. I live alone here. My wife is dead these four years now. How may I be of help to you?"

"You were fond of the princess?"

"Race did not appear to be an issue for her," he said politely. He looked down at the toast, which he was still holding. He appeared to have no further appetite for it. He excused himself and ducked into a doorway beneath the stairs. This led into a kitchen that looked even smaller than the sitting room. Through a window there, bare branches of a tree suggested a garden to the back of the house.

He returned to them, tightening the belt of his boxer's robe. He said formally and with considerable dignity, "I hope you have not come about that house-breaking in Clapham once again. At the time, I told the officers everything I knew, which was little enough, and when I did not hear from them again, I assumed the matter was at an end. But now I must ask: Did no one among you phone the good nuns?"

"May we sit down, Mr. Masoud?" Lynley asked. "We've a few questions to ask you."

The man hesitated, as if wondering why Lynley hadn't answered his question. Finally, he said thoughtfully, "Yes indeed," and he gestured to the sofa. There was no other seat in the room.

He fetched a chair from the kitchen for himself, and he placed it squarely opposite them. He sat, his feet flat on the floor. They were bare, Lynley saw. One toe was missing its nail. Masoud said, "I must tell you. I have never broken a law of this country. This I told the police when they came to speak with me. I do not know Clapham nor do I know any neighbourhood south of the River Thames. Even if I did know those things, on nights when I do not see my children, I go to Victoria Embankment. This is where I was on the night of that break-in in Clapham about which the police have questioned me."

"Victoria Embankment?" Lynley said.

"Yes. Yes. Near the river."

"I know where it is. What do you do there?"

"Behind the Savoy Hotel many people sleep rough all seasons of the year. I feed them."

"Feed them?"

"From my kitchen. Yes. I feed them. And I am not the only one to do this," he added, as if feeling the need to counter what he saw as Lynley's scepticism. "The nuns are there. And another group, which hands out blankets. When the police asked me about my van being in Clapham on a night when someone was burgled there, I explained this to them. Between half past nine and midnight I am far too busy to concern myself with burgling houses, Superintendent."

It was, he told them, the way of Islam, and he added, "as it is meant to be practised," with gentle emphasis on the word *meant*, perhaps to differentiate between the old ways and the militant forms of Islam sometimes espoused round the globe. The Prophet—blessed be his name—instructed his followers to care for the poor, Masoud explained. The mobile kitchen was how this one humble servant of Allah complied with that instruction. He took himself to Victoria Embankment all the year round, although the need for him was greatest in winter when the cold dealt harshly with the homeless.

Nkata was the one to jump on the words. "*Mobile* kitchen, Mr. Masoud. You don't use your kitchen here to fix up meals?"

"No, no. How could I keep the food hot for such a journey as it is from Telford Way to Victoria Embankment? My van is kitted out with what is necessary to prepare the meals within it. A cooker, a work space, a small refrigerator. This is all that I need. Of course, I could serve them sandwiches, which would not require the effort of cooking, but they need hot food, those poor souls in the street, not cold bread and cheese. And I am grateful that I can provide it."

"How long have you operated this mobile kitchen?" Lynley asked the man.

"Since I began taking my pension from British Telecom. That would be nearly nine years now. You must ask the nuns. They will confirm this."

Lynley believed him. Not only because the nuns would probably confirm it along with everyone else who saw Muwaffaq Masoud along the embankment on a regular basis but also because there was an air of honesty about the man that commanded one's trust. *Righteous* was the word Lynley thought would describe him best.

Nonetheless, he said, "My colleague and I would like to look at your van. Outside and inside. Will you approve of that?"

"Of course. If you will wait . . . ? Let me dress and I shall take you to it." He quickly mounted the stairs, leaving Lynley and Nkata to glance at each other in silent evaluation of what he'd had to say.

"What's your assessment?" Lynley asked.

"Telling the truth or a sociopath. But look at this, guv." Nkata turned his small leather notebook round on his knee so that it faced Lynley, and Lynley glanced at what he'd written:

waf
bile
chen
873-61

while beneath it he'd added:

Muwaffaq's
Mobile
Kitchen
8579-5479

Nkata said, "That's what I can't suss out. What'd he do, then? Serve those meals behind the Savoy, hang about in Central London for whatever, then cruise over to St. George's Gardens in the middle of the night afterwards, where he gets caught on the video we saw? Why?"

"Assignation?"

"With who? Drug dealer? That bloke does drugs like I do drugs. Prostitute then? His wife's dead, so he's wanting some, okay, but why would he take a tart to St. George's Gardens?"

"Terrorist?" Lynley offered. It seemed like a complete nonstarter, but he knew that nothing could be discounted.

"Gunrunner?" Nkata said. "Bomb maker?"

"Someone with contraband to hand over?"

"Not the killer, but meeting the killer," Nkata said. "Handing over something. A weapon?"

"Or taking something from him?"

Nkata shook his head. "Handing over something. Or someone, guv. Handing over the kid."

"Kimmo Thorne?"

"That works." Nkata glanced at the stairs, then back to Lynley. "He goes to the embankment, but how far're we talking from Leicester Square? From Hungerford Footbridge if that's how Kimmo and his mate got over the river? This bloke could know Kimmo from f'rever past, and he's biding his time to decide what to do with him."

Lynley considered this. He couldn't conceive of it. Unless, as Nkata himself had pointed out, the Asian man was a sociopath.

"Please then follow me," Masoud said as he descended the stairs. He'd put on not the traditional *shalwar qamis* of his countrymen, but rather baggy jeans and a flannel shirt over which he was zipping a leather flying jacket. He had trainers on his feet. He was suddenly much more of their country than of his own. The transformation did give one pause to consider him differently, Lynley realised.

The van was parked inside one of a string of garages that stood together at the end of Telford Way. There was no way to inspect the vehicle easily without moving it from the structure, and Masoud did this without being asked. He rolled the van back to give Nkata and Lynley access. It was red, like the van that had been seen by their witness from her flat above Handel Street, just outside St. George's Gardens. It was also a Ford Transit.

Masoud turned off the engine and jumped out, opening the sliding panel door to show them the inside of the vehicle. It was kitted out exactly as he'd said: a cooker had been fixed along one side. There were also cupboards, a work surface, and a small fridge. One could use the vehicle for camping, as there was room to sleep in the middle if necessary. One could also use it as a mobile murder site. There was little doubt of that.

But it hadn't been used in such a manner. Lynley knew that much before Masoud leapt out and opened the Ford for them to look over. The van was of recent vintage, and on its side "Muwaffaq's Mobile Kitchen" and the relevant phone number glistened pristinely.

Nkata spoke, asking the question as Lynley opened his own mouth to do so. "You had 'nother van before this one, Mr. Masoud?"

Masoud nodded. "Oh yes. But it was old and it had many times failed to start when I needed to use it."

"What happened to that van?" Lynley asked.

"I sold it."

"With the interior in place?"

"You're speaking of the cooker? The cupboards? The fridge? Oh yes, it was just like this one."

"Who bought it, then?" Nkata's voice held the sound of hope-against-hope. "When?"

Masoud thought about both questions. "This would be . . . seven months ago? Towards the end of June? I believe that was it. The gentleman . . . I regret I cannot remember his name . . . He wanted it for the August bank holiday, he told me. I assumed he intended to take it on a little journey, although he did not say as much."

"How did he pay?"

"Well, of course I was not asking a great deal for the van. It was old. It was not reliable, as I've already said. It needed work done upon it. And painting as well. He wished to give me a personal cheque, but as I did not know him, I required the payment to be made in cash. He departed but returned with the money the very same day. We concluded our transaction, and that was the end of it." Masoud put the pieces together himself as he finished his explanation. "That would be the van you seek. Of course. This gentleman bought it expressly for an illegal purpose, so he did not register his name upon it. And the purpose was . . . He is the Clapham burglar?"

Lynley shook his head. The burglar was a teenage boy, he told Masoud. The purchaser of the van was probably that boy's killer.

Masoud took a stricken step backwards. He said, "My van . . . ?," and could say no more.

"Can you describe this bloke?" Nkata asked. "Anything about him that you remember?"

Masoud's expression looked dazed, but he answered slowly and thoughtfully. "It was so long ago. An older gentleman? Younger than myself, perhaps, but older than you. He was a white man. English. Bald. Yes. Yes. He was bald because the day was hot and his head perspired and he wiped it with a handkerchief. An odd sort of handkerchief, as well, for a man. Lace on the edge. I remember that because I noticed and he said it had sentimental value. His wife's handkerchief. She made lace on things."

"Tatting," Nkata murmured, and to Lynley, "like that piece got left on Kimmo, guv."

"He was a widower like myself," Masoud said. "That was what he meant by sentimental value. And yes, I remember this: He was not very well. We walked from the house to this garage here and that short distance took his breath. I did not wish to comment on this, but I thought that a man of his age should not be so breathless as he was."

"Anything else you c'n remember about his looks?" Nkata asked. "He's bald and what else? Beard? Moustache? Fat? Thin? Marks on him anywhere?"

Masoud looked at the ground as if he'd be able to see a mental picture of the man there. He said, "There was no moustache or beard." He meditated on this, his forehead wrinkled with the strain of remembering. Finally he said, "I cannot say more."

Bald and breathless. There was nothing to go on. Lynley said, "We'd like to arrange an e-fit of this man. We'll send someone out to work with you."

"To draw his face, do you mean?" Masoud said doubtfully. "I will do what I can, but I fear . . ." He hesitated as he appeared to look for a polite way to say what he wanted to say. "So many English look similar to me. And he was very English, very . . . ordinary."

Which, Lynley thought, most serial killers were. It was their special gift: They faded into a crowd with no one the wiser about their presence. Only in fantasy chillers had they been born werewolves.

Masoud returned his van to the garage. They waited for him and walked back to his house. It was only when they were about to part that Lynley realised another question needed to be asked. He said, "How did he get here, Mr. Masoud?"

"What do you mean?"

"If he planned to drive your van home, he would have needed transport here in the first place. There's no railway station nearby. Did you see what his method of transport was?"

"Oh yes. That would have been the minicab. It remained in the street—parked just outside this house, in fact—during our transactions."

"Did you get a look at the driver of that cab?" Lynley exchanged a glance with Nkata.

"I'm sorry, no. He merely sat in the car outside my house and waited. He certainly did not appear interested in our transaction."

"Was he young or old?" Nkata asked.

"Younger than any of us, I should say."

FU DIDN'T take the van to Leadenhall Market. It wasn't necessary. He didn't like removing it from the carpark during daylight hours and, besides, He had other means of transport that would seem—at least to the casual observer—more logical for the area.

He tried to tell Himself that the last days had finally *proved* to Him His power. But even as others began to see Him as He'd long intended Himself to be seen, it appeared to Him that control of the situation was beginning to slip from His grasp. This concern bore no sense, but still He found Himself wanting to shout from a public place, "I am here, the One you seek."

He knew the ways of the world. As the knowledge spread, so did the risk. He had embraced that possibility from the first. He had even sought it. What He had not expected was how the need within Him would be fueled once He'd been finally acknowledged. He'd begun to feel consumed by it now.

He entered the old Victorian market from Leadenhall Place, where the freakishly modern Lloyds of London provided Him the cover of the commonplace: His presence here would not be remarked upon, and if one of the countless CCTV cameras along the way caught His image, no one would think anything of it in this place at this time of day.

Inside the market and beneath its vaulted ceiling of iron and glass, the great dragons loomed over him from every corner: long clawed and red tongued, with their silver wings unfurled for flight. Beneath them, the old cobbled central street was closed to traffic and the shops that lined it offered their wares to the daytime workers of the City as well as to tourists who—at other, more clement times of year—made this place part of their trips to visit the Tower or Petticoat Lane. It was designed for exactly that sort of custom, with narrow passageways offering everything from pizza to one-hour photo developing, cheek by jowl with butchers and fishmongers selling fresh items for that night's dinner.

In midwinter, the site was very nearly perfect for what Fu had in mind. It was virtually deserted in the daytime aside from during the City workers' lunch hours, and at late nighttime with the traffic bollards removed from either end of the main route through, what few vehicles rolled through it did so intermittently.

Fu strolled through the market towards its main entrance on Gracechurch Street. The shops were open, but they were sparsely peopled, while the most business being transacted appeared to be happening inside the Lamb Tavern, behind whose translucent windows the shapes of drinkers moved periodically. In front of this establishment, a shoe-shine boy did desultory business, buffing the black shoes of a banker type who was reading a broadsheet as his footwear was seen to. Fu glanced at this newspaper when he passed the man. One would expect a type like him to be perusing the *Financial Times*, but this was the *Independent* instead, and it carried on its front page the sort of headline that broadsheets generally reserved for royal superdramas, political nightmares, and acts of God. The words "Number Six" comprised it. Below that, a grainy photograph appeared.

Fu felt a different sort of need at the sight of this. It was one directed not towards fulfilling His growing desire but one that—had He lacked control—would have otherwise propelled Him towards that banker and that broadsheet like a starving hummingbird to the embrace of a flower. To proclaim Himself, to be understood.

He diverted His eyes instead. It was too early, yet He recognised in Himself the same sensation He'd experienced while watching the television programme about Him on the previous night. And how odd to name the sensation for what it was, because it was not at all what He'd expected it to be.

Anger. The heat of it, searing the muscles of His throat until He would cry out. For the one who truly sought Him had made no appearance before the television cameras, sending minions instead, as if Fu were a spider easily crushed beneath his heel.

He'd watched and there the maggot had found Him, slithering up the chair in which He sat, crawling in through His nose, curling behind His eyes till His vision went blurry, and then residing within His skull, where he remained. There to taunt. There to prove . . . *pathetic, pathetic, pathetic, pathetic. Stupid little wanker, nasty little swine.*

Think you're someone? Think you'll ever *be someone? Useless piece . . . Don't you ever turn your face from me when I'm talking to you.*

Fu tossed from it, turned from it. There it stayed.

You want fire? I'll show you fire. Give me your hands. I said give me your sodding hands. Here. You like how it feels?

He'd leaned His head against the back of the chair and He'd closed His eyes. The maggot ate greedily at His brain, and He tried not to feel or acknowledge it. He tried to remain where He was, doing what He alone had been able to do.

You hear me? You know me? How many people do you intend to send to the grave before you're satisfied?

As many as it takes, He'd thought at last. Till I am sated.

He'd opened His eyes then to see the sketch on the television screen. His face, and not His face at all. Someone's memory trying to coax an image out of the ether. He evaluated the depiction of Him, and He'd chuckled. He'd loosed His shirt and exposed Himself to the hate that would be directed towards that image from every corner of the country.

Come, He'd told it. Eat through my tissue.

That's what you think they'll do? For you? *Shite, you're full of it, aren't you, boy. I never did see a case like you.*

No one had, Fu thought. No one would again. Leadenhall Market made the promise of that.

He stood opposite a string of three shops just inside the Gracechurch Street entrance: two butchers' shops and a fishmonger's, all red, gold, and cream, like a Dickens Christmas. Above each shop and extending the entire length of it hung three tiers of nineteenth-century iron rails with myriad hooks reaching out from them. It was upon these that game birds had been displayed one hundred years ago, turkey upon turkey and pheasant upon pheasant, tempting the passerby to make a purchase during the appropriate season. Now they were only an antique remnant of a time long passed. But they were designed to serve Him.

It was here that He would bring them both. Proof and witness simultaneously. It would, He decided, be a crucifixion of sorts, with arms stretched wide along the game rails and the rest of the bodies wedged within the spaces between the rails themselves. It would be the most public of His displays. It would be the most bold.

He walked the area as He laid His plans. There were four separate ways to come into Leadenhall Market, each of them posing a different kind of challenge. But all of them shared one commonality, and it was the commonality of virtually every street within the City itself.

There were CCTV cameras everywhere. Those in Leadenhall Place guarded Lloyd's of London; in Whittingdon Avenue they watched over a Waterstone's and the Royal & Sun Alliance across the street; in Gracechurch Street they guarded Barclays Bank. The best possibility was in Lime Street Passage, but even here a smaller camera hung above a greengrocer's that He would have to pass when making His way into the market itself. It was much like choosing the Bank of England as the spot where He'd make His next "deposit." But the challenge of it all was half the pleasure. The other half came with the commission itself.

He would use Lime Street Passage, He decided. Its small and insignificant camera would be the easiest to get to and to render useless.

Having made this decision, He felt at peace. He retraced His steps, into the market and then in the direction of Leadenhall Place and Lloyds of London beyond it. That was when He heard the call.

"You, sir. Beg pardon, sir, if you'll just hang on . . ."

He paused. He turned. He saw a pear-shaped man coming towards Him, official epaulets broadening his shoulders. Fu allowed His face to fall into the slack expression that seemed to put people at ease in His presence. He offered a quizzical smile as well.

"Sorry," the man said as he joined Him. He was out of breath, which wasn't a surprise. He was overweight, and his trousers and shirt did not fit him properly. He wore the uniform of a security guard and his name badge said he was called B. Stinger. Fu wondered how often he was teased about that name. Or if it was a real name at all.

"It's the times," B. Stinger said. "Sorry."

"Something going on?" Fu looked round as if for an indication of this. "Is something wrong?"

"It's just that . . ." B. Stinger gave a rueful grimace. "Well, we saw you on the telly screens . . . in security, you know? You seemed to be . . . I told that lot you were probably looking for a shop, but they said . . . Anyway. Sorry, but can I help you find something?"

Fu did what seemed natural in response. He looked round for cameras, for more cameras than He'd seen outside the market itself. He said, "What? Did you see me on CCTV?"

"Terrorists," the man said with a shrug. "IRA, Muslim militants, Chechens, other assorted louts. You don't look like one of them, but when we see someone hanging about . . ."

Fu widened His eyes, an oh-wow sort of look. He said, "And you thought that I . . . ?" He smiled. "Sorry. I was having a look round. I come past here every day and I'd never actually been inside. It's fantastic, isn't it?" He pointed to the features He declared especially to His liking: the silver dragons, the gold-lettered signs with their deep maroon backgrounds, the decorative plasterwork. He felt like a bloody art appreciationist, but He babbled enthusiastically. At the end, He said, "Anyway, I'm glad I didn't bring my camera. You lot might've had me in the nick for that. But you're doing your job. I know that. D'you want my ID or something? I was just leaving, by the way."

B. Stinger held up his hands, palms outward, as if to say *enough.* "I just needed to have a word. I'll tell them you're clear." And then he added, like a confidential aside, "Paranoid, that lot. I'm up and down those stairs at least three times an hour. It's nothing personal."

Fu spoke affably. "I didn't think it was."

B. Stinger waved Him off and Fu nodded good-bye. He went on His way back to Leadenhall Place.

But there He paused. He felt the tension riding down his neck and across His shoulders, like a substance that was pouring out of His ears. This had all been for nothing, and a waste of His time when time was crucial now . . . He wanted to track down the security guard and take *him* as a prize, no matter how foolhardy such an act would be. Because now He would have to start again, and starting again when His need was this great was a dangerous proposition. It put Him in the position of being driven to carelessness. He couldn't afford that.

Think you're special, gobshite? Think you've got something anyone *would want?*

He tightened His jaw. He forced Himself to look at the cold, hard facts. This place would not do for His purpose, and He was blessed by the appearance of the security guard to demonstrate that fact. Obviously, there were more cameras within the market itself than He'd accounted for, hidden high in the vaulted ceiling, no doubt, tucked beneath an outspread dragon wing, made to look part of the elaborate plasterwork. . . . It made no difference. What counted was what He knew. And now He could seek another place.

He thought about the television programme. He thought about the newspaper articles. He thought about pictures. He thought about names.

He smiled at how simple the answer was. He knew the spot He had to seek.

BY THE TIME Lynley and Nkata returned to New Scotland Yard, Barbara Havers had done the work on Minshall's background. She had also viewed the Boots tapes to scan the queue behind Kimmo Thorne and Charlie Burov—aka Blinker—to see if any familiar face appeared there, and she'd additionally done her best with what other customers she could see in the shop from the CCTV footage. There was no one, she reported, who bore any resemblance to anyone she'd seen at Colossus. Barry Minshall was also not among the customers, she added. As to the e-fit from Square Four Gym and whether anyone in Boots looked like that individual. . . . She'd been less than enthusiastic about that sketch from the first.

"Whole thing's a nonstarter," she said to Lynley.

"What about Minshall's background?"

"He's kept his nose clean up to now."

She'd handed the photos of the boys in magician costumes over to DI Stewart, and he'd given them to officers who were in the process of showing them to the dead boys' parents for possible identification. She said, "If you ask me, I don't think that's going to get us anywhere either, sir. I compared them to the photos we've already got of the dead boys, and no one looks like a match to me." She sounded unhappy with this development. She definitely fancied Minshall for the killer.

Lynley told her to carry on digging in the background of the bath-salts vendor from the Stables Market, the bloke called John Miller who'd seemed overly interested in the goings-on at Barry Minshall's stall.

In the meantime, John Stewart had assigned five constables—this was all he could spare, the DI told Lynley—to handle the post-*Crimewatch* phone calls about the e-fit sketch and other information. Countless viewers apparently knew someone who bore a marked resemblance to the baseball-capped man who'd been seen in Square Four Gym. The constables had the job of sorting the wheat from the chaff among the callers. Cranks and crackpots loved the opportunity to make themselves important or to have a bit of revenge on a neighbour they were rowing with. What better way than to inform the police that one person or another "wants checking out."

Lynley went from the incident room to his office, where he found a report from SO7 sitting on his desk. He had fished his spectacles from his jacket pocket and started to read it when the phone rang and Dorothea Harriman's hushed voice told him that AC Hillier was heading in his direction.

"He's got someone with him," Harriman said *sotto voce*. "I don't know who it is, but he doesn't look like a cop."

A moment later, Hillier entered the room. He said, "I'm told you're holding someone."

Lynley removed his reading glasses. He glanced at Hillier's companion before he replied: a thirtyish man wearing blue jeans, cowboy boots, and a Stetson. Definitely, he thought, not a cop.

He said to the man, "We've not met . . . ?"

Hillier said impatiently, "This is Mitchell Corsico, *The Source*. Our embedded reporter. What's this about a suspect, Superintendent?"

Lynley carefully set the report from SO7 facedown on his desk. He said, "Sir, if I could have a private word?"

"That," Hillier told him, "is not going to be necessary."

Corsico said hastily, with a glance from one man to the other, "Let me just step outside."

"I said—"

"Thank you." Lynley waited till the journalist had gone into the corridor before he went on to Hillier, "You said forty-eight hours before the journalist would come onboard. You've not given me that."

"Take it above my head, Superintendent. This is not down to me."

"Then who?"

"The Directorate of Public Affairs made a proposal. I happen to think it's a good one."

"I've got to protest. This is not only irregular, it's also dangerous."

Hillier didn't look pleased with this remark. "You listen to me," he said. "The press can't get much hotter. This story is dominating every paper and every news outlet on television as well. Unless we get lucky and some hothead Arab group decides to bomb Grosvenor Square, we don't have a prayer of escaping scrutiny. Mitch is on our side—"

"You can't possibly think that," Lynley countered.

"And you assured me the reporter would come from a broadsheet, sir."

"And," Hiller went on, "his idea has merit. His editor phoned the DPA with it and the DPA gave it the go-ahead." He turned to the door and called out, "Mitch? Come back in here, please," which Corsico did, Stetson shoved to the back of his head.

Corsico echoed Lynley's sentiments. He said, "Superintendent, God knows this is irregular, but you're not to worry. I want to begin with a profile piece. To bring the public into the picture about the investigation through the people involved in it. I want to start with you. Who you are and what you're doing here. Believe me, no detail about the investigation proper will be in the story if you don't want it there."

"I've no time to be interviewed by anyone," Lynley said.

Corsico held up a hand. "Not to worry," he said. "I've considerable information already—the assistant commissioner has seen to that—and all I ask of you is your permission to be the fly on your wall."

"I can't give you that."

"I can," Hillier told him. "Can and do. I have confidence in you, Mitch. I know you're aware of how delicate this situation is. Come along and I'll introduce you to the rest of the squad. You've not seen an incident room, have you? I think you'll find it interesting."

With that, Hillier left with Corsico in tow. Incredulous, Lynley watched them go. He'd stood when the assistant commissioner and the journalist had entered the room, but now he sat. He wondered if everyone in the Directorate of Public Affairs had gone mad.

Who to phone? he asked himself. How to protest? He thought about Webberly, wondering if the superintendent could intercede from his convalescence. He didn't see how. Hillier was being used by the higher-ups now, and he didn't appear able to question that.

The only person who might put the brakes on this lunacy was the commissioner himself, but what would that gain in the long run save Lynley most likely being pulled from the case?

Profiles of the investigators, he said to himself in derision. God in heaven, what would it be next? Glossy photos in *Hello!* or an appearance on some inane chat show?

He took up the SO7 report, knowing only that the squad of investigators would be just about as happy with this development as he was. He put on his glasses to see what forensics had for him.

Davey Benton's fingernails had yielded skin beneath them, product of his desperate fight with his killer. The sexual assault had yielded semen. There would be DNA evidence from both of these results, the first DNA evidence to be gleaned from any one of the bodies.

The corpse had also yielded an unusual hair—Lynley's heart leapt when he read the word *unusual* and his thoughts went at once to Barry Minshall's—and this was currently undergoing analysis. It did not, however, appear to be a human hair, so consideration would have to be given to whether it might have come from the location in which the body had been dumped.

Finally, the shoe prints at the site in Queen's Wood had been identified. They were from a Church's, size nine. The style was called Shannon.

Lynley read this last bit gloomily. That narrowed the point of purchase down to every high street in London.

He punched in the extension for Dorothea Harriman. Would she get a set of this latest SO7 paperwork over to Simon St. James? he asked her.

Ever efficient, she'd already done so, adding that he had a phone call coming in from the Holmes Street station. Did he want to take it? And, by the way, was she meant to ignore this Mitchell Corsico bloke when he asked questions about what it was like to have an aristo for a guv? Because, she confessed, when it came to having an aristo for a guv, she'd been thinking that there *was* a way to hoist the assistant commissioner upon . . . "his own whatever," was how she put it.

"Petard," Lynley said, and he saw her point. That was the answer, and it was simplicity itself, requiring no higher-up to do anything at all. "Dee, you're a genius. Yes. Feel free to give him grist by the bushel. That should keep him occupied for days on end, so ladle it on. Mention Cornwall. The family pile. A row of servants playing Manderley under the direction of a brooding housekeeper. Phone my mother and ask her to arrange to have my brother look suitably drug addled should Corsico appear on her doorstep. Phone my sister and warn her to bolt her doors lest he show up in Yorkshire and want to examine her dirty linen. Can you think of anything else?"

"Eton and Oxford? A rowing blue?"

"Hmm. Yes. Rugby would have been better, wouldn't it? More laddish. But let's stay with the facts, the better to keep him occupied and away from the incident room. We can't rewrite history no matter how much we'd like to."

"Shall I call you his lordship? The earl? What?"

"Don't go too far or he'll see what we're doing. He doesn't seem stupid."

"Right."

"Now for Holmes Street station. Put them through, if you will."

Harriman did so. In a moment, Lynley found himself talking not to one of the officers or specials but rather to Barry Minshall's solicitor. His message was brief and welcome.

His client, James Barty said, had thought things over. He was ready to talk to the detectives.

Chapter Twenty-one

Ulrike Ellis told herself that there was no reason to feel guilty. She was sorry for the death of Davey Benton, as she would have been sorry for the death of any child whose corpse had been found like so much discarded rubbish in the woods. But the truth was that Davey Benton was not a Colossus client, and she celebrated the lifting of suspicion that had to go along with the revelation that an adult from Colossus was not involved in his killing.

Of course, the police had not said as much when she phoned. This was her own conclusion. But the detective inspector to whom she'd spoken had said, "Very well, madam," in a way that suggested he was crossing something important off his list, and that could *only* mean a cloud had been lifted, that cloud being the suspicion of an entire murder squad at New Scotland Yard.

She'd phoned there earlier and requested the name of the boy whose body had been found in Queen's Wood. She'd phoned once again with the delighted—although she'd tried very hard not to show it—information that they had no record of a Davey Benton registered as a client at Colossus. In between the two calls, she'd trolled the records. She'd looked through the hard copies of files, and she'd scrolled through everything

Colossus kept stored on its computers. She'd gone through the index cards they kept, filled out by kids expressing an interest in Colossus at outreach programmes the organisation had offered throughout London in the last year. And she'd phoned Social Services with the boy's name, to be told they had no record of him and had never recommended him for Colossus's intervention.

At the end of all this, she felt relief. The horror of the serial killings was not about Colossus after all. Not that she'd ever thought for a moment that it *actually* was . . .

A phone call from that unattractive female constable with the broken teeth and bad hair provided a blip on the screen of Ulrike's liberation from anxiety, however. The police were now working on some other connection. Had Colossus ever provided entertainment for clients? the detective constable wanted to know. For a special occasion, perhaps?

When Ulrike asked the woman—Havers, she was called—what sort of entertainment, she said, "Like a magic show, f'r instance. You lot ever do something like that?"

Ulrike said, as helpfully as she could manage, that she would have to research this detail. For the kids did indeed go on outings—that was part of the assessment course—although the outings were of the physically adventurous kind like boating, hiking, biking, or camping. Still, there was always a chance, and Ulrike wished to leave no stone of possibility unturned. So if she could get back to Constable Havers . . . ?

She set about finding out. Another troll through the records was called for. She also queried Jack Veness because if anyone knew what was going on in every nook and cranny at Colossus, it would be Jack, who'd been there before Ulrike's arrival on the scene.

Jack said, "Magic?," and raised one of his scraggly ginger eyebrows. "Like pulling rabbits out of hats or something? What're the cops on to now?" He went on to tell her that he'd never heard of magic shows being performed at Colossus or any of the assessment groups going out to see such a show either. He said, "This lot," with a jerk of his head towards the inner reaches of the building where the kids were busy with their assessment courses or other classes, "they're not the sort to go for magic in a big way, are they, Ulrike?"

Of course they weren't and she didn't need telling that by Jack Veness. She also didn't need to see Jack smirk, either at the thought of their kids sitting in a breathlessly spellbound semicircle to watch a magician perform or at the thought of her—Ulrike Ellis, the supposed head of the organisation—even considering that their hard-core clients might enjoy such entertainment. He needed putting in his place every few days, did Jack. She did the honours.

She said, "Do you find the search for a killer amusing, Jack? And if you do, why might that be?"

That wiped the smirk from his face. It was replaced with hostility. He said, "Why don't you chill, Ulrike?"

She said, "Watch yourself," and went on her way.

Her way was to dig for further information to offer the cops. But when she phoned with the message that no one at Colossus had brought in a magician or taken a group to see a magician, they seemed unimpressed. The constable who took her call merely echoed his miserable colleague, like someone reading from a script. He said, "Very well, madam," and told her he'd pass the information along.

She said, "You do see this has to mean—" but he'd already rung off, and she knew what that signified: It was going to take even *more* to get the cops off the metaphorical back of Colossus, and she was going to have to dig for it.

She tried to come up with a way to do it that was not so obvious it might garner future employee problems or even a group action against her. She knew an effective leader had to be unworried about the opinions of others, but that leader also had to be a political animal who knew how to twist an action taken into a reasonable step in the right direction, no matter what that action was. But she could not come up with a way to make her next move look like anything other than a declaration of her distrust. The very effort it took to plan out an approach actually made her teeth start aching till she wondered if she'd gone too long without a visit to the dentist. She searched in her desk for a packet of paracetamol, and she swallowed two with a gulp of cold coffee that had been sitting next to her telephone for God only knew how long. Then she went in search of . . . she decided to call it exoneration. Not for herself, but for the others. She told herself that *whatever* she uncovered she would report back to the cops. There was no doubt in her mind that Colossus did *not* harbour a killer. But she knew she had to seem reasonable to the cops, especially in light of having lied to them earlier about Jared Salvatore's being one of their clients. She had to appear cooperative. She had to demonstrate change. She *had* to get them away from Colossus.

She sidestepped Jack Veness for the moment and went in search of Griff. She saw through the window of the assessment room that he was in session with his new group of kids, and the flip chart he was using indicated that they were evaluating their last activity. She made a gesture when she caught his eye. May I talk to you? it said. He gave her five fingers and a half smile that communicated his mistaken belief about the topic she wished to pursue. No matter, she thought. Let him think she meant to cajole him back to her bed. That might make him less wary of talking to her, which was all to the good. She nodded and went to look for Neil Greenham.

She found Robbie Kilfoyle instead, in the practice kitchen, setting up for a cookery class. He was taking bowls and pans out of the classroom cupboards, working off a list provided him by the instructor. Ulrike decided to start with him. What the hell did she *really* know about Robbie anyway aside from the fact that he'd been in trouble with the law long ago? Peeping Tom, the CRB check upon him had revealed. She'd taken him on anyway as a volunteer. God knew they needed him, and volunteers had never been leaking out of the woodwork. People change, she'd assured herself at the time. But now she looked at him more critically, and she realised he had a baseball cap on . . . just like the e-fit of the serial killer.

God, God, *God*, she thought. If she had been the one to bring a killer into their midst . . .

But if *she* knew what the e-fit of the possible killer looked like because she'd seen it in the *Evening Standard* and on *Crimewatch* as well, didn't it stand to reason that Robbie Kilfoyle also knew? And *if* he knew and was the killer, why in God's name would he show up here, wearing that EuroDisney hat? Unless, of course, he was wearing it because he knew how odd it would appear if he *stopped* wearing it immediately after *Crimewatch* was broadcast. Or perhaps he truly *was* the killer and so cocky about not getting caught that he'd decided to be in her face and everyone else's with the EuroDisney cap on his head, like a red rag waving in front of a bull . . . Or even still, perhaps he was incredibly stupid . . . or didn't watch television or read the newspapers or . . . God . . . *God* . . .

"Something wrong, Ulrike?"

His question forced her to bring herself round. The ache in her teeth had moved to her chest. Her heart again. She needed a thorough checkup, stem to stern or whatever.

She said, "Sorry. Was I staring?"

"Well . . . yeah." He placed mixing bowls on the work top, spacing them out to accommodate the kids in the class. "They're doing Yorkshire pud," he told her, with a nod to the list he'd posted for himself on a corkboard right above the sink. "My mum used to make it every Sunday. What about you?"

Ulrike took the opening. "I never had it till we got to England. Mum didn't make it in South Africa. I don't know why."

"No roast beef?"

"I can't recall, actually. Probably not. Can I help you there?"

He looked round. He seemed wary of her offer. She could well understand, as she'd never made it before. She'd never even talked to him—*really* talked to him—aside from at the beginning when she'd taken him on at Colossus. She made a mental note to talk to *everyone* at least once every day henceforth.

He said, "There's not much to do, but I guess I could cope with some conversation."

She went to the corkboard and looked at his list. Eggs and flour. Oil. Pans. Salt. Yorkshire pudding certainly did not require genius to put together. She made a second mental note to talk to the instructor about challenging the kids a bit more.

She riffled through her mind to think of something she knew about Robbie, other than the fact he was a former prowler. "How's the job going?" she asked him.

He gave her a sardonic look. "Sandwich deliveries, you mean? It's a living. Well"—with a smile then—"it's *nearly* a living. I could do with something a bit better, frankly."

Ulrike took this as a hint. He was angling for permanent employment at Colossus. For paid employment. She couldn't blame him for that.

Robbie seemed to read her mind. He paused in the act of pouring flour from a bag into a large plastic bowl. "I can be a real team player, Ulrike," he said. "If you'd give me half a chance."

"Yes. I know that's what you want. It's under consideration. When we open the branch across the river, you're tops on the list to do assessment."

"You're not having me on, are you?"

"Why would I?"

He set the bag of flour on the work top. "Look, I'm not stupid. I know what's going on round here. The cops talked to me."

"They talked to everyone."

"Yeah, okay. But they've talked to my neighbours as well. I've lived there forever, so the neighbours told me when the cops came round. I expect they're one step away from surveillance."

"Surveillance?" Ulrike tried to make it sound casual. "On you? Surely not. Where do you go that they'd want to watch you?"

"Exactly nowhere. Oh, there's a hotel nearby, and they've got a bar. It's where I go when I need a break from my dad. You'd think it was a crime or something."

"Parents," she said. "Sometimes you need to get away from them, eh?"

He frowned. He stopped what he was doing. He was silent for a moment before he said, "'Get away'? What's this really about?"

"Nothing. It's just that Mum and I row, so I guess I thought . . . well, the same-sex thing, I suppose. Two adults of the same sex, in the same house? You start to get on each other's nerves."

"As long as we just watch the telly, Dad and I are fine," he informed her.

"Oh. Lucky you. Do that a lot? Watch telly, that is."

"Yeah. The reality shows. We're hooked on those. The other night, in fact, we—"

"Which night was this?" She saw she'd asked the question too quickly. His face took on a sudden sharpness she'd not seen before. He fetched eggs from the fridge, counting them out carefully, as if intent upon displaying his diligence. She waited to see if he would answer.

"The night before that boy was found in the woods," he finally said. He was terribly polite about it. "We watched the show with the yacht. *Sail Away*. Do you know it? It's on cable. We bet each other about who was going to get voted off. Have you got cable, Ulrike?"

She had to grudgingly admire the way he had put away affront in order to cooperate. She owed him something. She said, "Sorry, Rob."

He took a moment before he shrugged, relenting. "It's all right, I guess. But I did wonder why you stopped to chat."

"You *are* on the list for a paying job."

"Whatever," he said. "I'd better finish up here."

She let him go back to what he'd been doing. She felt ill at ease but concluded that people's feelings couldn't be allowed to matter, even her own. Later, when things were back to normal, she'd make more complete amends. Now, there were far more pressing concerns.

So she decided to abjure the circuitous approach. She found Neil Greenham and went directly for the jugular.

He was alone in the computer room, working on one of the kids' Web pages. Typical of the Colossus client, the page was black and featured Gothic graphics.

She said, "Neil, what were you doing on the eighth?"

He made a note on the yellow pad next to the mouse. She saw a muscle work in his fleshy jaw. He said, "Let me see, Ulrike. You must want to know was I murdering some poor kid in the woods."

She didn't say anything. Let him think what he would.

"Have you checked with the others?" he asked her. "Or am I the only favoured one?"

"Can you just answer the question, Neil?"

"*Can*, of course. But *will* is another matter."

"Neil, this is nothing personal," she told him. "I've already spoken to Robbie Kilfoyle. I'm intending to speak to Jack as well."

"What about Griff? Or doesn't he come onto your radar screen for murder? Now that you're playing at copper's nark, I'd think you'd want to start practising objectivity."

She felt herself colour. Humiliation, not anger. Oh, she'd thought they'd been so circumspect. No one can know, she'd told Griff. But in the end it hadn't mattered. When one allowed the besotted to overcome the cautious, a billboard wasn't exactly necessary. She said, "Do you plan to answer my question?"

"Sure," he said, "when I'm asked by the cops. And I expect I will be. You'll make certain of that, won't you?"

"This isn't *about* me," she told him. "It isn't *about* anyone. It's about—"

"Colossus," he finished for her. "Right, Ulrike. It's always about Colossus, isn't it? Now if you'll excuse me, I've work to do. But if you want a shortcut, phone my mum. She'll alibi me. 'F course I'm her darling blue-eyed boy, so I may have told her to lie when someone comes snooping round to ask questions. But that's the chance you'll be taking with all of us, anyway. Have a nice day."

He went back to the computer. His ruddy face was ruddier. She could see a pulse pounding in his temple. Outraged innocence under scrutiny? she wondered. Or something else? Fine, Neil. Have it your way.

Jack Veness was easier. He said, "Miller and Grindstone. Shit, Ulrike, it's where I always am. Why the hell are you doing this, anyway? Don't we have enough aggro around here?"

They did. She was making things worse, but that couldn't be helped. She *had* to have something to give to the cops. Even if it meant checking every alibi herself: Robbie's dad, Neil's mum, the publican at the Miller and Grindstone . . . She was willing to do it. She was able, as well. And she wasn't afraid. She'd do it because there was so much at stake—

"Ulrike? What happened? I thought I said five minutes."

Griff had come out to reception. He looked confused, as well he might, since any other time he'd told her when to show up in his orbit, she'd been there like a dependable satellite.

"I need a word," she said. "Have you got the time?"

"Sure. The kids're editing the trust circle. What's going on?"

Jack spoke up. "Ulrike's taking up where the cops left off."

Ulrike said, "That'll do, Jack," and to Griff, "Come with me."

She led the way to her office and shut the door. Neither the oblique approach nor the direct approach had succeeded without offence being taken, so she reckoned it didn't matter which way she went with Griff. She opened her mouth to speak, but he began first.

He said, running a hand back through that hair of his, "I'm glad you asked to talk, Rike. I've wanted to talk."

She said, "What?," before she thought it through. Rike. He'd murmured that in her ear. A groan with orgasm: Rike, *Rike*.

"I've missed you. I don't like the way things seem to have ended between us. I don't like *that* things seem to have ended. What you said about me . . . that I've been a good fuck. That went to the bone. I never thought of myself like that with you. It wasn't about fucking, Rike."

"Really? What was it about, then?"

He'd been standing by the door, she in front of the

desk. He moved, but not to her. Rather he went to the bookshelves and seemed to peruse them. He finally picked up the photo of Nelson Mandela standing between Ulrike—much younger and so much more innocent of life—and her dad.

He said, "This. This kid in the picture and everything she believed back then and still believes now. The passion of her. The life inside her. Connecting to both because I want them both myself: passion and life. That's what it was about." He replaced the picture and looked at her. "It's still there in you. That's what's so mesmerising. Was from the beginning, still is now."

He drove his hands into the back pockets of his blue jeans. They were tight, as always, moulding the front of him. She could see the mound where his penis lay. She averted her eyes.

"Things are insane at home," he went on. "I haven't been myself, and I'm sorry. Arabella's hormones up and down, the baby's colic. The silk-screen business isn't doing well just now. There's been too much on my mind. I started to think of you as one more thing I had to contend with, and I didn't treat you well."

"Yes. That's right."

"But it didn't mean—I didn't mean—that I didn't want you. Just then, the complication . . ."

"Life doesn't have to be complicated," she told him. "You've made it that way."

"Rike, I can't leave her. Not yet. Not with a new baby. If I did that, I wouldn't be good for you or anyone. You've got to see that."

"No one asked you to leave her."

"We were heading for that, and you know it."

She was silent. She knew that she needed to get them back on the track of why she'd wanted to speak to him in the first place, but his dark eyes diverted her and as they did so, they also dragged her back into the past. The feel of him near her. The heat of his body. That heady moment when he entered her. More than flesh to flesh, it was soul to soul.

She resisted the pull of memory and said, "Yes. Well. Maybe we were."

"You know we were. You could see what I felt. What I *feel* . . ."

He approached. She could feel the pulse light and rapid in her throat. Heat built within her and descended to her genitals. She felt the maddening moistening in spite of herself.

She said, "That was animal stuff. Only a fool would mistake it for the real thing."

He was close enough that she caught the scent of him. No lotion, was this. No cologne or after-shaving splash. It was just *his* scent, the combination of hair, skin, and sex.

He reached out and touched her: his fingers on her temple, describing a quarter circle to her ear. He touched the lobe. One finger traced the path of her jaw. Then he dropped his hand.

"We're still okay, aren't we?" he said. "At the heart of it?"

She said, "Griff, listen," but she could hear the lack of conviction in her tone. He would hear it as well. He would know what it meant. Because it *did* mean . . . Oh the closeness of him, the scent and the strength. Holding her down, his two hands imprisoning hers on the mattress, and his kiss, his kiss. Her hips in the rhythmical, rotating dance and then tilting tilting because nothing mattered then or even later but wanting, having, and satiation.

She knew that he felt it as well. She knew that if she dropped her gaze—which she would *not* do—she would see the evidence behind the tight denim.

Griff said roughly, "Listen to what, Rike? My heart? Yours? What they're telling us? I want you back. It's crazy. Stupid. I can't offer you one bloody thing just now except the fact that I want you. I don't know what tomorrow might bring. We could both be dead. I just want you now."

When he kissed her, then, she did not move away from his embrace. His mouth found hers and then his tongue coaxed her own mouth to open. She moved back against the desk, and he moved with her so that she felt the hard, hot demand of him pressing against her.

"Let me back, Rike," he murmured.

She slipped her arms round his neck and kissed him hungrily. There was danger everywhere, but she didn't care. For beyond the danger—above it and hindering its ability to harm her—there was this. Her hands in his hair, feeling the rough silk of it between her fingers. His mouth on her neck as his hands sought her breasts. The pressure of him grinding against her and the desire to have him, combining with the absolute indifference to discovery.

They would be quick, she told herself. But they could not part until . . .

Zips, knickers, and the gasp of pleasure on both their parts as he slid her up on the desk and entered. Her mouth on his, her arms clinging, his arms holding her hips in position, and the brutal thrust of him that could never be hard or brutal enough. And then she felt the blessed contraction and its release and a moment later his own groan of pleasure. And they were clasped together as they were meant to be, safe and secure, in less than sixty seconds.

They parted slowly. She saw he was flushed. She knew she was too. He was breathing rapidly, and he looked stunned.

"I didn't mean that to happen," he said.

"I didn't either."

"It's what we are together."

"It is. I know."

"I can't let it end. I tried. But it doesn't work because I see you and—"

"I know," she said. "I feel it too."

She pulled her clothes back on. She could feel him leaking out of her already, and she knew the smell of their sex was all over her. She was meant to care about that, but she didn't.

He felt the same. He had to because he pulled her back to him and kissed her.

Then, "I'm *going* to find a way."

She kissed him. The rest of Colossus didn't exist, out there beyond her office door.

He finally tore his mouth from hers with a laugh. He held her to him, pressed her head against his shoulder. He said, "You'll be there for me, won't you? You'll always be there, won't you, Rike?"

She raised her head. She said, "It seems I'm not going anywhere."

"I'm glad. We're together now. Always."

"Yes."

He caressed her cheek. He returned her head to his shoulder and held her. "Will you say that, then?"

"Hmmm."

"Rike? Will you . . . ?"

She raised her head. "What?"

"That we're together. We want each other, we know it isn't right, but we can't stop ourselves. So when we have the chance, nothing else matters. The time, the day, whatever. We do what we *have* to do."

She saw his earnest eyes—how closely they watched her—and she felt a coolness come into the air. "What're you talking about?"

Griff gave a lover's chuckle, tender and indulgent. She pulled away. He said, "What's wrong?"

She said, "Where were you? Tell me where you were."

"Me? When?"

"You know when, Griffin. Because that's what this"—she gestured at the two of them, the office, the interlude they'd just created—"is all about. You. My God. It's always about you. Having me so besotted that I'll say *anything*. The cops come calling and the last person I want them looking at closely is the man I'm fucking on the side."

He produced an expression of incredulity, but she was not taken in. Nor was she moved by the wounded innocence that replaced it. Wherever he'd been on the eighth, he needed an alibi for it. And he'd blithely assumed that she would provide it, secure in the knowledge that they were the star-crossed lovers that fate—or whatever it was—had intended them to be.

She said, "You bloody self-centred bastard."

"Rike—"

"Get out. Get out of my life."

He said, "What? Are you sacking me?"

She laughed, a harsh sound whose humour was directed only at herself and her stupidity. "It always comes down to that, doesn't it?"

"Down to what?"

"Down to you. No, I'm not sacking you. That would be far too easy. I want you here, right under my thumb. I want you jumping when I say frog. I intend to keep an eye on you."

Incredibly, he still said, "But will you tell the cops . . . ?"

"Believe me, I'll tell them whatever they want to know."

LYNLEY DECIDED he owed it to Havers to let her in on the second interview with Barry Minshall, since she'd been the one to collar him in the first place. So he fetched her from the incident room where she was in the midst of looking into the background of the bath-salts vendor in the Stables Market. He told her only to come with him. As they took the stairs down to the underground carpark, he put her in the picture.

"He's looking for a deal, I'll wager," she said when he told her that Barry Minshall was ready to talk. "That bloke's got so much dirty laundry, he's going to need a Persil factory to clean it all. Mark my words. Will you play, then, sir?"

"These are boys, Havers. Just out of childhood. I won't make their lives less valuable by giving their killer any option but the one that faces him: life residence in a very unpleasant environment where child molesters are the least popular of the denizens."

"I can live with that," Havers told him.

Despite her agreement, he found he needed to say more, as if he were in debate with her. It seemed to him that only by striking hard would anyone ever be able to extirpate the sickness that had begun to plague their society. He said, "Somewhere along the line, Havers, we've *got* to become a country without throwaway children. We've got to move beyond being a place where anything goes and nothing matters. Believe me, I'm happy enough to start by using Mr. Minshall as an object lesson for those who think of twelve- and thirteen-year-old boys as disposable items akin to take-away curry cartons." He paused on one of the landings, then, and looked at her. "Preaching," he said ruefully. "Sorry."

"No problem. You're entitled." She lifted her head to indicate the upper floors of Victoria Block. "But, sir . . ." She sounded hesitant, which was completely unlike her. She barreled forward. "This Corsico bloke . . . ?"

"Hillier's embedded reporter. We can't get round it. He's not listening to reason any more than he's listened to it all along."

"The bloke's staying in bounds," she reassured him. "It's not that. He's not looking at a thing, and the only questions he's asking are about you. Hillier said he's going to be profiling people, but I'm thinking . . ." She looked restless. Lynley could tell she wanted a cigarette, which had long been Havers' form of Dutch courage. He finished her thought.

"It's not a good idea. Bringing the investigators into the picture in a public forum."

"It's just not on," she said. "I don't want this bloke fingering through *my* knicker drawer."

"I've told Dee Harriman to give him enough of an earful about me that he'll be kept busy for days tracking down details from my disreputable past, which she's been instructed to gild as much as she likes: Eton, Oxford, Howenstow, a score of love affairs, upper-crust pursuits like yachting, pheasant shooting, fox-hunting—"

"Bloody hell, do *you*—"

"Of course not. Well, once when I was ten, and I loathed it. But Dee can talk about that as well as dozens of dancing girls performing at my whimsy if that's what it takes. I want this bloke kept out of everyone else's way for a while. God willing—and if Dee does her job and everyone else Corsico talks to catches on—we'll have this case wrapped up before he even gets on to profiling anyone else."

"You can't want your mug on the front page of *The Source,*" she said as they continued down the stairs. " 'The Earl Who's a Cop.' That sort of rubbish."

"It's the last thing I want. But if putting my face on the front of *The Source* keeps everything else about this case *out* of *The Source*, I'm willing to put up with the embarrassment."

They made their way to their separate vehicles, the day growing late and the Holmes Street station being close enough to Havers' bungalow to make it logical for her to return home at the end of their conversation with Barry Minshall. She trailed Lynley across London in her sputtering Mini, after a few breathless moments in the carpark wondering if the car would start at all.

At the Holmes Street station, they were expected. James Barty—the duty solicitor—had to be fetched, which took some twenty minutes while they cooled their heels in an interview room and declined an offer of late-afternoon tea. When Barty finally showed up, with crumbs from a scone studding the corner of his mouth, it shortly became evident that he had no idea why his client had decided to talk. It certainly wasn't something that the solicitor had urged Minshall to do. He preferred to wait until he saw what the police had to offer, Barty informed them. There was generally something behind it all when a charge of murder was as swift as this one had been, didn't the superintendent agree?

Barry Minshall's advent in their midst precluded a reply on Lynley's part. The magician came in, brought from his cell by the duty sergeant. He had on his dark glasses. He was much the same as he'd been on the previous day, save for his cheeks and his chin, which showed white stubble.

"How d'you like the accommodation?" Havers asked. "Growing on you yet?"

Minshall ignored her. Lynley switched the tape recorder on, giving the date, the time, and the people present. He said, "You've asked to speak to us, Mr. Minshall. What is it you'd like to say?"

"I'm not a murderer." Minshall's tongue came out and licked his lips, a lizard movement of colourless flesh against colourless flesh.

"D'you actually think that van of yours isn't going to give us fingerprints from here to Friday?" Havers asked. "Not to mention your flat. When was the last time you cleaned that place, anyway? I reckon it's got more evidence inside it than an abattoir."

"I'm not saying I didn't know Davey Benton. Or the

others. The boys in the pictures. I knew them. I *know* them. Our paths crossed and we became . . . friends, you can call it. Or teacher and pupil. Or mentor and . . . whatever. So I admit to having them over to my flat: Davey Benton and the boys in the pictures. But the reason was to teach them magic so that when I was invited to a children's party, there would be no question of . . ." He swallowed loudly. "Look, people aren't trusting, and why should they be? Someone dressed up like Father Christmas pulls a child on his knee and puts his hand up her knickers. A clown goes into the children's ward at the local hospital and takes a toddler into a linen room. It's everywhere you look, and I need a way to show parents they've nothing to fear from me. A boy assistant . . . He always puts the parents at ease. That's what I was training Davey to do."

"To be your assistant," Havers repeated.

"That's correct."

Lynley leaned forward, shaking his head. He said, "I'm concluding this interview . . ." He glanced at his watch and gave the time. He switched off the recorder and stood, saying, "Havers, we've wasted our time. I'll see you in the morning."

Havers looked surprised, but she got up as well. She said, "Right then," and followed him towards the door.

Minshall said, "Wait. I haven't—"

Lynley swung round. "You wait, Mr. Minshall. You listen as well. Possession and transmission of child pornography. Child molestation. Paedophilia. Murder."

"I didn't—"

"I'm not about to sit here and listen to you claim you were operating a training school for child magicians. You were seen with that boy. In the market. At your home. God knows where else, because we're just beginning. Traces of him will be everywhere associated with you, and traces of you will be all over him."

"You're not going to find—"

"We bloody well will. And the barrister who's even willing to take your case will have the devil of a time explaining it all away to a jury hungry to send you down for putting your filthy hands on a little boy."

"They *weren't* little . . ." Minshall stopped himself. He fell back in his chair.

Lynley said nothing. Neither did Havers. The room was suddenly as silent as a crypt in a country church.

James Barty said, "Would you like a moment, Barry?"

Minshall shook his head. Lynley and Havers remained where they were. Two more steps and they'd be out of the room. The ball was sailing into Minshall's court, and he was no fool. Lynley knew he had to see it.

"It meant nothing," he said. "That word. *Weren't.* It isn't the slip you think it is. Those boys who've died—the others, not Davey—you won't find a thing that connects me to them. I swear to God I didn't know them."

"Are we talking biblically?" Havers asked.

Minshall threw her a look. Even from behind his glasses, he transmitted the message: *As if you'd understand.* Next to him, Lynley felt her bristle. He touched her arm lightly, directing her back to the table. He said, "What have you got to tell us?"

"Turn on the recorder," Minshall replied.

Chapter Twenty-two

"It isn't what you think," were Barry Minshall's first words when Lynley had the tape recorder going. "Your sort have an idea fixed in the head, and then you mould the facts to make sure your idea plays out. But how you think it was . . . ? You're wrong. And how Davey Benton was . . . ? You're wrong about that as well. But I'll tell you straightaway, you won't be able to face what I have to say, because if you do, it topples the way you've probably always seen the world. I want some water. I'm parched and this will take a while."

Lynley hated to give the man anything, but he nodded to Havers and she disappeared to fetch Minshall his drink. She was back in less than a minute with a single plastic cup of water that looked as if she'd taken it directly from the ladies' toilet, which she probably had. She placed it in front of Minshall and he gazed from her to it as if checking to see if she'd spat in it. Finding it passable, he took a sip.

"I can help you," he said. "But I want a deal."

Lynley reached towards the recorder another time, preparatory to switching it off and ending the interview once again.

Minshall said, "I wouldn't do that. You need me just

as much as I need you. I knew Davey Benton. I taught him some elementary magic tricks. I dressed him up as my assistant. He rode in my van, and he visited me in my flat. But that's the end of it. I never put a hand on him in the way you're thinking, no matter what he wanted."

Lynley felt his mouth going dry. "What the hell are you implying?"

"Not implying, saying. Telling. Informing. Whatever you want to call it, it comes out the same. That boy was bent. At least, he *thought* he was bent, and he was looking for proof. A first time to show him what it was like. Male to male."

"You can't intend us to believe—"

"I don't care what you believe. I'm telling you the truth. I doubt I was the first bloke he tried because he was damned direct in his approach. Hands on my crotch the instant we were out of public view. He saw me as a loner—which I am, let's face it—and to his way of thinking, it was safe to try things out with me. That's what he wanted to do, and I set him straight. I do *not* have underage kids, I told him. Come back on your sixteenth birthday."

"You're a liar, Barry," Barbara Havers said. "Your computer's filled with child pornography. You were carrying it in your van, for God's sake. You're shagging your fist in front of your computer screen every night, and you want us to believe Davey Benton was after *you* and not the reverse?"

"You can think what you want. You obviously do. Why not, when I'm such a flipping freak? And *that's* running through your head as well, isn't it? He looks like a ghoul, so he must be one."

"Use that move often?" Havers asked. "I expect it works wonders out there in the world. Turn people's aversion in on themselves. That must work specially well on kids. You're a sodding genius, you are, boy-o. High marks for sorting out a way to play your appearance to your advantage, mate."

Lynley said, "You don't appear to understand your position, Mr. Minshall. Has Mr. Barty"—with a nod at the solicitor—"explained what happens when you're charged with murder? Magistrates' court, remand, coming to trial at the Old Bailey—"

"All those lags and screws just *waiting* to welcome you into Wormwood Scrubs with open arms," Havers added. "They have a special greeting for child molesters. Did you know that, Bar? It requires you to bend over, of course."

"I am *not*—"

Lynley switched off the recorder. "Apparently," he said to James Barty, "your client needs more time to think. Meanwhile, the evidence mounts up against you, Mr. Minshall. And the moment we confirm that you were the last person to see Davey Benton alive, you can feel free to consider your fate well sealed."

"I did *not*—"

"You might try to convince the CPS about that. We collect the evidence. We turn it over to them. At that point, things are out of our hands."

"I can help you."

"Think about helping yourself."

"I can give you information. But the only way you're going to get that from me is through a deal because *if* I give you anything, I'm not going to be a particularly popular man."

"If you don't give us something, you're being sent down as Davey Benton's," Barbara Havers pointed out. "And that's not going to do much for your popularity, Barry."

"What I suggest," Lynley said, "is that you tell us what you know and pray to God we're more interested in that than in anything else. But make no mistake about it, Barry, you're facing at least one murder charge currently. Any other charge you might come to face in the future as a result of what you tell us now about Davey Benton isn't going to carry the same stretch in prison. Unless it's another count of murder, of course."

"I didn't kill anyone," Minshall said, but his voice was altered now, and for the first time it seemed to Lynley that they might be getting through to the man.

"Convince us," Barbara Havers said.

Minshall thought for a moment and finally said, "Turn the recorder on. I saw him the night he died."

"Where?"

"I took him to a . . ." He hesitated, then went for more water. "It's called the Canterbury Hotel. I had a client there and we went to perform."

"What d'you mean, 'perform'?" Havers asked. "What kind of client?" In addition to the tape that Lynley was making, she was taking notes, and she looked up from her writing.

"Magic. We were doing a private show for a single client. At the end of it, I left Davey there. With him."

"With whom?" Lynley asked.

"With the client. That was the last I saw of him."

"And what was this client's name?"

Minshall's shoulders sagged. "I don't know." And as if he expected them to walk out of the interview room, he went on hastily. "I knew him only by numbers. Two-one-six-oh. He never told me his name. And he didn't know mine. He knew me only as Snow." He gestured at his hair. "It seemed appropriate."

"How did you meet this individual?" Lynley asked.

Minshall took another sip of water. His solicitor asked him if he wanted a conference. The magician shook his head. "Through MABIL," he said.

"Mabel who?" Havers asked.

"M-A-B-I-L," he corrected. "It's not a person. It's an organisation."

"An acronym standing for . . . ?" Lynley waited for the answer.

Minshall gave it in a tired voice. "Men and Boys in Love."

"Bloody *hell*," Havers muttered as she wrote in her notebook. She gave the acronym a vicious underscoring that sounded like the scrape of rough sandpaper on wood. "Let us guess what *that's* all about."

"Where does this organisation meet?" Lynley asked.

"In a church basement. Twice a month. It's a deconsecrated place called St. Lucy's, off the Cromwell Road. Down the street from Gloucester Road station. I don't know the exact address, but it's not hard to find."

"The scent of sulphur's no doubt a big hint when you get in the area," Havers pointed out.

Lynley shot her a look. He felt the same aversion to the man and his story, but now that Minshall was finally talking, he wanted him to continue talking. He said, "Tell us about MABIL."

Minshall said, "It's a support group. It offers a safe haven for . . ." He seemed to search for a word that would elucidate the purpose of the organisation at the same time as it depicted its members in a positive light. An impossible task, Lynley thought, although he let the man attempt it anyway. "It offers a place where like-minded individuals can meet, talk, and learn they're not alone. It's for men who believe there is no sin and should be no social condemnation in loving young boys and wanting to introduce them to male-male sexuality in a safe environment."

"In a *church*?" Havers sounded as if she couldn't restrain herself. "Like some sort of human sacrifice? On the *altar*, I expect?"

Minshall took off his glasses and shot her a withering look as he polished them on the leg of his trousers. He said, "Why don't you put a cork in it, Constable? It's people like you who head witch-hunts."

"You listen to me, you piece of—"

"That'll do, Havers," Lynley said. And to Minshall, "Go on."

The magician gave Havers another look, then shifted his body as if to dismiss her. He said, "There are no young boys who are members of the association. MABIL does *nothing* but provide support."

"For . . . ?" Lynley prompted.

He returned his dark glasses to his nose. "For men who're . . . conflicted about their desires. Those who've already made the leap help along those who want to make it. This help is offered in a loving environment, with tolerance for all and judgement of none."

Lynley could see Havers getting ready to make another remark. He cut her off with, "And two-one-six-oh?"

"I saw him straightaway, the first time he showed up. He was new to it all. He could barely look anyone in the eye. I felt sorry for the bloke and offered to help him. It's what I do."

"Meaning?"

And here Minshall stalled. He was silent for a moment and then asked for time with his solicitor. For his part, James Barty had been sitting there sucking on his lower teeth so hard that it looked as if he'd swallowed his lip. He burst out with, "Yes. Yes. Yes," and Lynley switched the recorder off. He nodded Havers towards the door, and they stepped out into the corridor of the Holmes Street station.

Havers said, "He's had *all* bloody night to cook this up, sir."

"MABIL?"

"That and the two-one-six-oh rubbish. D'you think for a moment there's going to *be* a MABIL at this St. Lucy's when we send Vice over there to sit in on their next 'meeting'? Not bloody likely, sir. And Bar will have the perfect comeback for that, won't he? Let me give it to you in advance: 'MABIL has members who're cops, you know. The Met's grapevine must've put those blokes in the picture, and they passed the word along. You know how it works: telephone, telegraph, tell-a-cop. They've gone to ground now. Too bad you can't find them . . .' And arrest their arses from here to Sunday," she added. "Sodding paedophiles."

Lynley observed her, righteous indignation personified. He felt it as well, but he also knew they had to keep the information flowing from the magician. The only way to sort out the truth from his lies was through encouraging him to talk for a length of time and listening for the snares he would ultimately set himself, which was the fate of all liars.

He said, "You know the drill, Havers. We need to give him the rope."

"I know, I know." She looked towards the door and the man behind it. "But he makes my skin crawl. He's in there with Barty coming up with a way to justify the seduction of thirteen-year-old boys, and you and I know it. What are we supposed to do about that? Sit there and seethe?"

"Yes," Lynley said. "Because Mr. Minshall's about to discover he can't have it both ways. He can't claim he rejected Davey Benton as too young to experience the love that dare not et cetera, while at the same time he provided the boy to a killer. I expect he's sorting out that little difficulty with Mr. Barty as we speak."

"So you *believe* there's a MABIL? That Minshall himself didn't murder that kid and all the others?"

Like Havers, Lynley looked towards the door of the interview room. "I think it's very likely," he said. "And there's part of it all that makes sense, Barbara."

"Which part is that?"

"The part that explains why we've now got a dead boy with no connection to Colossus."

She was with him, as usual, making the leap with,

"Because the killer had to find new ground once we showed up in Elephant and Castle?"

"From everything we know, he's not stupid," Lynley said. "Once we got on to Colossus, he had to find a new source of victims, didn't he. And MABIL *exactly* fills the bill, Havers, because no one would even suspect him there, especially not Minshall, who's just waiting to take him under his wing, eager and ready to hand over the victims, apparently believing—or at least telling himself that he believes—in the sanctity of the whole damned project."

"We need a description of two-one-six-oh," Havers said, with a nod at the interview room.

"And more," Lynley told her as the door opened and James Barty bade them enter once again.

Minshall had finished his water and was setting to the destruction of the plastic cup that had held it. He said he wanted to clarify things. Lynley told him that they were ready to listen to whatever the magician wished to tell them, and he activated the tape recorder as Havers sat and scraped her chair noisily against the lino.

"My first time was at the hands of my paediatrician," Minshall said quietly, his head lowered to direct his gaze—ostensibly, since he was wearing his dark glasses—on his hands as they tore apart his plastic cup. "He called it 'seeing to' my condition. I was a kid, so what did I know? Groping round between the legs to make sure my 'condition' didn't cause sexual problems in the future, like impotence or premature ejaculation. He eventually raped me right there in his surgery, but I kept quiet. I was that scared." Minshall looked up. "I never wanted other boys' first time to be like that. Do you understand? I wanted it to come out of a loving and trusting relationship so that when it happened to them, they'd be ready for it. They'd want it as well. They'd understand what was happening and what it meant. I wanted it to be a positive experience, so I empowered them."

"How?" Lynley kept his voice calm and reasonable, although what he wanted to do was howl. How they excelled when they had to justify, he thought. Paedophiles lived in a parallel universe to the rest of mankind, and one could do virtually nothing to blast them out of it, so immovably had they placed themselves there through years of rationalisation.

"Through openness," Barry Minshall said. "Through honesty."

Lynley heard Havers restrain herself. He saw how tight her grip was on her pencil as she took notes.

"I talk to them about their sexual urges. I allow them to see what they feel is natural and nothing to be hidden or ashamed of. I show them what all children need to be shown: that sexuality in all of its manifestations is something God given, to be celebrated rather than hidden away. There are actual tribes, you know, where children are *initiated* into sex as a rite of passage, guided there by a trusted adult. This is part of their culture, and if we ever manage to loose the chains of our Victorian past, it will be part of ours as well."

"That's what MABIL aims at, eh?" Havers asked.

Minshall didn't directly answer her. "When they come to see me in my flat," he said, "I prepare them for magic. To assist me. This takes some weeks. When they're ready, we perform for an audience of one: my client. From MABIL. What you need to know is that no boy has *ever* refused to go with the man to whom he was given at the end of our performance. They've been eager for it, in fact. They've been ready. They've been, as I've said, empowered."

"Davey Benton—" Havers began, and from the heat in her voice, Lynley knew he had to stop her.

He said, "Where did these 'performances' occur, Mr. Minshall? At St. Lucy's?"

Minshall shook his head. "They were private, as I said."

"At the Canterbury Hotel, then. Where you last saw Davey. Where is this place?"

"Lexham Gardens. Off the Cromwell Road. One of our members runs it. Not for this. Not for men and boys together. It's a legitimate hotel."

"I'll bet," Havers murmured.

"Take us through what happened," Lynley said. "At this performance. It was in a room?"

"A regular room. The client is always asked to book himself into the Canterbury in advance. He meets us in the lobby and we go upstairs. We do the show—the boy and I—and I get paid."

"For supplying the boy?"

Minshall wasn't about to admit to pandering. He said, "For the magic show at which the boy assisted."

"Then what?"

"Then I leave the boy. The client will take him home . . . afterwards."

"All those boys whose pictures we found in your flat . . . ?" Havers asked the question.

"Former assistants," Minshall said.

"You mean you handed *every* one of them over to be done by some bloke in a hotel room?"

"No boy went unwillingly. No boy stayed against his will at the end of the performance. No boy later came to me with a complaint about how he'd been handled."

"Handled," Havers said. "*Handled*, Barry?"

Lynley said, "Mr. Minshall, Davey Benton was murdered by the man you handed him over to. You understand that, don't you?"

He shook his head. "I know only that Davey was murdered, Superintendent. There's nothing that tells me my client did it. Until I hear from him otherwise, I remain convinced that Davey Benton went off on his own later that night, once he was driven home."

"What d'you mean, 'until you hear otherwise'?" Havers asked. "Are you expecting a serial killer to phone you up and say 'Thanks, mate. Let's have a second go of the same so I can kill another'?"

"You're saying my client killed Davey. I'm not. And yes, I'm expecting a second request from him," Minshall said. "There usually is one. And a third and a fourth if the boy and the man haven't reached a separate agreement on the side."

"What sort of agreement?" Lynley asked.

Minshall took his time about coming up with an answer. He glanced at James Barty, perhaps trying to recall how much the solicitor had advised him to say. He went on carefully. "MABIL," he said "is about love, Men and Boys in Love. Most children are eager for that, for love. Most *people* are eager for that, in fact. This isn't about—this has never been about—molestation."

"Just pandering," Havers said, obviously able to restrain herself no longer.

"No boy," Minshall plunged doggedly on, "has *ever* felt used or abused from an interaction I bring about through MABIL. We want to love them. And we *do* love them."

"And what do you tell yourself when they turn up dead?" Havers asked. "That you loved the life right out of them?"

Minshall gave his answer to Lynley, as if believing Lynley's silence implied tacit approval of his enterprise. "You have no proof that my client . . ." He decided to make a different point. "Davey Benton wasn't meant to die. He was ready to have—"

"Davey Benton fought his killer," Lynley cut in. "In spite of what you thought about him, Mr. Minshall, he wasn't bent, he wasn't ready, he wasn't willing, and he wasn't eager. So if he went with his killer at the end of your 'performance,' I doubt he did it willingly."

Minshall said hollowly, "He was alive when I left

them together. I swear it. I've never harmed a hair on a single boy's head. No client of mine has done that either."

Lynley had heard enough of Barry Minshall, his clients, MABIL, and the great project of love in which the magician apparently saw himself involved. He said, "What did this man look like? How did you contact each other?"

"He isn't—"

"Mr. Minshall, just now I don't care if he is or isn't a killer. I mean to find him and I mean to question him. Now how did you contact each other?"

"He phoned me."

"Land line? Mobile?"

"Mobile. When he was ready, he phoned. I never had his number."

"How did he know when you had all the arrangements in place, then?"

"I knew how long it would take. I told him when to phone again. He kept in touch that way. When I had things set up, I just waited for him to phone and I told him when and where to meet us. He went first, paid for the room in cash, and we met him there. Everything else happened as I said. We performed, and I left Davey with him."

"Davey didn't question this? Being left alone in a hotel room with a stranger?" That didn't sound like the Davey Benton that his father had described, Lynley thought. There had to be a missing ingredient to the mixture Minshall was describing. "Was the boy drugged?" he asked.

"I have never drugged one of the boys," Minshall said.

Lynley was used to the man's way of dancing round by this time. He said, "And your clients?"

"I do not drug—"

"Plug it, Barry," Barbara cut in. "You know exactly what the superintendent is asking."

Minshall looked at what he'd done to his plastic cup: rendered it into shreds and confetti. He said, "We're generally offered refreshments in the hotel room. The boys are free to take them or not."

"What sort of refreshments?"

"Spirits."

"Not drugs? Cannabis, cocaine, Ecstasy, the like."

Minshall actually reared up in offence at this question, saying, "Of *course* not. We're not drug addicts, Superintendent Lynley."

"Just buggerers of children," Havers said. Then, she shot *Sorry, sir* in a look to Lynley.

He said, "What did this man look like, Mr. Minshall?"

"Two-one-six-oh?" Minshall thought about it. "Ordinary," he said. "He had a moustache and goatee. He wore a peaked cap, like a countryman. Spectacles as well."

"And did you *never* put all this down as a disguise?" Lynley asked the magician. "The facial hair, the glasses, the cap?"

"At the time, I didn't think . . . Look, by the time a man's ready to stop fantasising about it and to make it real, he's *beyond* disguises."

"Not if he plans to kill someone," Havers pointed out.

"How old was this man?" Lynley asked.

"I don't know. Middle-aged? He must have been because he wasn't in very good shape. He looked like someone who doesn't take exercise."

"Like someone who might easily get out of breath?"

"Possibly. But look, he didn't have on a disguise. All right, I admit that some blokes wear them at first when they show up at MABIL—the wig, the beard, the turban, whatever—but by the time they're ready . . . We've built trust between us. And no one does this without trust. Because for all they know, I could be a cop undercover. I could be anyone."

"And so could they," Havers said. "But you never

thought about that one, did you, Bar? You just handed Davey Benton to a serial killer, waved good-bye, and drove off with the money in your pocket." She turned to Lynley. "I'd say we have enough, wouldn't you, sir?"

Lynley couldn't disagree. For now, they had enough from Minshall. They'd want a list of the calls he'd received on his mobile, they'd want to get over to the Canterbury Hotel, and they'd want to arrange for another e-fit to see if the one from Square Four Gym matched whatever image Minshall came up with of his client. From his description of two-one-six-oh, though, the points of comparison seemed to be not with the e-fit they already had from the gym, but rather with the description they'd been given earlier by Muwaffaq Masoud of the man who'd come to purchase his van. There hadn't been a moustache and a goatee, to be sure. But the age was right, the lack of physical fitness was right, and the bald head Masoud saw could easily have been hidden by the peaked cap Minshall was familiar with.

For the first time, Lynley considered an altogether new idea.

"Havers," he said to the constable when they were out of the interview room again, "there's another way to go with this. It's one that we've not looked at yet."

"Which is?" she asked, stowing her notebook in her bag.

"Two men," he said. "One procures and the other kills. One procures to give the other the *opportunity* to kill. The dominant and the submissive partners."

She thought about this. "It wouldn't be the first time," she said. "A twist on Fred and Rosemary, on Hindley and Brady."

"More than that," Lynley said.

"How?"

"It explains why we've got someone buying that van in Middlesex while someone else waits for him in a 'minicab' just outside Muwaffaq Masoud's house."

* * *

WHEN LYNLEY arrived home, it was quite late. He'd stopped in Victoria Street for a word with TO9 about MABIL, and he'd given the child-protection-team officers what information he had about the organisation. He told them about St. Lucy's Church, near Gloucester Road underground station, and he asked what the possibilities were of closing the group down.

The news he received in return was grim. A meeting of like-minded people to discuss their like-mindedness did not constitute a breach of the law. Was there something else going on besides talk in the basement of St. Lucy's Church? If not, Vice had too few officers and too many other ongoing illicit activities with which they had to contend.

"But these *are* paedophiles," Lynley countered in frustration upon hearing this assessment from his colleague.

"May be," was the reply. "But the CPS aren't going to drag anyone into court based on his conversation, Tommy." Still, TO9 would send someone undercover to a meeting of MABIL when their burdens were lighter round the Yard. Barring a complaint or hard evidence of criminal activities, that was the best TO9 could do.

So Lynley was feeling gloomy when he drove into Eaton Terrace. He parked in the garage in the mews and trudged down the cobblestone alley and round the corner to his home. The day had left him with the distinct sensation of being unclean: from his skin right through to his spirit.

Inside the house, the ground floor was mostly dark, with a dim light shining at the foot of the stairway. He climbed up and went to their bedroom to see if his wife had gone to bed. But the bed was undisturbed, so he went on, first to the library and ultimately to the nursery. There he found her. She'd bought a rocking chair for the room, he saw, and she was sitting in it, asleep, with an oddly shaped pillow in her lap. He recognised it from one of their many trips to Mothercare in the past few months. It was meant to be used when nursing a baby. The infant rested on it beneath the mother's breast.

Helen stirred as he crossed the room to her. She said, as if they'd only just been speaking moments before, "So I decided to practise. Well, I suppose it's more like seeing what it will feel like. Not the actual feeding, but just having him here. It's odd when you think about it, I mean when you actually stretch the thought out."

"What is?" The rocking chair was beneath the window, and he leaned against the sill. He watched her fondly.

"That we have actually *created* a little human being. Our own Jasper Felix, happily floating round inside me, waiting for his introduction to the world."

Lynley shuddered at the latter part of her thought: introducing their son to a world that often seemed filled with violence and was indeed a place of great uncertainty.

Helen must have seen this because she said, "What is it?"

"Bad day," he told her.

She extended her hand to him and he took it. Her skin was cool, and he could smell the scent of citrus upon her. She said, "I had a phone call from a man called Mitchell Corsico, Tommy. He said he was from *The Source*."

"God," Lynley groaned. "I'm sorry. He is from *The Source*." He explained how he was attempting to thwart Hillier's plan by keeping Corsico occupied with the minutiae of his own personal life. "Dee should have warned you he might be in touch. I didn't think he'd be quite that fast. She was intent upon giving him an earful to keep him away from the incident room."

"Ah." Helen stretched and yawned. "Well, I did assume there was something going on when he called me *Countess*. He'd spoken to my father as well, as things turn out. I've no idea how he tracked him down."

"What did he want to know?"

She began to get to her feet. Lynley helped her rise. She set the pillow into the baby's cot and put a stuffed elephant on top of it. "Daughter of an earl, married to an earl. Obviously, he loathed me. I tried to amuse him with my astounding mindlessness and my sad, fading It-girl proclivities, but he didn't seem as charmed as I would have liked. Lots of questions about why a blue blood—this is you, darling—would become a cop. I told him I hadn't the slightest idea as I'd much prefer it if you were available to lunch with me daily in Knightsbridge. He asked to come and visit me here at home, a photographer in tow. I drew the line at that. I hope that was the right thing to do."

"It was."

"I'm glad. Of course, it was hard to resist the idea of posing artfully on the drawing-room sofa for *The Source*, but I managed it." She slipped her arm round his waist and they headed for the door. "What else?" she asked him.

"Hmmm?" He kissed the top of her head.

"Your bad day."

"God. It's nothing I want to talk about now."

"Have you had dinner?"

"No appetite," he said. "All I want is to collapse. Preferably on something soft and relatively pliant."

She looked up at him and smiled. "I know just what you need." She took his hand and led him towards the bedroom.

He said, "Helen, I couldn't manage it tonight. I'm done for, I'm afraid. I'm sorry."

She laughed. "I never thought I'd hear that from

you, but fear not. I have something else in mind." She told him to sit on the bed, and she went to the bathroom. He heard the *snick* of a match. He saw its flare. A moment later, water began to run in the tub, and she returned to him. "Do nothing," she said. "Avoid thinking, if you can. Just be," and she began to undress him.

There was a ceremonial quality to how she did it, in part because she removed his clothes without haste. She set his shoes carefully to one side, and she folded trousers, jacket, and shirt. When he was nude, she led him into the bathroom, where the bathtub's water was fragrant and the candles she'd lit cast a soothing glow that was doubled by the mirrors and arced against the walls.

He stepped into the water, sank down, and stretched out until he was covered to his shoulders. She fixed a towelling pillow for his head, and she said, "Close your eyes. Just relax. Don't do a thing. Try not to think. The scent should help you. Concentrate on that."

"What is it?" he asked.

"Helen's special potion."

He heard her moving round the bath: the door swinging shut, the sound of garments dropping to the floor. Then she was next to the tub and her hand was dipping into the water. He opened his eyes. She'd changed into a soft towelling dressing gown, its olive colour warm against her skin. She held a natural sponge and she was applying a bathing gel to it.

She began to wash him. He murmured, "I've not asked about your day."

"Shhh," she replied.

"No. Tell me. It'll give me something to think about that's not Hillier or the case."

"All right," she said, but her voice was low and she ran the sponge the length of his arm with a gentle pressure that made him close his eyes once again. "I had a day of hope."

"I'm glad someone did."

"After much research, Deborah and I have targeted eight shops for the christening clothes. We've a date tomorrow, devoted entirely to the excursion."

"Excellent," he said. "An end to conflict."

"That's what we think. May we use the Bentley, by the way? There may be more packages than can fit in my car."

"We're talking about a baby's clothes, Helen. An infant's clothes. How much room can they take up?"

"Yes. Of course. But there may be other things, Tommy . . ."

He chuckled. She took his other arm. "You can resist anything but temptation," he told her.

"In a good cause."

"What else would it be?" But he told her to take the Bentley and to enjoy the excursion. He himself settled in to enjoy her ministration to his body.

She did his neck and kneaded the muscles of his shoulders. She told him to lean forward so that she could see to his back. She washed his chest and she used her fingers to press at points on his face in a way that seemed to drain all tension from him. Then she did the same on his feet till he felt like warm putty. She saved his legs for last.

The sponge glided up them, up them, up them. And then it was not the sponge at all but her hand, and she made him groan.

"Yes?" she murmured.

"Oh yes. Yes."

"More? Harder? How?"

"Just do what you're doing." He caught his breath. "God, Helen. You're a very naughty girl."

"I can stop if you like."

"Not on your life." He opened his eyes and met hers to see she was smiling gently and watching him. "Take off the robe," he said.

"Visual stimulation? You hardly need it."

"Not that sort," he replied. "Just take off the robe." And when she did so, he shifted so that she could join him in the water. She put a foot on either side of him and he reached for her hands to help her down. "Tell Jasper Felix to move over," he said.

"I think," she replied, "that he'll be happy to."

Chapter Twenty-three

Barbara Havers turned on the television to accompany her morning ritual of Pop-Tarts, a fag, and coffee. It was cold as the dickens in her bungalow, and she went to the window to see if snow had fallen during the night. It hadn't, but a sheen of ice on the concrete path from the front of the house gleamed with black menace in the security light that hung from the roof. She returned to her crumpled bed and considered dropping back into it while the electric fire did something to ward off the chill, but she knew she couldn't spare the time, so she ripped the top blanket off and wrapped it round herself before she shivered her way to the kitchen and put the kettle on.

Behind her, *The Big Breakfast* was regaling its viewers with the latest celebrity gossip. This mostly involved who was currently who else's partner—always a burning question for the British public, it seemed—and who had thrown over whom for whom else.

Barbara scowled and poured boiling water into the coffee press. She bent over the sink and tapped her finger against the fag that dangled from her lips, dislodging ash in the vicinity of the drain. God, they were obsessed, she thought. Partner this, partner that. Did anyone stay alone for five minutes . . . other than she herself, of course? It seemed that the national pastime was moving from one relationship to the next with as little downtime in between as possible. A single woman was an accepted failure as a human being, and everywhere you looked, the message blasted you between the eyes.

She carried her Pop-Tart to the table and went back for the coffee. She directed the remote at the television screen and she punched it off. She felt raw, far too close to the point of having to think of her partnerless life. She could hear the remark Azhar had made about whether she would ever find herself in the fortunate position of having children, and she did not want to venture within fifty yards of thinking of that. So she took a large bite of Pop-Tart and went in search of something to distract her from the consideration of her neighbour, his comment about her marital and maternal state, and the memory of that front door which had not opened when she had last knocked upon it. She found this distraction in her man from Lubbock. She put the CD on and cranked up the volume.

Buddy Holly was still raving on at the end of her second Pop-Tart, and her third cup of coffee. Indeed, he was celebrating his short life with such passion—and at such a volume—that as she headed for the bathroom and her morning shower, she nearly missed hearing the telephone's ring.

She quieted Buddy and answered, to find a familiar voice saying her name. "Barbara, dear, is that you?" It was Mrs. Flo—Florence Magentry, to the general public—at whose Greenford home Barbara's mother had been living for the past fifteen months with several other elderly ladies in similar need of care.

"Me and none other," Barbara said. "Hi, Mrs. Flo. You're up and about early. Everything okay with Mum?"

"Oh it is, it is," Mrs. Flo said. "We're all dandy out

here. Mum's asked for porridge this morning, and she's tucked right into it. Lovely appetite, she's got today. She's been mentioning you since yesterday lunchtime."

It was not Mrs. Flo's way to induce guilt in the relatives of her ladies, but Barbara felt it anyway. She hadn't been out to see her mum in several weeks—she looked at the calendar and realised it had actually been five—and it didn't take much to make her feel like a selfish cow who'd abandoned her calf. So she felt the need to excuse herself to Mrs. Flo and she said, "I've been working on these murders . . . the young boys? You might have read about it. It's been a rough case, and time's dead crucial. Has Mum—"

"Barbie, dear, you're not to go on like that," Mrs. Flo said. "I just wanted you to know Mum's had a few good days. She's been *here*, and she still is. So I thought that *as* she's a bit more in the present and out of the Blitz, it might be good to take time for an examination of her personals. We might be able to do it without sedating her, which I always think is preferable, don't you?"

"Bloody hell, yes," Barbara said. "If you'll make the appointment, I'll take her."

"Of course, dear, there's no guarantee that she'll be herself when you have to take her. As I said, there have been a few good days recently, but you know how it is."

"I do," Barbara said. "But make the appointment anyway. I can cope if we have to sedate her." She could steel herself to it, she told herself: her mum slumped into the passenger seat of the Mini, slack of jaw and bleary of eye. That would be nearly unbearable to behold, but it would be infinitely preferable to trying to explain, to her disintegrating ability to understand, what was about to happen to her when she was asked to put her legs into the ghastly stirrups in the doctor's surgery.

So Barbara and Mrs. Flo reached an agreement,

which consisted of a range of days when Barbara could drive out to Greenford for the appointment. Then they rang off, and Barbara was left with the rueful knowledge that she wasn't as childless as she looked to the outside world. For certainly her mother stood in place of progeny. Not exactly what Barbara had in mind for herself, but there it was. The cosmic forces governing the universe were always willing to give you a *variation* of what you thought your life was meant to be like.

She headed for the bathroom again, only to have the telephone ring a second time. She decided to let her answer machine take the call, and she left the room to turn the shower on. But from the bathroom, the voice she heard was male this time, which suggested the night had brought another development in the case, so she hurried back out in time to hear Taymullah Azhar saying, ". . . the number up here should you need to get in touch with us."

She snatched up the receiver, saying, "Azhar? Hello? Are you there?" And where was there? she wondered.

"Ah, Barbara," he said. "I hope I did not awaken you? Hadiyyah and I have come to Lancaster for a conference at the university, and I realised that I did not ask anyone to collect our post prior to our leaving. Could you—"

"Shouldn't she be at school? Is she on holiday? Half-term?"

"Yes, of course," he said. "That is to say, she should be at school. But I could not leave her alone in London, so we've brought her schoolwork with us. She does it here in the hotel room while I'm at my meetings. It is, I know, not the best arrangement, but she's safe and she keeps the door locked while I'm gone."

"Azhar, she shouldn't . . ." Barbara stopped herself. That way led to disagreement. She said instead, "You could have left her with me. I would have been happy to have her here. I'd always be happy to have her here. I knocked you up the other morning. No one came to the door."

"Ah. We would have been here in Lancaster," he said.

"Oh. I heard music—"

"My meagre attempt to thwart burglars."

Barbara felt unaccountably relieved by this information. "D'you want me to check the flat, then? Have you left a key? Because I could collect the post and go in and . . ." She realised how bloody *happy* she was to hear his voice and how much she wanted to accommodate him. She didn't like this at all, so she stopped herself from going on. He was, after all, still the man who thought her unfortunately unpartnered in life.

He said, "You are very kind, Barbara. If you would claim our mail, I'd ask nothing more of you."

"Will do, then," she said cheerfully. "How's my mate?"

"I believe she misses you. She is still asleep or I would bring her to the phone."

Barbara was grateful for the information. She knew he hadn't needed to give it to her. She said, "Azhar, about the CD, about the row . . . you know . . . what I said about your . . . about Hadiyyah's mum being gone . . ." She wasn't sure where to go with this, and she didn't want to reiterate her remarks in order to remind him of what she was about to apologise for. She said, "I was out of order with what I said. Sorry."

There was a silence. She could imagine him in some hotel room in the north, frost on the window and Hadiyyah a small lump in the bed. There would be two beds, with a nightstand between them and he would be sitting on the edge of his. A lamp would be on, but not on the nightstand because he wouldn't want its light to shine on his daughter and awaken her. He'd be wearing . . . what? Dressing gown? Pyjamas? Or was he dressed for the day? And were his feet bare or clothed in socks and shoes? Had he combed his dark hair? Shaved? And . . . And bloody *hell*, dolly, get a *grip*, for God's sake.

He said, "I was not offering a response to your words, as it turns out, Barbara. I was merely reacting to what you said. This was wrong of me, this reacting and not simply replying. I felt . . . No, I thought, She doesn't understand, this woman, nor can she possibly understand. Without the facts, she judges, and I'll set her straight. This was wrong of me, so I apologise as well."

"Understand what?" Barbara heard the water gushing freely in her shower and she knew she ought to turn it off. But she didn't want to ask him to hold on while she did that because she feared he'd be gone altogether if she did.

"What it was about Hadiyyah's behaviour . . ." He paused, and she thought she could hear the sound of a match being lit. He would be smoking, putting off his answer in that way they'd been taught by society, culture, films, and the telly. He finally said, very quietly, "Barbara, it began . . . No. Angela began with lies. Where she was going and whom she was seeing. She ended with lies as well. A trip to Ontario, relatives there, an aunt—her godmother, in fact—who was ill and to whom she owed much . . . And you will have guessed—have you not?—that none of that is the case at all, that there is someone else, as I was someone else for Angela once. . . . So for Hadiyyah to lie to me as she did . . ."

"I understand." Barbara found that she wanted only to stop the pain that she could hear in his voice. She didn't need to know what Hadiyyah's mother had done and with whom she'd done it. "You loved Angela, and she lied to you. You don't want Hadiyyah to learn to lie as well."

"For the woman you love more than your life," he

said, "the woman you have given up everything for, who has borne your child . . . the third of your children with the other two lost to you forever . . ."

"Azhar," Barbara said, "Azhar, *Azhar.* I'm sorry. I didn't think . . . You're right. How could I possibly know what it's like? Damn. I wish . . ." What? she asked herself. That he was there, she answered, there in the room so that she could hold him, so that something could be transferred from her to him. Comfort, but more than comfort, she thought. She'd never felt lonelier in her life.

He said, "No journey is easy. This is what I've learned."

"That doesn't help the pain, I expect."

"How true. Ah, Hadiyyah is stirring. Would you like to—"

"No. Just give her my love. And Azhar, next time you have to go to a conference or something, think of me, all right? Like I said, I'm happy to look after her while you're away."

"Thank you," he said. "I think of you often." And he gently rang off.

At her end, Barbara held on to the receiver. She kept it pressed to her ear, as if this would maintain the brief contact she'd had with her neighbour. Finally she said to no one, "'Bye, then," and replaced the phone. But she rested her fingers on it, and she could feel her pulse beating in the tips of them.

She felt lighter, warmer. When she finally made her way to the shower, she hummed not "Raining in My Heart" but rather "Everyday," which seemed more appropriate to her altered mood.

Afterwards, the drive to New Scotland Yard didn't bother her. She passed the journey pleasantly, without a single cigarette to buoy her. But all this good cheer faded once she arrived in the incident room.

The place was abuzz. Small knots of people gathered

round three different desks, and all of them were focussed on a tabloid opened upon each. Barbara approached a group that Winston Nkata was part of, standing to the rear with his arms crossed on his chest, as was his fashion, but none the less riveted.

She said to him, "What's up?"

Nkata inclined his head towards the desk. "Paper's done their piece on the guv."

"Already?" she asked. "Holy hell. That was fast." She looked round. She noted the grim expressions. She said, "He wanted to keep that bloke Corsico occupied. Didn't that work, or something?"

"He was occupied, all right," Nkata said. "Tracked down his house and ran a picture of it. He doesn't say what street, but he says Belgravia."

Barbara's eyes widened. "The *sod*. That's bad."

She worked her way forward as other of her colleagues moved off, having had their look at the paper. She flipped it to the front page to see the headline: "His Lordship the Cop" and an accompanying photo of Lynley and Helen, arms round each others' waists and champagne glasses in their hands. Havers recognised the picture. It had been taken at an anniversary party the previous November. Webberly and his wife, celebrating their twenty-fifth, just days before a killer had attempted to make him another of his victims.

She skimmed the accompanying article as Nkata joined her. She saw that Dorothea Harriman had done her part, as Lynley had described it to her, encouraging Corsico to pursue information left, right, and centre. But what they had all failed to anticipate was the speed with which the reporter would be able to put together his facts, mould them into the usual breathless prose of the typical tabloid story, and combine them with information that was more than the public had a right to know.

Like the approximate location of the Lynleys'

house, Barbara thought. There was going to be hell to pay for that.

She found the photograph of the Eaton Terrace house when she made the jump to page four for the continuation of the story. She found there, in addition to that picture, another photo, of the Lynley family pile in Cornwall, along with one of the superintendent as an adolescent in his Eton togs as well as one with him posing with his fellow oarsmen at Oxford.

"Flipping, flaming hell," she muttered. "How in God's name did he *get* this stuff?"

Nkata's response was, "Makes you wonder what he's going to unearth when he gets to the rest of us."

She looked up at him. If he could have looked green, he would have looked green. Winston Nkata would not want his background offered up for public consumption. She said, "The guv will keep him away from you, Winnie."

"Not the guv I'm worried about, Barb."

Hillier. That would be Winnie's concern. Because if Lynley made excellent fodder for the papers, what would the tabloids do when they got their teeth into the "Former Gang Member Makes Good" variety of tale? What Nkata's life was worth in Brixton was a moot issue at the best of times. What it would be worth should the story of his "redemption" hit the papers was a frightening one.

A sudden silence hit the room, and Barbara looked up to see that Lynley had joined them. He looked grim, and she wondered if he was castigating himself for having made himself the sacrificial lamb that *The Source* had offered on the altar of its circulation figures.

What he said was, "At least they haven't got on to Yorkshire yet," and a nervous murmur greeted this remark. It was the single but indelible blight on his career and his reputation: his brother-in-law's murder and the part he'd played in the ensuing inquiry.

"They will, Tommy," John Stewart said.

"Not if we give them a bigger story." Lynley went to the china board. He looked at the photographs assembled on it and the list of activities assigned to the team members. He said, as he usually did, "What do we have?"

The first report came from the officers who had been gathering information from the commuters who parked on Wood Lane and then walked the path down the hill, through Queen's Wood, and up to the Highgate underground station on Archway Road. None of these people on their way to work had seen anything unusual on the morning of the day that Davey Benton's body had been found. Several of them mentioned a man, a woman, and two men together—all of them walking dogs in the woods—but that was the extent of what they had to offer, and it did not include any descriptions, of either man or beast.

From the houses along Wood Lane leading up to the park, similarly nothing had been gleaned. It was a quiet area in the dead of night, and nothing had apparently altered that silence on the night of Davey's murder. This information was disheartening to everyone on the team, but better news came from the officer who'd taken the assignment to interview everyone in Walden Lodge, the small block of flats on the edge of Queen's Wood.

It was nothing to celebrate, the officer told everyone, *but* a bloke called Berkeley Pears—"There's a name for you," one of the other constables muttered—had a Jack Russell terrier that had started barking at three forty-five in the morning. "This was inside his flat, not outside," the constable added. "Pears thought someone might be on the balcony, so he took up a carving knife and went to see. He's sure he saw a flash of light down the hillside. On and off and on again, but shielded, like. He thought it was taggers or someone making their way to or from Archway Road. He got the dog quiet, and that was the end of it."

"Three forty-five explains why none of the commuters saw anything," John Stewart said to Lynley.

"Yes. Well. We've known from the first that he operates in the small hours," Lynley said. "Anything else from Walden Lodge, Kevin?"

"A woman called Janet Castle says she thinks she heard a cry or a shriek round midnight. Operative word *thinks*. She watches a lot of telly, crime dramas and the like. I think she's a frustrated DCI Tennison, without the sex appeal."

"Just one cry?"

"That's what she said."

"Man, woman, child?"

"She couldn't tell."

"The two men in the woods . . . those who were walking the dog in the morning . . . they're a possibility," Lynley said. He didn't elucidate but rather told the reporting constable to go back for further information from the commuter who'd sighted them. "What else?" he asked the others.

"That old bloke the tagger saw in the allotments?" came the reply from another of the Queen's Wood constables. "Turned out to be seventy-two years old and no way the killer. He can barely walk. Talks, though. I couldn't shut him up."

"What did he see? Anything?"

"The tagger. That's all he wanted to talk about as well. Seems he's phoned the cops over and over again about the little bugger but, according to him, they never do a damn thing because they have better things to occupy their time than catching vandals who happen to be defacing public property that's enjoyed by all."

Lynley turned to the Walden Lodge constable curiously. "Anyone inside talk about that tagger, Kevin?"

Kevin shook his head. He glanced at his notes, however, and said, "I only talked to residents of eight of the flats, though. As to the other two, one is newly empty and for sale and the other belongs to a lady taking her annual holiday in Spain."

Lynley considered this and saw the possibility. "Get on to the estate agents in the area. See who's been shown that empty flat."

He shared with the team a further report from SO7 that had been waiting for him on his desk when he'd arrived that morning. The hair on Davey Benton's body belonged to a cat, he told them. Additionally, there was no match between the tyres of Barry Minshall's van and the tracks left in St. George's Gardens. But there *was* a van out there that they were still seeking, and it looked as if it may have been purchased precisely for the use to which it was being put: a mobile killing site.

"At the time of Kimmo Thorne's death, it appears that the van was still registered to the previous owner, Muwaffaq Masoud. Someone out there has possession of that vehicle, and we've got to find it."

"You want the details released now, Tommy?" It was John Stewart who asked the question. "If we put that van in the public eye . . ." He made a gesture that said, You can figure out the rest.

Lynley thought it over. The reality was that van was going to contain a treasure trove of evidence. Find it and they had their killer. But the trouble was that the situation remained unchanged: Publicising the van's exact description, its number plates, and the writing on its side also allowed the killer to see their hand. He would either hide the vehicle in any one of the thousands of lockups round the city or he would clean and abandon it. They had to pursue the middle course in this matter.

He said, "Get the details out to every station in town."

He made additional assignments, then, and Barbara received hers with as much good grace as she could muster, considering that the first half of the assignment required her to compile her report on John Miller, the bath-salts vendor at the Stables Market. The second half got her out in the street where she preferred to be, however. Canterbury Hotel in Lexham Gardens. Find the night clerk and talk to him about who paid for a room for a single night on the evening that Davey Benton died.

Lynley was going on to the other assignments—everything from obtaining Minshall's mobile phone records to tracing the attendees at the last meeting of MABIL in St. Lucy's Church, by fingerprints if necessary—when Dorothea Harriman ushered Mitchell Corsico into the incident room.

She looked apologetic about it. Her expression clearly said, Orders from above.

Lynley said, "Ah. Mr. Corsico. Come with me please," and he left the squad to get back to work.

Barbara heard the steel in his voice. She knew that Corsico was about to get an earful.

LYNLEY HAD A copy of *The Source*. It had been supplied him by the guard in the kiosk when he'd arrived a short while earlier. He'd looked it over and had seen the error of his ways: How much hubris had he actually demonstrated, he wondered, in assuming he could outsmart a tabloid? The tabloids' bread and butter was produced through the means of digging up useless information, so he'd expected the lordship business, the Cornwall business, and the Oxford and Eton business as well. But he hadn't expected to see a photograph of his London home gracing the paper, and he was determined that the reporter would put no other officers in jeopardy by giving them the same treatment.

"Ground rules," he said to Corsico when he and the reporter were alone.

"You didn't like the profile?" the young man asked, hitching up his jeans. "There wasn't even the ghost of a suggestion about the incident room or what you've got on the killer. Or haven't got," he added with a sympathetic smile that Lynley wanted to smear across his face.

"These people have wives, husbands, and families," Lynley said. "Back off from them."

"Not to worry," Corsico said helpfully. "You're by far the most interesting of the lot. How many cops can boast an address a stone's throw from Eaton Square? I had a phone call this A.M. from a DS up in Yorkshire, by the way. Can't give you his name, but he said he had some information we might want to print as a follow-up to today's piece. Care to comment?"

That would be DS Nies, Lynley thought, of the Richmond police. He would no doubt have loved to bend the reporter's ear about time spent rubbing elbows with the Earl of Asherton in the nick. And the rest of Lynley's squalid past would come oozing out of the woodwork as well: drink driving, a car wreck, a crippled friend, all of it.

He said, "Listen to me, Mr. Corsico," and the phone rang on his desk at that moment. He snatched it up, said, "Lynley. What?"

He heard in reply: "I don't look at all like that sketch, you know." It was a man's voice, perfectly friendly. Some sort of tea-dancing music played in the background. "The one on telly. And what is it that you prefer to be called: superintendent or m'lord?"

Lynley hesitated, a deadly calm come over him. He was all too aware of Mitchell Corsico's presence in the room. He said to his caller, "Would you wait a moment please," and was about to tell Corsico to give him a few minutes' privacy when the voice continued.

"I'll ring off if you try that, Superintendent Lynley. There. I suppose I've made my decision about what to call you, haven't I."

"Try what?" Lynley asked. He looked towards his office door and the corridor, fixed upon flagging someone down. Failing that, he reached for a yellow pad on his desk to write the necessary note.

"Please. I'm not a fool. You won't be able to trace this call because I won't be on long enough for you to do it. Just listen."

Lynley waved Corsico over to his desk. Corsico feigned misunderstanding, pointing at his own chest and frowning. Lynley wanted to strangle the man. He waved him over again, "Fetch DC Havers" on the paper he finally shoved at him. "*Now*," he said, covering the mouthpiece of the phone.

"You'll get the computer records of this call anyway, won't you?" the voice asked him pleasantly. "That's how you work. But by the time you do it, I will have already impressed you once again. Indeed, I'll have absolutely dazzled you. You've a beautiful wife, incidentally."

Although Corsico had already gone for Havers, Lynley said to his caller, "I've a reporter in my office. I'd like to usher him out. Will you hang on while I do that?"

"Come now, Superintendent Lynley, you can't expect me to fall for that."

"Shall I put him on the line to convince you? He's called Mitchell Corsico and—"

"And unfortunately I can't get a glimpse of his identification, although I'm sure you'd like to arrange that. No. There's no need. I intend to be brief. First, I've signed a letter to you. The mark of Fu. The reason for this doesn't matter, but does the information itself suffice to convince you who I am? Or shall I add a reference to navels as well?"

Lynley said, "I'm convinced." Those details were among the few which the papers had no knowledge of. They identified the caller as the real thing or as someone close to the investigation, in which case Lynley knew the voice would have been familiar to him, which it was not. He *had* to get a trace on this call. But a single wrong move on his part and he knew that the killer would break the connection before Havers got to the room.

"Good. Then hear me, Superintendent Lynley. Out I went looking for a spot to thrill you another time. It was difficult to find, but I wanted you to know I have it now. Sheer inspiration. A bit risky, but it'll make a real *splash*. I'm planning an event you won't soon forget."

"What are you—"

"I've already made my selection too. I thought you'd like to know that, fair being completely fair."

"May we talk about this?"

"Oh, I don't think so."

"Then why have you—"

"Few words, much action, Superintendent. Trust me. It's better this way."

He rang off. Just as Havers came into the room with Corsico half a step behind her.

Lynley said to Corsico, "Get out."

"Hang on. I've done what you—"

"What follows is none of your business. Get out."

"The assistant commissioner—"

"Will survive the news that I've escorted you from my office for the moment." Lynley took the reporter by the arm. "I suggest you follow up on the information from Yorkshire. Believe me, it will make good reading for your next edition." He thrust him into the corridor and shut the door. He said to Havers, "He's phoned."

She knew. "When? Just now? Is that why . . . ?" She jerked her head towards the door.

"Get on to the records. We need to find out where he phoned from. He's got another victim."

"In his possession? Sir, those records . . . It's going to take—"

"Music," Lynley said. "I could hear dance music in the background. But that was it. Tea-dancing music. That's what it reminded me of."

"*Tea* . . . Not at this hour of the day. Are you thinking—"

"Period music. Thirties or forties. Havers, what does that suggest to you?"

"That he could have phoned from inside a lift with Muzak playing above his head and that could be bloody anywhere in town. Sir—"

"He knew about Fu. He said it as well. Christ, if that reporter hadn't been in the room . . . This has to be kept away from the press. He wants it. Corsico and the killer as well. They both want it front and centre. Page one with the accompanying headline. And he's got the victim, Havers. Picked out, already with him, or whatever. And the place as well. Christ, we can't be sitting ducks for this."

"Sir. *Sir.*"

Lynley brought himself round. He could see the anxiety on Havers' pale face. She said, "Something more, right? There's something more. What is it? Tell me. Please."

Lynley didn't want to give it words because then he knew he would have to face them. And face his responsibility as well. "He mentioned Helen," he finally said. "Barbara, he mentioned Helen."

Chapter Twenty-four

As Barbara Havers came back to the incident room, Nkata clocked the expression on her face. He saw her go to DI Stewart and have a few words, after which the DI left the room in a tearing hurry. This, in conjunction with Corsico's having come from Lynley's office to fetch Havers, told Nkata something was up.

He didn't approach Havers to be brought into the picture just yet. Instead he watched her go to the computer on which she'd been digging round for information on the bath-salts bloke from the Stables Market. She did a credible job of setting herself back to the task at hand, but from across the room, Nkata could see that more than bath salts was on her mind. She stared at the computer screen for at least two minutes before she roused herself and picked up a pencil. Then she stared at the screen for two minutes more before she gave up the effort and got to her feet. She headed out of the incident room, and Nkata saw she'd dug her fags from her bag. Sneaking off for a smoke in the stairwell, he thought. This would be a good time for a chat.

But instead of heading for the stairs to light up, she went for coffee, plugging coins into the machine and dismally watching the brew dribble into a plastic cup.

She fished a fag out of her packet of Players as well, but she didn't light it.

He said, "Company?," and felt round in his pocket for change for the coffee machine.

She turned and said tiredly, "Winnie. Come up with anything?"

He shook his head. "You?"

She did likewise. "The bath-salts bloke—John Miller?—turns out to be squeaky clean. Pays his council tax on time, has a credit card he pays off once a month, has his telly licence squared away, has a house and a mortgage and a cat and a dog, a wife and three grandkids. Drives a ten-year-old Saab and has bad feet. Ask me anything. I've become his Boswell."

Nkata smiled. He plugged his own coins into the coffee machine and punched white with sugar. He said, with a nod back in the direction of the incident room, "Corsico coming for you like that, earlier? I reckoned he picked you for the next profile in the paper. But it's something else, i'n't it. He came to get you from the super's office."

Barb didn't even try to misdirect him, another reason Nkata liked her. She said, "He phoned. Guv had him on the line when I got there."

Nkata knew whom she meant at once. He said, "Tha's what Stewart got on to?"

She nodded. "He'll get the records." She took a sip of her coffee and didn't grimace at the flavour of the brew. "For what good it'll do. This bloke's not stupid. He's not going to phone from a mobile and he's not going to ring us up from his bedroom land line, is he? He's in a call box somewhere and he's damn sure not going to make it in front of his home, his work, or anywhere else we're likely to connect him to."

"Has to be done, though."

"Right." She examined the cigarette she'd been intending to light up. She made up her mind and shoved it into her pocket. It broke in half. Part fell to the floor. She looked at it, then gave it a kick under the coffee machine.

"What else?" Nkata asked her.

"This bloke mentioned Helen. Super's cut up, and who can blame him."

"Tha's from the paper. He's trying to unnerve us."

"Right. Well. He's managed that." Barbara downed her coffee and crumpled the cup with a crunch. She said, "Where is he, anyway?"

"Corsico?" Nkata shrugged. "Digging through someone's personnel file, I expect. Typing everyone's name online and seeing what he can come up with next for a good story. Barb, this bloke—Red Van—what'd he say 'bout her?"

"About Helen? I don't know the details. But the whole idea of anything being printed in the paper about anyone . . . This isn't good. Not for us and not for the investigation. How're you with Hillier, by the way?"

"Avoiding him."

"Not a bad idea."

Mitchell Corsico appeared from out of nowhere then, his face brightening when he saw them by the coffee machine.

The reporter said, "DS Nkata. I've been looking for you."

Barb said under her breath to Nkata, "Rather you than me, Winnie. Sorry," and started back for the incident room. She and Corsico passed each other without a glance. A moment later, Nkata found himself alone with the reporter.

"Could I have a word?" Corsico purchased a tea for himself from the machine: milk and extra sugar. He slurped when he drank it. Alice Nkata would have disapproved.

"Work to do," Nkata said and made a move to go.

"It's about Harold, actually." Corsico's voice remained as friendly as ever. "I wonder if you'd just like to make a comment about him. The contrast between two brothers . . . It'll be a brilliant lead for the story. You're next, as you've probably gathered. You on the one hand and Lynley on the other. It's sort of an alpha and omega situation that'll make good reading."

At the mention of his brother's name, Nkata had felt his whole body stiffen. He would not talk about Stoney. And a comment about him? Like what? Anything he said—even if he said he had no comment at all—would come back to haunt him. Defend Stoney Nkata and it would go down to blinkers and blacks supporting blacks no matter what. Make no comment and it would go down to a cop disowning his past, not to mention his family.

Nkata said, "Harold"—and how odd his brother's Christian name sounded when he'd never called him that in his life—"he's my brother. Tha's right."

"And would you like to—"

"I just did," Nkata said. "Just confirmed it for you. If you'll 'scuse me, then, I've got work to do."

Corsico followed him down the corridor and into the incident room. He pulled up a chair next to Nkata's and took out his notebook, referring to the page on which he'd taken down information in what looked like old-fashioned shorthand.

He said, "I began that all wrong. Let me try it again. Your dad's called Benjamin. He drives a bus, right? How long has he worked for London transport? Which route would he be on, DS Nkata?"

Nkata tightened his jaw and began to sort through the papers on which he'd been recording information earlier.

Corsico said, "Yes. Well. It's Loughborough Estate, South London, isn't it? Have you lived there long?"

"All my life." Still, Nkata did not look at the reporter. His every movement he designed to say, I'm busy, man.

Corsico wasn't buying. He said with a glance at his notes, "And your mother? Alice? What does she do?"

Nkata swung round in his chair. He kept his voice polite. He said, "Super's wife ended up in the paper. Tha's not happening to my fam'ly. No way."

Corsico apparently took this as a welcome into Nkata's psyche, which seemed to be of more interest to him anyway. He said, "Tough being a cop with your background, Sergeant? Is that how it is?"

Nkata said, "I don't want a story 'bout me in the paper. I can't make it any more clear 'n that, Mr. Corsico."

"Mitch," Corsico said. "And you're looking at me as an adversary, aren't you? That's not how it should be between us. I'm here to do the Met a service. Did you read the piece about Superintendent Lynley? Not a bit of negativity to it. He was depicted in the most positive light I could manage. Well yes, all right, there's something more to be said about him . . . The affair in Yorkshire and his brother-in-law's death . . . but we don't need to get into that anytime soon, so long as the rest of the officers cooperate when I want to feature them."

"Hang on, man," Nkata said. "You threatening me? With what you'll do to the super 'f I don't play your game?"

Corsico smiled. Casually, he waved the questions off. "No. *No.* But information comes to me via the newsroom at *The Source,* Sergeant. That means someone else likely gets the information before I do. And *that* means my editor's twigged that there's more to a story than I've printed so far and he wants to know why, not to mention when I'm going to do a follow-up. Like this Yorkshire information: 'Why aren't you going with the murder of Edward Davenport, Mitch?' he's going to ask. I tell him that I've got a better story in hand, a sort of rags-to-riches or rather Brixton-Warriors-to-the-Met story. Believe me, I tell him, when you see this you'll understand why I moved on from Lynley. How'd you get that scar on your face, Sergeant Nkata? Is it from a flick knife?"

Nkata said nothing: not about Windmill allotments and the street fight that had ended up with his disfigurement and certainly nothing about the Brixton Warriors, who were as active as ever south of the river.

"Besides," Corsico said, "you know this comes from higher up than me, don't you? Stephenson Deacon—not to mention AC Hillier—drives a hard bargain with the press. I expect they'll drive a harder bargain with you if you don't jump onboard and help out with the profiles."

At this, Nkata made himself nod in a friendly fashion as he pushed back from his desk. He picked up his notebook and said with as much dignity as he could manage, "Mitch, I got to talk to the super right now. He's waiting for this"—with a gesture towards his notes—"so we'll have to do . . . whatever we have to do later on."

He left the incident room. Lynley didn't need the information he had—it was useless anyway—but there was no way in hell he was going to sit there and listen to the journalist's polite, implied threats. If Hillier blew a fuse as a result of Nkata's lack of cooperation, so be it, he decided.

Lynley's office door was open, and the superintendent was on the phone when Nkata entered. Lynley acknowledged him with a nod, indicating the chair in front of his desk. He was listening and writing on a yellow pad.

When he was finished with his call, Lynley said to him presciently, "Corsico?"

"He started off with Stoney. Straightaway. Man, I do not want this bloke digging into my fam'ly. Mum's got enough on her shoulders without Stoney ending up in the papers again." He surprised himself with his own passion. He hadn't thought he still felt the betrayal, the outrage, the . . . the whatever it really was, because he could not name it at the moment and he knew he couldn't afford to try.

Lynley took off his spectacles and put his fingers to his forehead, pressing hard. He said, "Winston, how do I apologise for all this?"

Nkata said, "You c'n take out Hillier, I guess. That'd do for a start."

"Wouldn't it just," Lynley agreed. "So you refused Corsico?"

"More or less."

"That was the right decision. Hillier won't like it. God knows he'll hear about it and have a seizure. But that won't happen at once, and when it does, I'll do my best to keep him away from you. I wish I could do more."

Nkata was grateful for that much, considering the fact that the super had already been profiled by the journalist. He said, "Barb says Red Van rang you . . ."

"Flexing his muscles," Lynley said. "He's trying to unnerve us. What've you got?"

"Sod all from the credit card purchases. That's a real nonstarter. Only connection between Crystal Moon and anyone we're looking at is Robbie Kilfoyle: the sandwich delivery bloke. Can we get surveillance on him?"

"Based on Crystal Moon? We're stretched too thin. Hillier won't authorise more officers on this, and those we have are already working fourteen- and eighteen-hour days." Lynley indicated his yellow pad. "SO7's done the comparison of everything inside Minshall's van to the rubber residue found on Kimmo Thorne's bike. No match. Minshall put in old carpet and not rubber lining. But Davey Benton's prints are all over that van. So are a score of other prints as well."

"The other dead boys?"

"We're doing the comparisons."

"You don't think they're there, do you?"

"The other boys? Inside Minshall's van?" Lynley put his reading glasses back on and looked at his notes before replying. "No. I don't," he finally said. "I think Minshall's telling the truth, much as I hate to believe it, considering his perversions."

"Which means . . ."

"The killer moved on from Colossus to MABIL once we showed up in Elephant and Castle asking questions. And now that Minshall's in custody, he's going to have to move on to yet another source of victims. We've got to get to him before he gets to them because God only knows where he's going to find them and we can't protect every boy in London."

"We need the meeting times of this MABIL, then. We got to alibi everyone for them."

"Back to square . . . if not square one, then square five or six," Lynley agreed. "You're right, Winston. It has to be done."

ULRIKE HAD no choice but to take public transport. The bike ride from Elephant and Castle to Brick Lane was a long one, and she couldn't afford the time it would take to pedal over there and back. It was suspicious enough that she was leaving Colossus without having a scheduled meeting both in her diary and on the calendar Jack Veness kept in reception. So she invented a phone call that had come in on her mobile—Patrick Bensley, president of the board of trustees, wanted her to meet him and a potential Big Money benefactor, she said—so she would be out. Jack would be able to find her on her mobile. She'd keep it on, as always.

Jack Veness had observed her, a half smile splitting his scraggly beard. He nodded knowingly. She didn't give him the chance to make a remark. He needed sorting once again, but she didn't have time to talk to him now about his attitude and the improvements in it that would be necessary should he ever want to advance in the organisation. Instead, she grabbed her coat, her scarf, and her hat, and she departed.

The cold outdoors was a shock that she felt against her eyeballs first and then in her bones. It was a quintessential London cold: so filled with damp that drawing air into her lungs was an effort. It prompted her to rush for the insufferable warmth of the underground. She crammed herself into a carriage heading for the Embankment and tried to keep away from a woman who was coughing wetly into the stale air.

At the Embankment, Ulrike disembarked and weaved through the other commuters. They were different here, their ethnicity changing from mostly black to largely white and far better dressed as she switched to the District line, which itself passed through some of the bastions of London's establishment employment scene. On her way, she dropped a pound coin into the open guitar case of a busker. He was crooning from "A Man Needs a Maid," sounding less like Neil Young and more like Cliff Richard with an adenoid problem. But at least he was doing something to support himself.

At Aldgate East, she purchased a copy of the *Big Issue*, her third in two days. She added an extra fifty pence to the price. The bloke selling it looked as if he needed it.

She found Hopetown Street a short distance along Brick Lane, and there she turned. She made her way to Griffin's house. It wasn't far into the estate, just across from a little green and some thirty yards from the community centre in which a group of children were singing as someone accompanied them on a badly tuned piano.

Ulrike paused just inside the gate that fenced off the tiny front garden. It was compulsively neat, as she'd thought it might be. Griff never spoke much about Arabella, but what Ulrike knew of her made the trimmed pot plants and the spotlessly swept stones on the ground exactly what she'd expected to find.

Arabella herself, however, was not. She came out of the house just as Ulrike started towards the door. She was guiding a pushchair over the threshold, its tiny occupant so heavily bundled against the cold that only a nose was showing.

Ulrike had expected someone utterly gone to seed. But Arabella had the look of someone quite trendy in her black beret and her boots. She wore a grey turtle-necked sweater and a black leather jacket. She was far too big in the thighs but was obviously working on it. She'd be back to form in no time.

Good skin, Ulrike thought as Arabella looked up. All her life in England exposed to the moisture in the air. You didn't find skin like that in Cape Town. Arabella was a regular English rose.

Griff's wife said, "Well, this is a first. Griff's not here, if you've come looking for him, Ulrike. And if he's not gone to work, he might be at the silk-screening business, although I rather doubt it, things being what they've been lately." And squinting like a woman making sure of the identity of her listener, she added in a sardonic tone, "It *is* Ulrike, isn't it?"

Ulrike didn't ask how she knew. She said, "I haven't come to see Griff. I've come to talk to you."

"That's another first." Arabella eased the pushchair off the single step that played the part of front porch. She turned and locked the door behind her. She made an adjustment to the baby's pile of quilts and then said, "I can't see what we have to talk about. Surely Griff hasn't made you promises, so if you think that you and I are going to have a reasonable discussion about divorce, swapping places, or whatever, I have to tell you you're wasting your time. And not only with me, but with him."

Ulrike could feel her face getting hot. It was childish, but she wanted to lay out a few facts in front of Arabella Strong, beginning with: Wasting my time? He fucked me in my office only yesterday, darling. But she restrained herself, saying only, "That's not why I've come."

"Oh, it's not?" Arabella said.

"No. I've recently booted his pretty little arse out of my life. He's all yours at last," Ulrike replied.

"That's just as well, then. You wouldn't have been happy had he chosen you permanently. He's not the easiest man to live with. His . . . His outside interests grow tiresome fast. One has to learn to cope with them." Arabella came across the front garden to the gate. Ulrike stepped aside but didn't open it for her. Instead, she let Arabella do it herself and afterwards she followed Griff's wife into the street. Closer to her, Ulrike got a better sense of who she was: the sort of woman who lived to be taken care of, who left school at sixteen and then acquired one of those wait-till-a-husband-comes-along kind of jobs that are utterly inadequate for self-support should the marriage break down and the wife need to make her own way in the world.

Arabella turned to her and said, "I'm going up to Beigel Bake, near the top of Brick Lane. You can come along if you like. I'm happy enough for the company. A friendly chat with another woman is always nice. And anyway, I've something you might want to see."

She started off, heedless of whether Ulrike was following. Ulrike caught her up, determined not to look as if she were tagging along like an undesirable appendage. She said, "How did you know who I was?"

Arabella glanced her way. "Strength of character,"

she said. "The way you dress and the expression on your face. The way you walk. I saw you come up to the gate. Griff always likes his women strong, at least initially. Seducing a strong woman allows him to feel strong himself. Which he isn't. Well of course, you know that. He never has been strong. He hasn't had to be. Of course he thinks he is, just as he thinks he's keeping secrets from me with all these . . . these serial trysts of his. But he's weak the way every handsome man is weak. The world bows to his looks and he feels he must prove something to the world *beyond* his looks, which he utterly fails to do because he ends up using his looks to do it. Poor darling," she added. "There are times I feel quite sorry for him. But we muddle along in spite of his foibles."

They turned into Brick Lane, heading north. A lorry driver was making a delivery of bolts of bright silk to a sari shop that stood on the corner, still decorated with Christmas lights as it was, perhaps, all year.

Arabella said, "I expect that's why you hired him, isn't it?"

"Because of his looks?"

"I expect you interviewed him, found yourself a bit dazzled to be on the end of that soulful expression of his, and didn't follow up a single reference. He'd have been depending upon that." Arabella gave her a look that seemed well practised, as if she'd spent days and months awaiting the opportunity to have her say in front of one of her husband's lovers.

Ulrike gave her that much. She deserved it, after all. "Guilty as charged," she said. "He gives good interview."

"I don't know how he'll cope when his looks fade," Arabella said. "But I suppose it's different with men."

"Longer shelf life," Ulrike agreed.

"Far more distant sell-by date."

They found themselves having a quiet chuckle and

then looked away from each other in embarrassment. They'd strolled some distance up Brick Lane. Across from a button-and-thread shop that looked as if it had done business on the spot since the time of Dickens, Arabella stopped.

She said, "There. That's what I wanted you to see, Ulrike." She nodded across the street, but not at Ablecourt and Son Ltd. Rather, she indicated the Bengal Garden, a restaurant that stood next to the button shop, its windows and front-door grilles closed and locked until nightfall.

"What about it?" Ulrike asked.

"That's where she works. She's called Emma, but I don't expect that's her real name. Probably something unpronounceable beginning with an *m*. So they added *uh* to Anglicise it. Or at least she did. Em-uh. Emma. Her parents probably call her by her given name still, but she's trying *very* hard to be English. Griff intends to help her along in that. She's the hostess. She's a real departure for Griff—he doesn't generally go in for ethnic types—but I think the fact that she's trying to be English in the face of parental objection . . ." Arabella glanced Ulrike's way. "He'd interpret that as strength. Or he'd tell himself so."

"How do you know about her?"

"I always know about them. A wife does, Ulrike. There are signs. In this case, he took me to the restaurant for dinner recently. Her expression when we walked in? He'd obviously been there before and laid the groundwork. I was phase two: the wife on his arm so Emma can see the situation her darling must contend with."

"What groundwork?"

"He has a particular pullover he wears initially when he wants to attract a woman. A fisherman's sweater. Its colour does something special to his eyes. Did he wear it round you? For a meeting you may have had, just the two of you? Ah. Yes. I see that he did. He's a creature of habit. But what works, works. So one can hardly blame him for not branching out."

Arabella walked on. Ulrike followed, casting one last glance at the Bengal Garden. She said, "Why do you stay with him?"

"Tatiana," she said, "is going to have a father."

"What about you?"

"My eyes are open. Griffin is who Griffin is."

They crossed a street and continued north, past the old brewery and into the region of leather shops and bargain prices. Ulrike asked the question she'd come to ask, although at this point she knew how unreliable Arabella's answer was probably going to be.

"The night of the eighth?" Arabella repeated thoughtfully, offering Ulrike the possibility that she was actually going to hear the truth. "Why, he was home with me, Ulrike." And then she added deliberately, "Or he was with Emma. Or he was with you. Or he was at the silk-screening business till dawn or later. I'll swear to any of them, whatever Griff prefers. He, you, and everyone else can absolutely depend upon that." She paused at the doorway to a large-windowed shop. Inside, customers lined up at a glass-fronted counter behind which an enormous blackboard listed the variety of bagels and the toppings on offer. She said, "I've no idea actually, but that's something I'll never tell the police, and *that* you can be sure of." She looked away from Ulrike to the interior of the shop, wearing the expression of a woman who suddenly sees where she is for the very first time. "Ah," she said, "here's the Beigel Bake. Would you like a bagel, Ulrike? It will be my treat."

He found a place to park that had *logic* written all over it. Beneath Marks & Spencer, there was an undergound carpark, and while it had a CCTV camera—

what else could one expect in this part of town?—should He ever be witnessed on film from this place, His presence possessed a rational explanation. Marks & Sparks had toilets; Marks & Sparks had a grocery. Either of those would serve as excuse.

To make sure, He went above to the store and put in an appearance in both facilities. He bought a chocolate bar in the grocery and stood wide legged at a urinal in the gents'. That, He thought, should satisfy.

He washed His hands thoroughly—at this time of year, one couldn't be too careful with all the head colds going round—and He ducked out of the store afterwards and headed in the direction of the square. It formed the intersection of half a dozen streets, the one whose pavement He walked along being the busiest of them, coursing upward in a glut of taxis and private vehicles all struggling southwest to northeast. When He got to the square itself, He crossed over with the traffic lights, breathing the fumes of a number 11 bus.

After Leadenhall Market, He'd been cheesed off, but now He was in a different frame of mind. Inspiration had struck Him, and He'd snatched it up, making a switch in His plans without anyone's intercession. As a result, there was no chant of ridicule from maggots. There was just the instant when He'd suddenly realised a new way was open to Him, broadcasting itself from every newsstand on every street corner that He passed.

In the square, He went to the fountain. It wasn't in the centre as design would dictate, but rather towards the southern corner. It was what He came to first, in fact, and He stood looking at the woman, the urn, and the trickle of water she was pouring into the pristine pool beneath her. Although trees lined the square at no great distance from the fountain, He saw that no remainder of their dead leaves decomposed in the water. Someone had long ago fished them out, so the trickle from the urn fell sonorously, without the *splat* that otherwise would suggest decay. In this part of town, that would be an unthinkable idea: death, decay, and decomposition. That was what made His choice so perfect.

He stood back from the fountain and observed the rest of the square. It was going to present an enormous challenge. Beyond the row of trees that lined a broad central path to a war memorial at the far end, a rank of taxis waited for fares and an underground station disgorged passengers onto the pavement. They made for banks, for shops, for a pub. They sat at window tables of a brasserie nearby or joined a line of ticket buyers at the box office of a theatre.

This was no Leadenhall Market: busy in the morning, at noon, and at the end of a workday, but otherwise not busy at all in the dead of winter. This was a place alive with people, probably well into the early hours of the morning. But nothing was insurmountable. The pub would close, the tube station would be locked and barred eventually, the taxi drivers would go home for the night, and the buses would run far less frequently. By three-thirty, the square would be His. All He had to do, really, was wait.

And anyway, what He had in mind for this location would not take long. He was regretful about the game rails in Leadenhall Market, which He now could not use to make the statement He wished to make, but this was far better. For benches lined the path from the fountain to the war memorial—wrought iron and wood gleaming in the milky sunlight—and He was actually able to *picture* how it was going to be.

He could see their bodies in this place: one of them redeemed and released and the other not. One of them the observer and the other the observed, so consequently, one of them laid out and the other positioned in an air of watchful . . . solicitude. But both of them deliciously, delightfully dead.

The plans were in motion inside His head, and He felt *filled*, as He always did. He felt free. There was no room for the maggot at a time like this. The wormlike thing shrank back, as if trying to escape the sun, which was represented to the hateful creature by His presence and His plan. See, *see*? He wanted to demand. But that could not come now, and it would have no reason to come till He had the two of them—observer and observed—within the circle that was His power.

All that remained was the waiting, now. Following and finding the moment to strike.

LYNLEY EXAMINED the e-fit, product of Muwaffaq Masoud's memory of the man who'd bought his van in the summer. He'd been looking at it for a good few minutes, trying to find points of comparison with the sketch they already had of the man who'd visited Square Four Gym in the days before Sean Lavery was murdered. He finally looked up—decision made—picked up the phone, and asked for an alteration in each drawing. On a copy of each, add a peaked cap, spectacles, and a goatee, he said. He wanted to see both individuals thus altered. He knew it was a stab in the dark, but there were times when a stab found flesh.

When that was in hand, Lynley finally had a moment to phone Helen. He'd thought much about his conversation with the serial killer, and he'd considered whether the best course of action was to send Helen home from her wanderings round London, with constables posted at front and back doors. But he knew how unlikely his wife was to embrace this move, and he also knew that overreacting to this could be playing into the killer's hands. At the moment, their man had no idea *where* the Lynley home actually was. Far better to put Eaton Terrace itself under surveillance—from rooftops, from the Antelope Pub—and cast out a net into which the killer might well wander. That would take several hours to set up. All he had to do was make sure that Helen took care in the meantime while she was out in the streets.

He reached her in a babble of noise: crockery, cutlery, and women's chatting. "Where are you?" he asked.

"Peter Jones," she said. "We've paused for sustenance. I'd no idea that hunting for christening garments would be so grueling."

"You've not made much progress if you've only got as far as Peter Jones."

"Darling, that's completely untrue." And then obviously to Deborah, "It's Tommy wondering how far we've managed to . . . Yes, I'll tell him." To Lynley, "Deborah says you might demonstrate a bit more faith in us. We've already made three stops and we've plans to go on to Knightsbridge, Mayfair, Marylebone, and a dear little shop Deborah's managed to unearth in South Kensington. Designer wear for infants. If we can't find something there, we'll not find it anywhere."

"You've a full day planned."

"At the end of it all, we intend to have tea at Claridge's, the better to look decorative among all that art deco. That was Deborah's idea, by the way. She seems to think I'm not getting out enough. And, darling, we've found one christening outfit already, did I say?"

"Have you?"

"It's terribly sweet. Although . . . well, your aunt Augusta *might* have a seizure watching her great-grandnephew—is that what Jasper Felix will be?—being ushered into Christianity in a miniature dinner jacket. But the nappies are so precious, Tommy. How could anyone complain?"

"It would be unthinkable," Lynley agreed. "But you know Augusta."

"Oh pooh. We'll search on. I do want you to see the

dinner jacket, though. We're buying every outfit we think suitable, so you can help decide."

"Fine, darling. Let me talk to Deborah."

"Now, Tommy, you aren't going to tell her to restrain me, are you?"

"Wouldn't think of it. Put her on."

"We're behaving ourselves . . . more or less," was what Deborah said to him when Helen handed over her mobile.

"I'm depending on that." Lynley gave a moment's thought to how he wanted to phrase things. Deborah, he knew, was incapable of dissembling. One word from him alluding to the killer and it would be written all over her face, in plain sight for Helen to see and to worry about. He sought a different tack. "Don't let anyone approach you while you're out today," he said. "People in the street . . . Don't let yourselves become engaged with anyone. Will you do that for me?"

"Of course. What's going on?"

"Nothing, really. I'm being a mother hen. Flu going round. Colds. God only knows what else. Just keep an eye out and take care."

She said nothing on the other end. He could hear Helen chatting to someone.

"Keep an adequate distance from people," Lynley said. "I don't want her falling ill when she's finally got beyond morning sickness."

"Of course," Deborah said. "I'll fend everyone off with my umbrella."

"Promise?" he asked her.

"Tommy, *is* there something—"

"No. No."

"You're certain?"

"Yes. Have a good day."

He rang off then, depending upon Deborah's discretion. Even if she told Helen exactly what he'd said, he knew it would seem to his wife that he was merely being overprotective about her health.

"Sir?"

He looked towards the door. Havers was standing there, her spiral notebook in hand. "What've you got?"

"Sod all in a bun," she said. "Miller's clean." She went on to report what she'd managed to unearth on the bath-salts vendor, which was, as she'd said, nothing at all. She finished with, "So here's what I've been thinking. P'rhaps we should consider him more carefully as someone likely to drop Barry Minshall in it. If he knows what we've got on Barry—I mean *exactly*—he might be willing to help. If nothing else, he could maybe identify some of the boys in the Polaroids we found in Barry's digs. We find those boys, and we've got a way to break up MABIL."

"But not necessarily a way to get the killer," Lynley pointed out. "No. Turn the MABIL information over to TO9, Havers. Give them Miller's name and his details as well. They'll give it all to the relevant Child Protection team."

"But if we—"

"Barbara," he said, stopping her before she could get into it, "that's the best we can do."

Dorothea Harriman came into the office as Havers groused about letting even part of the investigation go. The departmental secretary had several pieces of paper in her hand, which she turned over to Lynley. She departed in a breeze of perfume, saying, "New e-fits, Acting Superintendent. Straightaway, I was told. He said to let you know he's done several since you couldn't tell him what the glasses were like or how thick the goatee was. The peaked cap, he said, is the same on them all."

Lynley thanked her as Havers approached his desk for a look. The two sketches were now altered: Both of the suspects wore hats, spectacles, and had facial hair. It was little enough to go on, but it was something.

He got to his feet. "Come with me," he told Havers. "It's time to go to the Canterbury Hotel."

Chapter Twenty-five

"Like I said from the first to you lot," Jack Veness declared, "I was at the Miller and Grindstone. I don't *know* till what time because sometimes I'm there till last orders and sometimes I'm not and I don't keep a fucking diary of it, okay? But I was there, and afterwards my mate and I went for a take-away. No matter *how* many times you ask me, I'm going to give you the same flipping answer. So what's the point of asking?"

"Point," Winston Nkata replied, "is that more in'eresting events keep piling up, Jack. More we learn about who's doing what to who in this case, more we have to check out who might've done something else. And when. It always comes down to when, man."

"It always comes down to cops trying to pin something on someone and not caring much who the someone is. You lot got a nerve, you know that? People locked up for twenty years, turns out they been framed, and you never change your approach, do you?"

" 'Fraid that's what's going to happen?" Nkata asked him. "Why would that be?"

He and the Colossus receptionist were facing off right inside the entrance, where Nkata had followed him from the carpark. There, Jack'd been cadging cigarettes from two twelve-year-olds. He'd lit one, put another in his pocket, and tucked a third behind his ear. At first Nkata had thought he was one of the organisation's clients. It was only when Veness had stopped him with an "Oy! You! What're you about?" as he went for the door that Nkata realised the scruffy young man was a Colossus employee.

He'd asked Veness if he could have a word, and he'd offered his identification. He had a list of dates when MABIL had met—helpfully provided by Barry Minshall upon the advice of his solicitor—and he was comparing it to alibis. Trouble was, Jack Veness's alibi was unchanging, as he'd taken pains to point out.

Now Jack stalked into the reception area, as if satisfied that he'd been cooperative. Nkata followed him. There, a boy was lounging on one of the mangy-looking sofas. He was smoking and trying unsuccessfully to blow rings in the direction of the ceiling.

"Mark Connor!" Veness barked at him. "What're you about besides getting ready for a boot in your bum? No smoking *anywhere* inside Colossus, and you know that. What're you thinking?"

"No one's here." Mark sounded bored. "'Nless you plan on grassing me to someone, no one knows."

"*I'm* here, got it?" Jack snapped in reply. "Get the fuck out or put out the fag."

Mark muttered, "Shit," and swung his legs over the side of the sofa. He got to his feet and shuffled out of the room, the crotch of his trousers hanging nearly to his knees in gangsta fashion.

Jack went to the reception desk and punched a few keys at his computer. He said to Nkata, "What else, okay? If you want to talk to the rest of this lot, they're out. One and all."

"Griffin Strong?"

"You have trouble hearing?"

Nkata didn't answer this. He locked eyes with Veness and waited.

The receptionist relented but made it clear by his tone that he wasn't happy. "Hasn't been in all day," he said. "Probably having his eyebrows plucked somewhere."

"Greenham?"

"Who knows? His idea of lunch is two hours and counting. So he c'n take Mummy to the *doctor,* he says."

"Kilfoyle?"

"He never shows up till he's made his deliveries, which I hope happens soon since he's got my salami-and-salad baguette on him and I'd like to eat it. What else, man?" He grabbed up a pencil and tapped it meaningfully against a telephone message pad. As if on cue, the phone rang and he answered. No, he said, she wasn't in. Could he take a message? He added pointedly, "Truth to tell, I thought she was meeting with *you*, Mr. Bensley. That's what she said when she left," and he sounded satisfied, as if a theory of his had just been proved right.

He jotted down a note and told the caller he'd pass the information along. He rang off and then looked up at Nkata. "What *else*?" he said. "I've got things to do."

Nkata had Jack Veness's background inscribed on his brain, along with the background of everyone else at Colossus who had piqued the interest of the police. He knew the young man had reason to be uneasy. Old lags were always the first to come under suspicion when a crime went down, and Veness knew it. He'd done time before—no matter it was arson—and he wouldn't be anxious to do time elsewhere. And he was right about the cops' tendency to set their sights on a culprit early on, based on his past and their past interactions with him. All over England, there were red-faced chief constables sweeping up the debris of dirty investigations into everything from bombings to murder.

Jack Veness was no fool to expect the worst. But on the other hand, positioning himself thus was a clever move.

"You got a lot of responsibility here," Nkata said. "With everyone gone."

Jack didn't reply at once. This change in gears obviously was cause for suspicion. He finally made a reply of, "I c'n handle it."

"Anyone notice?"

"What?"

"You handling it. Or are they too busy?"

This direction appeared doable. Jack went for it, saying, "No one notices much of anything. I'm low man on the totem pole, not counting Rob. He leaves, I'm done for. Doormat time."

"Kilfoyle, you mean?"

Jack eyed him and Nkata knew he'd sounded too interested. "I'm not going there with you, mate. Rob's a good lad. He's been in trouble, but I expect you know that like you know I've been in trouble as well. That doesn't make either one of us a killer."

"You hang about with him much? Miller and Grindstone, f'r instance? That how you got to know him? He the mate you been talking about?"

"Look, I'm giving you sod all on Rob. Do your own dirty work."

"All goes back to this Miller and Grindstone situation we got," Nkata pointed out.

"I don't see it that way, but shit, *shit*." Jack grabbed a paper and scrawled a name and a phone number, which he then handed over. "There. That's my mate. Ring him and he'll tell you the same. We're at the pub, then we're off for a curry. Ask him, ask at the pub, ask at the take-away. 'Cross from Bermondsey Square, it is. They'll tell you the same."

Nkata folded the paper neatly and slid it into his notebook, saying, "Problem, Jack."

"What? *What*?"

"One night tends to fade into 'nother when you always go to the same place, see? A few days—or weeks—after the fact, how's someone s'posed to know which nights you were in the pub and buying take-away chicken tikka afterwards and which nights you skipped 'cause you were doing something else?"

"Like what? Like killing a few kids, you mean? Fuck it, I don't *care*—"

"Trouble here, Jack?"

Another man had entered, a somewhat rounded bloke with hair too thin for his age and skin too ruddy even for someone recently exposed to the cold. Nkata wondered if he'd been listening just outside the reception door.

"Help you with something?" the man asked Nkata with a glance that took the DS in from head to toe.

Jack didn't seem pleased to see the bloke. He apparently believed he needed no rescue. "Neil," he said. "Another visit from the Bill."

This would be Greenham, Nkata concluded. Just as well. He wanted a word with him too.

Jack went on. "More alibis needed. He's got a list of dates this time. Hope you keep a diary of your every move 'cause that's what he's looking for. Meet DS Whahaha."

Nkata said to Greenham, "Winston Nkata," and reached for his warrant card.

"Don't bother," Neil said. "I believe you. And this is what you need to believe. I'm going in there"—he indicated the inner reaches of the building—"and I'm ringing my solicitor. I'm finished answering questions or having friendly chats with the cops without legal advice. You lot are bordering on harassment now." And then to Veness, "Watch your backside. They don't plan to rest till they get one of us. Pass word round." He headed for the doorway to the interior of the building.

There was, Nkata concluded, nothing more to be gained on this side of the river aside from corroborating the Miller and Grindstone tale and the take-away curry situation. If Jack Veness was slip-sliding round London in the small hours, depositing bodies in the vicinity of the homes of his fellow Colossus workers, he'd not have announced that fact to anyone he knew at the pub or the take-away through obvious behaviour. Still, if he'd selected MABIL as his next source of young boys, he might not have been as circumspect about disguising his absence from the pub and the take-away on the nights of MABIL meetings. It was little enough to go on, but it was something.

Nkata left the building, telling Veness to have Robbie Kilfoyle and Griffin Strong phone him when they finally showed their faces. He went across the carpark at the rear of the building and slid into his Escort.

Across the street, tucked into the dismal and heavily graffitied railway arches leading out of London from Waterloo Station, four car-repair shops faced Colossus, along with a radio-controlled minicab and parcel service and a bicycle shop. In front of these establishments, young people of the area hung about. They mingled in groups and as Nkata watched, an Asian man emerged from the bicycle shop and shooed them off to another location. They exchanged words with the man, but nothing came of it. They began to slouch off towards New Kent Road.

When Nkata followed in his car, he saw more of them beneath the railway viaduct, and more strung out like African beads in twos, threes, and fours along the way to the grubby shopping centre, which took up the corner of Elephant and Castle. They shuffled along on a pavement spotted with discarded chewing gum, cigarette ends, orange juice cartons, food wrappers, crushed Coke cans, and half-eaten kebabs. Among themselves, they passed a fag . . . or more likely a spliff. It was difficult to tell. But they apparently had no worry of being stopped in this part of town, no matter what they did. There were more of them than there were outraged citizens to prevent them from doing whatever they liked, which seemed to be listening to deafening rap music and giving aggro to the kebab maker whose tiny establishment stood between the Charlie Chaplin Pub and El Azteca Mexican Products and Catering. They had nothing to do and nowhere to go: out of school, without the hope of employment, waiting aimlessly for the current of life to carry them wherever it would.

But none of them, Nkata thought, had started out this way. Each of them had once been a slate on which nothing had been written. This made him think of his own good fortune: that combination of humanity and circumstance that had brought him to where he was on this day. And had, he thought, also brought Stoney to where he was . . .

He wouldn't think of his brother, beyond his help now. He would think of helping where he could. In memory of Stoney? No. Not for that. Rather, in acknowledgement of deliverance and in blessing of his God-given ability to recognise it when it had come.

THE CANTERBURY HOTEL was one of a series of white Edwardian conversions that curved north along Lexham Gardens from Cromwell Road in South Kensington. Long ago, it had been an elegant house among other elegant houses in a part of town made desirable by the proximity of Kensington Palace. Now, however, the street was only marginally appealing. It was a spot that catered to foreigners with minimal needs and on very tight budgets, as well as to couples looking for an hour or two in which to do sexual business together with no questions asked. The hotels had names relying heavily on the use of *Court*, *Park*, or locations of historical significance, all of which suggested opulence but belied the condition of their interiors.

From the street, the Canterbury Hotel looked as if it was going to live up to Barbara's grim expectations of it. Its dingy white sign bore two holes that had renamed the establishment *Can bury Hot,* and its draughts-board marble porch gaped with missing pieces. Barbara stopped Lynley as he reached for the door handle.

"You see what I mean, don't you?" She waved at him the revised e-fits that she'd been carrying. "It's the one thing we haven't talked about."

"I don't disagree," Lynley told her. "But in the absence of something more—"

"We've got Minshall, sir. And he's starting to cooperate."

Lynley nodded at the door to the Canterbury Hotel. "The next few minutes will tell the tale on that. Right now what we know is that neither Muwaffaq Masoud nor our Square Four Gym witness has anything to gain by lying. You and I both know that's not the case for Minshall."

They were talking about the e-fits they'd obtained. Barbara's point was their unreliability. Muwaffaq Masoud had last seen the man who'd purchased his van many months earlier. The Square Four Gym observer had seen the individual following Sean Lavery—"and he didn't know if the bloke was *really* following Sean Lavery, admit it," Barbara had said—more than four weeks previously. What they had right now in the sketches was entirely dependent upon the memory of two men who, at the precise moment they'd seen the person in question, had no reason to memorise a single detail about him. The e-fits thus could be worth sweet FA to the police, while one generated by Barry Minshall could set them straight.

If, Lynley's point had been, they could rely upon Minshall to give them an accurate description in the first place. That was open to doubt until they saw how truthful his account was of the goings-on at the Canterbury Hotel.

Lynley led the way in. There was no lobby, just a corridor with a worn turkey runner and a pass-through window in a wall that seemed to open upon a reception office. The sound of aerosol spraying was emanating from this location, as was the heady eye-stinging odour of a substance that would have sent a huffer into raptures. They went to investigate.

There were no paper bags involved in what was going on. Instead, a twentysomething girl with what looked like a small chandelier dangling from one earlobe was squatting on the floor on an open tabloid, waterproofing a pair of boots. Hers, by the look of things: Her feet were bare.

Lynley had taken out his warrant card, but the receptionist did not look up. She was virtually ensconced in her position on the floor, fast becoming a victim of her aerosol can's fumes.

"Hang on," she said and sprayed away. She swayed dangerously on her heels.

"Bloody hell, get some *air* in this place." Barbara strode back to the door and slung it open. When she returned to the reception office, the girl had dragged herself up off the floor.

"Whoa," she said with a woozy laugh. "When they say do it in a ventilated place, they're not kidding." She reached for a registration card and plopped it on the counter along with a biro and a room key. "Fifty-five for the night, thirty by the hour. Or fifteen if you aren't particular about the sheets. Which I wouldn't recommend, by the way—the fifteen-pound option—but don't mention I said that." At that point, she finally took in the two people who'd come calling. It was clear she didn't twig they were cops—despite Lynley's identification dangling in plain sight from his fingers—

because her glance went from Barbara to her companion to Barbara again, and her expression said of Lynley, Whatever floats your boat.

Barbara saved Lynley the embarrassment of having to disabuse the girl of her notion about their presence in the Canterbury Hotel. As she dug out her police identification, she said, "When we do it, we prefer the backseat of a car. Bit cramped to be sure, but definitely cheap." She thrust her ID at the girl. "New Scotland Yard," she said. "And dead dee-lighted to know you're helping the neighbourhood cope with its ungovernable passions. This is Detective Superintendent Lynley, by the way."

The girl's eyes took in both warrant cards. She reached up and fingered the chandelier that dangled from her earlobe. "Sor-*ry*," she said. "You know, I didn't actually *think* the two of you—"

"Right," Barbara cut in. "Let's begin with the hours you work here. What are they?"

"Why?"

Lynley said, "Are you on duty at night?"

She shook her head. "I'm off at six. What's going on? What's happened?" It was clear that she'd been prepped on what to do should the rozzers ever come calling: She reached for the phone and said, "Let me get Mr. Tatlises for you."

"He works reception at night?"

"He's the manager. Hey! What're you doing?" This last she said as Barbara reached over the reception counter and broke the connection on the phone.

"The night clerk will do just fine," she told the girl. "Where is he?"

"He's legal," she said. "Everyone who works here is legal. There's not a *single* person without papers, and Mr. Tatlises makes sure they all enroll in English classes as well."

"A real upright member of society, he is," Barbara said.

"Where can we find the night clerk?" Lynley asked. "What's his name?"

"Asleep."

"I've not heard that name before," Barbara said. "What nationality is it?"

"What? He's got a room here . . . That's why. Look, he won't want to be woken up."

"We'll do those honours for you, then," Lynley said. "Where is it?"

"Top floor," she said. "Forty-one. It's a single. He doesn't have to pay. Mr. Tatlises takes it out of his wages. Half price as well." She said all this as if the information might be enough to keep them from speaking to the night clerk. As Lynley and Barbara headed for the lift, the girl reached for the phone. There was little doubt she was phoning either for reinforcements or to warn room 41 that the cops were on their way up.

The lift was a pre–World War I affair, a grilled cage that ascended at the dignified pace necessary for mystical assumptions into heaven. It was suitable for two individuals without luggage. But possession of luggage did not appear to be one of the qualifications for filling out a registration card in this hotel.

The door to 41 was open when they finally got there. The occupant was waiting for them, pyjamas on body and foreign passport in hand. He looked to be round twenty years old. He said, "Hello. How do you do. I am Ibrahim Selçuk. Mr. Tatlises is my uncle. I speak English little. My papers are in order."

Like the words of the receptionist below, all of what he said was rote: lines you must recite if a cop asks you questions. The place was probably a hotbed of illegal immigrants, but that was something they were not concerned about at the moment as Lynley made clear to the man when he said, "We're not involved in immigration. On the eighth, a young boy was brought to this hotel by an odd-looking man with yellow-white hair and dark glasses. An albino, we call him. No colour in his skin. The boy was young, blond—" Lynley showed Selçuk the picture of Davey Benton, which he took from his jacket pocket along with the mug shot taken of Minshall by the Holmes Street police. "He may have left in the company of another man who'd already booked a room here."

Barbara added, "And this song and dance—young boys being brought to this place by the albino man and leaving later with some other bloke?—it's supposedly happened over and over, Ibrahim, so don't let's try to pretend you haven't seen the action." She thrust the two e-fits at the night receptionist then, saying, "He might look like this. The man the young boy left with. Yes? No? Can you confirm?"

He said uneasily, "My English is little. I have passport here." And he danced from one foot to another like someone needing to use the toilet. "People come. I give them card to sign and keys. They pay in cash, that is all." He gripped the front of his pyjamas, in the area of his crotch. "Please," he said, casting a look back over his shoulder.

Barbara muttered, "Bloody hell." And to Lynley, " 'I'm about to wet myself' is probably not part of his English lessons."

Behind the man, his room was dark. In the light from the corridor, they could see that his bed was rumpled. He'd definitely been sleeping, but he'd also been prepared by someone at some point to keep his answers minimal at all times, admitting to nothing. Barbara was about to suggest to Lynley that forcing the bloke to hold his bladder for a good twenty minutes might go some distance towards loosening his tongue when a diminutive man in a dinner suit came trundling towards them from round the corner.

This had to be Mr. Tatlises, Barbara thought. His look of determined good cheer was spurious enough to act as his identification. He said in a heavy Turkish accent, "My nephew, his English wants repair. I am Mr. Tatlises and I'm happy to help you. Ibrahim, I will handle this." He shooed the boy into his room again and he closed the door himself. "Now," he said expansively, "you need something, yes? But not a room. No no. I've been told that already." He laughed and looked from Barbara to Lynley with a we-boys-know-where-we-want-to-plant-it expression that made Barbara want to invite the little worm to take a bite of her fist. Like someone would want to have a shag with *you*? she wanted to ask him. Puhh-leez.

"We understand that this boy was brought here by a man called Barry Minshall." Lynley showed Tatlises the relevant photos. "He left in the company of another man who, we believe, resembles this individual. Havers?" Barbara showed Tatlises the e-fits. "Your confirmation of this is what we require at this point."

"And after that?" Tatlises inquired. He'd given a scant glance to the photos and the drawings.

"You're not really in a position to wonder what happens after that," Lynley told him.

"Then I do not see how—"

"Listen, Jack-o-mate," Barbara broke in. "I expect your handmaiden of the boots downstairs put you in the picture that we're not here from your local station: two rozzers looking round their new patch for a nice bit of dosh from the likes of you, if that's how you keep this operation going. This's just a bit bigger than that, so if you know something about what's been going on in this rubbish tip, I suggest you unplug it and give us the facts, okay? We've got it from *this* individual"—she stabbed her finger onto Barry Minshall's mug shot—"that one of his mates from a group called MABIL met a thirteen-year-old boy right in this hotel on the eighth. Minshall claims it's a regular arrangement, since someone from here—and let me guess it's you—

belongs to MABIL as well. How's this all sounding to you for a lark?"

"MABIL?" Tatlises said, with some fluttering of eyelashes to approximate confusion. "This is someone . . . ?"

"I expect you know what MABIL is," Lynley said. "I also expect that if we asked you to join an identity parade, Mr. Minshall would have no trouble picking you out as the fellow member of MABIL who works here. We can avoid all that, and you can confirm his story, identify the boy, and tell us whether the man he left with looks like either one of these two sketches, or we can prolong the entire affair and haul you over to Earl's Court Road police station for a while."

"*If* he left with him," Barbara added.

"I know nothing," Tatlises insisted. He rapped on the door of room 41. His nephew opened it so quickly that it was obvious he'd been standing directly behind it listening to every word. Tatlises began speaking to him rapidly in their language. His voice was loud. He pulled the boy over by his pyjama jacket, and he snatched the sketches and the pictures, forcing the young man to study them.

It was a nice performance, Barbara thought. He actually meant them to believe that his nephew, and not himself, was the paedophile here. She glanced at Lynley, seeking permission. He nodded. She stepped up to business.

"Listen to me, you little wanker," she said to Tatlises, grabbing his arm. "If you think we're going to jump on the wagon you're driving, you're even stupider than you look. Leave him bloody alone and tell him to answer our questions and you can answer them as well. Got it? Or do I need to help you with your understanding?" She released him, but not before she ended her question with a twist of his arm.

Tatlises cursed her in his language, or so she assumed he was doing from the passion of his words and the expression on his nephew's face. He said finally, "I will report you for this," to both of them, to which Barbara answered, "I'm wetting my knickers in terror. Now translate this for your 'nephew' or whatever the hell he really is. This kid . . . Was he here?"

Tatlises rubbed his arm where Barbara had manhandled it. She expected him to start shouting something meaningful, like "Unconscionable brutality!," so assiduous were his ministrations to his limb. He finally said, "I do not work nights."

"Brilliant. He does, though. Tell him to answer."

Tatlises nodded at his "nephew." The younger man looked at the picture and nodded in turn.

"Fine. Now let's get on to the rest, okay? Did you see him leave the hotel?"

The nephew nodded. "He leaves with the other. I see this. Not the albin one, how you named him?"

"Not with the albino man, the man with yellowish hair and white skin."

"The other, yes."

"And you saw this? Them? Together? The boy walking? Talking? Alive?"

The last word set them both off in a babble of their own language. Finally, the nephew began to keen. He cried, "I did not! I did not!," and a damp spot appeared in the crotch of his pyjama bottoms. "He leaves with the other. I see this. I *see* this."

"What's going on?" Lynley demanded of Tatlises. "Have you accused him—"

"Worthless! Worthless!" Tatlises broke in, smacking his nephew round the head. "What evil are you using this hotel for? Did you not think you would be caught?"

The boy sheltered his head and cried, "I did not!"

Lynley pulled the men apart, and Barbara planted

herself between them. She said, "Get this straight and tattoo it on your eyeballs, both of you. *This* bloke brought the boy to the hotel, and *this* bloke left with him. Point the finger at each other and everyone in between, but there's not a rat in this place not going down for pimping, pandering, paedophilia, and anything else that we can make stick to you. So I suggest you might want 'cooperative as the dickens' to be what gets written in red across your paperwork."

She saw she'd got through. Tatlises backed off from his nephew. His nephew shrank back into his room. Both of them were reborn before their eyes. Tatlises might have had a dodgy arrangement with his MABIL friends about the use of the Canterbury Hotel, and he might have also collected a trunkful of lolly from allowing its rooms to be used for underage homosexual trysts, but it did seem he drew the line at murder.

He said, "This boy . . ." and took up the picture of Davey Benton.

"That's right," Barbara said.

"We're fairly certain he left here alive," Lynley told the man. "But he might have been killed in one of your rooms."

"No, no!" Nephew's English was improving miraculously. "Not with the albino. With the other man. I see this." And he turned to his putative uncle and spoke at some length in their mutual tongue.

Tatlises translated. The boy in the picture had come with the albino and they had gone up to room 39, which had been booked earlier and checked in to by another man. The boy left with that man some hours later. Two, perhaps. No more than that. No, he had not appeared ill, drunk, drugged, or anything else for that matter, although Ibrahim Selçuk had not studied the boy, to tell the truth. He'd had no reason to. It was not the first time a boy had come with the albino man and left with another man.

The night clerk added that the identity of the boys changed and the identity of the men booking the room changed, but the man who coupled them was always the same: the albino from the picture that the police had with them.

"That is all he knows," Tatlises finished.

Barbara showed the night clerk the sketches again. Was the man who booked the room either of these two blokes? she wanted to know.

Selçuk studied them and chose the younger of the two. "Maybe," he said. "It is something like."

They had the confirmation they needed: Minshall was apparently telling the truth insofar as the Canterbury Hotel went. So there was a slim hope that the hotel itself still had more it could reveal. Lynley asked to see room 39.

"There will be nothing," Tatlises said hastily. "It has been thoroughly cleaned. As is every room once it has been used."

Lynley was firm on this point, however, and they descended a floor, leaving Selçuk behind them to return to his sleep. Tatlises brought a master key from his pocket and admitted Lynley and Havers to the room in which Davey Benton had met his killer.

It was a dismal enough chamber of seduction. A double bed was its centrepiece, covered with the sort of quilted floral counterpane that would hide a multitude of mankind's transgressions, from liquids spilt to bodily fluids leaked. Against one wall, a blond wooden chest served double duty as a desk, with a kneehole into which a mismatched chair was thrust. On top of this, a plastic tray held the requisite tea-making equipment, with a grubby tin pot to use for the brew and a grubbier electric kettle for boiling the water. Dingy curtains covered the single transom window, and brown fitted carpet bore streaks and stains, stretching across the floor.

"The Savoy must be in real agony over the competition," Barbara remarked.

Lynley said, "We'll want SOCO over here. I want a thorough going-over."

Tatlises protested. "This room has been cleaned. You will find nothing. And nothing occurred in here that—"

Lynley swung on him. "I don't particularly care to have your opinion at this point," he said. "And I suggest you don't care to give it." And to Barbara, "Phone SOCO. Stay in this room till they get here. Then get whatever registration card was signed for this"—he seemed to seek a word—"place and check the address on it. Put Earl's Court Road into the picture about everything going on here, if they aren't already. Talk to their chief super. No one less."

Barbara nodded. She felt a rush of pleasure, both at the sensation of progress being made and at the responsibility given her. It was almost like old times.

She said, "Right, will do, sir," and took out her mobile as he directed Tatlises from the room.

LYNLEY STOOD outside the hotel. He tried to shake off the sensation that they were blindly swinging their fists at an enemy more adept at dodging than they were at forcing him into submission.

He phoned Chelsea. St. James would have had time to read and to assess the next group of reports he'd sent over to Cheyne Row. Perhaps, Lynley thought, there would be something uplifting he had to share. But instead of his old friend answering, it was Deborah's voice Lynley heard. No one at home. Leave a message at the tone, please.

Lynley rang off without doing so. He phoned his friend's mobile next and had luck there. St. James answered. He was just heading into a meeting with his banker, he said. Yes, he'd read the reports and there were two interesting details. . . . Could Lynley meet him in . . . what, about half an hour? He was up in Sloane Square.

Arrangements made, Lynley set off. By car, he was five minutes from the square if traffic was moving. It was, and he wove down towards the river. He came at the King's Road from Sloane Avenue and chugged up to the square in the wake of a number 11 bus. The pavements were crowded with shoppers at this time of day, as was the Oriel Brasserie, where he took timely possession of a table the size of a fifty-pence coin just as three women with approximately twenty-five shopping bags were leaving it.

He ordered coffee and waited for St. James to conclude his business. His table was one in the Oriel's front window, so he would be able to see his friend as he crossed the square and came down the neat, tree-lined walk that stretched past the Venus fountain to the war memorial. Right now, the centre of the square was empty save for pigeons that were scouting round for crumbs beneath the benches.

Lynley took a call from Nkata while he waited. Jack Veness had provided a friend to corroborate whatever alibi he chose to come up with, and Neil Greenham had latched on to his solicitor. The DS had left word for both Kilfoyle and Strong to phone him, but they'd no doubt hear from their mates at Colossus that alibis were being asked for, which would give both of them plenty of time to cook some up before speaking again to the cops.

Lynley told Nkata to carry on as best he could, and he picked up his coffee and downed it in three gulps. Scalding hot, it attacked his throat like a surgeon. Which was fine, he thought.

At last he saw St. James coming across the square.

Lynley turned and ordered a second coffee for himself and one for his friend. The drinks arrived as did St. James, who shed his overcoat by the door and worked his way over to Lynley.

"Lord Asherton at rest," St. James said with a smile as he pulled out a chair and carefully folded himself into it.

Lynley grimaced. "You've seen the paper."

"It was hard to avoid." St. James reached for the sugar and began his usual process of rendering his coffee undrinkable for any other human being. "Your photo is making quite a statement on the newsstands round the square."

"With follow-ups to come," Lynley said, "if Corsico and his editor have their way."

"What sort of follow-ups?" St. James went for the milk next, just a dollop, after which he began stirring his brew.

"They've apparently heard from Nies. Up in Yorkshire."

St. James looked up. He'd been smiling, but now his face was grave. "You can't want that."

"What I want is to keep them away from the rest of the squad. Particularly from Winston. They've set their sights on him next."

"With you willing to have your dirty linen aired for public consumption instead? Not a good idea, Tommy. Not fair on you and certainly not fair on Judith. Or Stephanie, if it comes to that."

His sister, his niece, Lynley thought. They shared in the story of the Yorkshire murder that had taken husband from one and father from the other. What rained on him as he tried to protect his team from exposure rained on his relations as well.

"I don't see any way round it. I'll have to warn them it's coming. I daresay they can cope. They've been through it before."

St. James was frowning down at his coffee. He shook his head. "Put them on to me, Tommy."

"You?"

"It'll work to keep them away from Yorkshire for a time and from Winston as well. I'm part of the team, if only tangentially. Play me up and set them on me."

"You can't want that."

"I'm not enthusiastic about it. But you can't want them delving into your sister's marriage. In this way, they'd only be delving into—"

"Driving drunk and crippling you." Lynley pushed his coffee away. "Christ but I've cocked so many things up."

"Not this," St. James said. "We were both drunk. Let's not forget that. And anyway, I doubt your reporter from *The Source* will even touch upon the subject of my . . . physical situation, let's call it. He'll be too politically correct. Unseemly to mention it: Why d'you happen to be wearing that appliance on your leg, sir? It's akin to asking someone when he stopped beating his wife. And anyway, if they do get on to it, I was out carousing with a friend and this is the result. An object lesson for today's wild adolescents. End of story."

"You can't want them homing in on you."

"Of course not. I'll be the laughingstock of my siblings, not to mention what my mother will say in her inimitable fashion. But look at it this way: I'm outside the investigation even as I'm inside the investigation, and there's an advantage to that. You can play it any way you want with Hillier. Either I'm part of the team—and he *did* say he wanted the team profiled, didn't he, sir?—or I'm ruthlessly self-serving and, as an independent scientist, I'm seeking the self-aggrandisement that only exposure in the press will afford me. Play it either way." Here he smiled. "I know you live only to torment the poor sod."

Lynley smiled also, in spite of himself. "It's good of

you, Simon. It keeps them away from Winston. Hillier won't like that, of course, but I can deal with Hillier."

"And by the time they get round to Winston or anyone else, God willing, this business will be finished."

"Have you anything with you?" Lynley nodded towards the briefcase that St. James had brought to the table with him.

"Dashed back for it, yes. I've had the advantage in several ways."

"Which means I've missed something. All right. I can live with it."

"Not missed exactly. I wouldn't say that."

"What would you say, then?"

"That I've the advantage of being some distance from the case while you're in the thick of it. And I don't have Hillier, the press, and God only knows who else breathing down my neck and demanding a result."

"I'll take the excuse as offered. With thanks. What did you find?"

St. James reached for the briefcase and opened it on a spare chair that he pulled from another table. He brought out the latest batch of paperwork he'd been sent.

"Have you found the source of the ambergris oil?" he asked.

"We have two sources. Why?"

"He's run out."

"Of the oil?"

"There was no trace of it on the Queen's Wood body. On all the others it was present, not always in the same place, but there. But on this one, it's not."

Lynley thought about this. He saw a reason the oil might have been absent. He said, "The body was naked. The oil might have been on his clothes."

"But the St. George's Gardens body was naked as well—"

"Kimmo Thorne's body."

"Right. *And* he still had traces of the oil on him. No,

I'd say there's a very good chance our man's run out of it, Tommy. He's going to need more, and if you've traced two sources, a watch on those shops might prove to be the key."

"You say there's a good chance," Lynley noted. "What else, then? There's something else, isn't there?"

St. James nodded slowly. He seemed undecided about the importance of his next revelation. He said, "It's *something*, Tommy. That's all I can say. I don't like to interpret it because it could take you in the wrong direction at the end of the day."

"All right. Accepted. What is it?"

St. James pulled another batch of documents out. He said, "The contents of their stomachs. Before this last boy, the Queen's Wood boy—"

"Davey Benton."

"Before him, the others had all eaten within an hour of their deaths. And in every case, the contents of the stomachs were identical."

"Identical?"

"Without a deviation, Tommy."

"But with Davey Benton?"

"He hadn't had anything in hours. Eight hours at least. Taken in conjunction with the ambergris-oil situation . . ." St. James leaned forward. He put his hand on the neat stack of documents for emphasis. "I don't need to tell you what this means, do I?"

Lynley turned from his friend. He looked to the square outside where, beyond the window, the grey winter day moved unceasing towards darkness and what darkness brought with it.

"No, Simon," he finally said. "You don't have to tell me a thing."

Chapter Twenty-six

The name on the registration card was Oscar Wilde. When Barbara Havers saw this, she looked up at Chandelier Earring, expecting a rolling of the eyes and an expression that said "What else would you expect?" But it was clear that the girl in reception was of the recent unschooled generation whose education was dependent upon music videos and gossip magazines. She hadn't made the connection any more than the night clerk had, but at least he had the excuse of being a foreigner. Wilde—in revival or otherwise—probably wasn't big in Turkey.

Barbara went on to the address: a number on Collingham Road. The hotel had a battered *A to Z*—purportedly for use by the hordes of tourists who stayed there—and she found the street not that far from Lexham Gardens. It was on the other side of Cromwell Road. She could hoof it there without any trouble.

Before descending to reception, she'd waited for the arrival of the SOCO team, having phoned for them from room 39. Mr. Tatlises had taken himself off somewhere in his dinner suit, doubtless to contact his fellow MABILians and give them the word that times were about to be a-changin'. He would then, she reckoned, make a vain attempt to destroy every bit of child pornography that he had in his possession. Stupid sod, Barbara thought. He wouldn't've been able to resist downloading that filth off the Net—none of them could ever resist that—and he was just enough of an idiot to think *delete* meant *gone but not forgotten.* The Earl's Court Road station would have a field day at this place. Once Tatlises was in their clutches, they'd find a way to squeeze him for everything he knew: about MABIL, about what was going on in the hotel, about little boys and money changing hands and everything else related to this disgusting situation. Unless, of course, some of them were involved in MABIL . . . some of the Earl's Court Road cops . . . but Barbara didn't want to think of that. Cops, priests, doctors, and ministers. One had to *hope,* if not to believe, that a moral core existed somewhere.

As ordered by Lynley, she spoke to the Earl's Court Road chief super. He set the wheels in motion. When the SOCO team arrived, she felt secure enough to leave.

With the address from the registration card in hand and the card itself turned over to the SOCO team for fingerprinting, she crossed over Cromwell Road and headed east, in the direction of the Natural History Museum. Collingham Road headed south some 100 yards from Lexham Gardens. Barbara made the turn and began searching for the correct address along the row of tall, white-fronted conversions.

Considering the name that had been on the registration card, she had little hope of the address being anything but another sham. She wasn't far from correct in this conclusion. Where Collingham Road met the lower half of Courtfield Gardens, an old stone church stood on the corner. A wrought-iron fence surrounded it, and inside the churchyard that the fence contained, a faded sign done in gold letters named the spot as St.

Lucy's Community Centre. Beneath this identification were the numbers of the street address. They corresponded identically to the numbers on the card from the Canterbury Hotel. How fitting it was, Barbara thought as she pushed through the gate and entered the churchyard. The address on the card was the address for MABIL: St. Lucy's, the deconsecrated church not far from the Gloucester Road underground station.

Minshall had said that MABIL met in the basement, so that was where Barbara headed. She went round the side of the building, following a concrete path through a small, overgrown cemetery. Toppling gravestones and ivy-choked tombs filled it to capacity, all of them untended.

A set of stone steps led down to the basement at the back of the church. A sign on the bright blue door called this portion of the centre "Ladybird Infant Daycare." This door stood partially open, and from within Barbara could hear the babble of children's voices.

She pushed her way inside and found herself in a vestibule, where a long rack of hooks at waist height held miniature coats, jackets, and macs, while below a row of pint-sized Wellingtons waited neatly for their owners. There appeared to be two classrooms opening off this little hall: one large and one small and both of them filled with enthusiastic children engaged in making paper Valentines (the small room) and an energetic conga line galloping about to the tune of "On the Sunny Side of the Street" (the large room).

Barbara was deciding which room to try for information when a sixtyish woman with spectacles on a gold chain round her neck came out of what seemed to be a kitchen, bearing a tray of ginger biscuits. Fresh ginger biscuits, by the smell of them. Barbara's stomach made an appreciative gurgle.

The woman looked from Barbara to the door. Her expression said that it was not meant to be left unlocked, which Barbara acknowledged was not a bad idea. The woman asked if she could be of help.

Barbara showed her identification and told the woman—who gave her name as Mrs. McDonald—that she'd come about MABIL.

Mabel? Mrs. McDonald said. They had no child named Mabel enrolled.

This was an organisation of men who met in the basement in the evenings, Barbara told her. M-A-B-I-L, it was spelled.

Ah. Well, Mrs. McDonald knew nothing about that. For that sort of information, the constable would have to talk to the letting agent. Taverstock & Percy, she informed Barbara. On Gloucester Road. They handled all of the lettings for the community centre. Twelve-step programmes, women's clubs, antiques and crafts fairs, writing classes, the lot.

Could she have a look round anyway? Barbara asked Mrs. McDonald. There was, she knew, nothing to find here, but she wanted to get a feel for the place where perversion was not only tolerated but encouraged.

Mrs. McDonald was less than happy about this request, but she said she'd show Barbara the facilities if she would wait right here while the biscuits got delivered to the conga line. She carried her tray into the larger room and handed it off to one of the teachers. She returned as the conga line disintegrated in a biscuit frenzy to which Barbara could only too well relate. She'd skipped lunch and it was already teatime.

She followed Mrs. McDonald dutifully from room to room. They blossomed with children—laughing, jabbering, fresh faced, innocent. Her heart felt sick at the thought of paedophiles defiling this atmosphere, even by their presence at night when these children were tucked up safely at home.

There was little enough to see, however. A large room with a dais at one end, a lectern pushed to one side, and chairs stacked up along walls decorated with rainbows, leprechauns, and an enormous, whimsical pot of gold. A small room with tot-sized tables where children created crafts that were then displayed along the walls in a riot of colour and imagination. A kitchen, a lavatory, a supply room. That was it. Barbara tried to picture the place filled with saliva-dripping child molesters, and it wasn't difficult. She could see them here easily enough, the miserable lot of them getting their rocks off at the thought of all the kids in these rooms every single weekday, just waiting for some monster to snatch them off the street.

She thanked Mrs. McDonald and left St. Lucy's. Although it seemed a dead end, she knew she couldn't leave the stone of Taverstock & Percy unturned.

The estate agent, she found, was back on the other side of Cromwell Road and up a distance. She passed a Barclay's—complete with drunken homeless beggar on the front steps—as well as a church and a string of nineteenth-century conversions—before she came to a smallish commercial area where Taverstock & Percy was bookended by a have-everything ironmonger and an old-fashioned take-away serving up sausage rolls and jacket potatoes to a line of road workers who were taking their tea break from a jackhammered hole in the middle of the street.

Inside Taverstock & Percy, Barbara asked to see the estate agent in charge of letting space in St. Lucy's Church, and she was shown to a young woman called Misty Perrin, who was apparently thrilled by the idea that custom for St. Lucy's was walking in off the street. She took out an application and fixed it to a clipboard, saying that of course there were certain rules and regulations that had to be met in order for anyone to have space in the former church or its basement.

Right, Barbara thought. That's what kept away the riffraff.

She took out her identification and introduced herself to Misty. Could she have a word about a group called MABIL.

Misty lowered the clipboard to her desk, but she didn't look concerned. She said, "Oh, of course. When you asked about St. Lucy's, I thought . . . Well, anyway . . . MABIL. Yes." She opened a filing drawer in her desk and fingered through its contents. She brought out a slim manila folder and opened it. She read through the material, nodding appreciatively and saying at the conclusion of her inspection, "I wish all tenants were as prompt as they are. Every month, they're right on time with the rent. No complaints about how they leave the premises at the end of their meetings. No problem in the neighbourhood with illegal parking. Well, of course the clamp takes care of that, doesn't it? Anyway, what would you like to know?"

"What sort of group is it?"

Misty looked back at her documents. "Support group, it appears. Men going through divorce. I'm not sure why they call it MABIL unless that's an acronym for . . . Men Against what?"

"Bloody Inconsiderate Litigation?" Barbara offered. "Whose name's on the contract?"

Misty read it to her. J. S. Mill. She recited the address as well. She went on to inform Barbara that the only *somewhat* odd thing about MABIL was that their fee always arrived in cash, brought in person by Mr. Mill on the first of the month. "He said it had to be cash because that's how they came up with the money, through a collection at their meetings. Well, it's a bit irregular and all that, but St. Lucy's said that was fine by them just so long as they got the money. And they've got it, every month on the first, for the last five years."

"Five years?"

"Yes. That's right. Is there something . . . ?" Misty looked anxious.

Barbara shook her head and waved off the question. What was the point? The girl was as innocent as the children in the Ladybird centre. She didn't depend on the promise of anything coming from it, but she showed Misty the two e-fits anyway. "J. S. Mill look like either of these blokes?" she asked.

Misty glanced at the sketches but shook her head. He was much older, she said—round seventy?—and he didn't have a beard or goatee or anything. He did wear an enormous hearing aid, if that was any help.

Barbara shuddered at the information. Someone's *granddad*, she thought. She wanted to find and strangle him.

She took the address of J. S. Mill as she left the estate agency. It would be bogus. She had little doubt of that. But she'd hand it over to TO9 nonetheless. Someone somewhere had to kick down the doors of the members of this organisation.

She was heading back in the direction of Cromwell Road when her mobile rang. It was Lynley asking where she was.

She told him, bringing him up to date on what little she'd managed to glean from her efforts with the registration card from the Canterbury Hotel. "What about you?" she asked him.

"St. James thinks our boy may need to buy more ambergris oil," Lynley told her and informed her of the rest of St. James's report. "It's time for you to take another trip up to Wendy's Cloud, Constable."

NKATA PARKED some distance along Manor Place. He was still thinking about the dozens of aimlessly sauntering black kids he'd seen in the vicinity of Elephant and Castle. No single place for them to go and very little for them to do. That wasn't the real truth of the matter—if nothing else, they could be at school—but he knew that was the way they themselves saw their situation, taught to think it by older peers, by disgruntled and disappointed parents, by lack of opportunity and too much temptation. It was easier for them, in the long run, not to care. Nkata had thought of them all the way to Kennington. He allowed them to become his excuse.

Not that he actually needed one. This journey was owed, not *to* him but *by* him. The time had definitely come.

He got out of the car and walked the short distance to the wig shop, still a hopeful sign of what was possible among the failed and boarded-up establishments in the neighbourhood. The pubs, naturally, were still doing business. But other than a dismal corner shop with heavy grilles on the windows, Yasmin Edwards' business was the only place open.

When Nkata entered, he saw that Yasmin was with a client. This was a skeletal black woman with a death's-head face. She was bald, and she sat slumped in a beauty chair before the long, mirrored wall and the counter at which Yasmin worked. On the counter, a makeup case was open. Three wigs stood near it: one comprising a head full of plaits; one close cropped like Yasmin's hair; one long and straight, of the sort worn by catwalk models.

Yasmin's glance went to Nkata and then away, as if she'd been expecting him and was unsurprised by his arrival. He nodded at her, but he knew she didn't see. She was focussed on her client and the brush on which she was applying blusher from a round tin box.

"I jus' can't see it," her client said. Her voice was as exhausted as her body looked. "Don't you bother with that, Yas-meen."

"You wait," Yasmin told her gently. "Le' me fix you,

luv, and in the meantime, study those wigs for the one you want."

"I'n't going to make a difference, is it," the woman said. "I don' know why I even came."

"'Cause you're pretty, Ruby, an' the world deserves to see that."

Ruby pooh-poohed her. "No more I'm pretty now," she said.

Yasmin didn't answer this remark, positioning herself instead in front of the woman in order to study her face. Yasmin's own was professional, devoid of the pity that the other woman would doubtless have been able to sense in an instant. Yasmin bent towards her and applied the brush along the ridge of her cheekbones. She followed this with a similar movement along her jaw.

Nkata waited patiently. He watched Yasmin work: the flick of a brush, a heightening of shading round the eyes. She finished her client off with lipstick, which she applied with a delicate paintbrush. She wore no kind of lipstick herself. The rose-bloom scar on her upper lip—long-ago gift of her husband—made this impossible.

She stood back and surveyed her work. She said, "Now you're something, Ruby. Which wig's goin' to finish off the picture?"

"Oh, Yas-meen, I dunno."

"Now come on. Your husband i'n't waiting out there for some *bald-headed* lady with a pretty new face. You want to try them again?"

"The short one, I guess."

"You sure? The long one made you look like whatsername the model."

Ruby chuckled. "Oh yeah, 'm ready for Fashion Week, Yas-meen. Maybe they'll put me in a bikini. I finally got the figger for it. Le' me do the short one. I like it good enough."

Yasmin removed the short wig from the stand. She lowered it gently onto Ruby's head. She stood back, then made an adjustment, then stood back again. "You're ready for a big night out," she said. "Make sure your man sees you get it." She helped Ruby out of the beauty chair and took the voucher that the woman held out to her. She gently pushed away an additional ten-pound note that Ruby tried to press upon her. "None 'f that," she said. "Buy some flowers for your flat."

"Flowers enough at the funeral," Ruby said.

"Yeah, but the corpse don't get to enjoy them."

They chuckled together. Yasmin saw her to the door. A car at the kerb waited for her, one door swinging open. Yasmin eased her inside.

When she returned to the shop, she went at once to the beauty chair where she began to repack her makeup supplies. Nkata said to her, "What's she got?"

"Pancreas," Yasmin said shortly.

"Bad?"

"Pancreas's always bad, Sergeant. She's doing chemo, but i'n't any point. What d'you want, man? I got work to do."

He approached her but still kept a safe distance between them. "I got a brother," he said. "He's Harold, but we called him Stoney. Cos he was stubborn as a stone in a field. A Stonehenge kind of stone, I mean. One you can't budge no matter what."

Yasmin paused in putting the makeup away, a brush in her hand. She frowned at Nkata. "So?"

Nkata licked his lower lip. "He's in Wandsworth. Life."

Her glance moved away, then back to him. She knew what that meant. Murder. "He do it?"

"Oh yeah. Stoney . . . Yeah. That was Stoney all the way through. Got a gun somewhere—he'd never say from who—and whacked a bloke in Battersea. He and his mate were trying to carjack his BMW and the bloke didn't cooperate like they wanted. Stoney shot him in the back of the head. An execution. His mate turned him in."

She stood there for a moment, as if evaluating this. Then she went back to work.

"Thing is," Nkata went on, "I could've gone the same way and was doing jus' that, 'cept I figured I was cleverer than Stoney. I could fight better, an' anyway I wasn't in'erested in ripping off cars. I had a gang, see, and they were my brothers, more brothers to me'n Stoney could've ever been anyway. So I fought with them cos that's what we did. We fought over turf. This pavement, that pavement, this newsagent's, that tobacconist. I end up in Casualty with my face split open"—he gestured to his cheek and the scar that ran down it—"and my mum faints dead on the floor when she sees it. I look at her and I look at my dad and I know he means to beat me bloody when we get home, with or without my face done up in stitches. And I see—all of a sudden, this was—that he means to beat me not for myself but cos I hurt Mum like Stoney hurt Mum. And then I really *see* how they treat her: doctors and nurses in Casualty, this is. They treat her like *she* did somethin' wrong, which is what they think she did cos one of her boys 's in prison and the other's a Brixton Warrior. And that's it." Nkata held out his hands, empty. "A cop makes conversation with me—this is about the fight that got me the scar—and he starts me off in another direction. And I cling to him and I cling to it cos I won't do to Mum what Stoney did."

"As easy as that?" Yasmin asked. He could hear the note of scorn in her voice.

"As simple as that," Nkata corrected her politely. "I wouldn't ever say it was easy."

Yasmin finished packing her makeup away. She closed the case with a snap and heaved it from the counter. She carried it to the back of the shop and shoved it on a shelf before she placed one hand on a hip and said, "That all?"

"No."

"Fine. What else?"

"I live with my mum and dad. Over on Loughborough Estate. I'm goin' to stay living with them no matter what cos they're getting older and the older they get, the more dangerous it is over there. For them. I won't have them facing aggro from smackheads an' dope dealers an' pimps. That lot don't like me, they don't wan' to be round me, they sure as hell don' trust me, and they keep their distance from my mum and my dad, long as I'm there. Tha's how I want it and I'll do what it takes to keep it that way."

Yasmin cocked her head. Her face maintained its distrustful, scornful expression, the same expression she'd worn since he'd met her. "So. Why're you telling me this?"

"Cos I want you to know the truth. An' thing is, Yas, the truth i'n't a road without curves and diversions. So you got to know that, yeah, I was 'tracted to you the first moment I saw you and who wouldn't be? So, yeah, I wanted you away from Katja Wolfe but not cos I believed you're meant for a man's love and not a woman's love cos I di'n't know that, did I, how could I. But cos I wanted a chance with you and the only way to *get* that chance was to prove to you Katja Wolfe wasn't worthy of what you had to offer. But at the same time, Yas, I liked Daniel from the first 's well. An' I could see Daniel liked me back. An' I bloody well know—knew it then and know it now—how life can be for kids on the street with time on their hands, specially kids like Daniel, without dads in the house. An' it wasn't cos I thought you weren't—aren't—a good mum, cos I could see that you were. But I thought Dan needed more—he still needs more—an that's what I came to tell you."

"That Daniel needs—"

"No. All of it, Yas. Beginning to end."

He still stood a distance from her, but he thought he could see the muscles move in her smooth dark neck as she swallowed. He thought he could see her heart beat in the vein on her temple as well. But he knew he was trying to think things into a reality defined by his hopes. Let it go, he told himself. Let it be what it is.

"What d'you want now, then?" Yasmin finally asked him. She returned to the beauty chair and picked up the two remaining wigs, holding one under each arm.

Nkata shrugged. "Nothing," he said.

"An' that's the truth?"

"You," he said. "All right. You. But I don't know if *tha's* even the truth, which is why I don't want to say it out loud. In bed? Yeah. I want you like that. In bed. With me. But everything else? I don't know. So tha's the truth, and it's what you're owed. You always deserved it, but you never got it. Not from your husband and not from Katja. I don't know if you're even getting it from your current man, but you're getting it from me. So there was you first an' foremost in my eyes. And there was Daniel afterwards. An' it's never been as simple as you thinking I'm using Dan to get to you, Yasmin. Nothin' is ever simple as that."

Everything was said. He felt empty of nearly all that he was: poured onto the lino at her feet. She could step right through him or sweep him up and dump him in the street or . . . anything, really. He was bare and helpless as the day he'd been born.

They stared at each other. He felt the wanting as he'd not felt it before, as if stating it blatantly had increased it tenfold till it gnawed at him like an animal chewing from the inside out.

Then she spoke. Two words only and at first he didn't know what she meant. "What man?"

"What?" His lips were dry.

"What current man? You said my current man."

"That bloke. The last time I was here."

She frowned. She looked towards the window as if seeing a reflection of the past in the glass. Then back at him. She said, "Lloyd Burnett."

"You di'n't say his name. He came in—"

"To get his wife's wig," she said.

He said, "Oh," and felt a perfect fool.

His mobile rang then, which saved him from having to say anything more. He flipped it open, said, "Hang on," into it, and used the blessed intervention as a means to his escape. He took out one of his cards and he approached Yasmin. She didn't raise the wig stands to defend herself. She wore only a jersey on top—no pocket available—so he slid his card into the front pocket of her jeans. He was careful not to touch her any more than that.

He said, "I got to take this call. Someday, Yas, I hope it's you ringing." He was closer to her than she'd ever let him get. He could smell her scent. He could sense her fear.

He thought, *Yas*, but he didn't say it. He left the shop and went towards his car, drawing the mobile to his ear.

THE VOICE ON the phone was unfamiliar to him, as was the name. "It's Gigi," a young woman said. "You told me to ring you?"

He said, "Who?"

She said, "Gigi. From Gabriel's Wharf? Crystal Moon?"

The association brought him round quick enough, for which he was grateful. He said, "Gigi. Right. Yeah. Wha's happened?"

"Robbie Kilfoyle's been in." Her voice lowered to a whisper. "He made a purchase."

"You got paperwork on it?"

"I got the till receipt. Right here in front of me."

"Hang on to it," Nkata told her. "I'm on my way."

LYNLEY SENT the message to Mitchell Corsico immediately after he talked to St. James: The investigation's independent forensic specialist would make a fine second profile for *The Source*, he told him. Not only was he an international expert witness and a lecturer at the Royal College of Science, but he and Lynley shared a personal history that began at Eton and had spanned the years since then. Did Corsico think a conversation with St. James would be profitable? He did, and Lynley gave the reporter Simon's contact number. This would be enough to remove Corsico, his Stetson, and his cowboy boots from sight, Lynley hoped. It would keep the rest of the investigation's team out of the reporter's mind, as well. At least for a time.

He returned to Victoria Street then, details from the past several hours roiling round in his head. He kept going back to one of them, one offered by Havers in their phone conversation.

The name on the letting agreement at the estate agency—the only name aside from Barry Minshall's that they could associate with MABIL—was J. S. Mill, Havers had told him. He'd supplied the rest, although she'd already got there: J. S. Mill. John Stuart Mill, if one wished to continue the theme set up at the Canterbury Hotel.

Lynley wanted to think that it was all part of a literary joke—wink wink, nudge nudge—among the members of the organisation of paedophiles. Sort of a slap in the collective face of the unwashed, unread, and uneducated general public. Oscar Wilde on the registration card at the Canterbury Hotel. J. S. Mill on the letting agreement with Taverstock & Percy. God only knew who else they would find on other documents relating to MABIL. A. A. Milne, possibly. G. K. Chesterton. A. C. Doyle. The possibilities were endless.

So, for that matter, were the million and one coincidences that happened every day. But still the name remained, taunting him. J. S. Mill. Catch me if you can. John Stuart Mill. John Stuart. John Stewart.

There was no use denying it to himself: Lynley had felt a quivering in his palms when Havers had said the name. That quivering translated to the questions that police work—not to mention life itself—always prompted the wise man to ask. How well do we ever know anyone? How often do we let outward appearances—including speech and behaviour—define our conclusions about individuals?

I don't need to tell you what this means, do I? Lynley could still see the grave concern on St. James's face.

Lynley's answer had taken him places he didn't want to go. No. You don't need to tell me a thing.

What it all really meant was asking that the cup be passed along to someone else, but that wasn't going to happen. He was in too far, truly "steep'd in blood so deep," and he couldn't retrace a single one of his steps. He had to see the investigation through to its conclusion, no matter where each single branch of it led. And there was decidedly more than one branch to this matter. That was becoming obvious.

A compulsive personality, yes, he thought. Driven by demons? He did not know. That restlessness, the occasional anger, the ill-chosen word. How had the news been received when Lynley—ahead of everyone else—had been handed the superintendent's position after Webberly was struck down in the street? Congratulations? No one congratulated anyone over anything in those days that had followed Webberly's attempted murder. And who would have thought to, with the superintendent fighting for his life and everyone else trying to find his assailant? So it was not important. It meant absolutely nothing. Someone had to step in, and he'd been tapped to do it. And it wasn't permanent, so it could hardly have been an important enough detail to make *anyone* want . . . decide . . . be pushed to . . . No.

Yet everything took him back inexorably to his earliest days among his fellow officers: the distance they'd originally placed between themselves and him who would never be one of the lads, not really. No matter what he did to level the playing field, there would always be what they knew about him: the title, the land, the public school voice, the wealth and the assumed privilege it brought, and who bloody cared except everyone did at the end of the day and everyone probably always would.

But anything more than that—dislike evolving to grudging acceptance and respect—was impossible to consider. It was disloyal, even, to entertain such thoughts. It was divisive and nonproductive, surely.

Yet none of this kept him from having a chat with DAC Cherson in Personnel Management, although his heart was at its heaviest when he did it. Cherson authorised the temporary release of employment records. Lynley read them and told himself they amounted to nothing. Details that could be interpreted any way one wanted: a bitter divorce, a ruthless child-custody situation, spirit-breaking child support, a disciplinary letter for sexual harassment, a word to the wise about keeping fit, a bad knee, a commendation for extra coursework completed. Nothing, really. They amounted to *nothing*.

Still, he took notes and tried to ignore the sense of betrayal he felt as he did it. We all have skeletons, he told himself. My own are uglier than those of others.

He returned to his office. From where he'd stowed it

on top of his desk, he read the profile of their killer. He thought about it. He thought about everything: from meals eaten and meals skipped, to boys disabled by an unexpected shot of electricity. What he thought was no. What he concluded was no. What he did was turn to the phone and ring Hamish Robson on his mobile.

He found him between sessions in his office near the Barbican, where he met with private clients away from the grim surroundings of Fischer Psychiatric Hospital for the Criminally Insane. It was a sideline dealing with normal people in temporary crisis, Robson told him.

"One can cope with the criminal element only so long," he confided. "But I expect you know what I'm talking about."

Lynley asked Robson if they could meet. At the Yard, elsewhere. It didn't matter.

"I've a full diary into the evening," Robson said. "Can we talk on the phone now? I've ten minutes before my next client."

Lynley considered this, but he wanted to see Robson. He wanted more than merely talking to him.

Robson said, "Has something more . . . Are you all right, Superintendent? May I help? You sound . . ." He seemed to shuffle papers on the other end of the line. "Listen, I might be able to cancel a patient or two, or move them round a bit. Would that help? I've also got some shopping to do and I'd blocked out time for that at the end of the day. It's not far from my office. Whitecross Street, where it intersects with Dufferin? There's a fruit and veg stall where I could meet you. We could talk while I make my purchases."

It would have to do, Lynley thought. But he could handle the preliminaries over the phone. He said, "What time?"

"Half past five?"

"All right. I can do that."

"If you wouldn't mind my asking . . . so that I might

think about it in advance? Is there a new development?"

Lynley considered it. New, he thought. Yes and no, he decided. "How confident are you in your profile of the killer, Dr. Robson?"

"It's not an exact science, naturally. But it's very close. When you consider it's based on hundreds of hours of detailed face-to-face interviews . . . when you consider the length and extent of the analyses of these interviews . . . the data compiled, the commonalities noted . . . It's not like a fingerprint. It's not DNA. But as a guide—even as a checklist—it's an invaluable tool."

"You feel that sure of it?"

"I feel that sure. But why are you asking? Have I missed something? Is there more information I ought to have? I can only work with what you give me."

"What would you say to the fact that the first five boys killed had all eaten something within the final hour of their lives, while the last boy had eaten nothing in hours? Would you be able to make an interpretation from that?"

A silence while Robson considered the question. He ultimately said, "Not out of context. I wouldn't like to."

"What about the fact that the food eaten by the first five boys was identical each time?"

"That would be part of the ritual, I'd say."

"But why skip it for the sixth boy?"

"There could be dozens of explanations. Not every boy was positioned identically after death. Not every boy had his navel removed. Not every boy had a symbol on his forehead. We're looking for markers that make the crimes related, but they won't be carbon copies of each other."

Lynley didn't reply to this. He heard Robson say to someone else, voice away from the phone, "Tell her a moment, please." His next client had arrived, no doubt. They had little enough time to conclude their conversation.

Lynley said, "Fred and Rosemary West. Ian Brady and Myra Hindley. How common was that? Could the police have anticipated it?"

"Male and female killers? Or two killers working as a team?"

"Two killers," Lynley said.

"Well of course, the problem was the disappearance factor in both of those examples, wasn't it? The lack of bodies and crime scenes to gather information from. When people simply disappear—bodies buried in basements for decades, hidden on the moors, what you will—there's nothing to interpret. In the case of Brady and Hindley, profiling didn't exist then, anyway. As for the Wests—and this would be the case for all serial-killing couples—there's one dominant partner and one submissive partner. One kills, one watches. One starts the process, one finishes it off. But may I ask . . . Is this where you're heading with the investigation?"

"Male and female? Two males?"

"Either, I suppose."

"You tell me, Dr. Robson," Lynley said. "Could we have two killers?"

"My professional opinion?"

"That's all you've got."

"Then, no. I don't think so. I stand by what I've already given you."

"Why?" Lynley asked. "Why stand by what you gave us originally? I've just given you two details you didn't have earlier. Why don't they change things?"

"Superintendent, I can hear your anxiety. I know how desperate—"

"You don't," Lynley said. "You can't. You don't."

"All right. Accepted. Let's meet at half past five. Whitecross and Dufferin. The fruit and veg man. He's the first stall you come to. I'll wait there."

"Whitecross and Dufferin," Lynley said. He rang off and carefully replaced the receiver.

He found that he was sweating lightly. His palm left a mark on the telephone. He took out his handkerchief and mopped his face. Anxiety, yes. Robson was right about that.

"Acting Superintendent Lynley?"

He didn't need to look up to know it was Dorothea Harriman, always appropriate with her appellations. He said, "Yes, Dee?"

She said nothing more. He did look up then. She had an expression asking for forgiveness in advance. He frowned. "What is it?"

"Assistant Commissioner Hillier. He's on his way down to see you. He rang me up personally and told me to keep you in your office. I said I would, but I'm happy to pretend you were already gone when I got here to tell you."

Lynley sighed. "Don't risk your own position. I'll see him."

"You sure?"

"I'm sure. God knows I need something to lighten up my day."

THE MIRACLE, Barbara Havers found, was that Wendy was not in the clouds this time round. In fact, when Barbara arrived at the woman's eponymous stall in Camden Lock Market, she was willing to wager that the aging hippie had actually taken the cure. Standing within the confines of her tiny establishment, Wendy still looked like hell on a tricycle—there was something about long grey locks, ashen skin, and multicoloured caftans fashioned from counterpanes of the subcontinent that simply did not appeal—but at least her eyes were clear. The fact that she didn't remember Barbara's earlier visit was something of a worry, but she seemed willing to believe her sister when Petula told her from behind the counter of her own establishment, "You were out of it, luv," at the time of their previous introduction to each other.

Wendy said, "Whoops," and gave a shrug of her fleshy shoulders. Then to Barbara, "Sorry, dear. It must've been one of those days."

Petula confided to Barbara with no small degree of pride that Wendy was "twelve-stepping it, again." She'd tried it before and it "hadn't taken," but the family had hopes it would this time round. "Met a bloke who gave her the ultimatum," Petula added under her breath. "And Wendy'll do anything for a length, you see. Always would. Has the sex drive of a she-goat, that girl."

Whatever it took, Barbara thought. She said, "Ambergris oil," to Wendy. "Have you sold any? This would be recently. Last few days, maybe?"

Wendy shook her grey locks. "Massage oil by the litre," she said. "I've six spas who're my most regular customers. They go in big for relaxants like eucalyptus. But no one's doing ambergris. Which's just as well, if you want to know my opinion. What we do to animals, someone out there will do to us eventually. Like aliens from another planet or something. They might like our fat just fine—the way we like whale blubber—and God only knows what they'll use it for. But just you wait. It's going to happen."

"Wendy, luv," Petula said, with one of those save-it-for-later chimes to her voice. She'd taken out a cloth and was using it to dust candles and the shelves they stood on. "It's okay, dear."

"I don't even know when I last had ambergris oil in stock," Wendy said to Barbara. "If someone asks for it, I tell them what I think."

"And has anyone asked for it?" Barbara brought out the e-fits of their possible suspects. She was finding this part of the routine rather tedious, but who really knew when she was going to strike that vein of gold? "One of these blokes, p'rhaps?"

Wendy looked at the drawings. She frowned and then dug a pair of wire-rimmed spectacles from deep within her copious cleavage. One of the lenses was cracked, so she used the other like a monocle. No, she told Barbara, neither of these blokes looked like anyone who'd come to the Cloud.

Barbara knew how unreliable her information would be—her drug use considered—so she showed the e-fits to Petula as well.

Petula made a study of both of them. Truth was, there were so many people coming into the market, especially at the weekends. She didn't like to say one of these blokes had been in, but at the same time, she didn't like to say neither of them had been in either. They looked a bit like beatnik poets, didn't they? Or clarinet players in a jazz band. One half-expected to see their sort in Soho, didn't one? Course one didn't—not that much any longer—but there was a time—

Barbara created a diversion on Memory Lane with a question about Barry Minshall. "Albino magician" certainly got Petula's attention—Wendy's as well—and there was a moment when Barbara thought that the mention of Minshall's name and a description of him was going to bear fruit. But no, an albino magician dressed in black and wearing dark glasses and a red stocking cap would be fairly memorable, even in Camden Lock Market. Minshall, they both said, was someone they definitely would have remembered.

Barbara realised that the tree of Wendy's Cloud was not going to produce, no matter how she attempted its pollination. She returned the e-fits to her shoulder bag and left the two sisters to close up for the day, pausing on the pavement outside to light up a fag and consider her next move.

Late afternoon, and she could have gone home, but

she had another route to explore. She hated the fact that all she kept turning down was one dead end after another, so she made her decision and went for her car. It was no great distance from Camden Lock to Wood Lane. And she could always go from there to the Holmes Street police station to see what more she could rattle out of Barry Minshall if things came to that.

She made her way north to Highgate Hill, doing a bit of rat-running in order to avoid the rush hour. It took her less time than she'd anticipated, and from there it was easy enough to negotiate the route to Archway Road.

She made one stop prior to taking herself to Wood Lane. A call to the incident room gleaned her the name of the estate agent who was selling the vacant flat in Walden Lodge that she'd heard about from one of the murder squad's meetings. In the no-stone-left-unturned category, she knew that he was probably a pebble with nothing beneath it, but she went there anyway and had a word with the bloke, waving her e-fits in his direction for good measure. Sod bloody all on a toasted tea cake was what she got for the effort. She felt like a Girl Guide selling biscuits in front of a Weight Watchers' meeting. There wasn't a taker anywhere.

She went on to Wood Lane. There, she found the street crowded with cars parked its entire length. These would be the vehicles of commuters who drove in to town from the northern counties and parked to take the underground for the rest of the journey. Among them, the police were still searching for someone who had seen something in the early morning hours of the day that Davey Benton's body had been found. Beneath the windscreen wiper of each car, a handout was tucked, and Barbara assumed it was this that asked for additional information from the daily commuters. For what it was worth. Perhaps a lot. Perhaps nothing at all.

At Walden Lodge, a descending drive led in the direction of an underground carpark. Barbara pulled her Mini into this drive. She was blocking access, but that couldn't be helped.

When she climbed the front steps of the squat brick structure—so out of place in a street of otherwise historical buildings—she found that the front door was propped open. A yellow bucket of water held it so, and "The Moppits" was printed in red upon this. So much for security, Barbara thought. She entered the building and called out a hello.

A young man popped his head round the first corner. He had a mop in hand, and he wore a tool belt from which cleaning implements dangled officially. One of the Moppits, Barbara concluded, as above her in the building someone began hoovering.

"Help you?" the young man inquired, hitching up his tool belt. "Not s'posed to let anyone in."

Barbara showed him her identification. She was working on the Queen's Wood murder, she told him.

He told her hastily that he knew nothing about *that*. He and his wife were merely a mobile cleaning service. They didn't live here. They came in once a week to do the sweeping, mopping, hoovering, and dusting of the common areas. And the windows as well, but only four times a year and today wasn't one of those days.

It was too much information, but Barbara put that down to nerves: A cop pops up on someone's horizon and suddenly everything can be open to interpretation. Best explain your life down to the minutest detail.

She had the flat number of the gent who'd seen the light flashing in the woods in the early morning hours when Davey's body had been found. She had his name as well: Berkeley Pears, which sounded like a brand of tinned fruit to her. She told the Moppit where she was heading and went for the stairs to seek him out.

When she knocked on his door, a dog began yapping

behind it. It was the kind of yapping she associated with a terrier in need of discipline, and she wasn't disabused of this notion when four different locks were released and the opening door allowed a Jack Russell to charge forward, intent upon her ankles. She pulled back and raised her bag to club the animal off, but Mr. Pears appeared in the terrier's wake. He blew on something that made no noise, but the dog apparently heard it. He—or was it she?—dropped to the floor at once, panting happily, as if a job had been well done.

"Excellent, Pearl," Pears told the loathsome beast. "Good dog. Treaties?" Pearl wagged her tail.

"She's supposed to do that?" Barbara said.

"It's the startle factor," the dog's owner replied.

"I could've clubbed her. She could've been hurt."

"She's fast. She'd've had you before you had her." He widened the door and said, "Bowl, Pearl. Now." The dog dashed inside, presumably to wait by her dish for a reward. "C'n I help you?" Berkeley Pears then asked Barbara. "How did you get into the building? I thought you were management. We're set to fight a legal battle over this, and she's trying to intimidate us out of it."

"Police." Barbara showed him her ID. "DC Barbara Havers. Could I have a word?"

"This's about the boy in the woods? I've already told them what little I know."

"Yeah. Got it. But another set of ears . . . ? You never know what's going to turn up."

"Very well," he said. "Come in if you must. Pearlie?"—this in the direction of the kitchen—"Come, darling."

The dog trotted out, bright eyed and friendly, as if she hadn't been a nasty little killing machine only moments before. She jumped into her master's arms and stuck her nose in the breast pocket of his tattersall shirt. He chuckled and dug in another pocket for her treat, which she swallowed without chewing.

Berkeley Pears was a type, there was no doubt of it, Barbara thought. He probably wore patent-leather shoes and an overcoat with a velvet collar when he left his digs. You saw his kind occasionally on the tube. They carried furled umbrellas, which they used as walking sticks, they read the *Financial Times* as if it meant something to them, and they never looked up till they reached their destination.

He showed her into his sitting room: three-piece suite in position, coffee table arranged with copies of *Country Life* and a *Treasures of the Uffizi* art book, modern lamps with metal shades at precise angles suitable for reading. Nothing was out of place in here, and Barbara assumed nothing dared to be . . . although three noticeable yellowish stains on the carpet gave testimony to at least one of Pearl's less than salubrious canine activities.

Pears said, "I wouldn't've seen a thing, you understand, if it hadn't been for Pearl. And you'd think I'd get a thank-you for that, but all I've heard is, 'The dog must go.' As if cats are less of a bother"—he said *cats* the way others said *cockroaches*—"when all the time that creature in number five howls morning and night like it's being skewered. Siamese. Well. What else would you expect? She leaves the little beast for weeks, while *I've* never left Pearl for so much as an hour. Not an hour, mind you, but does that count? No. One night when she barks and I can't quieten her quick enough and that is *it*. Someone complains—as if they don't all have contraband animals, the lot of them—and I get a visit from management. No animals allowed. The dog must go. Well, we intend to fight them to the very death, I tell you. Pearl goes, I go."

That, Barbara thought, might have been the master plan. She wedged her way into the conversation. "What did you see that night, Mr. Pears? What happened?"

Pears took the sofa, where he cradled the terrier like

a baby and scratched her chest. He indicated the chair for Barbara. He said, "I assumed it was a break-in at first. Pearl began . . . One can only describe it as hysterical. She was simply hysterical. She woke me from a perfectly sound sleep and frightened me to bits. She was flinging herself—believe me, there is *no* other word for it—at the balcony doors and barking like nothing I've ever heard from her before or since. So you can see why . . ."

"What did you do?"

He looked marginally embarrassed. "I rather . . . well, I armed myself. With a carving knife, which was all I had. I went to the doors and tried to see out, but there was nothing. I opened them, and that's what caused the trouble because Pearl went outside on the balcony and continued barking like a she-devil and I couldn't get a grip on her and keep hold of the knife, so it all took a bit of time."

"And in the woods?"

"There was a light. A few flashes. It's all I saw. Here. Let me show you."

The balcony opened off the sitting room, its large sliding window covered by a set of blinds. Pears raised these and opened the door. Pearl scrambled from his arms onto the balcony and commenced barking, much as described. She yapped at an ear-piercing volume. Barbara could understand why the other residents had complained. A cat was nothing in comparison with this.

Pears grabbed the Jack Russell and held her snout. She managed to bark anyway. He said, "The light was over there, through those trees and down the hill. It has to have been when the body . . . well, you know. And Pearl knew it. She could sense it. That's the only explanation. Pearl. Darling. That *is* enough."

Pears stepped back inside the flat with the dog and waited for Barbara to do likewise. For her part, though,

Barbara remained on the balcony. The woods began to dip down the hillside directly behind Walden Lodge, she saw, but that would be something one would not know from looking at the lodge from the street. The trees grew in abundance here, offering what would be a thick screen in summer but what was now a cross-hatching of branches bare in midwinter. Directly below them and right up to the brick wall that defined the edge of the lodge's property, shrubbery grew unrestrained, making access from Walden Lodge into the woods a virtual impossibility. A killer would have had to thrash through everything from holly to bracken in order to get from here to the spot where the body had been dumped, and no killer worth his salt—let alone a bloke who'd so far managed to eliminate six youths and leave virtually no evidence behind when he dumped their bodies—would have attempted that. He would have deposited a treasure trove of useful clues in his wake. And he hadn't done so.

Barbara stood there thoughtfully, surveying the scene. She considered everything that Berkeley Pears had told her. Nothing he'd reported was out of place, but there was one detail that she didn't quite understand.

She reentered the flat, pulling the balcony door closed behind her. She said to Pears, "There was a cry of some sort heard sometime after midnight from one of the flats. We've had that information from the interviews we've done with all the residents in this building. You've not mentioned it."

He shook his head. "I didn't hear it."

"What about Pearl?"

"What about her?"

"If she heard the disturbance in the woods at this distance—"

"I suggest she *sensed* it rather than heard it," Pears corrected.

"All right. We'll say she sensed it. But then why didn't she sense something wrong in the building round midnight when someone cried out?"

"Possibly because no one did."

"Yet someone heard it. Round midnight. What d'you make of that?"

"A desire to help the police, a dream, a mistake. Something that didn't happen. Because if it did, and if it was out of the ordinary, Pearl would have reacted. Good grief, you saw how she was with you."

"That's how she always is when there's a knock at the door?"

"Under some conditions."

"What would those be?"

"If she doesn't know who's on the other side."

"And if she does know? If she hears a voice or smells a scent and recognises it?"

"Then she makes no noise. Which was why, you see, her barking at three forty-five in the morning was so unusual."

"Because if she doesn't bark, it means she knows what she's seeing, hearing, or smelling?"

"That's right," Pears said. "But I don't actually see what this has to do with anything, Constable Havers."

"That's okay in the scheme of things, Mr. Pears," Barbara said. "Fact is, I do."

Chapter Twenty-seven

Ultimately, Ulrike decided to soldier on. She had little choice. Upon her return from Brick Lane, Jack Veness had handed her the telephone message from Patrick Bensley, president of the board of trustees. With a knowing smirk, he'd said, "Have a good meeting with the *prez*, did you?," as he'd passed her the slip of paper, and she'd said, "Yes, it went very well," before lowering her gaze to see upon the phone message the name of the man whom she'd claimed she was leaving Colossus to meet.

She didn't try to pretend anything. She was too caught up in trying to decide what to do with the information she had from Arabella Strong to quickstep into giving Jack a reason why Mr. Bensley had phoned her while she was supposedly meeting him. So she merely folded the message into her pocket and leveled a look at Jack. She said, "Anything else?," and endured yet another insufferable smirk. Nothing at all, he told her.

So she decided she *had* to continue, no matter what it looked like to the police and no matter how they might react if she handed over information to them. She still had the hope that the Met would respond in a quid pro quo fashion, defined by keeping any mention of Colossus away from the press. But it didn't really matter whether they did or did not because, regardless, now she *had* to finish what she'd started. That was the only way she was going to be able to excuse her journey to Griffin Strong's house should the board of trustees get wind of it from someone.

As far as Griff himself went—as far as Arabella's vow to lie for him went—Ulrike didn't want to dwell on this, and Jack's reactions gave her a reason not to. They moved him directly to the top of her list.

She didn't bother with an excuse when she left Colossus a second time late in the day. Instead, she took up her bicycle and headed along the New Kent Road. Jack lived in Grange Walk, which opened off Tower Bridge Road, less than ten minutes by bicycle from Elephant and Castle. It was a narrow one-way street across from Bermondsey Square. One side of it comprised a newish housing estate, while the other bore a terrace of homes that had probably stood in the spot since the eighteenth century.

Jack had rooms in one of these houses: number 8, a building distinguished by its fanciful shutters. Painted blue to match the rest of the woodwork on the sooty building, they had heart-shaped openings at the top to let in the light when they were closed and secured. They were open now, and the windows that they would otherwise cover were hung with lace curtains looking several layers thick.

There was no bell, so Ulrike used the door knocker, which was shaped like an old-time cine-camera. To compensate for the noise from Tower Bridge Road, she applied some force to the knocking. When no one answered, she bent to the brass letter box in the middle of the door and lifted it to peer inside the house. She saw an old lady lowering herself carefully down the stairs, two-stepping it sideways and with both hands on the railing.

The woman evidently saw Ulrike peering in, for she shouted, "I do *beg* your pardon!," and she followed this with, "I be*lieve* this is a private residence, whoever you are!," which prompted Ulrike to drop the hinged lid on the letter box and wait, chagrined, for the door to open.

When it did, she found herself confronted by a crumpled and very peeved face. This was framed by tight white curls and, along with her thin-framed body, they shook with indignation. Or so it seemed at first, until Ulrike dropped her gaze and saw the zimmer frame to which the old lady held. Then she realised it wasn't so much anger as it was palsy or Parkinson's or something else that was causing the tremors.

She apologised hastily and introduced herself. She mentioned Colossus. She said Jack's name. Could she have a word with Mrs. . . . ? She hesitated. Who the hell *was* this woman? she wondered. She should have sussed that one out before barreling over here.

Mary Alice Atkins-Ward, the old lady said. And it was Miss and proud to be so, thank you very much. She sounded stiff—a pensioner who remembered the old days when people had manners defined by courteous queues at bus stops and gentlemen giving up seats to ladies on the underground. She held the door open and manoeuvred herself back from it so that Ulrike could enter. Ulrike did so gratefully.

She found herself immediately in a narrow corridor much taken up by the stairway. The walls were jammed with photos, and as Miss A-W—which was how Ulrike began thinking of her—led the way into a sitting room overlooking the street, Ulrike took a peek at these. They were, she found, all photos taken from television shows: BBC1 costume dramas mostly, although there were also a smattering of gritty police programmes as well.

She said in as friendly a fashion as she could, "You're a fan of the telly?"

Miss A-W cast a scornful look over her shoulder as she crossed the sitting room and deposited herself in a ladder-backed wooden rocking chair sans a single softening cushion. "What in heaven's name are you talking about?"

"The photos in the corridor?" Ulrike had never felt so out of step with someone.

"Those? I wrote them, you ninny," was Miss A-W's retort.

"Wrote?"

"Wrote. I'm a screenwriter, for heaven's sake. Those are my productions. Now what do you want?" She offered nothing: no food, no drink, no fondly reminiscent conversation. She was a tough old bird, Ulrike concluded. It was going to be no easy feat to pull the wool here.

Nonetheless, she had to try. There was no alternative. She told the woman that she wanted to have a few words about her tenant.

"What tenant?" Miss A-W asked.

"Jack Veness?" Ulrike prompted her. "He works at Colossus. I'm his . . . well, his supervisor, I suppose."

"He's not my tenant. He's my great-nephew. Worthless little bugger, but he had to live somewhere once his mum chucked him out. He helps with the housework and the shopping." She adjusted herself in her chair. "See here, I'm going to have a cigarette, missy. I hope you're not one of those flag-waving ASHers. If you are, too bad. My house, my lungs, my life. Hand me that book of matches, please. No, no, you ninny. Not over there. They're right in front of you."

Ulrike found them among the clutter on a coffee table. The book was from a Park Lane hotel where, Ulrike imagined, Miss A-W had doubtless terrified the staff into handing matches over by the gross.

She waited till the old lady had extracted a cigarette from the pocket of her cardigan. She smoked unfiltered—no surprise there—and she held the burning fag like an old-time film star. She picked a piece of tobacco from her tongue, examined it, and flicked it over her shoulder.

"So, what's this about Jack?" she asked.

"We're considering him for promotion," Ulrike replied with what she hoped was an ingratiating smile. "And before someone's promoted, we talk to those people who know him best."

"Why do you suppose I know him any better than you do?"

"Well, he does live here . . . It's just a starting point, you understand."

Miss A-W was watching Ulrike with the sharpest eyes she had ever seen. This was a lady who'd been through it, she reckoned. Lied to, cheated on, stolen from, whatever. It must have come from working in British television, notorious home of the thoroughly unscrupulous. Only Hollywood was meant to be worse.

She continued to smoke and evaluate Ulrike, clearly unbothered by the silence that stretched between them. Finally she said, "What sort?"

"I beg your pardon?"

"No, you don't," she said. "What sort of promotion?"

Ulrike did some quick thinking. "We're opening a branch of Colossus across the river. The North London branch? He may have told you about it. We'd like Jack to be an assessment leader there."

"Would you now. Well, he doesn't want that. He wants community outreach. And I'd expect you'd know that if you'd talked to him about it."

"Yes, well," Ulrike improvised, "there's a hierarchy involved, as Jack's no doubt mentioned. We like to place people where we think they'll . . . well, blossom actually. Jack's probably going to work his way up to community outreach eventually, but as for now . . ." She made a vague gesture.

Miss A-W said, "He'll be in a snit about that when he hears. He's like that. Sees himself persecuted. Well, his mum didn't help with that any, did she. But why can't you young people just get *on* with things instead of sniveling when you don't get what you want when you want it? That's what I'd like to know." She cupped her hand and flicked ash into it. She rubbed this into the arm of her rocking chair. "What does this assessment leader do?"

Ulrike explained the job, and Miss A-W picked up on the most relevant part. "Young people?" she said. "Working with them to build trust? Not exactly up Jack's street. I'd suggest you move right along to another employee if that's what you want, but if you tell him I said that, I'll call you a filthy liar."

"Why?" Ulrike asked, perhaps too quickly. "What would he do if he knew we were talking?"

Miss A-W dragged in on her cigarette and let out what smoke wasn't otherwise adhering to her doubtless blackened lungs. Ulrike did her best not to breathe in too deeply. The old lady seemed to consider what she wanted to say because she was silent for a moment before she settled on, "He can be a good enough boy when he sets his mind to it, but he generally has his mind on other things."

"Such as?"

"Such as himself. Such as his lot in life. Just like everyone else his age." Miss A-W gestured with her cigarette for emphasis. "Young people are whingers, and that's the boy's problem in a teacup, missy. To hear him talk, you'd think he's the only child on earth who grew up without a dad. *And* with a loose-knickered mum, who's flitted from man to man since the boy was born. Since before that, as a matter of fact. From the womb, Jack was probably listening to her try to recall the name of the last bloke she slept with. So how could it be a surprise to anyone that he turned out bad?"

"Bad?"

"Come now. You know what he was. He went to Colossus from borstal, for heaven's sake. Min—that's his mum—says it's all to do with her never being quite sure which lover was actually his dad. She says, 'Why can't the lad just *cope*? I do.' But that's Min for you: blaming anyone and anything before she'd ever take a real look at herself. She chased men all her life, and Jack chased trouble. By the time he was fourteen, Min couldn't cope with him any longer and her mum didn't want to, so they sent him to me. Until that arson nonsense. Stupid little sod."

"How do you get on with him?" Ulrike asked.

"We live and let live, which's how I get on with everyone, missy."

"What about with others?"

"What about what about?"

"His friends. Does he get on with them?"

"They'd hardly be friends if he didn't get on with them, would they?" Miss A-W pointed out.

Ulrike smiled. "Yes. Well. D'you see them much?"

"Why d'you want to know?"

"Well, because obviously . . . Jack's interactions with them indicate how he'd interact with others, you see. And that's what we're—"

"No, I don't see," Miss A-W said tartly. "If you're his superior, you see him interacting all the time. You interact with him yourself. You don't need my opinion on the matter."

"Yes, but the social aspects of one's life can reveal . . ." What, she thought? She couldn't come up with an answer, so she cut to the chase. "Does he go out with friends, for instance? In the evenings. Pubbing or the like?"

Miss A-W's sharp eyes narrowed a degree. She said carefully, "He goes out as much as the next lad."

"Every night?"

"What on earth difference does it make?" She was sounding more and more suspicious, but Ulrike plunged on.

"And is it always the pub?"

"Are you asking if he's a dipso, Miss . . . who?"

"Ellis. Ulrike Ellis. And no, it's not about that. But he's said he's in the pub every night, so—"

"If that's what he's said, that's where he is."

"But you don't believe that?"

"I don't see how it matters. He comes and he goes. I don't keep tabs on him. Why should I? Sometimes it's the pub, sometimes it's a girlfriend, sometimes it's his mum when they're on good terms, which happens whenever Min wants him to do something for her. But he doesn't tell me and I don't ask. And what I want to know is why *you're* asking. Has he done something?"

"So he doesn't always go to the pub? Can you recall any time recently when he didn't? When he went somewhere else? Like to his mum's? Where does she live, by the way?"

At this, Ulrike saw she'd gone too far. Miss A-W heaved herself to her feet, cigarette dangling from her lips. Ulrike thought fleetingly of the word *broad* as applied to women by American tough guys in old black-and-white films. That was what Miss A-W was: a broad to be reckoned with.

The old lady said, "See here, you're prowling round for information and don't pretend this is *anything* but a fishing expedition. I'm not a fool. So you can lift your tight little bum off that sofa and leave my house before I call the police and ask them to assist you in the act."

"Miss Atkins-Ward, please. If I've upset you . . . It's only part of the job . . ." Ulrike found herself floundering. She needed a delicate touch, and that was what she was lacking. She simply did *not* possess the Machiavellian manner that her position at Colossus occasionally required. Too honest, she told herself. Too up front with people. She *had* to shed that quality or at least be able to shrug it off occasionally. For God's sake, she needed to practise lying if she was going to acquire *any* useful information.

She knew that Miss A-W would report her visit to Jack. Try as she might, she couldn't see how she could avoid that happening unless she hit the old lady over the head with a table lamp and put her in hospital. She said, "If I've offended . . . used the wrong approach . . . I should have been more delicate with the—"

"*Is* there something wrong with your hearing?" Miss A-W cut in, shaking her zimmer frame for emphasis. "Are you leaving or do I have to take matters a step further?"

And she would, Ulrike saw. That was the insanity of it. One had to admire a woman like this. She'd taken on the world and succeeded, owing no one a thing.

Ulrike had no further choice but to hustle herself from the room. She did so, making noises of apology in the hope they would suffice to keep Miss A-W from phoning the police or telling Jack that his supervisor had come round checking up on him. She had little confidence in either of these possibilities actually happening. When Miss A-W threatened, she followed through with the proposed action.

Ulrike hurried out of the house and into the street. She rued her plan and her ineptitude. First Griff, now Jack. Two down and shot to smithereens. Two to go and God only knew the mess she'd make of *them*.

She climbed on her bike and wheeled her way into Tower Bridge Road. Enough for today, she decided. She was going home. She needed a drink.

* * *

IT WAS FADING daylight, and the overhead lights were already crisscrossing Gabriel's Wharf when Nkata got there. The cold was keeping people indoors, so aside from the haberdasher sweeping the pavement in front of her fanciful shop, no one else hung about. Most of the shops were still open, however, and Nkata saw that Mr. Sandwich appeared to be one of these despite its posted hours: Two middle-aged white ladies in voluminous aprons seemed to be cleaning behind the counter.

In Crystal Moon, Gigi was waiting for him. She'd closed for the day, but when he knocked on the door, she appeared from the back immediately. Casting a look round, as if she expected to be spied upon, she came to the door, unlocked it, and gestured him inside conspiratorially. She relocked it behind him.

What she said made Nkata wonder why he'd come. "Parsley."

He said, "What about it? I thought you said—"

"Come here, Sergeant. You need to understand."

She urged him over to the till and she indicated the large book open next to it. Nkata recognised the antique volume from his first visit, when Gigi's gran had been in charge of the place.

"I didn't think anything of it when he came in," she said. "Not at first. Because parsley oil—which is what he bought—has more than one use. See, it's a bit of a miracle herb: diuretic, antispasmodic, stimulant of the uterine muscles, breath freshener. If you plant it next to roses, it even improves their scent, no joking. And that doesn't begin to take into account all its uses in cooking, so when he bought it, I didn't think . . . except I knew that you had your eye on him, didn't I, so the more I thought about it—even though he didn't even *mention* ambergris oil—I decided to have a look in the book and see what else it might be used for. It's not like I have them memorised, you understand. Well, maybe

I ought, but there are zillions and it's just too much for one brain to hold on to."

She went behind the counter and swung the herb book round so that he could see it. Even then, she seemed to feel the need to prepare him for what he was about to read.

She said, "Now it may be nothing, and it probably is, so you must swear to me you won't tell Robbie I rang you about it. I have to work next door to him, and bad blood between neighbours is the worst. So can you promise me you won't tell him about this? That you know about the parsley oil, I mean. And that I told you?"

Nkata shook his head. "'F this bloke's our killer, I can't promise you a thing," he told her honestly. "You got something we can use at someone's trial, it goes to the CPS and they want to interview you as a potential witness. That's the truth of it. But I don't see how parsley relates to anything so far, so I reckon you're the one to decide what you want to tell me 'bout it."

She cocked her head at him. "I like you," she said. "Any other cop would've lied just then. So I'll tell you." She pointed out the entry for parsley oil. In herbal magic, it was used for triumph. It was also used to drive away venomous beasts. Sown on Good Friday, the plant itself would nullify wickedness. Its power was in its root and its seeds.

But that wasn't all.

"Aromatic oil," Nkata read. "Fatty oil, balsam, medicinal, culinary, incense, and perfume." Nkata pulled thoughtfully at his chin. Interesting as it was, he didn't see how they could use any of this data.

"Well?" Gigi's voice bore a low-wattage undercurrent of excitement. "What d'you think? Was I right to ring you? He hadn't been in in *ages*, see, and when he walked into the shop I . . . well, to be honest, I nearly bricked it. I didn't know *what* he was likely to do, so I tried to act like everything was normal, but I watched him and I kept waiting for him to go for the ambergris oil, in which case I s'pose I might've passed out on the spot. Then when he bought the parsley oil instead, like I said, I didn't think too much about it. Till I read this stuff about triumph and demons and evil and . . ." She shuddered. "I just *knew* I had to tell you. Because if I didn't and if something happened to someone somewhere and if it turned out Robbie's the . . . not that I *think* he is for a minute and God, you must *never* tell him 'cause we've even had drinks together like I told you before."

Nkata said, "You got a copy of the receipt and all that?"

"Oh abso*lute*ly," Gigi told him. "He paid cash and the oil was the *only* thing he bought. I've got the till copy right here." And she rang up something on the till to open it, whereupon she pulled up the tray that held the notes separate from one another, and from beneath this, she took a slip of paper which she handed over to Nkata. She'd written "Rob Kilfoyle's purchase of parsley oil" on this. She'd underlined "parsley oil" twice.

Nkata wondered how they could possibly make use of the fact that one of their suspects had purchased parsley oil, but he took the receipt from Gigi and folded it inside his leather notebook. He thanked the young woman for her vigilance and told her to be in touch with him should Robbie Kilfoyle—or anyone else—stop in for ambergris oil.

He was about to leave when the thought struck him, so he paused in the doorway to ask her a final question. "Any chance he nicked the ambergris oil while he was in here?"

She shook her head. She hadn't taken her eyes off him *once*, she assured Nkata. There was no *way* he'd taken anything that he'd not presented to her and paid for. No way at all.

Nkata nodded thoughtfully at this, but he wondered all the same. He left the shop and stood outside, casting a look towards Mr. Sandwich, where the two aproned women were still at work. A "closed" sign now hung in the window. He took out his police identification and went to the door. There was one possibility for the parsley oil that he needed to check out.

When he knocked, they looked up. The plumper of the two women was the one who opened the door to him. He asked her if he could have a word, and she said yes, of course, do come in, officer. They were just about to go home for the day and he was lucky to catch them still at it.

He stepped inside. At once he saw the large yellow cart parked in a corner. "Mr. Sandwich" was painted neatly on it, along with a cartoon figure of a filled baguette with crusty face, top hat, spindly arms, and legs. This would be Robbie Kilfoyle's delivery cart. Kilfoyle himself, along with his bicycle, would be long gone for the day.

Nkata introduced himself to the two women who told him in turn they were Clara Maxwell and daughter Val. This bit of information was something of a surprise, since the two looked more like sisters than they did parent and child, a circumstance caused not so much by Clara's youthful looks—of which there were none to speak of—as by Val's dowdy dress sense and drooping figure. Nkata adjusted to the information and nodded in a friendly fashion. In return, Val kept her distance behind the counter, where she did as much lurking as she did cleaning. Her glance kept shifting from Nkata to her mother and back again, while Clara established herself as spokeswoman for the two.

"C'n I have a word with you 'bout Robbie Kilfoyle?" Nkata asked. "He works for you, right?"

Clara said, "He's not in trouble," as a statement of fact and cast a look at Val, who nodded in apparent agreement with this remark.

"He delivers your sandwiches, i'n't that the case?"

"Yes. Has done for . . . what is it, Val? Three years? Four?"

Val nodded again. Her eyebrows knotted, as if in a display of concern. She turned away and went to a cupboard from which she took a broom and dustpan. She began using this on the floor behind the counter.

"Must be nearly four years, then," Clara said. "Lovely young man. He carries the sandwiches round to our clients—we do crisps, pickles, and pasta salads as well—and he returns with the cash. He's never been out by so much as ten pence."

Val looked up suddenly.

Her mother said, "Oh yes, I'd forgotten. Thank you, Val. There *was* that one time, wasn't there?"

"What time?"

"Shortly before his mum died. This would have been December, year before this last one. We were ten pounds short one day. Turned out he'd borrowed them to buy Mum flowers. She was in a home, you know." Clara tapped her skull. "Alzheimer's, poor soul. He took her . . . I don't know . . . tulips? Would there've been tulips at that time of year? Perhaps something else? Anyway, Val's right. I'd forgotten about that. But he confessed straightaway when I asked him about it, didn't he, and I had the money in my hand the very next day. After that, nothing. He's been good as gold. We couldn't run the business without him because mainly what we do is delivery, and there's no one but Rob to do it."

Val looked up from her sweeping once again. She brushed a lank lock of hair from her face.

"Now, you know that's the truth," Clara chided her

gently. "You couldn't make those deliveries, no matter what you think, dear."

"Does he buy supplies for you as well?" Nkata asked.

"What kind of supplies? Paper bags and such? Mustard? Wrapping for the sandwiches? No, we mostly have all that delivered."

"I had in mind . . . p'rhaps ingredients," Nkata said. "He ever get parsley oil for you?"

"*Parsley?*" Clara looked at Val as if to register her level of incredulity. "Parsley *oil*, you say? I never knew there was such a thing. Of course, I suppose there must be, mustn't there? Walnut oil, sesame oil, olive oil, peanut oil. Why not parsley oil as well? But no, he's never bought it for Mr. Sandwich. I wouldn't know what to do with it."

Val made a sound, something like gurgling. Her mother, hearing this, leaned over the counter and spoke directly into her face. Did she know something about parsley oil and Robbie? Clara inquired. If she did, dearest, then she needed to tell the policeman straightaway.

Val's glance went to Nkata. She said, "Nuffink," which was the extent of her intelligible comments during the entire interview.

Nkata said, "I s'pose he could be using it for cooking. Or for his breath. How's his breath?"

Clara laughed. "It's nothing I've ever noticed, but I daresay our Val's got close enough for a whiff now and then. How is it, darling? Nice? Bad? What?"

Val scowled at her mother and skulked off into what seemed to be a storeroom. Clara said to Nkata that her daughter had "a bit of a crush." Not that anything could come of it, naturally. The sergeant had probably noticed that Val had a few problems with her social skills.

"I'd thought Robbie Kilfoyle might be *just* the ticket

to bring her out of herself," Clara confided in a lower voice, "which is part of the reason I hired him. He'd never had much of an employment record—that's owing to the mum being ill for so long—but I rather saw that as something of an advantage in the romance department. Wouldn't have his sights set so high, I thought. Not like other lads for whom Val, let's face it, poor love, wouldn't exactly be a prize. But nothing came of it. No spark between them, you see. Then when his mum passed on, I thought he'd come round a little bit. But he never did. The life just went out of the lad." She glanced back in the direction of the storage room and then added quietly, "Depression. It will do you in if you aren't careful. I felt it myself when Val's dad died. It wasn't sudden, of course, so at least I had some time to prepare. But you feel it all the same when someone's gone, don't you? There's that void, and there's no getting round it. You're staring into it all day long. Val and I opened this shop because of it."

"Because of . . . ?"

"Her dad's dying. He left us well enough off, I mean with enough to get by on. But one can't sit home and stare at the walls. One has to keep living." She paused and untied her apron. As she folded it carefully and laid it on the top of the counter, she nodded as if she'd just revealed something to herself. "You know, I think I'll have a word with our Robbie about that very subject. Life must go on." She cast a last, furtive look at the storage room. "And she's a good cook, our Val. That's not something a young man of marriageable age ought to turn his nose up at. Just because she's the quiet type . . . After all, what's more important at the end of the day? Conversation or good food? Good food, correct?"

"Won't get an argument from me," Nkata said.

Clara smiled. "Really?"

"Most men like to eat," he told her.

"*Exactly*," she said, and he realised she'd begun looking at him with entirely new eyes.

Which told him it was time to thank her for her information and to depart. He didn't want to think of what his mum would say if he showed up at home with a Val on his arm.

"I WANT AN EXPLANATION," were the assistant commissioner's words to Lynley as he walked through the door. He hadn't waited for Harriman to announce him, instead allowing a simple and terse, "Is he in here?," to precede him into the office.

Lynley was seated behind his desk, comparing forensic reports on Davey Benton with those from the killings that had gone before his. He set the paperwork aside, took off his reading spectacles, and stood. "Dee said you wanted to speak to me." He motioned towards the conference table at one side of the room.

Hillier didn't accept that wordless invitation. He said, "I've had a talk with Mitch Corsico, Superintendent."

Lynley waited. He'd known how likely it was that this would come once he thwarted Corsico's intentions of doing a story on Winston Nkata, and he understood the workings of Hillier's mind well enough to realise he had to let the assistant commissioner have his say.

"Explain yourself." Hillier's words were regulated, and Lynley had to give him credit for descending into enemy territory with the intention of holding on to his temper as long as he could.

He said, "St. James has an international reputation, sir. The fact that the Met is pulling out all the stops on this investigation—by bringing in an independent specialist to be part of the team, for example—was something I thought should be highlighted."

"That was your thought, was it?" Hillier said.

"In brief, yes. When I considered how far a profile of

St. James could go to boost public confidence in what we're doing—"

"That wasn't your decision to make."

Lynley went doggedly on. "And when I compared that increase in confidence with what could be gained by profiling Winston Nkata instead—"

"So you admit you moved to block access to Nkata?"

"—then it seemed likely that we could make more political hay from letting the public know we've an expert witness on our team than we could make by putting a black officer on display and washing his dirty linen in public."

"Corsico had *no* intention—"

"He went straight to questions about Winston's brother," Lynley cut in. "It sounded to me as if he'd even been briefed on the subject, so he'd know what angle he ought to take when he wrote the interview. Sir."

Hillier's face took on deep colour. It rose from his neck like a ruby liquid just beneath his skin. "I don't want to think what you're implying."

Lynley made an effort to speak calmly. "Sir, let me try to be clear. You're under pressure. I'm under pressure. The public's stirred up. The press is brutal. Something's got to be done to mould opinion out there—I'm aware of that—but I can't have a tabloid journalist sniffing round the background of individual officers."

"You're *not* going to be naying or yeaing decisions made above your head. Do you understand?"

"I'll be doing whatever naying or yeaing is necessary and I'll be doing it every time something occurs that could affect the job done by one of my men. A story on Winston—featuring his pathetic brother because you and I know *The Source* was intending to put Harold Nkata's face right there next to Winston's . . . Cain and Abel, Esau and Jacob, the unreturned and unreturnable prodigal . . . whatever you want to call him . . . And a story on Winston just at the moment when he's already got to contend with being on public display at press conferences . . . It's just not on, sir."

"Are you daring to tell me that you know better than our own people how to manage the press? That you—speaking no doubt from the great height you alone happen to occupy—"

"Sir." Lynley didn't want to get into mudslinging with the AC. Desperately, he sought another direction. "Winston came to me."

"*Asking* you to intervene?"

"Not at all. He's a team player. But he mentioned that Corsico was going after the good brother-bad brother angle on the story, and his concerns were that his parents—"

"I don't care about his God damn parents!" Hillier's voice rose precipitately. "He's got a story and I want it told. I want it seen. I want that to happen and I want you to ensure that it does."

"I can't do that."

"You bloody well—"

"Wait. I've said it wrong. I *won't* do that." And Lynley went on before Hillier had a chance to respond, telling himself to stay calm and to stay on message. "Sir, it was one thing for Corsico to dig round about me. He did it with my blessing and he can go on doing it if that's what it'll take to help our position here at the Met. But it's another thing for him to do that to one of my men, especially one who doesn't want that happening to himself or to his family. I've got to respect that. So do you."

He knew he shouldn't have said that last, even as his lips formed the words. It was just the remark Hillier had apparently been waiting for.

"You're God damn out of order!" he roared.

"That's your way of seeing it. Mine is that Winston Nkata doesn't want to be part of a publicity campaign designed to soothe the very people who've been betrayed by the Met time and again. I don't blame him for that. I also won't fault him. Nor will I order him to cooperate. If *The Source* intends to smear his family's trouble across the front page some morning, then it's—"

"That's enough!" Hillier was teetering on the edge. Whether what he fell into was rage, a seizure, or an action they both would regret remained to be seen. "You God damn bloody disloyal piece of . . . You come in here from a life of privilege and you dare . . . you bloody well dare . . . *you* to tell *me* . . ."

They both saw Harriman at the same time, standing white faced in the doorway that had been left open when Hillier entered. No doubt, Lynley thought, every ear on the floor was being assaulted by the strength of the animosity that the AC felt for him and he for the AC.

Hillier shouted at her, "Get the hell out of here! What's wrong with you?" And made a move to the door, likely to slam it in Harriman's face.

Incredibly, she put out a hand to stop him, doing just that as they both reached for the door at once.

He said, "I'll see you in—"

Which she interrupted with, "Sir, sir. I need to speak to you."

Lynley saw, unbelievably, that she was talking not to him but to Hillier. The woman's gone mad, he thought. She means to intervene.

He said, "Dee, that's not necessary."

She didn't look at him. She said, "It is," with her eyes fixed on Hillier. "It *is*. Necessary. Sir. Please." The last word came from somewhere in her throat, where it caught and seemed nearly to lodge.

That got through to Hillier. He grabbed her by the arm and took her from the room.

Then things moved, both quickly and incomprehensibly.

There were voices outside his office and Lynley headed for the door to see what in God's name was going on. He got only two steps in that direction, though, when Simon St. James came into the room.

St. James said, "Tommy."

And Lynley saw. Saw and somehow understood without wanting to begin to understand. Or to give St. James's purpose in his office—arriving unannounced to him but certainly announced and fully forewarned to Harriman . . .

He heard a cry of "Oh my God" from somewhere. St. James flinched at this. His eyes, Lynley saw, were fixed upon him.

"What is it?" Lynley asked. "What's happened, Simon?"

"You must come with me, Tommy," St. James said. "Helen's . . ." Then he faltered.

Lynley would always remember that—that his old friend faltered when it came to the moment—and he would always remember what the faltering meant: about their friendship and about the woman whom both of them had loved for years.

"She's been taken to St. Thomas' Hospital," St. James said. His eyes reddened at the rims, and he cleared his throat harshly. "Tommy, you must come with me at once."

Chapter Twenty-eight

Outside Berkeley Pears' flat, Barbara Havers considered her next move. It appeared to be a nice little visit with Barry Minshall in the Holmes Street station to see what else she could scoop out of the cesspool that was his brain.

She was heading off to do just that, making her way along the corridor towards the stairs, when she heard the sound. It was something between a howl and the cry of someone in the throes of death by strangulation, and it stopped Barbara in her tracks. She waited to hear if the cry would repeat itself, and in due course it did. Throaty, desperate . . . It took a moment for her to realise that she was listening to a cat.

"Bloody hell," she murmured. It had sounded *exactly* like . . . She attached the sound to the shriek that someone in the building had heard the night of Davey Benton's murder, and when she made that leap, she realised that *everything* about her journey to Walden Lodge might well have been an exercise in pure futility.

The cat cried again. Barbara knew little enough about felines, but it sounded like one of those cracked-voice Siamese types. Malevolent little furballs though they were, they still had a right—

Furballs. Barbara looked towards the door behind

which the cat sounded another time. Cat fur, she thought, cat hair, what*ever* the bloody hell it was. There'd been cat hair on Davey Benton's body.

She went in search of the building manager. A question to one of the Moppits directed her to a ground-floor flat. She knocked on the door.

After a moment, a woman's voice called out, "Who is it, please?" in a tone that suggested she'd opened the door more than once to an unexpected visitor.

Barbara identified herself. Several locks were disengaged and the building manager stood before her: Morag McDermott, she was called. What did the police want this time round because God only knew she'd told them everything she could think of last time they'd come seeking information about "that dreadful nasty business in the woods."

Barbara saw she'd interrupted Morag McDermott in the midst of an afternoon snooze. Despite the time of year, she wore a thin dressing gown through which her skeletal body showed, and her hair was pancaked on one side. The unmistakable pattern of a chenille counterpane had lumped her cheeks like facial cellulite.

She added sharply, "How on earth did you get into the building? Let me see your identification at once."

Barbara fished it out and explained the situation with the front door and the Moppits. In response to this, the building manager pulled a sticky pad from a tabletop nearby and scribbled furiously upon it. Barbara took this as invitation to enter, and she did so as Morag McDermott slapped her note onto the wall next to the door. This was already aflutter with two score similar notes. The wall resembled a prayer board in a church.

It was for her monthly report to the management firm, Morag informed Barbara as she replaced the little yellow pad in a drawer. Now, if the constable would step this way, into the sitting room . . .

She made it sound as if the room in question required

directions to get to when in fact it was less than five feet from the front door. The flat's floor plan was identical to that of Berkeley Pears but reversed so that it faced not the woods but the street. Its decor, however, was utterly dissimilar to the flat Barbara had been in earlier. Where Berkeley Pears would have passed a drill sergeant's inspection, Morag was a poster child for clutter and sheer bad taste. Mostly, this was due to horses, of which there were hundreds on display, on every surface, in all sizes, and of all possible composition: from plastic to rubber. She was *National Velvet* gone berserk.

Barbara edged her way past a tea stand of Lippizaners poised to perform their airs above the ground. She trod the sole path available into the room, which led to a sofa burdened with perhaps a dozen equine cushions. There she deposited herself. She'd begun to perspire, and she understood why the building manager was wearing so thin a dressing gown in the middle of winter. It felt like a Jamaican summer in the flat, and it smelled as if the place hadn't been aired since the day of Morag's advent in the building.

Cutting to the chase was the best option for personal survival, Barbara concluded, so she went directly to the subject of the cat. She'd been about to leave the building, she said, when she'd heard the sound of an animal in distress. She wondered if Morag ought to know about that. It certainly sounded—to her admittedly unschooled ears since she'd never owned anything more than a gerbil—serious. A Siamese cat perhaps, she added helpfully. This would be in flat number 5.

"That's Mandy," Morag McDermott told her promptly. "Esther's cat. She's on holiday. I mean Esther, of course, not the cat. She'll quiet soon enough when Esther's boy comes to feed her. There's nothing for you to worry about."

Worry for the animal was the last thing on Barbara's mind, but she went with the flow of the conversation.

She needed to get inside that flat, and she didn't want to wait for a warrant to do it. Mandy sounded dead frantic, she told the building manager solemnly. True, she didn't know much about felines, but she thought the situation wanted checking into. And by the way, Berkeley Pears had told her that cats weren't allowed in the building. Had he been playing fast and loose with the truth?

"*That* man will say anything," Morag replied. "Of *course* cats are allowed in the building. Cats, fish, and birds."

"But not dogs?"

"He knew that before he moved in, Constable."

Barbara nodded. Yes, well, people and their animals . . . It took all kinds, didn't it? She brought Morag round to flat number 5 once again. "This cat . . . Mandy? She sounds . . . well, is there any chance the son hasn't come round to feed her for a while? Have you seen him here? Entering or leaving?"

Morag thought about this, drawing the neck of her dressing gown more tightly closed at her throat. She admitted that she hadn't exactly *seen* the son in the vicinity lately, but that didn't mean he hadn't been there. He was completely devoted to his mum. *Everyone* should have such a son.

Nonetheless . . . Barbara offered a smile she hoped was ingratiating. Perhaps they ought to have a look . . . ? For the sake of the cat? Something could have happened to prevent the son from coming round, couldn't it? Car crash, heart attack, kidnap by aliens . . . ?

At least one of Barbara's suggestions seemed to work because Morag nodded thoughtfully and said, "Yes, perhaps we ought to see . . ." before she went over to a corner cupboard and opened it to reveal the back of its door covered with hooks from which keys dangled.

Still attired in her dressing gown, Morag led the way to flat number 5. There was silence behind the door and for a moment Barbara thought that her ruse to get inside was going to fail. But as Morag said, "I don't actually hear—" Mandy howled cooperatively once more. With an "Oh, my dear," the building manager hastily unlocked the door and opened it. The cat escaped like a lag given an unexpected opportunity. She melted round the corner of the corridor, going for the stairs and doubtless heading for the freedom of the front door, which the Moppits still had propped open.

This would not do. Morag took off after her. Barbara stepped inside the flat.

The first thing she noted was the overpowering smell of urine. Cat urine, she assumed. No one had changed the poor creature's litter for days. The windows were closed and the curtains drawn over them, which greatly exacerbated the matter. It was no wonder the cat had bolted for the outdoors. Anything to get a breath of fresh air.

Barbara closed the door despite the odour, the better to give herself warning when Morag returned and would have to insert the key in the lock another time. That done, the flat was even gloomier, so she opened the curtains and saw that flat number 5, like that of Berkeley Pears, faced the woods at the back of the property.

She turned from the window and surveyed the room. The furniture came to her straight out of the sixties: vinyl sofa and chairs, side tables once called Danish modern, coy figurines in the shape of animals with anthropomorphic expressions on their faces. Bowls of potpourri—ostensibly attempting to rid the air of the foetid odour of cat—sat on lacy antimacassars that were now being used as mats. Barbara saw those last with a rush of happiness: Kimmo Thorne's loincloth in St. George's Gardens. Things were definitely looking up.

She prowled round for signs of recent occupation—of deadly occupation—and she found the first of them in the kitchen: one plate, one fork, one glass in the sink.

Did you feed him something before you raped him

then, you bugger? Or did you have a bit of sustenance yourself while the kid entertained you with one more magic trick which you applauded and for which you told him you had a *very* nice reward? Come over closer to me, Davey my lad. God, but you're a lovely boy. Did anyone ever tell you that? No? Why not? It's plain to see.

On a floor in the corner, the cat's dry food spilled out of a container and a large bowl next to it was empty of water. Using a dishcloth to hold it by its edges, Barbara carried this to the sink and filled it. Wasn't the cat's fault, she told herself. No point in letting it suffer any longer. And suffer Mandy had done since the night of Davey Benton's murder. There was no way in hell that the killer could have afforded to return to this place once Davey was dead, not with the street crawling with cops intent upon finding a witness.

She went from the kitchen back into the sitting room, looking for signs. He'd have raped and strangled Davey Benton somewhere in here, but the rest he would have done when he got the body into the woods.

She went to the bedroom, where, as she had done in the sitting room, she opened the curtains and turned back to survey the scene illuminated by the fast-fading daylight. A bed with covers and counterpane in place; side table with an old-fashioned wind-up alarm clock and lamp; chest of drawers with two framed photos sitting on top.

It all looked so ordinary, save for one detail: The clothes-cupboard door hung partially open. Inside, Barbara could see a flowery dressing gown askew on a hanger. She took it out. The belt was missing.

Let me show you how to do a knot trick, he'd said, and Barbara could *hear* his coaxing voice. It's the only trick that *I* know, Davey, and believe me, it'll make your mates stand up and take notice when they see how easily you can escape even if they tie your hands behind your back. Here. You tie me first. See how it works? Now I'll tie you.

Something like that, she thought. *Something* like that. He had done it that way. And then bent the boy over the bed. No shouting, Davey. No wiggling about. Okay. All right. Don't panic, lad. I'll untie your hands. But no trying to get away from me now because . . . God damn, you *scratched* me, Davey. You *bloody* well scratched me and now I'll have to . . . I *told* you not to make a sound, didn't I? Didn't I, Davey? *Didn't* I, you miserable filthy little sod?

Or maybe he had used handcuffs on the boy. Glow-in-the-dark handcuffs just like those that Barry Minshall had given Davey. Or maybe he hadn't needed to restrain him at all or hadn't *thought* to restrain him because Davey had been so much smaller than the rest of the boys and there had, after all, been no mark of restraints on his wrists, not like the others . . .

Which gave Barbara pause. Which made her admit how *desperately* she wanted this place on Wood Lane to be the answer. Which told her she was on dangerous ground, weaving place to fit circumstance in the worst kind of reckless police work, of the sort that landed innocent people in prison because the cops were just so bloody tired and so anxious to get home for supper one night in ten because their wives were complaining and their kids were misbehaving and some serious sorting needed to be done and why did you even *marry* me, Frank or John or Dick, if you meant to be gone day and night for months on end. . . .

That was how it happened, and Barbara knew it. That was how cops made deadly mistakes. She returned the dressing gown to the clothes cupboard and forced her mind to stop painting pictures.

Out in the sitting room, she heard Morag's key scratching at the lock. There was no time for anything else but a quick look at the bedsheets beneath the counterpane, catching the faint scent of lavender upon them. They offered no visible secrets to her, so she moved to the chest of drawers on the other side of the room.

And there it was: everything she needed. In one of the two photographs, a woman posed in her wedding gown with her bespectacled groom. In the other, a much older version of the same woman stood on Brighton Pier. With her was a younger man. He was bespectacled like his father.

Barbara picked this latter picture up and took it over to the window for a better look. In the sitting room, Morag's voice called out, "Are you in here, Constable?" and Mandy gave her Siamese yowl.

In the bedroom, Barbara murmured, "Bloody hell," at what she was looking at. Hastily, she shoved the Brighton Pier photograph into her shoulder bag. She composed herself as best she could and called out, "Sorry. Having a look round. Got reminded of my mum. She goes for this sixties stuff in a very big way."

Complete casuistry but it couldn't be helped. Truth was, in her present state, Mum wouldn't know the sixties from a basket of potatoes.

"She'd run out of water," Barbara said helpfully when she joined the building manager in the sitting room. The sound of Mandy lapping came from the kitchen. "I refilled her bowl. She's got plenty of food, though. I think she'll be set for a while."

Morag gave Barbara a shrewd look, which suggested she wasn't entirely convinced of the constable's heartfelt concern for the cat. But she didn't make a move to frisk Barbara's person, so the end result was a round of farewells after which Barbara hotfooted it outside and dug round in her shoulder bag for her mobile.

It rang just as she was about to punch in the numbers for Lynley. A Scotland Yard extension was calling.

"Detective Con . . . *Con*stable Havers?" Dorothea Harriman was on the other end. She sounded terrible.

"Me," Barbara said. "Dee, what's wrong?"

Harriman said, "Con . . . Detect . . ." And Barbara realised she was sobbing.

She said, "Dee. Dee, get a *grip*. For the love of God, what's going on?"

"It's his wife," she cried.

"Whose wife? What wife?" Barbara felt the fear coming upon her in a rush because there was only one wife that she could conceive of in that moment, one woman only about whom the department's secretary might be calling her. "Has something happened to Helen Lynley? Has she lost her baby, Dee? What's going on?"

"Shot." Harriman keened the word. "The superintendent's wife has been shot."

LYNLEY SAW that St. James had come to him not in his old MG but in a panda car, driven from St. Thomas' Hospital with lights flashing and siren blaring. He assumed this much because that was how they returned to the other side of the river, riding in the back with two grim-faced Belgravia constables in the front, the entire journey made in a matter of minutes which nonetheless felt like hours to him, all the time with traffic parting like Red Sea waters before them.

His old friend kept a hand on his arm, as if expecting Lynley to bolt from the car. He said, "They've got a trauma team with her. They've given her blood. O-negative, they said. It's universal. But you'll know that, won't you. Of course you will." St. James cleared his throat and Lynley looked at him. He thought at that moment, unnecessarily, that St. James had once loved Helen, had so many years ago intended to be her husband himself.

"Where?" Lynley's voice was raw. "Simon, I *told* Deborah. . . I *said* that she was to—"

"Tommy." St. James's hand tightened.

"Where, then? Where?"

"In Eaton Terrace."

"At *home*?"

"Helen was tired. They parked the car and unloaded their parcels at the front door. Deborah took the Bentley round to the mews. She parked it, and when she got back to the house—"

"She didn't *hear* anything? See anything?"

"She was on the front step. At first, Deborah thought she'd fainted."

Lynley raised his hand to his forehead. He pressed in on his temples as if this would allow him to understand. He said, "How *could* she have thought—"

"There was virtually no blood. And her coat—Helen's coat—it was dark. Is it navy? Black?"

Both of them knew the colour was meaningless, but it was something to cling to and they *had* to cling to it or face the unthinkable.

"Black," Lynley said. "It's black." Cashmere, hanging nearly to her ankles, and she loved to wear it with boots whose heels were so high that she laughed at herself at the end of the day when she hobbled to the sofa and fell upon it, claiming she was a mindless victim of male Italian shoe designers with fantasies of women bearing whips and chains. "Tommy, save me from *myself*," she would say. "Only foot binding could be worse than this."

Lynley looked out of the window. He saw the blur of faces and knew they'd made it as far as Westminster Bridge, where people on the pavements were caught in their own little worlds into which the sound of a siren and the sight of a panda car zooming by caused them only an instant of wondering, Who? What? And then forgetting because it didn't affect them.

"When?" he said to St. James. "What time?"

"Half past three. They'd thought to have tea at Claridge's, but as Helen was tired, they went home instead. They'd have it there. They bought . . . I don't know . . . tea cakes somewhere? Pastries?"

Lynley tried to absorb this. It was four forty-five. He said, "An hour? More than an hour? How can that be?"

St. James didn't reply at once, and Lynley turned to him and saw how drawn and gaunt he looked, far more than normal for he was a gaunt and angular man by birth. He said, "Simon, why in God's name? More than an hour?"

"It took twenty minutes for the ambulance to get to her."

"Christ," Lynley whispered. "Oh God. Oh Christ."

"And then I wouldn't let them tell you by phone. We had to wait for a second panda car—the first officers needed to stay at the hospital . . . to speak to Deborah . . ."

"She's there?"

"Still. Yes. Of course. So we had to wait. Tommy, I couldn't let them phone you. I couldn't do that to you, say that Helen . . . say that . . ."

"No. I see." And then he said fiercely after a moment, "Tell me the rest. I want to know it all."

"They were calling in a thoracic surgeon when I left. They haven't said anything else."

"Thoracic?" Lynley said. "Thoracic?"

St. James's hand tightened on his arm once again. "It's a chest wound," he said.

Lynley closed his eyes, and he kept them closed for the rest of the ride, which was mercifully brief.

At the hospital, two panda cars stood at the top of the sloping entrance to Accident and Emergency, and two of the uniformed constables who belonged to them were just coming out as Lynley and St. James entered. He saw Deborah at once, seated on one of the blue steel chairs with a box of tissues on her knees and a middle-aged man in a crumpled mackintosh talking to her, notebook in hand. Belgravia CID, Lynley thought. He didn't know the man, but he knew the routine.

Two other uniforms stood nearby, affording the detective privacy. Apparently, they knew St. James by sight—as they would, since he'd already been at the hospital earlier—so they let both of them approach the interview that was going on.

Deborah looked up. Her eyes were red. Her nose looked sore. A pile of sodden tissues lay on the floor next to her feet. She said, "Oh, Tommy . . . ," and he could see her try to pull herself together.

He didn't want to think. He couldn't think. He looked at her and felt like wood.

The Belgravia man stood. "Superintendent Lynley?"

Lynley nodded.

"She's in the operating theatre, Tommy," Deborah said.

Lynley nodded again. All he could do was nod. He wanted to shake her, he wanted to rattle the teeth in her head. His brain shouted that it was *not* her fault, how could it be this poor woman's fault, but he needed to blame, he wanted to blame, and there was no one else, not yet, not here, not now . . .

He said, "Tell me."

Her eyes filled.

The detective—somewhere Lynley heard him say his name was Fire . . . Terence Fire, but that couldn't be right because what sort of name was Fire, after all?—said that the case was well in hand, he was not to worry, all stops were being pulled out because the entire station knew not only what had happened but who she was, who the victim—

"Don't call her that," Lynley said.

"We'll be in close contact," Terence Fire said. And then, "Sir . . . If I may . . . I am so terribly—"

"Yes," Lynley said.

The detective left them. The constables remained.

Lynley turned to Deborah as St. James sat next to her. "What happened?" he asked her.

"She asked would I park the Bentley. She'd been driving, but it was cold and she'd got tired."

"You'd done too much. If you hadn't done too much . . . those God damn bloody christening clothes . . ."

A snaking tear spilled over the rim of Deborah's eye. She brushed it away. She said, "We stopped and unloaded the parcels. She asked me to take care parking the car because . . . You know how Tommy loves his car, she said. If we put a scratch on it, he'll have us both for dinner. Watch the left side of the garage, she said. So I took care. I'd never driven . . . You see, it's so big and it took me more than one try to get it into the garage . . . But not five minutes, Tommy, not that even. And I assumed she'd go straight into the house or ring the bell for Denton—"

"He's gone to New York," Lynley said, unnecessarily. "He isn't there, Deborah."

"She didn't tell me. I didn't know. And I didn't think . . . Tommy, it's *Belgravia*, it's safe, it's—"

"No where is God damn safe." His voice sounded savage. He saw St. James stir. His old friend raised a hand: a warning, a request. He didn't know nor did he care. There was only Helen. He said, "I'm in the middle of an investigation. Multiple murders. A single killer. Where in the name of heaven did you get the idea any place on earth is safe?"

Deborah took the question like a blow. St. James said his name, but she stopped him with a movement of her head. She said, "I parked the car. I walked back along the mews."

"You didn't hear—"

"I didn't hear a sound. I came round the corner back into Eaton Terrace and what I saw was the shopping bags. They were spread on the ground, and then I saw her. She was crumpled . . . I thought she'd fainted, Tommy. There was no one there, no one nearby, not a single soul. I thought she'd fainted."

"I told you to be sure *no* one—"

"I know," she said, "I know. I know. But what was I meant to make of that? I thought of flu, someone sneezing in her face, Tommy being a fuss pot husband because I *didn't* understand, don't you see that, Tommy? How would I know because this is Helen we're talking about and this is Belgravia where it's supposed to be . . . and a gun, why would I *ever* think of a gun?"

She began to weep in earnest then, and St. James told her that she'd said enough. But Lynley knew she never could have said enough to explain how his wife, how the woman he loved . . .

He said, "What then?"

St. James said, "Tommy . . . "

Deborah said, "No. Simon. Please." And then to Lynley, "She was on the top step and her door key was in her hand. I tried to rouse her. I thought she'd fainted because there was no blood, Tommy. There was *no* blood. Not like what you would think if someone is . . . I'd never seen . . . I didn't know . . . But then she moaned and I could tell something was terribly wrong. I phoned triple nine and then I cradled her to keep her warm and that's when . . . On my hand, there was blood. I thought I'd cut myself at first and I looked for where and how but I saw it wasn't me and I thought the baby, but her legs, Helen's legs . . . I mean, there was no blood where one would think . . . And this was a different sort of blood anyway, it looked different because I know, you see, Tommy . . ."

Even in his own despair, Lynley felt hers, and that was what finally got through to him. She would know what the blood of a miscarriage looked like. She'd suffered how many . . . ? He didn't know. He sat, not next to Deborah and her husband, but across, on the chair that Terence Fire had been using.

He said, "You thought she'd lost the baby."

"At first. But then I finally saw the blood on her coat.

High up, here." She indicated a spot beneath her left breast. "I phoned triple nine again and I said, There's blood, there's *blood*. Hurry. But the police got there first."

"Twenty minutes," Lynley said. "Twenty God damn minutes."

"I phoned three times," Deborah told him. "Where *are* they, I asked. She's bleeding. She's bleeding. But I still didn't know she'd been shot, you see. Tommy, if I'd known . . . If I'd told them that . . . Because I didn't think, not in Belgravia . . . Tommy, who would shoot someone in Belgravia?"

Lovely wife, Superintendent. The sodding profile in *The Source.* Complete with photographs of the smiling superintendent of police and his charming wife. Titled bloke, he was, not your garden variety sort of cop at all.

Lynley rose blindly. He would find him. He would *find* him.

St. James said, "Tommy, no. Let the Belgravia police . . ." And only then did Lynley realise he'd said it aloud.

"I can't," he said.

"You must. You're needed here. She'll come out of theatre. They'll want to speak to you. She's going to need you."

Lynley headed in the direction of the door but this, apparently, was why the uniformed constables had been hanging about. They stopped him, saying, "It's in hand, sir. It's top priority. It's well in hand," and by that time St. James had reached his side as well.

He said, "Come with me, Tommy. We won't leave you," and the kindness in his voice felt like a crushing weight on Lynley's chest.

He gasped for breath, for something to cling to. He said, "My God. I've got to phone her parents, Simon. How am I going to tell them what's happened?"

* * *

BARBARA FOUND that she couldn't bring herself to leave even as she told herself she wasn't needed and probably wasn't wanted either. People milled about everywhere, each one of them in a personal hell of waiting.

Helen Lynley's parents, the earl and countess of whatever because Barbara couldn't remember if she'd ever heard the title so many generations in their family, were huddled in misery and they looked frail, more than seventy years old and unprepared to face what they were facing now.

Helen's sister Penelope rushing in from Cambridge with her husband at her side, tried to comfort them after herself crying out, "How is she? Mum, my God, how *is* she? Where's Cybil? Is Daphne on her way?"

They all were, all four of Helen's sisters, including Iris on her way from America.

And Lynley's mother was tearing up from Cornwall with her younger son, while his sister hurried down from Yorkshire.

Family, Barbara thought. She was neither needed nor wanted here. But she could not bring herself to leave.

Others had come and gone: Winston Nkata, John Stewart, other members of the team, uniformed constables and plainclothes officers whom Lynley had worked with through the years. Cops were checking in from stations in every borough in town. Everyone save Hillier had seemed to put in an appearance during the course of the night.

Barbara herself had arrived after the worst sort of journey from North London. Her car had refused to start at first up on Wood Lane, and she'd flooded its engine in a panic trying to get the bloody thing running. She'd sworn at the car. She'd vowed to reduce the Mini to rubble. She'd strangled the steering wheel. She'd phoned for help. She'd finally got the engine to sputter into life, and she'd sat on the horn trying to clear traffic out of the way.

She'd got to the hospital just after word had been given to Lynley about Helen's condition. She'd seen the surgeon come to fetch him and she'd watched as he'd received the news. It's killing him, she'd thought.

She wanted to go to him, to say she'd bear the weight of it with him, as his friend, but she knew she didn't have that right. Instead, she watched as Simon St. James went to him, and she waited until Simon had returned to his wife to share with her what he had learned. Lynley and Helen's parents disappeared with the surgeon, God only knew where, and Barbara understood that she could not follow. So she crossed the room to speak to St. James. He nodded at her and she was furiously grateful that he did not exclude her or ask why she was there.

She said, "How bad is it?"

He took a moment. From his expression, she prepared herself to hear the worst.

"She was shot beneath the left breast," he said. His wife leaned into him, her face against his shoulder as she listened along with Barbara. "The bullet evidently went through the left ventricle, the right atrium, and the right artery."

"But there was no blood, there was almost no blood." Deborah spoke into the jacket he was wearing, into his shoulder, shaking her head.

"How can that happen?" Barbara asked St. James.

"Her lung collapsed at once," St. James told her, "so the blood began filling the cavity that was left in her chest."

Deborah began to cry. Not a wail. Not an ululation of grief. Just a shaking of her body that even Barbara could see she was doing her best to control.

"They would have put a tube in her chest when they first saw the wound," St. James told Barbara. "They would have got blood from it. A litre. Perhaps two.

They would have known then that they had to go in at once."

"That's what the surgery was."

"They sutured the left ventricle, did the same for the artery and the exit wound in the right ventricle."

"The bullet? Have we got the bullet? What happened to the bullet?"

"It was under the right scapula, between the third and fourth rib. We have the bullet."

"So if she's repaired," Barbara said, "that's good news, isn't it? Isn't it good news, Simon?"

She saw him withdraw inside himself then, to a place she could not know or imagine. He said, "It took so long to get to her, Barbara."

"What do you mean? So long? Why?"

He shook his head. She saw—inexplicably—that his eyes grew cloudy. She didn't want to hear the rest, then, but they'd waded too far into these waters. Retreat was not an option.

"Has she lost the baby?" Deborah was the one to ask the question.

"Not yet."

"Thank God for that, then," Barbara said. "So the news is good, right?" she repeated.

St. James said to his wife, "Deborah, would you like to sit down?"

"Stop it." She raised her head. The poor woman, Barbara saw, looked like someone with a wasting disease. She felt, Barbara realised, like she'd pulled the trigger on Helen herself.

"For a while," St. James said, his voice so low that Barbara had to lean in to him to make out his words, "she had no oxygen."

"What do you mean?"

"Her brain was deprived of oxygen, Barbara."

"But now," Barbara said, insistent still. "She's all right, yes? What about now?"

"She's on a ventilator now. Fluids, of course. A heart monitor."

"Good. That's very good, yes?" It was surely excellent, she thought, reason to celebrate, terrible moment but they'd all passed through it and everything was going to sort itself out. Right? Yes. Say the word *yes*.

"There's no cortical activity," St. James said, "and that means—"

Barbara walked away. She didn't want to hear more. Hearing more meant knowing, knowing meant feeling, and that was the *last* bloody God damn thing . . . Eyes fixed on the lino, she paced rapidly out of the hospital into the cold night air and the wind, which struck her cheeks so surprisingly that she gasped and looked up and saw them gathered. The carrion feeders. The journalists. Not dozens of them, not as she'd seen them behind the barriers at the Shand Street tunnel and at the end of Wood Lane. But enough, and she wanted to hurl herself at them.

"Constable? Constable Havers? A word?"

Barbara thought it had to be someone from inside the hospital, coming out to fetch her with a piece of news, so she turned, but it was Mitchell Corsico and he was approaching with his notebook in his hand.

She said, "You need to clear out of here. You especially. You've done enough."

His brow furrowed as if he couldn't quite make out what she was saying to him. "You can't think . . ." He paused, clearly regrouping. "Constable, you can't think this has anything to do with *The Source*'s story on the superintendent."

Barbara said to him, "You know what I think. Get out of my way."

"But how is she? Is she going to be all right?"

"Get out of my bloody *way*," she snarled. "Or I won't answer for the consequences."

Chapter Twenty-nine

Preparations had to be made, and He set about them with His usual care. He worked quietly. He caught Himself smiling more than once. He even hummed as He measured for the span of a grown man's arms and when He sang, He did so quietly because it would be idiocy to take an unnecessary and stupid risk at this point. He chose tunes from who-only-knew-where, and when He finally burst into "A Mighty Fortress Is Our God," He had to chuckle. For inside the van, it was indeed a fortress: a place where He would be safe from the world, but the world would never be safe from Him.

The second set of leather restraints He fixed opposite the sliding panel door of the van. He used a drill and bolts to do the job, and He tested the result with the weight of His body, hanging from them as the observer would hang, struggling and twisting as the observer would do. He was satisfied with the result of His efforts, and He went on to catalogue His supplies.

The cylinder for the stove was full. The tape was cut and hanging well within His reach. The batteries in the torch were fresh. The implements for a soul's release were sharp and prepared for use.

The van had petrol, a full supply. The body board was perfectly pristine. The clothesline ligatures were neatly coiled. The oil was in its proper place. This would, He thought, be His crowning achievement.

Oh yes, too right. You think *that, do you? Where'd you learn to be such a fool?*

Fu used the back of His tongue to change the pressure against His eardrums, eliminating the maggot's voice for a moment, that insidious planting of the seeds of doubt. He could hear the *whoosh* of that pressure changing: Crinkle and crack against His eardrums and the maggot was gone.

Only to return the instant He ceased the movement of His tongue. *How long're you planning to occupy space upon the planet? Was there ever on earth a more useless bit of gobshite than you? Stand there and* listen *when I'm talking to you. Take it like a man or get out of my sight.*

Fu hastened His work. Escape was the key.

He left the van and made for safety. There was nowhere, really, where the maggot left Him in peace, but there were still distractions. Always had been and always would be. He sought them. Quickly now, quickly quickly. In the van, He used judgement, punishment, redemption, release. Elsewhere, He used more traditional tools.

Do something useful with your time, little sod.

He would, He would. Oh yes He would.

He made for the television and punched it on, raising the volume until everything else might be driven away. On the screen, He found Himself looking at a building's entrance, figures coming and going, a female reporter's mouth moving, and words that He could not connect to meaning because the maggot would not leave His brain.

Eating at the very essence of Him. *You hear me, gobshite? Understand what I say?*

He raised the volume higher still. He caught snatches of words: *yesterday afternoon . . . St. Thomas' Hospital . . . condition critical . . . who is nearly five months pregnant . . .*

and then He saw *him*, the detective himself, witness, observer. . . .

The sight brought Fu round and banished the maggot. He focussed on the television screen. The man Lynley was coming out of a hospital. He had a uniformed constable on either side of him and they were shielding him from reporters who were shouting questions.

". . . any connection to . . . ?"

"Do you regret—"

"Is this in any way related to the story that *The Source . . .*?"

". . . decision to embed a journalist . . . ?"

Lynley walked through them, away, beyond. He looked like stone.

The reporter on-screen said something about an earlier news conference, and the scene switched to that. A surgeon in operating gown stood behind a lectern, blinking in the television lights. He spoke about the removal of a bullet, the repairing of damage, a foetus that was moving but that's all they could report at the moment, and when questions were asked by the unseen listeners, he would say no more, merely removing himself from behind the lectern and from the room. The scene then went back to outside the hospital, where the reporter stood, shivering in the morning's wind.

"This is," she said gravely, "the first time that a family member of a police detective has been struck down in the midst of an investigation. The fact that this crime should fall so quickly on the heels of a tabloid's profile of that same detective and his wife brings into question the wisdom of the earlier and highly irregular Scotland Yard decision to allow a journalist unprecedented access to a criminal investigation."

She ended her report but for Fu, the image of Lynley was what stayed with Him when the viewer was returned to the television studio where the presenters managed to look suitably grave as they went on with the morning's news. Whatever they said was lost to Him at that point because He saw only the police detective: how he walked and where he looked. What struck Fu the most was that the man was not the least bit wary. He had no defence.

Fu smiled. He flicked off the television with a snap. He listened intently. No sound in the house. The maggot was gone.

DI John Stewart took immediate charge, but it seemed to Nkata that he was merely going through the motions, his mind on other things. Everyone's mind was elsewhere as well: either mentally at St. Thomas' Hospital where the superintendent's wife lay fighting for her life or with the Belgravia police who were handling the investigation into her shooting. Still, Nkata knew there was only one reasonable way for any of them to proceed, and he told himself to keep moving forward because he owed it to Lynley to do the job. But his heart wasn't in it, and this was a bloody damn dangerous place to be. How simple a matter it was to let a crucial detail slip when one was in this state, because he—along with everyone else—was distracted by an external concern.

His carefully plotted and altogether irritating multicoloured outline in hand, DI Stewart had made assignments that morning and then began to micromanage every one of them in his inimitable fashion. He paced maddeningly round the room and when he wasn't doing that, he was liaising with the Belgravia police. This consisted of demanding to know what progress they'd made on the attack on the superintendent's wife. In the meantime, detectives in the incident room made reports and PCs typed them. Occasionally someone asked in a hushed voice, "Does anyone know how she is? Is there any word?"

The word was *critical*.

Nkata reckoned Barb Havers would know more, but

she hadn't put in an appearance so far. No one had made mention of this fact, so he'd concluded Barb was either still at the hospital, or on an assignment Stewart had given her earlier, or going her own way in things, in which case he wished she'd get in touch with him. He'd seen her briefly at the hospital on the previous night, but they hadn't spoken more than to exchange a few terse words.

Now, Nkata tried to force his thoughts to travel in a productive direction. It seemed like days had passed since he'd last received an assignment. Making himself adhere to it was like swimming through refrigerated honey.

The list of dates for the MABIL meetings—helpfully provided by James Barty to demonstrate the extent to which his client Mr. Minshall was willing to cooperate with the police—covered the last six months. Using this list as a jumping-off point, Nkata had already spoken to Griffin Strong by telephone, and he had received the man's meaningless assurance that he had been with his wife—never left her side and she would be the first to confirm that, Sergeant—whenever an alibi was called for. So Nkata had gone on to talk to Robbie Kilfoyle, who'd said he didn't exactly keep records of what he did every night, which was little enough, since, besides watching the telly, all he ever did was drop by the Othello Bar for a pint and perhaps they could confirm that at the bar, although he doubted even they would be able to say when he'd been in and when he'd not. From there, Nkata had conversed with Neil Greenham's solicitor, with Neil himself, and ultimately with Neil's mother who said that her lad was a good lad and if he said he was with her *whenever* he said he was with her, then he was with her. As for Jack Veness, the Colossus receptionist declared that if his great-aunt, his mate, the Miller and Grindstone Pub, and the Indian take-away were not good enough to clear his name, then the cops could God damn arrest him and have done with it.

Nkata immediately discounted any alibi given by a relative, which consequently made Griffin Strong and Neil Greenham look good in the role of member of MABIL and serial killer. The problem for him was that both Jack Veness and Robbie Kilfoyle seemed to fit the profile far better. This made him in turn decide he needed to have a closer look at the profile document that had been provided for them weeks ago.

He was about to conduct a search for it in Lynley's office when Mitchell Corsico turned up in the incident room, escorted there by a minion of Hillier's whom Nkata recognised from their earlier press conferences together. Corsico and the minion had a word with John Stewart, at which point the minion left for points unknown and the journalist sauntered over to Nkata. He deposited himself on a chair near the desk where Nkata had been studying his notes.

"I got the word from my guv," Corsico told him. "He's axed the St. James direction. Sorry, Sergeant. You're my next man."

Nkata looked at him, frowning. "What? You crazy? After what's happened?"

Corsico removed a small tape recorder from his jacket pocket, along with a notebook, which he flipped open. "I was set to do that forensic bloke next, the expert witness you lot have working outside the Yard? But the big cheeses over on Farringdon Street gave the project thumbs down. I'm back to you. Listen, I know you don't like this, so I'm willing to compromise. I get inside to talk to your parents, I leave Harold Nkata out of the story. Sound like a deal to you?"

What it sounded like was a decision made by Hillier and his DPA cronies and passed along to Corsico, who'd probably already planted a bug in his editor's ear about . . . what did they call it? . . . the natural *angle* that a story on Winston Nkata had. Human interest, they would describe it, without a thought where the *last* human interest tale had got them.

"*No* one's talking to my mum and dad," Nkata said. "No one's putting their pictures in the paper. No one's looking them up at home. No one's getting inside their flat."

Corsico made an adjustment to the volume on his tape recorder and nodded thoughtfully. "That does bring us to Harold then, doesn't it? He shot that bloke in the back of the head, as I understand. Made him kneel at the edge of the pavement, then put the barrel of the gun to his skull."

Nkata reached for the tape recorder. He dropped it onto the floor and slammed his foot into it.

"Hey!" Corsico cried. "I am *not* responsible—"

"You listen to me," Nkata hissed. Several heads turned their way. Nkata ignored them. He said to Corsico, "You write your story. With or without me, I c'n see you're set on doing it. But my brother's part of it, my mum's or my dad's picture in that paper, one word 'bout Loughborough Estate . . . and I'm coming after you, unnerstan? And I 'xpect you know enough about me already to get what I mean."

Corsico smiled, completely unfazed. It came to Nkata that this was the reaction the reporter had been seeking. He said, "Your speciality was the flick knife, as I understand it, Sergeant. You were what? Fifteen years old? Sixteen? Did a knife seem less traceable to you than . . . say . . . a pistol of the sort your brother used?"

Nkata wouldn't take the bait this time. He got to his feet. "This isn't going to be part of my day," he told the reporter. He slid a pen into his jacket pocket, preparatory to heading for Lynley's office to get back to what he'd intended to do.

Corsico got to his feet as well, perhaps with the intention of following. But that was when Dorothea Harriman came into the room, looked round for someone, and chose Nkata.

She said, "Is Detective Constable Havers—?"

"Not here," Nkata said. "What's wrong?"

Harriman gave a glance to Corsico before she took Nkata by the arm. She said meaningfully to the reporter, "If you don't *mind* . . . Some things are personal," and she waited until he retreated to the other side of the room. Then she said, "Simon St. James just phoned. The superintendent's left the hospital. He's meant to go home and rest, but Mr. St. James thinks he may head here at some point today. He's not sure when."

"He's coming back to work?" Nkata couldn't believe this was the case.

Harriman shook her head. "If he comes here, Mr. St. James thinks he'll go to the assistant commissioner's office. He thinks someone needs to . . ." She hesitated, her voice uncertain. She raised a hand to her lips and said in a more determined tone, "He thinks someone needs to be ready to look after him when he gets here, Detective Sergeant."

BARBARA HAVERS cooled her heels in the interview room at the Holmes Street station while the solicitor serving the interests of Barry Minshall was rounded up. A sympathetic special constable in reception had taken one look at her and said, "Black or white?," when she'd first entered the station. Now she sat with the coffee—white—in front of her, her hands curved round a mug that was shaped into the caricatured visage of the Prince of Wales.

She drank without tasting much of the brew. Her tongue said *hot, bitter*. That was it. She stared at her hands, saw how white her knuckles were, and tried to loosen her grip on the mug. She didn't have the information she wanted and she didn't like being in the dark.

She'd phoned Simon and Deborah St. James at the most reasonable hour she could manage. She'd ended up listening to their answer machine, so she reckoned they'd either never left the hospital on the previous night or had returned there before dawn to wait for further news about Helen. Deborah's father wasn't in, either. Barbara told herself he was walking the dog. She'd rung off on the answer machine without leaving a message. They had better things to do than phone her with news, which she might be able to get in another way.

But ringing the hospital was even worse. Mobile phones could not be used inside, so she was left having to speak to someone in charge of general information, which was no information at all. Lady Asherton's condition was unchanged, she was told. What did that mean? she asked. And what about the baby she was carrying? There was no reply to this. A pause, a shuffling of papers, and then, Terribly sorry, but the hospital was not allowed . . . Barbara had hung up on the sympathetic voice, mostly because it *was* sympathetic.

She told herself that work was the anodyne, so she gathered her things and left her bungalow. At the front of the house, however, she saw that lights were on in the ground-floor flat. She didn't pause to ask the *should*s of herself. At the sight of movement behind the curtains covering the French windows, she changed direction and crossed to them. She knocked without thinking, merely knowing that she needed something and that something was real human contact, no matter how brief.

Taymullah Azhar answered, manila folder in one hand and briefcase in the other. Behind him somewhere in the flat, water ran and Hadiyyah sang, off-key but what did it really matter: "Sometimes we'll sigh, sometimes we'll cry . . ." Buddy Holly, Barbara realised. She was singing "True Love Ways." It made her want to weep.

Azhar said, "Barbara. How good to see you. I'm so very glad . . . Is something wrong?" He set down his briefcase and put the manila folder on top of it. By the time he'd turned back to her, Barbara had got a better grip on herself. He wouldn't necessarily know yet, she thought. If he hadn't looked at a newspaper and if he hadn't turned on the radio or seen the television reports . . .

She couldn't bring herself to talk about Helen. She said, "Working hard. Bad night. Not much sleep." She remembered the peace offering she'd bought—it seemed like another lifetime to her—and she dug round in her shoulder bag till she found it: the five-pound-note trick meant for Hadiyyah. Astound your friends. Amaze your relations. "I picked this up for Hadiyyah. Thought she might like to try it out. It'll take a five-pound note to do it. If you've got one . . . She won't hurt it or anything. At least not when she gets good. So in the beginning I s'pose she could use something else. For practice. You know."

Azhar looked from the magic trick in its plastic covering back to Barbara. He smiled and said, "You are very good. To Hadiyyah. And *for* Hadiyyah. This is not something I have told you, Barbara, and I apologise for that. Let me get her now so that you—"

"No!" The intensity of her word surprised both of them. They stared at each other in some confusion. Barbara knew she'd puzzled her neighbour. But she also knew she couldn't explain to Azhar how the kindness of his words had seemed like a blow from which she felt in sudden danger. Not from what the words implied but from what her reaction to them told her about herself.

She said, "Sorry. Listen, I've got to go. About a dozen things on my plate and I'm juggling them all at once."

"This case," he said.

"Yeah. What a way to earn a living, eh?"

He observed her, dark eyes set in skin the colour of pecans, expression grave. He said, "Barbara—"

She cut him off. "I'll talk to you later, okay?" Despite her need to escape the kindness in his tone, though, she reached out and clasped his arm. Through the sleeve of his neat white shirt she could feel the warmth of him and his wiry strength. "I'm dead chuffed you're back," she said, the words coming thickly. "See you later."

"Of course," he replied.

She turned to go, but she knew he was watching. She coughed and her nose began to run. She was God damn falling *apart*, she thought.

And then the blasted Mini wouldn't start. It hiccuped and sighed. It spoke to her of arteries hardening with oil too long unchanged in its system, and she saw that from the French windows Azhar was still observing her. He took two steps outside and in her direction. She prayed and the god of transport listened. The engine finally sprang to life with a roar and she reversed down the drive and into the street.

Now she waited in the interview room for Barry Minshall to give her the word: *Yes* was all she required of him. *Yes* and she was out of there. *Yes* and she was making an arrest.

The door finally opened. She pushed her Prince of Wales mug to one side. James Barty preceded his client into the room.

Minshall wore his dark glasses, but the rest of him was strictly incarceration-issue garb. He needed to get used to it, Barbara thought. Barry would be going away for a good many years.

"Mr. Minshall and I are still waiting to hear from the CPS," his solicitor said by way of prefatory remarks. "The magistrate's hearing was—"

"Mr. Minshall and you," Barbara said, "ought to be thanking your stars we still need him hanging round this end of town. When he gets to remand, he's likely to find the company not quite as accommodating as it is here."

"We've been cooperative thus far," Barty said. "But you can't expect that cooperation to extend into infinity, Constable."

"I don't have deals to offer and you know it," Barbara told him. "TO9 is dealing with Mr. Minshall's situation. Your hope"—and this to Minshall himself—"is that those boys in the Polaroids we found in your flat enjoyed their experience at your hands so much that they wouldn't dream of testifying against you or anyone else. But I wouldn't count on that. And anyway, face it, Bar. Even if those boys don't want to be put through a trial, you've still supplied a thirteen-year-old to a killer and you're going down for that one. If I were in your position, I'd want it known to the CPS and everyone else concerned that I started cooperating the moment the rozzers asked my name."

"It's only your belief that Mr. Minshall supplied a boy to someone who murdered him," Barty said. "That has never been our position."

"Right," Barbara said. "Have it any way you want, but the laundry gets wet no matter what order you put it into the machine." From her bag she brought out the framed photograph she'd taken from flat number 5 in Walden Lodge. She laid it on the table at which they were sitting, and she slid it across to Minshall.

He lowered his head. She couldn't see his eyes behind the dark glasses, but she noted his breathing and it seemed to her he was making an effort to keep it steady. She wanted to believe this meant something important, but she didn't want to get ahead of herself. She let the moments stretch out between them while inside she repeated two words: *Come on. Come on. Come on.*

Finally, he shook his head, and she said to him, "Take off your glasses."

Barty said, "You know that my client's condition makes it—"

"Shut up. Barry, take off your glasses."

"My eyesight—"

"Take off your *bloody* glasses!"

He did so.

"Now look at me." Barbara waited till she could see his eyes, grey to the point of altogether colourless. She wanted to read the truth in them, but even more than that she wanted just to *see* them and to have him know that she was seeing them. "At this precise moment, no one's saying you handed over any boys in *order* to get them killed." She felt her throat trying to close on the words, but she forced herself to say them anyway because if the only way to get him to move in her direction was to lie, cheat, and flatter, she would lie and cheat and flatter with the best of them. "You didn't do that to Davey Benton and you didn't do that to anyone else. When you left Davey with this . . . this bloke, you expected the game to be played the way it had always been played. Seduction, sodomy, I don't know what—"

"They didn't tell me what—"

"*But*," she broke in because the last thing she could bear was to hear him justify, protest, deny, or excuse. She just wanted the truth and she was determined to have it from him before she left the room. "You didn't mean him to die. To be used, yes. To have some bloke touch him up, rape him even—"

"No! They were never—"

"Barry," his solicitor said. "You needn't—"

"Shut *up*. Barry, you offered those boys for cash to your slimeball mates at MABIL, but the deal was always sex, not murder. Maybe you had the boys yourself first or maybe you just popped your cork by having all those other blokes depending on you to supply them with new flesh. The point is, you didn't mean anyone to die.

But that's what happened and you're either going to tell me that the bloke in this picture is the one who called himself two-one-six-oh or I'm going to walk out of this room and let you go down for everything from paedophilia to pandering to murder. That's it. You're going down, Barry, and you can't escape it. It's up to you how far you want to sink."

She had her eyes locked on his and his skittered wildly in their sockets. She wanted to ask him how he'd come to be the man he was—what forces in his own past had brought him to this—but it didn't matter. Abused in childhood. Molested. Raped and sodomised. Whatever had turned him into the malevolent procurer he was, all that was water under the bridge. Boys were dead and a reckoning was called for.

"Look at the picture, Barry," she said.

He moved his gaze to it another time and he looked at it long and hard. He finally said, "I can't be sure. This is old, isn't it? There's no goatee. Not even a moustache. He's got . . . his hair is different."

"There's more of it, yes. But look at the rest of him. Look at his eyes."

He put his glasses back on. He picked up the picture. "Who's he with?" he asked.

"His mum," Barbara said.

"Where'd you get the picture?"

"From her flat. Inside Walden Lodge. Just up the hill from where Davey Benton's body was found. Is this the man, Barry? Is this two-one-six-oh? Is this the bloke you gave Davey to at the Canterbury Hotel?"

Minshall set the photograph down. "I don't . . ."

"Barry," she said, "take a nice, long look."

He did so. Again. And Barbara switched from *Come on* to prayer.

He finally spoke. "I think it is," he said.

She let out her breath. *I think it is* wouldn't cut the

mustard. *I think it is* wouldn't get a conviction. But it was enough to spawn an identity parade, and that was good enough for her.

HIS MOTHER had finally arrived at midnight. She'd taken one look at him and opened her arms. She didn't ask how Helen was because someone had managed to catch her en route from Cornwall and tell her. He could see that from her face and from the way his brother hung back from greeting him, gnawing on his thumbnail instead. All Peter managed to say was, "We rang Judith straightaway. She'll be here by noon, Tommy."

There should have been comfort in this—his family and Helen's family gathering at the hospital so that he did not have to face this alone—but comfort was inconceivable. As was seeing to any simple biological need, from sleeping to eating. It all seemed unnecessary when his being was focussed on a single pinpoint of light in the midnight of his mind.

In the hospital bed, Helen was insignificant in comparison to the machinery round her. They had told him the names, but he recalled only their individual functions: for breathing, to monitor the heart, for hydration, to measure oxygen in the blood, to maintain watch over the foetus. Aside from the whir of these instruments, there was no other sound in the room. And outside the room, the corridor was hushed, as if the hospital itself and every person within it already knew.

He didn't weep. He didn't pace. He made no attempt to drive his fist through the wall. So perhaps that was why his mother ultimately insisted he had to go home for a while when the next day dawned and found them all still milling round the hospital corridors. A bath, a shower, a meal, anything, she told him. We'll stay right here, Tommy. Peter and I and everyone else. You must make an attempt to take care of yourself.

Please go home. Someone can go with you if you like.

There were volunteers to do that: Helen's sister Pen, his brother, St. James. Even Helen's father although it was easy to see that the poor man's heart was in shreds and he'd be no help to anyone while his youngest daughter was where she was . . . as she was. So at first he'd said no, he would stay at the hospital. He couldn't leave her, they must see that.

But finally, sometime in the morning, he consented. Home for a shower and a change of clothes. How long could that take? Two constables ushered him through a small gathering of reporters whose questions he neither understood nor even heard very well. A panda car drove him to Belgravia. He dully watched the streets roll by.

At the house they asked did he want them to stay? He shook his head. He could cope, he told them. He had a live-in man in the house. Denton would see that he had a meal.

He didn't tell them that Denton was off on a long-awaited holiday: bright lights and big city, Broadway, skyscrapers, theatre every night. Instead, he thanked them for their trouble and took out his keys as they drove off.

The police had been. He saw signs of them in the scrap of crime-scene tape that still clung to the narrow porch's railing, in the fingerprint dust that still powdered the door. There was no blood, Deborah had said, but he found a spot of it on one of the draughts-board marble tiles that comprised the top step just before the door. She'd been so close to getting inside.

It took him three tries to get his key properly in the lock, and when he'd managed the whole operation, he felt light-headed. He expected the house to be different somehow, but nothing had changed. The last bouquet of flowers she'd arranged had lost a few petals to the marquetry top of the table in the entry, but that was it. The rest was as he'd last seen it: one of her winter scarves hanging over the railing of the stairs, a magazine left open on one of the sofas in the drawing room, her dining-room chair sitting at an angle and not replaced the last time she'd sat upon it, a teacup in the kitchen sink, a spoon on the work top, a binder of fabric samples for the baby's room on the table. Somewhere in the house, the bags of christening clothes were probably stowed. Mercifully, he did not know where.

Upstairs, he stood beneath the shower and let the water beat upon him endlessly. He found he couldn't exactly feel it, and even when it struck his eyeballs, he didn't blink nor did he feel pain. Instead, he relived individual moments, silently imploring a God he could not say he believed in to give him a chance to turn back time.

To what day? he asked himself. To what moment? To what decision that had led them all to where they now were?

He stood in the shower until there was no hot water left in the boiler. He had no idea how long he'd been there when he finally emerged. Dripping and shivering, he remained undried and unclothed till his teeth were castanets in his skull. He couldn't face walking back into their bedroom and opening the wardrobe and the drawers to search out clean clothes. He was nearly air-dried before he summoned the will to pick up a towel.

He moved to the bedroom. Ridiculously, they were babes in arms without Denton there to sort them out, so their bed was badly made, and consequently the impression of her head was still in her pillow. He turned from this and forced himself over to the chest of drawers. Their wedding picture accosted him: hot June sunshine, the fragrance of tuberoses, the sound of Schubert from violins. He reached out and toppled the frame so it fell facedown. There was fleeting mercy when her image was gone and then quick agony when he could not see her so he righted it again.

He dressed. He gave the procedure the sort of care she herself would have taken. This allowed him to think about colours and fabrics for a moment, to search out shoes and the proper tie as if this were an ordinary day and she still in bed with a cup of tea on her stomach, watching to see he didn't make a sartorial faux pas. His ties were the thing. They had always been. Tommy darling, are you *absolutely* certain about the blue one?

He was certain of little. He was certain, in fact, of only one thing, and that was that he was certain of nothing. He went through motions without complete knowledge of making them, so he found himself dressed at last and staring at himself in the mirrored wardrobe door wondering what he was meant to do next.

Shave, but he couldn't. The shower had been difficult enough, labeled as it was "the first shower since Helen" and he couldn't do more. He couldn't have more labels because he knew the very weight of them would kill him in the end. The first meal since Helen, the first tank of petrol since Helen, the first time the post dropped through the door, the first glass of water, the first cup of tea. It was endless and it was burying him already.

He left the house. Outside, he saw that someone—most likely one of the neighbours—had left a bunch of flowers on his doorstep. Daffodils. It was that time of year. Winter faded to spring and he needed desperately to stop time altogether.

He picked up the flowers. She liked daffodils. He'd take them to her. They're so cheerful, she'd say. Daffodils, darling, are flowers with spunk.

The Bentley was where Deborah had carefully parked it, and when he opened the door, Helen's scent floated out to him. Citrus, and she was with him.

He slid into the car and closed the door. He rested his head on the steering wheel. He breathed in shallowly because it seemed to him that deep breaths would dissipate the scent more quickly, and he needed the fragrance to last as long as it possibly could. He couldn't bring himself to adjust the car seat from her height to his, to sort out the mirrors, to do anything that would erase her presence. And he asked himself how, if he couldn't do this much, this very simple and essential thing because, for the love of God, the Bentley wasn't even the car she regularly drove, so what did it matter, then how could he possibly walk through what he had to walk through now?

He didn't know. He was operating on rote behaviors that he hoped could carry him from one moment to the next.

Which meant starting the car, so that was what he did. He heard the Bentley purr beneath his touch and he reversed it out of the garage like a man performing keyhole surgery.

He glided slowly along the mews and into Eaton Terrace. He kept his eyes averted from his front door because he didn't want to imagine—and he knew he *would* imagine, how could he help it?—what Deborah St. James had seen when she'd walked round the corner having parked the car.

As he drove to the hospital, he knew he was taking the same route the ambulance had taken when bearing Helen to Casualty. He wondered how much she'd been aware of what was going on around her: drips being established, oxygen seeping into her nose, Deborah somewhere nearby but not as close as those who listened to her chest and said her breathing was laboured on the left side now, nothing going into a lung that had already collapsed. She'd have been in shock. She wouldn't have known. One moment she'd been on the front steps, searching out her door key, and the next she'd been shot. Short range, they'd told him. Less than ten feet away, probably closer to five. She'd seen him, and he'd seen the shock on her face, the surprise to find herself suddenly vulnerable.

Had he called her name? Mrs. Lynley, have you a moment? Countess? Lady Asherton, isn't it? And she'd turned with that embarrassed, breathless laugh of hers. "Drat! That silly story in the paper. All of it was Tommy's idea, but I expect I cooperated more than I should have done."

And then the gun: automatic pistol, revolver, what did it matter? A slow, steady squeeze on the trigger, that great equaliser among men.

He found it difficult to think and even more difficult to breathe. He struck the steering wheel as a means of bringing himself round to the moment he was in and not one of the moments already lived through. He struck it to distract himself, to cause himself pain, to do *anything* to keep from fracturing beneath everything that assaulted him from memory and imagination.

Only the hospital could save him, and he hurried in the direction of its refuge. He wove round buses and dodged cyclists. He braked for a crocodile of tiny schoolchildren on the kerb waiting to cross the street. He thought of their own child among them—his and Helen's: high socks, scabby knees, and miniature brogues, a cap on his head, a name tag fluttering round his neck. The teachers would have printed it for him, but he'd have been the one to decorate it any way that he liked. He'd have chosen dinosaurs because they'd taken him—he and Helen—to the Natural History Museum on a Sunday afternoon. There he'd stood beneath the bones of the T. rex with his mouth agape in wonder. "Mummy," he would have said, "what is it? It's tremendously big, isn't it, Dad?" He'd have used words like that. *Tremendously*. He'd have named constellations, he'd have known the musculature of a horse.

A horn honked somewhere. He roused himself. The children were across the street now and on their way, heads bobbing and shoes scuffling along, three adults—fore, mid, and aft—keeping a careful eye on them.

Which was all that had been required and he'd failed: keeping a careful eye. Instead, he'd as good as provided a map to his own front door. Photographs of him. Photographs of Helen. Belgravia. How difficult could it have been? How tough a proposition even to ask a few questions in the neighbourhood?

And now he reaped the result of his hubris. There are things we don't know, the surgeon had said.

But can't you tell . . . ?

There are tests for some conditions and no tests for others. All we can do is make an educated guess, a deduction based on what we know about the brain. From that we can extrapolate. We can present the facts as we know them and we can tell you how far those facts can take us. But that's it. I'm sorry. I wish there were more . . .

He *couldn't*. Think about it, cope with it, live with it. Anything. The horrible day after day of it. A sword piercing his heart but neither fatally, quickly, nor mercifully. Just the tip of it at first and then a bit more as days became weeks became the necessary months in which he waited for what he already knew was the very worst.

A human being can adapt to anything, yes? A human being can learn to survive because as long as the *will* to endure remained, the mind adjusted and it told the body to do the same.

But not to this, he thought. Not ever to this.

At the hospital, he saw that the journalists had finally dispersed. This was not a twenty-four/seven story for them. The initial incident and its relationship to the investigation of serial murders had mobilised them at first, but now they would check in only sporadically. Their focus would be on the perpetrator and the police from this point on, with passing references made to the victim and canned footage of the hospital used—a shot of a window somewhere, behind which the wounded was ostensibly languishing—should that be required by the producers. Soon even that would be considered a rehash of a twice-told tale. We need something fresh and if you haven't got a new angle on this situation, bury it inside. Page five or six ought to do it. They had, after all, the meat of the matter: scene of the crime, press conference from the doctor, the image of himself—nice, good, a suitable reaction shot—leaving the hospital earlier in the day. They would be given the name of the press officer from the Belgravia station as well, so that was it, really. The story could just about write itself. On to other things. There were circulation figures to concern them and other breaking news to bolster those figures. This was business, merely business.

He parked. He got out of the car. He moved towards the hospital entrance and what waited for him inside: the unchanging and unchangeable situation, the family, his friends, and Helen.

Decide, Tommy darling. I trust you completely. Well . . . all except in the matter of ties. And that's always been a puzzle to me because you're generally a man of impeccable taste.

"Tommy."

He stirred from his thoughts. His sister Judith was coming towards him. She was looking more like their mother every day: tall and lithe with close-cropped blonde hair.

He saw she was holding a folded tabloid, and he would later think it was this that set him off. Because it wasn't the most recent edition but rather the one in which the story about him, his personal life, his wife, and his home had appeared. And suddenly what he felt was shame in such a wave that he thought he'd actually drown beneath it and the only way to struggle to the surface was to give in to the rage.

He took the tabloid from her. Judith said, "Helen's sister had it stuffed in her bag. I hadn't seen it yet. I actually didn't know about it, so when Cybil and Pen mentioned—" She saw something, surely, for she came to his side and put her arm round him. She said, "It isn't that. You *mustn't* think so. If you start to believe—"

He tried to speak. His throat didn't allow it.

"She needs you now," Judith said.

He shook his head blindly. He turned on his heel and left the hospital, returning to his car. He heard her voice calling after him and then a moment later he heard St. James, who must have been near when he'd first seen Judith. But he couldn't stop and speak to them now. He had to move, to go, to deal with things as they should have been dealt with from the first.

He made for the bridge. He needed speed. He needed action. It was cold and grey and damp outside, and there was clearly a rainstorm on its way, but when the first drops finally fell as he turned into Broadway, he saw them only as minor distractions, splatters on the windscreen on which was already written an unfolding drama, of which he wanted no part.

In the kiosk, the officer waved him through, his mouth opening to speak. Lynley nodded to him and drove on, descending to the carpark, where he left the Bentley and stood for a moment in the dim light, trying to breathe because it felt to him as if he'd been holding air in his lungs since he'd left the hospital, left his sister, returned the accusing tabloid to her hands.

He made for the lift. What was wanted was Tower Block, that aerie from which the sight of the trees in St. James's Park marked the changing of the seasons. He made his way there. He saw faces emerge as if from a mist, and voices spoke, but he wasn't able to make out the words.

When he reached AC Hillier's office, the assistant commissioner's secretary blocked his path to the door. Judi MacIntosh said, "Superintendent . . . ," in her most officious voice and then apparently read something or understood something for the first time because she altered to, "Tommy, my dear," in a tone so rich with compassion that he could hardly bear it. "You don't belong here. Go back to the hospital."

"Is he in there?"

"Yes. But—"

"Then step aside please."

"Tommy, I don't want to have to ring for anyone."

"Then don't. Judi, step aside."

"Let me at least tell him." She made a move for her desk when any sensible woman would have simply charged into Hillier's office ahead of him. But she did things by the book, which was her downfall because with the path unblocked, he accessed the door and let himself in, shutting it behind him.

Hillier was on the phone. He was saying, ". . . many so far? . . . Good. I want the stops pulled out . . . Bloody right it's to be a special task force. *No* one strikes at a cop—" And then he saw Lynley. He said into the phone, "I'll get back to you. Carry on."

He rang off and stood. He came round the desk. "How is she?"

Lynley didn't respond. He felt his heart slamming against his ribs.

Hillier gestured to the phone. "That was Belgravia. They're getting volunteers—these're men off duty, on rota, whatever—from all over town. Asking to be assigned to the case. They've a task force in place. It's top priority. They went into action late yesterday afternoon."

"It doesn't matter."

"What? Sit down. Here. I'm getting you a drink. Have you slept? Eaten?" Hillier went for the phone. He punched in a number and said he wanted sandwiches, coffee, and no it didn't matter what kind, just get it to his office as soon as possible. Fetch the coffee first. And to Lynley again, "How is she?"

"She's brain dead." The first time he'd actually said the words. "Helen is brain dead. My wife is brain dead."

Hillier's face went slack. "But I was told a chest wound . . . How is that possible?"

Lynley recited the details, finding that he needed and wanted the pain of telling them one by one. "The wound was small. They didn't see at first that—" No. There was a better way to say it all. "The bullet went through an artery. Then through parts of her heart. I don't know the order, the actual path of it, but I expect you get the general idea."

"Don't—"

Oh, he would. He *would*. "But," he said forcefully, "her heart was still beating at this point, so her chest began to fill with blood. But they didn't know that in the ambulance, you see. Everything took them too long. So when they finally got her to hospital, she had no pulse, she had no blood pressure. They put a tube down her throat and they shoved another into her chest and that's when the blood started coming out of her—pouring out—so they knew, you see, at that point they knew." When he breathed, he could *hear* it grinding into his lungs and he knew Hillier could hear it as well. And he *hated* that fact for what it revealed, and for how it could be used against him.

Hillier said, "Sit down. Please. You need to sit down."

Not that, he thought. Never that. He said, "I asked what they did for her in Casualty. Well, one would ask that, don't you agree? They told me they opened her up right there and saw one of the holes the bullet had made. The doctor actually stuck his finger in it to stop the flow of blood, if you can picture that, and I wanted to be able to picture it because I had to know, you see. I had to understand because if she was breathing even shallowly . . . But they said the blood flow was inadequate to her brain. And by the time they controlled it . . . Oh, she's breathing now on the machine and her heart's back to beating, but her brain . . . Helen's brain is dead."

"God in heaven." Hillier went to the conference table. He pulled out a chair and indicated he meant Lynley to sit. "I'm so sorry, Thomas."

Not his name, he thought. He could not bear his name. He said, "He found us, you see. You understand that, yes? Her. Helen. He found her. He *found* her. You see that. You know how it happened, don't you?"

"What do you mean? What are you talking—"

"I'm talking about the story, sir. I'm talking about your embedded journalist. I'm talking about putting lives into the hands—"

"Don't." Hillier raised his voice. It didn't seem like something done in anger, though, rather in desperation. A last-ditch effort to stem a tide he could not stop from rising.

"He phoned me after that story appeared. He mentioned her. We gave him a key, a map, whatever, and he found my wife."

"That's impossible," Hillier said. "I read the story myself. There was no way he could have—"

"There were a dozen ways." His own voice was louder now, his anger fueled by the other's denial. "The moment you started playing with the press, you *created* ways. Television, tabloids, radio, broadsheets. You and Deacon—the two of you—thought you could use the media like two crafty politicians, and see where it's brought us. See where it's brought us!"

Hillier held up both his hands, palms out: the universal sign to stop. He said, "Thomas. Tommy. This isn't—" He stopped. He looked towards the door and Lynley could almost read the question in his mind: Where is that bloody coffee? Where are the sandwiches? Where is a useful distraction, for God's sake, because I have a madman in my office. He said, "I don't want to argue with you. You need to be at the hospital. You need to be with your family. You need your family—"

"I have no God damn family!" Finally the weir gave

way. "She's dead. And the baby . . . The baby . . . They want her on machines for at least two months. More if possible. Do you understand? Not alive, not dead, with the rest of us watching . . . And you . . . God damn you. You've brought us to this. And there is no way—"

"Stop. *Stop*. You're mad with grief. Don't do and don't say . . . Because you'll regret—"

"What the hell else do I *have* to regret?" His voice broke horribly and he *hated* the breaking and what it revealed about how he had been reduced. Man no longer, but something like an earthworm exposed to salt and to sun and writhing, writhing, because this was the end this was surely the end and he hadn't expected . . .

There was nothing for it but to lunge for Hillier. To reach him, to grab him, to force him . . . somewhere . . .

Strong arms caught him. From behind, these were, so it wasn't Hillier. He heard a voice in his ear.

"Oh Jesus, man. You got to get away. You got to come with me. Easy, man. Easy."

Winston Nkata, he thought. Where had he come from? Had he been there all along, unnoticed?

"Take him away." It was Hillier speaking, Hillier with a handkerchief to his face, held by a hand that was shaking.

Lynley looked at the detective sergeant. Nkata seemed to be behind a shimmering veil. But even then, Lynley could still see his face in the moment before his arms went round him.

"Come with me, guv," Winston murmured in his ear. "You come with me now."

Chapter Thirty

It was late in the afternoon by the time Ulrike decided the next approach she wanted to take, having learned from her encounter in Bermondsey with Jack Veness's aunt that prevarication wasn't going to serve her purpose. She began with the list of dates she'd got earlier from New Scotland Yard. She took this list and fashioned a multicolumn document from it, using the dates, the victims' names, and the names of the police's potential suspects as the columns and the rows. She allowed herself plenty of space to fill in any pertinent fact that came to light about everyone who looked questionable to her.

10 September, she wrote first. *Anton Reid.*

20 October came after that. *Jared Salvatore.*

25 November was next. *Dennis Butcher.* And then more quickly,

10 December, Kimmo Thorne.

18 December, Sean Lavery.

8 January, Davey Benton, who was—she thanked God—not one of theirs. Nor, if it came down to it, was the detective superintendent's wife, and *that* had to mean something, didn't it?

But just *supposing* what it meant was a killer moving further afield because the heat was too much at Colossus. That was highly possible, and she couldn't discount it because to discount it—to anyone—could be construed as an attempt to direct suspicion elsewhere. Which was what she wanted to do, of course. But not while looking as if she was doing it.

She realised it had been completely ludicrous to pretend she was interviewing Mary Alice Atkins-Ward in order to see if Jack Veness was ready to be promoted to a more responsible position with Colossus. She couldn't think how she'd actually come up with such a plan, and she certainly understood why Miss A-W had seen through it. So now she was going to opt for the direct approach, one that had to begin with Neil Greenham, the only individual who'd called in a solicitor, cavalrylike, with the Indians looming. She decided to accost Neil in his classroom, a glance at the clock telling her he'd still be there giving kids the individual help for which he was noted.

He was having a tête-à-tête with a black boy whose name escaped her for the moment. She frowned as she watched and heard Neil say something about the boy's attendance. Mark, he called him.

Mark Connor, she thought. He'd come to them via Youth Offenders in Lambeth, perpetrator of a common street mugging gone wrong when he pushed an old lady and she fell, breaking her hip. Just the sort of kid Colossus was designed to save.

Ulrike watched as Neil put a hand on the boy's slender shoulder. She saw Mark flinch. She went immediately on the alert.

She said, "Neil, could I have a word?," and took note of how he then reacted. She was looking for *any* sign that she could interpret, but he appeared careful not to give her one.

He said, "Let me finish up here. I'll be along directly. Your office?"

"That's fine." She'd have preferred to have him here in his own environment, but her office would do. She went on her way.

He turned up exactly fifteen minutes later, cup of tea in hand. He said, "I didn't think to ask you if you wanted . . . ?" and gestured with the cup to indicate his offer.

This seemed to signal a truce between them. She said, "That's fine, Neil. I don't want any. Thanks. Come in and sit down, won't you?"

As he sat, she got up and closed the door. When she returned to her desk, he lifted an eyebrow. "Special treatment?" he asked, with a soundless sip of Darjeeling or whatever it was. It *would* be soundless, naturally. Neil Greenham was not the sort of bloke who slurped. "Should I be flattered or warned by the sudden attention?"

Ulrike ignored this. She'd thought about an entrée to the conversation she needed to have with Neil, and she decided she had to keep the goal in mind no matter where she began. That goal was cooperation. The time for stonewalling had long since passed.

She said, "It's time we talked, Neil. We're getting close to the moment when we open the North London branch of Colossus. You know that, don't you?"

"Hard not to know it." He looked at her steadily over the rim of his cup. His eyes were blue. There was a suggestion of ice about them that she had not noticed before.

"We'll be wanting someone who's already in the organisation to head that branch. D'you know that as well?"

He shrugged noncommittally. "That makes sense," he said. "Not much learning curve involved for someone who already works here, right?"

"There's that, and it's a compelling reason. But there's loyalty as well."

"Loyalty." Not a question, but a statement. He made it in a reflective tone.

"Yes. Obviously, we'll be looking for someone whose first loyalty is to Colossus. It has to be that way. We've enemies out there, and meeting them head-on requires not only perspicacity but the spirit of a warrior. You know what I mean, I daresay."

He took his time before replying, lifting his tea and having a thoughtful—and silent—sip. He said, "As it happens, I don't."

"What?"

"Know what you mean. Not that *perspicacity*'s beyond my ability to comprehend, mind you. It's the spirit of a warrior bit that has me confused."

She gave a gentle laugh, of the self-directed kind. "Sorry. I was thinking of the image of the warrior leaving home—wife and kids behind him—and setting off to do battle. That willingness of the warrior to set the personal to one side when a battle has to be fought. The needs of Colossus in North London will have to come first to its director."

"And in South London?" Neil inquired.

"What?"

"What about the needs of Colossus in South London, Ulrike?"

"The North London director isn't going to be responsible—"

"That's not actually what I meant. I was just wondering if the way South London Colossus is being run is a model for how North London ought to work."

Ulrike gazed at him. He looked mild enough. Neil always had seemed a bit fuzzy round the edges, but now she had the distinct sensation of flint beneath the soft, boyish surface. And not just the flint of the anger problem that had cost him his erstwhile teaching job, but something else. She said, "Why don't you speak a bit more directly?"

"I didn't know I wasn't," Neil said. "Sorry. I guess what I'm saying is that it seems a little hypocritical, all this."

"All what?"

"All this talk about loyalty and Colossus first. I'm . . ." He hesitated, but Ulrike knew the pause was for effect. "In other circumstances I'd be delighted to be having this confab with you. I'd even flatter myself by concluding that you're considering recommending me to head the North London branch when it opens."

"I thought I *did* imply—"

"But the loyalty to Colossus bit rather gives you away. Your own loyalty hasn't exactly been impeccable, has it?"

She knew he was waiting for her to ask him to clarify his statement and she wasn't about to give him that pleasure. She said, "Neil, everyone has a moment now and again when they're distracted from their primary concern. No one at any level of administration expects anyone else to have tunnel vision in the loyalty department."

"Which is good for you, I expect. Your own secondary concerns being what they are."

"I beg your pardon?" She wanted to grab the question back the instant she said it, but it was too late because he snatched it up like a fisherman netting a hooked trout.

"Discretion is as discretion does. Which is to say that sometimes discretion doesn't at all. Doesn't do, I mean. Or perhaps 'doesn't work' is a better way of putting it. It's one of those 'best-laid plans of mice and men' kind of things, if you know what I mean. Which in it*self* is to say that when there's a plan to cast stones, it's always a good idea that the thrower live in a house of bricks. Do you want me to be any more direct, Ulrike, or do you get my meaning? Where's Griff, by the way? He's been flying under the radar for a bit, hasn't he? Is that on your advice?"

So now they'd come to it, Ulrike thought. They were at a take-off-the-gloves moment. Perhaps it was time. Her personal life was none of his business, but he was going to be made to see that the reverse was not the case.

She said, "Get rid of the solicitor, Neil. I don't know why you've hired him, and I don't want to know. But I'm telling you to get rid of him straightaway and speak to the police."

Neil changed colour, but the way he adjusted his body told her he was not blushing with embarrassment or shame. He said, "Am I hearing you . . . ?"

"Yes. You are."

"What the *hell* . . . Ulrike, you can't tell me . . . You of all people . . ."

"I want you to cooperate with the police. I want you to tell them where you were for every date they question you about. If you'd like to make it easier on yourself, you can begin with telling me and I'll convey the information to them." She picked up her pen and held it poised above the paper on which she'd created her three-column data sheet. She said, "We'll start with last September. The tenth, to be precise."

He stood. "Let me see that." He reached for the paper. She put her arm across it. "Is your name on that as well?" he asked her. "Or is the bonking-Griff alibi going to serve as your answer to any question they ask you? And anyway, how does it all work, Ulrike, you fucking a suspect on the one hand and acting the role of copper's nark on the other?"

"My life—" she began, but he cut in.

"Your life. Your life." His voice was a scoff. "All Colossus all the time. That's how it's supposed to look, right? Butter wouldn't melt, and in the meantime, you don't even know when a kid goes missing. Have the cops cottoned on to that? Have the board of trustees? Because I think they'd be rather interested, don't you?"

"Are you threatening me?"

"I'm stating a fact. Take it however you like. In the meantime, don't tell me how to react when the cops start trawling through my life."

"Are you aware of how insubordinate—"

"Bugger *off*." He reached for the door. He jerked it open. He shouted, "Veness! Get in here, will you?"

Ulrike stood then. Neil was crimson with fury and she knew she matched him colour for colour, but this was intolerable. She said, "Don't you dare start ordering round other employees. If this is an example of how you take or don't take direction from a superior, then believe me, it's going to be noted. It's already noted."

He swung round. "D'you think I actually *believed* you'd consider me for anything other than bum wiper of this lot? Jack! Get in here."

Jack arrived at the door, saying, "What's going on?"

"Just want to make sure you know Ulrike's grassing to the cops about us. I've had my sit down with her, and I expect you're next on the list."

Jack looked from Neil to Ulrike, and then his gaze dropped to the desk and the fact sheet upon it. He said an eloquent, "Shit, Ulrike."

Neil said, "She's found a second calling." He adjusted the chair he'd been sitting in and gestured to it. "Your turn," he said to Jack.

"That'll do," Ulrike told him. "Go back to work, Jack. Neil's giving in to his predilection for temper tantrums."

"While Ulrike's spent a good long time giving in to—"

"I said that'll do!" It was time to wrest control from the snake. Pulling rank was the only way, even if it meant he would make good his threat and put the board of trustees into the picture about her carrying on with Griff. She said, "If you want to keep your job, I suggest you get back to it. Both of you."

"Hey!" Jack protested. "I only came in here—"

"Yes, I know," Ulrike said calmly. "I'm speaking largely to Neil. And what I'm saying remains the same, Neil. Do what you intend to do, but in the meantime drop the solicitor."

"I'll see you in hell first."

"Which makes me rather wonder what you're hiding."

Jack looked from her to Neil and back again. He said, "Holy shit," and left them together.

"I won't forget this," was Neil's final comment.

"I don't expect you will," was hers.

NKATA HATED the moment, the activity, and himself: sitting at Hillier's side before a newly energised collection of journalists. There was nothing like the drama of trauma to get them motivated. Nothing like bringing that trauma home and giving it a human face to make them momentarily sympathetic to the Met.

He knew this was what AC Hillier was thinking as he fielded their questions after having made his statement. *Now* they had the press where they wanted them, the AC's demeanor seemed to suggest. They were going to think twice before they went after the Met while an officer's wife was fighting for her life in hospital.

Except she wasn't fighting for her life. She wasn't fighting for anything because she *wasn't* any longer.

He was immobile. He wasn't attending to what was being said, but he knew that this was fine with Hillier. All he needed to look was fierce and ready. Nothing more would be asked of him. He hated himself for complying.

Lynley had insisted. Nkata had got him out of the AC's office by grabbing him round the shoulders in an embrace of insistence but also one of devotion. He'd known in that instant that he would do anything for this man. And that had startled him because for years he'd told himself that the *only* important fact of his life was to succeed. Do the job, and let everything else slide right off you because it is *not* important what anyone thinks. It is only important what you know and who you are.

Lynley had seemed to understand this about him without their ever having spoken about it. He'd continued to understand it even in the midst of what he was going through.

Nkata had taken him from Hillier's office. As they left, he'd heard the AC punching numbers on the telephone. He reckoned Hillier was trying to reach building security to escort Lynley from the premises, so he made for a spot they'd not be likely to look: the library on the twelfth floor of the building, with its sweeping views of the city and the silence into which Lynley had told him the worst.

And the worst was actually more than the superintendent's wife being dead. The worst was what they were asking of him.

He'd said dully, staring out at the view, "The machines can keep her breathing for months. Long enough to deliver a viable . . ." He stopped. He rubbed his eyes. *Looking like hell* was such a common expression, Nkata had thought as he'd stood there. But this was real hell, he realised. This wasn't looking like. This was living in. "There's no way to measure the exact amount of brain damage to the baby. It's there. They can be . . . what was it . . . ninety-five percent certain of that because she'd gone without sufficient oxygen for twenty minutes or more and if that destroyed her brain, it only stands to reason . . ."

"Man, it's . . . You don't have to . . ." Nkata hadn't known what else to say.

"There's no test, Winston. Just the choice. Keep her on the machines for two months—although three would be ideal . . . well, at least as ideal as anything could be at this point—and then go in for the baby. Cut her open, take the baby, and then bury the body. Because there is no *her* any longer. Just the body. The breathing corpse, if you will, from which they could cut the living—albeit permanently damaged—child. You'll have to make this decision, they say. Think about it, they say. No real hurry, of course, because it's not as if a decision either way is going to affect the corpse."

Nkata knew they probably hadn't used the word *corpse*. He could see that Lynley himself was using it because it was the brutal truth of the matter. And he also could see what a story it would make and was already making: the earl's wife dead, her body reduced to incubator and incubator's inhabitant, the eventual birth—could they even call it a birth?—featured on the front page of every tabloid in town once it happened, because what a story it was, and then the follow-ups ever after, perhaps one a year in a deal that would have to be made with the press: Give us our privacy to cope with this situation now and occasionally we'll tell you how the child is doing, perhaps allow a photo to be taken, only leave us alone, please leave us alone.

All Nkata could say was, "Oh," a sound that escaped him in a groan.

Lynley looked at him. "I made her the sacrificial lamb. How do I live with that?"

Nkata knew what he was talking about. Although he didn't quite believe his own words, he said, "Man, you did *not* do that. You *never* think that. You are *not* responsible." Because for Lynley to believe that this tragedy was down to him, a chain would be forged and its links would lead inexorably to Nkata himself, and he couldn't stand that, he knew he couldn't. For he also knew that part of the superintendent's plan had been to occupy Mitchell Corsico so thoroughly with a story about himself that he would be kept away from everyone else and from Nkata especially, who had perhaps the most attention-grabbing past of everyone involved in the serial-killing investigation.

Lynley seemed to know what he was thinking because he'd replied with, "It's down to me. Not to you, Winston."

And then he'd left. He'd said, "Do your bit. Something has to come out of all this. Don't take my side. It's over. All right?"

Nkata responded with, "I can't—" but Lynley cut him off.

"Don't bloody make me responsible for anything else, for God's sake. Promise me, Winston."

So here he was at Hillier's side, playing the part.

Dimly he could hear the press briefing drawing to a conclusion. The only indication Hillier gave of his own inner state was in the direction he sent Mitchell Corsico afterwards. The reporter would return to the press pool, to his paper, to his editor's side, to wherever he wanted to go or to be. But he wouldn't be writing any further profiles of anyone in the investigation.

Corsico protested with, "But you *can't* be thinking the story on the superintendent had anything to do with what's happened to his wife. Jesus God, there was *no* way this bloke could have found her. No *way*. I made certain of that. You know I made certain. That story was vetted by everyone but the pope."

"You've had my last word on the matter," Hillier said.

Other than that, he spoke nothing about Lynley and what had happened in his office. He merely nodded at Nkata and said, "Get on with it," and went on his way. Solitary, this time. No minion accompanied him.

Nkata returned to the incident room. He saw he had a message to phone Barb Havers on her mobile, and he made a mental note to do it. But first he tried to remember what he'd been engaged in so much earlier when Dorothea Harriman had given him the word about Lynley's possible arrival in Victoria Street.

The profile, he thought. He'd intended to have another look at the profile of the killer in the hope that something therein would relate to one of the suspects . . . if they were indeed suspects at all because the only thing that appeared to connect them to the killings was proximity to some of the victims, which was seeming more and more like nothing to build anything upon at all, not sand beneath the foundation but ice, ready to crack under the burden of proof.

He took himself to Lynley's office. On the superintendent's desk, there stood a photograph of his wife, Lynley at her side. They were both perched on a sun-drenched balustrade somewhere. His arm was round her, her head rested on his shoulder, they both were laughing into the camera while in the background a blue sea glittered. Honeymoon, Nkata thought. He realised they'd been married less than a year.

He averted his eyes. He made himself look through the stack of paperwork on Lynley's desk. He read Lynley's notes. He read a recent report by Havers. And at last he found it, identifiable by the cover-sheet stationery from Fischer Psychiatric Hospital for the Criminally Insane. He slid the report out from the stack in which Lynley had placed it. He carried it to the conference table, sat, and tried to clear his mind.

"Superintendent," a neat sample of cursive on the covering stationery said, "while you may not be a believer, I hope you'll find this information helpful." No signature, but the profiler himself must have written it. No other person would have a reason to.

Before he turned to the report beneath the stationery,

Nkata gave thought to where the hospital was located. He admitted to himself that he was thinking of Stoney, even now. It always came down to his brother in the end. He wondered if a place like Fischer could have helped his brother, eased his anger, cured his madness, removed the urge to strike out and even to kill . . .

Nkata realised he was reading the heading on the creamy paper over and over. He frowned. He focussed. He read again. He'd been taught that there were no coincidences at the end of the day and he'd just, after all, seen Lynley's notes and Havers' report. He reached for the phone.

Barbara Havers burst into the office. She said, "Didn't you get my message? Bloody hell, Winnie. I phoned. I asked you to ring me back. I've got . . . What the hell's going *on* round here?"

Nkata handed the report to her. "Read this," he said. "Take your time."

WITH REASON, everyone not only wanted a part of him but also needed a part of him. Lynley accepted this even as he knew he could do next to nothing to accommodate anyone. He could barely accommodate himself.

When he returned to the hospital, he was aware of virtually nothing. He found his family and hers where he'd left them, along with Deborah and St. James. *Holding the fort* came ridiculously into his mind. There was no fort to hold and nothing to hold it for.

Helen's sister Daphne had arrived from Italy. Her sister Iris was due from America, anticipated at any moment, although no one knew when that moment might be. Cybil and Pen were tending to their parents, while his own siblings sat with their mother, no stranger to hospitals, certainly no stranger to sudden and violent death.

The room they'd been allotted was small, and they crowded it, perched uncomfortably on whatever chairs and settees had been scavenged, sent to this particular place to shield them from the other families of other patients because of their numbers, because of the sensitivity of the situation, and because of who they were. Not who they were by class but who they were by occupation: the family of a cop whose wife had been shot in the street. Lynley was aware of the irony of it all: being granted this privacy because of his career and not because of his birth. It seemed to him that this was the only moment in his life that was honestly defined by his chosen occupation. The rest of the time, he'd always been the earl, that odd bloke who'd eschewed life in the country and mingling among his own kind for work of the commonest sort. Tell us why, Superintendent Lynley. He couldn't have done so, especially now.

Daphne, the latest arrival, came to him. Gianfranco, she told him, had wanted to be there as well. But that would have meant leaving the children with—

"Daph, it's fine," Lynley said. "Helen wouldn't have wanted . . . thank you for coming."

Her eyes—dark like Helen's, and it came to him how much Helen looked like her eldest sister—grew bright, but she did not weep. She said, "They've told me about . . ."

"Yes," he replied.

"What're you . . . ?"

He shook his head. She touched his arm. "Dear heart," she said.

He went to his mother. His sister, Judith, made a spot for him on the settee. He said, "Go to the house, if you'd like. There's no need for you to stay here hour after hour, Mother. The spare room's available. Denton's in New York, so he won't be there to do a meal for you, but you can . . . in the kitchen . . . I know there's something. We've been fending for ourselves, so in the fridge there're cartons—"

"I'm fine," Lady Asherton murmured. "We're all

fine, Tommy. We don't need a thing. We've been to the café. And Peter's been fetching coffee for everyone."

Lynley glanced at his younger brother. He saw that Peter still could not look at him for longer than a second. He understood. Eyes upon eyes. Seeing and acknowledging. He himself could barely stand the contact.

"When does Iris get here?" Lynley asked. "Does anyone know?"

His mother shook her head. "She's in the middle of nowhere over there. I don't know how many flights she's had to take or even if she's taken them yet. All she said to Penelope was that she was on her way and she'd be here as soon as possible. But how does one get here from Montana? I'm not even sure where Montana is."

"North," Lynley said.

"It's going to take her forever."

"Well. It doesn't matter, does it?"

His mother reached for his hand. Hers was warm but quite dry, which seemed to him an unlikely combination. And it was soft as well, which was also strange because she loved to garden and she played tennis every day the Cornwall weather allowed it, every season of the year, so why were her hands still soft? And God in heaven, what did *that* matter?

St. James came over to him while Deborah watched from across the room. Lynley's old friend said, "The police have been, Tommy." He glanced at Lynley's mother and then said, "Do you want to . . . ?"

Lynley rose. He led the way out of the room to the corridor. "By the worst means the worst" came to him from somewhere. A song? he wondered. No, it couldn't be that.

"What is it?" he asked.

"They've determined where he went after he shot her. Not where he came from, although they're working on that, but where he went. Where they went, Tommy."

"They?"

"It appears there may have been two. Males, they think. An elderly woman was walking her dog along the north end of West Eaton Place. She'd just come round the corner from Chesham Street. Do you know where I mean?"

"What did she see?"

"From a distance. Two individuals were running round the corner from Eaton Terrace. They seemed to have seen her and they ducked into West Eaton Place Mews. A Range Rover was parked alongside a brick wall there. It took a dent in the bonnet. Belgravia think these blokes—individuals, whoever they were—jumped onto the Range Rover and leapt into the garden beyond that brick wall. Do you know where I'm talking about, Tommy?"

"Yes." Beyond the brick wall a line of gardens—each one defined by yet another brick wall—comprised the back of the houses on Cadogan Lane, itself another mews that was one of hundreds in the area, once housing stables for the sumptuous dwellings nearby, now housing homes converted from garages that themselves had been converted from the stables. It was a complicated area of streets and mewses. Anyone could fade into the woodwork there. Or make good an escape. Or anything.

St. James said, "It's not what it sounds like, Tommy."

"Why is that?" Lynley asked.

"Because an au pair on Cadogan Lane also reported a break-in, shortly after Helen . . . shortly after. Within the hour. She's being interviewed. She was home when the break-in occurred."

"What do they know?"

"Just about the break-in at the moment. But if it's related—and good God, it *has* to be related—and if whoever broke in went out of the front of the house, then there's further good news. Because one of the larger houses along Cadogan Lane has two CCTV cameras mounted on the front of it."

Lynley looked at St. James. He wanted desperately to care about this because he knew what it meant: If the au pair's housebreaker had gone in that direction, there was a chance the closed-circuit television cameras had caught him on film. And if he'd been caught on film, that was a step in the direction of bringing him to whatever justice there was, which was little enough, and what did it matter at the end of the day?

Lynley nodded, however. It was expected of him.

St. James said, "The house with the au pair?"

"Hmm. Yes."

"It's quite a distance from where the Range Rover was, in the mews, Tommy."

Lynley struggled to think what this meant. He could come up with nothing.

St. James went on. "There're perhaps eight—maybe fewer, but still a number of them—gardens along the route. Which means whoever went over the wall where the Range Rover stood had to continue going over walls. So Belgravia are doing a search of every one of the gardens. There'll be evidence."

"I see," Lynley said.

"Tommy, they're going to come up with something. It's not going to take long."

"Yes," Lynley said.

"Are you all right?"

Lynley considered this question. He looked at St. James. All right. What did it really mean?

The door opened, and Deborah joined them. "You must go home now," Lynley said to her. "There's nothing you can do."

He knew what he sounded like. He knew she would misread him, hearing the blame, which was there but not directed towards her. Seeing her merely reminded him that she'd been with Helen last, heard her talk last, laughed with her last. And it was the *last* of it that he couldn't stand, just as earlier he'd not been able to tolerate the *first* of anything else.

She said, "If you like. If it'll help you, Tommy."

"It will," he said.

She nodded and went to collect her things. Lynley said to St. James, "I'm going to her now. Do you want to come? I know you've not seen . . ."

"Yes," St. James said. "I'd like to, Tommy."

So they went to Helen, dwarfed in her bed by everything that kept her working as a womb. She looked waxen to him, Helen yes but even more Helen no and never again. While within her, damaged beyond hope or repair but who knew how much—

"They want me to decide," Lynley said. He took his wife's lifeless hand. He curled her flaccid fingers into his palm. "I can't stand it, Simon."

WINSTON DROVE, and for this Barbara Havers was grateful. After a day in which she'd determinedly not thought about what was happening at St. Thomas' Hospital, she felt she'd been punched in the gut with the news about Helen Lynley. She'd known it was going to be a grim prognosis. But she'd told herself that people survived being shot all the time, and medicine being as advanced as it was meant Helen's chances had to be good. But there was no current advance in medicine that compensated for a brain deprived of oxygen. A surgeon didn't just go in and repair that damage like the Messiah laying hands on a leper. There was literally no coming back once the word *vegetative* was applied to a situation. So Barbara hunched against the door in Winston Nkata's car and clenched her teeth so hard together that her jaw was pulsing and sore by the time they reached their destination in the darkness.

Funny, Barbara thought as Nkata parked the car with his usual quasi-scientific precision, she'd never thought of thc City as a place people lived. They worked here, true. They went to events at the Barbican. Tourists came here to visit St. Paul's Cathedral, but after hours the place was supposed to be a ghost town.

That was not the case at the corner of Fann and Fortune Streets. Here Peabody Estate welcomed home its residents at the end of their working day, a pleasant, upmarket area with blocks of flats that faced a perfectly groomed garden of winter-pruned rosebushes, shrubbery, and lawn across the street.

They'd phoned first. They'd decided they would go in the back door on this one, no storm-trooping but rather a collegial approach. There were facts to check and they'd come to check them.

The first thing Hamish Robson said to them when he answered the door was, "How is Superintendent Lynley's wife? I've seen the news. They've apparently got a witness. Did you know? There's some sort of film footage as well, although I don't know from where. They say they may have an image to broadcast . . ."

He'd come to the door wearing rubber gloves, which seemed odd till he ushered them into the kitchen where he was doing the washing up. He appeared to be something of a gourmet cook, because there were pots and pans on the work top in amazing abundance, and crockery, cutlery, and glassware for at least four people, already standing wetly in the dish drainer. Suds galore mounded in the sink. The place looked like a set for a Fairy Liquid commercial.

"She's brain dead." Winnie was the one to tell him. Barbara could not bring herself to use the term. "They got her hooked up to machines because she's pregnant. You know she was pregnant, Dr. Robson?"

Robson had plunged his hands into the sink, but he took them out and rested them on the edge of it. "I'm so sorry." He sounded sincere. Perhaps he was at some level. Some people were good at creating compartments for the various parts of themselves. "How is the superintendent? He and I had made an arrangement to meet the day . . . the day this all occurred. He never turned up."

"He's trying to cope," Winston said.

"How can I help?"

Barbara brought out the profile of the serial killer that Robson had provided for them. She said, "Can we . . . ?" and indicated a neat chrome-and-glass table that defined a dining area just beyond the kitchen.

"Of course," Robson said.

She laid the report on the table and pulled out a chair. She said, "Join us?"

Robson said, "You don't mind if I carry on with the washing up?"

Barbara exchanged a glance with Nkata, who'd joined her at the table. He gave an infinitesimal shrug. She said, "Why not. We can talk from here."

She sat. Winston did likewise. She gave the ball to him. "We took some second and third looks at this profile," he told Robson, who went back to washing a pot he brought forth from the suds. He was wearing a cardigan and he hadn't bothered to roll the sleeves up, so where the gloves ended, the wet began, weighing down the wool of his sweater. "I had a look at some of the guv's handwritten notes 's well. We got some conflicting information. We wanted to sort that with you."

"What kind of conflicting information?" Robson's face was shiny, but Barbara put that down to the steamy water.

"Le' me put it this way," Nkata said. "Why'd you come up with the age of the serial killer as twenty-five to thirty-five?"

"Statistically speaking—" Robson began, but Nkata interrupted.

"Beyond statistics. I mean, the Wests wouldn't've fitted that part of a statistical description. And tha's just for starters."

"It's never going to be foolproof, Sergeant," Robson told him. "But if you've doubts about my analysis, I suggest you bring in someone else to do another. Bring in an American, an FBI profiler. I'd bet the results—the report you get—is going to be nearly the same."

"But this report here—" Nkata gestured to it, and Barbara slid it across the table to him. "I mean, come down to it, all we got is your word that it's even authentic. I'n't that right?"

Robson's glasses winked in the overhead lights as he looked from Nkata to Barbara. "What reason would I have to tell you anything but the truth of what I saw in the police reports?"

"That," Nkata said, with a lift of his finger to stress the point, "is one very good question, innit."

Robson went back to his washing up. The pot he was scrubbing didn't appear to need the attention he was giving to it.

Barbara said to him, "Why don't you come over here to the table, Dr. Robson? It'll be a little easier to talk."

He said, "The washing up . . ."

"Right. Got it. Only there's a hell of a lot of washing up, isn't there? For just one bloke? What'd you fix up for dinner?"

"I admit to not washing up every night."

"Those pots don't look used to me. Take off the gloves and join us, please." Barbara turned to Nkata. "You ever see a bloke wear rubber gloves to do the washing up, Winnie? Ladies do, sometimes. *I* do, being a lady myself. Got to keep the manicure manicured. But blokes? Why d'you think . . . ? Ah. Thanks, Dr. Robson. It's cozier like this."

"I'm protecting a cut," Robson said. "There's no law against that, is there?"

"He's got a cut," Barbara said to Nkata. "How'd you get that, Dr. Robson?"

"What?"

"The cut. Let's have a look at it, by the way. DS Nkata here is something of an expert on cuts, as you can probably tell by his mug. He got his . . . How'd you get that impressive scar, Sergeant?"

"Knife fight," Nkata told her. "Well, I used the knife. Other bloke had a razor."

"Ouch in a lifeboat," Barbara said, and again to Robson, "How'd you say you got yours?"

"I didn't say. And I'm not sure it's any of your business."

"Well, it can't be from pruning the rosebushes because the time to do that's come and gone, hasn't it. So it has to be from something else. What?"

Robson said nothing, but his hands were clearly visible now and what was on them wasn't a cut at all but rather a scratch, several scratches, in fact. They'd been deep by the look of them and possibly infected, but they were healing now and the flesh was new and pink.

Barbara said, "I can't sort out why you won't answer me, Dr. Robson. What's going on? Cat got your tongue?"

Robson licked his lips. He took off his glasses and polished them on a cloth that he removed from his pocket. He was nobody's fool; he must have learned at least something from his years of dealing with the criminally insane.

"See," Nkata said to the man, "way the constable and I look at it, we got only one thing tells us your report i'n't a bucketful of cock, and that's your word on the matter, unnerstan?"

"As I've said, if you don't believe me—"

"An' we realised—this is the constable and me—that we been running six ways to Sunday looking for someone who fits that profile. But what if—this's what the constable and me've been thinking cos we do think on occasion, you know—the real bloke we're looking for had a way to make us think we were looking for someone else? 'F we were—" He turned to Barbara. "What was that word, Barb?"

"Predisposed," she said.

"Yeah. Predisposed. What if we were predis*posed* to think one way while the truth was the other? Seems to me, then, the killer could go on doing his thing, pretty safe knowing who we were looking for wasn't anything in the world like him. It'd be clever, don't you think?"

"Are you trying to suggest . . . ?" Robson's skin was shiny. But he wouldn't remove his cardigan. He'd probably donned it before letting them into the flat, Barbara thought. He'd have wanted to cover his arms.

"Scratches," Barbara said. "Always nasty. How'd you get yours, Dr. Robson?"

"Look," he replied, "I've a cat that—"

"Would that be Mandy? The Siamese? Your mother's cat? She was a bit thirsty when we were introduced this afternoon. I took care of that, by the way. You're not to worry."

Robson said nothing.

"The thing about Davey Benton that you didn't expect was that he was a fighter," Barbara went on. "And how would you know? How would anyone know because he didn't look like a fighter, did he? He looked just like his brothers and sisters, which is to say he looked like . . . well, he looked like an angel, didn't he? He looked fresh. Untouched. Nice boyflesh there for the taking. I can almost understand why a bloody sick bastard like you might've wanted to carry things further with *this* one and rape him, Dr. Robson."

"You haven't a shred of evidence to back up that statement," Robson said. "And I suggest you take yourselves out of this flat straightaway."

"Really?" Barbara nodded thoughtfully. "Winnie, the doctor would like us to leave."

"Can't do that, Barb. Not without his shoes."

"Oh right. You left two footprints at the final crime scene, Dr. Robson."

"One hundred thousand footprints wouldn't mean a thing and all of us know it," Robson told her. "How many people do you expect buy the same ordinary pair of shoes each year?"

"Millions, probably," Barbara said. "But only one of them leaves his footprint at the scene of a murder where the victim—this is Davey, Dr. Robson—also has DNA evidence under his fingernails. Your DNA, I expect. From those nice scratches you've been protecting. Oh, and the cat's, by the way. The cat's DNA. That's going to be a difficult one to talk your way out of at the end of the day." She waited for a reaction from Robson and she got it in the movement of his Adam's apple. "Cat hair on Davey's body," she said. "When we link that to little Mandy the squalling Siamese—God, that cat makes a bloody racket when she's thirsty, doesn't she—you're done for, Dr. Robson."

Robson was silent. Nice, Barbara thought. He had less and less to argue about. He'd hedged his bets with the profile and he'd given 2160 as his moniker when he'd moved on from Colossus to Barry Minshall at MABIL. But there was the phone number of Fischer Psychiatric Hospital for the Criminally Insane right on the letterhead of the stationery that covered his lying report: with 2160 the final four numbers that a credulous caller—like the Inspectors Plod whom Robson no doubt believed worked at the Met—could punch in to be connected to the place.

She said, "Two-one-six-oh, Dr. Robson. We've had Barry Minshall—but I think you know him as Snow—locked up for a bit in the Holmes Street station. We took this over and let him study it for a while." She removed the photo of Robson and his mother that she'd found in Esther Robson's flat. "Our Barry—that's your Snow, remember—turned it this way and that but he always came up with the same conclusion. This is the bloke he handed Davey Benton over to, he tells us. At the Canterbury Hotel. In Lexham Gardens where the registration card's going to hold interesting fingerprints and the clerk will be only too happy—"

"You damn well listen to me. I *didn't*—"

"Oh right. I damn well expect you *didn't*."

"You've got to see—"

"Shut up," Barbara said. She shoved herself away from the table in disgust. She walked out of the room and left Winston Nkata the pleasure of reciting the caution before they arrested the piece of filth.

HE WATCHED first from across the street. Rain had fallen while He'd made His way across town, and now the lights from the hospital shone against the pavement. They made streaks of gold and when He squinted, He could almost think it was Christmas again: gold and then the red of tail lights on the cars as they passed by.

Not that Father Christmas'll be coming to visit the likes of you, you know.

He groaned. He did the tongue thing again, pressure against His eardrums. *Whoosh whoosh*. Safe again, gone again. He could breathe as normal because normal is as normal does.

The reporters were gone, He saw. And wasn't that nice? Wasn't that a mark of the meant-to-bes? The story was still a sensational one, but now it could be covered from a distance. Profiles of all the principals, if you will. Because what, after all, needed to be said about a body in a bed? Here we are in front of St. Thomas' Hospital on day number whateveritwas and the victim still lies within, so back to you in the studio for the weather report, which is far more interesting to the general public than *this* nonsense, so why don't you give me a bloody new assignment please. Or words to that effect.

But for Him, it was endlessly fascinating. Events had conspired to illustrate over and over again that supremacy was more than a chance of birth. It was also a miracle of timing, embraced by the willingness to seize the moment. And He was the god of moments. In fact, it was He who *made* moments. This was the quality—one among many—that made Him different from everyone else.

Think you're special? That it, little sod?

He used his tongue. *Whoosh* and *whoosh*. Release the pressure to check and—

You get away from him, Charlene. Jesus, it's time he learned his lesson because special is as special God damn does and what the hell *has ever been special about . . . I said step* away. *Who wants some of this? Bugger the both of you. Get out of my sight.*

But in His sight was the future. It lay before Him in the streak of gold from the hospital lights. And in what the lights meant, which was broken. *Broken*. One of them was broken. One of them was destroyed. One of them was a shell that had cracked at first and now lay smashed in a hundred pieces. And He'd been the one to crush that egg beneath the heel of His shoe. He and no other. Look at me now. Look. At. Me. Now. He wanted to crow, but there was danger in this. And equal danger in remaining silent.

Attention? That it? You want attention? Develop some personality, and that'll give you attention, if that's what you want.

Lightly, He hit His fist against His forehead. He forced the air against His eardrums. *Whoosh whoosh*. If He didn't take care, the maggot would eat away His brains.

At night in bed, He'd started plugging orifices against the invasion of the worm—cotton in ears and nostrils, plasters across His arsehole and at the end of His prong—but He still had to breathe and that was where He failed in His prophylactic measures. The worm got in with the air He took into His lungs. From His lungs, it crawled into His bloodstream where it swam like a deadly virus to His skull and munched and whispered and munched.

Perfect adversaries, He thought. You and I and who would've thought it when all of this started? The maggot chose to feast upon the weak, but He . . . Ah, He'd chosen an opponent worthy of the struggle for supremacy.

And that's *what you think you've been doing, little bugger?*

Maggots ate. That was simply what maggots did. They operated solely on instinct and their instinct was to eat until they metamorphosed into flies. Blowflies, bluebottles, horseflies, houseflies. It didn't matter. He merely had to wait out the period of eating, and then the maggot would leave Him in peace.

Except there was always the chance that *this* particular maggot was an aberration, wasn't there, a creature that would never sprout wings in which case, He did have to rid Himself of it.

But that was not why He had begun. And that was not why He was here just now, across the street from the hospital, a shadow waiting to be dispersed by light. He was here because there was a coronation that needed to happen, and it would happen soon. He would see to that.

He crossed the street. This was chancy, but He was ready and willing to take that chance. To show Himself was to make a mark of preeminence upon a time and a place, and that was what He wanted to do: to begin the process of carving history from the stone of now.

He walked inside. He did not seek His adversary, nor did He even try to locate the room in which He knew he would be found. He could walk directly to it if He'd wanted to, but that was not His purpose in coming here.

At this hour of night breaking into morning, there were few enough people in the hospital corridors and those who were present did not even see Him. From this He knew that He was invisible to people in the way that gods were invisible. Moving among ordinary men and knowing that He could smite them at any moment illustrated irrefutably to Him what He was and would always be.

He breathed. He smiled. It was soundless in His skull.

Supremacy is as supremacy does.

Chapter Thirty-one

Lynley remained with her throughout the night and long into the day that followed. He used the time largely to disengage her face—so pale upon the pillow—from what she was now, from the body to which she had been reduced. In this, he tried to tell himself that it was not Helen he was looking upon. Helen was gone. In that instant in which everything had been transformed for them both, she had fled. The Helen of her had soared from the framework of bone, muscle, blood, and tissue, leaving behind not the soul, which defined her, but the substance, which described her. And that substance alone was not and could never be Helen.

But he couldn't make a go of that because when he tried, what came to him were images, for he had known her simply far too long. She'd been eighteen years old and not his in any way but rather the chosen mate of his friend. Meet Helen Clyde, St. James had told him. I'm going to marry her, Tommy.

D'you think I'll do for a wife? she had asked. I haven't a single wifely talent. And she'd smiled a smile that had engaged his heart, but rather in friendship than in love.

Love had come later, years and years later, and in between the friendship and the love what had bloomed was tragedy, change, and sorrow, altering all three of them unrecognisably. Madcap Helen no more, St. James no longer the fervent batsman in front of the wicket, and himself knowing he'd been the cause. For which sin there was no forgiveness. One did not alter lives and simply walk away from the damage.

He'd been told once that things are at any given moment just as they are supposed to be. There are no mistakes in God's world, he'd been told. But he could not believe that. Then or now.

He saw her in Corfu, a towel spread beneath her on the beach and her head thrown back so that the sun could strike her face. Let's move to a sunny climate, she'd said. Or at least let's disappear into the tropics for a year.

Or thirty or forty?

Yes. Brilliant. We'll Lord Lucan it. With less cause, of course. What do you think?

That you'd miss London. The shoe sales if nothing else.

Hmm, there is that, she said. I am a lifelong victim of my feet. The perfect target for male designers with ankle fetishes, I'm the first to admit it. But have they no shoes in the tropics, Tommy?

Not the sort you're used to, I'm afraid.

The silly stuff of her that made him smile, the very maddening Helen of her.

Can't cook, can't sew, can't clean, can't decorate. Honestly, Tommy, why *do* you want me?

But why did one person ever want another? Because I smile with you, because I laugh at your banter, which you and I both know very well is designed just for that . . . to make me laugh. And the why of *that* is that you understand and have done from the first: who I am, what I am, what haunts me most and how to banish it. That's why, Helen.

And there she was in Cornwall, standing before a portrait in the gallery, his mother at her side. They were looking upon a grandfather with too many greats in front of him to know exactly how far back he was in time. But that didn't matter because her concern was centred on genetics and she was saying to his mother, D'you think there's *any* chance that terrible nose could pop up again somewhere along the line?

It's rather ghastly, isn't it? his mother murmured.

At least it shades his chest from the sun. Tommy, why didn't you point this picture out to me before you proposed? I've never seen it before.

We kept it hidden in the attic.

That was very wise.

The Helen of her. The Helen.

You cannot know someone for seventeen years and not have a swarm of memories, he thought. And it was the memories that he felt might kill him. Not that they existed but that there would be no more of them from this point forward and that there were others he'd already forgotten.

A door opened in the room, somewhere behind him. A soft hand took his, shaping his fingers round a hot cup. He caught the scent of soup. He looked up to see his mother's tender face.

"I don't know what to do," he whispered. "Tell me what to do."

"I can't do that, Tommy."

"If I let her . . . Mum, how can I let her . . . them? And if I do that, is it ego? Or is it ego if I don't? What would she want? How can I know?"

She came close to him. He turned back to his wife. His mother curved her hand round his head so she cradled his cheek. "Dearest Tommy," she murmured. "I would take this from you if I could."

"I'm dying. With her. With them. And that's what I want, actually."

"Believe me. I know. No one can feel what you feel, but all of us can *know* what you feel. And, Tommy, you must feel it. You can't run away. It won't work like that. But I want you to try to feel our love as well. Promise you'll do that."

He felt her bend and kiss the top of his head, and in that action, although he could hardly bear it, he also knew there was healing as well. But that was even worse than what lay before him in the immediate future. That he might stop feeling this agony someday. He didn't know how he could live through that.

His mother said, "Simon's come back. Will you speak to him? I think he has news."

"I can't leave her."

"I'll stay. Or I'll send Simon to you. Or I can get the message if you'd like."

He nodded numbly and she waited in silence for him to make up his mind. He finally handed the cup back to her, the soup untouched. "I'll go to him," he said.

His mother took his place at the bed. He turned at the door and saw her lean towards Helen's head and touch the dark hair that fell back from her temples. He left her to maintain a vigil over his wife.

St. James was just outside in the corridor. He looked less haggard than the last time Lynley had seen him, which suggested he'd gone home for some sleep. Lynley was glad of this. The rest of them were operating on nerves and caffeine.

St. James suggested they find the café and when they reached it, the smell of lasagne suggested the hour of the day to be somewhere between noon and eight o'clock at night. Inside the hospital, Lynley had long since lost track of time. Where Helen was, the lights were dim, but elsewhere it was forever fluorescent daytime, with only the changing faces of staff members with each new shift suggesting that hours were passing normally for the rest of the world.

Lynley said, "What time is it, Simon?"

"Half past one."

"Not in the morning, though."

"No. Afternoon. I'm getting you something." He nodded to the stainless steel and glass of the buffet. "What would you like?"

"It doesn't matter. A sandwich? I'm not hungry."

"Consider it medicinal. It'll be easier that way."

"Egg mayonnaise, then, if they have it. Brown bread."

St. James went to fetch it. Lynley sat at a small table in the corner. Other tables were occupied by staff, by members of patients' families, by ministers, and in one case by two nuns. The café reflected the sombre nature of what went on in the building it served: Conversation was hushed; people seemed careful not to clatter their crockery and cutlery.

No one glanced his way, for which Lynley was grateful. He felt raw and exposed, as if he had no protection from the knowledge of others and the judgements that they could pass upon his life.

When St. James returned, he brought egg sandwiches on a tray. He'd bought one for himself as well, and he'd picked up a bowl of fruit and a Twix bar along with two cartons of Ribena.

They ate first, in companionable silence. They'd known each other for so many years—from their very first day at Eton, in fact—that words would be superfluous at the moment. St. James knew; Lynley could tell that in his face. Nothing needed to be said.

St. James nodded his approval when Lynley finished the sandwich. He moved the bowl of fruit in his direction and followed that with the chocolate bar. When Lynley had eaten as much of both as he could stand, his friend finally relayed his information.

"Belgravia have the gun. They found it in one of the gardens, along the route from the mews where that

Range Rover had been dented, to the house where the au pair reported a break-in. They had to leap one brick wall after another to get away. They lost the gun along the route in some shrubbery, evidently. They wouldn't have had time to go back for it, even if they knew it was missing."

Lynley looked away from St. James's face because he knew his friend was watching him carefully and gauging him with every word. He'd want to make sure he told Lynley nothing that might push him over the edge again. This told Lynley he knew about Hillier and New Scotland Yard, in what seemed now like another lifetime.

"I won't storm the Belgravia station," he said. "You can say the rest."

"They're fairly certain the gun they found is the one that was used. They'll do the ballistics study on the bullet they took from . . . from Helen, naturally, but the gun—"

Lynley turned back to him. "What kind is it?"

"Handgun. Twenty-two calibre," St. James said.

"Black-market special."

"It looks that way. It hadn't been there long, in the garden. The home owners claimed to know nothing about it, and a look at the shrubbery supported their claim. It was freshly broken up. In the other gardens along the way as well."

"Footprints?"

"Everywhere. Belgravia are going to catch them, Tommy. Soon."

"Them?"

"There were definitely two of them. One of them was mixed race. The other . . . They're not sure yet."

"The au pair?"

"Belgravia have spoken to her. She says she was with the baby she looks after when she heard a window being broken down below, at the back of the house. By the time she got down to see what was going on, they were inside and she met them at the bottom of the stairs. One of them was already at the front door, heading out. She thought they'd burgled the house. She started screaming, but she also tried to stop them from getting away, God only knows why. One of them lost his hat."

"Is someone getting an e-fit made?"

"I'm not sure that's going to be necessary."

"Why?"

"The house on Cadogan Lane with the CCTV cameras? They've got images. They're being enhanced. Belgravia are going to run them on television and the papers will print the best of the lot. This is . . ." St. James raised his head ceilingward. Lynley saw how difficult this was for his friend. Not only the knowledge of what had happened to Helen but also the gathering of information to pass on to Helen's husband and her family. The effort left him no time for grief. "They're putting everything they have into this, Tommy. They've more volunteers than they can use, from stations all over town. The papers . . . You've not seen them, have you? It's been an enormous story. Because of who you are, who she is, your families, everything."

"Just the sort of thing the tabloids love," Lynley said bitterly.

"But they're carrying the public along with them, Tommy. Someone is going to see the pictures from the CCTV camera and turn the boys in."

Lynley said, "The boys?"

St. James nodded. "At least one of them, apparently, was a boy. The au pair says he looked about twelve years old."

"Oh my God." Lynley looked away, as if this would prevent his mind from making the inescapable connection.

St. James made it anyway. "One of the Colossus

boys . . . ? In the company of the serial killer but without knowing his companion is the serial killer?"

"I gave him—them—an invitation to my home. Right in the pages of *The Source*, Simon."

"But there was no address, no street name. A killer looking for you couldn't have found you through that article. It's impossible."

"He knew who I was, what I look like as well. He could have followed me home from the Yard on any day. And then all that would be left for him was laying his plan and waiting for an appropriate time."

"If that's the case, why take a boy with him?"

"To give him a sin. So he could be his next victim when the job on Helen was done."

THEY'D DECIDED to let Hamish Robson stew for a night in lockup. It would be something of a taste of the future. So they'd taken the profiler to the Shepherdess Walk police station which, while it wasn't the closest lockup to his flat near the Barbican, allowed them to avoid negotiating a route which would take them deeper into the City to get to the Wood Street station.

Search warrant in hand, they spent most of the following day in Robson's flat, building their case against the psychologist. One of the first bits of evidence they found was his laptop computer squirreled away in a cupboard, and Barbara made short work of tripping along the trail of electronic bread crumbs that Robson had left upon it.

"Kiddy porn," she said to Nkata over her shoulder when she found the first of the images. "Boys and men, boys and women, boys and animals, boys and boys. He's a real piece of work, our Hamish."

For his part, Nkata found an old *A to Z* with the location of St. Lucy's Church circled on the corner of Courtfield Road. And tucked into its pages was the name and address of the Canterbury Hotel as well as a business card with "Snow" and a phone number printed on it.

This, along with Barry Minshall's earlier identification of Robson's photograph and 2160 as part of the phone number of the doctor's employer, was enough to bring a SOCO team onto the scene and to send another to Walden Lodge. The first would be looking for further evidence in Robson's car. The second would be gathering what it could from his mother's flat. It seemed unlikely that he'd have brought Davey Benton or anyone else into his digs here near the Barbican. But at least Davey would have ridden over to Wood Lane with Robson and, once there, he would have left his mark inside Esther Robson's flat.

When they had enough to put him away as a paedophile if nothing else, they went to the station. He'd already phoned for his solicitor, and after a wait for her to turn up from the magistrate's court, Barbara and Nkata met them both in an interview room.

It was, Barbara thought, a nice touch for Robson to employ a female solicitor. She was called Amy Stranne, and she appeared to have achieved an advanced university degree in impassivity. She matched her utter lack of expressive reaction with a severe, short haircut, an equally severe black suit, and a man's tie knotted at the throat of her white silk shirt. She took a pristine legal pad from her briefcase, along with a manila folder whose contents she consulted before speaking.

"I've advised my client of his rights," she said. "He wishes to cooperate with you in this interview because he feels there are significant aspects of the current investigation that you don't understand."

Too right, Barbara thought. Bless his black little heart. The psychologist knew he was going to be locked up for years. Like Minshall, the slimy sod was already trying to position himself for a lesser sentence.

Nkata said, "We got SOCO sifting through your vehicle, Dr. Robson. We got SOCO sifting through your mum's flat. We got a team at the Yard searching for the lockup you got to have somewhere in town, because we 'xpect that's where you got the van hidden, and we got 'bout half a dozen officers treading through your background to find anything anyone else might miss."

Robson's haggard face suggested that his accommodation in Shepherdess Walk hadn't been to his liking. He said, "I didn't—"

"Please," Barbara said. "If you didn't kill Davey Benton, we'd be happy to hear what actually happened to him between the time you raped him and the time he ended up a body in the woods."

Robson flinched at the baldness of the statement. Barbara wanted to point out to him that there was actually no palatable way to portray what had happened to the thirteen-year-old. Robson said, "I didn't mean to hurt him."

"Him?"

"The boy. Davey. Snow told me they always went willingly. He said they were well prepared."

"Like a joint of beef?" Barbara asked. "All salt-and-peppered?"

"He said they were ready and they wanted it."

"It?" Nkata said.

"The encounter."

"The rape," Barbara clarified.

"It wasn't . . . !" Robson looked to his solicitor. Amy Stranne was taking notes, but she appeared to sense his glance in her direction, because she looked up. She said, "It's up to you, Hamish."

"You've got healed scratches on your hands and arms," Barbara noted. "And we've got skin under Davey's fingernails. We've evidence of forcible sodomy as well. So what is it about this scenario that we ought to be taking as a voluntary sexual encounter . . . not that sex with thirteen-year-olds is legal, by the way. But we're willing to set that aside for a moment if only to hear your version of the romantic seduction which apparently—"

"I didn't intend to hurt him," Robson said. "I panicked. That's all. He'd been cooperative. He'd been enjoying . . . Perhaps he was hesitant, but he wasn't telling me to stop. He *wasn't*. I swear he was liking it. But when I turned him round . . ." Robson's face was grey. His thin hair drooped across his forehead. Spittle dried at the corners of his mouth, buried within his nicely trimmed goatee. "I just tried to keep him quiet after that. I told him the first time was always a little frightening, even a little painful, but he wasn't to worry."

"How nice of you," Barbara noted. She wanted to rip the sorry bugger's eyes out. Next to her, Nkata stirred. She told herself to back off, which she knew her colleague was also telling her through his body language. But she didn't want this sod to think that their silence—*her* silence—implied approval, even though she knew her silence was crucial in order to keep him talking. She pressed her lips together and bit down to keep them in place.

"I should have stopped then," Robson said. "I know it. But at the moment . . . I thought if he would just be quiet, it would be over quickly enough. And I wanted . . ." Robson looked away, but there was nothing in the room for him to fix upon save the tape recorder making a history of his words. "I didn't intend to kill him," he said again. "I just wanted him to keep quiet while . . ."

"While you finished with him," Barbara said.

"You strangled him with your bare hands," Nkata pointed out. "How was that supposed to—"

"I didn't know how else to get him silent. He was only struggling at first, but then he began to scream and I didn't know how else to quieten him. And then as things were . . . were building for me . . . I didn't realise why he'd gone so silent and limp. I thought he was cooperating."

"Cooperating." Barbara couldn't help herself. "With sodomy. Rape. A thirteen-year-old. You thought he was cooperating. So you finished the job, only you found you were plugging away at a corpse."

Robson's eyes reddened. "My whole life," he'd said, "I tried to ignore . . . I told myself it didn't matter: my uncle, the wrestling and the touching. My mother wanting to sleep with her little man and the arousal that was *natural* to any boy only how could it have been natural when she was making it happen? So I ignored it and I eventually married, but I didn't want her, you see, the woman, fully formed and making demands of me. I thought pictures would help. Videos. Dodgy things that no one would know about."

"Kiddy porn," Barbara said.

"I could get aroused. Easily at first. But then later . . ."

"Takes more," Nkata said. "Always takes more, like a drug. How'd you get on to MABIL?"

"Through the Internet. A chat room. I went at first just to see, just to be round men who felt as I felt. I'd borne the burden so long. This obscene need. I thought it would cure me if I went and saw the sorts of men who . . . who actually engage in it." He brought a tissue out of his pocket and used it to scrub at his face. "But they were just like me, you see. That was the hell of it. They were like me, only happier. At peace. They'd arrived at a spot where they'd come to believe there is no sin in bodily pleasure."

"Bodily pleasure with little boys," Barbara said. "And why would that be? The no sin part of it."

"Because the boys learn to want it as well."

"Do they now. And how is it that blokes like you measure the wanting, Dr. Robson?"

"I can see you don't believe . . . that you think I'm—"

"A monster? A freak? A genetic mutant who needs to be wiped from the surface of the earth along with the rest of your ilk? Why the hell would I think that?" Finally, it was all too much for her.

"Barb," Nkata said.

He was *so* like Lynley, she thought. Capable of keeping cool when that was called for, the one thing she'd never been able to do because she'd always associated keeping cool with letting your insides get eaten by the horror you felt when you had to deal with monsters like this.

"Tell us about the rest," Nkata said to Robson.

"There's nothing more to tell. I waited as long as I could, far into the night. I carried the . . . his body into the woods. It was three . . . four in the morning? There was no one anywhere."

"The burning, the mutilation. Tell us about that."

"I wanted to make it look like the others. Once I saw I'd accidentally killed him, that was the only thing I could think. Make it look like the others so you would conclude the same killer was at work on Davey as on them."

"Hang on. Are you trying to claim you didn't kill the other boys?" Barbara asked.

Robson frowned. "You haven't thought . . . You haven't been sitting there thinking I'm the serial killer? How on earth can that be? How could I even have had access to those other boys?"

"You tell us."

"I *did* tell you. From the profile, I told you."

They were silent. He made the leap to what the silence implied.

"My God, the profile's *real*. Why would I ever have made that up?"

"Most obvious reason in the world," Nkata said. "Lays a nice trail away from yourself."

"But I didn't even know those boys, those dead boys. I didn't *know* them. You must believe—"

"What about Muwaffaq Masoud?" Nkata asked. "You know him?"

"Muwaf . . . ? I've never . . . Who is he?"

"Someone who might be able to pick you out of an identity parade," Nkata said. "Been a while since he's seen the bloke who bought a van off him, but I 'xpect having the man in front of him might do to jog his memory a bit."

Robson turned to his solicitor then. He said, "They can't . . . Can they do this? I've cooperated. I've told them everything."

"So you say, Dr. Robson," Barbara put in. "But we've found liars and killers're cut from similar cloth, so don't mind us for not taking your word as gospel."

"You've got to listen to me," Robson protested. "The one boy, yes. But it was an accident. I didn't intend it to happen. The others, though . . . I am not a murderer. You're looking for someone . . . Read the profile. *Read* the profile. I am not the person you're looking for. I know you're under pressure to bring this case to a close, and now that the superintendent's wife has been assaulted—"

"The superintendent's wife is dead," Nkata reminded him. "You forget that for some reason?"

"You're not suggesting . . ." He turned to Amy Stranne. "Get me away from them," he said. "I won't speak to them further. They're trying to make me something I'm not."

"That's what they all say, Dr. Robson," Barbara told him. "In a pinch, blokes like you always whistle the exact same tune."

TWO MEMBERS of the board of trustees came to see her, which told Ulrike that trouble was not just brewing, it was steaming in the carafe. The president of the board, dressed to the nines with everything but the requisite gold chain to illustrate his authority, had the board secretary in tow. Patrick Bensley was doing the talking, while his cohort tried to look like someone more substantial than an entrepreneur's socialite wife, her recent face-lift on tight display.

It didn't take long for Ulrike to understand that Neil Greenham had made good on the threats he'd uttered the last time they'd spoken. She'd reached that conclusion when Jack Veness told her that Mr. Bensley and Mrs. Richie were unexpectedly in reception, asking for a word with the Colossus director. What took her longer was sorting out exactly which one of the threats Neil had acted upon. Was she to be taken to task for her affair with Griffin Strong or for something else?

She'd seen Griff only briefly in the past few days. He'd kept himself busy with his new group of assessment kids and when he wasn't involved with them, he was out of the way and busily engaged in outreach work, silk-screening work, or the sort of social work he'd been asked to do a thousand times since signing on at Colossus. He'd always been too busy to see to that latter aspect of his job before now. It was astounding how tragedies managed to illustrate for people exactly how much time they'd in fact had for preventing tragedies in the first place. In Griff's case, it was taking the time to connect with his assessment clients and their families outside the regular Colossus hours. He was good about that now, or so he claimed. Truth was, he could have been bonking Emma the Brick Lane Bengali hostess every time he was gone from Colossus, for all Ulrike knew. Or cared, for that matter. She had larger concerns now. And wasn't that an additionally intriguing twist in life? A man one would have sacrificed nearly everything for turned out to have the value of a dust mote when one's head finally cleared.

But the clearing had come at too great a cost. And it turned out that was why Mr. Bensley and Mrs. Richie had come to call. Which visit in and of itself wouldn't have been so bad had she not already been visited that day by the police.

This time it was Belgravia, not New Scotland Yard. They turned up in the form of an unfriendly detective inspector called Jansen with a constable in attendance, who remained nameless and wordless throughout the interview. Jansen had produced a photograph for Ulrike to inspect.

In the picture, which was grainy but not impossible to make out, two individuals were caught in the act of apparently jogging down a narrow street. The identical houses along it—all of them only two and three floors tall—suggested the action had occurred in a mews. The subjects of the photo were in an affluent part of town, as well: There was no rubbish or litter visible, no graffiti, no dead plants in decrepit window boxes.

Ulrike reckoned she was meant to say whether she recognised the individuals who were rushing by the CCTV camera that had produced their photo. So she studied them.

The taller of the two—and he seemed to be male—had sussed out the presence of the camera and wisely averted his face. He wore a hat pulled low over his head. He had his jacket collar turned up, wore gloves, and was otherwise dressed completely in black. He might as well have been a shadow.

The smaller one had not had the same foresight. His image, while not crisp, was still clear enough for Ulrike to be able to say with certainty—and no small measure of relief—that she didn't know him. There was nothing about him that was recognisable to her, and she knew she would have been able to name him had they been acquainted because he had masses of unforgettably crinkly hair and enormous splotches—like monstrous, unrestrained freckles—on his face. He looked to be round thirteen years old, perhaps younger. And he was a mixed-race boy, she decided. White, black, and something in between.

She handed the picture back to Jansen. "I don't know him," she said. "The boy. Either one of them, although I can't say for sure because of how the taller one is hidden. He saw the CCTV camera, I expect. Where was it?"

"There were three," Jansen told her. "Two on a house, one across the street from it. This is from one of the cameras on the house."

"Why're you looking . . . ?"

"A woman was gunned down on her doorstep. It may be down to these two."

That was all he told her, but Ulrike made the leap. She'd seen the newspapers. The wife of the Scotland Yard superintendent, who'd come to Colossus to speak to Ulrike about the deaths of Kimmo Thorne and Jared Salvatore, had been shot on her doorstep in Belgravia. The hue and cry over this had been deafening, broadsheets and tabloids especially. The crime had been inconceivable to the inhabitants of that part of town, and they'd been making their feelings known in every venue they could find.

"He isn't one of ours, this boy," Ulrike replied to DI Jansen. "I've never seen him before."

"Are you sure about the other?"

He had to be joking, Ulrike thought. No one would be able to recognise the taller man. If it even *was* a man. Still, she took another look at the picture. "I *am* sorry," she said. "There's just no way—"

"We'd like to show this round the place, if you don't mind," Jansen told her.

Ulrike didn't like what this implied—that she was somehow out of the loop at Colossus—but she had no choice. Before the officers left to flash the photo round, she asked them about the superintendent's wife. How was she?

Jansen shook his head. "Bad," he said.

"I'm sorry. Will you—" She nodded at the photo. "Do you expect to catch him?"

Jansen looked down at it, a slim slip of paper in his large chafed hands. "The kid? That'll be no problem," he replied. "This is in the *Evening Standard*'s latest right now. It'll make the front of every paper tomorrow morning and it'll be on the news tonight and again tomorrow. We'll get him, and I expect it'll happen soon. And when we get him, he'll talk and then we'll have the other. Absolutely no bloody doubt about it."

"I'm . . . That's good," she said. "Poor woman."

And she *did* mean that. No one—no matter how rich, how privileged, how titled, how fortunate, or how anything else—deserved to be gunned down in the street. But even as she told herself this and assured herself that the milk of human kindness and compassion had not *utterly* drained out of her when it came to the upper class of this rigid society in which she lived, Ulrike still felt relieved that Colossus could not be attached to this new crime.

Only now, here were Mr. Bensley and Mrs. Richie and they were sitting with her in her office—another chair having been procured from the reception area—intent upon talking about the one subject she had done everything in her power to keep from them.

Bensley was the one to introduce it. He said, "Tell us about the dead boys, Ulrike."

She could hardly act the innocent with a "What boys would this be?" sort of reply. There was nothing for it but to tell them that five boys from Colossus had been murdered from September onward, their bodies left in various parts of London.

"Why weren't we informed?" Bensley asked. "Why

did this information have to come to us from someone else?"

"From Neil, you mean." Ulrike could not keep herself from saying it. She was caught between the desire to let them know she was perfectly aware of her Judas's identity and the equal need to defend herself. She went on with, "I didn't know myself till after Kimmo Thorne was murdered. He was the fourth victim. The police came round then."

"But otherwise . . . ?" Bensley did one of those tie-adjustment moves, of the kind meant to illustrate an incredulity that might otherwise strangle him. Mrs. Richie accompanied this with a click of her teeth. "How is it you didn't know the other boys were dead?"

"Or even missing," Mrs. Richie added.

"We're not organised to keep attendance tabs on the clients," Ulrike told them, as if they hadn't had this explained to them a thousand times or more. "Once a boy or girl gets beyond the assessment course, they're free to come and go as they like. They can participate in what we have to offer or they can drop out. We want them to stay because they want to be here. Only those who're here as a probationary measure are monitored." And even then, Colossus didn't tattle on the kids straightaway. There was a certain amount of leeway given even to them, once they had completed the assessment course.

"That," Bensley said, "is what we expected you to say."

Or were told to expect, Ulrike thought. Neil had done his best: She'll make excuses, but the fact remains: the director of Colossus damn well ought to know what's going on with the kids Colossus is meant to be helping, wouldn't you agree? I mean, how much work are we talking about: to look in on the courses and ask the instructors who's there and who's fallen by the wayside? And wouldn't it be wise for the director of Colossus to place a phone call and try to locate a child who's dropped out of a programme designed—and funded, let's not forget that—to prevent him from dropping out in the first place? Oh, he'd done his very best, had Neil. Ulrike had to give him high marks for that.

She found she had no ready response to Bensley's comment, so she waited to see what the board president and his companion had really come to see her about, which she reckoned was only tangentially related to the death of the Colossus boys.

"Perhaps," Bensley said, "you were too distracted to know that boys had gone missing."

"I've been no more distracted than usual," Ulrike told him, "what with the plans for the North London branch and the associated fund-raising going on." *On your instruction, by the way,* was what she did not add, but she did her best to imply it.

Bensley, however, didn't make the inference she wished him to make. He said, "That's not exactly how we understand it. There's been another distraction for you, hasn't there?"

"As I said, Mr. Bensley, there's no easy way to approach this work. I've tried to keep my focus spread evenly on all the concerns a director would have in running a place like Colossus. If I missed the fact that several boys stopped coming, it was due to the number of concerns that I had to deal with related to the organisation. Frankly, I feel terrible that none of us"—with delicate emphasis on the word *none*—"managed to see that—"

"Let me be frank," Bensley interrupted. Mrs. Richie settled herself in her chair, a movement of the hips spelling out *Now we've got to the point.*

"Yes?" Ulrike folded her hands.

"You're under review, for want of a better word. I'm sorry to have to tell you this, Ulrike, because overall your work for Colossus has seemed unimpeachable."

"Seemed," Ulrike said.

"Yes. Seemed."

"Are you sacking me?"

"I didn't say that. But consider yourself under scrutiny. We'll be conducting . . . Shall we call it an internal investigation?"

"For want of a better word?"

"If you will."

"And how do you intend to carry out this internal investigation?"

"Through review. Through interviews. Let me say that I believe you've largely done a fine job here at Colossus. Let me also say, personally, that I hope you emerge unscathed from this look at your employment and personal history here."

"My personal history? What does that mean, exactly?"

Mrs. Richie smiled. Mr. Bensley hemmed. And Ulrike knew her goose was in the oven.

She cursed Neil Greenham, but she also cursed herself. She understood to what extent she was going to be cooked if she didn't bring about a significant alteration to the status quo.

Chapter Thirty-two

"Put him through two identity parades," was how DI Stewart had initially greeted the news that Hamish Robson had cooperated as far as the Davey Benton murder was concerned but had refused to admit to anything else. "Have Minshall *and* Masoud both look at him."

To Barbara's way of thinking, two identity parades was a waste of time since Barry Minshall had already tentatively identified Robson from the photograph she'd nicked at his mother's flat. But she tried to see it as DI Stewart would: not as the compulsion towards overkill that had long made the DI a notorious and tiresome personality at the Yard but as a tremor in the earth designed to rattle Robson into further admissions. The very act of standing in a line of men and waiting to learn if an unseen witness would finger you as the perpetrator of a crime was unnerving. Having to do it twice and hence understanding that there was yet *another* witness to God only knew what . . . At the end of the day, that was actually a very nice touch, and Barbara had to admit it. So she made the arrangements to have Minshall carted over to the Shepherdess Walk station, and she stood behind the two-way mirror while the magician picked out Robson in an instant, saying, "That's the man. That's two-one-six-oh."

Barbara had the pleasure of saying to Robson, "That's one down, mate," so as to leave him dangling in the wind of suspense. Then she cooled her heels while Muwaffaq Masoud worked his way from Hayes into the City via a wasted eternity on the Piccadilly line. Even though she understood the game plan that Stewart was following, at that point she would have preferred that Stewart follow it with someone other than her. So she still tried to work her way out of having to hang about the Shepherdess Walk station waiting for Masoud to turn up. He was, she told DI Stewart, going to say the same as Minshall, so wouldn't her time be better spent looking for the lockup where Robson'd left the van? There was going to be a mountain of evidence against the sod when they found that lockup, wasn't there?

Stewart's response had been, "Set about the job you've been assigned, Constable," whereupon he doubtless returned to his list of to-dos. He was a great one for making lists, was Stewart. Barbara could only imagine how his day began at home as he consulted his self-made schedule to see what time he was meant to clean his teeth.

Her own day had begun with *Breakfast News* on the telly. They ran the best of the CCTV footage that they'd managed to get off a house in a street not far from Eaton Terrace, and to this they added a more ill-defined image that they'd got from Sloane Square underground station. These were the individuals wanted for questioning in the shooting of Helen Lynley, Countess of Asherton, the presenters told their early morning audience. Anyone who recognised either one of them was asked to phone the incident room at the Belgravia Street police station.

Once the presenters had said her name, they then

kept referring to Helen as Lady Asherton. It was as if the individual she was had been completely engulfed by her marriage. The fifth time the presenters used her title, Barbara turned off the telly and tossed the remote into a corner. She couldn't cope with any more of it.

Despite the hour, she wasn't hungry. She knew that there was no way she was going to be able to face something even vaguely resembling breakfast, but she also knew she had to have something, so she forced herself to eat a tin of unheated American sweet corn followed by half a plastic container of rice pud.

When she'd worked herself up to it, she picked up the phone and tried to get real news of Helen. She couldn't bear the thought of talking to Lynley, and she didn't expect him to be at home anyway, so she phoned St. James's number. This time she managed to get a real person on the line and not a voice on an answer machine. That person was Deborah.

When she had her there, Barbara wasn't quite sure what to ask. *How is she?* was ludicrous. *How's the baby?* was just as bad. *How's the superintendent coping?* was the only query even remotely reasonable, but it was also unnecessary because how the hell was the superintendent *supposed* to be coping, knowing the decision that faced him: a modest proposal of keeping his wife a dead body in a bed for the next few months, with air pumping mechanically in and out of her, while their child was reduced to . . . They just didn't know. They knew it was bad. They just didn't know how bad. How close to disaster was close enough?

Barbara settled on saying to Deborah, "It's me. I just wanted to check in. Is he . . . ? I don't know what to ask."

"Everyone's arrived," Deborah told her. Her voice was very quiet. "Iris—that's Helen's middle sister, she lives in America, did you know?—she was the last to get here. She made it, finally, last night. She had a terrible time getting out of Montana; they've had so much snow. Everyone stays at the hospital in a little room they've set up. It's not far from hers. They go in and out. No one wants to leave her alone."

She meant Helen, of course. No one wanted Helen left alone. It was an extended vigil for all of them. How could anyone decide? she wondered. But she couldn't ask. So she said, "Has he talked to anyone? A priest, a minister, a rabbi, a . . . I don't know, anyone?"

There was a silence. Barbara thought perhaps she'd intruded too far. But finally Deborah spoke again, and her tone had changed to such careful tightness that Barbara knew she was crying.

"Simon's been there with him. Daze—that's his mother—she's there as well. There's a specialist supposed to fly in today, someone from France, I think, or perhaps it's Italy, I don't really remember."

"A specialist? What sort?"

"Neonatal neurology. Something like that. Daphne wanted it done. She said if there's the slightest possibility that the baby wasn't harmed . . . She's taking this very badly. So she thought that an expert on babies' brains . . ."

"But Deborah, how's that going to help him *cope*? He needs someone to help him deal with what he's going through."

Deborah's voice dropped. "I know." She gave a broken laugh. "It's exactly what Helen hated, you know. All this soldiering on that people do. Stiff upper lips and just getting *on* with things. God forbid anyone should sound like a whinger. She hated that, Barbara. She'd prefer to have him screaming from the rooftop. At least, she would say, that's real."

Barbara felt her throat tighten. She couldn't talk any longer. So she said, "If you see him, tell him . . ." What? I'm thinking of him? Praying for him? Going through the motions of bringing all this to an end when she knew it was only beginning for him? What was the message, exactly?

She needn't have worried.

"I'll tell him," Deborah said.

On her way to her car, Barbara saw Azhar watching her somberly from the French windows of his flat. She raised a hand but she didn't stop, not even when Hadiyyah's solemn little face appeared next to him and his arm went round her thin shoulders. The parent-child love of it was too much at the moment. Barbara blinked away the image.

When Muwaffaq Masoud finally arrived at the Shepherdess Walk station those hours later, Barbara recognised him mostly by his confusion and unease. She met him in reception and introduced herself, thanking him for coming such a distance to help with the inquiry. He smoothed his beard unconsciously—she was to see that he did this a lot—and he polished his spectacles once she took him to the room from which they'd view the line of men.

He gazed upon them long and hard. They turned for him, one at a time. He asked that three of them step forward—Robson was one of them—and he took a lengthier look at them. Finally he shook his head.

"The middle gentleman resembles him," he said, and Barbara felt a rush of pleasure since he'd fingered Robson. But the pleasure died when he went on. "But I must say it is only a resemblance based on the shape of his head and the type of body. The robustness of it. The man I sold the van to was older, I think. He was bald. He had no facial hair."

"Try to think of this bloke here without the goatee," Barbara said. She didn't add that Robson could have shaved his thinning hair off before he went out to Hayes to purchase a van.

Masoud tried to do as she asked. But his conclusion

remained unchanged. He could not say for certain that the man he was looking at was the same man who'd purchased a van from him in the summer. He was terribly sorry about that, Constable. He sincerely wished to be of help.

Barbara took this news back to New Scotland Yard. She kept her report to Stewart brief. It was yes on Minshall and no on Masoud, she told the DI. They needed to find that sodding van.

Stewart shook his head. He was going over someone's report—red pencil in hand like a frustrated schoolteacher—and he tossed it down on his desk before he said, "That whole line's a nonstarter, as things turn out."

"Why?" Barbara asked.

"Robson's telling the truth."

She gawped at him. "What d'you mean?"

"I mean copycat, Constable. C-o-p-y and c-a-t. He killed the kid and arranged it to look like one of the other murders."

She said, "What the *hell*?," and shoved her hand through her hair in sheer frustration. "I just spent four bloody hours putting this bloke into identity parades. D'you mind telling me why you had me waste my time like that if you *knew* . . ." She couldn't even finish.

The DI said with his usual finesse, "Christ, Havers. Don't get your knickers caught in the crack, all right? No one's keeping secrets from you. St. James only just rang us with the details. He'd told Tommy it was likely, nothing else. Then the attack on Helen happened, and Tommy never passed the information on to us."

"What information?"

"The dissimilarities revealed by the postmortem exam."

"But we always *knew* there were dissimilarities: the manual strangulation, the lack of a stun gun, the rape.

Robson himself pointed out that things escalate when—"

"The boy hadn't eaten in hours, Constable, and there was no trace of ambergris oil on him."

"That could be explained—"

"Every other boy had eaten within an hour of his death. Every other boy had consumed the identical thing. Beef. Some bread. Robson didn't know that and he didn't know about the ambergris oil. What he did to Davey Benton was based on what he knew of the crime, which was superficial: what he saw in the preliminary report and in the photographs of the scene. That's it."

"Are you saying Minshall had nothing to do . . . Robson had nothing . . . ?"

"They're responsible for what happened to Davey Benton. End of story."

Barbara sank heavily into a chair. Round her, the incident room was muted. Obviously, everyone knew about the dead end they'd all just run headlong into. "Where does that leave us?" she asked.

"Back to alibis, background checks, prior arrests. Back, I daresay, to Elephant and Castle."

"We've *damn* well done—"

"So we do it again. Plus every other man whose name has come up in the course of the investigation. They're all going under the microscope. Make yourself part of that."

She looked round the room. "Where's Winnie?" she asked.

"Belgravia," Stewart said. "He's having a closer look at the CCTV tapes they got off Cadogan Lane."

No one said why, but no one had to. Nkata was looking at the CCTV tapes because Nkata was black and a mixed-race boy was featured on them. God, but they were so obvious, Barbara thought. Have a look at these snaps of the shooter, Winnie. You know how it is. All of them look the same to us and, besides, if this is gang related . . . You get the picture, don't you?

She picked up a phone and punched in the numbers of Nkata's mobile. When he answered, she heard voices babbling in the background.

"Masoud said Robson's not our bloke," she told him. "But I expect you're up to speed on that."

"No one knew till St. James phoned Stewart, Barb. This was . . . Must've been round eleven this morning? Wasn't personal."

"You know me too well."

"Not like I don't go through the same dance."

"How're you doing? What d'they expect you to be able to tell them?"

"From looking at the tapes? I don't think *they* know. They're trying everything at this end. I'm just another source."

"And?"

"Sweet FA. Kid's mixed race. Mostly white, some black, and something else. Don't know what. Th'other bloke in the picture? He could be anyone. He knew what he was doing. Kept himself covered, face away from the camera."

"Well, that was one excellent use of your time, wasn't it?"

"I can't blame them, Barb. Doing what they can. They got a decent lead, though. Not five minutes before you rang. Came through by phone."

"What is it? Where'd it come from?"

"Over West Kilburn. Harrow Road station's got a snout in the community they depend on reg'larly, some black bloke with a big street rep and a nasty disposition, so no one messes with him. 'Cording to Harrow Road, this bloke saw the pictures in the paper from the CCTV, and he phoned them up and gave them a name. Could be nothing, but Harrow Road seem to think it's worth looking into. Could be, they say, we got the shooter we're looking for."

"Who is it?"

"Didn't get the name. Harrow Road are picking him up for questions. But if he's the one, he's going to crack. No doubt about it. He's going to talk."

"Why? How can they be so sure?"

"'Cause he's twelve years old. And this i'n't the first time he's been in trouble."

ST. JAMES GAVE Lynley the news. They met not in the corridor this time but rather in the small room that the family had been occupying for what seemed to Lynley like months on end. Helen's parents had been talked into decamping, going in the company of Cybil and Daphne to a flat they owned in Onslow Square, where Helen herself had once lived. Penelope had returned to Cambridge to check on her husband and her three children. His own family were taking a few hours for rest and for a change of scene in Eaton Terrace. His mother had phoned when they'd arrived, saying, "Tommy, what shall we do with the flowers?" Scores of bouquets on the front porch, she said, a coverlet of them that descended the steps and went onto the pavement. He had no suggestions to give her. Offerings of sympathy could not touch him, he found.

Only Iris remained, stalwart Iris, the least Clydelike of all the Clyde sisters. Not a hint of elegance anywhere about her, her long hair no-nonsense and pulled back from her face with slides in the shape of horseshoes. She wore no makeup, and her skin was lined from the sun.

She'd wept when she'd first seen her youngest sister. She'd said fiercely, "This is *not* supposed to happen here, God damn it," and he'd understood from that that she meant violence and death brought about by a gun. The provenance of this was America, not England. What was happening to the England she'd known?

She'd been gone too long, he wanted to tell her. The England she'd known had been dead for decades.

She'd sat with Helen for hours before she spoke again, and then it was to say to him quietly, "She's not here, is she?"

"No. She's not here," Lynley agreed. For the spirit of Helen was gone entirely, now moved onward to the next part of existence—whatever that was. What remained was just the housing for that spirit, kept from putrescence by the questionable miracle of modern medicine.

When St. James arrived, Lynley took him to the waiting area, leaving Iris with Helen. He listened to the news about the Harrow Road police and their snout, but what he took in was a single piece of information: *trouble with the law prior to this.*

He said, "What sort of trouble, Simon?"

"Arson and bag snatching, according to Youth Offenders up there. He's had a social worker attempting to counsel the family for some time. I spoke with her."

"And?"

"Not much, I'm afraid. An older sister doing community service for a street mugging and a younger brother no one knows much about. They all live with an aunt and her boyfriend on a council estate. That's all I know."

"Youth Offenders," Lynley said. "He has a social worker, then."

St. James nodded. His gaze stayed on Lynley and Lynley could feel him making a study of him, evaluating him even as he too drew together the facts like strands of a web whose centre was always and forever the same.

"Youth at risk," Lynley said. "Colossus."

"Don't torture yourself."

He gave a bleak laugh. "Believe me, I don't need to. The truth is doing the job well enough."

TO ULRIKE, given the current circumstances, there were no two uglier words than *internal investigation.* That the board of trustees intended to gather information about her was bad enough. That they intended to do it through interviews and reviews was worse. She had enemies aplenty at Colossus now, and three of them were going to be happy as the dickens to take the opportunity to throw a few tomatoes against the image of herself that she'd tried to build.

Neil Greenham headed the list. He'd probably been storing his rotten little informational fruit grenades for months now, just waiting for the appropriate time to hurl them. For Neil was fighting for complete control of Colossus, and this was something that Ulrike had not realised till the latest development of Bensley and Richie turning up in her office. Of course, he'd never been a team player, had Neil—witness him actually *losing* a teaching job in a climate where the government was begging for teachers!—and while that had always been something of a red flag that Ulrike now admitted she should have noted, it was nothing compared to the insidious side of him that had been revealed with the unexpected advent in Elephant and Castle of two of the board members, not to mention the questions they had asked upon their arrival. So Neil was going to revel in the chance to tar her with a brush he'd no doubt been dipping in pitch since the first time she'd looked at him sideways.

Then there was Jack. The whole what-had-she-been-*thinking* of Jack. Her errors with Jack didn't have to do with trotting off to talk to his landlady aunt, however. They had more to do with giving him a paid position at Colossus in the first place. Oh yes, that was supposed to be the whole theory about the organisation: to build the sense of self in malefactors till they didn't have to malefact any longer. But she'd let fall by the wayside a critical piece of knowledge that she'd always possessed about individuals like Jack. They didn't take kindly to others' suspicions about them, and they were especially nasty when it came to the idea—however mistaken—that someone had grassed them up or was considering doing so. So Jack would be looking for payback, and he'd get it. He wouldn't be able to think things through to the point of understanding how taking part in the facilitation of her demise at Colossus might come back and bite him in the arse once a replacement for her was found.

Griff Strong, on the other hand, understood that only too well. He would do what it took to preserve his position in the organisation, and if that meant making ostensibly reluctant allegations of sexual harassment from a female superior who couldn't keep her hands off his delectable albeit married and oh-so-hesitant body, then that was what he would do. So what Neil Greenham planted in the minds of the board of trustees and what Jack Veness watered, Griff would cultivate. He'd wear that blasted fisherman's sweater for the interview, as well. If he told himself anything, he would list the reasons why they'd come to a situation of every man for himself. Arabella and Tatiana would top that list. "Rike, you know I've got personal responsibilities. You always knew that."

The only person Ulrike could come up with who *might* speak up in support of her was Robbie Kilfoyle, and that was merely because as a volunteer and not a paid employee, he'd have to be careful when interviewed. He'd have to walk a fine line of neutrality because he'd have no other way to protect his future and move himself along in the direction he wanted, which was paid employment. He couldn't want to deliver sandwiches for the rest of his life, could he? But he had to be positioned, had Rob. He had to see himself as a player on her team and no one else's.

She went in search of him. It was late in the day. She didn't check the time, but the darkness outside and the emptiness of the building told her it was long after six and probably closer to eight. Robbie often worked later into the evenings, putting things back in order. There was a good chance he was still in the back somewhere, but if he wasn't, she was determined to track him down.

He was nowhere in the building, however. The kit room was compulsively neat—something to compliment Rob on when she saw him, Ulrike thought—and surgery could have been performed in the practice kitchen so tidy was it. The computer lab had been seen to as well, as had the assessment meeting room. Rob's careful marks were evident everywhere.

Rational thought told Ulrike to wait till the next afternoon to speak to Robbie. He would turn up round half past two as always, and she could thank him and forge a bond with him then. But anxiety suggested she start forging straightaway, so she looked up Rob's phone number and rang his house. If he wasn't there, she reckoned, she could leave a message with his dad.

But the double ringing went on and on. Ulrike listened to it for a good two minutes before she rang off and went on to plan B.

She was, of course, flying by the seat of her jeans, and she knew it. But the part of her that was saying, Relax, go home, have a bath, drink some wine, you can do all this tomorrow was outshouted by the part of her exclaiming that time was flying and the machinations of her enemies were well under way. Besides, her stomach had been riding above her lungs, it seemed, for most of the day. She was *never* going to be able to breathe, eat, or sleep with ease till she did something to alter that.

And anyway, she was a *doer*, wasn't she? She'd never sat round and waited to see how events unfolded.

In this instance, that meant corralling Rob Kilfoyle so he'd be ready to take her part. The only way she could see to do that was to get on her bicycle and find him.

It took the *A to Z* to accomplish the first part of the plan, since she had no clue where Granville Square was once she had Rob's address in hand. She found it tucked to the east of King's Cross Road. This was a definite plus. She would merely have to work her way up to Blackfriars Bridge, cross the river, and head north. It was simple, and its simplicity told her the journey to Granville Square was meant to be.

She saw it was later than she'd thought once she was outside and aboard her bicycle. The commuter traffic had long since thinned out, so the trip up Farringdon Street—even in the vicinity of Ludgate Circus—wasn't as white knuckling as she'd expected.

She made good time to Granville Square, a four-sided terrace of simple Georgian town houses in various states of disrepair and renovation, typical of so many neighbourhoods in London. In the centre of the square was the ubiquitous patch of nature, this one not locked off, barred, and otherwise kept private to all but paying residents of the nearby houses, but rather open to anyone who wanted to walk, read, play with a dog, or watch children romp in the miniature playground along one side. Rob Kilfoyle's house faced the middle of this playground. It was dark as a tomb, but Ulrike parked her bike by the railing and went up the steps anyway. He could be in the back, and now that she'd come, she wasn't about to leave without making an attempt to roust him out of there if he was within.

She knocked but gained no reply. She rang the bell. She tried to peer in the front windows, but she had to resign herself to the admission that other than affording her exercise, the ride across town to this borderland between St. Pancras and Islington had been wasted.

"He isn't home, our Rob," a female voice declared behind her. "No surprise in that, though, poor lad."

Ulrike turned from the door. A woman was watching her from the pavement. She was shaped like a barrel, with a similarly shaped, wheezing English bulldog on a lead. Ulrike went back down the steps to join her.

"D'you happen to know where he is?" She introduced herself as Rob's employer.

"You that sandwich woman?" The woman said she was, "Sylvia Puccini. Missus. No relation by the way, if you're musical. Live three doors down. Known our Rob since he was a toddler."

"I'm Robbie's other employer," Ulrike said. "At Colossus."

"Didn't know he *had* another employer," Mrs. Puccini said, eyeing her carefully. "Where'd you say?"

"Colossus. We're an outreach programme for youth at risk. Robbie's not strictly an employee, I suppose. He volunteers in the afternoons. After he does his sandwich round. But we consider him one of us all the same."

"Never mentioned it to me."

"You're close to him?"

"Why d'you ask?"

Mrs. Puccini sounded suspicious, and Ulrike could sense that they might easily head into Mary Alice Atkins-Ward territory if she pursued this route. She smiled and said, "No particular reason. I thought you might be since you've known him so long. Like a second mum or something."

"Hmm. Yes. Poor Charlene. God rest her dear tormented soul. Alzheimer's, but Rob would have told you that, I expect. She went off early winter last year, poor thing. Didn't know her own son from shoe leather at the end. Didn't know *anyone,* if it comes down to it. And then his dad. He hasn't had an easy time of it for the last few years, our Rob."

Ulrike frowned. "His dad?"

"Dropped like a stone. Last September, this was. Setting off to work like always and drops like a hundredweight. Falls straight down the Gwynne Place Steps right over there." She indicated the southwest end of the square. "Dead before he ever hit the ground."

"Dead?" Ulrike asked. "I didn't know Rob's dad was also . . . He's dead? You're sure?"

In the light of a streetlamp, Mrs. Puccini cast her a look that indicated how bizarre she thought the question was. "If he's not, luv, we all stood round and watched someone else get sent off to be cremated. And that's not very likely, is it?"

No, Ulrike had to agree, it certainly wasn't. She said, "I suppose it's just that . . . You see, Rob's never mentioned his dad passing away." On the very much contrary, she added to herself.

"Well, he wouldn't, I expect. I can't say Rob'd ever be the sort to go shopping for pity, no matter how bad he felt about his dad's passing. Vic was one who didn't ever tolerate whingers, and you know what they say: as the sapling's bent. But make no mistake about it, my dear. That boy felt deeply when he found himself alone."

"There are no other relations?"

"Oh, there's a sister somewhere, a lot older than Rob, but she took off years ago and didn't show up to either funeral. Married, kids, Australia or who knows where. Far as I know, she's not been in touch since she was eighteen." Mrs. Puccini gazed at Ulrike more sharply then, as if evaluating her. When she next spoke, it was apparent why. "On the other hand, dear, between you, me, and Trixie here"— she indicated the dog with a shake of the lead, which the animal apparently took as a sign to resume her walk because she lumbered to her feet from where she'd been squatting gustily at Mrs. Puccini's ankles —"he wasn't a very nice bloke, that Victor."

"Rob's father."

"As ever was. A real shocker when he went like that, true, but not a lot of hearts were breaking at the thought of it in *this* neighbourhood, if you must know."

Ulrike heard this, but she was still attempting to process the first bit of information: that Robbie Kilfoyle's dad was in fact dead. She was comparing this to what Rob had told her recently . . . Sky Television, wasn't it? Something called *Sail Away*? All she said to Mrs. Puccini was, "I do wish he'd told me. It helps to talk."

"Oh, I expect he's talking." Unaccountably, Mrs. Puccini nodded once again towards the Gwynne Place Steps. "There's always a friendly ear when you're paying for it."

"Paying?" Friendly ears and paying suggested one of two things: prostitution, which seemed about as much Rob's style as armed robbery, or psychotherapy, which seemed equally unlikely.

Mrs. Puccini appeared to know what she was thinking because she gave a hoot of laughter before she explained. "The *hotel,*" she said. "At the base of the steps. He goes to the bar there most nights. I expect that's where he is right now."

This proved to be the case when Ulrike bade Mrs. Puccini and Trixie good night and headed across the square and down the steps. She found that they led to an unassuming and unmistakably postwar tower block, heavily given over to chocolate-coloured bricks and minimal exterior decoration. Inside, however, it boasted a lobby done up in faux art deco, its walls hung with paintings depicting well-heeled men and women lounging and partying between the two world wars. At one end of this lobby, a door marked the entrance to the Othello Bar. It seemed strange to Ulrike that Robbie—or anyone from the neighbourhood—would choose a hotel rather than a nearby pub in which to do his drinking, but she decided that the Othello Bar had one quality to recommend it, at least on this night: There was virtually no one present. If Robbie wished to bend the sympathetic ear of the barman, that individual was entirely available. There were seats at the bar to boot, another feature making the Othello perhaps more welcoming than the corner pub.

Robbie Kilfoyle was at one of these seats. Two of the tables were occupied by businessmen working at laptops with their lagers before them; one other table was taken up by three women whose enormous bums, white trainers, and choice of drink at this time of night—white wine—suggested they were American tourists. Otherwise the bar was empty. Thirties music played from speakers in the ceiling.

Ulrike slid onto the stool next to Robbie. He glanced her way once, then again when the sight of her registered with him. His eyes widened.

"Hi," she said. "One of your neighbours said you might be here."

He said, "Ulrike!," and looked round her as if to see if she was accompanied by someone. He was wearing a snug black jersey, she noted, which emphasised his physique in a way that his usual neatly ironed white shirt had never done. Lessons from Griff? she wondered. He had *quite* a nice body.

The barman heard Rob exclaim and came to take her order. She said she'd have a brandy, and when he fetched it for her, she told Rob that Mrs. Puccini had suggested she look for him here. "She said you'd been coming here regularly since your dad died," Ulrike added.

Robbie looked away and then back at her. He didn't attempt to obfuscate, and Ulrike had to admire him for that. He said, "I didn't like to tell you about it. That he'd died. I couldn't think of a *way* to tell you. It seemed like it would've been . . ." He thought about it, it appeared, as he turned his pint of lager between his hands. "It would have been like asking for special treatment. Like hoping someone'd feel sorry for me and give me something as a result."

"Whatever gave you that idea?" Ulrike asked. "I hope nothing anyone's done at Colossus would make you feel you had no friends to confide in."

"No, no," he said. "I don't think that. I s'pose I just wasn't ready to talk about it."

"Are you now?" This was, she saw, an opportunity to forge the loyalty bond with Robbie. While she had bigger concerns than the death of a man that had taken place months ago—a man she had never even met—she wanted Robbie to know that he had a friend at Colossus and that friend was sitting right next to him in the Othello Bar.

"Am I ready to talk about it?"

"Yes."

He shook his head. "Not really."

"Painful?"

A glance in her direction. "Why d'you say that?"

She shrugged. "It seems obvious. You apparently had a close relationship with him. You lived together, after all. You must have spent a great deal of time together. I remember your telling me about how the two of you watched tele—" She stopped, the words cut off by the realisation. She twirled her brandy glass slowly and made herself finish. "You watched television with him. You did say you watched television with him."

"And we did," he replied. "My dad was a bugger and a half on good days, but he never went after anyone when the telly was on. I think it hypnotised him.

So whenever we were alone together—especially after Mum finally went into hospital—I turned on the telly to keep him off my back. Force of habit when I was talking to you about watching the telly with him, I guess. That's all we ever really did together." He drained his beer. "Why'd you come?" he asked.

Why *had* she come? Suddenly, it seemed rather unimportant. She sifted through topics to find one that was simultaneously believable and innocuous. She said, "Actually, to thank you."

"What for?"

"You do so much round Colossus. Sometimes you don't get acknowledged enough."

"You came round here for that?" Robbie sounded incredulous, as any reasonable person might.

Ulrike knew the ground was treacherous here, so she decided that opting for the truth was wise. "More than that, really. I'm being . . . well . . . investigated, Rob. So I'm sorting out who my friends are. You must have heard."

"What? Who your friends are?"

"That I'm being investigated."

"I know the cops've been round."

"Not that investigation."

"Then what?"

"The board of trustees are looking into my performance as director of Colossus. You must have known they came round today."

"Why?"

"Why what?"

"Why must I have known? I'm pond scum over there. Least important and last informed."

He said it casually, but she could tell he was . . . what? Frustrated? Bitter? Angry? *Why* hadn't she seen this before? And what was she supposed to do about it now, other than apologise, make a vague promise about things changing round Colossus, and go on her way?

She said, "I'm going to try to change that, Rob."

"If I take your part in the coming conflict."

"I'm not saying—"

"It's okay." He shoved his pint glass away, shaking his head when the barman offered him another. He settled his bill and hers and said, "I understand it's a game. I get the politics of everything. I'm not stupid."

"I didn't mean to suggest you were."

"No offence's been taken. You're doing what you have to do." He slid off his stool. "How'd you get here?" he asked. "You didn't bike over, did you?"

She told him she had done. She finished off her brandy and said, "So I'd better set off."

He said, "It's late. I'll take you home."

"Take me? I thought you cycled as well."

"To work," he said. "Otherwise, no. I got Dad's van off him when he died in the summer. Poor sod. He bought himself a camper for his pension years and dropped dead the next week. Never even had a chance to use it. Come on. We can fit your bike inside. I've done it before."

"Thanks, but that's really not necessary. It puts you to trouble, and—"

"Don't be stupid. It's not any trouble." He took her arm. He said, " 'Night, Dan," to the barman and he guided Ulrike not to the door through which she'd come but towards a corridor. This led, she found, to the toilets and, beyond them, to the kitchen, which he entered. Only a single cook remained, and he said, "Rob," with a nod of hello as they passed through. She saw there was another exit here, an escape route for the kitchen workers should a fire start, and this was the door that Robbie chose. It took them to a narrow carpark behind the hotel, canyoned on one side by the building itself and on the other side by a slope at the top of which was Granville Square. In a far dark corner of the carpark, a van stood waiting. It looked old and harmless, with rust spots pitting the faded white lettering on its side.

"My bike," Ulrike began.

"Up in the square? We'll sort that out. Get in. We'll drive round to pick it up."

She looked round the carpark. It was dimly lit and otherwise deserted. She looked at Robbie. He shot her a smile. She thought of Colossus and how hard she'd worked and how much would fall into ruin if she was made to hand it over to someone else. Someone like Neil. Someone like Griff. Anyone, in fact.

Some things needed a leap of faith, she decided. This was one of them.

At the van, Robbie opened the door for her. She climbed inside. He shut the door. She felt for the seat belt but couldn't find it anywhere above her shoulder. When Robbie joined her and saw her searching, he started the van up and said, "Oh, sorry. That's a bit tricky. It's lower than you'd expect. I've got a torch here somewhere. Let me give you some light."

He rustled round on the floor next to his own seat. Ulrike watched him bring up a torch. He said. "This should be of some help," and she turned back to reach over for the belt once again.

Everything happened in less than three seconds after that. She waited for the light to shine from the torch. She said, "Rob?," and then felt the jolt run through her body. She gasped for breath.

The first spasm shook her. The second rendered her semiconscious. The third teetered her on the edge from which she slid into the dark.

Chapter Thirty-three

Harrow Road's reputation as a police station wasn't a good one, but cops had a lot to contend with in West Kilburn. They were dealing with everything from the usual social and cultural conflicts one found within a multiethnic community, to street crime, drugs, and a thriving black market. They found themselves perpetually coping with gangs as well. In an area dominated by housing estates and grim tower blocks built in the sixties when architectural imagination was moribund, legends abounded of cops being outrun, outmanoeuvred, and outsmarted in places like the interlocking and tunnel-like corridors of the notorious Mozart Estate. The police had been outnumbered forever in this part of town. They knew it, which didn't improve their tempers when it came to meeting the needs of the public.

When Barbara and Nkata arrived, they found a heated argument going on in reception. A Rastafarian accompanied by a hugely pregnant woman and two children was demanding action of a special constable—"I wan' that fuckin' car *back*, man. You t'ink dis woman plan on giving birth in the street?"—who claimed things to be "out of my power, sir. You'll have to talk to one of the officers who're working on the case."

The Rasta said, "*Shit*, then," and turned on his heel. He grabbed his woman's arm and made for the door, saying, "Blood," to Nkata with a nod as he passed him.

Nkata identified himself and Barbara to the special constable. They were there to see Detective Sergeant Starr, he said. Harrow Road had a boy in lockup, fingered as the shooter in a street crime in Belgravia.

"He's 'xpecting us," Nkata said.

Harrow Road had reported to Belgravia, who'd reported, in turn, to New Scotland Yard. The snout in West Kilburn had proved reliable. He'd named a kid who resembled the one seen on the CCTV films from Cadogan Lane, and the cops had found him in very short order. He hadn't even been on the run. The job on Helen Lynley done, he'd merely repaired to his home, via underground to Westbourne Park because his mug had been visible on their CCTV tapes as well, sans companion this time. Nothing could have been easier. All that remained was matching his fingerprints to those on the gun found in the garden near the scene of the crime.

John Stewart had told Nkata to take it. Nkata had asked Barbara to accompany him. By the time they got there, it was ten o'clock at night. They could have waited till morning—they'd been working fourteen hours at that point and they were both knackered—but neither one of them was willing to wait. There was a chance that Stewart would hand this job over to someone else, and they didn't want that.

Sergeant Starr turned out to be a black man, slightly shorter than Nkata but bulkier. He had the look of a pleasant-faced pugilist.

He said, "We've already had this yob in for street brawling and arson. Those times, he's pointed the finger elsewhere. You know the sort. It wasn't *me*, you fucking pigs." He glanced at Barbara as if to ask pardon for his language. She waved a weary hand at him. He went on. "But the family's got a whole history of trouble. Dad got shot and killed in a drug dispute in the street. Mum toasted her brain with something, and she's been out of the picture for a while. Sister tried to pull off a mugging and ended up in front of the magistrate. The aunt they live with hasn't been willing to hear shit about the kids being on the fast track to trouble, though. She's got a shop down the road that she works in full-time and a younger boyfriend keeping her busy in the bedroom, so she can't afford to see what's going on under her nose, if you know what I mean. It was always just a matter of time. We tried to tell her first time we had the kid in here, but she wasn't having it. Same old story."

"He talked before, you said?" Barbara asked. "What about now?"

"We're getting sod all out of him."

"Nothing?" Nkata said.

"Not a word. He'd probably not've told us his name if we hadn't already known it."

"What is it?"

"Joel Campbell."

"How old?"

"Twelve."

"Scared?"

"Oh yeah. I'd say he knows he's going away for this. But he also knows about Venables and Thompson. Who bloody doesn't? So six years playing with bricks, finger-painting, and talking to shrinks and he's finished with the criminal-justice system."

There was some truth in this. It was the moral and ethical dilemma of the times: what to do with juvenile murderers. Twelve-year-old murderers. And younger.

"We'd like to talk to him."

"For what good it'll do. We're waiting for the social worker to show."

"Has the aunt been here?"

"Come and gone. She wants him out of here directly or she'll know the reason why. He's going nowhere. Between her position and ours, there wasn't a hell of a lot to discuss."

"Solicitor?"

"I expect the aunt's working on that angle now."

He gestured for them to follow him. On their way to the interview room, they were met by a worn-out looking woman in a sweatshirt, jeans, and trainers, who turned out to be the social worker. She was called Fabia Bender, and she told Sergeant Starr that the boy was asking for something to eat.

"Did he ask or did you offer?" Starr inquired. Which meant, of course, had he opened his mouth to say something at last?

"He asked," she replied. "More or less. He said, 'Hungry.' I'd like to fetch him a sandwich."

"I'll organise it," he said. "These two want a word. You see to that."

Arrangements made, Starr left Nkata and Barbara with Fabia Bender, who didn't have much more to add to what the detective had already told them. The boy's mother, she said, was in a mental hospital in Buckinghamshire, where she'd been a repeat patient for years. During this most recent round of institutionalisation, her children had been living with their grandmother. When the old lady decamped for Jamaica with a boyfriend who was being deported, the children got passed off to the aunt. Really, it was no surprise that kids found their way into trouble when their circumstances were so unsettled.

"He's just in here," she said and shouldered open a door.

She went in first, saying, "Thank you, Sherry," to a uniformed constable who apparently had been sitting with the boy. The constable left, and Barbara entered the room behind Fabia Bender. Nkata followed, and they were face-to-face with the accused killer of Helen Lynley.

Barbara looked at Nkata. He nodded. This was the boy he'd seen on the CCTV film taken in Cadogan Lane and in the Sloane Square underground station: the same head of crinkly hair, the same face blotched with freckles the size of tea cakes. He was about as menacing as a fawn caught in the headlamps of a car. He was small, and his fingernails had been bitten to the quick.

He was sitting at the regulation table, and they joined him there, Nkata and Barbara on one side and the boy and the social worker on the other. Fabia Bender told him that Sergeant Starr was fetching him a sandwich. Someone else had brought him a Coke although it remained untouched.

"Joel," Nkata said to the boy. "You killed a cop's wife. You know that? We found a gun nearby. Fingerprints on that'll turn out to be yours. Ballistics'll show that gun did the killing. CCTV film places you on the scene. You and 'nother bloke. What d'you got to say, then, blood?"

The boy slid his gaze over to Nkata for a moment. It seemed to linger on the razor scar that ran the length of the black man's cheek. Unsmiling, Nkata was no teddy bear. But the boy drew himself in—one could almost see him call upon courage from another dimension—and he said nothing.

"We want a name, man," Nkata told him.

"We know you weren't alone," Barbara said.

"Th' other bloke was an adult, wasn't he? We want a name out of you. It's the only way to go forward."

Joel said nothing. He reached for the Coke and closed his hands round it, although he did not attempt to pop it open.

"Man, where you think you're going for this one?"

Nkata asked the boy. "You think we send blokes like you to Blackpool for a holiday? Going away is what happens to the likes of you. How you play it now determines how long."

This wasn't necessarily true, but there was a chance that the boy wouldn't know it. They needed a name, and they would have it from him.

The door opened then and Sergeant Starr returned. He held the triangle of a plastic-wrapped sandwich in his hand. He unwrapped it and passed it over to the boy. The child picked it up but did not take a bite. He looked hesitant, and Barbara could tell he was struggling with a decision. She had the sensation that the alternatives he was considering were ones that none of them would ever be able to understand. When he finally looked up, it was to speak to Fabia Bender.

"I ain't grassing," he said and took a bite of his sandwich.

That was the end of it: the social code of the streets. And not only of the streets, but the code that pervaded their society as well. Children learned it at the knees of parents because it was a lesson essential to their survival no matter where they went. One did not sneak on a friend. But that alone told them volumes in the interview room. Whoever had been with the boy in Belgravia, there was a strong possibility that he was considered—at least by Joel—a friend.

They left the room. Fabia Bender accompanied them. DS Starr remained with the boy.

"I expect he'll tell us eventually," Fabia Bender assured them. "It's early days yet, and he's never been inside a youth facility before. When he gets there, he'll have another think about what's happened. He isn't stupid."

Barbara considered this as they paused in the corridor. "He's been in here for arson and a mugging, though, hasn't he? What happened about that? A wrist slapping by the magistrate? Did things even go that far?"

The social worker shook her head. "Charges were never brought. I expect they didn't have the evidence they wanted. He was questioned, but then he was released both times."

So he was, Barbara thought, the perfect candidate for some sort of social intervention, of the kind provided in Elephant and Castle. She said, "What happened to him then?"

"What do you mean?"

"When he was released. Did you recommend him to any special programme?"

"What kind of programme?"

"The kind designed to keep kids out of trouble."

"You ever send a kid over to a group called Colossus?" Nkata asked. "'Cross the river, this is. Elephant and Castle."

Fabia Bender shook her head. "I've heard of it, of course. We've had their outreach people here for a presentation as well."

"But . . . ?"

"But we've never sent any of our children over to them."

"You haven't." Barbara made this a statement.

"No. It's quite a distance, you see, and we've been waiting for them to open a branch closer to this part of town."

LYNLEY WAS ALONE with Helen and had been so for the last two hours. He'd made the request of their respective families, and they'd agreed. Only Iris protested, but she'd been here at the hospital the least amount of time, so he understood how impossible she felt it that she would be asked to part from her sister.

The specialist had come and gone. He'd read the charts and the reports. He'd studied the monitors.

He'd examined what little there was to examine. In the end, he'd met everyone because Lynley had wanted it that way. As much as a person could ever be said to belong to anyone, Helen belonged to him by virtue of being his wife. But she was a daughter as well, a beloved sister, a loving daughter- and sister-in-law. The loss of her touched every one of them. He did not suffer this monstrous blow alone, nor could he ever claim to grieve it alone. So all of them had sat with the Italian doctor, the neonatal neurologist who told them what they already knew.

Twenty minutes was not a vast span of time. Twenty minutes described a period in which very little could generally be accomplished in life. Indeed, there were days when Lynley couldn't even get from his house to Victoria Street in under twenty minutes, and other than showering and dressing or brewing and drinking a cup of tea or doing the washing up after dinner or perhaps dead-heading the roses in the garden, one-third of an hour didn't provide the leisure necessary to do much of anything. But for the human brain, twenty minutes was an eternity. It was forever because that was the nature of the alteration it could bring upon the life depending upon its normal functioning. And that normal functioning depended upon a regular supply of oxygen. Witness the victim of the gunshot, the doctor had said. Witness your Helen.

The difficulty, of course, was in the not knowing, which arose from the not seeing. Helen could be seen—daily, hourly, moment by moment—lifeless in the hospital bed. The baby—their son, their amusingly named, for want of a permanent decision by his indecisive parents, Jasper Felix—could not. All they knew was all the specialist knew and what he knew was dependent upon what was common knowledge about the brain.

If Helen had no oxygen, the baby had no oxygen. They could hope for a miracle, but that was all.

Helen's father had asked, "How likely is that 'miracle'?"

The doctor shook his head. He was sympathetic. He seemed generous and good hearted. But he would not lie.

None of them looked at one another at first, once the specialist left them. All of them felt the burden, but only one of them experienced the weight of having to make a decision. Lynley was left with the knowledge that everything rested with him and upon him. They could love him—as they did and as he knew—but they could not move the cup from his hands to theirs.

Each one of them spoke to him before they left for the night, somehow knowing without being told that the moment for resolution had arrived. His mother remained longer than any of them, and she knelt before his chair and looked up into his face.

"Everything in our lives," she said quietly, "leads up to everything else in our lives. So a moment in the present has a reference point, both in the past and in the future. I want you to know that you—as you are right now and as you ever will be—are fully enough for this moment, Tommy. One way or the other. Whatever it brings."

"I've been wondering how I'm meant to know what to do," he said. "I look at her face and I try to see on it what she'd want me to do. Then I ask myself if even that is a lie, if I'm merely telling myself that I'm looking at her and trying to see what she'd want me to do when all the time I'm just looking at her and looking at her because I can't face the coming moment when I won't be able to look at her at all. Because she'll be gone. Not only gone in spirit but gone in flesh as well.

Because right now, you see, even in this, she's giving me a reason to keep going on. I'm prolonging that."

His mother reached up and caressed his face. She said, "Of all my children, you were always the hardest on yourself. You were always looking for the right way to behave, so concerned you might make a mistake. But, darling, there are no mistakes. There are only our wishes, our actions, and the consequences that follow both. There are only events, how we cope with them, and what we learn from the coping."

"That's too easy," he said.

"On the contrary. It's monumentally difficult."

She left him then and he went to Helen. He sat at her bedside. He knew that no matter how he disciplined his mind to this moment, the image of his wife as she was just now would fade with time, just as the image of her as she had been days ago would also fade, had indeed already begun to fade, until ultimately, there would be nothing of her left in his visual memory. If he wanted to see her, he'd be able to do so only in photographs. When he closed his eyes, however, he'd see nothing but the dark.

It was the dark that he feared. It was everything that represented the dark, which he could not face. And Helen was at the centre of it all. As was the not-Helen that would come about the instant he acted in the only way he knew his wife would have wanted.

She'd been telling him that from the first. Or was even *that* belief a lie?

He did not know. He lowered his forehead to the mattress and he prayed for a sign. He knew he was looking for something that would make the road an easier one for him to walk. But signs did not exist for that purpose. They served as guides, but they did not smooth the way.

Her hand was cool when he felt for it where it lay at her side. He closed his fingers round it and he summoned hers to move as they might have done had she only been what she looked, asleep. He pictured her eyelids fluttering open and he heard her murmured "Hullo, darling," but when he raised his head, she was as before. Breathing because medical science had evolved to that extent. Dead because it had evolved no further.

They belonged together. The will of man might have wished it otherwise. The will of nature was not so vague. Helen would have understood that even if she had not phrased it that way. *Let us go, Tommy* would have been how she put it. At the heart of matters, she had always been the wisest and most practical of women.

When the door opened some time later, he was ready.

"It's time," he said.

He felt his heart swelling, as if it would be torn from his body. The monitors deadened. The ventilator hushed. The silence of parting swept into the room.

BY THE TIME Barbara and Nkata arrived back at New Scotland Yard, the news was in. The gun bore the boy's prints on the barrel and on the grip, and ballistics showed the bullet to have come from the same pistol. They made their own report to John Stewart, who listened stone faced. He looked as if he believed his own presence in the Harrow Road station might have made a difference, shaking the name of the other perpetrator out of the kid. Sod all he knew, Barbara thought, and she told him what they'd learned from Fabia Bender about the boy and about Colossus.

At the end, she said, "I want to tell the superintendent, sir." When Stewart's expression suggested that he smelled something bad, she altered her declaration to, "I'd like to tell him, that is. He thinks Helen's shooting has to do with this investigation, with that profile in *The Source* as the way the shooter found her.

He needs to know . . . It'll give him one less thing to think about, I expect."

Stewart appeared to look at this from every angle before he finally agreed. *But*, he told her, she was to do the paperwork related to their call in Harrow Road, and she was to do that before setting off for St. Thomas' Hospital.

It was past one in the morning, then, when she finally staggered down to her car. Then the blasted Mini choked on her, and she sat with her head on the steering wheel, willing the damn engine to turn over properly. In her head, she heard that same admonition from some mystical automotive dimension suggesting that she might want to get the car seen to before it conked out altogether. She muttered, "Tomorrow. All right? To*mor*row," and hoped that promise was enough.

It was. The engine finally started.

At this time of night, the streets of London were virtually empty. No sane taxi driver was out, trying to get a fare in Westminster, and the buses ran far less frequently. An occasional car was passing by, but largely the streets were as vacant as the pavements where the homeless tucked themselves into doorways. So she made quick time to the hospital.

As she drove, she realised that he might not be there, that he might have gone home and tried to get some sleep, in which case she would not disturb him. But when she arrived and pulled into a drop-off point directly down from Lambeth Palace Road, she saw his Bentley at the far end of the carpark. He was with Helen, then, as she'd reckoned he would be.

She gave passing thought to the risk of shutting the Mini's engine off after she'd finally got it going. But the risk was necessary because she wanted to be the one to tell Lynley about the boy. She felt a need to relieve at least some small portion of the guilt he was carrying round, so she turned the key in the ignition and waited for the Mini's hiccupping to come to an end.

She grabbed up her shoulder bag and got out of the car. She was just about to walk towards the entrance when she saw him. He'd come out of hospital, and the look of him—how he walked and how he held his shoulders—told her how permanently altered he was. She hesitated, then. How to approach a dearly loved friend . . . How to approach him in such a time of devastation? At the end, she didn't think she could. Because, after all, what difference did it actually make with his life now, as it was, in ruins?

He trudged across the carpark to the Bentley. There he looked up. Not at her but at a spot in the carpark out of her range of vision. It was as if someone had called his name. And then a figure quickly emerged from the darkness and things happened very swiftly after that.

Barbara saw that the figure wore all black. He moved over to Lynley. There was something in his hand. Lynley looked round. Then he turned in a flash back to his car. But he got no farther. For the figure reached him and pressed the object that he carried into Lynley's side. Not even a second passed before Barbara's superintendent was on the ground and the hand that held the object pressed to him again. His body jerked and the figure in black looked up. Even from a distance, Barbara saw she was gazing on Robbie Kilfoyle.

It had all taken three seconds, perhaps less. Kilfoyle grabbed Lynley by his armpits and dragged him quickly to what Barbara should have bloody well *seen*, she thought, if she hadn't been so focussed on Lynley. A van was parked deeply in the shadows, its sliding door open. In another second, he'd got Lynley inside.

Barbara said, "Bloody sodding *hell*," weaponless and for a moment utterly directionless. She looked to the Mini for something she could use . . . She reached for her mobile to phone for help. She punched in the first nine as, across the carpark, the van roared to life.

She dived for her car. She threw her bag and her mobile inside, phone call incomplete. She would punch in the last two nines in a moment, but in the meantime she had to get going, had to get on his tail, had to follow and shout the direction she was traveling into the mobile so that an armed unit could be sent on its way because the van, the bloody van, was moving, it was coming across the carpark now. It was red, as they'd suspected, and on its side were the faded letters they'd seen in the film.

Barbara shoved her key into the ignition and turned it. The engine ground. It did not engage. Across from her, the van was rumbling towards the exit. Its lights swept her way. She ducked because he *had* to think he had an all clear so he'd keep his pace slow, steady, and unsuspecting. She could follow then and ring for the men with the nice big guns to take down this useless piece of human excrement before he did something to someone who meant everything to her to someone who was her friend her mentor and who at this moment would not fight back would not care to fight back and would think Do with me as you will and she could not let that happen to Lynley.

The car did not start. It *would* not start. Barbara heard herself shriek. She leaped out. She slammed the door behind her. She dashed across the carpark. She thought how he'd been heading to the Bentley, had been near to the Bentley, so there was a chance . . .

And he'd dropped the keys as he'd fallen. He'd *dropped* the keys. She grabbed them up with a sob of gratitude that she forced herself to quell and then she was in the Bentley. Her hands were shaking. It took a century to get the key into the ignition but then the car was starting and she was trying to get the damn seat into a place where she could reach the accelerator and the brake because his legs were long because he was nearly a foot taller than she. She jerked the car into gear and reversed it and prayed that the killer was being careful careful careful because the last thing he would want was to attract attention to his driving.

He'd turned left. She did the same. She revved the engine of the huge car, and it leapt ahead like a well-trained thoroughbred and she swore as she gained control over it control over her reactions control over her exhaustion which was no longer exhaustion at all but raging adrenaline and the need to stop this bugger in his tracks arrange a little surprise for the bastard bring out a hundred cops if necessary and all of them armed so that they could storm his bloody little mobile killing site and he *couldn't* hurt Lynley while the van was in motion so she knew she was all right until it stopped. But she needed to let the cops know where she was heading, so the moment she finally caught sight of Kilfoyle's van crossing Westminster Bridge, she reached for the mobile. And realised it was back in the Mini along with her bag, left where she'd thrown them when she'd leapt into her car, her call to 999 incomplete.

She shouted, "Shit! *Shit!*," and knew that, barring a miracle, she was on her own. *You and me, babe.* Lynley's life in the balance because that was it, wasn't it, this was going to be the pièce de résistance, you bloody sod, *this* was going to put your miserable name in lights—you would kill the cop who was looking for you and you would do to him what you'd done to the others and as he was he could not fight back and as he'd been in the carpark he wouldn't care about fighting to save himself and you know that, don't you, just as you knew where to find him, you sod, because you'd read the papers and you'd watched the telly and now you were going to have real fun.

She didn't know where they were. The bugger was good when it came to rat runs but he'd be good, wouldn't he, because he bicycled and he knew the streets he knew the byways he knew the whole flaming town.

They were heading northeast. That was all she could tell. She stayed behind as far as she dared without losing him altogether. She drove without headlights, which he could not do if he wanted to look normal casual just going from point A to point B in all innocence at whatever time it was, which felt like two in the morning or later. She couldn't risk stopping at a phone box or grabbing up a pedestrian—had there even been one—and demanding the use of his mobile. All she could do was remain in pursuit and think feverishly of what she could do when she got to wherever the hell they were going which she knew would be the spot where he'd killed the others. And then transported their bodies so where do you plan to place Lynley's, you piece of filth? But that would not happen even if the superintendent welcomed it in his present state because she would not allow it because although that bugger had the weapons she had surprise and she bloody well intended to use it. Only what *was* it that was the surprise other than her presence which was going to mean sweet FA to this bastard with his stun gun his knives his duct tape his restraints his bloody sodding oils and his marks on the forehead.

Wheel brace in the boot of the Bentley. That was what it boiled down to and what the hell was she supposed to do with that? Don't you fucking touch him or I'll swing this thing at your miserable head while I'm dodging your stun gun and you're leaping upon me with your carving knife? How was *that* going to work?

Up ahead, he turned once more and it looked like a final time. They'd been driving and driving, at least twenty minutes and possibly longer. Just before the turn, they'd crossed over a river which damn well wasn't the Thames way up here when way up here was far north and east of where they'd begun. Then they'd passed an outdoor storage facility at the northeast edge of the river and she'd thought, He's got a bloody lockup where he does the job, just like we'd thought at some point along the route that's brought us to this miserable moment. But he passed the storage facility with its neat row of lockups lined up along the river and instead he pulled into a carpark just beyond. It was large, vast when she compared it to where he'd been parked at St. Thomas' Hospital. Above it was a sign that finally told her where they were, Lea Valley Ice Centre. Essex Wharf. They were at the River Lea.

The ice centre was an indoor skating rink looking like an antique Quonset hut. It sat some fifty yards off the road, and Kilfoyle drove to the left of it where the carpark made a dogleg that possessed two distinct advantages for a killer: It was overgrown with evergreen shrubbery and the streetlamp above it was broken. When the van was parked there, it was completely in shadow. No one driving by would see it from the street.

The van's lights went out. Barbara waited for a moment to see if Kilfoyle planned to emerge. If he dragged his victim out and did his stuff in the bushes . . . only how the hell could he burn someone's hands in the bushes? No, she thought. He'd do it inside. He had no need to depart his mobile execution site. He just had to find a spot where no one was likely to hear any noise coming from the van, a spot where no one was likely ever to see the van. He'd do his stuff and then go on his way.

Which meant she had to do her business first.

She'd been idling the Bentley at the kerb, but now she slowly pulled into the carpark herself. She watched and waited for some sort of sign, like the slight motion of the vehicle as Kilfoyle moved round inside it. She got out of the car, although she left it running. She looked for something . . . for anything she could use. Surprise was the only thing she had, she reminded herself. What then constituted the biggest surprise she could give the sodding freak?

She went over the details feverishly. What they knew and everything they had tried to guess. He restrained them, so he'd be doing that now. For the drive, he'd have placed Lynley where he could zap him with the stun gun whenever he seemed to be coming to his senses. But now he'd be restraining him. And in the restraint came the hope of salvation. For as the restraints immobilised Lynley, so did they protect him. And that's what she wanted.

Protection gave her the answer she needed.

LYNLEY WAS aware of his inability to order his body to move. What was gone from him was the message-to-action workings of his brain. Nothing was natural. He had to think about moving his arm instead of just moving it, but it didn't move anyway. The same for his legs. His head felt unduly heavy, and somewhere his muscles were being told to short-circuit. It felt as if his nerve endings were in warfare.

He was aware also of darkness and movement. When he managed to focus his eyes on something, he was also aware of warmth. The warmth attached itself to movement—not his, unfortunately—and through a haze he saw that he was not alone. A figure lay in the gloom and he was sprawled upon it, half on a body and half on the floor of the van.

He knew it was a van. He knew it was *the* van. In the instant in which his name was called quietly from the shadows, in which he'd turned and thought it was a reporter who'd come to be the first to interview the nonhusband and nonfather he had just become, one part of his brain told him something wasn't right. Then he'd seen the torch in the extended hand, and he'd known whom he was looking at. After that, he'd been struck by the bolt of current and it was over.

He didn't know how many times he'd been hit with the stun gun during the journey to wherever they were when the van finally stopped. What he did know was that the bolts hit him with a regularity that suggested the administrator knew how long a victim's disorientation was likely to last.

When the van stopped and its engine shut off, the man who had called himself Fu climbed into the rear, stun-gun torch in his hand. He applied it to Lynley another time in the businesslike manner of a doctor administering a necessary injection, and the next time Lynley came to his senses and finally felt as if his muscles might be his own once more, he found that he was bound to the inside wall of the van, hanging downward by his armpits and his wrists, legs bent so that his ankles could also be bound to the wall behind him. The bindings felt like leather straps, but they could have been anything. He couldn't see them.

What he could see was the woman, source of the earlier warmth he'd felt. She lay bound on the floor of the van, arms stretched out to either side in the manner of a horizontal crucifixion. The cross itself was there as well, represented by a board on which she was lying. She had duct tape patched across her mouth. Her eyes were open wide in terror.

Terror was good, Lynley managed to think. Terror was much better than resignation. As he looked at her, she seemed to sense his gaze. She turned her head. He saw that she was the woman from Colossus, but in his present state, he couldn't recall her name. That suggested to him that Barbara Havers had been right all along, in her inimitable, stubborn, bloody-minded way: The killer in the van with them was one of the men who worked for Colossus.

The man Fu was getting everything ready, primarily

himself. He'd lit a candle and stripped, and he was anointing his naked body with a substance—this would be the ambergris, wouldn't it?—that he took from a small brown vial. Next to him was the cooker that Muwaffaq Masoud had described to them in Hayes. It was heating up a large pan from which the scent of previously burnt meat gave off a faint odour.

He was actually humming. It was all in a night's work for him. They were in his power, and the manifestation of power and the execution of power were what he wanted out of life.

On the floor of the van, the woman made a pitiful sound from beneath the duct tape. Fu turned at this, and in the light Lynley saw that he looked vaguely familiar, that he possessed that quintessential and very English face of substantial pointed nose, rounded chin, and bread-dough cheeks. He could have been a hundred thousand men on the street, but in him the strain had mutated somehow, so he was not a bland little individual working at an ordinary job and going home to the wife and the children every evening in a terrace house somewhere but, rather, he was who circumstances in life had altered him to be: someone who liked to kill people.

Fu said, "I wouldn't have chosen you, Ulrike. I rather like you. It was actually my mistake ever to mention Dad. But when you started asking for alibis—and it was fairly obvious that was what you were doing, by the way—I knew I had to tell you *something* you'd be happy with. Sitting home alone would never have cut the mustard, would it? The *alone* part would have made you curious." He looked down on her, completely friendly. "I mean, you would have been all over that, p'rhaps even telling the coppers about it. And then where would we be?"

He brought out the knife. He took it from the little work top where the propane cooker was merrily heating not only the pan but the van itself now. Lynley could feel the warmth undulating across to him.

Fu said, "It was meant to be one of the boys. I thought Mark Connor. You know him, don't you? Likes to hang round in reception with Jack? Little rapist in the making, you ask me. He needs sorting, Ulrike. They all need sorting. Proper little gobshites, they are. Need discipline and no one gives that to them. Makes one wonder what kind of parents they have. Parenting, you know, is essential to development. Will you excuse me for a moment?"

He turned back to the cooker. He took up the candle and held it to various points on his body. It came to Lynley that this was a hieratic ritual he was watching. And he was *meant* to be watching, like a worshipper at church.

He wanted to speak, but his mouth too was covered with tape. He tested the bindings that held his wrists to the side of the van. They were immovable.

Fu turned again. He stood there quite naturally in his nudity, his body glistening where he'd used the oil on it. He held up the candle and saw that Lynley was watching him. He reached for something on the work top again.

Lynley thought it would be the torch to stun him once more, but it was instead a small brown bottle, not the one he'd been using but another that he took from a little cupboard and held up so that Lynley would be sure to see it.

"Something new, Superintendent," he said. "After Ulrike, I'll switch to parsley. Triumph, you see. And there'll be much cause for it. For triumph. For me, that is. For you? Well, I don't expect you've much to feel grand about at this moment, have you? But you're curious, still, and who can blame you? You want to *know*, don't you? You want to understand."

He knelt by Ulrike, but he looked at Lynley. "Adultery. Nowadays it's nothing she'd actually go to gaol for, but it'll do nicely. She would have touched him—intimately, Ulrike? It *would* have been intimately, wouldn't it?—so, like the others, her hands bear the stain of her sin." He looked down at Ulrike. "I expect you're sorry for that, aren't you, darling?" He smoothed her hair. "Yes, yes. You're sorry. So you'll be released. I promise you that. When it's over, your soul will fly to heaven. I'll keep a bit of you with me . . . snip snip and you're mine . . . but at that point, you won't feel it. You won't feel a thing."

Lynley saw that the young woman had begun to cry. She struggled wildly against her restraints but the effort only exhausted her. Fu watched her, placid, and smoothed her hair once again when she was finished.

"It has to happen," he said kindly. "Try to understand. And do know that I *like* you, Ulrike. Actually, I quite liked them all. You have to suffer, of course, but that's what life is. Suffering through whatever we're handed. And this is what's been handed to you. The superintendent here will bear witness. And then he'll pay for his own sins as well. So you're not alone, Ulrike. You can take comfort from that, can't you?"

The toying with her, Lynley saw, was giving the man pleasure, actual physical pleasure. This, however, seemed to embarrass him. It would doubtless make him feel like one of the "others" and he wouldn't like that: the indication that he too was of warped human stock like every other psychopath who had gone before him, getting a sexual kick from another's terror and pain. He picked up his trousers and donned them, pushing his phallus out of view.

But it seemed that the *fact* of his arousal altered him. He became all business, the friendly chat put behind him. He sharpened the knife. He spat into the pan to test the heat of it. From a rack, he took a length of thin line that he held—one end in each hand—and snapped expertly as if to test its strength.

"Down to work, then," he said when he was fully prepared.

BARBARA STUDIED the van from the farthest end of the carpark, some sixty yards away. She tried to think what the inside might be like. If he'd killed the boys and sliced them open within the vehicle—which she was certain he'd done—that called for space, space in which to lay someone out, which meant the back of the van. Obvious, no? But how exactly was one of these bloody vehicles structured? she wondered. Where were its most vulnerable points and where the most secure? She didn't know. And she didn't have the time to find out.

She climbed back into the Bentley and she adjusted the seat, far back now, as far as it would go. This would make it difficult for her to drive, but she wasn't going a great distance.

She fastened her safety belt.

She revved the motor.

She said, "Sorry, sir," and changed the car from park to drive.

FU SAID to Ulrike, "We've had judgement already, haven't we? And I can see both admission and repentance in your tears. So we'll go on directly to punishment, darling. From punishment, you see, purification comes."

Lynley watched as Fu removed the pan from the stove. He saw him smile kindly down at the struggling woman. He too struggled but it was to no avail. "Don't," Fu told them both. "It'll make everything worse." And then directly to Ulrike, "Anyway, darling, trust me on this. It's going to hurt me far worse than it'll ever hurt you."

He knelt beside her and placed the pan on the floor.

He reached for her hand, untied it, and held it tight. He considered it for a moment, then kissed it.

And the side of the van exploded.

THE AIRBAG DEPLOYED. Smoke filled the car. Barbara coughed and fumbled frantically with the fastening on her safety belt. She managed to release it and she stumbled from the car, sore of chest and hacking to clear her lungs. When she got her breath back, she looked at the Bentley and realised then that what she'd thought was smoke was actually some sort of powder. The airbag? Who knew. The important thing was that nothing was on fire, neither the Bentley nor the van, although neither was the same as it had been.

She'd aimed for the driver's door. She'd hit it dead centre. Thirty-eight miles an hour had done the job. The speed had destroyed the front of the Bentley and sent the van spinning into the shrubbery. What faced her now was the rear of the van, its single window staring and black.

He had the weapons, but she had surprise. She went forward to see what surprise had wrought.

The sliding door was on the passenger's side. It was open. Barbara yelled, "Cops, Kilfoyle. You're finished. Step outside."

Nothing in response. He had to be unconscious.

She moved carefully. She looked round her as she went. It was dark as pitch, but her eyes were adjusting. The shrubbery was thick, gnarling from the ground right into the carpark, and she made her way along it to the open van door.

She saw figures, unaccountably two of them and a candle guttering on its side on the floor. She righted this and it shed light in a glow that allowed her to find him. Lynley hung limply from his arms and his wrists, bolted like a piece of meat to the side of the van. On the floor, Ulrike Ellis lay bound. She'd wet herself. The smell of piss was rank in the air.

Barbara stepped over her and got to Lynley. He was conscious, she saw, and she sent a broken prayer of gratitude heavenward. She ripped the piece of duct tape from his mouth, crying, "Did he hurt you? Are you hurt? Where *is* he, sir?"

Lynley said, "See to the woman, the *woman*," and Barbara left him to go to her. She saw that a heavy frying pan lay next to Ulrike and for a moment she thought the bastard had bashed her with it and she was finished altogether. But when she knelt and felt for a pulse, it was fast and steady. She ripped the duct tape from Ulrike's mouth. She unbound her left hand.

She said, "Sir, where is he? Is he here? Where—"

The van lurched.

Lynley shouted, "Barbara! Behind you!"

And the bastard was there. Back in the van and coming towards her and God *damn* but didn't he have something in his hand. It looked like a torch but she couldn't believe it was a torch since it wasn't on and anyway he was storming at her and—

Barbara grabbed the only thing within reach. She leaped to her feet just as he lunged. He missed her, fell forward.

She was more fortunate.

She swung the frying pan and brained him on the back of the head.

He fell over Ulrike, but that didn't matter. Barbara brained him a second time for good measure.

Chapter Thirty-four

Nkata arrived at the police station on Lower Clapton Road in record time. He found it not overly far from Hackney Marsh, in an area of town he'd never before seen. An old redbrick Victorian affair, the station looked like something Bobby Peel might emerge from at any moment, and at this early hour, it was still lit up as if for night, exterior lights thwarting the would-be terrorists unheard of in the 1800s.

What had awakened him was his mobile phone ringing, with Barb Havers on the other end. She'd said tersely, "It's Kilfoyle, Winnie. We've got the bugger. Lower Clapton Road if you want to be in on things. Do you?"

He'd said, "*What*? I thought you went to tell the super—"

"Kilfoyle was there. He snatched him out of the carpark. I followed and . . . bloody hell, I wrecked his Bentley, Win, but it was the only way—"

"You telling me you saw the guv get snatched and d'in't ring for help? Fuck all, Barb—"

"I couldn't."

"But—"

"Winnie. Stuff a sock in it. If you want to be in on things, get over here now. They've got him in a cell while they wait for John Stewart to get here, but they'll let us talk to him in advance if the duty solicitor gets here first. So d'you want in?"

"I'm on my way."

He'd banged round in the dark in his haste to be gone, which had roused his mother. She'd come storming out of her bedroom with a tatting hook held aloft—God only knew what she'd intended to do with it—and when she'd seen him, she demanded to know what in the name of Jamaica he was doing out here at four thirty-two o'clock in the morning?

"You just gettin *in*?" she'd cried.

Just going out, he'd said.

"Without your *breakfast*? You sit down and let me do a proper fry-up for you."

Can't, Mum. Case is closing and I want to be there for it. Only so much time before I get muscled aside by the higher-ups.

So he'd grabbed his coat, kissed her cheek, and he'd taken off, sprinting down the corridor, hurtling down the stairs, dashing to his car. He had a general sense of where the police station was. Lower Clapton Road was just north of Hackney.

Now he hustled into reception, where he gave his name and showed his identification. The special on duty placed a call somewhere, and in less than two minutes, Barb Havers came to fetch him.

She brought him into the picture quickly: what she'd seen in the carpark of St. Thomas' Hospital, her miserable wreck of a flaming worthless Mini breaking down, her appropriation of Lynley's Bentley, the Lea Valley Ice Centre, the hurried plan, the crash of the Bentley into the van, finding Lynley and Ulrike Ellis within it, the brief confrontation with the killer himself.

"He didn't count on the frying pan," Barbara concluded. "I could've hit him round six times more, but the super shouted I'd bashed him enough."

"Where is he?"

"The guv? In casualty. That's where we all went when triple nine got these blokes"—with a gesture round her to indicate their colleagues from the Lower Clapton Road station—"over there. Kilfoyle'd hit him with the stun gun so much, they wanted to watch him for a while. Same for Ulrike."

"And Kilfoyle?"

"Bugger's head's like a brick wall, Winnie. I didn't break anything, more's the pity. He's probably got concussion, a contusion, whatever, but his vocal cords are operable, so he's doing just fine 's far as we're concerned. Oh, and I got him with the stun gun 's well." She grinned. "Couldn't resist."

"Police brutality."

"And proud to have it written on my tombstone. Here we are." She shouldered open the door to an interview room. Inside, Robbie Kilfoyle sat with a duty solicitor who was speaking to him urgently.

Nkata's first thought was that Kilfoyle didn't, in fact, look very much like any e-fit they'd come up with during the course of the investigation. He bore only a mild resemblance to the man seen lurking round Square Four Gym, where Sean Lavery worked out, and he bore no resemblance at all to the man who'd bought the van from Muwaffaq Masoud late the previous summer, had he, in fact, even been that man. So much for people's memories, Nkata thought.

Robson, on the other hand and for his sins, had been fairly close to the mark from the start with his profiling of the serial killer, and the meagre facts they were able to glean from Kilfoyle—when the duty solicitor wasn't telling him to mind what he said or to plug his mug altogether—confirmed this. Kilfoyle's age of twenty-seven was dead within range and his circumstances weren't far off either. Mum deceased, he'd lived with his dad till the older man had dropped dead in late summer. That would've been the stressor, Nkata reckoned, because the first of the killings started not long afterwards. They already knew that his past fit the profile, with truancy problems, peeping Tom allegations, and AWOL concerns in his record. But in the limited time they had with him prior to DI John Stewart's arrival to take over, they saw that the rest of the details were going to come from the evidence that would be gleaned from his home, possibly from the environs of the ice-rink carpark, and from his van.

The van was waiting for the arrival of SOCO. The environs of the ice-rink carpark were waiting for full daylight. That left his house in Granville Square. Nkata suggested they check it out. Barb was reluctant "to leave the bloody sod," but she agreed to do so. They met DI Stewart on the way out. He already had his clipboard in hand, and the parting in his razor-cut hair might have been put there with a straight edge. There were still comb marks in it as well.

He nodded at them both. He directed his comments to Barb. "Well done, Havers. Doubtless you'll be reinstated now. Back to rank. For what it's worth, I approve. How is he?"

Nkata knew the DI wasn't referring to Kilfoyle. Barb answered the question. "In casualty. For now. I expect they'll release him in a few hours. I phoned his mum. She'll fetch him. Or his sister will. They're both here in London."

"And otherwise?"

Barb shook her head. "He's not saying much."

Stewart nodded and looked bleakly at the police building. Barb's face altered and Nkata could see she was thinking she could almost like the bloke for the instant in which he'd actually evidenced a modicum of compassion. "Poor bloody sod," Stewart murmured. And then to them in his usual tone, "Carry on. Have something to eat. I'll see you later."

A meal was not of interest to them. They made their way instead to Granville Square. By the time they got there, it had come to life. A crime-scene van parked out front hailed SOCO's presence within, and curious neighbours gathered on the pavement. Nkata flashed his ID at the constable at the front door, explained why Barb didn't have hers, and got them both inside.

Within, more of the pieces of the killer's personality became revealed. In the basement, a neat stack of newspapers and tabloids displayed stories that chronicled Kilfoyle's exploits, and an *A to Z* sitting on a nearby table x-marked-the-spots he'd carefully selected to deposit bodies. Upstairs, the kitchen contained a wide variety of knives—all being tagged and bagged by SOCO—while over the chairs in the sitting room lay the same sort of tatting-edged mats that had been used to fashion a flimsy and respectful codpiece for Kimmo Thorne. Everywhere, tidiness reigned. The place was, in fact, a testament to tidiness. Only in one room were there signs—other than with the newspapers and the *A to Z*—that an extremely unsteady mind was at work: In a bedroom upstairs, a dated wedding picture had been defaced, with the shaggy-haired groom disemboweled by means of pen and ink and the same mark upon his forehead as had been made as the signature of the letter Kilfoyle had sent to New Scotland Yard. In the wardrobe as well, a disturbed hand had slit every male garment down its centre.

"Didn't care for Dad much by the looks of things, did he?" Barb remarked.

A voice spoke from the doorway. "Thought you two might want to see this before we cart it off." One of the white-suited forensic-team members stood there, an urn in his hands. It was a funeral urn by the look and the size of it, suitable for containing human ashes.

"What've you got?" Nkata asked.

"His souvenirs, I'll wager." He carried the urn to the

chest of drawers on which the wedding picture stood. He tipped off its top. They looked inside.

Human dust formed the majority of the contents, along with several ash-covered lumps. Barb was the one who twigged what they were.

"The navels," she said. "Whose ashes d'you expect those are? Dad's?"

"Could be the Queen Mum's for all I care," Nkata remarked. "We got the bastard."

The families could be given the news now. There would be no satisfactory justice for them; there never was. But there would be a conclusion.

Nkata drove Barb back to St. Thomas' Hospital to arrange for her car to be towed away and put into running order again. There, they parted, and when they did, neither of them looked at the hospital itself.

Nkata headed towards New Scotland Yard. It was nine in the morning by then, and traffic was slow. He was negotiating Parliament Square when his mobile rang. He reckoned it was Barb, all attempts at coping with her car a failure. But a glance told him the number was not one he knew, so he said, "Nkata," and nothing else.

"You arrested him, then. It was on the news this morning. Radio One." A woman's voice spoke, familiar, but not one he'd heard on the phone before.

"Who's this?"

"I'm glad it's over. And I know you meant good towards him. Towards us. I know that, Winston."

Winston. "Yas?" he said.

"I knew it before but I d'in't want to look at what that meant, unnerstan? I still don't. Want to look at it, I mean."

He considered this, considered the fact she'd phoned at all. "C'n you give it a glance, you think?"

She was silent.

"A glance's not much, innit. Just a flick when you

move the eyes. Tha's all. Not looking at nothin, really, Yas. Just *sneaking* a look. Tha's it. Tha's all."

"I don't know," was what she finally said.

Which was better than things had been before. "When you do know, you ring me, then," he told her. "Waitin's not a trouble to me."

LYNLEY RECKONED that one of the reasons they forced him to stay in Casualty was their worry that he would do something to Kilfoyle if they released him. And the truth was that he *would* have done something, although not what they obviously thought he would do. Instead, he would merely have asked a question of the man: Why? And perhaps that question would have led to others: Why Helen and not me? And why in the *way* he had done it, with a boy in his company? What sort of statement did that make? Power? Indifference? Sadism? Pleasure? To destroy as many lives as possible in as many ways as possible in one swift blow because he knew the end was coming? Was that why? He'd be famous now, infamous, notorious, with all the attendant bells and whistles. He'd be up there with the best of the best, those names like Hindley that would forever light the firmament of iniquity. Avid followers of crime would flock to his trial and writers would document him in their books and he would thus never fade from public memory like an ordinary man or, for that matter, like an innocent woman and her unborn child, both dead now and soon to become yesterday's news.

Obviously, those in power had believed that Lynley would spring to the attack if he came face-to-face with the monster again. But springing to the attack suggested a life force within, driving one forward. That was gone from him now.

They said they would release him to a relative and, since they had his clothing tucked away somewhere, he was forced to wait until a member of his family arrived. They had no doubt suggested in their phone call to Eaton Terrace that that person take as long as possible in making the trip to the hospital, so it was midmorning when his mother came to fetch him. She had Peter with her. A taxi, she said, was just outside.

"What's happened?" She looked older to him than she had days earlier. He understood from this that the experience in living chaos, which they all were enduring, was taking a toll on her as well. He hadn't thought of that before. He wondered what it meant that he thought of it now.

Beyond their mother, Lynley's brother stood, lanky and ill at ease, as always. They'd been close once, but that was years in the past, with cocaine and alcohol and fraternal abandonment leering like spectres in the space between them. Too much disease ran through his family, Lynley thought, part of it of the body, the rest of it of the mind.

Peter said, "You all right, Tommy?," and Lynley saw his brother's hand reach out, then drop uselessly to his side. "They wouldn't tell us on the phone . . . just to fetch you, they said. We thought . . . They said you'd come from near the river. But up here . . . What river? What were you—"

His brother was afraid, Lynley thought. Another possible loss in his life and Peter did not know how he'd cope with that if he had no crutch to lean upon: up the nose, in a vein, out of the bottle, whatever. Peter didn't want that, but it was always out there, beckoning to him.

Lynley said, "I'm all right, Peter. I didn't try anything. I won't try anything," although he knew that latter statement was neither a promise nor a lie.

Peter chewed on the inside of his lip, a habit from his childhood. He gave a nervous nod.

Lynley explained what had happened in two simple sentences: He'd had an encounter with the killer. Barbara Havers had taken care of matters.

"Remarkable woman," Lady Asherton said.

"She is," Lynley replied.

He discovered that Ulrike Ellis had been released to the police several hours earlier to make her statement. She was shaken, he learned, but otherwise unharmed. Kilfoyle had done nothing save stun her, gag her, and restrain her. That was bad enough but so far from what it could have been that it was ludicrous to suggest she would not recover.

In the taxi, he sank into a corner, his mother next to him and his brother perched on the jump seat opposite. He said to Peter, "Tell him Scotland Yard," and his mother protested with, "You're to come straight home."

He shook his head. "Tell him," and nodded towards the driver.

Peter leaned to the opening in the shield between driver and passengers. He said, "Victoria Street. New Scotland Yard. And after that, Eaton Terrace."

The driver swerved into the street with the flow of traffic and headed in the direction of Westminster.

"We should have stayed with you, at the hospital," Lady Asherton murmured.

"No," Lynley said. "You did what I asked." He looked out of the window. "I'll want to bury them at Howenstow. I think that's what she would have wanted. We never discussed it. There was no need. But I'd like—"

He felt his mother's hand take his. "Of course," she said.

"I don't know when yet. I didn't think to ask when they'd release the . . . her body. There are all sorts of details . . ."

"We'll handle things, Tommy," his brother said. "All of them. Let us."

Lynley looked at him. Peter was leaning forward, closer to him than he'd been in ages. Slowly he nodded his agreement. "Some of them, then," he said. "Thank you."

They rode the rest of the way in silence. When the taxi made the turn from Victoria Street into Broadway, Lady Asherton spoke again. She said, "Will you let one of us come in with you, Tommy?"

"There's no need," he told her. "I'll be all right, Mum."

He waited till they drove off before he entered. Then he went inside, not to Victoria Block but to Tower Block. He made his way to Hillier's office.

Judi MacIntosh looked up from her work. Like his mother, she seemed to be able to read him, and it appeared that what she read was accurate, for he had not come for a confrontation. She said, "Superintendent, I . . . All of us here . . . I can't imagine what you're going through." She held her hands at her throat, as if beseeching him to relieve her of saying anything more.

He said, "Thank you," and he wondered how many more times he would have to thank people in the coming months. Indeed, he wondered what he was even thanking them for. His breeding called for this expression of gratitude when he wanted instead to raise his head and shriek into the eternal night that was falling round him. He despised good breeding. But even despising it, he relied upon it again when he said, "Would you tell him I'm here? I'd like a word. It won't take long."

She nodded. Rather than phone into Hillier's office, however, she went through the door. She closed it softly behind her. A minute passed. Another. They were probably phoning someone to come up. Nkata again. Perhaps John Stewart. Someone capable of restraining him. Someone to escort him from the premises.

Judi MacIntosh returned. "Do go in," she said.

Hillier wasn't in his usual position, behind the desk. He wasn't standing at one of the windows. Instead, he'd come across the carpet to meet Lynley halfway.

He said quietly, "Thomas, you must go home and get some rest. You can't continue—"

"I know." Lynley couldn't recall the last time he'd slept. He'd been running on anxiety and adrenaline for so long he no longer remembered what it felt like to be doing otherwise. He removed his warrant card and every other vestige of police identification that he had upon him. He extended them to the assistant commissioner.

Hillier looked at them but did not take them. "I won't accept this," he said. "You've not been thinking straight. You're not thinking straight now. I can't allow you to make a decision like this—"

"Believe me, sir," Lynley cut in, "I've made far more difficult decisions." He passed Hillier then and went to his desk. He lay his identification upon it.

"Thomas," Hillier said, "don't do this. Take some time off. Take compassionate leave. With everything that's happened, you can't be in a position to decide your future or anyone else's."

Lynley felt the hollowness of a laugh rising in him. He could decide. He had decided.

He wanted to say that he didn't know any longer how to be, let alone who to be. He wanted to explain he was good for no one and nothing now and he did not know if things would ever be any different. Instead what he said was, "For my part of what went between us, sir, I am most deeply regretful."

"Thomas . . ." The tone of Hillier's voice—was it pained? It actually sounded so—stopped him at the door. He turned. Hillier said, "Where will you go?"

"To Cornwall," he said. "I'm taking them home."

Hillier nodded then. He said something more as Lynley opened the door. He couldn't have been certain what the words were, but later he would think they'd been "Go with God."

Outside, in the anteroom, Barbara Havers was waiting. She looked done in, and it came to Lynley that at this point she'd been working more than twenty-four hours straight. She said, "Sir . . ."

"I'm fine, Barbara. You needn't have come up."

"I'm to take you somewhere."

"Where?"

"Just . . . They're suggesting I drive you home. I've a car on loan, so you won't have to cram yourself into my heap."

"That's fine, then," Lynley said. "Let's go."

He felt her hand on his elbow, guiding him from the office to the lift. She spoke to him as they went along, and he gathered from her words that there was evidence aplenty to link Kilfoyle to the deaths of the Colossus boys.

"And the rest?" he asked her as the lift doors opened on the underground carpark. "What about the rest?"

And she spoke of Hamish Robson and then of the boy in lockup at the Harrow Road station. Robson's was a crime of necessity and opportunity, she said. As for the boy in Harrow Road, he wouldn't say.

"But there's no connection at all between him and Colossus," Havers said as they reached the car. They continued talking over its roof, her on one side and him on the other. "It looks like . . . Sir, it looks to everyone like a one-off street crime. He won't talk . . . this kid. But we're thinking it's a gang."

He looked at her. She seemed underwater to him, and at a great distance. "A gang? Doing what?"

She shook her head. "I don't know."

"But you have an idea. You must. Tell me."

"Car's unlocked, sir."

"Barbara, tell me."

She opened her door but didn't climb inside. "It could've been an initiation, sir. He needed to prove something to someone, and Helen was there. She was just . . . there."

Lynley knew from this there was supposed to come absolution for himself, but he could not feel it. He said, "Take me to Harrow Road, then."

She said, "You don't need to—"

"Take me to Harrow Road, Barbara."

She gazed at him and then got into the car. She started it up. She said, "The Bentley . . ."

"You put it to good use," he told her. "Well done, Constable."

"It's to be Sergeant again," she said. "Finally."

He said, "Sergeant," and he felt his lips curve slightly. "Well done, Sergeant Havers."

Her own lips trembled and he saw her chin dimple. She said, "Right. Well." She got them out of the carpark and on their way.

If she worried that he was going to do something rash, she gave no sign of it. Instead she told him how Ulrike Ellis had got herself into the company of Robbie Kilfoyle, and from there she went on to say that the announcement of the arrest had been handed over to John Stewart to make before the media once Nkata refused to do it. "Stewart's moment of glory, sir," was how she concluded. "I think he's been waiting for stardom for years."

"Keep on his good side," Lynley told her. "I don't want to think of you with enemies in the future."

She glanced at him. He could see what she feared. He wished he could tell her the situation was otherwise.

In the Harrow Road station, Lynley told her what he wanted. She listened, nodded, and in an act of friendship he welcomed with gratitude, she did not try to talk him out of it. When strings had been pulled and arrangements had been made, she came to fetch him. As she'd done in Victoria Street, she walked along at his side, her hand lightly upon his elbow.

She said, "In here, sir," and opened a door to a dimly lit room. Beyond it, on the other side of the two-way mirror, Helen's killer sat. They'd given him a plastic bottle of juice, but he hadn't opened it. He had his hands clasped round it, and his shoulders were slumped.

Lynley felt a large breath leave him. All he could say was, "Young. So young. Good Christ in heaven."

"He's twelve years old, sir."

"Why."

There was no answer and he knew she knew he did not expect one. He said, "What's happened to us, Barbara? What in God's name?" And he also knew she knew he wanted no reply.

Still, she said, "Will you let me take you home now?"

He said, "Yes. You can take me home."

IT WAS LATE in the afternoon when he went to Cheyne Row. Deborah answered the door. Wordlessly, she held it open for him to enter. They stood facing each other—long-ago lovers that they were—and Deborah gazed as if to make a study of him before she straightened her shoulders in what seemed to be resolve and said, "In here, Tommy. Simon's not home."

He didn't tell her he'd come to see her, not his friend, because she seemed to know this. She took him into the dining room where, in what seemed like another century, she'd been wrapping the baby gift for Helen. On the table, folded neatly upon the carrier bags which had held them, lay the christening outfits that Deborah and Helen had bought. Deborah said, "It seemed to me that you'd want to see them before I . . . well, before I took them back to the shops. I don't know why I thought that. But as it was the last thing she did . . . I hope I was right."

They were Helen, all of them: her whimsical statement about what was truly important and what was decidedly not. Here was the tiny dinner jacket she'd spoken of, there a miniature clown costume, next to it white velvet dungarees, an impossibly tiny three-piece suit, an equally tiny BabyGro fashioned into a bunny costume . . . The assortment was appropriate to anything but a christening, but that had been Helen's point. We'll start our own tradition, darling. Neither side of our subtly battling families can possibly be offended by that.

Lynley said, "I couldn't let them do what they wanted to do. I couldn't face it. She'd become a specimen to them. A few months on life support, sir, and we'll see how everything turns out. Could be bad, could be worse, but in the meantime we'll have pushed the envelope of medical science. One for the journals, this will be. One for the books." He looked at Deborah. Her eyes were bright, but she gave him the gift of not weeping. He said, "I couldn't do that to her, Deborah. I *couldn't*. So I shut things down. I shut them down."

"Last night?"

"Yes."

"Oh, Tommy."

"I don't know how to live with myself."

"Without blame," she said. "That's how you must do it."

"You as well," he told her. "Promise me that."

"What?"

"That you won't live a single moment thinking that this was your fault, that you could have done something to stop what happened, to prevent it, to anything. You were parking a car. That's all you were doing. Parking a car. I want you to see it that way because it's the truth. Will you do that for me?"

"I'll try," she said.

WHEN BARBARA HAVERS arrived home that evening, she spent thirty minutes cruising up and down streets, waiting for someone to vacate a parking space at a time of day when most people were at home for the duration of the night. She finally found a space in Winchester Road, nearly all the way to South Hampstead, and she took it gratefully despite the fact that a lengthy slog awaited her once she locked up and began plodding back to Eton Villas.

As she walked, she realised how much she ached. Her muscles were sore from her legs up to her neck, but particularly in her shoulders. The wrecking of the Bentley had had a greater impact than she'd felt in the immediate aftermath. Clubbing Robbie Kilfoyle with the frying pan hadn't helped. Had she been a different sort of woman, she would have decided a nice massage was in order. Steam room, sauna, whirlpool, the whole experience. Throw in a manicure and pedicure as well. But she was not that sort of woman. She told herself that a shower would do. And a good night's sleep, since she'd gone without for some thirty-seven hours and counting.

She kept her mind on that. Up to Fellows Road and along the way, she fixed her thoughts on showering and dropping into bed. She decided she wouldn't even turn on the lights in her bungalow lest anything keep her from her appointed rounds, which were defined by a journey from front door to dining table (drop off one's belongings), from dining table to bathroom (turn on the shower, shed clothes onto the floor, let water beat upon throbbing muscles), and from bathroom to bed (the embrace of Morpheus). This allowed her not to think of what she didn't want to think about: that he hadn't told her, that she'd had to learn it from DI Stewart.

She lectured herself about the way she felt, which was cut off and drifting into space. She told herself that his private life was none of her bloody business anyway. She pointed out to herself that his pain would have been intolerable, and to *speak* of it—to confide that he had ended things and with them his life as he'd known it and seen it weaving a future for him, for her, for them as a little family—would probably have finished him off. But all her self-talk did was provide a thin patina of guilt over her other feelings. And all the guilt did was momentarily silence the child within her who kept insisting they were supposed to be friends. Friends *told* each other things, important things. Friends leaned on each other because they were friends.

But the news had come to the incident room via Dorothea Harriman, who'd asked for the ear of DI Stewart, who'd then made a sombre general announcement. No one knew about funeral arrangements, he'd said in conclusion, but he'd keep them informed. In the meantime, though, carry on, you lot. There're reports to be made to the CPS on more than one front, so let's make them because I want this signed, sealed, and delivered in such a way that no doubt exists in anyone's mind what kind of verdict the jury's intended to hand down.

Barbara had sat there and listened. She'd been unable to prevent herself from thinking that they'd been together from Hillier's office to Harrow Road and from Harrow Road to Eaton Terrace, and Lynley had never said he'd turned off his wife's life support. She *knew* it was not what she ought to be thinking. She *knew* his decision to keep the information to himself was not about her. Yet still she felt a sorrow renewed rush over her. That child inside her kept insisting, We're meant to be friends.

Why they were not, and could never be at the end of the day, was the fault not of who they were—man, woman, colleagues—but of who they *were* beneath all that. This had been both determined and defined before either one of them had seen the first light of day. She could rail against it till the end of time, but she could not change it. Certain strands of certain fabrics made the fabric itself too strong to be torn.

In Eton Villas at last, she turned up the drive and in through the gate. Hadiyyah, she saw, was heaving a rubbish sack along the path to the bins at the back of the building, and Barbara watched her struggling with it for a moment before she said, "Hey, kiddo. C'n I help?"

"Barbara!" Her voice was bright as ever. Her head lifted and her plaits swung round. "Dad and I have cleaned out the fridge. He says spring's coming and this's our first step to welcome it. Cleaning the fridge, that is. 'Course that means that we're going to be cleaning the rest of the flat next, and I'm not much looking forward to that. He's making a list of what we're to do. A *list*, Barbara. And washing walls is at the top of it."

"That sounds pretty bad."

"Mummy used to wash them every year, so that's why we're doing it. So when she comes home, everything'll be nice and sparkling for her."

"Coming home, then, is she? Your mum?"

"Oh my goodness, eventually. One can't be on holiday forever."

"No. I expect you're right." Barbara handed over her shoulder bag to the little girl and took the rubbish from her. She heaved it like a duffel and manoeuvred it to the bins. Together they heave-hoed it to join the rest of the rubbish.

"I'm going to have tap lessons," Hadiyyah told her as they brushed themselves off. "Dad said so tonight. I'm ever so pleased, because I've wanted them for ages. Will you come to watch me when I do my exhibition?"

"Front-row centre," Barbara said. "I love exhibitions."

"Brilliant," she said. "P'rhaps Mummy'll be there as well. If I get good enough, she'll come. I know it. 'Night, Barbara. Got to get back to Dad."

She scooted off, round the corner of the house. Barbara waited till she heard a door shut, telling her her little friend was safely inside. Then she went to her own digs and unlocked the door. True to her decision, she turned on no lights. She merely walked to the table, dumped her belongings, and turned to head for the shower and its blessed heat.

The damn answering machine stopped her with its blinking light. She thought about ignoring it but knew she couldn't. She sighed and made her way across to it. She punched the button and heard the familiar voice.

"Barbie, dear, I've got the appointment." Mrs. Flo, Barbara thought, her mother's keeper. "My Lord, it wasn't easy to get one, the NHS being what it is these days. Now I do have to tell you that Mum's gone back to the Blitz, but I don't want you to *worry* about it. If we must sedate her, we simply must, my dear, and that's all there is to it. Her health—"

Barbara cut off the message. She would listen to the rest another time, she vowed. But not tonight.

A hesitant knock sounded on her front door. She crossed back to it. She'd not switched on a single interior light, so she reckoned only one person knew she was finally at home. She opened the door, and he stood before her, a covered pan in his hand.

Azhar said, "I believe you have not had your dinner, Barbara," and extended the pan in her direction.

She said, "Hadiyyah told me you were cleaning out the fridge. Are these leftovers? If yours are anything like mine, Azhar, I'd be taking my life in my hands to eat them."

He smiled. "This is freshly made. *Pilau*, to which I've added chicken." He lifted the lid. In the dim light, she couldn't see the contents, but she could smell their fragrance. Her mouth watered. Hours, days, weeks since she'd had a decent meal.

She said, "Cheers. Sh'll I take it, then?"

"If I might set it down?"

"'Course." She held the door open wider but still did not turn on the light. At this point it had more to do with the terminal disarray of her digs than with a desire for sleep. Azhar, she knew, was akin to a neat freak on steroids. She didn't trust the strength of his heart if he saw the mess she'd not dealt with in weeks.

He placed the pan in the kitchen area, on the work top. She waited by the door, assuming he'd leave after that. He didn't.

Instead he said, "Your case is concluded, then. The news is full of it."

"This morning, right. Or last night. Or somewhere in between. I don't actually know. Things start running together after a while."

He nodded. "I see."

She waited for more. More did not come. A silence hung between them. He finally broke it.

"You have worked long with him, haven't you?"

His voice was kind. Her insides gave warning. She said lightly, "Lynley? Yeah. Few years. A decent enough bloke if you can get past that voice. He finished school in the days before estuary English, when they turned out toffs who did world tours and spent the rest of their lives chasing foxes round the countryside."

"Things are very bad for him."

She didn't reply. Instead she saw Lynley at the front door to his house in Eaton Terrace. She saw the door open before he could put his key in the lock, his sister framed in the light from inside. She waited, thinking he might turn and wave a farewell, but his sister put her arm round his waist and drew him within.

"Terrible things happen to very good people," Azhar said.

"Well yeah. Right."

She couldn't—and wouldn't—talk about it. Too fresh, too sore, vinegar washing over open wounds.

She ran her hand back through her chopped-up hair and gave a big sigh that he was meant to read as tired-woman-needing-her-rest-thank-you. But he'd been a fool only once in his life, and he'd learned to be a wiser man from that experience. So she couldn't drive him off with theatrics. She would have to be direct or stand there and tolerate what he had to say.

"Such a loss. One does not recover completely from that."

"Yeah. Well. I reckon that's right. He's got a row to hoe and I don't envy him it."

"His wife. And the child. There was a child, the papers said."

"Helen was pregnant, yeah."

"And did you know her well?"

She. Would. Not. She said, "Azhar . . ." and took an unsteady breath. "You see, I'm knackered. Absolutely done in. Pickled. Dead on my—"

The word. The word itself and she stopped herself on it. She strangled back a cry. Tears sprang to her eyes. She brought a fist to her mouth.

Leave, she thought. Please go. Bloody *leave*.

But he didn't do that, and she saw that he wouldn't, that he'd come for a reason beyond what she could, at that moment, comprehend.

She waved a hand at him, waved him off and away, but he didn't do as she hoped he would do. Instead he crossed the small room to her, said only, "Barbara," and took her into his arms.

She began to weep, then. Like the child she'd been and the woman she'd become. It seemed the safest place to do so.

Acknowledgments

When an American attempts to write a novel set in London, various forces and personalities come into play. For this book, a little volume called *City Secrets*, edited by Robert Kahn, set me off on my journey to find locations suitable for the action in this story. My editor at Hodder and Stoughton in London as well as my publicist there—Sue Fletcher and Karen Geary—made numerous helpful suggestions, and my fellow writer Courttia Newland introduced me firsthand to the immediate environs of West Kilburn. South of the river, Fairbridge opened its doors to me, and there I learned of the work that organization does to make a difference in the lives of young people at risk. My efforts to capture the flavor of the sort of police work that goes into the investigation of a serial killing were aided by David Cox of the Metropolitan Police and Pip Lane, retired and formerly of the Cambridge constabulary. Bob's Magic, Novelties, and Gags in the Stables Market at Camden Lock stood in for Barry Minshall's magic stall, and Bob himself was most kind to speak to me about the market and magic. *Mind Hunter* by John Douglas and Mark Olshaker and *The Gates of Janus* by—astoundingly—Ian Brady formed the background of my creation and understanding of the serial killer in this novel. And the ever resourceful and infinitely patient Swati Gamble of Hodder and Stoughton provided me with information on everything from schools to bus schedules to the floor coverings of vans.

In America, my editor at HarperCollins—Carolyn Marino—offered support and encouragement throughout the lengthy process of creating this novel. My longtime reader Susan Berner weighed in on the second draft with a fine critique. My fellow writer Patricia Fogarty graciously read a third draft. My assistant, Dannielle Azoulay, did everything from research to walking the dog in order to free my time to write. My husband, Tom McCabe, heroically put up with five A.M. wake-up calls for months on end—including on ski trips, hikes in the Great Smokies, and Seattle getaways—without a word of complaint. My students kept me sharp and honest. And my dog always kept me human.

To all these individuals, I owe a debt of gratitude. Mistakes found herein are not due to them but to myself.

Additionally, I must acknowledge the Man behind the Career: my literary agent, Robert Gottlieb. Every time he begins a sentence with, "Now, you know, Elizabeth . . . ," I realize it's time to listen up.